# DANCING
## WITH DARKNESS
### OF ASTRAL AND UMBRAL BOOK THREE

Editing by Kaelan Rhywiol of Chimera Editing

https://kaelanrhywiol.com/

http://www.chimeraediting.com/


First Edition

ISBNs

E-Book: 978-0-9992067-9-9

Paperback: 978-1-951235-01-7

Hardback: 978-1-951235-00-0

# TABLE OF CONTENTS

# FOREWORD

**PLEASE NOTE:** This book begins immediately after the events of *Courting Balance*. If you have not read the first two books in this series, I highly recommend doing so before reading this book.
*Of Astral and Umbral* volumes are <u>not</u> standalone stories.

I want to take a moment to say THANK YOU to everyone for being so patient while waiting for more OAU to release. 2019 has been a rough year for my wrist health, forcing me to take a long hiatus from all my work while I heal.

No one wants a broken author, right?

Here's hoping that 2020 is a much better year for us all!

As always, the images above, paired with the voice of the chapter, will be your guide to perspective in this book.

The new, third, icon designates chapters written from Darius' point of view.

Keep in mind that Devillians are not Human and their behavior will often reflect as such. Their culture is their own, and it is something you will learn together with Arianna!

And a final note, there are some references to slavery in this book. Some of the BDSM kind, and some of the *real* kind. There will be mentions of the distinctions between the two, as well as Arianna and Nalithor's shared distaste for true slavery.

# CHAPTER ONE
*Bruised but Not Broken*

*'Dehsul!'* I lowered my bruised body into the springs and grit my teeth, attempting to make no sudden movements. *'So many beasts! Are they what we skipped by flying the rest of the way to Ceilail?'*

I failed to bite back a whimper as I waded deeper into the hot water, stopping once it was up to my chin. Spasms ran through my bruised muscles, making it difficult for me to relax. Even not moving at all couldn't stop it. Thankfully, I had avoided breaking anything, but beasts ramming me and tossing me into trees wasn't how I had envisioned ending the day. The 'lesser' beasts in Rilzaan were both stronger and more intelligent than I wanted to give them credit for.

*'At least I get to sleep on a bed and not the ground tonight...'* I flinched, muttering curses as the hot water ran through a wound I

must've missed healing. *'Maybe I should have let Nalithor—'*

*"Rely'ric, are you certain you can't check on Her Highness?'* A female voice questioned from somewhere by the entrance to the springs. *"She looked like she was in such rough shape, yet she wouldn't let us perform hyrzan to help—"*

*"You know men are not allowed to intrude on* any *of the bathing areas meant for women,"* Nalithor cut her off, his tone firm. *"I, for one, do not want to be at the other end of Amakiir's claws—do you?"*

Several women attempted to argue with him. I shook my head and then tuned them out so that I could clean off the grime of both travel and battle. My muscles and joints protested every movement, but I was filthy. I gnawed my lower lip in frustration. Few things that *didn't* hurt at this point, but I refused to let the Varjior women assist me.

'Hyrzan,' as they called it, sounded too intimate for my liking. Their brief description of it came down to a ritual of incense, strong liquor, and an herb-infused full-body massage. While I appreciated their concern, I had no interest in such questionable, intimate, or hands-on methods. I didn't know these people and had no reason to trust them touching me.

*'Didn't you heal your wounds?'* Nalithor's voice broke my train of thought, making me pout and sink until the water bubbled up my nose. *'The village women seem terribly concerned. They said you wouldn't allow them to join you?'*

*'I healed the cuts, not the bruises,'* I grumbled, dipping fully underwater to soak my hair. *'I still can't seem to grasp how to heal bruises*

*for the life of me. I'll be fine though.'*

*'I'll wait for you at our tents. You should let me heal you,'* Nalithor stated.

I frowned and glanced toward the spring's entrance, listening as Nalithor and the Varjior women walked away. His concerned demeanor struck me as strange, though I couldn't claim it was a bad thing. Still, it was a relief that they had left. I'd be able to finish my bath in peace.

After perching on a low rock, I scrubbed the grime and blood from my hair with cleansers that smelled faintly of cherries. I was thankful that we'd arrived in the Varjior village so late at night; I really didn't feel like dealing with the giggling groups of single women *again*, nor was I in the mood for people to pester me about the bruises I'd sustained.

Clambering out of the springs proved to be even more difficult than climbing in had been. My muscles screamed in protest when I pulled myself onto the stone ledge. The pain brought tears to my eyes, but I shook it off. I dried myself with a towel instead of magic, deciding that using my power seemed like too much effort. My hair received the same treatment, and I left both slightly damp.

*'Ugh, I'm turning purple.'* I grimaced and looked down at my arms, eyeing the mottled patches of purple and yellow that had formed. *'By how my back feels…that's probably worse. Maybe I will take Nalithor up on that offer after all.'*

After dressing in lightweight clothing and an over-robe I slipped through the maze of tents and crude buildings that made up the majority of the village. Amakiir had assigned us tents around the village's outer ring, near where many of the warriors' tents were. Most people were asleep already by the sound of things, but that came as no surprise.

A little over a day of travel by foot had left the former captives exhausted, and it was late enough that most of Amakiir's people were asleep as well. We were lucky that none of the captives were ill, but most weren't physically fit. The children and teenagers, in particular, had struggled to maintain pace. Most of the people were captured for use as pleasure slaves, not for working mines or farms. Some were even the sons and daughters of noble or otherwise wealthy families; others were common folk or temple servants that happened to be 'above average' in appearance.

I found Nalithor perched on a stump near my tent, his spear settled across his lap while he cleaned the blade. Several patches of grass around his feet were rotted from where beast blood had dripped onto them. As I drew near, Nalithor dismissed the weapon and cleaning kit into a shrizar before turning to look at me with concern.

"Will you let me heal you?" Nalithor questioned.

"You don't have to...but it would help," I grumbled, fidgeting with one of my sleeves.

"You weathered some rough blows," Nalithor murmured in a troubled tone, following me into my tent. "At the very least you should have accepted some help in and out of—"

Nalithor cut himself off with a sharp intake of breath, followed by a growl, when I plopped down on a stool and tugged my over-robe off. I sat with my back to him and held the dark fabric over my bare chest. The Magelights inside my tent flickered, threatening to disappear entirely, as the Adinvyr muttered curses.

*'He's...upset?'* I chose to keep the question to myself, then glanced over my shoulder at Nalithor when he placed his hand on my back.

"You should have let me handle more of the beasts," Nalithor spoke softly.

I flinched in response to the sudden warmth of magic flowing from his hand and across my skin.

"Someone had to keep the rescues calm and together," I countered, clenching my hands in the fabric of my robe. "They're less scared of you than they are of me. It made more sense to let me handle the beasts."

"Arianna..." Nalithor sighed, drawing his magic down my back. "I would say they respect you now, not fear you." He paused when I tensed. "Ah... Sorry, did I hurt you?"

"It's kind of hard *not* to hurt me with this much bruising," I pointed out, flinching again as he trailed his fingers and magic down my spine. "We're leaving for Dauthrmir in the morning, right?"

"Yes, the rest of the airships will arrive early in the morning." Nalithor recoiled, removing his hand from my back when I flinched yet again. "The academy sent word ahead to inform me that I'm expected to resume my duties after I report to Lucifer. I was going to ask if you would join me, but with these wounds…"

"I'll be fine as long as you take the edge off the bruising," I mumbled, gripping my robe tighter.

"You're certain?" Nalithor asked, his voice full of concern. "Aren't you still recovering from releasing Ceilail? I would understand if you prefer to rest instead of overseeing classes with me."

"I'm sure. I'll go crazy if I have to stay in the house all day." I nodded once, then twitched and shot Nalithor a look. "Don't you think your hands are wandering a little too low, Nalithor?"

"You are bruised *everywhere*," Nalithor huffed. "While I'm happy you're willing to accompany me, I'm just…concerned for your wellbeing."

*'Happy? Concerned for me?'* I bit back an amused smile. I stayed silent while Nalithor's darkness flowed through my skin. It seemed as though he got the hint about his wandering hands, but his wandering magic was just as distracting. *'Maybe I really did overdo it.'*

"Arianna… If you were Human, you would likely be dead." Nalithor sighed and rested his cheek against the back of my shoulder, his hands gripping my waist while his magic subsided. "I'm going to go get you something for the pain. You're not going to have a restful sleep in this state."

"That's not nec—" I stopped myself when Nalithor shook his head against my shoulder and dug his claws into my waist.

"You are fidgeting too much for me to heal you properly." Nalithor released me. A moment later, I heard him rise to his feet. "I need you to be still, and you need to rest."

"So, you're getting me a sedative?" I frowned and shifted so that I could look at him over my shoulder.

"Yes. You're heavily bruised and you've torn quite a few muscles. I would rather not have you tear more in the course of squirming." Nalithor paused, realization followed by discomfort spreading across his features. He averted his gaze, his body tensing. "Ah…if you do not trust me, then I can get—"

"That's not it!" I exclaimed, surprising even myself. "I *do* trust you, it's just—"

"Then let me fetch you some toryn'xir. It's strong enough to make you sleep, but weak enough that you should wake up in the morning." Nalithor smiled and placed his hand on top of my head. "Part of our duty as warriors is to make sure we recover as quickly as possible. Since we're working as partners…we're responsible for each other's wellbeing. Let me do my part."

"Fine…" I mumbled, pivoting away from him.

*'I need to take my own advice.'* I tugged my clothing back into place with a wince. *'I told him he doesn't need excuses to speak with me or get to know me—the same should work in reverse, right? I don't need to endure this ache just to— Ow…'*

"Toryn'xir is quite strong. I recommend taking it in one gulp," Nalithor informed me as he returned with a shot glass of opalescent lavender liquid. "Into bed with you."

I bit back a quip and hopped off my seat with a low grumble

instead. Nalithor came to stand in front of me as I perched on the edge of the bed, then shot me a stern look when I opened my mouth to speak. Pouting, I accepted the glass from him and sniffed at the liquid. It didn't smell bad per se, but I didn't recognize the scent either. The concerned Adinvyr didn't look as though he was in the mood to answer such questions.

"Sweet dreams." Nalithor chuckled as I tilted my head back and downed the pale liquid.

"Aren't you saying that a little earl—" I swayed on the edge of the bed and grasped the edge to brace myself. "When you said…strong…"

"I didn't mean the taste." Nalithor caught me by my shoulders when I pitched forward.

His chest rumbled beneath my cheek as my consciousness slipped, but I couldn't make out what he said. My mind was gone almost the instant he caught me.

---

"A-Ari? Hair? Mask?!" Darius yelped when I strode into the classroom, causing Nalithor to shoot my brother a filthy look from behind his desk. "Nali? What did you do?"

I perched on the chair waiting beside Nalithor's desk and crossed my legs, glancing between my twin and the angered Adinvyr.

"I *healed* her, firstly," Nalithor spoke with a low growl, "second, I decided that she is not allowed to adhere to the Old Ways any longer. Do you have a problem with that, *Prince Black*?"

"We're still *X'shmiran* citizens!" Darius exclaimed, slamming his hands down on the desk and standing up in protest. "And what do you mean she's *'not allowed?'* She's not *yours* to—"

Nalithor bared his fangs and snarled at my twin. His tail snapped into the corner of the desk with a resounding crack. I studied him for a moment and then switched my attention to Darius—he was too frustrated to realize that he'd made a *deity* angry.

"My mask is far from wearable," I added dryly, before motioning in the direction of the door. "Unless *you* would like to venture outside the Barrier and search for the many pieces—"

"The one that tore her mask nearly took her face with it!" Nalithor rumbled, heat radiating from him. I glanced over to examine the glare he'd settled on Darius. "You should worry about your sister's wellbeing *before* outdated traditions!"

"If it wasn't for Nalithor's healing capabilities, I would be stuck in bed for the next few days due to yesterday's beasts as well," I added as my brother opened his mouth to protest further. "No matter how you try to deny it, Darius, fighting beasts isn't 'safe' by any stretch. Armor gets torn, weapons break, and bodies get damaged."

*'Thank you again, by the way,'* I offered to Nalithor while Darius mouthed a few times.

*'Don't you have other masks?'* Nalithor smirked at me.

*'He doesn't know that,'* I replied innocently.

"But I—!" Darius started.

The corner of my eye twitched. I rounded on my brother and summoned ice over his mouth with a subtle motion of my hand.

"Darius. This is a *classroom*." I reprimanded him. "Nalithor is your *professor* and *a deity*. He should be afforded the proper respect. He isn't your partner, your plaything, or your fuck toy.

"Even if he were, this is still *his* classroom. Kindly remember your manners and stop disrupting class. I'm already of half a mind to hang you from the clock tower by your ankles."

*'You're cute when you're frustrated,'* Nalithor teased, smiling when I shot him a disgruntled look. *'He did say he would like to speak with you about something after class.'*

*'You have that smug look on your face again,'* I informed him, huffing as I turned my attention away from him and back to the class. *'Is it my imagination...or have they grown worse?'*

*'They've gotten worse.'* Nalithor grabbed the back of my chair and pulled it so that it was beside his. *'Your brother managed to convince the other Archmagi to test him again* and *rush the new results... He scored worse than before.'*

*'He does have a habit of getting his way.'* I sighed, readjusting myself. *'Unfortunately, he fits the role of spoiled prince quite well, most of the time. It wouldn't surprise me if they indulged him just to silence him... I'll admit I'm the same way at times.'*

*'Your time would be better spent by indulging* me.*'* Nalithor purred, nudging me. I looked at him again, this time in surprise. *'I believe I'm much more pleasant, and I can assure you that I am* much *more rewarding.'*

*'You are more pleasant. I'll give you that,'* I replied with a small smile.

*'As much as I enjoy the attention, I probably shouldn't let you get away with neglecting your students.'*

*'One of these days I will take a bite out of you as* payment *for refusing to distract me from such boring tasks,'* Nalithor informed me, sighing as he rose to his feet. He squeezed my shoulder and then moved around the desk to oversee his students. *'Alas, you are right. Keeping this lot from blowing up their homes or countries is rather important...I guess.'*

I fell silent, satisfied that Nalithor's attentions had been redirected for the moment. I returned to observing the class as the surprisingly patient Adinvyr *attempted* to teach his students to control their powers. Darius, and a handful of other students, comprised the group of most fearful students.

Glancing around, I realized that Darius' partner didn't appear to be part of this class. *'Aren't similar mages paired? Why is Vivus in none of my brother's classes?'*

Almost all the students seemed terribly distracted by Nalithor even though his Dauthrmiran-styled robes covered his skin from the throat down. He had also carefully resealed most of his aura upon returning to the city. Nalithor seemed as though he was determined to reduce the amount of unwanted attention he gained for being both an Adinvyr and a deity, but none of his methods seemed to be helping.

"Professor, the crystal cylinders during our exams were meant to represent the ten elements, right?" An Elven student asked, his brow furrowing in confusion.

"That's correct, Edth'y." Nalithor nodded.

"Why were there eleven?" Edth'y frowned. "Is it just to provide more space for powerful mages to spread their power, or something else?"

"Occasionally we discover mages with unusual power," Nalithor began, crossing his arms while he contemplated something. "The cylinders are enchanted with sigils to draw each of the elements from the person being tested. Anomalies such as wood, metal, and most magic appear in response even though they are not accepted as primary elements.

"The practice originated as a way to discover mages who were utilizing forbidden magics, such as Blood Magic, and inadvertently led to the discovery of other types of magic."

Another student leaned forward. "Wouldn't wood and metal magics fall under earth magic?"

"Wood Mages can *only* work with wood and trees." Nalithor shook his head and pivoted to address the second student. "Likewise, Metal Mages can only work with metal. It isn't unusual for them to have control over one of the primary elements alongside, but their affinity for wood or metal allows them to do things an Earth Mage cannot; such as forging permanent blades or armor out of raw metal without the use of a forge."

"As fascinating as this is," I began with an amused smile, "I hope you two didn't bring this topic up in order to distract from your assigned tasks."

Both students turned burgundy. Nalithor shook his head and

sighed at them. I watched while Nalithor paced among the rows of students once more, redirecting each of the students to focus on their control exercises. The ones affiliated with light were incapable of sustaining so much as a pinpoint of it, while the ones allied with darkness couldn't even shape or draw on their own shadow.

Lucky for me, none of the Light or Astral Mages bore the type of presence that made me want to run and hide…but I got the feeling that was due to their poor abilities more than anything else. That, or perhaps Nalithor's dark presence simply overshadowed them all.

*'Control over their magic seems like it isn't the only area they're lacking in,'* I commented after a while, watching as Nalithor's tail twitched in response, though he didn't turn. *'They all want a taste of their teacher, don't they?'*

*'Yes. Well, aside from the few who have been looking at you like you're meat,'* Nalithor muttered. *'My power—'*

*'Your power isn't to blame!'* I laughed. *'You've hidden your aura, your scent, and even your skin, almost completely! You distract them because you're nice on the eyes, Nalithor, and that isn't something so easily hidden.'*

*'Adinvyr or not, deity or not, I'm rather certain their libidos would have this lot distracted regardless.'*

*'You sound terribly amused.'* Nalithor shot me a smirk over his shoulder. *'Nice on the eyes, am I?'*

*'Like you don't know,'* I countered, watching his smirk transform into a broad grin. *'It's almost time to give them their homework and prepare for your next class, isn't it?'*

'*Aye, it is,*' Nalithor replied, turning to approach me and return to his desk. I leaned out of my chair a little, watching the student's reactions. '*I get the feeling you aren't admiring my ass this time.*'

'*This time...?*' I snorted, flushing. '*They just seem...unusually entranced by your tail.*' I bit back a laugh when Nalithor made a sharp flourish with his tail. Most of the students turned scarlet in the face and glanced away as if they'd seen something naughty. '*Oh, I see...*'

'*What is it?*' Nalithor shot me a look, then tugged on my curls and passed me. '*You look like a fox stalking its prey.*'

'"*Prey*" *is all they're good for...*' I murmured, sitting back in my chair. '*They've just recently learned of Adinvyr anatomy, haven't they?*'

'*Anatomy...? Ah...*' Nalithor arched an eyebrow at me before turning his attention to one of the shelves behind his desk. '*You think they are trying to ascertain what manner of things I can do to them with my tail?*'

'*Can you think of another reason for them to be so mesmerized by it?*' I countered, tilting my head. '*That and the fact that you seem to be fond of squeezing me with your tail must have the gears in their heads turning.*'

'*If anyone is going to look at me like* that, *I would prefer it be* you.' Nalithor teased, striding past me once more. '*That said, you should join your brother on his way out. I'd imagine he's at least a little concerned by your prolonged absence.*'

'*The rest of my classes for the afternoon are of the physical variety, if you wish to join me. I'm sure you'd enjoy giving some of the students a good thrashing.*'

'*They'd be too easy!*' I laughed, rising to my feet; though I didn't miss the brief look of disappointment that flashed across Nalithor's face. '*Seeing your frustration with them does have its own appeal though.*'

I shot Nalithor a smirk as I moved out of the classroom and into the hallway to wait for Darius. It wasn't long before the disheartened students filed out. My twin promptly latched onto my arm, his expression firm, and dragged me outside of the academy. He seemed upset about something, but I wasn't sure what.

"Ari! Why did it take so long for you and Nali to come back?" Darius demanded. "Eyrian and the others said the two of you would be a few hours behind, but it's been almost two weeks!"

"Nalithor had business in another part of Abrantia Valley and invited me to hunt with him." I shrugged, turning to look at my twin. "Is *that* why you wanted to speak with me?"

"Nothing happened between you two then?" Darius narrowed his eyes at me, concerned. "You and he didn't fu—"

"Darius," I sighed, clamping my hand over his mouth, "I am far more picky than you are when it comes to such things. Nothing happened between Nalithor and me aside from some good old-fashioned bloodshed.

"There were *a lot* of things to kill."

"If you say so..." Darius grumbled, shooting me a suspicious look. In a matter of seconds, he switched gears and adopted a cheerful grin. "Are you coming to the party tonight, Ari?"

"Party? What party?" I frowned. '*Wait... Don't tell me—*'

"The party to celebrate your successful hunts!" Darius beamed. "Since you played a big role, they decided to wait until you and Nali returned. Everyone but that Elf chick will be there! I hear she got sent home for some reason.

"There'll be food, drink, and lots of hot men! You really should come—"

"She was sent home because she tried to kill me," I stated, causing Darius' eyes to widen. "I don't know about this party, though. It sounds noisy, and I—"

"Nalithor, Eyrian, Xander, and Azhar will all be there!" Darius continued as if I hadn't spoken. "I'm sure they're all quite hungry— and well, *hungry*—after all the fighting you did. Especially Nali, it's been so long after all! You should—"

"Not interested." I dismissed him as an unwanted pang of jealousy stabbed through my heart. Heat rose within my chest in response to the anger that my jealousy made me feel. There was no reason for me to be jealous…but that didn't stop it from happening. I hated it. "I don't share your fascination with their feeding practices, Darius. Now then… Don't you have a class you should be going to?"

Darius sighed heavily and then stalked back into the academy. I shook my head at his back. What a pain in the ass he could be at times. *'He did that on purpose, didn't he? He could have just said he didn't want me to come.'*

Before I could turn and stalk back to our house, Nalithor's arms wrapped around my waist and pulled me back against his chest. His scent filled my senses, but I just shot him an annoyed glare over my shoulder.

"Your brother truly has no tact." Nalithor chuckled. "He certainly did succeed in eliciting a rather nice spike of jealousy from you, my dear, while simultaneously insulting my honor… Quite the feat on his part.

"I do hope you will reconsider the matter of the party, however. I was hoping to convince you to attend as my *date*."

"D-date?" I asked slowly, feeling my face ifnite. I wasn't certain I'd heard him right. Nalithor's mischievous chuckle as he nuzzled my shoulder only made it worse. "Are you seri—"

"Quite serious, my dear." Nalithor purred, giving me a firm squeeze. "I decided that I want exclusive rights to your company for the evening, even though we are *both* expected to join the celebration. Also, I don't intend to 'dine' on *anyone* at the party…though if you decide to offer yourself, I certainly won't object."

"Hmmm…" I pondered for a moment while he nuzzled me again. A smirk crept across my face when I felt him tense. "I'll join you. Be forewarned that I will refuse to share you with any of the other 'guests.'"

"Mmm… *You* won't share *me*?" Nalithor lifted his fingers to my chin, turning my face slightly.

"That's right," I confirmed, adopting a self-satisfied smile in hopes it would do something to hide how flustered I felt. "Djialkan wasn't wrong when he said that I don't like to share *anything*. That goes doubly so if you intend to claim *'exclusive rights'* to my company, Nalithor."

"I'm certainly not complaining." Nalithor chuckled, releasing a roll of power for emphasis. I bit my lip to hold back a shiver. "I will pick you up tonight. Will you still join me for the remainder of today's classes?"

"Sure," I replied with a slight nod. "Let's show the rookies why they're still rookies."

Nalithor grinned down at me, released me, then offered me his arm. After a moment, I accepted and let him lead me to the academy's training areas. More than once I glanced to the side at him as we walked. He had put quite the damper on his power and scent alike. It actually irritated me on some level. Not because he had hidden power, but because he *needed* to hide it.

*'Actually... No. It* is *because he hid it.'* I realized with a small frown. *'His power and scent are both so comforting. I don't like it being diluted.'*

I perched on top of the fence surrounding our designated training field and remained silent as Nalithor approached his waiting students. Most of them attempted to look imposing or 'strong' as the Adinvyr approached them. Smirking to myself, I let a brief spike of power and bloodlust roll over them. Each and every one of them lost their composure in an instant and grew pale.

Nalithor, however, shot me a smirk before returning his attention to the shaken greenlings.

I probably found it more entertaining than I should have to watch

Nalithor deal with the students and their inflated egos. In actuality, he was a very good teacher. However, this particular lot was wearing on his patience fast. Most of them didn't even know how to hold a weapon properly. Nalithor was so incredibly displeased it was almost cute.

"Need some help?" I inquired after quite some time had passed, then smirked as Nalithor's tail switched back and forth a few times.

"You have something in mind?" Nalithor pivoted to look at me, narrowing his eyes.

"They're not going to understand how to hold a weapon unless they actually *hit* something with incorrect grips," I offered. Motioning with my left index finger, I summoned thirty pillars of ice in the training arena. "If they hit these… I think they'll understand quicker, don't you?"

"Learning through experience, hmmm?" Nalithor mused.

"Well if you *really* want to, you can just stand there for another half-hour and correct their grips individually," I spoke with mock innocence. "Or, they could spend a few minutes, at most, smacking these for understanding. If they sprain or break something, either one of us can repair them with ease."

"We'll try it your way," Nalithor replied dryly, turning his sharp gaze to the confused students. "You heard Her Highness! Strike the pillars."

*'Maybe you've suppressed too much of your power. They don't seem like they're taking you seriously,'* I commented, tracking Nalithor as he

approached me and then leaned back on the fence beside me. *'Or…is it normal for the academy greenlings to be so belligerent?'*

*'No, they aren't usually this problematic.'* Nalithor chuckled and slipped an arm around my hips, scooting me closer to him. *'You look like you're considering lecturing them as you did with your brother.'*

*'It's either that or I leave you with uncooperative students.'* I motioned at the academy clock tower. *'I'm not going to dinner in* this *after all.'*

*'You have that scheming look to you again,'* Nalithor remarked, moving to stand in front of me. He rested his hands on the beam to either side of my hips and smirked. *'Should I be concerned, my dear?'*

*'Only if you think someone in Dauthrmir actually has a chance of competing against you,'* I replied innocently, returning his smirk. *'For now, though… I can't exactly get up with you blocking my way, now can I?'*

*'I was considering stealing another kiss.'* Nalithor chuckled at me. *'Very well, I'll let you scamper off. Reining in this bunch shouldn't be an issue.'*

Nalithor took a step back and then returned to his unruly and whining students, allowing me to slide off my perch. While making my way back to the house, I realized that I was *disappointed*, of all things, that Nalithor had chosen against kissing me. *'Was he…was he teasing me?'*

# CHAPTER TWO
### A Questionable Outing

*'Damn it, where did I put them?'* I chewed on my lower lip while overturning my room in search of hair ornaments. *'I know I didn't leave them in Abrantia... Where the hells are they?!'*

Thankfully, I had made it back to the house before Darius, so I was able to bathe and get dressed in peace. I knew *exactly* what I wanted to wear to the party, and had decided that getting a reaction out of Nalithor far outweighed the headache my twin would give me for wearing such a seductive dress. If the ensemble didn't draw Nalithor's interest, it'd be a strong sign for me to move on.

I had considered, for all of maybe thirty seconds, wearing something that wasn't black. However, it was just too perfect for me to pass up. The contrast with my skin was nice, but that wasn't the only reason I chose it. The thing that made the dress stand out most to me were the lace panels running down either side of the plunging neckline. My nipples were hidden by the pattern of the lace, while the rest of my skin peeked through here and there. The wrist-length sleeves were the same black lace, but the rest of the bodice and flowing skirt were solid black satin.

*"You are going to give them a heart attack and more if you insist on wearing that,"* Djialkan commented dryly from his perch, watching me search my vanity. *"If you put your hair up, he will steal your hair sticks."*

Alala warbled her agreement, causing me to turn and shoot them both a disgruntled glare.

"I'm not going to put *all* of my hair up," I grumbled, rummaging around in the back of the drawer. Upon finding them, I pulled them out and splayed them between my fingers with a triumphant grin. "Just some of—

"Hey! Give those back!"

*"You may have them back when you return tonight."* Djialkan snorted and flew out of the window with my hair sticks clamped in his mouth. *"Do try not to get into too much 'trouble' with the Adinvyr?"*

I shot a scowl after Djialkan and then turned back to my vanity with a heavy sigh. Alala's warbling made it sound like she was laughing at me, and I wouldn't have been surprised if that was the case. Although I still couldn't communicate with her through telepathy or speech, she'd been underfoot and making happy-sounding noises almost constantly since my return to Dauthrmir.

In all honesty, I hadn't thought I would be wearing anything other than mages' robes for another few months at least—if ever. Even though almost two weeks had passed since the beast shredded my mask, even *thinking* about leaving my room without a mask and hood struck me as strange. It wasn't until my mask was destroyed that I truly realized that such things had become security blankets for me. With them, I could hide my emotions and reactions from most people. However, without them…

I shook my head and then leaned toward the mirror, painting my lips a deep scarlet. After applying sultry makeup around my eyes, I decided the look was finished, and slid my feet into black satin high heels. I rose to my feet and readjusted my dress to make sure everything was in place, then made my way to the door.

Darius had been home for nearly an hour, if the sounds of movement downstairs were anything to go by. It seemed likely that he would be ready soon, and he was in for a shock when he realized *why* I was wearing such a provocative dress. I smirked to myself as I neared the staircase. My brother was going to be *so* frustrated.

"Oh, Ari, so you *are*…home…" Darius blinked up at me as I descended the stairs. "I thought you weren't going to the party? And…you're wearing that? Isn't it a little—"

"I received an invitation I couldn't refuse." I brushed my hair over one shoulder and shot Darius a sly smile. "If you're ready you can go ahead without me."

"An invitation you couldn't refuse?" Darius' face wrinkled in confusion, then he pointed at my chest. "Is it really appropriate for you to wear something like *that*?"

"The lace hides what it needs to hide." I shrugged and glanced down at my breasts. "*I* think I look quite nice."

"How have you adapted so quickly to Vorpmasian ways?" Darius sighed, grabbing me by the shoulders. "You seem like you're fitting in with them so well already—and wearing a dress like *that* you look like one of them. But you're *not* one of—"

"You're over-thinking it, Darius. I'm just combat-oriented like they are." I shook my head at him. "I get along with the ones who are hunters or warriors like myself, and I have no interest in the ones who aren't. Most of the ones *you* get along with are probably healers, politicians, and other types of non-combat mages, right?"

Darius opened his mouth to protest but I ignored him and moved away to pull a long brocade coat on over my dress. I fastened the silvery clasps all the way up to my throat, earning another confused look from my twin. I met his look with a mischievous grin. Before Darius could think of something else to say, the doorbell rang and he took off at a run down the hall, mumbling something about fetching his coat.

I did my best to stifle my amusement before making my way to the foyer to answer the door.

*"Ari, wait for me!"* Darius yelled from deep within the house as I opened the door to reveal Nalithor.

The Adinvyr released an amused chuckle as he looked down at me, his tail swishing as he took a moment to examine me.

"Going to make me wait to see what's underneath?" Nalithor teased, reaching up to tug at the high collar of my coat.

"Oh, Nali!" Darius exclaimed from behind me. I had to bite back my laughter as Nalithor pulled me from the doorway and to his side. "You're... *Ari*, you didn't tell me that your invitation was from *Nalithor*."

"I'm her *date*," Nalithor corrected, chuckling when my brother mouthed a few times.

"Date?" Darius' expression cycled through anger, jealousy, and confusion before settling into a frown. "Why a date when you could just fuck—"

"One of these days, Darius, you will understand that the *chase* is half the fun," Nalithor interrupted. "Furthermore, most Adinvyr don't just *bed* whatever strikes their fancy. We can be quite particular, I'll have you know."

"I don't understand. What's the point in *dating* or *courting* when you can have as many people as you want in your bed?" Darius huffed, exasperated. I just laughed in response, though Nalithor twitched.

"Do you truly think that a race known for jealousy and possessiveness would want to engage in frivolous relationships?" Nalithor countered in disbelief, confusing my poor twin even further. "Even those of my kind who desire more than one lover *do not* do so lightly. I will see to it that cultural classes are added to your workload. It appears that your knowledge of Devillian cultures is still just as lacking as your knowledge of Below.

"Shall we, Arianna?"

"Ari, you're really going in *that*?!" Darius yelped.

"Then you really *do* have something interesting hidden under your coat," Nalithor mused, looking down at me as he led me away from the house. "Your *dear* brother seems quite distressed."

"The question is what he's distressed *by*. My attire, or because his *favorite* teacher is giving me his undivided attention?" I countered innocently, earning a fang-filled grin from Nalithor.

The sound of fast-approaching footsteps from behind us made me turn slightly to listen.

"So wait, are you like," Darius began as he dashed in front of us, then started walking backward so he could face us, "her *date-date*, or just her escort since you two've been working together?"

"To put it bluntly…" Nalithor shot my brother a haughty look. "Arianna belongs to *me* for the evening."

"*B-belongs*?!" Darius yelped as my face ignited. "But she's a *girl* in case you haven't noticed! Wouldn't you rather have a man in your—"

"Arianna is a *woman*, firstly," Nalithor corrected my twin, his tone frigid. He coiled his tail around my waist and gave Darius a dangerous look. "Were she not, then I would have no interest. I have no interest in men, and even less interest in *boys* like yourself. I do, however, have *plenty* of interest in your sister here. Was *that* clear enough for you?"

Darius made a noise somewhere between a huff and an indignant shriek, whirled around, and stormed off through the streets of Dauthrmir without us. I almost couldn't contain my laughter, so I redirected my attention to my date instead. "He won't believe you for long. If everyone else reacts to my attire the way Darius did, I may just have to wear my coat all night."

"You are a tease." Nalithor laughed, squeezing me. "That you're in *heels* already piqued my curiosity *before* seeing how flustered Darius is. Between my interest and the chill in the air tonight, I think it's in our best interest to be on our way. Shall we?"

"Sure, let's go." I grinned. "I'm not so cruel as to make you wait unnecessarily."

Nalithor chuckled and led me through the city once more. Although he'd released his tail's grip on me, one of his arms stayed around my waist in a possessive fashion. I didn't mind being tucked up against his side as we walked, though some of the looks and greetings shot our way flustered me. Nalithor expertly deflected the calls and beckoning of the citizens we passed, sometimes going as far as to shield me from view when questionable individuals tried to wander too close.

*'I guess it's a good thing I wore a coat, if all the attention we're getting is any indication,'* I commented as we approached a building that was at least five stories tall, and near the Scarlet District. Lavender lanterns and a myriad of blooming foliage surrounded the lacquered building, hiding much of it from the street's view. *'Oh? Draemiran cuisine again?'*

*'You sound eager.'* Nalithor smiled, pulling me past the thick wall of hedges that lined the property. *'I hope your attire will allow you to kneel at the table with us. At least this time there will be plusher cushions*

*available.'*

*'I like Draemiran food and drink.'* I pouted at him, earning a low chuckle. *'As for the seats, I will be fine. I can slip off my shoes if need be.'*

"Welcome, Nalithor-y'ric, Arianna-z'tar." A Rylthra man bowed and slid the doors open for us. "Your party is waiting in your usual room, Nalithor-y'ric."

Nalithor nodded to the dark-haired Rylthra and escorted me to a small lift that carried us to the fifth floor. I caught the sound of our waiting comrades and my indignant brother as we strode down the hallway. My companion shook his head, an amused smile playing on his face, and then slid the door of the room open, motioning for me to enter first.

"There you two are!" Eyrian grinned at us when we entered. "I was wondering if there'd been a change of plans since Darius came on ahead."

"I just don't understand why *she* is his *date!*" Darius snapped, shooting the Draekin a glare. "Ari, keep your coat on!"

"I won't allow it." Nalithor shook his head, tracking me as I moved to the coat rack on our left. I began undoing the clasps as I walked, noting that the Adinvyr was watching my movements with more care than usual. "My own selfish reasons aside, it is much too warm in here for a coat—let alone one as heavy as she's wearing."

I smirked, watching Nalithor hang up his coat. He wore dark brocade clothing in the Draemiran style as per usual, leaving a portion of his torso exposed before the cloth met and tucked into an armored waistband. It was quite similar to kimonos I had seen him wear in the past, but there was something...*courtly*...about this one.

Nalithor looked much like he was stalking prey as he tracked my movements. Perhaps some people, like my brother, would have been intimidated by his intensity. I found it amusing. Nalithor's startled expression and *blushing*, of all things, when I slipped my coat off my shoulders made the effort I'd put into my appearance well worth it. He remained silent and just watched me for a moment as I hung up my coat.

"I can always put my coat back on if you don't like it," I teased.

"Definitely *not* necessary." Nalithor closed the distance between us and smoothed his palms down my sides and to my hips, then shot a glare somewhere over my head. "Darius, I should *eviscerate you* for suggesting she hide this from me."

"B-but it's so inappropriate!" Darius protested, continuing to stutter as Nalithor led me to our seats.

"Looking like...*that*..." Eyrian gaped, flushing scarlet. After a moment he yanked his eyes away from me and looked at Nalithor with a dangerous glint in his eyes. "I'm tempted to challenge you for her myself."

"Ahhh... Which *reminds* me." Nalithor smirked, watching me perch on the cushion beside him. Once I was settled, Nalithor released the seals on his power and shot a sideways look at Eyrian. "Do you *still* want to challenge me, Eyrian?"

"Tch, even I'm not stupid enough to get between an Adinvyr and his prey!" Eyrian snorted, raising his hands in defeat.

*'Prey, hmmm?'* I arched an eyebrow at Nalithor.

*'I am inclined to agree with him now that I've seen what you decided to tease me with.'* Nalithor shook his head. *'How am I supposed to be a gentleman and keep my hands to myself when you look so* appetizing?'

"Is it really appropriate for you to wrap your tail around her like that?" Darius demanded from his seat across the table.

I had to bite the inside of my cheek to keep myself from laughing when Nalithor growled at Darius. My brother's lack of a response to the aggressive sound made it even more difficult to suppress my amusement. A quick glance around the table revealed the others felt much the same, aside from Vivus—he looked more upset with Darius than anything.

"I'm sure my *date* can decide for herself whether or not it's appropriate," Nalithor countered, glaring at Darius. An involuntary twitch shot through him when I made a show of running my fingertips and nails along the hot scales of his tail. *'Tsk, tsk, tsk. What am I going to do with you?'*

*'With a smirk like that?'* I inquired, watching him pour a cup of tea for me. *'I think the better question is what you* don't *want to do to me.'*

*'I assure you that my thoughts are…mostly appropriate,'* Nalithor offered, a hint of color rising to his face again as he offered me my tea. *'I should say that, at the moment, I'm more* triumphant *than anything.'*

*'Ah yes, I suppose I've indulged you once again, haven't I?'* A small smile crept across my lips as I accepted the drink from him. I took a

brief sip and then set it down, deciding to let it cool further. It seemed likely we would be here for a while.

'*You really are quite beautiful, you know,*' Nalithor commented, causing my face to burn scarlet in response to both his blunt compliment *and* his warm smile. '*I'm going to have to make sure I don't lose sight of you. Xander looks as though he's already plotting to take a bite out of you, and I can't have that.*'

'*That's…probably more pleasant than what my brother is thinking about doing to* you, *at least.*' I shot him a sly look. '*I can't say I blame him, though. You can be quite distracting.*'

'*Me? Distracting?*' Nalithor laughed, pulling me closer to his side. '*How does that work, exactly? You're still not affected by my power.*'

'*You're attractive and you smell good. That's plenty to make you distracting,*' I replied, resisting the urge to roll my eyes. '*The regal attire and exposed skin exacerbate the matter of course… As do those smirks of yours.*'

"Okay, Ari, what do I have to do to get you to let me have him?" Darius demanded, pointing at Nalithor. "Obviously you cast some sort of spell on him to make him—"

"Why should I *let* you have him?" I interjected, shifting on the cushions so that I could slip one arm behind Nalithor's back and placed my free hand on Nalithor's lower abdomen. "It would be rather rude of me to *let* someone he *doesn't want* have him, don't you think?"

'*And you called* me *a scoundrel.*' Nalithor chuckled as I rested my cheek against his chest. He seemed amused, and took the opportunity

31

to coil more of his tail around my hips, then rested his left hand on my thigh. *'Not that I'm complaining, mind you. I could certainly get used to this.'*

"I *want* him!" Darius protested. "Get your hands off him! If you don't agree, I'll kick you out of the house!"

*'He thinks* that *is a valid argument?'* Nalithor shook his head.

"Mmm…too bad. Mine." I dismissed my brother's protests and rubbed my cheek against Nalithor's chest, listening to the rumble of his chuckle as his tail tightened around me. "Or…are you going to *challenge* me again, Darius?"

Darius and the others froze in place with wide eyes when I released a ripple of intermingled power and bloodlust. Despite their fear, Nalithor seemed to approve. He let out a throaty laugh and stroked my thigh, his fingers dancing in just *barely* an acceptable area. I found it *very* distracting, but not at all unpleasant.

"Whether you kick her out or not doesn't matter," Nalithor began, his voice full of amusement while my brother grew angrier at each consecutive pet. "Your lodgings are temporary, and you have been told this time and time again. You and Vivus will be relocated soon, as will Arianna. If you kick her out prematurely…I will simply take her under my wing since I intend to make her my partner anyway.

"Aside from that… You have already challenged Arianna once before, Darius. You know that she can and *will* wipe the floor with you, and that she doesn't even have to lift a finger to do it."

"Darius-*zir*, this is supposed to be a *celebration* of successful hunts," Eyrian added, clamping a hand on Darius' shoulder and narrowing his eyes. "If you can't accept that Arianna is Nalithor's date, your choices are challenge her…or shut your mouth and sit down. You were invited because you're her brother. If you aren't going to act like it, I will be happy to remove you—if Nalithor doesn't beat me to it."

*'Ahhh… I'm glad you're so different from your twin,'* Nalithor mused, walking his fingers along my thigh. *'I do hope you realize that I'm not going to let you out of this position any time soon, my dear.'*

*'You do seem to enjoy the attention,'* I commented dryly, before glancing to the side at my silently fuming brother. *'At this point I'm almost certain that Darius would've been furious regardless of what I wore.'*

*'I enjoy* your *attention,'* Nalithor correct me with a purr. *'That said, I hope you aren't just trying to rile up that* boy.*'*

*'The answer to that should be rather obvious.'* I huffed, shifting to look up at Nalithor. *'I don't have to do or even* say *anything to rile Darius up when it comes to you. I could sit still, keep my hands to myself, and remain silent all night…and he would still attempt to wrest you away from my "shameful influence."*

*'Besides, it would be rather insulting to treat a warrior*—let alone my date—*in such a reprehensible fashion.'*

"Didn't you say she's *yours* for the night, Nalithor? Not the other way around?" Darius inquired, his brow wrinkled with confusion. "If you're *really* a dominant, doesn't that mean she's way out of line?"

*'He genuinely doesn't understand?'* Nalithor paused, his hand resting

fully on my upper thigh. *'Or do both of you—'*

*'Darius was almost* never *allowed outside the palace,'* I offered, shifting to fetch my tea. *'X'shmiran novels are just as poorly informed as our educational literature. However... There isn't exactly anything in our culture comparable to what* he *is thinking about. I would wager that Darius has been mulling over romance novels in our absence instead of his textbooks and schoolwork.'*

"If he were to own her, she would own him," Xander spoke oh-so-helpfully, pointing at my brother. The Vampire grinned when Darius turned scarlet. "And that's *assuming* they wanted the kind of relationship *you're* thinking about. Not everyone 'Below' wants to have such a—"

"Darius, at this rate you're going to have so many classes to attend and so many books to read that you won't have time for *anything* else!" I interjected before the conversation could wander further. "Whether or not you 'understand' is irrelevant. We're here for good drink, good food, and pleasant company—right?"

*'Just give up already!'* I kept my thoughts private, settling a firm glare on my brother. *'Even if Nalithor liked us both... There's no way in the hells I will share him. I refuse.'*

"But..." Darius frowned, his gaze shifting over my head and to Nalithor. "Nalithor, you're an Adinvyr. If you wanted her, couldn't you just 'charm' her, or whatever it is your race does? Assuming you at least want to feed from her or bed her—"

I released a small sigh. As usual, fucking seemed to be the only thing my brother cared about. It was like any other possibility vacated his thick skull—especially when it came to Nalithor, for some reason. No matter how far back I searched my memory, I couldn't recall a time when I'd seen Darius so dead-set on 'obtaining' a specific individual before. *'Does Nalithor's power as an Adinvyr affect my brother? Or is something else going on?'*

"Arianna is immune to the 'charms' of an Adinvyr. I have to earn her attentions the hard way, as it were." Nalithor chuckled and picked me up by the waist, startling a yelp out of me as he settled me in his lap. "As for what I would like to *do* to her... Well, first is the matter of releasing whatever seals are keeping her in this Human form. I'm rather certain I would *break* her otherwise. Quite literally."

"B-break?" Darius choked on his drink, both of us turning scarlet. Though, I had to stifle my laughter when I spotted *his* priceless expression. "Fine, fine! I give up. I'm going to need a *lot* more drinks now after *that*. Thanks."

*'Not going to run away?'* Nalithor teased, wrapping his arms around my waist and pulling me back against his chest.

*'It doesn't seem necessary,'* I replied with a small smile. *'However, I have to admit that I'm a little concerned that Darius is this upset. Threatening to kick me out of the house is questionable. Even for him.*

*'Ah! Before I get sidetracked though, I wanted to ask you if there's any way I can help with studying the samples you collected from the beasts.'*

Nalithor leaned down to nuzzle my shoulder, his tone curious, *'You would like to help? Ahhh... We have been procrastinating about teaching each other as well, haven't we? A week and a half mostly to ourselves, yet...'*

*'Well I* am *supposed to provide you with information about X'shmir and its beasts,'* I replied, biting back a whimper when Nalithor's fangs grazed the side of my throat.

*'Mmm... I'll make you a deal then.'* Nalithor let out a playful laugh and straightened himself. *'After you've submitted to the remainder of your medical examinations, you're welcome to come find me—wherever it is I happen to be working.'*

*'Humph... Better not be any needles involved,'* I grumbled, pouting. A twitch ran through me as Nalithor smoothed his hands over my thighs, prompting me to shoot him a look over my shoulder. *'You really* are *enjoying this too much, aren't you?'*

*'A* normal *woman would be a quivering mess on the floor by now,'* Nalithor informed me, his tone a little too serious. *'I think you underestimate just how strongly my kind affects their prey.'*

"Ari, have you figured out where you're going to work?" Darius inquired out of the blue. "I found this cute little bar that's hiring, we should both—"

"I'm not sure if I'm suited for something that doesn't involve killing things," I pointed out with a small frown, attempting to tune out Nalithor's laughter. "Granted, I suppose neither of us are truly suited for work."

"I don't think we're *that* bad." Darius pouted.

"I'm sure there are plenty of people in Dauthrmir who would be willing to *train* you," Nalithor commented casually. Something about his tone made Darius and I both turn brilliant red, and I bristled.

"You're having too much fun, Nali." Eyrian pointed at Nalithor, drink in hand.

"Oh, that reminds me!" Darius flashed me a bright grin and leaned forward in his seat. "What were your results for the DSO test, Ari? You never told me."

"Still not telling," I muttered, crossing my arms.

Several of our companions shot me questioning looks, so I just 'humphed' and glanced away.

"I still think you must have tested as an alpha female," Darius pointed out, causing me to burst into laughter. "What? Are you saying that *isn't* the case?"

"Someone being an 'alpha' doesn't mean what you seem to *think* it means, Darius." Azhar snorted in disbelief, finally breaking his prolonged silence. "She can be an alpha *and* a slave. It is not unusual for two alphas to—"

"*Pet*," Nalithor corrected with a growl, causing me to glance over my shoulder at him again. He grinned at me and added, "I like the term 'pet' better than 'slave.' It suits my tastes more accurately and does not carry the same negative weight as 'slave' has come to carry in the common tongue."

"So, Nali, you're a 'pet' then, right?" Darius's blunt question made me almost choke on my tea. My poor brother was even more oblivious than I thought.

"Quite the opposite." Nalithor chuckled. He raised a hand to my throat and squeezed gently, summoning darkness around it. "I think *this one* would make an *excellent* pet, however."

"You haven't earned the right to collar me yet!" I barked as Nalithor nuzzled into the right side of my throat. His lips curled into a grin against my skin as he chuckled.

"'*Yet?*'" Nalithor purred before flicking his tongue up my neck, then nibbled on my earlobe. '*Your inner Adinvyr is showing again.*'

'*Even if I couldn't hear your heartbeat, I can certainly feel it.*' He paused to run one of his claws down the left side of my throat. '*All things considered, I'm rather surprised you can keep your thoughts tame.*'

I suppressed a shiver. '*At least I can't claim you're boring. Still…this isn't conducive to ordering dinner, let alone having it.*'

'*Perhaps I should have* you *for dinner,*' Nalithor teased, even as he loosened his grip on me and let his hand fall from my throat. '*You really are going to be a fun chase, aren't you?*'

"How was your hunt in Ceilail?" Eyrian spoke up, drawing Nalithor's attention from me. "You were gone for so long I thought I'd have to come bail you two out myself. Were there more beasts than our contacts implied?"

"Ah… No." Nalithor shook his head, his gaze flicking to my brother briefly and then to Eyrian. "The situation worsened while we were on our way to the forest; I had to fly us both there in order to stop our prey before they could leave. As such—"

"You *flew?*" Eyrian sighed, holding his fingers to his temples for a moment. "That was reckless, Nalithor, even for us! What would you have done if you were unable to move after?"

"I'm quite certain the feisty one here could have handled our prey by herself had the situation called for it." Nalithor interjected with a chuckle, ruffling my hair. "Arianna destroyed the beasts herself, allowing me to focus solely on our prey and rescues. She was still raring to go even after I let her have so much of our—"

"*Let* me?" I shot him a look. "I would have *taken* them from you if you pushed me."

"You could try." Nalithor smirked.

"I would succeed." I crossed my arms.

"As I was saying," Nalithor laughed, "after our prey were dealt with, my energy was spent. We remained in the forest while I regained my strength, and ended up having to deal with some other matters while there. You'll learn of them when I get to make my full report."

Eyrian settled a challenging gaze on Nalithor for a moment, but the Adinvyr clearly wouldn't budge. Nalithor glanced toward my brother again and then back to Eyrian, earning a small sigh from the Draekin. Eyrian looked disappointed, but nodded his head and muttered something in a language I didn't recognize.

*'Didn't you report in this morning?'* I prodded the back of one of Nalithor's hands as it crept up my leg.

*'Our time was limited, I only managed to give them a briefing before I had to make my way to the academy,'* Nalithor replied, giving me a brief squeeze with his tail. *'He's unhappy that he didn't get to join us. I usually take the time to regale him of the details when I hunt without him,*

*so he's cross that I haven't yet done so—and that I claimed you for myself tonight.'*

*'If Darius wasn't here—'*I started, but Nalithor just shook his head.

*'We can't rightfully ask him to leave unless he makes a scene again.'* Nalithor lifted me off his lap and set me to the side, shooting me a small smile. *'Eyrian and I have been friends for a long time. He never stays cross with me for long, and I'll soon have my opportunity to fill him in. Don't worry.'*

"So, you said you 'let' her deal with the beasts?" Eyrian tilted his head to the side, looking at me for a moment then back to Nalithor. "That's unlike you."

"*He* would have become my prey if he'd interfered," I pointed out, causing the Draekin to arch an eyebrow at me. "Unlike you lot, I've always hunted alone. I don't like to share. My prey is *my prey*, and anyone that interferes can expect—"

"She is more than capable of handling herself," Nalithor interjected dryly, nudging me. *'Are you ever satisfied, my dear? You should permit me to help with that.'*

*'Cheeky.'* I shot him a look.

"Isn't hunting scary, though?" Darius frowned at us. "The beasts in X'shmir are huge, and they're so dangerous! Are the beasts on the Rilzaan Continent weaker, or are Devillians truly just that accustomed to battle?"

"For mortals, certainly," Azhar murmured, gripping his chin in thought. "Elves have some chance against the lesser beasts, as do

Humans—if they outnumber the beasts. Both are useless against the more powerful Duxes. We haven't fought enough X'shmiran beasts to know, yet, whether one is stronger than the other."

"A hundred mortals wouldn't stand a chance against a single Dux," Xander added, likely having noticed Darius' confusion. "Both empires typically utilize demigods—such as Eyrian, Azhar, and I—against Duxes. If the situation is desperate, the empires will send an army of mortals to deal with a Dux, but we avoid it best as possible.

"All that aside, I think we need to get a few more drinks in you if you're still thinking about serious things."

"That's an idea I can get behind!" Eyrian grinned, lifting his tankard.

*Now, now, no pouting.* Nalithor chuckled, brushing a stray curl off my shoulder. *You're still a little drained from helping Ceilail, and fighting the beasts... You should relax. Get to know our companions, make friends...or lavish me with attention. I certainly won't complain if you decide to focus on* me *for the evening.*

*I'm sure you get more than enough attention as it is.* I shook my head at him.

*Not from anyone as interesting as you.* Nalithor chuckled. *Truly, Arianna. You needn't be so guarded while in the city. Enjoy yourself.*

*Hunting* is *how I enjoy myself,* I pointed out, glancing to the side at him as he sighed. *I'm not accustomed to the company of other people, but I will try. Just hope a beast doesn't wander near.*

*If a beast* does *draw near... We can see who kills it first.*

Several hours later I sunk into the steaming bath at my house and released a shaky sigh. Once Darius' had settled down, and consumed more drinks, dinner had been quite pleasant. Eyrian, Xander, and Azhar seemed like interesting people, but I wasn't quite sure how to converse with them. Any attempt at conversation on my part usually involved killing beasts, and those three seemed to view that as 'work.'

*Nalithor*, however, had been…testing. All night. There had been little serious conversation between us, and an *incredible* amount of teasing on his part throughout dinner and after. It was like he was trying to determine what it would take for his power to affect me. The Adinvyr was proficient at dancing the line between inappropriate and not.

Despite my supposed 'immunity' to him, I was so damned aroused I could barely think straight.

*'I can't believe I almost invited him back to…'* I crossed my arms on the edge of the bath and buried my face in them, shutting my eyes. I had to calm down. *'My bloodlust and physical lust are getting worse. I'm starting to think those "inner Adinvyr" jokes of his aren't jokes at all.*

*'How am I supposed to take care of this problem when every damned Adinvyr in the city can probably sense my thoughts if I—'*

I twitched, losing my train of thought when I recalled the sensation of his lips traveling along the side of my throat. The sensation of fingers trailing down my spine made me tense and check to make sure I was still alone. Since coming Below I'd scarcely felt him reaching out to me in such a manner, but now it was even more distracting. I shivered and dug my nails into my arm hard enough to draw blood, growling in frustration.

My desire was spiraling out of control. I wanted to call Nalithor back to my rooms and have him pin me to the nearest surface. The mere *thought* of having him buried inside of me sent another shudder through me and elicited a whimper.

Shrieking my frustration, I stalked through the water and headed for the steps leading out of the bath. I couldn't take it anymore, I had to do *something* about my arousal before I lost my damned mind or the Adinvyr's wandering power lured me into his clutches. There was no way I could function like this, and I was beyond caring if every Adinvyr in the city noticed my lust-driven thoughts.

Something had to be done, and my instincts screamed that calling on Nalithor didn't seem like the right move.

# CHAPTER THREE
*Demands*

"Nalithor, do you have anything to add about the X'shmiran princess?" Lucifer narrowed his eyes at me. "Eyrian, Xander, and Azhar all reported that her desire for bloodshed is unlike anything they've seen from a Human before. You had the opportunity to work with her for longer, so what are your observations?"

"'X'shmiran' princess, huh?" I leaned back in my seat and glanced at the ceiling for a moment. "I know neither of you believe that. Even for a second."

Eyrian tensed, but Lucifer just continued to look at me with an expectant expression. I wanted nothing more than to leave our morning meeting and go find the princess in question, but I knew better than to shirk my duties...especially when her father appeared cross with me. Sighing, I shifted in my seat to lean on one arm rest. Without a word, I summoned a barrier around the throne room and then settled my gaze on Lucifer, waiting.

"Leave us," Lucifer spoke, turning to look at the members of the Imperial Guard who waited by the door. "Eyrian will inform you when you may return."

"Nalithor?" Eyrian glanced at me, tilting his head slightly.

I gave them an unamused glare. "Both of you can dispense with the 'X'shmiran' drivel."

"You're the one claiming she was a fake." Eyrian snorted, crossing his arms at me.

"And yet she can speak to both Onyre and Aleri," I reminded him. "And the Elders didn't recognize her—not as *her*, not as a fake."

"*Them...*" Lucifer muttered with distaste. "What do you mean *the Elders* didn't recognize her? I know you aren't so foolish as to bring her to them yourself."

"They stopped us on our way to Ceilail, thinking that'd I'd decided on a Chosen without informing them." I raised a hand to calm the fuming emperor. "*They* offered to find Djialkan a new ward... Needless to say, he didn't take to it kindly. He told Arianna, who told me, that Djialkan didn't 'recognize these gods.' I'm to understand that he's consulted Onyre and Aleri on the matter.

"To address your original question, Arianna is a whirlwind of death. She lives and breathes for battle. Even when she was injured, or otherwise weakened, I had a difficult time convincing her to give herself time to rest and heal. Her bloodlust is something else entirely."

Eyrian frowned at me. "Even when we were children, we rarely saw the princess ever *truly* weakened."

I sighed, slumping back in my chair. Even if I didn't want to do it, I had to let them know what happened with Ceilail—and the part Arianna had played in freeing the Lari'xan. It was unlike anything we had seen from her when she was a child in Dauthrmir.

That sort of power and blind instincts were something I would have expected out of…myself. I should have been able to sense that something that dangerous was out of balance, yet I'd been oblivious.

The next hour, to my displeasure, was spent giving them a detailed account of the past two weeks.

"Have the Oracles assign Arianna as my partner," I spoke up after giving them time to process the information I'd given them about Ceilail. "No one else is—"

"You know damn well she should be *my* partner." Eyrian growled, clenching his fists. "Had she not been taken by those bastards—"

"Eyrian would be in charge of Arianna's personal army, while you would be in charge of the Imperial Guard, Nalithor." Lucifer finished as Eyrian trailed off into a slew of curses. "Enough, both of you. I won't have you brawling over *my daughter* in the throne room. You have both been like sons to me. I won't have you tearing each other apart.

"Nalithor, you know as well as I do that the Oracles won't just *let* you claim Arianna as your partner. They're far too cross with you, and you've resisted a partner for *decades*. Nor are her results in. Be patient.

"Eyrian, *you* know that times have changed. Nalithor is bound by his status as a god—he can't enter my service as a member of the Imperial Guard. That the Elders permitted him to remain a general is already a minor miracle. We shouldn't push them further, especially knowing their...'distaste' for Arianna. Nalithor, at least, has a chance to protect her if the Elders move against her—the same cannot be said for you, Eyrian."

"Oracles be damned," I muttered, shaking my head. "There aren't many Devillians who would be able to work with her, Lucifer. Eyrian stands a chance, perhaps, but I can't think of anyone else who *might* be able to stand their ground against Arianna's wrath."

"What of other Adinvyr?" Eyrian shot me an odd look. "I know you said that she's resistant to *your* power, but..."

"My concern is that other people won't be able to resist *her* power." I shook my head. "You felt her combined rage and excitement when we first went to Abrantia, yes? What she emitted upon sensing the beasts and slavers in Ceilail was many times that. Even I was almost swept away by her bloodlust—had I been, the slavers might have been able to slip away. She cleared the beasts out by herself in half an hour, perhaps less."

"Her powers haven't waned after all this time?" Lucifer murmured, stroking his chin. "I will speak with the Oracles and make certain they're not planning to partner Arianna with someone weak. It wouldn't do for her to enthrall anyone—even if temporarily—and especially if the Oracles attempt to partner her with a Beshulthien.

"Now, what of Darius? He *is* in several of yours classes, is he not?"

"Something strikes me as strange about the boy, but I can't determine what," I answered after a moment of thought. "He's selfish, certainly, but I feel that we're missing something. I struggle to believe that his experiences in X'shmir are solely responsible for his behavior or his fears."

"It's odd that his tests came back as *worse*," Eyrian added, nodding his agreement. "Xander didn't know what to make of it. He said that Darius *felt* powerful when they tested the boy's power again, but the results the equipment gave them were far removed from how the boy made the Archmagi present feel."

"If you are both comfortable with Arianna's intentions, and ability to protect herself, I think it's time we have our spies shift to look after Darius." Lucifer shifted in his seat, looking between Eyrian and I. "We are agreed that we should keep their identities quiet for now?"

"Of course." Eyrian nodded. "We still need to wait before Nalithor can make good on his promise to conquer X'shmir. Considering the Elders' strange behavior, and past actions, it's best we keep this information to ourselves for now.

"Are we certain we shouldn't assign Her Highness a protective detail? At the very least—"

I laughed, shaking my head. "She'd probably slay them herself if we tried. I want to keep her safe as well, Eyrian, but she's even more headstrong than we remember. Arianna has acted as a solitary huntress for too long. It will take some work before we can convince her to accept a partner, I feel, let alone help her relax enough to make friends."

"Make friends?" Eyrian arched an eyebrow at me. "You sure you aren't plotting to keep her away from everyone? *Again?*"

"Give me *some* credit." I shot him a glare. "She *needs* people in her life. You've seen her at dinner twice now—she doesn't know what to do with herself when she's in pleasant company."

"She's been alone for too long." Lucifer sighed, his expression one of sadness. "I expect the two of you to keep an eye on her. We may not be able to move against X'shmir yet, but at the very least we can make sure there aren't too many prying eyes around Arianna. I'll make sure Xander understands he isn't to say anything to the Beshulthiens about Arianna's identity."

After I finished regaling Lucifer and Eyrian both with the details of my extended stay in Abrantia, I made my way through the palace with the Draekin alongside. I could already sense Arianna's presence moving around in the Sapphire Quarter, along with her growing irritation, but it didn't look like Eyrian was done with me yet.

"What changed your mind?" Eyrian nudged me. "You seemed unmovable, yet now you're just…accepting it?"

"Wouldn't it be more foolish for me to accept it without question?" I countered, coming to a stop. "We shouldn't talk about this here. Suffice to say… I can't bring myself to try fooling myself any longer. If we're somehow *wrong*…"

"Tch, it'd be kinda impressive if we're wrong." Eyrian ran a hand back through his hair. "That bloodlust is unmistakable, but I never thought I'd see the day where she turned it against her brother."

"I can agree with you there," I murmured, crossing my arms. "You're going to go give the spies their new orders?"

"Aye. Lucifer is right—we need to keep an eye on him." Eyrian nodded, grimacing. "He just…doesn't make sense. There haven't been any further assassination attempts, but I get the feeling it has more to do with Arianna's absence than anything. Those blubbering fools still haven't talked aside from ranting about how 'the Evil Mage must die.'"

"Wonderful." I snorted. "Keep me informed."

"You're going to go hunt the princess?" Eyrian narrowed his eyes at me, tensing.

"Learning more about the beasts should serve as a good excuse to keep an eye on her, no?" I smirked when he growled at me. "Times have changed, Eyrian. You are bound by duty to serve and guard Lucifer directly, unless he finds some other task for you. I'm better suited to keep an eye on *her*."

"Is that what your 'date' was? An excuse to 'keep an eye on her?'" Eyrian demanded, baring his fangs. "I haven't seen you put that much effort into your appearance in ages—and by the gods her *dress*. If you're leading her along, I swear to the gods I will—"

"Do you really think I would do that to her?" I snapped, grabbing Eyrian by the front of his robes. "Even if we disregard all that she did for me in Ceilail, do you truly think that I—"

Eyrian's fist connected with my jaw, causing me to stagger back into the wall. The seething Draekin didn't make another move to hit me, but his tail thrashed behind him. Electricity crackled around his arms as he struggled to calm himself. After a few deep breaths, Eyrian's magic subsided and he released a sigh.

"Promise me that you won't try to shelter or isolate her like you did when we were kids," Eyrian spoke in a defeated tone. "I know we were just kids back then, Nalithor, but you always made it difficult for anyone else to come near her. Our families scarcely remember that I was affected by her...'death'...too."

"I know, Eyrian, I know." I sighed, grabbing my friend by the shoulders. "I'm not the foolish child I once was. You, of all people, should know that. My reluctance to believe in her identity was...a means to protect myself. Surely you can understand how her existence is...frightening, at times. She seems to know nothing of our past. We must all get to know her again but... Even before I accepted who she is..."

"You're a dolt." Eyrian smacked me lightly upside the head. "What would Erist and Arom say if someone *happened* to let them know you've been such an idiot about a woman, hmmm? I can just hear them now, they—"

"Don't you *dare*!" I shook him by his shoulders. "I'll skin you if you say a *word* to either of them!"

"We both have work to do, right?" Eyrian laughed, brushing me off. "You should go find and question the girl before she gets any angrier. Contact me if you think of any additional orders for our spies.

As you said, times have changed. It's going to take *both* of us to keep her safe."

The Draekin turned and dispersed into the wind and out of view, leaving me alone in the palace hallway. I stared after him for a moment then sighed, slumping back against a windowsill. Eyrian hadn't hit me that hard in a while, but I had deserved it.

When wallowing in self-pity it was easy to forget that Eyrian had been close to Arianna too, and that he had also witnessed her 'death.' That I had attempted to keep most people our age away from Arianna back then only worsened my guilt. *'Why did I always feel like keeping others away from her was the only way to protect her? Was I truly that foolish or…have I forgotten something?'*

# CHAPTER FOUR
*Business as Usual*

*'Why did I let Nalithor talk me into more medical exams?!'* I fidgeted with my bangles and growled as I stalked through the streets of Dauthrmir. *'I should skin them and tan their hides if I ever see them again!'*

A shiver ran down my spine when I considered it, causing me to bite my lower lip. I mulled the idea over for a moment, wondering if perhaps I should return to the Sapphire Quarter to make good on it. The jolt of arousal was enough to make my nipples stiffen and my pulse quicken. I desperately needed something to kill, yet there wasn't anything inside the city I could shred without getting into massive trouble. *'I'm really losing it, aren't I? I should have calmed down a little after last night…but just* thinking *about killing something…'*

I dug my fingers into one arm, hoping the sudden pressure would snap me to my senses. Thinking, let alone *acting*, like a bitch in heat would only go to prove those women correct in their wild assumptions about me. *'Really. Did they have to act like I'm some sort of sex-crazed creature? Tch, how could they even begin to claim that Humans are worse than Adinvyr? They're a race that has everything to do with sex!'*

After calming myself, I continued my way to the Merchant's Plaza and wandered through the labyrinth of shop-streets. The city bustled with more activity than usual, making everything a tight squeeze. Most of the Devillians appeared to be in good spirits, both smiling and speaking in elated tones. Many of the women wore hair ornaments with flowers woven into, or dangling from, them. They wore elegant attire made of brightly colored silk, brocade, and sometimes a translucent material I didn't recognize.

Even the female warriors were wearing more decorative armor and accessories.

The men, in comparison, looked more rugged and were showing more skin than normal. They wore varying styles of armor adorned with arcane trinkets and jewelry. None of them carried visible weapons, but their poise made it clear they were genuine warriors. Their eyes were alert, even though their stances and conversations seemed relaxed.

It still struck me as strange that female warriors were so common in Vorpmasia. Most branches of the military seemed to have women in their ranks, and I had yet to hear anyone speak ill of such practices.

It was so far removed from what I was accustomed to in X'shmir that I had no idea what to make of it.

What truly had me curious was the number of younger Devillians and their elegant attire. The majority of them appeared to be Adinvyr, but many other Devillian races wore similar attire, arcane accessories, and flowers. I felt a little out of place in comparison, and certainly underdressed.

*'Ugh, they're giving me a headache already.'* I bit back a grimace and strengthened my barriers as I passed a group of arguing Sizoul women. Buy food, then retreat to my house in the Sapphire Quarter; that was my plan, but it was starting to feel like it wasn't going fast enough. *'Are the Adinvyr really to blame for the knocking on my barriers? They barely even give me a second glance.'*

Thankfully, the store I chose was much less crowded than the streets outside it. I released a relieved sigh and strode through the dim store in search of things to buy, adopting a slow pace. The longer I could delay returning to the streets, the better.

Being without my mask made me so nervous, yet I received fewer stares without it. The number of people skulking around my barriers hadn't changed much, but I was content with the disappearance of the myriad of displeased, distrusting, and concerned looks the masks and hoods had earned me.

*'Maybe I was lucky and kept my...uh...'frustration' to myself last night.'* I pulled a few bags of herbs and spices down from a shelf, then shook my head. *'Though, the books implied that it's impossible to hide*

*such things from Adinvyr. Hmmm. I hope the books are wrong.'*

"Arianna-jiss, this is an awful lot of food!" The Human storeowner exclaimed, pointing to the veritable mountain of items I'd selected. "Just how much do you and that boy eat?!"

"We're completely out of *everything*, and Darius didn't restock while I was gone." I sighed, running a hand through my curls. "Somehow he managed to devour *all* the leftovers he brought home too."

"Your brother is taking classes with a partner at the academy now, isn't he?" The woman inquired while helping me pack all the food into boxes. "What about you? I heard you went to hunt with Generals Il'thar and Vraelimir. Have you partnered with one of them? Feisty lads, those two. Could use a feisty lass to keep them in line."

"My results aren't back yet, so I haven't been paired with anyone." I shook my head, feeling an odd strike of pain through my chest. "They…they just needed an extra pair of blades for the hunt. I was asked to come along since I'm familiar with the type of beasts they were hunting."

"We didn't *'just'* need an extra pair of blades," Nalithor spoke from behind me. I flushed, stiffening, as the storeowner giggled at me. "I was wondering where you went, Arianna, when I discovered you weren't at the house. We have work to do."

*'He came to find me?'* I glanced over my shoulder at him before returning to packing up my purchases. *Just how in the hells does he manage to find me in a city this large? And so easily? The spies have been*

*absent today, so they're not to blame… Hmmm.'*

"Oh? Did you hire her to work at *The Little Orchid* Nalithor-zir?" The woman asked slyly. "I'm sure that pretty face of hers would draw in *many* new customers."

"That's actually a good idea…" Nalithor murmured, tracking me as I moved the boxes into a shrizar. "What do you think, Arianna? As much as these kimonos suit you, I'm sure a maid uniform would be just as fetching."

"I refuse to call anyone 'master' or 'mistress' if they aren't—" I started to protest, then trailed off when I realized what I was implying. Nalithor's smirk didn't help matters in the slightest.

"Comments such as *that* lead me to believe you've spent as little time studying as Darius has." Nalithor smirked and placed a hand on top of my head. "Do I need to make sure your books are on the appropriate subjects and *not* erotic novels, Arianna?

"Ah…but, pleasurable matters aside, we have the matter of beasts to discuss."

I paid the giggling storeowner before moving out of the shop and onto the busy street with Nalithor. A handful of citizens shot us curious looks, but the majority seemed oblivious to our presence. It made me feel as if I'd grown more paranoid since leaving X'shmir. *'When did I start caring about whether or not people looked?'*

"What kind of beasts?" I glanced up at Nalithor only to find he was examining my kimono with intense interest.

"Where did you get this?" Nalithor slipped an arm around my

corseted waist and pulled my right arm up by the sleeve with his free hand. "It has faint energy clinging to it like—"

"The Guardians of Sihix made it for me," I replied, glancing between him and the soft fabric for a moment. "Is something wrong with—? H-hey! What are you doing?"

"You look *delicious*." Nalithor purred, dipping down to nuzzle my throat briefly. Once he released me, he smiled and continued, "If you keep dressing in such an alluring way, I'm going to start thinking that you're *trying* to draw my interest, Arianna."

*'Draw his interest?'* I stared at him as he beckoned for me to follow him through the city streets. While walking alongside him, I glanced at him, studying his pleased expression for a moment, before reaching out to him telepathically. *'Because you like this style of clothing, or…?'*

*'You could have easily chosen to revert to your X'shmiran attire, or even your armor, upon returning.'* Nalithor shot me another smile and then focused forward once more.

*'Still struggling to figure out what I think of you?'* I arched an eyebrow at him.

*'You can be quite confusing at times.'* Nalithor chuckled. *'Let's have a race, shall we?'*

*'A race?'* I tilted my head. *'What kind of race?'*

*'To see who can flow through the shadows faster. That would be a much more entertaining way to return to the Sapphire Quarter, don't you think?'* Nalithor grinned and grabbed me around the waist with both arms, pulling me into the shadow of a building with him.

'*Hey, I didn't agree—*' I cut myself off with a shiver as his darkness wrapped around my senses and drowned the city itself out.

'*Race me.*' Nalithor chuckled, his voice sending waves through the darkness as if it were a sea. '*Is the vixen less confident in her affinity than I thought?*'

'*Fine, I'll—*' I sighed as Nalithor shot off ahead, his laughter echoing all around me. Resigned, I propelled myself through the darkness after him. '*I guess even deities are childish sometimes too.*'

Nalithor's behavior reminded me of children that wanted to have a swimming race, except the myriad of shadows cast by Magelights were our lake. We were melded with the shadows, indiscernible to most people. The darkness fought itself over whose power to emulate more. We were raw power, bouncing into each other and spiraling ever-upwards to the Sapphire District above. Occasionally leaping out of one shadow and into another if we ran into the end of our current vessel.

After the first few hundred feet my competitive streak kicked in and I twisted through the shadows with a new burst of speed. Nalithor's darkness snapped out to impede me, but I just laughed and slipped out of his reach. Once I reached our destination I leapt out of the shadows and slid several feet across the grass. I laughed, feeling Nalithor's power rapidly catching up behind me.

Before I could turn and flaunt my victory, Nalithor lifted me up by my waist with a cheerful laugh, spinning me around once before setting me down. When I turned, I found that Nalithor looked *delighted*, not defeated. The huge, boyish grin stretched across his features was incredibly endearing.

"And here I thought you were going to just let me win!" Nalithor laughed, ruffling my curls.

"Of course I wasn't going to just *let* you win!" I huffed, pawing displaced hair from my eyes. "You *challenged* me to—!"

"Next time we should have a prize for the winner." Nalithor put his arm around my shoulders and steered me toward the house. "Pity I didn't consider that sooner."

"I still would've won." I nudged his ribs with my elbow.

"That depends on what the prize was," Nalithor replied in a devious tone, running his hand down the side of my torso. "I could always make *you* the prize."

"I'd make a *terrible* prize." I rolled my eyes.

"No, I think you would make an *exquisite* prize," Nalithor interjected. He slowed his pace and lowered his tone when we caught sight of my twin on the porch outside the house. "What a pity... Looks like I have to share you already."

*'Well, at least Darius is reading a textbook.'* I kept the thought to myself, examining my twin's furrowed brow and then the book itself. *'Ah...advanced material. Is he ever going to focus on the basics first?'*

Nalithor gave me a small squeeze before releasing me and allowing me to ascend the porch steps unaided. Darius finally glanced up from his book and looked between us a few times before dropping his gaze back to his book and sighing.

"Ari, I'm *starving*," Darius whined. "Hi, Nali…"

"Aren't you supposed to be in class?" I frowned at him and then nudged the front doors open, glancing over my shoulder at Nalithor. "You can come in, we don't bite."

"Much," Darius corrected, motioning at me before rising to his feet. "My classes were all canceled today, and Vivus is busy. So, I'm bored and hungry."

"He thinks he's being subtle about wanting me to cook breakfast." I jammed my thumb in Darius' direction and then continued down the hallway.

"You *do* owe me breakfast as well." Nalithor chuckled from somewhere behind me. "We can discuss the beasts over breakfast, if you like."

"Beasts?" Darius piped up. "You guys killed a ton of them in Abrantia, right?"

I walked into the kitchen and made my way to the pantry so I could store my purchases, then carried what I'd need for breakfast over to one of the kitchen counters. Nalithor's eyes wandering down my back as he tracked my movements, making me feel a little more nervous than usual. Something about his gaze seemed rather piercing…or perhaps I was overthinking it. *'Hopefully overthinking it…'*

"We did," Nalithor finally replied to my brother as he perched on a chair at the kitchen table. "There were a few strange things about the beasts we found—and the creatures they were with. I took samples from the ones we killed on our first day out so that we can study them."

"Did you start analyzing them already, Nalithor?" I arranged the ingredients on the counter. "Or did you want to ask me about X'shmiran beasts?"

"Before that, can I ask a serious question?" Darius interrupted before Nalithor even had a chance to respond. "Why do you believe that we aren't Human, Nali?"

*'Why can't he just go away?'* I grimaced, tensing as I looked down at the bowls in front of me. *'I shouldn't be thinking like that. Maybe. Fuck.'*

"Pointed ears, fangs, slit pupils..." Nalithor murmured as if he was reading a list. "Neither of you carry the same unpleasant stench that Humans do. Then of course there's Arianna's black blood. That's a telltale sign that—"

"Ari? Your blood is black?!" Darius yelped, earning a brief glance from me.

"We'll know soon enough if I'm 'Human' or not." I shrugged. "The exceptionally *rude* healers who examined me this morning took all manner of tests, including blood samples."

"But you hate needles," Darius pointed out, making me twitch.

"I cut myself with a dagger instead," I snapped. "Fuck needles!"

"So, the vixen *does* have a weakness," Nalithor teased.

"I have plenty of weaknesses; you're just not privy to them!" I huffed, earning laughter from them both.

"Darius, you truly believe that you and Arianna are Human?" Nalithor inquired. He paused to shoot me a knowing smile when I placed a pot of tea and three cups on the table in front of him. I wasn't sure what to make of it, so I returned to making our food.

"I don't know how we could be *anything* else." Darius snorted. "We're twenty-five. We were five when the X'shmiran Royal Family adopted us. For us to be something else, even Elven, we would be *children* still."

"Unless something or *someone* bound us in Human form," I pointed out, shaking my head.

"Bah! As if anything is strong enough to do that to me!" Darius blustered.

"*I* could probably do that to you since your grasp on your magic is so weak," I countered, rolling my eyes.

"Still, Arianna's strength is anything but Human," Nalithor interjected, chuckling. "I've checked time and time again; Djialkan isn't using his power to enhance or supplement Arianna's abilities.

"There's also the matter of Humans—including their deities— being stripped of magic," I commented while piling food onto platters. "No mortal can be born with power that their patron deities don't possess. The deities 'evolve' before their people do…so, if we really are Human, all Nalithor would have to do is seek out the Human god and goddess to determine it."

"You aren't." Nalithor smiled as he watched me approach. "None of us have been able to determine what the two of you are, aside from 'anomalies.' That said, if you are sealed into Human forms as I believe, it's possible that those seals would interfere with determining your species. Magic capable of *that* is…powerful."

"I'm honestly not that concerned about what Darius and I are," I stated while placing a large platter of lemon-raspberry pancakes on the table, followed by platters of meats and of fruits. "Regardless of the outcome, we're still mages and we're still 'us.' It might be a little strange if we suddenly sprout new limbs or acquire a taste for blood, or something like that, but I'm sure we'll adapt."

"As if you don't already have a taste for blood!" Darius pointed his fork at me.

"I'm talking about a different type of bloodlust." I pouted, catching the smirk Nalithor shot me. "What's *that* look for, Nalithor?"

"Well, you *did* mention that the young ones seem fascinated by the idea of you drinking from them," Nalithor replied sweetly, his tail swishing. "There *must* be a reason for that, seeing as they should be thinking of drinking *you*… Are both of you still being bothered by 'interested' parties?"

"It's not really a bother. Makes it easier to get laid." Darius shrugged, ignoring the sour look I shot him.

"I've been tuning it out." I motioned at my temples. "I don't like the idea that *anyone* can hear whatever lewd thoughts might cross my mind, regardless of what barriers I put up."

"It's probably *because* of your lewd thoughts that they won't leave you alone!" Darius snorted, causing my face to grow hot. "*Please!* You had a whole wing of the palace all to yourself. I'm sure you've at least— Ow!"

"Good girl, 'lala." I grinned as the fox ran off with part of Darius' pant leg in her mouth.

"Trying to avoid unwanted attention by not thinking at all?" Nalithor inquired with a playful smirk, watching Alala run circles around the kitchen table for a moment before shifting his gaze to me. "How is *that* working for you, I wonder?"

*'D-did he...'* I felt my face growing even hotter as I tried to read the Adinvyr's expression. *'I swear, if he caught any of my thoughts last night, I may just throw myself off the city's edge.'*

"It doesn't seem like it's working well," I muttered, bristling at his sultry expression. "I'm surprised by how many of them can't seem to take the hint that I'm uninterested."

"They're too young to understand that you're genuinely resistant." Nalithor grinned. "Still, it *is* considered terribly rude for them to clamor for the attention of someone who doesn't want them or their advances. They should have challenged you by now. You'd be well within your rights to put them in their place, if you so desire."

"Bah! That would require hunting down *so many* people." I sighed, shaking my head. "They aren't even worth a fraction of the time that would take. If they were beasts, then maybe. At least then they would be fun."

"In that case, they won't leave you alone until someone stronger makes it clear they intend to pursue you." Nalithor frowned, settling back in his seat. "It frustrates me that they're behaving this way. They're piss-poor examples of Adinvyr."

"Well, it's probably a good thing we don't use the public baths then," Darius remarked, staring down at his plate for a moment. "None of them know if she's a dominant, submissive, or 'other'…but they all know she doesn't have a partner yet. So, seeing her nude would just get *everything* chasing her tail, right?"

"While I would like to say no… You may be right in this case." Nalithor shifted to examine me for a moment. "You do seem quite proficient in attracting unwanted attention, Arianna."

"Enough about me and the gaggle of ill-mannered cretins who want a taste!" I released an exasperated sigh. "Beasts are much more pleasant to talk about, and that's what you came to find me for, isn't it?"

*'I hope my attentions don't fall into the same category,'* Nalithor commented, shooting me an amused smile. "We've discovered that the X'shmiran beasts are capable of passing through the barriers we've erected around the individual Vorpmasian territories. We captured footage of one such beast passing from the Suthsul Desert and into Draemir.

"Something about the beasts must be inherently different from their Rilzaan brethren. We need to determine what that is so we can reinforce the barriers accordingly. The one that stumbled into Draemir was 'drunk,' as the ones we slew were, so our men were able to take it on without issue. However, we can't risk this becoming a common occurrence."

*'Footage? Some type of Magitech or something? Does it have something*

*to do with feet?'* I bit back my questions for the moment and tapped my nails against the table. "Hmmm, I haven't encountered a Rilzaan Dux yet. It will be difficult for me to determine any differences. I assume you want to take the direct approach and poke around inside my head for information instead?"

"Isn't that dangerous?" Darius protested, looking between Nalithor and me with unease. "Surely there's a better option?"

"Actually, I had a different idea." Nalithor grinned broadly. "If I take you to a *'specimen'* we've captured, would you be able to determine the differences *without* killing it?"

"You would have to restrain me," I responded flatly, earning a strange look from them both. "That I haven't already wandered off to kill it just means you have it hidden behind powerful barriers. If I'm to examine it, then—"

"Then I'll need to keep you from entering a killing frenzy and destroying everything that so much as *smells* like a beast?" Nalithor finished with a warm smile, nodding. "What if I have to bite you in order to calm you down?"

*'I still don't understand why he's so approving of my desire to kill!'* I bit back a frustrated sigh. *'I've seen enough of Vorpmasian culture to know it's not* just *a cultural thing. Does it have something to do with his role?'*

"How does *biting her* come anywhere *close* to calming her down?!" Darius snapped, scowling.

"Your venom, I'm guessing?" I rolled my eyes and then turned to look at Nalithor.

"Yes—unless you happen to be immune to that as well." Nalithor chuckled. "While it is *technically* an aphrodisiac… A few drops are enough to keep someone tame and pliable for a few days, up to a week if your mental or magical fortitude is lacking."

"Just a few *drops* does that?" Darius exclaimed, shaking his head hard. "There's gotta be a better option!"

"In this case, I'm not allowed to use my power as a deity to stop her. This isn't a matter regarding the balance, so I'm expected to act with restraint." Nalithor shook his head. "Arianna—"

"You have my permission to do what's necessary to stop me, if it comes to that." I shrugged. "I'm not certain how a Rilzaan Dux will affect me in comparison to X'shmiran ones, so it would be best for us to act with caution."

"Very well. After breakfast we will get to work." Nalithor nodded at me, then turned to Darius. "As for *you*, Darius, you should be studying the books your various professors assigned you. A tome on healing techniques employed by Archmagi is of no use to you in your current state."

I fell silent while consuming breakfast and a few cups of tea, listening as Nalithor and Darius conversed about study materials. Perhaps, if the reprimand came from his crush, Darius would finally listen. After all, it was clear that he didn't plan to listen to Djialkan, Fraelfnir, or me. I doubted that Nalithor would tolerate Darius' ignorance for much longer—especially when it came to the matter of his species.

A short while later I found myself somewhere deep within academy grounds, examining the massive Dux-class beast that the Vorpmasians had trapped behind layers of barriers. The creature was covered in charcoal-colored fur, its build like a fusion between a wolf and an ape. The scent wasn't even *close* to the same as a X'shmiran Dux, but was still objectionable. I wasn't sure why, but the researchers and mages present were all giving Nalithor and I a wide berth.

"You look confused," Nalithor remarked, watching as I prodded the barrier with tendrils of my darkness.

"Its strange scent gave me a thought," I murmured distractedly, examining the bony spines that ran along the beast's arms. *These barriers are very weak... Who erected them?'*

*'The Dauthrmiran and Beshulthien Archmagi both designed and constructed the barriers,'* Nalithor replied dryly, tracking me with an amused smile. *'I don't even need to tell them to lower the barriers for you, do I?'*

I crossed my arms and stared up at the dozens of layers of magical runes, unable to determine the language they were written in. That the runes weren't Angelic came as a relief, but that didn't change the fact there was a severe problem with the magics. An oily-brown substance had fused itself to the floating runes, and was a clear, alarming, sign that the barriers wouldn't hold for much longer.

*'One of them has been drinking from the beast. Their magic reeks and*

*is weakening the barrier,'* I grumbled, sensing Nalithor stiffen beside me. *'Still, such unpleasant things aside, I get the feeling that you'll find similarities if you compare this creature's blood and venom to the samples we took in Abrantia. The scents are too similar to ignore. I'm sure you noticed.'*

*'What are you thinking, hmmm?'* Nalithor inquired, sliding an arm around my waist. He gripped my hip tightly, digging his claws into me. *'I can sense your bloodlust spinning out of control already, Arianna.'*

*'I want to kill the bastard that's been drinking the beast.'* I shivered, motioning at the beast. *'That idiot's magic needs to be stripped from the barriers, then the trustworthy ones need to reconstruct them.'*

*'That's right...you can see magic, can't you?'* Nalithor murmured, causing me to shoot him a questioning look. *'Let me see what you're seeing.'*

*'You can't see...?'* I trailed off as Nalithor shook his head, a small smile on his face. *'Hmmm... Alright, here.'*

I wanted to question why a *god* of all people couldn't see magic, but I chose to focus on his request for now. I offered him my right hand and, once he accepted it, I closed my eyes. For a few moments I concentrated, opening a single door in my mind for Nalithor to pass through. Once I opened my eyes, he could see through me. His grip flinched when I focused my gaze on the barrier in front of us. He let out a rather displeased growl upon spotting the putrid, oily magic that had intertwined with the otherwise pure power that formed the barriers.

'*How did you learn to see magic?*' Nalithor asked after a moment.

'*Well, it is rather hard to see from behind those masks,*' I pointed out with a grin as Nalithor withdrew his hand and stalked toward the nearby scholars. '*Do you think the corrupted barrier is why they're keeping their distance?*'

'*They're keeping their distance because word of your ferocity is spreading.*' Nalithor purred, glancing over his shoulder to shoot me a chilling smile. '*Am I going to have to fight you for the pleasure of killing this one, my dear?*'

'*I'll let you have him; you can make it up to me later,*' I replied, placing my palms on the railing that sat between me and the beast.

The sound of a shriek and the scent of blood soon caught my attention, making me glance over my shoulder again. Nalithor had already torn the offending individual in half. The former Elf's blood stained the floor the same oily brown color that a beast's would. '*Mmm... It's a shame they can't die twice.*'

"Take a sample of *that*." I pointed down at the growing pool of blood. "It doesn't smell right."

"You're right; it doesn't smell like an Elf's blood *or* a beast's." Nalithor nodded, striding toward me in a way that made it look like he was hunting prey. However, his predatory demeanor wasn't what had my attention anymore.

"You *let* him cut you?" I asked, reaching up to Nalithor's face with a huff of disapproval. "Were you so excited to have something to kill that you got careless?"

"You're not going to leap off to kill *that*?" Nalithor inquired with a smile, motioning at the beast. I ignored it and healed the slice across his face instead. "If you keep looking at me like that, Arianna, I'm going to think that you want to take a taste of me instead of heal me."

*'A taste…maybe.'* The thought came unbidden, making my fingers twitch and my pulse quicken. *'Tch, I need to focus on healing him. Something like* that *can wait. Maybe I can redirect his attention?'*

"Do I really seem like I have that type of bloodlust?" I tilted my head slightly and withdrew my hands, but he caught my bloodied hand and brought it to his lips instead, lapping his blood off my fingers slowly. "Y-you're…"

"Now if you want a taste, your options are more limited." Nalithor teased, slipping his tail around my waist and pulling me to him with it. "As much as I enjoy teasing you… Have you examined the beast sufficiently?"

"You're certain I can't kill it?" I inquired after a moment of consideration, glancing at the creature again. *'I want to tear it apart. Why bother keeping something like this here? It needs to* die.*'*

*"If you would like me to take a bite out of you…you don't have to look for an excuse."* Nalithor purred quietly, nuzzling into the left side of my throat. He released a shaky sigh, squeezing me closer. "Especially not when you smell *this* good… Mmm, you really are difficult to deal with."

"*I'm* difficult?" I huffed as Nalithor tightened his grip and lifted me off the floor. "But…yes, I think I've examined it enough."

My pulse raced at an uncontrollable pace, and I had no doubts that Nalithor could feel it beneath his cheek. Keeping the tremble out of my voice was almost impossible. Nalithor's power had already wrapped so tightly around me that I wouldn't have been surprised if I could look down and see it with normal vision.

As much as Nalithor claimed that I was 'resistant' or 'immune' to him... I was beginning to feel quite the opposite.

"Perhaps I should taste you anyway..." Nalithor adjusted his grip on me, his voice husky as he kissed the side of my throat. "Or...am I still *earning* it?"

"You're...still earning it," I managed to reply, feeling him smirk into my skin; clearly, he'd noticed my hesitation. "Are you really so hungry that you're—"

Nalithor cut me off with a firm kiss and pinned me back against the wall. My mind threatened to go blank as he pressed himself between my legs and pulled them up around his waist. The idea of resisting didn't even cross my mind when I felt his tongue flick across my lips; I was all-too willing to give in to him at this point.

His taste was irresistible, and the blood on his tongue made it even more mesmerizing.

I lost myself to his passion, his taste, and his power. Despite the fact we weren't alone, I seriously considered pulling Nalithor's clothes off then and there. His desire was palpable, even when he drew back slightly moments later, his lips still hovering over mine. I was surprised I could even hear his devious chuckle over the roar of my pulse.

"Ahhh... Sometimes you make it so difficult to focus, Arianna," Nalithor mused, running his thumb down the front of my throat. "I suppose we should get to work compiling your findings, however..."

Nalithor chuckled when I failed to think of a response. He drew one of his hands along my thigh and nipped down my throat. When his mouth roamed over a certain spot, I twitched and barely held back a whimper, digging my heels into his back. At least I *thought* I had held it back.

'Oh? *Did I find one of those "weaknesses" you claimed I wasn't privy to?'* Nalithor questioned, running his tongue over the spot again. *'You shouldn't hold back on* my *account if it feels good... In fact, I encourage you not to.'*

"N-Nalithor-zir, such a display with a *foreign* princess in a place of *work* is—" One of the older researchers exclaimed, causing Nalithor to pause with his lips parted and fangs against my throat.

Nalithor tensed and released a feral snarl, turning away from my throat so that he could glare at the researchers. Darkness snapped out from his shadow and lashed toward them, making several shriek and stagger backward.

"I'd be lying if I said I minded..." I grumbled, feeling my face flush darker. "You know, I'm pretty sure Nalithor-*y'ric* can decide for himself what is or isn't appropriate."

Much to my dismay, Nalithor pulled me away from the wall and slung me over his shoulder. Without so much as another word to the researchers, he carried me out of the room and through the sterile network of tunnels that had led us to the beast in the first place. He didn't seem to have *any* qualms about keeping his hand on my ass.

"People do tend to question whether or not we're 'appropriate' with each other, don't they?" Nalithor chuckled, squeezing my butt for emphasis. "I do hope you don't mind too terribly much. You're just *so* irresistible, you know."

"You sound smug," I mumbled, watching his tail sway. *'Venom is carried in…all of their bodily fluids, right? Is that why I feel so… Ugh, that has to be it, right? More…I want more…'*

"Mmm, *victorious*," Nalithor corrected me, drawing the fingertips of his free hand along my inner thigh, making me twitch. "If you want another taste… I think I will have you *beg me* next time."

"If you insist on carrying me like this, I'm going to fall out of my top!" I growled at him, attempting to clutch my kimono closed over my chest. "I don't know about *you*, but *I* don't want to flash the entire campus with my—"

Before I could even finish, Nalithor pulled me over his shoulder and settled me in his arms instead. His smirk made it clear that he was even more pleased with himself than I had first thought. The swishing of his tail was a mere *fraction* of just how self-satisfied the Adinvyr was feeling.

"You really are incredibly easy to manhandle, you know." Nalithor grinned at me. "Now then… Let's see what we can learn of the beasts, preferably *before* I decide that a more *thorough* taste of you is in order— and before you decide to take a bite out of me."

*'A more thorough…?'* The corner of my eye twitched, heat rising in my body again. "L-let me down. I can walk, Nalithor."

"I will. When it suits me," Nalithor countered.

The 'victorious' Adinvyr chuckled at my frustrated sigh and continued through the labyrinth of underground passages. It amazed me that there was so much space carved out beneath the academy, especially when taking into account that Dauthrmir hovered in the air above a lake. A few scholars we passed offered respectful greetings to Nalithor, and all of them seemed perplexed by his decision to carry me. Even so, Nalithor maintained his firm grip as we passed dozens of hidden laboratories and other rooms I could only guess the purpose of.

*'I don't know what I want more; to kill that beast, or to have another taste of Nalithor…'* I suppressed a grimace, considering both options. *'Fuck. I need to distract myself with something else.'*

"Where are we going?" I shot Nalithor a frown as he carried me out of the tunnels and into the Sapphire Quarter. "I'm not going to run off and kill that—"

"Yes, you are." Nalithor cut me off, his tone dry. "Your desire to kill it is making *me*…"

Nalithor sighed and shook his head, his grip tensing. Instead of finishing his sentence, he hastened his pace and carried me in the direction of the palace district. He didn't stop to utter a single word to anyone we passed, and instead made his way straight for his wing of the palace. A few guards and servants shot him questioning looks, but none spoke up to inquire.

Upon reaching his laboratory-library combination, Nalithor set me down and waved the double doors shut. I caught a brief shimmer of magic around the room as he turned and made his way toward a nearby desk, pulling off his overrobe as he went. *'He erected a barrier? Is he trying to keep us in or others out?'*

"You should get comfortable, we're going to be here a while," Nalithor called, shooting me a glance over his shoulder. "As much as I would like to quiz you about X'shmir, it will have to wait. Strengthening our defenses against the beasts is much more important."

"Yes... It wouldn't be good to have the beasts attacking Vorpmasian cities directly," I murmured, crossing my arms as I tried *not* to stare at his muscular torso. "How can I help?"

"Have you calmed enough to focus?" Nalithor asked, striding toward me with a book and pen in hand.

I gave him an unamused glance. "Do I *look* like I'm going to run off and eviscerate something?"

"Well, you are a rather dangerous woman." Nalithor grinned crookedly. "I would like to spar with you so that we can both work out our frustration, but it will have to wait as well. Would you be willing to compile your observations for me? While you do that, I can begin prepping my share of the samples for analysis."

"Sure." I nodded, accepting the book and pen from him. *'"Our" frustration, huh?'*

Nalithor smiled and ruffled my curls before retreating to the second level of the laboratory. With a small sigh, I turned and moved to a nearby sofa. Before sitting, I dismissed my kimono and corset in favor of black breeches and a loose blouse. I could always summon an overrobe if I needed to keep up appearances as an Umbral Mage, after all.

*'Let's see... Differences between X'shmiran and Rilzaan Dux-class Chaos Beasts...'* I pondered, pulling on my headphones, turning the volume down a few notches so that I could hear Nalithor if he returned. *'Should I include physical differences as well?'*

Pursing my lips, I spun the pen a few times and stared at the blank page before me. I wasn't sure what to write, let alone what would be helpful. After a few minutes of consideration, I decided it would be best if I was as detailed as possible. Even if the information on the X'shmiran beasts was old news to me, it wasn't common knowledge to the Vorpmasians. My hope was that Nalithor could glean anything that I overlooked.

I nudged off my sandals and then pulled my legs up on the sofa, using my thighs to brace the book. Nalithor's presence nearby made it difficult for me to focus, but I did my best. Gnawing my lip, I pushed the Adinvyr from my thoughts to the best of my ability and began writing in Draemiran.

*'Was it...was it really necessary to kiss me like that?'* I wondered, frustrated upon realizing that I could still taste the Adinvyr. *'I want more...'*

Shutting my eyes, I took several calming breaths to help me focus on my task. I wanted to tell myself that the problem was the brief exposure to his venom, but I knew better than that. At dinner the previous night I hadn't been exposed to his venom, yet I had considered inviting him to my bed. I tensed my jaw and curled my free hand into a fist.

*'This isn't the time to be worrying about things like that!'* I began writing again, this time faster in hopes of distracting myself from Nalithor. *X'shmiran beasts appear to be made of dead and decaying things, whilst Rilzaan beasts appear to be animalistic...'*

I wasn't sure how much time had passed before I caught the scent of food and tea, rousing me from my writing. Apparently, I had become so absorbed that I didn't even notice Nalithor return to the first floor, let alone the fluctuation in his barrier.

*'When did I become comfortable enough to let my guard down around him?'* I wondered, glancing between Nalithor and the meek servant. *'Maybe if I eat real food, I'll stop craving him. Well, his blood anyway...* Dehsul*!'*

Nalithor pivoted to look at me when I snapped my book shut, "Finished?"

"Probably. I can't think of anything else to add." I swung my legs off the sofa and set my headphones aside before padding over to the cart of food, barefoot. The servant fidgeted and flushed darker the closer I got. "Hmmm, smells good..."

"P-p-please help yourself, A-Arianna-jiss." The servant bowed so low that her torso was parallel to the floor. "I-if you need anything, d-don't hesitate to call!"

Before I could thank her, she fled from the room with a startled squeak. I tilted my head, watching for a moment as the panicky Devillian disappeared from view. I shifted my gaze up to the chuckling Adinvyr beside me, utterly confused.

"Am I scary or something?" I frowned.

"My dear, I could argue that you would frighten anyone who isn't a deity." Nalithor laughed, tugging at my curls. "Do you mind conversing while we eat?"

"Sure," I mumbled while piling food onto my plate. "What would you like to—? Hey!"

"Mmm, I wish you had stayed in your kimono." Nalithor purred, slipping an arm around my waist as he kissed me where my blouse had slipped off my shoulder. "Although…this is cute too."

"*I'm* not for lunch, you know!" I grumbled as his arm slipped from my waist, his hand trailing down to my hip.

"*Yet*." Nalithor smiled, straightening. He pulled my blouse back up onto my shoulder for me then continued, "Let's take a look at what you've compiled for me."

"Aside from their obvious physical differences, and the differences in their scents, I honestly didn't notice anything that different." I shook my head, carrying my plate and a cup of tea back to the sofa. "However, I'm almost positive that the 'drunken' beasts were altered by something related to your 'captive.' The scent was—"

"You're getting carried away, again," Nalithor commented when I cut myself off to take a deep breath. An amused smile played on his lips as he joined me on the sofa. "Am I going to have to stop you, Arianna?"

"No… I just want to get back to hunting and training already." I sighed, setting my tea on the coffee table before settling onto the sofa once more. "I wrote down everything I know about the X'shmiran beasts, along with the few differences that I *did* notice. You've hunted Rilzaan beasts for a long time, right? So, you'll probably—"

Nalithor pulled me closer with one arm, wrapping his tail around my hips. He shot me a smile when I gave him a questioning look. "This seems like a good way to keep you from running off to hunt without me."

"Now the concern is whether or not I'll bring you to hunt the beast with me?" I arched an eyebrow.

"Hunting with you is a vast improvement over hunting alone." Nalithor grinned. "Let's eat. After, I will take a look at what you wrote. We need to determine if the X'shmiran beasts are truly capable of passing through the barriers, or if…"

"Or if there's a meddler to kill?" I finished with a little too much excitement, shifting to look up at him. "That could be more fun than beasts! They all seem so weak, after all. Maybe—"

"*Calm down.*" Nalithor squeezed me again and wrapped his dark aura around me like a snug blanket, threatening to overwhelm all else. "One thing at a time, my dear. Perhaps, if you're a good girl, I will consider bringing you to hunt with me later."

"Fine." I pouted, returning my attention to the plate I was holding. *'He'd better mean that...'*

# CHAPTER FIVE
*Filthy Rats!*

I stumbled through the house, grumbling to myself, while making my way to the kitchen. Everything seemed like too much effort this morning, but I'd managed to pull on training clothes at least. Researching the beasts had taken longer than expected, so I hadn't gotten to return to the house until the wee hours of the morning. Nalithor and I hadn't made much headway the prior night. I planned to seek the Adinvyr out later—after taking out my frustration on training dummies.

*'Tea, tea, I need tea…'* I held my forehead in one hand for a moment and winced when the kitchen's Magelights blinded me temporarily. *'What's that noise…?'*

Frowning, I looked around the kitchen in search of what was

making the muffled sounds. There was no one there, but the sound itself was familiar. A chill shot down my spine when I realized it was *Darius*. If I could hear him sobbing from the kitchen, he was either nearby or he was severely distressed. I grit my teeth and strode out of the kitchen to look for my brother.

*'I know that sound.'* I clenched my fists, struggling to quell my bubbling anger. *'What made him snap? Are his professors or therapists pushing him too hard? Did something happen while I was gone last night?'*

"A-Ari!" Darius wailed at me when I rounded a corner. "I-I don't wanna!"

"Don't want…to what?" I shielded my eyes, waiting for them to adjust to the golden and white light swirling around my brother. It cut through the otherwise comfortable darkness in our house like a blade, making me bristle. *'Ugh, his light… I hate it. I want to snuff it out. It feels like—'*

"O-our parents are here f-for some reason!" Darius shrieked. "I-I'm expected to come and m-meet with them and t-the Vorpmasians in an hour!"

Time stopped, my blood running cold. Shivers ran through my body and my skin prickled into waves of goosebumps. What were *they* doing in Vorpmasia? Why was Darius' presence required? Hadn't the Vorpmasians claimed that they would keep Darius separated from the bastards?"

*'Can I… Can I get away with killing them here?'* I bit down on my lower lip, shivering while I considered it. *'No, no. Unlikely…'*

"A-Ari?" Darius' whimper snapped me out of it, making me turn to look at him. "Y-you'll come with me, right? D-don't leave me alone w-with those—"

"Didn't you just say you don't want to go?" I blinked at him as he scrambled out of the corner and clung to my leg. His tear-stained face soaked my pant leg. "Darius…"

I sighed and placed a hand on Darius' head, patting his curls while he sobbed. The light swirling around him hissed and retreated away from my hand, slinking away to observe from afar. As much as I hated the light… I hated *those people* more. Darius was my only sibling, light affinity or not, and those people had hurt him so many times. It was unforgivable.

*'Did Nalithor know they were coming here?'* I gnawed on the inside of my cheek. *'I think he would tell me if he knew, but…'*

"I-I need to go b-because it's really important to the treaty between X'shmir and Vorpmasia!" Darius' grip on my leg grew painfully tight while he continued to shake, small sobs wracking his body. "I-I know t-the Vorpmasians said they'd keep me s-safe b-but…"

"You want me to come along and look imposing?" I sighed, patting his head again. "And if I…lose control and kill them?"

"Nali will stop you!" Darius exclaimed, shaking his head.

*'Nalithor is just as likely to lose it and kill them as I am… I think.'* I grimaced, my shoulders slumping. *'If he hasn't killed them already, there must be some reason, right? They represent so many things that he loathes. I doubt he would leave them alive without good reason.'*

"Let's get dressed then, Darius," I relented, tugging gently at his curls. "You're still in your pajamas, and I'm in my training clothes. I'm sure you need to wear formal finery, right? And, if I'm going to look imposing, I'll need to change too."

Darius hesitated before releasing my leg and pulling himself to his feet. He mumbled his acceptance and retreated to his room to get dressed. I let out a shaky sigh and then turned to stalk back upstairs. Darkness swirled around my bare feet as I padded down the hallway and into my rooms. Both Alala and Djialkan both jerked awake when I slammed the door.

*"You look murderous,"* Djialkan spoke, lifting his head to watch me as I summoned trunks of clothing from my shrizar. *"What are you looking for?"*

"The X'shmiran filth are at the palace," I snapped, opening one of the trunks to rummage through it. "I'm escorting Darius. I need something that makes me look imposing."

Alala ran under the bed and geckered at the shadows around my feet, while Djialkan simply flew over to perch on my shoulder. If I was going to have to deal with those fucking bastards from X'shmir, then I was going to make myself look like a goddess of death. I wouldn't be satisfied until their heads were rolling at my feet but, for now, I would have to be content with frightening them.

*"Nalithor will have to subdue you if you do not calm down,"* Djialkan warned me, nudging my cheek with his snout. *"Alala says that you should dress like one of the Vorpmasians, not as a X'shmiran. I agree with*

*her."*

I paused mid-reach for a X'shmiran robe and cut my eyes to the side at my companions, "Dauthrmiran…or Draemiran?"

Alala scooted out from beneath the bed and pawed at the side of one of the unopened trunks. I flipped the lid open for her, then sat back on my heels to wait. She seemed like she had something in mind, so I allowed her to paw through the contents in peace. After a few moments, Alala pulled several items from the trunk and then yipped at me.

"You're sure?" I arched an eyebrow.

*"I agree with her."* Djialkan snorted and leapt off my shoulder, gliding over to curl up on the bed. *"You had best hurry, lest Darius grow too skittish and leave without you."*

I nodded and pulled off my training clothes, replacing them with the partially armored robes that Alala had selected. The layers beneath the platinum-plated overrobe conformed to my curves and revealed a questionable amount of cleavage, but that had its own unique appeal to me at the given moment. I could piss off the X'shmirans while simultaneously flaunting my cleavage for Nalithor. It seemed like a win-win situation for me.

*'Oh, for fuck's sake!'* I snapped at myself while pulling on the clothing. *'I should be focused on protecting Darius right now, not thinking about that* delicious *taste of Nalithor's blood that I—'*

Bristling, I bit my cheek hard and ground it between my teeth while I finished getting dressed.

The layers beneath the overrobe left my throat, cleavage, and shoulders bare because the embroidered fabric hung just off my shoulders. My leather overrobe swept around the outer section of my bust to clasp beneath my chest, framing my cleavage.

"Alala, are you *trying* to show me off?" I sighed, glancing over at the fox. She just pounced around in a circle on the floor, warbling the entire time. "Bah, whatever. I'm going to get going. Watch the house for me, you two."

I swept downstairs with a smirk on my face and pinned up a portion of my hair while walking. My armored boots made a satisfying click on the floor with each step.

Darius was pacing around in the foyer and wringing his hands, his white, gold, and jade robes fluttering around him. Fear came off him in waves, his emerald eyes were wide.

"S-still no mask?" Darius stuttered, looking up from the floor when I descended the last few steps. "D-don't you think t-that will be a problem?"

"Why, I'm just abiding by our hosts' traditions," I replied innocently, placing a hand over my chest as if offended.

Darius cracked a smile and let out a nervous laugh before falling into step with me. The sweet morning air outside carried a chill that relieved me of my temper and bloodlust. However, the reprieve was brief. Darius' sheer terror made my blood boil again in seconds.

The few people who crossed our path on the way to the palace all gave us a wide berth and shot me wary glances. I wondered if my anger was truly that palpable, or if my darkness had manifested around me again. Either way, it didn't matter much to me. My least favorite type of monster was currently in Dauthrmir, yet I couldn't hunt it. I had every right to be livid.

*'I don't want to do this, Ari.'* Darius whimpered, clinging to my sleeve. His trembling grew worse with every step we took through the Sapphire Quarter. *'Why are t-those people here and not in X'shmir? I thought they'd signed the treaty! I don't wanna—'*

*'It will be worse if we don't go, right?'* I glanced to the side at Darius, having caught the sound of his teeth chattering. *'Do you really think that the Dauthrmirans will just let the rats do as they please?'*

*'N-no... But what happens if they say something to piss the Dauthrmirans off?'* Darius' grip on my arm clamped down hard, likely bruising me. *'O-or worse, if they upset Nali. He's...he's higher ranking than Lucifer, isn't he? What'll happen i-i-if...'*

*'I actually kind of want to see him that pissed off...'* I kept the thought to myself before answering my twin. *'Darius, calm down. There's no point in worrying about what-ifs. We knew that they would probably have to come Below for political reasons at some point, and we also know that the Vorpmasians intend to keep you safe—and out of those bastard's clutches.'*

*'I-I feel terrible for it, but I wish Nali had j-just gone and conquered X'shmir without w-waiting for us to become Dauthrmiran citizens...'* Darius mumbled, startling me. *'L-let's hurry before I c-change my mind.'*

Several of Nalithor and Eyrian's men fell into step with us when we neared the palace gates, informing us that the generals had assigned them to work as Darius' bodyguards for the day. I could tell a few of them were Astral Mages like Darius. The crisp stink of light affinity mages wore at my patience almost as much as the X'shmirans did.

*'Kill.'*

My instincts revved into action when I sensed intense bloodlust channeled at my brother. Instead of speaking, I grabbed my brother by his shoulder and shoved him toward Maric. Darius yelped his confusion as darkness swept outward from me like a shockwave when I drew my scythe. *'Filth. Human* fucking *filth. They really brought assassins with them to the palace?!'*

"Keep Darius out of my way," I commanded, spinning my scythe into position. Taking a deep breath, I let my vision blur and grow unfocused while I searched out the source of the bloodlust with my darkness. "Keep yourselves out of my way too while you're at it."

"G-General Black?" One of the younger soldiers stuttered, only to be hushed by Maric.

*"Kill the witch, then kill him!"* A manic voice screeched.

"Fool." I spun my scythe behind me as my darkness snatched the voice's owner.

A blood curdling scream ripped through the air when I dragged the assassin out of his hiding place. His blubbering grew more and more desperate as I strode across the grass toward them. I smiled at the bastard before swinging my blade through him at an angle, severing him from his shoulder to his opposite hip. Blood splashed across my skin, hair, and clothes. I didn't care. There were more to kill.

"They always die too fast..." I tilted my head to the side, examining the severed corpse. "Oh well. Who wants to be next?"

*'Fear. I smell fear. Not Darius'.'* I glanced around, letting my darkness rush along the ground. *'More... How many more? Hmmm, not enough to be interesting. I see.'*

I swept across the courtyard and extended darkness into every nook and cranny I sensed. Eight. Eight more bastards needed to die. I ripped them out of hiding and dragged them into open view. My darkness hoisted them into the air around me in a circle while I smiled at them. Their terrified whimpering and begging sent a shiver down my spine. The poor fools didn't understand what they had gotten themselves into.

"Who sent you?" I asked sweetly, leaning against my weapon. Looking between the filthy rats, I sighed; I was already bored. "Ah... Or have the King and Queen grown so dense that they're willing to bring assassins here themselves?"

"Don't talk!" One of the more ragged looking males snapped to another.

"O-ho?" I grinned savagely and turned to the ragged one, burying the tip of my scythe in his abdomen. He screamed in agony, which only served to make me twist it more. "Resistant ones? I like resistant ones. You're more fun— Ah... You broke already."

I sighed in disappointment and shook my head at the unconscious man. An upward swing of my blade cut him in half, my darkness releasing him. His comrades screamed in terror, several soiling themselves as they stared at the ruined corpse. *'This is why I prefer beasts…they don't break as easily.'*

"J-just tell her what she wants to hear!" The sole female assassin screeched. "M-maybe she'll hand us over to the D-Dauthrmirans and—"

"T-the king and queen sent us!" Another male offered hurriedly. "T-they said their heir h-has been tainted by the Devillian ways—"

*'Lying? Really?'* I spun my scythe and rested it against my shoulder while I examined the man. *'Unexpected…'*

"W-we've all seen her face! We're going to die anyway!" One howled in despair.

"Arianna-jiss, we're going to be late at this rate," Maric offered, his tone full of amusement. "We should get going. Do you want to capture them, or…?"

"They won't talk," I stated, watching with interest as the assassins began their struggle against my shadows anew. They spewed curses amid their incoherent screaming, eyes wide with fear. *'Die.'*

With a few wide swings of my scythe I severed the assassins into several chunks each. Blood soaked my hair and clothes as I watched their remains drop to the ground, lifeless. My grip twitched when I considered tearing them into finer chunks, but the unpleasant smell of their vacated bowels and burst organs made me reconsider. I sighed, relaxing slightly now that their murderous presences were gone.

"A-Ari, aren't you going to c-clean all of *that* off?" Darius yelped, shying away from my darkness as it flowed back to me. "Y-you're—"

My brother cut himself off and turned to dry heave. Perhaps it was a good thing that we hadn't stopped to have tea or breakfast before making our way here. Getting vomit out of Darius' white clothing would have been an utter pain.

"No, I think it's about time I made a fucking point to those 'people,'" I replied coolly, stepping over a tangle of intestines and portions of severed limbs. "Maric, why are you laughing?"

"Some of our men were worried you wouldn't be able to handle working with Devillians—especially one like Nalithor!" Maric slapped his thigh as he howled with laughter. "You're just as vicious as he can be!"

"I apologize, Arianna-jiss." Another soldier snickered, tail snapping back and forth as he failed to restrain his laughter. "S-seeing a tiny thing like you do *that* is just—"

I rolled my eyes and placed one of my bloodied fists on my hip. "Yes, yes. A tiny 'Human' princess ravaging the bodies of her enemies has some entertainment value for your kind that I still fail to grasp. Didn't you say we were going to be late? Let's go."

'Tch. *Human blood smells and tastes* awful.' I grimaced, spitting out a mouthful of blood.

When we entered the palace, the servants grew pale and scurried away upon spotting my blood-coated body. Even a few of the Imperial Guard looked queasy, though I had a feeling it was because of the foul metallic scent of Human blood. I doubted any of Eyrian's men would find the sight of blood and gore nauseating.

"Darius-zir, we will wait for you outside the throne room," Maric informed my brother. "We have been ordered to accompany you everywhere until the X'shmiran king, queen, and their guests have left Vorpmasia."

"W-what about Ari?" Darius whimpered, his gaze flicking to me as we came to a halt in front of the throne room doors.

"Arianna-jiss will continue to work with General Vraelimir on a classified matter," Maric stated in a rather formal tone, before pivoting to shoot me a crooked grin. "You sure you don't want to clean up first, General?"

I nodded and shifted my attention to the ebony doors, tilting my head when I caught the sound of a vaguely familiar instrument. It sounded similar to a violin, and I had heard several songs on my headphones that used the same instrument. Though I didn't know the name of it, I *did* know that the way it was being used sounded much like the first time I heard Nalithor playing a violin in X'shmir. It had to be him playing the song. *'Is he bored?'*

*"I apologize if we have offended you, Lucifer."* I heard Dilonu wheeze. *"However, is the Umbral Mage's presence here necessary? He wears neither a mask nor a hood!"*

*"Why would a god be among mortals?"* Tyana added ever-so-helpfully. *"Everyone knows that deities are ethereal beings!"*

"A-Ari, don't—" Darius groaned, covering his face with one hand when I grinned at the door.

"They're really that dense?" Maric turned to look at me.

I laughed, finally dismissing my scythe. "Oh, you don't even know the *half* of it."

*"We understand that your gods are important to you of course, but we see no reason to erect temples to your gods in our city."* Dilonu continued. His tone made me want to roll my eyes.

"Ari—" Darius started, but it was too late.

"So!" I kicked the throne room doors open, leaving a bloody outline of my booted foot. "Which one of you fuckers sent assassins after Darius, hmmm?"

The air grew still when I strutted into the throne room with darkness swirling about my feet. I smirked at the X'shmiran royals and nobles while they shrieked and brought their hands up to cover their eyes. Several caught enough of a glimpse of my bloodied form to turn green. In contrast, the Devillians in the room—including the representatives of the Vorpmasian Families—appeared fascinated.

"What is the meaning of this?" Tyana shrieked, holding one hand over her eyes and pointing at me with the other. "Why is the whore without her mask?!"

I glanced toward the dais at the back of the throne room when the music abruptly ceased, a glimpse of rage rippling across Nalithor's face. He shot the X'shmiran queen a murderous look but, lucky for her, she missed it. She likely would have pissed herself had she seen it. Several of the Vorpmasian royals shot Nalithor wary looks, but he seemed as if he didn't notice.

"Darius," Dilonu barked, making my twin flinch. "Explain yourself at once!"

"H-her mask was d-destroyed while hunting." Darius whimpered, shrinking away from the bastard king. "S-since we're in foreign lands, and she has no replacements, I thought it would b-be alright for her to adhere to t-their ways—"

"Arianna." Nalithor's firm, enraged demeanor made me focus again on him with a startled expression, only to find he was already sweeping across the floor toward me. He left the stone frozen in his wake. "What is this about *assassins*?"

"Nine assassins were waiting for us in the courtyard." I shook my head when my bloodlust threatened to rise again. "They were all from X'shmir. I—"

I fell silent when Nalithor grabbed my face in both of his hands and pulled me abruptly to him, making me brace myself against his chest. His skin was hot like fire, a stark contrast to the icy floor around us. His rage rippled through him beneath my hands. The expression in his eyes was so intense that I decided to remain silent, unsure of what to say. For the life of me, I couldn't determine the source of his anger.

"S-she's still a princess of X'shmir! Unhand her!" Tyana demanded.

"I don't remember giving you permission to wear someone else's blood." Nalithor growled at me, swiping his thumb roughly across my lower lip. His muscles tensed and his tail snapped into the floor behind him, breaking both the ice and several of the stone tiles. "Such *unworthy* blood should be cleansed ***immediately***."

"Oh? I thought I was making a good point for *them*," I murmured quietly in Draemiran, flicking my gaze to the X'shmirans and then back to the growling Adinvyr. "Are you going to let—"

Nalithor's power slammed through me, ripping every last drop of blood from my skin, hair, and clothes. The Humans present shrieked and whimpered, cowering away from the wild darkness he had summoned. I simply remained silent and attempted to restrain myself. His power threatened to draw me in, sliding over every inch of my skin and dulling my awareness of the others present.

Once every trace of blood was gone, Nalithor's pale eyes drifted down my form. His gaze was predatory and penetrating. I could hear my brother attempting to stutter some kind of excuse from behind me, but Darius couldn't formulate a coherent thought. *'Darius is concerned about what Nalithor might do?'*

"She may be an Evil Mage, but she's still the First Princess of X'shmir!" Dilonu bellowed. "Unhand her, Adinvyr."

"The word you were looking for is '*Rely'ric,*' not 'Adinvyr'. Unless you're *trying* to die, that is." I shot Dilonu a condescending look.

"F-Father, Nalithor-y'ric is a *god!*" Darius stressed, stomping one foot in indignation. "Arianna has been working with—"

*'Can you play along?'* Nalithor's question made me turn my attention back to him.

*'They're causing even more trouble than I thought?'* I asked as he traced my lower lip again.

*'That...and the fact that we shouldn't kill them.* **Yet**.*'* Nalithor confirmed, his gaze drifting from my lips, down my throat, and to my cleavage.

*'I'll play along but, if you keep looking at me like that, I'm going to grow worried,'* I replied dryly.

*'Their blood is unworthy of you,'* Nalithor reiterated with a growl, bristling as his eyes snapped up to mine. *'Did you leave any of them alive? I should shred them for tainting—'*

"Let's pretend, for a moment, that he *is* a god. What would he want with an Evil Mage like her?" Tyana argued with Darius, sending Nalithor's tail cracking into the floor as another shudder of rage ran through him.

"I have chosen Arianna-jiss to work for me," Nalithor stated, shifting to glare at the X'shmiran royals. "As a X'shmiran mage, she's in a unique position to inform us about the beasts that plague both our lands and yours." Nalithor paused to pull me fully against his chest and made a show of nuzzling his face into the side of my neck. "Furthermore...*she tastes delicious*."

*'Play...along.'* Nalithor released a shaky sigh and then coiled his tail around my hips lazily. *'We need them to think you're...a little* more *than "just" working with me.'*

"How *dare* you!" Dilonu snapped as Nalithor pulled my overrobe from my shoulder and exposed my bare neck and shoulders for all to see. "Arianna, kill him!"

"Why should I?" I drawled, shifting my shoulder downwards to offer a longer stretch of my throat to Nalithor. "Our very own texts dictate that obeying a *god* is more important than— Ahhhnn..."

*'So, you're sensitive here too?'* Nalithor asked with a devious chuckle, drawing me completely against him. He planted kisses and sharp nips along my throat and pressed one arm firmly against my back. His power danced around both of us like a lazy fog of darkness and frost, luring my darkness out from where I kept it. *'I think they can do with a little more* fear.*'*

"H-how do you know he's a god?" Tyana demanded while I struggled to separate my darkness from Nalithor's. "What proof do you have?"

*'Nnngh... Come here.'* Nalithor released a feral rumble into the side of my throat and then lifted me off the floor. He stalked back toward his chaise at the back of the room and addressed the X'shmiran's as he walked, "All you need to know is that I chose to work with Arianna-jiss over Darius-zir... Or would you prefer that I feast on *his* body over hers?"

"F-feast..." One of the Human nobles muttered.

*"If our Holy Mage was tainted in such a way by an Evil Mage..."*

*"Your Majesties, it may be for the best to—"*

"Fine, we will sell her to you," Dilonu stated flatly. "I'm sure we can come to an agreement on the price."

*'Nalithor, calm down.'* I placed a hand against Nalithor's chest, having sensed his rage snap. He moved to turn on the Human king but hesitated when I touched him. *'They're not supposed to die*

*yet…right?'*

**'That bastard is trying to sell you!'** Nalithor bared his fangs and set me down on his chaise. His masculine features twisted with anger as he flicked his gaze to glare over his shoulder at the Humans. Yet he still hesitated to move. For that, I was thankful.

*'Would you really risk being Exiled over a Human's blustering idiocy?'* I countered, catching him by his wrist when he turned. *'There's also the matter of my curse to consider.*

*'Besides… I already want to kill them bad enough as is. If both of us lose control…'*

"Nalithor," Lucifer finally spoke up, shifting his bi-colored gaze between Nalithor and me a few times. "I believe you told me that you and Arianna-jiss have not concluded your research as of yet…*right?* Feel free to see to important matters such as those instead. We need to remedy the beast problems in Vorpmasia, Beshulthien, *and* X'shmir as soon as possible."

*'Will Darius be alright without you here?'* Nalithor turned to look down at me again. He twisted his hand out of my grip so that he could grasp my hand instead, shooting me a concerned look. *'I may detest the boy, but…'*

The Adinvyr trailed off with an odd expression on his face as he examined me. Instead of waiting for my reply he tugged me to my feet and slipped an arm behind my back. Nalithor maintained a brisk pace and led me past the X'shmirans, my twin, and out of the throne room past Darius' waiting escort. Maric called a greeting to his commanding officer, but Nalithor was unresponsive.

*'Where are we going?'* I frowned up at Nalithor when he began leading me out of the palace instead of to his laboratory.

*'We are going to hunt...'* Nalithor trailed off as he led me into a courtyard, his lips parting in surprise while he examined the bloody mess I had left behind. *'You did this to them and yet you're still raring for more?'*

*'Hunting?'* I asked excitedly, turning to press myself up against his side and grin up at him. *'Where? What are we looking for? Can we grab breakfast first?'*

*'What am I going to do with you?'* Nalithor sighed, tightening his grip on my waist. *'Let's find you some breakfast. After, we can find something to rip apart.'*

*'What if we can't find anything?'* I pouted, watching him cast a displeased look at the Human blood and gore everywhere. *'Wha— Hey!'*

*'I did say their blood is* **unworthy**.*'* Nalithor bristled, lifting me off the ground again. He didn't set me back on my feet until we had cleared the courtyard entirely. *'We will find something to hunt. That I can assure you.'*

# CHAPTER SIX
## *Bloodlust*

"Haa… How many have you killed so far?" I slumped back against a huge tree, attempting to catch my breath.

"Sixty-four," Nalithor answered after taking a deep swig from his waterskin. "And you?"

"Ha! I'm still winning!" I grinned at him. "Sixty-eight!"

"I *will* win." Nalithor turned away from me to search for more beasts. "You may be cute, but I refuse to lose to you."

I laughed at him as he disappeared through the underbrush. Turning our hunt into a competition had certainly made it more interesting. At first, we had set out with the intention of collecting samples from a few beasts and killing a few extra to alleviate our mutual anger with the X'shmirans. However, Nalithor had eagerly accepted my challenge and seemed determined to prove himself as the better hunter.

*'Well, this is one Draemiran quirk that I can understand at least,'* I mused, taking a few sips of water.

Smiling, I rose to my feet and stalked through the forest once more. We were still in Vorpmasian territory, but this place was situated between the barriers around the Dauthrmiran Crater and Draemir, leaving it open to the beasts and all manner of other creatures. Thus far the two-hour airship ride had proved to be well worthwhile.

As much as I enjoyed ripping the beasts apart, I actually found more amusement in Nalithor's desire to prove that he was 'worthy' of hunting with me.

I summoned a longsword in one hand and slipped through the trees in search of more beasts. My darkness flowed around me freely in search of prey. My brow furrowed when I failed to sense any more beasts nearby. Nalithor, however, was close.

*'We should delay our competition.'* Nalithor's voice was strangely singsong, causing me to arch an eyebrow and glance off in the direction of his presence. *'I found something fun.'*

*'Fun...?'* I trailed off with a shiver as the Adinvyr's bloodlust hit me, then took a sharp turn to join him. *'Tch, what could you possibly have found that would make you want to delay our contest?'*

*'Just come help kill it already!'* Nalithor laughed.

*'Help?'* I arched an eyebrow as I rushed toward Nalithor's presence. *'I don't smell any more beasts. What could he have— Oh.'*

I skidded to a stop upon entering an open field and looked from Nalithor to the colossal beast and back a few times. The creature stood at least eight stories high but wasn't moving. The slow, steady expansion and contraction of its torso was the only indication that the beast was even breathing. Corpses of other beasts, ranging from the smallest peons to a few Duxes, littered the ground around Nalithor, staining the soil and grass a putrid mixture of oil-brown and yellow.

Darkness whirled around Nalithor's armored form wildly. He leveled his spear at the remaining beast, pale blue-white flames licking along the edge of the blade. Nalithor's tail snapped back and forth behind him in excitement as he waited for his prey to make a move. The air crackled with his combined elements, frost even beginning to join in the elemental dance.

"Are you sure you're the God of Balance? Not the God of Death?" I quipped before summoning a heavier set of armor around myself.

"I'll take that as a compliment." Nalithor shot me a smirk over his shoulder.

Something about the look in his eyes made my heart skip several beats as the feeling of something constricting it passed through. It startled me enough to make my grip on my sword twitch, nearly causing me to drop the weapon. Nalithor's power, intermingled with bloodlust, continued to rush through me even when he returned his gaze to the waiting monstrosity.

'W-what was that?' I clenched my teeth and tried to brush off the lingering sensation. 'That wasn't fear. F-fuck. His bloodlust is...'

"And you've chastised *me* for getting too excited." I groaned, covering my face with one hand as I shrugged off his murderous intent. "Has the damned thing made a move at all?"

"You noticed, didn't you?" Nalithor purred once I drew closer.

"That they have no scent?" I offered, tilting my head.

"Either that, or *something* is concealing it. They should reek—especially the dead ones." Nalithor cast a sideways glance at me when I came to stand beside him. "I think you will need a larger weapon than that, my dear."

"You're probably right." I dismissed my longsword and drew a claymore instead. "How…have you not rushed it already?"

"Give me *some* credit." Nalithor smirked, then shifted his attention back to our prey. "*Let's kill it.* You can keep up with me, right?"

Nalithor sprung across the bloody field with a wild grin plastered across his face, his pale eyes alight with bloodlust, excitement, and something else I couldn't quite identify. His power rippled through the air as he swung his blade through the beast's legs. A torrent of dark yellow blood gushed from the wounds like a wave.

'*Damn it all.*' I laid the flat of my claymore on my shoulder and darted forward, summoning platforms of darkness around the beast. '*Did he feed recently? He's much more exuberant than when we were in Abrantia.*'

I grimaced at the thought. That was unacceptable. Even if I wasn't willing to let him feed from me, yet, the idea of him feeding from someone else pissed me off more than the presence of the stupid Chaos

Beast did. If Nalithor had fed on someone... I would kill them. Then, I would see to it that he understood he was *mine*.

*'Ugh, why am I thinking like that?'* I bit the inside of my cheek, hard. *'He only kissed me like that in order to keep me from killing their precious specimen...right?'*

"What do you think, Arianna? X'shmiran or Rilzaan?" Nalithor's sensual tone snapped me out of my self-pity. I glanced at him from my perch and resisted the urge to roll my eyes. How he managed to be catlike, bloodthirsty, and sensual all at the same time was beyond me.

"It doesn't look like it was made from corpses, so I would argue that it's native to Rilzaan," I replied, returning my gaze to the beast. Pausing for a moment, I examined its leathery hide and the multitude of black spines that ran along many sections of its body. Even if it was from Rilzaan, I couldn't identify what sort of animal it could have possibly resembled. "I'm more concerned about why it isn't moving."

"I want to shred it and yet it's *so* uncooperative..." Nalithor sighed, leaping lightly to my platform. He looked down at me with a mischievous glint in his eyes. "At this rate we will have *another* party thrown in honor of our successful hunt."

"Don't invite Darius this time." I huffed, leaping from the platform.

I sped through the air toward the beast and cocked my arms, pulling the claymore back. Perhaps if I impaled the thing deep enough it would finally respond to us. Unmoving prey was *so* unexciting. I needed it to roar, to scream. I wanted it to bleed, for it to try to flee in terror. I wanted—

*'Ahhhnnn, has "The White Fox" grown serious?'* Nalithor teased, making me twitch as I buried my claymore hilt-deep in the beast's flesh.

*'Does he really have to make such an erotic sound?'* I bristled as Nalithor's darkness swarmed around me. *'Shouldn't you be trying to kill it as well, Nalithor?* Hmmm?'

I grimaced and tugged at my claymore, attempting to pull it from the beast's flesh. The blade must have wedged into one of the beast's ribs, because I couldn't get it to budge at all. After a few yanks I grew frustrated and summoned all four of my elements around the length of the sword without a buffer. The elements collided with each other and caused an explosion around the length of the sword, blowing a massive hole in the beast's flesh and shattering a portion of its rib.

*'That's better!'* I grinned when the monster roared with pain. Visible shudders ran through the beast's body as blood poured from the wound and streamed to the ground like a putrid waterfall.

"Mmm... Who lost themselves to the other's desire *this time*, I wonder?" Nalithor chuckled, plucking me off the beast's side and back to one of the shadowy platforms. "We should still exercise *some* caution."

"Rely'ric, Arianna-jiss!" A voice called from somewhere below. "We heard the roaring! What—"

"By the Elders! What is *that*?!" A second voice exclaimed.

*'Nnngh, they just* had *to interrupt.'* Nalithor growled, his hand

twitching against my waist. "*That* is an unclassified type of Chaos Beast. It is much too large for us to bring back to Dauthrmir as a specimen...and too unknown."

'*Those soldiers are just going to get in our way,*' I pointed out, dismissing my claymore as I examined the whimpering beast's hide. '*We're going to have to get creative if we want to kill this damned thing.*'

'*You're* quivering *with the desire to kill it...*' Nalithor teased with a purr. '*One of these days... I will have* you *trembling with desire for* me *instead. Stronger than your desire to kill, if I have my way...*'

'*Now who's lost themselves?*' I bit back a shiver as the Adinvyr's power stroked down my back. '*At this rate neither of us will kill our prey. Or...do you want me to* make you *let me go?*'

'*You could try. I would win,*' Nalithor stated, glancing down at me before returning his focus to the monster. "Arianna-jiss and I will tear the creature apart with our magic. The two of you should retreat to the ship—you do not have protection against beast blood. This...*thing*...bleeds more than one might expect.

"Send word back to Dauthrmir. I want the academy's scholars and an escort sent here to examine the creature immediately."

The soldiers scampered away to do as ordered, and Nalithor finally released my waist. I felt his bloodlust spiraling out of control while he examined the beast...or at least, his bloodlust was at a point that would have made me lose any semblance of control. Nalithor's pulse and breathing were both calm, while his gaze was both excited and calculating.

I just wanted to rush the damned thing and tear into it.

"Am I going to have to put you on a leash?" Nalithor laughed when I shot him a flushed glare. "Do you remember how you killed the monster in Abrantia? I think it is safe to assume that this one should share similarities."

"It had some sort of core powering it, I think," I grumbled, crossing my arms. "I felt something shatter when I pierced it, more fragile than bone."

"Very well. Let's execute this one and then return to Dauthrmir," Nalithor murmured, darkness swirling out from him to prod at the monster. "I think dinner and drinks are in order before we return to more mundane tasks."

*'I'm going to need more than a few drinks to deal with his teasing!'* I sighed, shaking my head as the Adinvyr leapt for the beast.

I watched in silence as Nalithor pelted the creature's open wounds with darkness, fire, and lightning. Strangely, the scent of burning flesh never reached my nose. I could detect Nalithor's scent and the scent of the forest just fine, but anything related to the beasts was beyond me. It unnerved me. *'What could possibly interfere with our senses in such a way? This many beast corpses should have us both running for cleaner air.'*

While Nalithor continued to tear into the beast, I decided to spread my darkness through the forest in search of whatever was interfering with our senses. My gaze snapped up to the sky when I sensed a new, unfamiliar, source of bloodlust. A familiar musty scent assaulted my nose moments later. I felt my lips curl into a ferocious snarl when I spotted just *what* was barreling toward Nalithor.

*'That fucking piece of trash! Why does it have a Godslayer?!'* I sprung from my perch and summoned clawed gauntlets around my hands, rushing to intercept the crazed Angel.

The corrupted bastard let out a screech of terror when I collided with it. I knocked the Godslayer from its hands and then, with a savage kick, broke one of its wings and sent it slamming into the thick pool of beast blood and gore that coated the field below. The Godslayer clattered haphazardly to the ground somewhere. I landed on the Angel's back and crouched, debating with myself what to do to the disgusting creature first.

"A sneak attack from a pathetic flappy-thing, huh…" I gripped one of the Angel's wings and twisted it at a sharp angle. "You may suck at surprise attacks…but you sure do scream well."

I ripped the Angel's left wing in half and grinned when he wailed and bucked beneath my feet. He tried to dislodge me from his back as I tossed his torn wing aside, but I just laughed and gripped his other wing, breaking a piece of it as well. The bastard blubbered and cursed at me, his words near-unintelligible through his pained sobs. His corrupted blood was indistinguishable from the blood of the beasts that surrounded us. It disgusted me.

How could creatures who were supposed to be powerful and regal, stoop so low?

"Ah, ah, ah." Nalithor purred, catching me around the waist and hoisting me off the Angel's back. "Don't kill him yet."

"But—" I growled at Nalithor when he placed me a few feet away from the Angel. "He was trying to kill you!"

"We've been over this; a Godslayer can't harm me." Nalithor chuckled. He took several steps toward the whimpering Angel and then lifted him by his ragged robes. "Ah... What would Gabriel think if she saw you like this?"

"No one cares about the Whore Queen!" The Angel snapped, clawing at Nalithor's hand. "We will overthrow her, and then we will purge every last Devillian from—"

"Aye, so your kind has said for centuries." Nalithor sighed, tossing the Angel aside like an uninteresting toy. An unseen force snapped the corrupted creature's neck before it even hit the ground. Nalithor pivoted to address me next, his expression one of amusement, "Arianna, where did the sword fall?"

"Over there, somewhere." I motioned to my right. "You could have let *me* kill it you know... You got the beast all to yourself!"

"Adorable." Nalithor smirked, tousling my hair as he passed. "Let's find the sword and then take our leave before the stench grows overwhelming...or before you run off and find something else troublesome."

I watched in silence as Nalithor lifted the discarded Godslayer. He grimaced while examining it and then, to my surprise, engulfed the weapon in flames. The liquid metal dripped to the ground with a hiss and ignited the beast blood. Nalithor let out a displeased huff and froze the surface off the blood, snuffing out the flames. He tossed the ruined weapon aside and then pivoted to return to me.

"Let's go." Nalithor nudged the small of my back. "Where there is one Angel, there is usually another. If they're bold enough to attack a god…" He sighed, shaking his head. "It wouldn't do for them to turn their blades against you instead."

Despite his words, Nalithor looked pleased and like he wanted to return to hunting. Neither of us dismissed our armor while we padded through the forest and back to the waiting airship. Although the waiting pilots and soldiers expressed worry upon seeing us, Nalithor dismissed their attentions and led me aboard with another heavy sigh.

"We could have hunted more if you're that disappointed with your prey," I commented dryly as I took my seat and allowed my armor to disappear into my jewelry. "I wouldn't mind thrashing a few dozen more beasts."

"Don't tempt me." Nalithor chuckled, taking a seat next to me. "Besides, I wanted to ask you to heal *this* for me."

He pulled back his sleeve to the elbow and offered me his wrist, revealing deep gouges and claw marks on the back of his hand and all the way up his forearm. The scent of his blood was intoxicating. I wanted another taste. *'I had best heal this quickly…and distract myself while doing so.'*

"Were you aware that Dilonu and Tyana were coming to Dauthrmir?" I asked, taking his arm in both hands.

"I would have *told* you, had I known!" Nalithor huffed in indignation. "They're here for the spring festivities, along with other dignitaries from the Rilzaan Alliance. Darius' escort has been ordered to remain by his side at all times, and—"

"You could have, you know, *told me.*" I motioned at my temples with one finger before returning to mending his wounds. I gave him a firm look and continued, "Darius was a wreck when I found him this morning. He was huddled in a corner with his light going out of control. When I found out *why*, I..."

"Trust me, I sensed that bloodlust of yours." Nalithor laughed, shifting so that he could bring his free hand up to my face. A devious grin settled on his features as he turned me to look at him. "I nearly lost myself to your desire, you know. I wanted their heads rolling at my feet, their bodies torn and broken. I..."

"Calm down, you're—!" I exclaimed as he lifted me onto his lap and nuzzled me, his elevated pulse making blood flow from his wounds faster. *'New subject, new subject. U-uhm... Why does he have to smell like dessert?'*

"How did it feel? Tearing those assassins apart?" Nalithor purred, coiling his tail around my hips. "You made such a mess of them, too..."

"How did it...feel?" I blinked at him for a moment as he chuckled. "They were too easy. Not really a challenge.

"Nalithor, your wounds. Stop fidgeting. Let me—"

"That's not what I meant," Nalithor interrupting, pulling me closer until my back was flat against his chest. "For you to have done *that* to them... You truly enjoy putting filth in their place, don't you?"

'*Filth...*' I tensed when my mind flipped back to the Humans I'd torn to shreds this morning. Their fear. Their pain, and the bright red blood I had painted the courtyard with. An involuntary shiver ran through me when I recalled, and I found myself glancing to the side, flushed with embarrassment.

"Ahhh... There it is." Nalithor laughed, startling me when he used his tail to pull my hips down against his. "You really are an *exquisite* huntress."

I couldn't think of anything to say after a comment like *that*, so I opted to focus on my work instead. While healing him, I realized the flow of blood from his wounds had slowed. They'd even begun to heal in places. I bristled and shot him an irritated glare over my shoulder, earning only a mischievous laugh in reply.

'*Really! He intentionally riled me up? Just so that he could draw on...*' I felt my face flush darker, so I refocused on his forearm. '*Ugh, really? Drawing on my "enjoyment" to heal himself? I don't know if I should be flattered or if I should kick his ass.*'

"Just what will it take for me to earn access to *this?*" Nalithor questioned, drawing a claw down the side of my throat. He laughed when I shivered in response to the contact. "You're quite flushed, my dear. I can't *imagine* why."

"The innocent act doesn't suit you." I shot him a glare, causing him to laugh again. "I should kick your ass."

"You're more than welcome to try. However, I will win." Nalithor purred, squeezing me with both his tail and his free arm. "Dinner, mri'lec, and then research when we return... You know, if we keep up this pattern, you may as well start staying in the palace with me."

*'I really don't know how to take a comment like that...'* I let out a small sigh and released his now-healed arm. "If I have to deal with the presence of *those people* in the palace, I'm going to need something much stronger than mri'lec."

"Anything stronger than that and you won't be able to focus on our work," Nalithor remarked, catching both of my wrists in his hands. He turned them over to reveal his blue-black blood staining my skin, the sight of which made my pulse race.

With a low chuckle, Nalithor used his magic to cleanse the blood from my skin, leaving a prickling sensation on my palms. After a moment of hesitation, he let me out of his lap so that I could fasten myself into a seat properly. I glanced to the side at him, discovering that he was sulking a little in his seat. His disappointed expression was adorable, and his tail was twitching alongside him at a languid pace.

"Are you...sure you shouldn't run home to Darius?" Nalithor asked, shifting his gaze to the side at me. "You said he was quite the mess this morning."

"It's not exactly a home if he threatened to kick me out of it. Nor do I claim to have a home to begin with," I pointed out with a half-shrug, smiling when Nalithor's tail smacked hard into the floor. "Although, as his sister, I should probably tend to him... I don't want to. Not with the way he's been behaving as of late. Besides, he's probably called some of his harem boys over to the house already."

"I hope you're prepared for another late night then," Nalithor remarked, sinking into his seat as he relaxed a bit. "We probably won't receive any data from the scholars for another six hours, minimum, so we may not get to factor our newest prey in."

"That's fine, I don't mind." I laughed, shaking my head. "Even when we're focused on work, your company is still pleasant. While hunting is preferable...taking it easy every now and then is alright too."

"We'll have to continue our competition some time." Nalithor grinned. "Taking a corrupted Angel out like *that* however... I would say you have won for today. You are far too cute when you go on a rampage."

"As much as I enjoy your acceptance of my 'questionable' nature, I still don't quite understand it." I sighed as he snatched up my hand and kissed it.

"You will understand once you have the opportunity to go to Draemir, I believe." Nalithor smiled, lowering my hand from his lips.

*'Draemir huh?'* I wondered, watching as Nalithor maintained his grip on my hand even as he nestled into his seat and shut his eyes. *'What does he want from me anyway? With his antics, I would think he's interested in me, but...'*

I bit back a sigh and shifted my attention away from the Adinvyr. There was no way in the hells I would outright ask him something like *that*. Becoming involved with a deity didn't seem appropriate...and yet I wanted to risk it anyway. I hated the idea of giving him up to someone else.

*'Am I a hypocrite?'* I glanced back to Nalithor's peaceful expression, then up to his platinum horns. *'Perhaps…I will wait and see if he makes his intentions clearer. I have a difficult time telling if he's truly interested, or if he just wants information out of me. Deities just…use people, right?'*

Looking away from him again, I stared out the window to my left and watched as the dense forests between Dauthrmir and Draemir blurred by. The glowing blooms reminded me of the starlight above but, sadly, clouds obscured the sky I had grown so fond of over the past few weeks. Rumbles in the distance indicated it would soon storm, likely bringing rain along with it.

*'Perhaps instead of mri'lec we can have something warm instead.'*

# CHAPTER SEVEN
*Invitation*

Another late night of research come and gone, and we still hadn't made much progress. Dinner had taken much longer than I expected, and while that seemed to suit Nalithor just fine, the academy's scholars weren't finished with their examinations of the unusual beast by the time we returned to the palace. We had so little information to work with that I was beginning to think Nalithor was just attempting to find ways to distract me from my brother, or perhaps keep an eye on me for himself.

I couldn't think of a way to teach Nalithor about X'shmiran beasts—short of taking him to X'shmir to fight them for himself. That didn't sound like it was an option though. *'Pity.'*

Once he'd finally deigned it time for me to return to my lodgings, he'd insisted on walking me home. I couldn't determine if it was to keep me from wandering off to slay Dilonu and Tyana...or if he genuinely wanted to accompany me. As far as I was concerned, figuring that man out was more difficult than researching the beasts.

*'Maybe I should use today to go through more cultural tomes.'* I leaned back in my seat and glanced toward the stove, impatient for my kettle of tea to be ready. *'One of those books must have* something *about the meaning behind all his nuzzling and stuff, right? The tomes on Devillian culture seem quite thorough, so I can't imagine it* wouldn't *be covered.*

*'Not to mention his distaste for "someone else's" blood on me... What's with that, anyway?'*

The whistling of the tea kettle broke my train of thought and prompted me to get out of my chair. After preparing my first cup of tea, I turned and then released a heavy sigh the moment Djialkan rounded the corner to enter the kitchen. He hadn't even said anything yet, but I knew by the expression on his face that I wouldn't like whatever it was.

*"Get dressed,"* Djialkan commanded, coming to hover in front of my face. *"Your presence is required at the academy. It sounds as if you should don a formal set of robes.*

*"It is cold, and it is still raining. I suggest wearing one of your coats— unless you intend to hang on Nalithor's arm all day."*

"Eh?" I glared at the fae-dragon, my grip twitching on my cup. "What about my breakfast? And...really? Hang on Nalithor's arm all day? Just what sort of woman do you—"

*"Have a snack,"* Djialkan interjected, snorting. *"Take Alala with you. I have business to attend to with Onyre and Aleri."*

Djialkan disappeared through the doorway before I could protest further, leaving me to sigh in frustration alone in the kitchen. I grimaced and then set my tea down so that I could pile a few slices of ham on a biscuit as breakfast, then nibbled at my food as I headed back upstairs in search of Alala and clothing. The fluffball was easy enough to find—she was already awake and running around my room recklessly, jumping on and off nearly every surface her dainty paws could reach.

*'You're supposed to be a nocturnal creature... How do you have so much energy in the morning?!'* I watched the fox for a moment and then shook my head. With a small motion of my free hand, I summoned my clothing trunks from a shrizar and let them drop to the floor. "Alala, we're going to the academy, and I need something formal to wear. What do you think, hmmm? Our choices already have Nalithor suspicious that I'm dressing for *him*."

*'Not that I can genuinely deny it,'* I added to myself, stuffing the remainder of my sandwich into my mouth. *'Getting a reaction out of him is fun, even if he's still difficult to deal with. Though...it would be nice to know what he actually thinks.*

*'I can't very well study cultural tomes while overseeing his class though, can I? Damn it!'*

I nibbled one of my fingers while thinking back on the past few days, unsure what to think. Soon enough my mind went back to the last time he'd kissed me, causing my face to grow hot and my pulse to speed up. I shook my head, hard, and then turned to rifle through my dresser in search of undergarments. This was no time for me to dwell on the Adinvyr or his antics.

*'Humph, something must be wrong with me. I shouldn't miss his attentions.'* I yanked my undergarments on while cursing under my breath. *'Least of all the phantom groping. That was just a sign of his hunger, right? So…why did it stop?'*

I paused, frowning. Had it truly stopped? He seemed to be appearing in my dreams more and more frequently as of late, yet I couldn't recall feeling him reaching for me in his sleep anymore. At the very least, if he was, it was nowhere near as strong or often as when I was still in X'shmir. Since coming Below, all of his attention seemed focused on me only when we were physically near each other.

*'I'm over-thinking it.'* I shook my head. *'We're practically on the same schedule now. I'm probably asleep if and when he's reaching for me.'*

Alala's teeth suddenly sank into my ankle, making me yowl and refocus my thoughts on the devilish little creature. I growled at her and she geckered back at me, fur standing on end. She moved to bite me again, and I danced out of reach.

"*What,* 'lala?! You have my attention!"

She warbled at me and pranced over to a pile of clothes she'd dragged from one of the chests, causing me to sigh. The shimmering pile of black and blue satin she'd pulled out was hardly formal as far as I was concerned. It would put a great deal of skin, especially my cleavage, on display. The plunging neckline would reveal at least a third of each breast, and a slit down one side of the skirt would reveal my leg to the hip—and the black outer layer didn't cover much more. The gradated sky blue-to-cobalt fabric was gorgeous, that I couldn't deny, but I had to question how it was an appropriate choice when "formal" had been specified.

"You're *trying* to pique his interest in me aren't you, Alala?" I put a hand on my hip and looked at the warbling fox. "I hope you know what you're doing... Wearing this, I'll *have* to switch to armor if anyone wants to fight me!"

I dressed quickly and pulled on a pair of thigh-high leather boots to go with the dress, followed by a hooded leather overrobe. After pulling my hair into a loose bun and flipping up the hood, Alala leapt up my torso, onto my shoulder, and settled around the back of my neck. Her nose just barely stuck out of my hood. I just laughed at her, shook my head, and then made my way downstairs.

Djialkan was right about one thing at least; the rain was making everything cold. *And dark.* With the clouds blotting out the light from the stars and triple moons, our only sources of light were the glowing plants scattered about the city and the blue-white Magitech lamps lining the roads. I glanced around and scanned the Sapphire Quarter for a moment. The crystalline roads had a dim glow as well, but it seemed as if the majority of the light cast throughout the district came from the plants growing everywhere.

*'Even with the lamps lining the street, and the fixtures on the*

*buildings...*' I pursed my lips and stepped off the porch into the pouring rain. *'I wonder, do they have so much green space in Dauthrmir because of how much light the plants provide?'*

While making my way toward the academy I wrinkled my nose, catching a set of unfamiliar and unpleasant scents in the air. The honeysuckle stench of that Elven *bitch*, Illyana, was mingled with a few new ones—one of which made me bristle. I frowned upon pulling open the main door to the academy; the smell was even stronger there.

A receptionist greeted me in the lobby and directed me in the direction of Nalithor's classroom. I mumbled my thanks to him and strode off in the direction of the nearest staircase.

*'Surprise, surprise.'* I rolled my eyes, clicking through the hallways with my hood still up. *'At this rate, I'll have to have his students call me "Professor" as well. Granted, it did seem unlikely that someone else would've requested my presence. Djialkan could have just* said *it was Nalithor. Tch.'*

Maric and a handful of other soldiers stood guard outside of Nalithor's classroom. They turned and saluted or otherwise bowed to me in silence as I approached. That unpleasant scent was even stronger here, as was the stench of that Elven bitch. Darius' escort looked more on-edge than normal, but I wasn't sure if it was appropriate for me to inquire.

*'How are you this morning, Darius?'* I paused outside the door.

*'Better... I hate having an escort,'* Darius muttered. *'They even have to come with me to the bathroom! I-I know it's necessary, but it really sucks.*

*And the political talks… Well, you saw how they acted yesterday. I can't believe the Vorpmasians didn't just kill our delegates. The Vorpmasian Royal Families aren't as violent as I thought they'd be.'*

*'I see,'* I murmured, crossing my arms. *'They must really respect Nalithor if they're restraining themselves.'*

"*She clearly requires more schooling, Nalithor,*" A male voice argued from somewhere beyond the door, making me frown again. This new voice sounded much like Nalithor, except not as deep and with no accent to speak of. "*I am aware that she jeopardized one of her comrades during your mission, but I cannot think of anyone better to teach her to tame her darkness.*"

"You don't '*tame*' darkness," I interjected, nudging the classroom doors open. "Darkness is an untamable, capricious substance. *Accepting* and *taming* are two very different things."

The man conversing with Nalithor confused me. A simple glance between the two was enough to determine they were closely related. I frowned within my hood while examining this new male. He stood several inches shorter than Nalithor and looked a little younger. His hair was bright electric blue and shoulder-length and hung in layers. His eyes were molten orange and gradated to crimson around his slit pupils. He wore pompous burgundy, gold, and garnet attire and, by the way they hung off his form, I could tell he was more slender than Nalithor.

What perplexed me most was that this unfamiliar, unpleasant-smelling man had no horns, no tail, no claws, and no black sclerae. He looked more like an oddly-colored Elf than anything.

*'Burgundy and gold... Beshulthien colors?'* My gaze shifted between the two men a few more times.

"Arianna, you haven't reverted to X'shmiran ways have you?" Nalithor asked with concern as I turned to shut the classroom doors behind me. When I turned to face him again, his worried expression was soon replaced by laughter. "Is that... Ahahaha, Alala, what are *you* doing *there?*"

"She didn't want to get rained on either," I replied dryly, lowering my hood. Alala leapt from my shoulder and over to Nalithor's. Shaking my head, I pivoted in place to examine the class for a moment. There were several new Elven students among the usual ones, along with Illyana, and they had all taken to glaring at me already.

"So, *this* is the fine young woman that my servants are so displeased with." The unfamiliar man took several steps toward me. A fake warm smile formed on his face as he offered me a hand. "I hope you will forgive them. My name is Rabere Inej Derkesthai. I'm the Emperor of Beshulthien."

"Don't tell me this tiny bitch has your interest too, Your Excellency?!" Illyana exclaimed, slamming her palms down on her desk. She appeared oblivious to the fact that even my *brother*, of all people, growled at her.

"I really should skin you," I murmured, making a small motion with my left hand. Darkness gripped the woman's wrists and ankles and hoisted her high above the classroom while I examined her. "Then again, I could simply quarter you. But...hmmm. I don't think Djialkan or Alala would be interested in what little meat you have to offer. Quite the scrawny one, aren't you?"

"Did you wake up on the wrong side of bed, my dear?" Nalithor purred from his seat, smirking when I shot him a look. "My *brother* here seems to believe that we should allow Illyana to attend our class."

*'Brother?'* I glanced at Rabere. *'Now I'm even more confused. He doesn't have any Devillian features!'*

"I rather dislike being ignored, *Your Highness*," Rabere spoke in a conversational tone, placing his hand on my shoulder. He released a ripple of pathetic, foul-smelling magic in a poor attempt to make me comply. "Kindly put my servant down."

Instead of obliging him, I turned and grabbed him by the wrist, tossing him face-first into the floor. I planted one of my stiletto heels on his spine and twisted his arm back at an unpleasant angle. Rabere's 'servants' let out angry shrieks. Nalithor, however, rose to his feet and walked around the side of his desk, an amused expression on his face.

"And *I* rather dislike being touched without permission!" I snapped hotly, twisting Rabere's arm further for emphasis. "'Kindly' keep your hands and your power to yourself, or I'll decide adding you to my list of prey is worth the hassle!"

"Now, now." Nalithor chuckled, running his hands down my sides before scooping me into his arms. He promptly turned and carried me toward his desk. "As you can see, Rabere, she's immune to Vampiric 'charms' as well, not just those of the Adinvyr. You can't simply command her to release Illyana."

"Yet she allows you to handle her like that?" Rabere countered with disdain as he pulled himself to his feet. He motioned to his brother as he set me down. "That crest… Don't tell me you've *claimed* her as your goddess already? Isn't that a little quick for an *Adinvyr*?"

"Unlike *you*, he has permission to touch me!" I bristled, pulling off my coat. Biting back curses, I hung my coat on the rack behind Nalithor's desk and then turned to examine both the Vampire Emperor and the uneasy students alike. "Now, you should explain to me why I shouldn't rip Illyana-tyir to shreds."

"I was so easily bested by a woman wearing something like *that*?" Rabere sighed, his eyes drifting down to my cleavage. His open ogling elicited a threatening snarl from Nalithor. "Judging by my older brother's growling, he *must* have claimed you.

"Nalithor, she's clearly itching to kill Illyana. Why isn't *she* also a student?"

"As if she could do anything to an Elven Princess of Beshulthien!" Illyana snapped. The corner of my eye twitched and I broke into a scowl. "That she has yet to do anything other than hold me here just goes to prove that she is a weak little *cunt* just like I—"

"Ah, ah, ah." Nalithor chuckled, moving in front of me. He caught both of my wrists when I went to motion the Elf into oblivion, a smile nestled on his face. "You have more self-control than that, *Reiz'tar*, and I won't have you ruining such *delicious* attire with that creature's blood."

The amused Adinvyr brought one of my hands up to his lips and kissed my knuckles before releasing me and turning to look at his brother. The contemptuous glare he settled on Rabere sent a shiver down my spine—I didn't want *anyone*, let alone Nalithor, to *ever* look at me like that. "Rabere, I recommend answering Arianna's question.

"As for why she isn't a student... It is because she has the necessary control and acceptance over her elements to be an *Archmagi*. You see, *this* is the princess that has been sparring with me so evenly."

*'Darius, are they brothers by blood? Do you know?'* I stretched my barriers around my twin's mind as well, watching as both Nalithor and Rabere twitched. Both of them shot me wary looks, unable to listen in.

*'Technically...yes,'* Darius replied uneasily, watching as the brothers returned to glaring at each other. *'A few decades ago, Rabere sought power. He wanted to surpass Nalithor. From what I understand, this was before Nali even became a god.*

*'Rabere was tricked by an Exiled God and made into the First Vampire. Xander was the first person that crossed paths with the new, very hungry, Vampire. The Emperor's panic when he realized what he'd done resulted in Xander becoming the Second Vampire. Unfortunately for them, the Exiled Gods were having fun at Rabere's expense. Vampires are weaker than any of the Devillian races and require blood to feed. They can't live off anything else.*

*'Even as a racial deity, Rabere was still weaker than Nalithor. Once Nalithor became a god, a little over twenty years ago, it only served to further the gap. Adding insult to injury, Devillians can't be turned, and*

*their blood is poison to Vampires.'*

I shot my brother a look—I wasn't expecting such a thorough answer. Perhaps he'd been studying, at least some, after all.

"There's only one woman you've *ever* called 'Reiz'tar.'" Rabere eyed his brother warily. "She *is* your goddess, then? With those Brands and that crest...

"Illyana! Why do you want to kill Arianna-jiss?"

"Because I'm an Elven princess! Nalithor should be mine!" Illyana snapped, somehow maintaining her haughty visage while squirming in the grip of my darkness. "That some little Human *whore* could be considered more worthy than I to work with him is unfathomable! As an Elf, *I* am more suited to—"

I rolled my eyes at the Elf and perched on the edge of Nalithor's desk, examining Illyana in an attempt to determine just what was making me so angry. She didn't even register as a threat to me. Even before she opened her mouth to speak, her mere presence was enough to make my blood boil and my pulse pound. Ripping her into tiny little pieces sounded like an *excellent* idea, and she was only making it worse by acting as if she had rights to *my* Nalithor.

*'She's on Chaos Beast blood,'* I remarked, prodding Nalithor with the thought while I continued to track the struggling Elf. Tilting my head, I tapped my foot against the air as if listening to music. *'I don't see or smell any changes in her... But could that be part of why she's so unreasonable?*

*'It seems like Elves don't like Humans much, sure, but her fellow*

*servants—and your Elven students—are nowhere near this belligerent.'*

"You...are looking at her like she's food." Rabere frowned, his tone nervous. He winced when I glanced at him and raised his hands as if in defeat.

"Arianna," Nalithor began with a devious chuckle. He placed his hands flat on the desk to either side of my hips and leaned down to look me in the eye. "Are you certain? If you're correct, this would be an *excellent* chance to educate our students, don't you think?"

"I'm certain." I pouted when Nalithor chuckled again and pressed his lips to my cheek briefly. "I wouldn't want to kill her *this* badly unless there was something wrong with her. On her own, she's just a buzzing insect."

"Rabere, sit down," Nalithor commanded, motioning toward a smattering of empty chairs by a wall. "Over there somewhere is fine.

"Arianna, cut her."

Without hesitation, I summoned a blade of ice and used a tendril of shadow to wield it, slashing Illyana's wrist. Bright red blood, tainted with tendrils of oily brown, streamed down her skin and to the floor. The Vampire released a displeased hiss in response to the sight, or perhaps the scent, of the woman's fouled blood. However, most of our students simply looked confused. I drew the bitch to the front of the classroom and dangled her there so the students wouldn't need to crane their necks.

*'You really are such a good girl—when you want to be.'* Nalithor teased, trailing his claws along my exposed thigh. "What you're seeing,

*class*, is the beginnings of corruption caused by beast blood. The blood of Chaos Beasts has been gaining popularity as a drug over the past century and is highly addictive.

"After too much consumption, the 'host' begins taking on aspects of beasts—eventually their blood completely turns. Once their blood is tainted in full, the only remaining option is to kill them; thus Arianna-jiss's desire to kill Illyana.

"Beast blood makes it difficult to control oneself. Power, emotions, desires… It's all subject to the whims of the vile blood they've consumed."

*'Can you show them what a corrupted Angel looks like?'* Nalithor asked, squeezing my thigh.

With a simple motion of my left hand, I conjured a statue of ice in the shape of the first corrupted Angel that came to mind—the bastard I had seen so many times while in Limbo. I felt Nalithor tense in response and, for a moment, I wondered if I should have chosen a different likeness instead. I wasn't sure if I wanted him to figure out just who I was…but it was too late to change the statue now. I bit back my panic and focused my attention on the startled students instead, watching as they shrieked and scrambled away.

Alala bristled and geckered at the statue from Nalithor's shoulder, but a few pats from the Adinvyr hushed her.

"Would you like to look like that, Illyana?" I tilted my head and examined the Elf's mortified expression. "I can't claim to be familiar with Elven beauty standards, but I'd imagine that this would *at least* fall short."

"Why would anyone take a drug that does *that* to them?!" Darius demanded in disbelief.

I glanced at my stunned twin and arched an eyebrow; *that* was the first thing he thought to ask?

"It's an illegal method of boosting one's power," Rabere replied uneasily, examining his captured servant. "It's popular among species that have little to no magical power. It enhances physical strength as well as amplifying spells. However, it is also insanely addictive—to the point that most people who resort to it are 'corrupted' in a single sitting."

"You should take Illyana to healers who are capable of cleansing minor corruption," Nalithor pointed out with a dismissive wave, earning an angry glare from his younger brother. "Arianna and I have a class to teach, and this one *hates* it when our class is interrupted."

Nalithor nuzzled into the side of my neck, smirking, and made a show of trailing his claws down the front of my throat. For some reason, Rabere looked incredibly pissed and rushed to collect the Elven bitch before storming out. The playful Adinvyr released a devious chuckle and nipped at my skin before standing tall and returning his attention to instructing the class.

*'I don't like how he was looking at me,'* I informed Nalithor, huffing as I watched him stride away from me and to an assortment of instruments at the back of the classroom. *'I assume you didn't deny his questioning for a reason?'*

*'Having you as my goddess isn't an unpleasant notion.'* Nalithor shot me a smirk over his shoulder. *'That aside, if he believes you haven't been claimed, he is liable to steal you away to Beshulthien and attempt to turn you into one of his Vampire whores. I don't intend to let that happen.*

*'He lost all of his instincts as an Adinvyr upon becoming a Vampire. He is incapable of determining whether you've been claimed.'*

"Nalithor-zir," one of our usual Elven students spoke shyly, holding up a familiar trinket. "W-would you accept this? I heard that Draemiran warriors often adorn their weapons for luck."

*'That looks like…'* I stared at the large platinum charm, taking in the crystals and intertwined scraps of brocade. *'It's very similar to what Corentine did with my crystal. If it's for luck, why is the girl so nervous— and why does Corentine want me to keep mine hidden?'*

"You have only heard half of the tale, then." Nalithor shook his head. "I'm afraid I cannot accept."

The young woman looked equal parts confused and crestfallen as Nalithor turned and continued about his task of distributing small instruments to each of his students. Before I could get a better look at the charm, the Elf had tucked it away and out of sight. I had seen many soldiers in Dauthrmir, thus far, with similar trinkets fastened to the shafts or hilts of their weapons. However, I was still unsure of their significance—luck made sense to me, but Nalithor's rejection and Corentine's warnings struck me as strange.

I could only assume that the Elf's gift was very inappropriate.

*'Half the tale?'* I asked, my curiosity getting the better of me.

Nalithor paused, his tail swishing a few times.

*'I'm unsure of what I could compare it to in X'shmiran culture,'* he finally replied in a dry tone. *'There are different types with different meanings. While they are all meant to bring luck, the* style *indicates whether it was given by family or by a lover. Seeing as she is neither, it isn't appropriate for me to accept. Did I seem cold?'*

'No, I was just curious,' I replied, glancing at the pouting girl and then to Nalithor's back. *'I noticed that quite a few of your men have similar adornments on their blades. It hadn't occurred to me that there might be some deep significance behind them.'*

*'Do you not have similar traditions in X'shmir?'* Nalithor asked, glancing at me over his shoulder curiously.

*'I can't think of anything comparable, no,'* I answered after a moment of contemplation. *'Humans don't often put thought into the gifts they give each other, and X'shmiran culture isn't complex by any stretch.'*

*'That dress of yours is distracting, you know,'* Nalithor commented, his abrupt change of topic causing me to arch an eyebrow at him and the new rhythm his tail had adopted. *'For a moment I thought that I was going to have to fight my brother for you.'*

*'If he tries to use his power on me again, I will kill him.'* I huffed, crossing one leg over the other. *'I get the distinct feeling that he isn't the sibling you're protective over.'*

*'I have three more younger brothers and a younger sister.'* Nalithor laughed. *'Rabere was disowned by our parents and cast out of Vorpmasia for what he did. The Elders' convoluted laws are the only reason he was*

raised to the status of a Lesser God instead of executed. Accepting an offer from, or working with, an Exiled God is usually a death sentence.'

'I find it a little strange that he couldn't determine whether I'm a goddess, or if you had "claimed" me—as you both put it.' I frowned, crossing my arms while I thought. 'You say that he lost his instincts as an Adinvyr, but shouldn't a god be able to determine whether or not someone else is also a deity?'

'He also couldn't determine if your brother is a god—only that he has a great deal of magic,' Nalithor stated, shooting me an amused smile. 'You and Darius have more power than I think you realize.

'As far as the matter of "claiming" goes… Even if you and I were lovers, and had exchanged power as is common among Devillian couples, it isn't something a Vampire would be capable of sensing. It would take a collar around one of our throats to make it clear to him, and even then, my brother thinks more similarly to Humans and Elves on that matter.'

'Let me guess—he thinks that submissives are there to be shared and used by the dominant's friends and whoever else?' I rolled my eyes, watching as Nalithor grimaced and his tail snapped into the floor.

'**I do not share.** But most non-Adinvyr dominants I have met seem to delight in the practice!' Nalithor's venomous tone and snapping tail made it difficult for me to hold back my laughter. 'You seem terribly amused.'

'I share your distaste,' I offered, still attempting to refrain from giggling at him. 'It's just highly amusing when you speak about something with so much contempt. Generally, you're quite calm by comparison.

*'You mentioned Adinvyr specifically—is this a quirk shared by your kind?'*

Nalithor crossed his arms, his expression thoughtful as he strode towards me. *'Ah... Plural relationships are not frowned on in my culture, though they are not what I, personally, desire. Due to our nature as Adinvyr, such relationships are incredibly complex.*

*'The problem that most of us have is this concept of...sharing. Humans and Elves, in particular, seem so keen on sharing with friends or strangers who are* outside of *the relationship. I struggle to understand the appeal. Adinvyr are possessive over whoever their partner—or partners—are.'*

"Professor, will Arianna-jiss be taking over our classes while you're in Draemir?" One of the Rylthra students questioned, leaning forward in his seat.

I tilted my head and shot Nalithor a questioning look. *'Draemir?'*

"Ahhh... Thank you for reminding me." Nalithor chuckled. He swept toward me and gripped my chin once in range, lifting my face toward his as a smirk settled across his features. "Arianna, can I convince you to accompany me to Draemir? Our spring festivities are stretched over the next few weeks, and I would enjoy your presence there."

"We'd love to, right, Ari?" Darius called out cheerfully. I grinned when Nalithor twitched and cast an irritated look at my brother from the corner of his eyes.

"The invitation is for Arianna *only*, Darius. *You* have a great deal of schoolwork to attend to!" Nalithor bristled. "Besides, I'm uncertain of whether you could handle the culture shock."

"I wasn't aware I was allowed outside Dauthrmir's borders," I remarked, drawing Nalithor's attention back to me. "I was under the impression that I had to stay here until my exam results are back, at the very least."

"You would be in *my* care," Nalithor stated with a self-satisfied smile.

"And which one of us is supposed to be keeping which out of trouble, exactly?" I arched an eyebrow at him as his tail slithered around my thigh. "However, I'd be *delighted* to go, if I'm allowed."

"I'll have to keep a close eye on you while we're there..." Nalithor murmured absentmindedly before leaning in and planting a soft kiss on my lips, much to the dismay of my brother and the other students. "It wouldn't do to have anyone trying to steal you from me, now would it?"

'A-Ari...is he implying what I think he's implying?' Darius blinked, looking between me and Nalithor with a startled expression on his face even as the Adinvyr in question moved away to oversee the students once more. 'I-I know he said he didn't like men, but...he just kissed you and—'

'Darius, focus on your task or you're going to hurt something—or someone.' I pointed at the small metal object in his hands.

'Your brother is bothering you again?' Nalithor questioned while weaving between desks. He chuckled and reached up to scratch Alala's chin as she hissed at my twin. 'I suppose Alala thinks so, at any rate.'

'He was asking me if "you're implying what he thinks you're implying,"' I offered, glancing around the room. 'I must say, after that, it doesn't look like any of them can focus on the task you gave them. Granted, my focus is a little lacking at the moment as well...'

'Alala mentioned that Djialkan didn't let you get breakfast.' Nalithor motioned at the fox riding on his shoulder. 'With my brother lurking in the city, I'm not inclined to let you wander off without me to escort you.'

I arched an eyebrow at him. A lack of breakfast was hardly the reason I was struggling to focus. *He* was to blame, yet he seemed oblivious.

'Strangely, I agree with you about the escort.' I bit back a grimace. 'I don't like the way he or his magic smells. That said, a lack of food isn't why—'

'I'll have someone from The Little Orchid bring you food,' Nalithor stated with a smile, turning to return to the front of the class. He walked over and lifted me off his desk, then placed me in his chair instead. 'You are a little too distracting for all of us when sitting there like that, my dear.'

'Distracting, huh?' I pondered, falling into silence as I settled into the oversized chair. Sighing, I crossed my legs and let my mind wander off. 'With how good he smells it's almost impossible for me to focus properly!'

Frowning, I contemplated the events of the past few weeks. Something about this place seemed to prod along the desires I *thought* I had managed to suffocate so long ago. I wanted to taste Nalithor's blood again so much that it hurt, and that was one of the more tame desires that had been running through my mind as of late. The fact that Adinvyr could sense lustful thoughts still made me hesitate, but there was no denying my libido wanted to spin out of control just as badly as my bloodlust did—if not more so.

*'Ari, you look like you're going to take a bite out of Nali!'* Darius snapped, causing my face to flush as I refocused my thoughts. *'You really have been spending too much time around the Devillians, haven't you?'*

*'I don't think it's that...'* I grumbled, shifting to switch which legs were crossed. *'Have you had any unusual urges while around these people? You've spent more time with a broader variety of non-Humans here than I have.'*

*'Unusual... I don't think so,'* Darius commented with a frown. *'I've never really been cautious about such things though. I haven't had to be.'*

*'What has you so distracted, hmmm?'* Nalithor suddenly spun the chair around so that the back of it was to the students. He looked down at me with an amused expression. *'You were regrettably unresponsive when I attempted to get your attention...and you are rather flushed, Arianna. Is your brother angering you again, or...?'*

I just looked up at Nalithor for a moment, startled and unsure of what to say. Actually telling him what Darius and I had been discussing seemed...embarrassing.

*'I still want to skin the foul-mouthed healers that oversaw my examinations the other day, and I still can't stand the presence of those*

*X'shmiran bastards!'* I huffed the first excuse that came to mind as Nalithor reached down and tilted my chin around as if looking for something wrong.

*'Foul-mouthed? You must have met Rylda and Rymia.'* Nalithor chuckled, running his thumb over my lips. *'They used to work for the Vraelimir Family—I can imagine that they must have been quite troublesome.'*

*'They seemed convinced that, because I'm Human, I would scamper off and breed with everything!'* I bristled and crossed my arms, growling. *'That was* before *they saw my blood is black, but it still pisses me off.'*

*'Those two have an intense dislike for Humans,'* Nalithor offered with an amused smile, finally releasing my chin. *'Humans are notorious for being disloyal, and the two of them learned the truth of it the hard way. They are likely concerned about what your intentions are whilst in Vorpmasia.*

*'You don't strike me as the disloyal sort…but then, you aren't very Human either.'*

"If you don't hurry, you are all going to be late for your next class," Nalithor spoke in a loud, firm voice. He straightened to glare at the students over the back of the chair and, moments later, I heard papers rustling and students rushing to obey.

I spent most of the following hours in silence, eating breakfast and then observing the remainder of Nalithor's classes. Something seemed to have changed about the way his students looked at me but, for the life of me, I couldn't determine *what*. I had managed to keep my mind off lusty thoughts for the most part, so I didn't think it was that. Even so, the way some of them looked at me made me concerned that my thoughts during "playtime" might have escaped my barriers after all.

*'When do we need to leave for Draemir?'* I asked, watching the last class of the day trickle out the door.

*'I'm required to leave for Draemir tomorrow,'* Nalithor began in a contemplative tone. *'You can either leave with me tomorrow, or wait until the festival is close to starting in earnest. That would be a week and a half from now.*

*'Despite my role as a god, I am still considered a prince in Draemir—and expected to act as one. My parents wish for me to fulfill my duties whilst there...and they are quite curious about you.'*

*'Me? Why me?'* I blinked up at him as he offered me a hand up.

*'They are startled by my pledge to conquer X'shmir for you.'* Nalithor smiled, pulling me to my feet and into his chest. *'Seeing as I've never seen fit to conquer* for *someone before... Perhaps they are concerned that you've cast a spell on me, hmmm?'*

*'I dislike the sound of "princely duties,"'* I informed him with a small growl, prodding his chest. *'Sounds like boring political dinners with cock-hungry noblewoman who are too—'*

*'You are correct.'* Nalithor laughed. He released me and pulled my overrobe from the nearby rack and offered it to me with a grin. *'As my guest, you are allowed to claim exclusive rights to my attention if you desire...but I can't promise that you won't be challenged for that right.'*

*'So, you have to rely on me to rescue you?'* I smirked at him and

shrugged on my overrobe.

*'I don't expect you to rescue me,'* Nalithor replied, slipping his arms around me. He leaned down and nuzzled into my shoulder, sighing. *'In fact...if you don't desire me, it would be quite inappropriate for you to do so.*

*'Regardless, there are some duties I must attend to that you can't pull me away from, such as my role as a general. Seeing as you are not my partner, I am not permitted to drag you into such affairs. Draemir differs from Dauthrmir in that regard.'*

*'And we won't know who my partner is for a while yet since my tests weren't rushed?'* I offered in understanding, pausing as Nalithor nuzzled me again. *'I get the feeling that this will be quite the learning experience.*

*'Still, I see no reason to wait. I'll admit that I'm curious to learn more about you and Draemir—and this seems like a prime opportunity to do so.'*

*'You would like to learn more about me?'* Nalithor questioned, intrigued, as he pulled me to the door and led me down the winding hallways of the academy. *'With the way you've been watching me all day, I was expecting you to say that you wish to take a bite of me.*

*'Though, I must admit, I've been concerned that you may have found yourself a lover already. You have been quite distracted.'*

*'A...?'* I shook my head and burst into disbelieving laughter. *'No. Don't you think I would have kicked your ass for kissing me if I had found someone?'*

Nalithor frowned. *'It's difficult to believe that no one else is* at least *pursuing you.'*

*'I think they're all scared of me,'* I replied dryly, placing one hand on my hip. Motioning with my free hand, I continued, *'You're the only one that's proved worthy of my interest, anyway. I— What? What's the surprised look for?'*

*'You aren't going to make me jump through elaborate hoops to prove myself?'* Nalithor asked, curious, as he stopped and turned to examine me. *'Most women would require... Ah, but I suppose you aren't "most women" are you?'*

*'I would like to think I'm not...'* I tilted my head. *'You treat me like a person and not like a "thing"—perhaps even as an equal. You've also shown me that you're more than capable both as a warrior and as a sparring partner. Perhaps you're a bit of a tease...but I can't really say that's a bad thing.*

*'Still, I do wonder why both you* and *Darius think I was considering taking a bite...'*

*'You're a very predatory woman, Arianna.'* Nalithor smiled, slipping his arm around me once more. *'Now then, I will see you home and make sure my brother doesn't intend to sink his fangs into you. I might say to the hells with the Elders' laws and kill him myself if he lays finger or fang on you.*

*'I will fetch you in the morning so that we may depart.'*

# CHAPTER EIGHT
## *Draemir*

The door to my room slammed open and startled me out of my deep slumber. My heart leapt into my throat as I tumbled out of bed, falling to the floor in a tangle of blankets. Before I could clear my bleary vision, the force of light slammed through me. Adrenaline flooded my system, sending my pulse into dizzying overdrive and making me tremble.

Djialkan and Alala both dashed in front of me and faced the door, snarling.

"Ari, get out of my fucking house!" Darius screamed at me.

I just sat on the floor and stared at him for a moment, my blood running cold. Darius looked hysterical, incensed, and had shimmering light swirling around his body. I heard armored feet rushing up the stairs, alongside orders barked in Draemiran. Whether they were coming to protect Darius or me was uncertain.

"What—" I shivered and pulled a few blankets over my nude form, shrinking away from the light. *'Hate it. Light... Snuff it out.* Snuff it out! *G-get rid of it.* **Kill**—'

"It's all *your* fault!" Darius screeched, stalking into the room fully. "Because of *you*, my friends think that I was lying about Nalithor being *mine*! They don't believe that Vivus and I got to fuck him! Because of *you*, I can't even fuck Vivus in my room! *My room*! This is ridiculous!"

"You *made* him kiss you and invite you to Draemir, didn't you? Fucking bitch!"

*'Nalithor? His?'* I twitched.

My Guardians both shifted, both growing to the size of a small pony. They blocked half the room, their threatening noises growing more agitated and bassy. Several soldiers and mages from Darius' escort skidded to a stop in the doorway, with Maric at the front. Most of them were looking from Darius and to my guardians, unsure of what to do.

"How is it *my* fault you lie your fucking ass off?!" I snapped at Darius. *'Kill it. That light, I hate it. Why won't you extinguish it?! M-maybe...if I snuff you out, then...'*

"**I said get out!**" Darius roared, forming his light into javelins. "I should have listened to our parents when they said that all an Umbral Mage like *you* wants is to make the life of an Astral miserable!"

Darius hurled his javelins at me. I jerked up a wall of darkness between us and cringed when the light slammed into it, releasing a shrill sound that reverberated through the air. The scent of light, its presence, the *look* of it—I hated it all. Especially *his* light. *'It's wrong, so wrong. Twisted. Extinguish it. Hate it, hate it, hate it! How is it* my *fault that* he *made such a stupid mistake?! Nalithor is* mine, *not his!'*

"M-Maric…" I curled my fists into the blanket, shaking with both rage and fear.

"Yes, General?" Maric stiffened in the doorway, though he shot me a concerned frown.

"G-get Darius out of m-my sight," I stuttered through clenched teeth. "Before I—"

"I *said* I'm kicking you out of the house!" Darius snapped, attempting to push past both Djialkan and Alala. "Why are you still sitting there? Get out!"

Djialkan's jaws clamped down on Darius' arm and, with a sharp motion of his head, the fae-dragon threw my raging twin at the wary soldiers. Maric shot me another concerned look before saluting me and beckoning for his men to restrain my brother. The Astral Mages in Maric's command blanketed Darius in warm golden light, before flinching and scrambling backward when I shot them a murderous glare.

*"Let Her Highness dress and gather her belongings in privacy!"* Djialkan bellowed, his voice making the windows rattle. *"If she does not slay you for the intrusion, Alala and I will!"*

Alala lowered her head and snarled at the Astral Mages to make her point, lips curling upwards to reveal fangs as long as my hand. The Astrals fled backward and dragged Darius from the room, having realized that my twin's kicking and screaming was the least of their worries at that given moment.

I wanted to kill them. Their fucking light wore at my patience.

"Arianna-jiss." Maric sighed, running a hand through his scruffy hair. "Will you be alright?"

"Just...keep Darius and your Astral Mages away from me," I replied, rising to my feet with a blanket clutched over my chest. "I need to meet up with Nalithor soon anyway, but—"

"I'm sure I don't have to tell *you* of all people to keep this spat from Nalithor until Dauthrmir is far behind you," Maric interjected, giving me a firm look. "You told us to take Darius out of your sight so *you* wouldn't kill him, right? Nalithor won't be so merciful."

I nodded in reply and watched as the rugged soldier left. Djialkan shambled over to the door and nosed it shut so that I could get dressed. Alala returned to her normal size with a puff of pale blue magic, but her fur still stood on end. She paced around the room, grumbling and growling, the entire time I was getting ready.

I couldn't stop trembling while throwing on a pair of low Susthulite sarouel and a matching cropped top. For the time being, I pulled a long coat on over the ensemble. It seemed likely to me that Draemir would be much warmer than Dauthrmir due to its proximity to the Suthsul Desert, and the lighter clothing meant I could dress faster—and get away from the damned light that was eating away at my sanity.

While I attempted to make myself look presentable, Djialkan went about the room returning all our belongings to my shrizars. Darius' light still raged freely around the house while I pinned my curls out of my face and applied some makeup. I dropped my tube of lipstick several times before managing to steady my hands enough to paint my lips.

*"Arianna, we should hurry,"* Djialkan returned to his cat-like size and perched on my shoulder. *"Fraelfnir says that Darius is struggling to come upstairs again."*

"C'mere, 'lala." I turned in my seat and beckoned to the irritable fox. "Let's go meet Nalithor."

Alala huffed and leapt from the bed to my arms. Her tail draped over my wrists and twitched in irritation. Sighing, I turned to look at the door to my room and hesitated. Wisps of golden light were pushing around the door's edges, corrupting what was once *my* territory with its crisp stink. I shook my head and moved to the balcony, choosing to leap into the yard below instead of walk downstairs.

Before walking away from the house, I glanced back at it one more time, watching the shimmer of light as it pressed against the first-floor windows from inside. I'd never seen my brother's power act in such a way before, but his escort seemed to be keeping him in check—for now.

*'Really... What's with him all of a sudden?'* I mumbled curses under my breath and turned to stalk through the Sapphire Quarter. *'Who in*

*the hells would believe him about Nalithor anyway?'*

Finding Nalithor wasn't difficult by any stretch of the imagination. He shot me a concerned look when he spotted me strolling down the street to meet him, but it looked as if he didn't plan to inquire about the situation just yet. Both Djialkan and Alala were *still* making angry noises, and Alala was still channeling her inner porcupine. *'She'd look a lot more threatening if she wasn't so soft...'*

"Shall we?" Nalithor shifted his attention from the grumbling fox and up to my face. "You have everything you need?"

"The sooner we get going, the sooner these two will stop grumbling—I hope," I replied with a small smile, looking up at the Adinvyr.

Nalithor opened his mouth as if to say something, then shook his head slightly and closed his mouth. He beckoned for me to follow him, and I hurried to oblige, releasing a relieved sigh. His presence and scent were already helping to calm me, though the uneasy glance he shot in the direction of "Darius'" house didn't go unnoticed. That he was uneasy didn't surprise me. Particles of gold and prismatic light had begun drifting around the entire property during our brief exchange and only seemed to be expanding.

*'Disgusting...'* I shivered, squeezing Alala for comfort. A hint of bloodlust rose again, so I tore my gaze away from the house and settled my gaze on Nalithor's back instead. *'If anyone else had tried that with me, they would be...'*

"Here, we'll be taking this airship to Draemir," Nalithor called to me a few minutes later, breaking me out of my self-pity. "The flight will take several hours, so—"

"*There had better be food!*" Djialkan huffed, leaping from my shoulders to fly past Nalithor.

Alala yipped her agreement and scrambled out of my grip to dart after Djialkan. The crew exchanged amused looks when the white fluffball and the fae-dragon sped past them, then resumed their pre-flight preparations. Returning my attention to Nalithor, I found that he looked expectant—but was waiting patiently by the ramp for me. I still wasn't exactly fond of the flying deathtraps by any stretch but, for now, getting away from Darius seemed more important than the unease the airships made me feel.

I leaned against the railing on one of the ship's outer decks and watched as the lush Draemiran forests rushed by beneath me. The Dauthrmir Crater was several hours behind us now, leaving me free of the disgusting light my brother wielded. The air here was comfortably warm and filled with the scents of the forests far below. I could make out massive ancient trees which bloomed with pale, glowing flowers in many colors. We were now close enough to the city itself that I could spot rolling farmland, lit by moonlight, on the horizon.

Nalithor had left Alala, Djialkan, and I to our own devices for the most part. Both of my Guardians were still in a foul mood, but *my* mood had been lifting since entering Draemiran territory. It was difficult for me to stay cranky when there was such beautiful, sweet-smelling scenery sprawled before me. The combination of ancient mrifon trees, others I didn't have a name for, and the starry sky above was just…breathtaking. Sparkling rivers and streams carved their way through the forests and past the farmland, heading far into the distance. Most of the country, thus far, seemed undisturbed by both people and beasts alike.

"I hope you aren't tense because going to Draemir worries you," Nalithor spoke from somewhere behind me, causing me to turn and watch him as he approached. He shot me a concerned frown, but I just smiled back.

"Djialkan and Alala haven't spouted off and vented to you already?" I questioned, tracking the concerned Adinvyr's movements as he walked over to me.

"Aren't you cold?" Nalithor frowned, his pale eyes wandering down my form for a moment, while I just blinked up at him in surprise. "I certainly don't mind the view but—"

"This is about as warm as a X'shmiran summer!" I laughed, shaking my head at him before turning to look out over the ship's railing again. "I'm not acclimated to the warmer temperatures Below, yet, and I assume it's only going to get warmer."

"Susthulite attire suits you…" Nalithor murmured, wrapping an arm around my waist. "I'm beginning to think there isn't anything you *wouldn't* look good in."

"Really though, neither of them told you?" I probed again as his hand came to rest over my stomach.

"They are both angrier than you are and refuse to speak with me." Nalithor shook his head, resting his free hand on the railing. He looked down at the forest below and sighed, continuing, "I get the feeling that I'm going to be very displeased by whatever has all three of you so angry on such a beautiful morning."

"Well, aside from almost every Adinvyr in the damn city pelting me with their fantasies all night, every night," I began dryly, smiling when Nalithor's grip twitched and growled. "Darius kicked us out of the house this morning. *Permanently.* We almost didn't have time to stow things in my shrizar."

"He...*what?*" Nalithor demanded furiously, turning away from the railing to bring a hand to my face. "Would you like me to put him in his place for you? That brat needs to learn some—"

"Not necessary. His reasoning for kicking me out is pathetic." I grinned, shaking my head. "Not only is he angry about being unable to bring Vivus to the house... He's angry because somehow it's *my* fault that his "friends" discovered he was lying about bedding you."

"He claimed to have done *what* to me, exactly?" Nalithor bristled, lowering his face toward mine. "And how is it *your* fault that they discovered his lies?"

"Supposedly I *made* you kiss me," I grumbled, glancing away from him as I flushed. "From what I understand, he's been claiming that he and Vivus both topped you."

"I'm of half a mind to kill your brother." Nalithor growled, pulling my face towards his until I had to stand on my tiptoes. "That he would

155

go as far as to blame you *and* kick you out of the house... He really is quite obsessed with me, isn't he?"

"He is. And he doesn't seem to realize it's pointless to..." I trailed off and blinked at the sight beyond the railing, staring at the sprawling city nestled on the shore of a large lake. "Wow."

Nalithor chuckled, released my face, and pulled me back against his chest. I stared at the expansive maze of tiered, lacquer-coated wooden buildings in awe. While Dauthrmir was built upon vertical tiers of floating stones, Draemir had instead chosen to build outward. The city curved around and out from a large lake, its most decorated buildings sitting along the lake's shore itself. It appeared to be built *around* nature instead of attempting to overtake it.

What truly stunned me was the shimmer of magic that ran through *everything*. Veins and orbs of many-colored lights twinkled or pulsated through everything in the city, the forests, and the surrounding farmland. Magic truly seemed to be part of everything in their lives and their surroundings.

"You're a little more fascinated than I expected." Nalithor squeezed me.

"Would you... Would you like to see what your home's magic looks like?" I offered after a moment, tilting my head back to look at the surprised Adinvyr.

"Isn't it quite a strain to share such vision with others?" Nalithor hesitated, glancing from me to the city and back.

"It's not that bad." I shook my head and then shot him a small, teasing smile. "Consider it a gift?"

I offered him my right hand and then bit back a grin when I saw a faint flush rise to his cheeks. Finally, he took my hand, and I refocused on the scenery before me. Nalithor's grip tensed briefly when I switched from my normal vision and back to seeing magic. I heard his breath catch in his throat as he gazed down at his city and the surrounding countryside below. After several long moments, he leaned down to nuzzle my shoulder, his arm tightening around me even as he withdrew from the connection that let him see.

"Thank you, Arianna." Nalithor purred into the side of my neck, squeezing me again as if for emphasis. "Ahhh... Now I find myself even more inclined to shirk my princely duties in favor of pampering you."

"Princely duties? Sounds like politics," I commented, suppressing a shudder when Nalithor's lips brushed against my throat. "Politics *does* tend to ruin everything."

"Yes, well, my parents did decide to be troublesome." Nalithor laughed. He planted a brief kiss on the side of my neck before straightening to his full height. "They likely mean to test me by throwing every noblewoman they can find my way. Or, perhaps they intend to test *you*. I am uncertain. Either way, they're not just going to let me get away with choosing to conquer for someone."

"Test *me*?" I inquired. Pursing my lips, I shook my head and glanced up at him again. "Are there more cultural nuances that you should be informing me of before we arrive? *Hmmm?*"

"As I mentioned yesterday, you have the right to claim my company for yourself because you're my guest. At the same time, it is not appropriate for you to '*intervene*' in such a way if you are not...interested," Nalithor replied, causing me to arch an eyebrow at his hesitation.

"So, I can only 'rescue' you if I'm sincerely interested?" I tilted my head a little when his grip twitched tense enough for his claws to bite into my stomach. "What else do I need to know? Are there any particular customs for clothing or speaking that I should abide by? Should I be concerned about challengers? What about *more* people prodding my barriers? Will—"

"While I would like to see you in more Draemiran attire," Nalithor began, smoothing his hands down my sides and to the low-rise waistband of my sarouel, "I can't deny that *this* has its charms as well. However, you're free to wear what you like in Draemir—we *celebrate* the male and female physiques in Draemir, unlike X'shmir. You could opt to walk around the city in lingerie, and it would still be considered appropriate. If anyone decides to shower you with unwanted attention, I would be happy to take care of them for you. Aside from that, I would recommend speaking in our native tongue while in Draemir."

"Rely'ric, we will be landing soon. You and Arianna-jiss should return to your seats," a voice called from behind us.

I bit back an amused smile when Nalithor growled at the soldier for interrupting our conversation. After a heavy sigh, Nalithor gave me a small tug and led me back inside the airship and to our waiting seats.

For several minutes we simply sat in silence, but Nalithor watched me with an unreadable expression the entire time. So, I chose to prod him for more information.

*'How should I handle honorifics?'* I glanced to the side at him. *'In X'shmir I'm not treated like a princess, but you said that* here *I should still be treated like one.'*

*'Even if you weren't the daughter of royalty, your Brands would elevate you to high status in Vorpmasia. Honorifics are not required for people of lower rank than you.'* Nalithor's expression shifted from unreadable to one of contemplation as he spoke. *'Might I convince you to don one of your emblazoned coats for the walk through the city? Call me selfish if you wish, but I would rather not share the sight of your skin with the residents of the Scarlet District. We will be passing through there on our way to the palace.'*

*'Selfish?'* I shot him a crooked grin, watching as he flushed. *'Were it for any other reason, I might be concerned you wished to hide me from view. Seeing as it's the* Scarlet *District, however, I can—'*

*'I would much rather show you off,'* Nalithor interjected firmly, reaching over to grasp my hand. He lifted it to his lips and kissed it, a playful twinkle dancing in his eyes. *'Those people and I have never seen eye-to-eye. They do not follow the same customs that the nobility and royalty do. As far as I'm concerned, they are not worthy enough to see any part of you.'*

*'You never answered me about challengers.'* I nudged him once before summoning one of my high-collared armored overrobes.

*'If any of them desire you they* should *challenge you,'* Nalithor replied, tensing his jaw. *'However, the same could be said for the Adinvyr in Dauthrmir. If they believed you to be close in power to them, they should have challenged you—otherwise, it is only polite to leave you alone. As such…my offer still stands to put them in their places for you.'*

Once the airship was fully settled into its dock on the outskirt of the city, Nalithor rose to his feet and offered me his hand. After pulling me to my feet, he shot me a brief smile and then moved away to speak with one of the nearby shoulders. I took the opportunity to shrug on my overrobe and fasten the buttons of the double-breasted bodice into place. Alala and Djialkan soon rounded a corner, seeming in better moods than before. The fae-dragon himself perched on one of my shoulders. Alala ran circles around my feet for a short while before allowing me to pick her up.

"Well then, I suppose we should be going," Nalithor remarked, turning away from the soldier to look between the warbling fox and me. "Hmmm…"

"Hmmm?" I questioned, tilting my head as the Adinvyr strode toward me.

"I'll be taking these." Nalithor smirked, plucking my hair sticks from their place. "Alala, are you really going to keep both of Arianna's arms to yourself?"

Alala warbled at him, swishing her tail in reply. Nalithor released a dejected sigh.

"Very well. Stay close, Arianna." Nalithor beckoned for me to follow him through the corridors of the airship.

"Concerned that some scoundrel will come whisk me away?" I teased, falling into step with the sulking Adinvyr. He glanced down at me, so I shot him a smile in return.

"Didn't you once call *me* a scoundrel?" Nalithor pointed out dryly, causing me to grin.

"I've decided you're not a scoundrel. You're just extremely mischievous and playful!" I laughed, following Nalithor out of the airship and into the temperate, sweet-smelling air of Draemir. *'Ah... I see you're even more popular here,* Your Highness.'

I glanced around at the dockyard, examining the throngs of waiting Adinvyr. They were all exuberant and attempting to get a better look at their prince. However, their reaction to me was almost instantaneous. Hushed murmurs swept through the crowd like a wave, followed by dozens of nudging and prodding at my barriers. Their thoughts remained tame while they expressed their curiosity and confusion, and I could only hope it would stay that way.

Almost all the women had mrifon in their hair to signal their availability and wore clothes that revealed their seductive figures. Some of them looked disappointed that Nalithor had brought a woman home with him, but a surprising number of them seemed more interested in *me* than in Nalithor. I wasn't quite sure what to make of it. It took most of my self-control to keep from hiding behind him.

"Shall we, Arianna-z'tar?" Nalithor smiled at me, expertly ignoring the clamoring crowd. "If we hurry, we should be able to spar before lunch."

"Only if you promise to show me around later." I grinned at him. "*If* you'll indulge me, of course."

'*-z'tar now, is it?*' I wondered privately as we escaped the crowd and made our way through the Scarlet District at a brisk pace. '*My distaste for such people aside, this district sure is lavish. Still. Calling me "Arianna-z'tar?" And in front of so many people? Is he trying to hint that he's that interested in me…or is he trying to rile up the crowd of strumpets? How am I supposed to—*'

My thoughts paused as the probing of my barriers worsened, causing my eye to twitch. Perhaps most of them had focused on Nalithor at first, but now I seemed to have their undivided attention. They appeared intent on figuring me out. While their collective presence was still tame, the sheer number of them alone threatened to give me a headache.

'*I didn't accidentally hide my power behind my shields again, did I?*' I fell into step with Nalithor while taking in my surprisingly ornate surroundings. Lavender and scarlet Magefire lanterns hung from the buildings or were otherwise affixed to posts, arches, and fences.

'*Bothering you already, are they?*' Nalithor inquired, a small frown tugging at his lips. '*Your power isn't hidden. However, your coat* does *obscure your Brands—aside from those on your hands. Perhaps they are confused.*'

'*I'll kick their asses later if needed.*' I shook my head, then moved a little closer to Nalithor. I didn't like some of the stares I was attracting.

*'I'm still not used to being noticed in a way that doesn't involve things being thrown at me...'*

*'I* must *think of a sufficient punishment for the X'shmirans,'* Nalithor muttered, bristling even as he continued to ignore everyone we passed. *'How would you like to spar with me today? Armed, unarmed, magic... Or perhaps you would like to work on those grappling skills of yours?'*

*'You mean my* lack *of grappling skills?'* I laughed. *'I should probably say that working on my grappling skills would be best. Though, I prefer not to script sparring matches.'*

*'You prefer them to be more chaotic and similar to actual battle?'* Nalithor shot me a knowing smile before slipping an arm behind my back, pulling me closer.

*'Yes, exactly.'* I confirmed, glancing to the side when several women released indignant shrieks; they didn't seem to approve of Nalithor's hand on my hip. *'You seem quite practiced at ignoring the people of this district, but they still appear quite enamored with you, Nalithor.'*

*'I disagree with most of our people about whether or not districts such as this are needed.'* Nalithor grimaced. *'Although the male and female prostitutes are all willing participants, treated well, and live their own lives outside of "work"... I strongly disapprove of such practices.*

*'They dislike me both because I won't bed them, and because I'm so dedicated to the* proper *methods that the nobles and the rest of the Royal Family adhere to. We prefer to hunt for our "food," and we prefer to* earn *the attentions of others.'*

*'So, they're like jealous, disgruntled children?'* I offered, attempting

to tune out a few whistles from above us. *I'll be honest; I half-expected to be met with animosity for being* Human *and accompanying their* precious *prince.'*

"Yo, Nali! You're back?" A vaguely familiar voice called from somewhere ahead of us.

I turned my attention forward to find a red-headed Adinvyr in armor. He was examining me curiously, but the look in his bright green eyes and the snapping of his bronze tail gave him away. In a blur, he dashed toward me with one of his fists pulled back. Before either of them could fully react, I palm-struck his wrist out of my way and then spun into a roundhouse kick.

My shin connected with the Adinvyr's armor with enough force to make him stumble. Alala let out a discontented huff and scrambled out of my arms to perch on Nalithor's shoulder. Djialkan remained with me and puffed darkness while peering at the Adinvyr that had rushed me.

"While I'm not a fan of bronze, I think I might take your horns and mount them on my wall," I remarked conversationally, shifting into an offensive stance. Nalithor just laughed while I examined the startled Adinvyr. "Aren't you the same one that tried to pick a fight with me back in X'shmir?"

"Still biting off more than you can chew I see, Sorr," Nalithor spoke with a broad grin. "Arianna, you didn't even bother to shield your leg, did you?"

"Beast hide is harder than his armor," I replied with a dismissive huff, pivoting to look at my smirking companion. "You two know each other well, then? I shouldn't make a trophy out of him?"

"She's serious, isn't she?" Sorr blinked at me, then looked to Nalithor who had begun laughing again. "If she kicks like *that*, I can see why you said you didn't need an escort!"

"Arianna, Sorr is one of the Draemiran Generals. I trained him." Nalithor chuckled, motioning to the red-headed Adinvyr. "His manners may be lacking, at times, but he's a good warrior."

"So, I shouldn't kill him? I suppose I'll have to find something else to hunt." I sighed, running a hand through my curls before pulling my hair over my shoulder. "Still…you declined an escort, Nalithor?"

"Seeing as we can both take on a Dux on our lonesome, I don't believe it necessary," Nalithor replied dryly, causing Sorr to look toward me with disbelief. "Let's go. The sooner we get through your introduction to my *doting* mother, the better."

"Erist'il and Arom'il already arrived too," Sorr spoke flatly. I watched with interest as Nalithor's tail smacked into the cobblestone streets with enough force to crack several of the stones. "Keeping Erist and Ellena away from *this* fine young woman will be difficult."

"Arianna, do *try* not to kill my mother or *that woman*, won't you?" Nalithor sighed, motioning for me to follow him. "Or at least leave me one of them…"

*'Now, now, cheer up.'* I hurried after him, grinning. *'A festival is supposed to be a* happy *occasion, isn't it?'*

*'Together, my mother and Erist are the real "scoundrels."'* Nalithor

huffed, bristling. *'I was hoping to be free of Erist's and Arom's pestering for this week at least. They are usually late to arrive... Ah. Mother must be plotting something. Wonderful.'*

Nalithor's face flushed when I giggled at him, but I couldn't help it. A *god* complaining about his mother's antics struck me as hilarious.

*'Draemir is quite beautiful,'* I informed him with a bright smile, attempting to change the subject. To my surprise, he flushed darker and didn't say anything, so I continued, *'I'm surprised you didn't choose to wear one of your kimonos home. Your clothing is distinctly Dauthrmiran.'*

*'I had hoped that my people would cease looking at me like meat if I wore something more...covering,'* Nalithor grumbled, running a hand through his hair. *'You seem fascinated.'*

*'Of course I am!'* I grinned. *'Though, I get the feeling you don't want me to wander off and explore on my own.'*

*'I don't trust anyone to keep their claws or fangs off you when you smell so damn good...'* Nalithor muttered, blushing darker. *'Once you've settled into your suite and we've had our sparring match, I'll take you into the city for lunch. How's that sound?'*

*'I'd like that,'* I answered, watching with curiosity as Nalithor's face remained rather pink. After a moment, I reached out to Djialkan. *'It isn't my imagination is it?'*

*'He's smitten.'* Djialkan snorted.

It was difficult for me to accept, but I couldn't think of any other reason for Nalithor's behavior. What else could possibly cause a *warrior* to blush? I didn't know how to feel about the matter and dwelling on it made me...anxious.

I found myself drawn in by Draemir's unusual landscaping, architecture, and people once more as we wandered through their mercantile districts. Everything was immaculate and artistic; even the buildings themselves were like works of art. Many of the younger Adinvyr roaming the city had enormous wolf-like creatures known as Vrandool accompanying them, with the youngest children being guarded by both their parents and what Nalithor referred to as Vrandool *puppies*.

How they could be a *puppy* and come up to my chest in height was beyond me.

*'They're really cute though... I want one.'* I pursed my lips, tracking a few of the creatures as they padded alongside their masters.

Off to one side of the central merchant district was a large building that, according to Nalithor, was Erist'il and Arom'il's temple. On the direct opposite side was a similar building which belonged to the God and Goddess of War. These temples were where they stayed during their visits to Draemir, and was where the faithful left gifts.

It appeared as though both pairs of deities had a great deal of influence on the Draemirans. Most of the decorations and artwork I spotted during our stroll reflected battle, war, hunting, romantic love, or physical love. Many young Adinvyr were sparring in the streets, while the children and their Vrandool played games to hone their tracking skills.

Hints of foreign cultures were limited in Draemir, and it didn't take long for me to realize that very few people here *weren't* Adinvyr. Most people that belonged to other species appeared to be tourists, and Nalithor informed me that they were likely here for Draemir's famous spring festivities.

When we arrived in the residential portion of the city, I immediately understood why Nalithor had mentioned that Draemir might come as culture shock to my brother.

There were several pairs of Adinvyr having sex out in the open, and it was rather obvious that this was normal behavior in Draemir. Passing soldiers and citizens were unfazed by the public displays. Uninterested, even.

For an outsider like me, it was difficult to ignore the passionate moaning and name-calling going on. Hells, it was hard enough not to stare at the men's rather startling…assets. Their sheer size was difficult for me to grasp despite my anatomy studies. Drawings versus the real thing were quite different.

Almost as shocking was the way the Adinvyr couples used their tails. While some simply intertwined their tails, others were using them for penetration purposes.

It was fascinating, in a way, but I felt as though it wasn't appropriate to stare or watch. Other Adinvyr were clearly ignoring the exchanges, not sparing them even a glance. Their indifference gave me the impression that, even though the displays were public, you weren't supposed to spectate or speak up.

'*I was expecting at least a quip, perhaps even disgust,*' Nalithor commented after a few minutes. '*Yet you seem mostly unfazed. Did Djialkan warn you?*'

'*No, he didn't warn me.*' I shook my head. '*I would say I'm startled, not "unfazed." However, it's obviously part of the norm here. Otherwise, the patrolling guards would be reprimanding or arresting them. Your culture is heavily influenced by both sex and war, isn't it? I can't be too surprised.*'

'*If I wasn't with you, they would be pleading for you to join them.*' Nalithor's blunt statement made my face flush hot, causing him to chuckle at me. '*It's mostly the commoners who partake of the more public displays of desire. Some of the nobles do as well, when they're younger. However, the nobles and royals are often more exacting and jealous both... We usually don't want to let anyone see the object of our interest nude.*'

'*I can't fathom why any of them would want to share—let alone just invite some random person off the street!*' I released an exasperated sigh, forcing myself to keep my eyes focused forward.

'*Aye, if you had a lover and he suggested a threesome you would have both his head and the head of the invitee.*' Djialkan snorted. I shot him a glare as my face grew hotter. He wasn't wrong, but he didn't need to share as much either! '*Your brother would certainly be happy to indulge the commoners himself, however.*'

'*Darius wouldn't know whether to accept their summons or if he should convert them to X'shmiran ways!*' I huffed, crossing my arms. Nalithor shot me a questioning look, so I added, '*Humans are sexual* creatures and don't like to admit it. X'shmirans, in particular, are quite bad about it.

'Many of our laws revolve around punishing sexual behavior; from the most "innocent" to the most "perverse." Seeing as such things are subject to opinion, I'm sure you can imagine how such a stance can go awry.'

'Ah yes, we never did finish regaling each other about the details of our respective cultures,' Nalithor mused while scratching Alala's chin. After a moment he pulled her off his shoulder and offered her back to me with a smile. 'I am relieved by your acceptance…and by your distaste for sharing, admittedly.'

'I'm not exactly sure what would be the polite way to decline potential invitations.' I sighed, taking Alala and holding her against my stomach with both arms. 'All of my knee-jerk reactions sound terribly rude. I don't want to be offensive… What are you laughing at?'

'It's terribly amusing to see such an imposing woman holding such an adorable animal like a stuffed toy.' Nalithor grinned, ruffling my curls. 'Let's make haste; Alala desires a nap, and Djialkan sounds like he needs one as well.'

Beyond the commoners' residential section were the estates belonging to the nobles. The sprawling estates, and the buildings on them, were massive. Each one was like a palace as far as I was concerned, and each estate was surrounded by several acres of lush land, streams, and gardens.

There weren't many people walking the streets there, but the few unspoken for Adinvyr we *did* pass seemed displeased when they spotted us but, strangely enough, I couldn't figure out if they were more jealous of Nalithor or of me.

*'Ah! The military district* here *is even larger than the one in Dauthrmir!'* I perked up as Nalithor led me past an incredible number of barracks, training grounds, and many groups of training soldiers. *'Does this have to do with Suthsul being directly to the south?'*

*'That and the proximity of an Aledacian Forest.'* Nalithor shot me an approving smile and reached over to ruffle my curls. *'We have dealt with more beasts than most parts of Vorpmasia, and are one of the few territories that have been loyal to Lucifer since the beginning.*

*'Most of the other territories had to be conquered in order to be brought under the Vorpmasian banner, and two of them are to our east and west. We had to establish ourselves as a people not to be trifled with, and that mindset has remained.'*

"Nalithor!" A female exclaimed, her voice chastising as we approached the outer rim of gardens that surrounded the palace grounds. "You should have accepted an escort, or at least transportation! You know I don't like to be kept waiting. We—"

"Now, now, Ellena!" A second woman grinned while I sized the pair up and listened to Nalithor's poorly contained growl. "Even if the girl doesn't bite, we know Djialkan sure does."

"*Both* of you were so impatient that you deigned it necessary to greet us at the gates?" Nalithor crossed his arms over his chest. He eyed the women with an uneasy expression.

The first woman, Ellena, stood at least six-foot-two and had long straight hair that shone a shade of blue that was almost white. She must have been where Rabere inherited his eyes from—they were an incredible molten orange. Except, as an Adinvyr, Ellena still had her black sclerae and slit pupils. She was shapely and wore a simple, lightweight gown in white. The intricate silver jewelry, forged by Aurelian, was more than enough decoration for the goddess. The adornments matched her twisting horns and her scaled tail almost perfectly, while the pumpkin-colored crystals matched the palest part of her eyes.

The second woman was around my height and had no Devillian traits to speak of. Her ears were pointed like an Elf, but she didn't carry herself like one. Her hair was a deep shade of auburn, and her eyes were golden. Like Ellena, she had a voluptuous figure and wore jewelry forged by Aurelian. Hers, however, was gold with pink crystals. The overall design was decidedly floral.

"Clearly they're just *overjoyed* to see you again," I teased, shooting Nalithor a look. Alala chirped and warbled her amusement, her tail wagging back and forth.

"I'm Ellena Vraelimir. Nalithor's *mother*," Ellena offered as the fox fled my arms to return to Nalithor's shoulder once more. "I do hope my son has been at least *attempting* to behave himself?"

"I'm Erist'il—most call me Erist," the second woman added with a broad grin while she examined me. She turned to look at Nalithor with a crooked grin after a moment. "Nalithor! Did you have her don a coat in an *attempt* to have her intimidate possible pursuers? *Hmmm*?"

"I'm Arianna Jade Black…but I suppose you both already know that," I commented dryly. Djialkan bristled on my shoulder and hissed at the women as they approached and snatched up both my hands. "I could remove my coat if you like, but I can't exactly do that if you're going to hold my hands like that."

"You have my permission to throw them if you like." Nalithor chuckled, placing a hand on top of my head. He shot both of the women a firm look. "At the very least, you two should *ask* Arianna if you may examine her Brands in such a fashion."

The pair of women exchanged strange looks before releasing my hands. Ellena instantly rounded on Nalithor.

"*You* have work to attend to immediately," Ellena informed Nalithor, her expression firm as she reached up to grip one of his shoulders. Her words earned an aggravated sigh from her son, but she continued, "Erist and I can see to it that Arianna settles into her rooms fine."

"I want to see what, under that coat, has drawn Nalithor's fancy," Erist added slyly, causing warmth to rise to my face. "You've obviously got a nice figure and full *assets* under there, but—"

"You are both incorrigible," Nalithor stated with disdain, shrugging his mother's hand from his shoulder. He took a step forward and lifted me off the ground by my waist so that he could nuzzle me without bending down. By the women's expressions, it was unusual behavior for him. "I expect you to kindly refrain from pestering Arianna with your usual sort of questions, Erist. Your inquiries are already inappropriate, to begin with, but even more so since Arianna hails from X'shmir."

"She's tiny," Ellena remarked thoughtfully, motioning down at my feet. "You let him pick you up like that, Arianna? You'll just inflate my son's ego even more."

"If I fought him over it, we would never have time for civilized conversation," I answered with a crooked grin. "My height seems to be a point of interest with many people in Dauthrmir...*this one* included."

"Nalithor, there's a rather large gathering of nobles who require your attention," Ellena stated flatly. I felt Nalithor twitch in response as he set me down. "I won't have you shirking your duty as a prince just because you're also the God of Balance! You're still the First Prince of Draemir!"

"Fine. *Fine.*" Nalithor released a heavy sigh and let go of my waist. He began walking toward the palace with Alala still curled up on his shoulder. "Do at least *try* to remain appropriate?"

I watched Nalithor walk away for a few seconds, examining his downtrodden demeanor and the dejected swishing of his tail. He was clearly displeased and didn't want to see to his duties in the slightest, regardless of his mother's demands. Under other circumstances, his disobedience would have amused me. However, in this case, I found myself rather dissatisfied with the thought of him tending to the needs of anyone else. Jealous would have been more accurate.

"I won't allow it," I muttered, brushing past the women. I quickly caught up to Nalithor and caught his hand in mine before he could turn to question me.

"You won't '*allow*' it?" Ellena demanded indignantly. "As a prince, he has duties he *must* fulfill! You may be his guest, but—"

"*If you want him to fulfill his duties so badly—then you can fight me for him!*" I snarled, pivoting to glare at Ellena. Darkness exploded outward from my feet when I released a wave of power and bloodlust to shove her back. "I don't intend to share his company with *anyone* while I'm here. If you don't like it, I'll be more than happy to crush you right now!"

"You heard the princess." Nalithor purred, lacing his fingers with mine. He pulled me into his chest, his free hand snaking around to the small of my back. "Arianna-z'tar and I have plans for sparring, and then lunch. If you intend to challenge her, then I suggest you do so now."

"You found a feisty one!" Erist cackled in delight. "In the presence of *three* gods and she makes a display like that? No wonder you decided to conquer for her!"

"Arianna, you aren't Human in the slightest are you?" Ellena questioned with an amused smile, her expression unfaltering even when I shot her another glare. "Nalithor's father *does* need to speak with him briefly. Let's compromise. Erist and I will show you to your suite while Nalithor speaks with his father. Afterward…he's all yours."

"Is it important?" I questioned begrudgingly, earning a rumbling chuckle from Nalithor.

"Yes, it's important," Ellena replied with a serious nod. She crossed her arms and shifted her attention over my head and to her son. "Nalithor, you've sparred with her before, I assume? Could she make good on her threat to 'crush' me?"

"I might be biased." Nalithor laughed, squeezing me. "But I'm certain she could wipe the floor with you and wouldn't need to draw her weapon to do so. She has bested me before…and *you* have *never* managed such a feat."

*'How can he just say that so casually?'* I wondered with a small sigh. *'Ellena is a Lesser God, and Erist'il is an Upper God. He's above* both… *I shouldn't be able to best either of them; let alone him.'*

"You're certain?" Erist inquired, arching her eyebrow. "When you're holding her there like that it's even more apparent how tiny she is."

"She kicks harder than Eyrian, and is faster. In a purely physical match, she was able to elude capture and proceeded to win against me," Nalithor confirmed, almost sounding as if he was bragging. He released me and looked down at me with a soft smile. "What will it be, Arianna? Will you compromise, or…?"

"I'll compromise. *This time.*" I pouted, feeling my face flushing brighter.

"Lysander is in his study, Nalithor." Ellena giggled while she and Erist each claimed one of my arms. "Take all the time you need. We have *plenty* of questions we want to pelt this one with!"

*"If you leave us with these women for too long, Nalithor, I will roast*

*you!"* Djialkan snapped from my shoulder. I couldn't help but laugh even as the two goddesses dragged us deeper into the palace grounds.

"Now I understand why he insisted that your rooms should be in *his* section of the palace!" Ellena exclaimed while tugging me along. "You must be driving the poor boys and girls in Dauthrmir mad. He hasn't killed any of them yet, has he?"

"Humph, with how much they've been nosing around my barriers... I wouldn't be cross if he had," I replied, disgruntled, as they pulled me past many lush gardens and toward a set of lacquered buildings on the southwestern shore of the lake.

"You gave me quite a fright, you know!" Ellena chastised. "Nalithor has never even *once* contemplated conquering for someone before—and he's meant to consult *us* first! When Lucifer contacted Lysander and me to let us know about the situation, I nearly flew out to Dauthrmir myself to find out just what sort of woman had stirred my son's inner conquerer in such a way!"

"They're *all* like this, you know." Erist jabbed her thumb in Ellena's direction.

"It's been too long since Lysander last conquered for me," Ellena contemplated aloud. "I should find another country to fix and have him take it for me."

"You would deal with that sort of political mess *willingly?*" I shook my head in disbelief. "If Lucifer contacted you to inform you of the situation, then surely you realize there are *many* reasons to conquer X'shmir."

The women pulled me into a wing of the palace that smelled strongly of Nalithor and led me down the hall.

"Oh, certainly." Ellena nodded, her voice filled with distaste. She switched to a more cheerful tone and continued, "I'm relieved to find that Nalithor's gift is for a *powerful* woman, however."

"I don't think either of us has seen Nalithor blush since— *Oooh...*" Erist trailed off, her eyes growing wide as she looked from me and then to Ellena. "He *did* say Arianna-'z'tar,' and her eyes... Ellena?"

"I think you're right." Ellena nodded. "Arianna, do you have anything to wear to formal parties? From what I understand, the X'shmirans do not treat *anyone* well, but especially you."

"It depends on how formal we're talking." I frowned, then nudged Djialkan. *'They realized who I am? So fast?'*

*'I believe Nalithor has as well,'* Djialkan answered with a yawn. *'Not until recently. Fear not.'*

"Let's get a look at your wardrobe then!" Erist beamed as Ellena slid a door to a suite open. "You use a *shrizar,* like most mages, right? Here—this room has a large walk-in. Is this enough space?"

The lavish suite was decorated with satins, silks, velvets, brocades, and leathers in scarlet and cream. All the furniture, pillars, and beams in the room were intricately carved dark reddish-brown wood. The floor was the same type of wood, but smooth and glossy underfoot. I couldn't decide whether the furniture seemed too pretty to sit on, or too comfortable-looking *not* to sit on. It seemed as if all the carvings and brocades depicted imagery like a story, but I had no idea of where to begin with trying to "read" whatever story the images told.

The adjacent wardrobe that the women seemed impatient for me to fill was ridiculous as far as I was concerned. It was easily the size of my room back in Dauthrmir. In the center of the wardrobe was a large counter with drawer upon drawer for smaller items like jewelry, and makeup. One wall appeared to be dedicated to weapon racks and even had a mannequin meant for armor.

"I can't even fill *half* of this!" I laughed in disbelief, shaking my head at the two women while I pulled my overrobe off. I hung it up, opened my collection of shrizar, and summoned all my clothing onto hangers in the room, then summoned the trunks from Sihix in one corner of the wardrobe.

"Oh? Secretly saucy are we?" Erist giggled, pulling down one of my lace-paneled dresses. "Has he seen you in *this* yet?"

"I wore that to the celebration dinner when we returned from hunting in Abrantia." I flushed, shifting in discomfort. "He was my date…and my twin brother was incredibly pissed off. Was sure worth it, though…"

"Twin brother? And he isn't with the two of you?" Ellena probed while looking through my clothing.

"The invitation was for me *only*." I shrugged. "Darius is attending the academy. He's rather smitten with Nalithor."

*"Darius kicked Arianna out of the house this morning because she is 'stealing Nalithor away!'"* Djialkan snapped in irritation. A moment later, he leapt from my shoulder and flew out of the wardrobe. *"I am*

*going to sleep."*

"The scaly one hasn't changed much." Erist shook her head, then motioned at my torso. "This...is a surprise, however. I can sense Nalithor hasn't made you his Chosen or his goddess, so that means your Brands of Divinity are naturally this way."

"Chosen?" I asked with a small frown. "I've heard the term before, but I'm still unsure what it means."

"Deities who are Middle or Upper Gods often take like-minded mortals under their wing, blessing them with power and the like," Erist replied while circling me. "Middle and Upper Gods have many responsibilities, as you can imagine, and we *need* the help of our 'Chosen' in order to properly do our jobs. The world is quite large, after all.

"Racial Gods—that is, Lesser Gods—such as Ellena here or her estranged son aren't capable of sensing such pacts, or even the lack thereof."

"Honestly, this selection is so limited!" Ellena finally exclaimed, turning away from my clothes to look at me. "Erist, I think we should have her attend the party tonight. I have the *perfect* kimono in mind for her too."

"I thought you were going to suggest that we take her shopping!" Erist laughed.

"That's a good idea too. However, I think it'd be much more amusing to have Nalithor take her shopping," Ellena replied, her expression one of contemplation. "If his blushing earlier was any indication, he's really got quite the soft spot for you, Arianna."

"A shopping excursion would require that I'm capable of *not* killing the multitudes of your people who seem intent on knocking on my barriers!" I huffed, placing a hand on one hip. "Since you're their *goddess*, Ellena-z'tar, any bright ideas on how to make them stop?"

"You mentioned people nosing around your barriers before," Ellena murmured. "The clueless children have already started here as well?"

"They can't seem to understand that they're of no interest to me." I pouted, pivoting to watch as the women strode past me and into the sitting room.

"Your best option would be to release a particularly strong shockwave of your power when you arrive at tonight's party," Ellena replied, tapping her fist against her cheek as she thought. "The party is for gods and demigods, but since you've decided to claim my son's attentions—and because I'm inviting you—you can come as Nalithor's date. I'll make sure he's aware.

"Erist and I will come by tonight to dress and fetch you. We can discuss the particulars of our customs then."

"Oh right, one more thing!" Erist clapped her hands together and grinned. "The bath is at the end of the hallway. The door on the *right* is Nalithor's suite. By the color you just turned, I guess you already know of Draemiran bathing traditions! Ha-ha!"

"Let's take care not to tease her *too* much." Ellena giggled as they made their way over to the sliding door and out of the room.

"Nalithor teases me *plenty* without the two of you pitching in!" I stalked over to the door and slid it closed behind them. *'Tch, I really can't stand women!'*

After a few moments of consideration, I flopped down on a chaise and decided to read a book on the Aledacian Forests while waiting for Nalithor to find me for a sparring match. Alas, his father must have had a lot to say. It was almost a full hour before Nalithor knocked lightly on my door and I heard Alala warble.

"They didn't trouble you, did they?" Nalithor inquired when I slid the door open and looked up at him.

"I was expecting your mother to be cross with me," I grumbled, watching as Alala leapt off Nalithor's shoulder and scampered into the rooms behind me. "They seemed more distressed by my wardrobe than anything else. Typical women."

"The power you released during your sudden proclamation has the entire city in a frenzy, you know." Nalithor chuckled, pulling me into the hallway with him. He smiled and lifted my face by the chin. "You can be quite fearsome when you want to be, it seems."

"Frenzy?" I blinked up at him, resting my palms against his abs as he pulled me closer.

"I don't know what you laced your power with...but they seem rather desperate to inspect *my* barriers," Nalithor replied, sliding his tail around my hips. "Are they still bothering you as well?"

"They are," I confirmed as he shifted his hand to cup my face. "I take it you haven't run into *those women* yet?"

"I sensed they were looking for me, and so I avoided them." Nalithor grimaced. "Did they have something important to say, for once?"

"Erist not so much," I commented thoughtfully, earning a laugh from the seemingly distracted man before me. "*Ellena*, however, wants me to join you for dinner tonight as your date. Apparently, they plan to come by tonight to dress me in *something*—I suppose they think I don't have anything suitable. They don't seem like they plan on giving us much choice in the matter, either."

"I certainly wouldn't mind the chance to show you off early..." Nalithor murmured, his eyes trailing down my throat and to my chest briefly as he paused. "She *must* be plotting something if she's willing to invite someone who isn't blatantly a god or demigod."

"She said it's alright since I've claimed exclusive rights to you during my stay," I pointed out, watching with amusement as Nalithor's face flushed a little. "Come now, did you really think I was going to let anyone else have you?"

"I'm never certain *what* to think when you're involved." Nalithor laughed, lifting me up so that I was level with his face. "Now then... We have a sparring match and lunch to get out of the way, don't we?"

"Are you going to let me walk, or are you planning to carry me?" I arched an eyebrow at him as he coiled his tail tighter around my hips. "This doesn't seem conducive to either option."

"I think I'll carry you," Nalithor replied with a smile, sliding one arm beneath my knees and bracing my shoulders with the other. "Your daintiness, combined with your power and bloodlust, never ceases to entertain me. That aside, it seems as though we may need to put my countrymen in their place."

"Your mother seems to think a 'strong' release of my power upon arrival tonight should fix the issue," I offered as his tail uncoiled from my hips and he began walking through the palace. "I'd like to know why they're pestering you as well now."

"Some of them must have pieced together what your 'outburst' was about." Nalithor chuckled, stroking the side of my thigh with his thumb. "Let's have an unarmed match with no use of magic, shall we? I would like to see how you fare *without* the presence of a beast egging you on."

"Outburst?" I pouted.

"You really surprised me, you know." Nalithor smiled as he carried me out of the palace and toward a nearby stretch of beach, which led to a nearby forest. "At the very least, you didn't leave any room for doubt regarding your sincerity."

"I meant what I said," I stated, earning a self-satisfied smirk from the Adinvyr.

"We should be able to spar in peace here," Nalithor informed me, setting me down on the sand. "If I win... Mmm, I think you'll owe me another kiss."

"And if *I* win?" I asked, my face growing hotter.

"If *you* win... Hmmm, what would you like?" Nalithor laughed, kicking off his shoes.

"If I win…. I get to choose what you wear tonight," I replied after a moment, causing Nalithor to arch an eyebrow at me.

"Are you that concerned I'll find something to tease you with?" Nalithor chuckled, tracking me as I removed my sandals and then adopted an offensive stance.

"I get the feeling that those two plan to put me in something teasing, or something that's meant to make the other guests jealous," I pointed out, examining Nalithor's exposed chest for a moment before smirking back at him. "It wouldn't be fair to let *you* be the only one flaunting their date now would it?"

"Ahhh, such a mischievous vixen you are." Nalithor grinned as he, too, adopted an offensive stance. "Perhaps if you perform well enough I'll grant your request despite your defeat."

At least two hours had passed since we had started sparring. However, I couldn't determine if a few seconds or several minutes had passed since Nalithor pinned me beneath him, and I was no longer sure if I cared. He had laced his fingers with mine and trapped my hands above my head with ease. However, it was his torso nestled between my legs that I found most distracting while he kissed me deeply. It was near-impossible for me to control my rising desire as both his passionate kiss and his power threatened to overwhelm me.

"Mmm… You're making it even more difficult for me to let you out of my sight, you know," Nalithor purred. He withdrew slightly to kiss down the side of my throat and, this time, I couldn't suppress a small shudder or bite back a small whimper. "Tsk, tsk.... Are you *sensitive*, Arianna? You're so excited from a kiss, despite your resistance to my power?

"As tempting as it is to make *you* my lunch, after that delicious whimper of yours... Well, that wouldn't be quite fair now, would it?"

Before I could even *attempt* to formulate a retort, Nalithor pulled me to my feet with a devious chuckle and then went to reclaim his discarded shoes. After a moment, I turned to do the same and brushed sand off both my sarouel and skin as I went. Regaining some semblance of self-control proved difficult with both his scent and taste still clinging to me. His presence so close made it even harder.

"You certainly made it difficult to defeat you this time," Nalithor commented, catching me around the waist. He smiled, pulling me to his side. "To think that you would make me work so hard for something you so very clearly enjoyed."

"Well, I never claimed I didn't *want* you to kiss me..." I grumbled, glancing away.

"And yet you made it more difficult than it had to be." Nalithor chuckled, his hand coming to rest low on my hip. One of his fingers slipped under the hem of my sarouel to stroke the skin just below my hipbone, making me twitch slightly.

"Bah! I wasn't going to just *let* you win!" I pointed out with a huff, attempting to ignore his distracting petting. "What are you thinking of for lunch...*aside* from me?"

"Still mostly you." Nalithor smirked, drawing a claw across my tender skin. "But... I don't have the proper time to *savor* you before we're expected at dinner in a few hours.

"I'll take you into the city for lunch so that you can see more of Draemir before tonight."

# CHAPTER NINE
*Troublesome*

Quite some time ago I had retreated into the bath and drifted over to a large wall of windows. A cool breeze wafted in off the lake and drifted into the massive room, stirring the steam that rose from the water. Beyond the windows was an unobscured view of the palace gardens, the shore, and the lake. I could even admire some of the mrifon forest that surrounded the lake, as well as the scent of their blooms that perfumed the air, from where I saw. As with Dauthrmir, everything in Draemir was lit by the soft glow of plants, the moons and stars above, and the occasional decorative lantern.

It was tranquil, but not enough to distract me from the never-ending knocking on my barriers.

I remained at the window with my arms crossed on the sill while relaxing into the bath. The water smelled of cherries, mrifon, and something else I didn't quite recognize. The pond-like baths were one of the things I enjoyed most about coming Below. I only wished that I had more things to hunt, and therefore more excuses to make use of the baths.

"So, you *are* still here." Nalithor's voice by my ear startled me, giving me no chance to react before he wrapped a large towel around my nude form and pulled me away from the window. His chest rumbled against my back when he spoke again, "You adapt quite quickly to other cultures, don't you?

"What were you thinking about, hmmm? You didn't respond to my knocking *or* when I called to you."

"I was admiring the view." I motioned to the row of open windows with one hand, then paused when Nalithor nuzzled my damp shoulder. *"Not thinking* seems like the best way to tune out your curious countrymen. They've grown more persistent since we went for lunch."

"I'll punish them for you later," Nalithor purred, pulling me to the shallow end of the bath. "For now… Erist and my mother are quite impatient for you to return to your rooms. They had the servants bring many boxes to your suite, and wouldn't allow me to see what they're attempting to dress you in. You should indulge them before they come to pull you from the baths themselves."

"I get the feeling that you would fight them for access to me at the moment," I commented when he hesitated to release me. Once he let go, I waded up the steps and then glanced over my shoulder at the smirking Adinvyr, only to find that he had a towel wrapped low around his waist. "You look smug."

"I *knew* you would try to steal a peek," Nalithor replied, grinning slyly. "You really are ador...able..."

Nalithor fell silent when I dropped my soaked towel to the floor around my feet. Smirking to myself, I strode to where my change of undergarments and a satin robe were draped over the back of a settee. I felt Nalithor's eyes tracing down my bare back while I wrung the water out of my long curls. After a moment of consideration, I chose to dry myself with magic and then snatched up a pair of black satin panties.

"Oh? The *smug* Adinvyr has no witty comment for me?" I inquired sweetly while I pulled my panties up my legs, taking care not to flash anything other than my round buttocks at him.

"I should take you right now for being such a damned tease," Nalithor replied with a frustrated growl, causing me to shoot a smirk over my shoulder at him.

Nalithor had moved over to the edge of the bath to watch me and had crossed his arms on the ledge. His chin rested on his forearms, while his tail cut back and forth in the water with a slow but rhythmic pattern like that of an agitated cat. He tracked my every movement as if he were waiting for an opportunity to pounce.

"I'm sure that, if you want to see more, you can earn it," I stated innocently, pulling on my bra and then my robe before turning to face him fully. "I'll see you at dinner. Do *try* not to let anyone else lay their filthy hands on you, alright?"

Without waiting for his response, I strode out of the bathroom and grinned when I heard him release another low growl. Getting a reaction out of the Adinvyr was incredibly satisfying. As I neared my suite, I smoothed my expression over and then slid the door open. I arched an eyebrow upon finding the two goddesses perched on sofas within the sitting room. They appeared to be arguing about something but weren't speaking in the common or Draemiran tongues.

"Isn't this a *lot* of boxes?" I spoke up, motioning at the slew of empty boxes in a corner before closing the door behind me.

"We couldn't decide which one to pour you into!" Erist laughed, pointing toward the wardrobe. "The servants placed your options on mannequins in there so you can pick one yourself."

"But first, drop the robe," Ellena stated flatly, earning a questioning look from me. "I want to get a good look at your Brands before you get dressed, and we both want to make sure that you have a *potent* birth control spell on you.

"We did some poking around your barriers to get an idea of just how much attention you've drawn, as well. If, at some point, you decide to indulge some of them, it would be for the best that there are no 'risks' to come alongside."

*Really? Birth control nonsense again? Do I really strike them as someone eager to give in to carnal desires?'* I bit back a sigh and pulled off my robe, tossing it over the back of a nearby chair. "I've been getting a lot of attention—or at least it seems like a lot to me."

"Hmmm... Your Brands of Divinity are really quite similar to both Lucifer's *and* Nali's..." Ellena muttered, hurrying over to circle me. "I take it that you and your twin aren't biologically related to the X'shmirans?"

"That's correct." I nodded as Erist joined us and examined me with a frown of her own. "Do I even *want* to know why the two of you are so concerned about whether or not I have a 'potent' birth control spell on me?"

"*We* created the spell," Erist spoke, motioning between herself and Ellena. "I'm sure I don't need to explain why Adinvyr need such a thing. We had to put a stop to the rather *prolific* amount of breeding happening among the Adinvyr during the early days of our world. The larger the clans grew, the more risk of attracting beasts.

"While there are versions of the spell for both men *and* women, it is safer to make sure that you have it on you as well. It wouldn't do for someone to 'oops' you.

"Even *if* you wanted to breed, I doubt your body could handle it when you're stuck between Human and...whatever you are. Hells, you probably couldn't even *handle* sex with most Devillian men. Perhaps a Rylthra or Sundreht—they are closer to Humans in size—but any other race is like to split you open."

*'She really does have a one-track mind, doesn't she?'* I sighed, shaking my head. *'Still, if Devillians are truly that well-endowed... I suppose that would explain why I haven't seen many Humans or Elves in the company*

*of Devillian partners.'*

"You really have quite the figure!" Ellena exclaimed with a brilliant grin. She grabbed one of my bra straps and stretched it for a moment before letting it snap back into my shoulder. "I never *imagined* you would grow up to look like this, Arianna."

"To be fair, we didn't even think she was *alive*," Erist pointed out, pressing a thumb low against my abdomen. A portion of my skin glowed in response to her touch, revealing a pale pink butterfly. "A butterfly hmmm? Rylda and Rymia must have been the healers who saw to you then?"

"I'll freeze them for not warning me ahead of time just *who* my son was bringing home!" Ellena huffed, coming to stand before me with crossed arms. "He told me about coming across you in Limbo decades ago, Arianna. I'm aware that your memory is…lacking.

"By the lack of surprise or confusion… I take it you really are the *same* Arianna? You're not… You're not a reincarnation?"

*"Arianna has more memory of Limbo than she has of Vorpmasia,"* Djialkan interjected even as I opened my mouth to state as much, so I sighed and motioned loosely at the fae-dragon instead. *"She is a woman now, not the child you once knew. It would be best if you pretend that she and her child self are two different people entirely. It is as if she has lived two different lives, and they are night and day by comparison."*

I raised an eyebrow at the fae-dragon. That wasn't the most meaningful of phrases in a land where both day and night were dark.

"You were such a cute kid, too!" Ellena informed me, hooking an arm around my shoulder. She led me toward the wardrobe, continuing, "You, Darius, and Rabere were always chasing after Nalithor's tail, but only you could actually keep up with my eldest. Does Darius still have some strange attachment to my son?"

"He wants Nalithor badly enough to have kicked me out of the house over it." I sighed after a moment, shelving the dozens of questions I wanted to bombard these women with. "It's strange to think that I once knew all of them—and a little upsetting. So, I have been attempting not to dwell on it.

"Ah… You want me to pick one of *these* to wear?"

Ellena's expression and tone became serious. "I intend to determine just how much my son desires you. He's never wanted to conquer for someone, and he's never brought home a guest who isn't simply one of his military friends. Yet, if he has realized *who* you are, he hasn't told any of us.

"That aside, a great deal of your wardrobe consists of Draemiran-inspired Umbral Mage attire. I think it's high time you wore a *proper* kimono!"

"*Proper?*" I asked in disbelief, motioning at the nearest garment. "So much of my tits will be exposed in *any* of these!"

"Precisely. Nalithor should receive plenty of challenges if you wear one of these!" Erist cackled, jabbing her thumb in the direction of the kimonos. "What'll it be? I think you're going to have to switch to a strapless bra no matter which you choose, so perhaps you should do that while you think."

I bit back an aggravated sigh and looked between the colorful yet *sultry* kimonos. Almost all of them would hang off my shoulders and just barely cover my bra when worn. The skirts would reveal one leg all the way up to the hip—perhaps even higher. I couldn't deny that the clothing was beautiful, but it was far removed from what I was accustomed to wearing.

The women were a pain in the ass, I had no doubts about that anymore, at least. As far as I was concerned, Nalithor didn't require more testing.

*'However, that red one…'* I examined the painted scarlet silk. *'As much as I love blue, this one stands out more. It also shows more skin, but…*

"Fine. I'll play your game. This one."

"You've grown up to be a tease as well then!" Ellena laughed, squeezing my shoulder. She nodded her head in approval, her expression delighted. "I win this round, Erist."

"I could have sworn she would have picked the blue one!" Erist exclaimed, latching onto my left arm. "Blue *is* still your favorite color, isn't it?"

"Yes, but the red one stands out more…" I pointed out with a small pout. "The blue one covers *too* much and looks like it would restrict my movement."

"Let's get you dressed!" Ellena grinned. "While we don't do the silly announcing of names and titles that mortals do at *their* parties, we do still give a sort of 'introduction' upon arriving. Tonight's party is being held on the lake, and we must cross a floating bridge to access it.

"When you first step foot on the bridge, release a nice big wave of your power, alright? Erist and I will be both walking across it first, so you'll get to see us do similar. Once we're halfway across, it's appropriate for you to 'startle' everyone with that power of yours and begin to walk."

*'What sort of tradition is that?'* I gnawed the inside of my cheek instead of rolling my eyes. *'I mean, really! We're not allowed to hide our power while in Vorpmasia anyway, so what's the point? How is that an "introduction?"'*

"You'll probably get challenged the moment you step onto the party floor," Erist added with a laugh while rummaging through my wardrobe for a bra. "Try not to hurt yourself *or* the kimono."

"I'm starting to feel like this 'party' will consist of more fighting than it will of dining," I muttered dryly, pulling on the bra that Erist offered me. "What about my jewelry? I'm not sure it matches the kimono."

"It's fine!" Ellena giggled and held up the first layer for me. "Ah, and don't worry about finding sandals or shoes to match. We'll all be barefoot."

"I think we should leave her lips unpainted too. What do you think, Ellena?" Erist remarked, watching as the Adinvyr goddess helped me into the layers of kimono. "Maybe some sultry makeup for her eyes and just gloss for her lips? Looks like we don't need to repaint her nails either."

"No lipstick?" I questioned, eyeing the Goddess of Love with unease. "Now that you mention it, I'm not sure if Nalithor's ever really seen me without my lips painted or stained…"

"I agree with Erist, their natural color is quite lovely. My son is likely to ruin your lipstick anyway if you choose to wear any." Ellena waved her hand dismissively, then lifted another layer of silk. "I'm of half a mind to put your hair up just so that Erist and I can bet on how long it will take for Nalithor to steal *all* of your hair ornaments."

"Did he make a habit out of *that* as a kid, too?" I rolled my eyes, motioning to my curls. "He's already snatched up two of my hair sticks that I'm aware of."

"Aye, he's always been fond of your hair." Erist laughed. "I suppose we all were. You were like a bloodthirsty porcelain doll when you were a child. Quite adorable, honestly."

"I'm starting to hate that word!" I grumbled, pouting as the woman scrounged through my belongings.

"Let's put part of her hair up in a bun," Ellena commented distractedly, pulling open several drawers. "We can leave the rest of her hair hanging down her back. Arianna, you don't have a fan?"

"We're already running late." Erist huffed while helping Ellena with my hair. "She can just contend with revealing her blushing. We don't have time to find her a fan."

*Why are they already assuming I'm going to be blushing about something?* I sighed, crossing my arms. *Hells, why does Ellena think that Nalithor will ruin my lipstick? He hasn't managed that yet, at least.*

Several minutes later the goddesses were finally satisfied with my appearance, and I found myself hurrying down the palace hallways to follow the impatient women. They barely even gave me a chance to examine myself before ushering me out of my rooms and toward the lake. Alala scampered alongside me as I jingled my way across the polished wooden floors. She appeared insistent on joining me.

When we exited the palace, my lips parted in surprise. Soft, glowing lights hung from many of the trees, were woven into trellises, or otherwise lined the stone pathways that wound through the palace grounds. Many more candles and lanterns danced on the surface of the peaceful lake. It was a breathtaking sight, but I had little time to appreciate it before Erist and Ellena rushed me along a walkway and toward the floating bridge.

Ellena released a burst of power that smelled of lavender and honey the moment she stepped onto the bridge. I bit back a small frown as her magic sent small ripples across the lake.

*'Hmmm, that's all the power she has?'* I wondered, watching as the Goddess of Adinvyr sashayed across the bridge and toward the marble construction that rose out of the lake offshore. *I can see why Nalithor was confident that I could best her. Even though she's a "Lesser" God, I feel as though she should have much more power than* that.

*'Really though—a* floating *bridge? If I fall in, I'm taking the heads of* all *the witnesses.'*

Erist went next, shooting me a grin before she stepped onto the bridge herself. I suppressed my distaste when her power burst forth.

Her magic took on the form of pink butterflies and flower petals, swirling around her feet and then scattering to the winds as she walked. It smelled of roses, musk, and something that made me think of the cheesy bath scenes in Darius' romance novels. Her power wasn't much more impressive than Ellena's even though she was an Upper God.

One thing I *did* notice, however, was that neither of them jingled quite as much as I did. I had much more jewelry than them both despite my "lower" rank, and neither of them appeared to have bell charms fastened to their jewelry.

*'You're coming too, Alala?'* I questioned, earning a yip from the small fox. *'Fine. You're a lady too, after all. Let's see if I can put enough power into my display to deter any further knocking, hmmm?'*

I took a deep breath to calm the nervous racing of my heard, then closed my eyes for a moment to center myself. When I opened my eyes again, I released a shockwave of power with enough force to create a sound like thunder. The entire visible surface of the lake froze in an instant as I began to strut down the bridge with Alala prancing beside me. Every flame in sight, be it a candle, a torch, or a lantern, flared cobalt when touched by my power. Shadows darkened, twisted, and then took on the form of foxes to watch the party guests.

The multitudes of Devillians skulking around my barriers collectively flinched before vanishing entirely, leaving my mind blissfully quiet. However, the grinning Goddess of Adinvyr soon drew my attention.

The moment I stepped foot onto the marble floor, several Devillian men and women leapt over Ellena's head with their weapons drawn. It was clear they intended to fight me, but...

My gaze flicked to the side when I sensed a ripple of power and rage that were both distinctly Nalithor's. He appeared between the attacking Devillians and me in an instant, his spear drawn. A single swipe was all it took for him to knock the challengers away from me, sending them skidding across the floor on their backs. Nalithor's muscles were coiled and tense, ready to spring after them at a moment's notice.

*"Kindly remember that Arianna-z'tar is my date."* Nalithor's dangerous, harsh growl made the challengers freeze and grow pale. I simply examined Nalithor's armored torso for a moment, intrigued by the platinum plates that seemed to conform and bend to each individual muscle of his back. "If anyone else wishes to challenge her, you will go through *me* first. I won't have her or her lovely attire being ruined by your pathetic attempts."

Nalithor's tail shattered several tiles beneath him when a younger demigod called out something in an unknown language. I watched, intrigued, as the angered Adinvyr shot a deadly glare in the direction of the other male. Finally, he turned to settle his rather intense gaze on me. Nalithor dismissed his spear and then offered me his hand. Once I accepted it, he bowed and kissed the back of my hand. His eyes flicked upwards as he shot me a victorious smirk. The expression was contagious, making it difficult for me to keep my expression passive.

No one else attempted to interfere as Nalithor began to escort me across the floor.

"Arianna-jiss, I see you've already christened our gifts to you with the blood of beasts!" An unfamiliar male voice cackled, drawing my attention to a burgundy-haired and golden-eyed monster of a man. His voice was practically like thunder. A slightly smaller woman with raven-colored hair sat beside him. They both had massive weapons resting on the floor beside them.

"My blades haven't drunk anywhere *near* enough blood, yet," I commented, examining the pair for a moment. *'That's the God and Goddess of War, then? Aurelian and Elise? I'd heard tales that he was a massive man—but I didn't expect he'd be even larger than the Devillians!'*

"*Patience.* I'm sure I can find more toys for you to play with soon enough," Nalithor purred, escorting me up the few steps of the dais that held the head table. "Mmm… What am I going to do with you? After a display like that…"

"Now I understand why you were *late*, Ellena," another male voice remarked, this one belonging to the pewter-haired man that sat at the center of the head table. He was a few inches shorter than Nalithor, but his frosty eyes and amused smirk made their relation all too clear. "My name is Lysander Vraelimir. I'm Nalithor's father, and Ellena's husband. I hope my wife's plotting didn't trouble you, Arianna-jiss."

Before I could answer him, Nalithor pulled me down onto a pile of pillows behind the head table. Nalithor wrapped both an arm and his tail around me in a possessive manner, growling as he glared somewhere down at the tables below us. His parents, to my surprise, both laughed and nodded their approval before turning to discuss something with their guests on the right-hand side of the table.

The possessive man beside me seemed uninterested in their conversation and instead opted to rest a hand on my thigh.

*'I wasn't going to slip off anywhere.'* I pointed out, amused as Nalithor's grip tightened. *'You don't like the way someone is looking at me, I take it?'*

*'Mmm... You just* had *to choose the most deliciously* troublesome *attire, didn't you?'* Nalithor sighed, nuzzling into my exposed shoulder. He wrapped both arms around my corseted waist and purred.

"Why does *she* get the right to His Highness's company?" A woman demanded, indignant. I arched an eyebrow and glanced in her direction, finding what must have been an Elven demigoddess. "Even with those Brands, she isn't a goddess or a demigoddess! She looks *Human*! She doesn't deserve Nalithor-zir."

*'I see. So, Illyana really isn't the only Elf that has issues with Humans.'* I watched as several more Elves at the woman's table nodded their agreement. Two more Elves, both men, rose to their feet to suggest challenging us as well. *'Humph. Even so, with that logic, they're nowhere near being "worthy" of a Devillian either. They aren't that much more powerful than Humans.'*

"It's always the weakest dogs who bark the loudest, isn't it?" I inquired with a bored tone, shifting to press myself up against Nalithor's side. I heard Nalithor's pulse quicken when my bust pressed against his exposed skin, so I took the opportunity to trail my nails down his muscular abdomen—much to the Elves' displeasure. "Unless you intend to challenge one of us...*you should sit down and keep that mouth of yours shut.*"

Nalithor chuckled in response to the power and murderous intent that I channeled at the Elven woman and the two men. The two men grew pale but stood their ground, while the woman shrieked in fear and ran to hide behind a man that must have been her father. It occurred to me that the man was likely the God of Elves...but I didn't care. He was even weaker than the Devillian deities present were.

Nalithor could squash him like an insect if necessary.

"Arianna-z'tar is my guest and my *date,*" Nalithor reiterated in a commanding tone, coiling his tail around my exposed thigh. "If any of you don't like it, you're welcome to challenge me. However, I can't promise that I will leave you in on piece when I'm through with you. **Learn your place.**"

Something about the unbridled power and bloodlust in Nalithor's aura was terribly arousing to me. Heat had risen in my body, and I couldn't seem to calm my pulse no matter how I tried. His hand and tail caressing my thigh did *not* help matters in the slightest, but it wasn't long before someone interrupted.

"I will challenge you for the right to Arianna-z'tar!" An unfamiliar Akor male rose from his seat and strode onto the open floor below the dais. His expression was one of rage as he leveled a claymore at Nalithor, his horns, and tail alight with flames to match his anger. "I won't stand idly by and let you claim such a powerful woman for yourself!"

Nalithor sprung clear over the table and struck the Akor's blade with his own. The force of his attack shattered the claymore, but Nalithor wasn't done and followed through with the motion. The edge of Nalithor's spear tore across the weaker Devillian's torso, spilling black blood onto the marble floor. Several more Devillian demigods shot to their feet, prepared to challenge Nalithor. Much to my surprise, several women voiced their desire to fight Nalithor for me as well.

"I told you it would be less than five minutes before our son drew blood," Lysander spoke, a pleased grin on his face as he glanced to his wife. He shifted his gaze to me as I pulled Alala into my lap. "I'll admit that I didn't believe him when he first told us that you were utterly resistant to his power as both an Adinvyr *and* as a god... But it appears that not a single one of our guests affects you. Why is that?"

"You're all weak compared to Nalithor," I replied simply, tracking Nalithor's movements as he tore into yet more challengers. "Is it normal for there to be this many challengers? Of both sexes?"

"*Weak?*" Lysander questioned, skeptical, so I glanced toward him and nodded. "I can see why he adores you. Not many would make such a bold statement in the presence of deities.

"I get the feeling that you wish to join him in hunting the X'shmirans but you can't, can you?"

"Unfortunately, no, I can't," I replied, returning my gaze to the fighting Devillians. I stroked Alala's fur while gauging the movements of the people *attempting* to challenge Nalithor. They were all well-practiced in combat, that much was certain, but they were no match for Nalithor. He was being utterly merciless, uncaring of how deeply he had wounded several of them. "If X'shmir were a matter I could tend to for myself, I would have done so long ago.

"These fools truly think they stand a chance if they team up against Nalithor?"

Ellena giggled, shifting to look at me. "Half of them are frustrated that he's never shown interest in them. The other half are angry that he's attempting to keep someone like *you* all to himself. You look like you want a piece of the action!"

"I'm not confident that I wouldn't kill them for their insubordination," I replied dismissively, tracing the path of Nalithor's spear as it tore into another demigod. The bastards weren't even a challenge for him. Hells, a beast would have probably given him more trouble than the pampered brats were. "Would it be inappropriate for me to intervene?"

"They won't stop challenging the two of you until *you* make it clear that you want exclusive rights to my son's company." Lysander laughed, shaking his head. "The way he greeted you indicated his plans to keep you to himself, but the young fools are too blinded by lust to determine *your* motives, Arianna-jiss. If you can intervene *without* killing them, then by all means—"

"Don't you think you fools have kept my companion from my side long enough?" I demanded. Without a movement, I froze everyone, aside from Nalithor, in place on the ballroom floor. Nalithor tensed and shot me a strange look while the other demigods and a handful of deities began muttering protests.

"I desire another Chosen as my slave girl, and *you* would make a fine addition!" One of the cheekier deities snapped, eliciting a snarl from Nalithor. The Adinvyr flipped his grip on his spear and leveled it with the other man's throat. I was a little disappointed that Nalithor didn't just behead the bastard then and there.

"I have no interest in joining your—or anyone's—harem." I waved my hand dismissively as I rose to my feet and swept around the table to approach Nalithor. "Disloyal, polyamorous, arrogant, and *weak* creatures like you disgust me. Nalithor or I could take your head without twitching a finger."

"You *bitch*!" The deity shrieked. "What would a stupid mortal whore like *you* know about taking the head of a *god*?!"

"Nalithor-*y'ric*," I purred teasingly, brushing Nalithor's spear out of my way before pressing myself up against his torso. I reached up and linked my hands behind his neck, shooting him a sly smile. "This filth isn't worth your time or mine. How about we return to our seats and enjoy each other's company, *hmmm*?"

"Get your hands off him!" A male Elf from my left snarled. I shot the man an icy glare, ignoring Nalithor's tail as it coiled over my hips and rump.

"He's *mine*," I stated, snarling at the young Elven demigod. "I would be happy to remove your tongue for you—"

Nalithor cut me off with a deep kiss, much to the dismay of many of the guests. His passion startled me, causing heat to rise to my face even as I submitted to his intense kiss. After a moment, he withdrew with a rather sultry glint in his eyes and bit his lower lip with a low purr.

"I do believe I still owe you a drink or two after all, but, dinner comes first—right?" Nalithor mused, smoothing one hand down my spine. He lifted his gaze to shoot a glare over the top of my head. "You heard her. I recommend returning to your seats, *peacefully*, before we decide to make good on Arianna-z'tar's threat."

Nalithor didn't bother waiting for their responses. Instead, he dipped down and scooped me into his arms before striding across the frozen floor with ease. Once we arrived at our seats, again, he set me down on his left. Everyone at the head table, even his parents, seemed just as startled as the guests did. I didn't care. If anyone else attempted to interfere, I was likely to kill them.

"Arianna-jiss, I'm beginning to think you would have intervened even if we *hadn't* said it was appropriate," Ellena remarked wryly, glancing at her son as he pulled me as close to his side as possible.

"They need to learn their place," I stated with a huff. Alala leapt onto my lap and began pouncing between my lap and Nalithor's repeatedly. After a moment, Alala stole a piece of bread off the table and scampered off to hide in a corner. I shook my head at the fox, then added, "Their unwillingness to accept their own weakness is *most* unattractive."

*'What am I going to do with you when you've taken to making such*

*bold proclamations, hmmm?'* Nalithor questioned. He slipped his tail under the folds of my kimono and ran it firmly over the front of my panties, almost startling a squeak out of me. He leaned down to nuzzle my throat and whispered, *"I want you in my bed."*

For a moment, I thought my heart was going to beat out of my chest while Nalithor nibbled at the side of my throat. I hastened to battle down, or at least hide, my already significant arousal. Watching him fight had already excited me far too much, and his teasing only served to make it worse. That he had finally given voice to his desires…I didn't know what to think. Someone—*him* of all people— wanted *me?* It was difficult to believe, but he left little room for doubt.

*'And here I thought you might be cross with me for interrupting your hunt,'* I managed to reply. He wrapped his tail around my left thigh several times, tight enough that I couldn't tell whose pulse I was feeling anymore. At least that location was more appropriate, even if only slightly.

*'I'm sure the noises you'll make as I claim you will more than make up for it,'* Nalithor replied, his fangs grazing across my throat. He paused, seeming thoughtful. *'Perhaps I should steal you away to my rooms* now— *'*

"Nalithor, has Arianna been assigned a partner yet?" Lysander interrupted with a cough. I bit back a laugh when Nalithor growled into my throat.

"Her results and her orders should arrive within the next few days," Nalithor replied tersely. He straightened himself and poured drinks for us both, still bristling. "If they pair her with someone other than me, I will hunt them down and then take her for myself."

"Ahhh, so the big scary God of Balance really *is* smitten!" Erist exclaimed, approaching the head table with a huge grin on her face. A golden-blonde male with dark green eyes followed her and released a sigh at her words. "Maybe we really didn't need to pour her into a kimono, after all, Ellena."

"Erist, *please*." The blonde male sighed again, raising his fingertips to his temples for a moment before bowing to Nalithor. "As always, I apologize for my wife's inappropriate behavior."

"So, which one of you chose *this* particular kimono for my date, hmmm?" Nalithor questioned, setting my drink down in front of me. *'I hope you're in the mood for tea—there's little else if you wish to delay spirits.'*

*'Tea is more than fine,'* I replied with a subtle nod. *'Thank you.'*

"*She* picked it." Erist pointed at me, her tone flat. My face ignited when Nalithor turned to shoot me a questioning look. "We gave her plenty of less revealing options but—"

"—she said something about this one 'standing out more,'" Ellena finished with a giggle. "*Arianna*, are you *trying* to seduce my son?"

"I don't need to '*try*'!" I retorted hotly, bristling as I shot the goddess a sharp glare.

"If anything, *I* have been trying to seduce *her*," Nalithor added, shooting the incorrigible goddess a glare of his own. "Must I whisk Arianna away to my private palace in order to save her from your meddling?"

*'Private palace?'* I wondered, watching as the women giggled at him. *'Tch, I can see why they frustrate him.'*

Erist and Ellena seemed to finally get the hint and switched to more pleasant conversation among themselves and their husbands. Nalithor, however, maintained his distracting and possessive grip on my thigh throughout dinner. I found that I didn't mind, even if it did force me to focus harder.

Few of the present deities and their children were foolish enough to challenge Nalithor again. The few who *were* stupid enough to do so learned their mistake in seconds. Nalithor seemed to have no patience for *anyone* attempting to "steal" me away from him. Every single one of the challengers had to be whisked away to the healers in order to ensure their wounds were properly cared for. It "wouldn't do" for the demigods to die, apparently. *'Pity. I suppose they'll have to learn of their foolishness in another fashion.'*

"General Vraelimir, I hate to interrupt—" A soldier rushed toward the table and dropped to one knee, bowing his head. He flinched when Nalithor growled at him but didn't back down. "*General*, it's urgent. Scouts have discovered a group of beasts moving through the forests to our south—*within the barrier.*

"The Elders have ordered you to deal with them. You're the closest and most experienced general."

"Beasts?" I inquired, my interest piqued. Nalithor maintained his possessive grip, his arms squeezing tight under my bust as I tilted my head back to look at him. "Can I come for the hunt? I want to kill—"

"I'm afraid that, *this time*, you must stay here." Nalithor chuckled when I pouted. He shifted me so that I was sitting sideways in his lap and then brought a hand up to my face. "This is a job for me as a *god*, my dear. It would be inappropriate for me to have you join unless you're my Chosen, my goddess, or my *partner*... As this is an *urgent* matter, I'll need to leave immediately."

Before I could open my mouth to protest, Nalithor kissed me firmly and enveloped me in his power. His tongue snaked past my lips to tease at mine for a moment before he saw fit to release me and rise to his feet, leaving me wanting for more.

*'You shouldn't deny yourself pleasure just because you're concerned about your thoughts being overheard.'* Nalithor teased as he walked away, summoning heavier armor and his spear as he swept across the marble floor. *'You are just making it worse for yourself the longer you wait.'*

I twitched, my face growing scarlet. I shot a brief glare at his back. I wasn't sure if I even *wanted* to know how he knew that I'd been denying myself pleasure—for the most part. *'Making it worse for myself? Tch.* He *makes it worse for myself!'*

Alala whined and leapt into my lap, watching as Nalithor disappeared into the shadows.

"Well!" Ellena exclaimed, causing me to glance to the side at her even as I struggled to keep the wiggling fox still. "Will you indulge us with your company for a little while longer, Arianna? Or are you too tired from your trip?"

"I think a bath and some sleep sounds like a better idea, for now."
I shook my head and rose to my feet, holding Alala tight to my
stomach.

After exchanging a few brief pleasantries, I swept off across the
marble floor and toward my suite. I wanted nothing more than to
follow Nalithor and join him in the hunt but... I bit back a dejected
sigh and shook my head, making my way across the palace grounds.
Something told me that I shouldn't chase after Nalithor and his prey.

The moment I opened the door to Nalithor's wing of the palace,
Alala wriggled from my grip and sped down the hall to Nalithor's
rooms instead of mine. Whether she was looking for him, or just
wanted to guard his "territory," I had no idea. In a way she seemed
more attached to him than she was to me.

I entered my suite and closed the door behind me with a small sigh.
*'Maybe after a quick bath and some...'* My thoughts trailed off into
blankness as I sunk to my knees with a shudder.

Nalithor's lust enveloped me so strongly that I couldn't even begin
to form a coherent thought. Images, sensations, and sounds of him
dominating me sped through my mind as his power slid across every
inch of my body. Another small shudder and a whimper ran through
me when the vision of Nalithor taking me from behind flipped
through my mind. Every notion, every sensation, sent a new jolt of
desire through me and weakened my resistance. Wetness leaked down
my thighs already as my breath came in short gasps.

This, whatever it was, was far "worse" than any time I'd felt him reaching for me before. His power was so strong it almost felt corporeal, leaving my skin hot wherever it touched. If this was even a *fraction* of what people experienced from the Adinvyr hunting them, I didn't know how the other races could control themselves when in Draemir.

I was so blinded by his lust—and mine—that removing my clothes took longer than it should have, causing me to spew curses at whoever designed a contraption as complicated as a corset. Once I had freed myself from the corset and kimono, I tore my undergarments off and left everything on the floor before stalking to my bed in a stupor. For a moment I was torn between the idea of killing the Elders for assigning Nalithor duties tonight or simply pleasuring myself.

My indecision didn't last. Another wave of lust engulfed me when Nalithor's power squeezed around my throat for a brief moment. That was all it took to break the remaining shreds of resistance and indecision. I collapsed on the bed and ran a hand between my legs with a whimper, my back arching as my mind was flooded with more imagery, sensations—fantasies. Whether they were mine or his, I didn't know anymore. I gave into Nalithor's lust, letting the simple visions and implied sensations sweep me away.

I was well beyond controlling myself *or* keeping Nalithor out of my thoughts now. I *felt* every little thing that he imagined, and it only served to stir my pent-up desire to new heights. I was desperate for release, desperate for him to return and do every damned thing his thoughts suggested. Between his near-constant teasing, the fact that I had been denying myself pleasure since arriving in Vorpmasia, and the imagery he had chosen to pelt me with—I couldn't take it anymore.

"N-not enough…" I panted, frustrated as the tremors subsided. "Nowhere *near*…enough. *Again.*"

I bit my lip hard in a failed attempt to stifle myself, letting Nalithor's lust *and* mine consume me again. I couldn't stop. Not until I was satisfied, or I passed out from exhaustion. Whichever one came first.

# CHAPTER TEN
## *Bloody Trails*

*'Something is wrong. I just know it.'* I frowned, swinging my legs back and forth while surveying the forest from high in the trees. *'What happened to it being a* short *mission? It's been three days!'*

From my perch, I could see the southern edges of the Draemir Barrier and the occasional glimpse of moonslit sands beyond it. Ellena had assigned this search area to me, and it had only taken a few hours for me to reach it. I should have caught the scent of Nalithor or his men by now, yet there was still nothing. Pursing my lips, I summoned my map and double-checked to make sure I was in the right location.

*'They should have come through this way.'* I gnawed on my lower lip, glancing from the map and to my surroundings a few times. *'No signs of travel here, let alone fighting. No sign of beasts. Did they cover their*

217

*tracks, or am I lost?'*

I slipped off the branch and landed in a crouch in the underbrush below. A small sigh escaped me. The footprints of the soldiers had led me this far, yet their tracks had disappeared the moment I entered the forest. I glanced up at the branches above me in thought for a moment. I didn't *think* men in full armor could leap through the branches, but the lack of other discernible tracks was making me reconsider. It was either that, or they had taken the time to cover their tracks.

*'Though, I suppose an Earth or Wilds Mage would make that easy enough.'*

Something felt wrong, still. Whatever it was, it felt "wrong" enough to keep my pulse from calming down. I couldn't stop fidgeting with the hems of my gloves or loose hair. When I left Draemir several hours prior, I had thought that I was simply excited to hunt—finally— and to find Nalithor. Now, however, it was clear to me that it was something *other* than that.

While I was still concerned that something may have happened to the Adinvyr, that wasn't even what had me nervous anymore.

Not long passed before I stepped out from the cover of the trees and looked out across the Suthsul Desert. Forests gave way and faded into sand, the barrier ending mere yards into the desert itself. So far from Vorpmasia's core, the sky was a little brighter—like twilight in X'shmir—except the glow on the horizon wasn't the same sickly violet I had grown up with. I doubted that I would actually get to see true daylight while scouting the barrier's rim—it was already midday.

I tilted my head and shifted my gaze away from distant dunes, refocusing my attention on the ground closer to me. A myriad of tracks surrounded me, but they were old. The winds had almost smoothed them over entirely. With a muffled grumble, I summoned an orb of cobalt flames and searched the surface of the sand around me for anything helpful.

*'Is that...?'* My heart stopped for a moment when the light of my flames reflected off something platinum.

I crouched down and pulled the section of platinum chain from the sand with a frown. Part of the chain was black with blood. A quick sniff told me it was, undoubtedly, Nalithor's. If I wasn't mistaken, it was a scrap of chain from his jewelry. It didn't look like it was part of armor. *'What in the hells could tear this off him? Hells! What on Avrirsa did they run into?'*

I surveyed my immediate surroundings with a grimace, my heart racing within my chest. Sure enough, there was still the occasional splash of blood here and there beneath a light coating of sand. The scents were already fading, but there had been a nasty fight here. Strangely, it didn't appear to have been against Chaos Beasts. I couldn't smell any such creatures or their blood. If the Draemirans had slain beasts, their corpses would have been visible in the sand still.

Rising to my feet, I tugged the hood of my cloak over my head and strode alongside the barrier, heading east. I followed the faint tracks and bloodstains, searching for any remnants of our missing soldiers and deity. With every step, I grew more uneasy. They had been sent to fight beasts, yet there wasn't a single track that belonged to one of those monsters. Even if their prey had been aerial beasts there would have been feathers or putrid blood spilled on the ground to indicate their presence.

I didn't make it far before something made me stop dead in my tracks. Fear, concern, and dread shot through my chest as I stared down at the blade of Nalithor's spear. I hesitated for a moment before rushing forward and kneeling by the spear. I grasped it just below the blade with one hand, using my other to dust sand off the remainder of the shaft.

Upon uncovering the spear I sat back on my heels with a sigh of relief, thankful that Nalithor wasn't attached to it. My heart continued to race in my throat while I stared down at the weapon in disbelief. I couldn't fathom what could have possibly made Nalithor leave it behind. He could have easily summoned it back to his jewelry instead, and no warrior worth his salt would leave his primary arm behind in the middle of a fight. Even had he been disarmed, recalling the spear would have been as easy as a simple thought for him.

I eyed the weapon, hesitant. Since it wasn't mine, and it was forged by Aurelian, I shouldn't have been able to touch it, to begin with. That much I knew. Aurelian and Elise cast potent seals on their creations to make sure they couldn't be wielded by someone they weren't bound to. Yet the spear hadn't burned or otherwise rejected me when I grabbed it.

*'Stupid, stupid, Ari!'* I chastised myself. *'Just* grabbing *it like that was*

*risky. But still…finding it again won't exactly be easy.'*

I reached for the spear again and grasped the heavy shaft. Nothing happened. I rose to my feet with a sigh and brought the spear along with me, balancing it on my shoulder once standing. There didn't appear to be anything else in the sands nearby that belonged to Nalithor. Hells, even the smallest of clues as to what had happened would have sufficed for me. Blood, bodies, weapons. Anything.

A sudden roar shook the ground, making me wince and flinch. When it stopped shaking, I glanced back the way I had come. My blood ran cold, my skin prickling into goosebumps. A *massive* Chaos Beast stalked along the barrier, grinding its shoulder into the flickering magic. It left a bloody smear against the magicked wall as it went. I simply stared at the creature in disbelief for a moment, watching as its blood trickled along the magic and down to burn holes in the sand.

The damned thing was craning its head around like it, too, was looking for something.

I grumbled several curses and broke into a sprint, eager to put more distance between me and the beast. The further I went, the more erratic the soldier's tracks became. Perhaps a hundred yards later, the tracks became strewn with corpses before veering back into the forest. Some of the bodies were that of Draemiran soldiers, but they weren't what worried me.

I slowed to a stop and nudged one of the corpses with the toe of my boot. There were many bodies in both Beshulthien and Elven armor as well. Every single one had pitch black veins popping out of their skin and appeared to have died while in severe pain—not by mortal injury. While their bodies and faces were contorted in agony, most of them had only suffered scrapes or bruises.

A handful of soldiers had sustained fatal wounds, but their veins had turned black just as those of their comrades had. They appeared to have died from the same thing, and not from their injuries, judging from their twisted positions. *'Not good.'*

Glancing around, I paused when my eyes fell on what appeared to be the corpse of an Angel. This one wasn't corrupted or twisted like the ones I had seen before. However, its veins had turned black as well, and he looked as if he had been crawling across the sand in search of something when he died. His arm was outstretched as if he had been reaching for something, but all I found were more footprints.

*'Easy now...'* I glanced toward my right hand when darkness trickled from the shaft of Nalithor's spear. The tendrils of power wrapped around my hand and wrist, making me bristle. *'I guess finding him comes first.'*

The beast behind me roared again, causing me to grit my teeth and glance over my shoulder. As much as I wanted to kill it, my concern for Nalithor outweighed my bloodlust. However, the damned thing did present me with a different sort of problem. I was under orders to send a burst of magic into the air to mark the location of the soldiers...but I also knew the Draemirans would struggle with the colossal creature. Getting them to let me help had already been difficult enough—I doubted I could convince them to request further assistance from the visiting demigods.

I shivered as darkness traveled up to encase my entire forearm. The spear seemed just as eager to tear into the beast as I was.

*'Djialkan, can you hear me from there?'* I pivoted to face the forest, examining the sets of tracks that led into the thick underbrush.

*'What is it, Arianna?'* Djialkan inquired, concerned. *'I thought you were going to be a good girl and follow your orders?'*

*'There's a "problem" stalking along the southern portion of the barrier.'* I grimaced when the damned thing roared again. *'The Draemirans need to steer clear of it, but I did find some of our missing Draemirans... And some other things I doubt are supposed to be here.'*

*'You are not going to take care of this "problem" yourself?'* Djialkan huffed at me.

*'I think finding our missing deity comes before that, don't you?'* I bristled, sensing Djialkan pause.

*'Then, the presence with you is not...?'*

*'I found his spear and part of his torn jewelry. I haven't found him yet.'*

Djialkan fell silent for several long moments, but I could feel his mind whirling in thought. I decided to let him think in silence and set myself to surveying my surroundings again in search of anything else that I might have missed. There had to be *something* to tell me what had happened.

*'I will guard your rooms. Alala is going to keep watch over Nalithor's,'* Djialkan finally spoke. *'I will tell Ellena and Lysander to withdraw their*

*men until you have contacted me to let us know it is safe to proceed. You are nervous, Arianna. Just what did you find?'*

*'I'm not sure.'* I shook my head, then glanced at the spear as it tugged at my hand again. *'The beast is catching up, and Nalithor's spear seems eager to rip into it. I'm going to follow the tracks I found and see if I can find the other missing men—and put some distance between the damned creature and myself.'*

*'Be careful, Arianna.'* Djialkan sounded uneasy. *'If you take too long, we will come find you for ourselves.'*

I launched into the forest with renewed vigor and followed the trail of corpses, blood, and broken branches. There were dozens of dead Draemirans, Beshulthiens, Elves, and several more Angels in the mix. Nalithor had lost his men, many of them, to…something. I wasn't sure if it was a poison, or perhaps a nasty magic technique, but whichever it was—it wasn't a good death. Not for a warrior.

*'Something must have kept him from taking revenge.'* I narrowed my eyes, catching moonslight peeking through the trees ahead of me. *'He wouldn't just stand by and let his men die in this way. Hells, he could have healed them! What could have forced him to put self-preservation first?'*

When I burst out of the trees, I skidded to a stop at the top of a waterfall and grimaced. The waterfall stood well over a hundred feet tall, and I couldn't spot an easy way to get down. I crouched on the edge of the granite rocks and frowned while I examined the shore fare below. Even from so high up I could see that the men who had escaped from the barrier's edge had fallen over the cliffs in their desperation to flee. The mangled remnants of their bodies below were testament to that.

'*I could summon platforms and leap down that way, but…*' I grimaced, watching the spray of water. '*There's no guarantee he went that way. I'd rather not risk slipping* twice *if I have to double back.*'

Scenting the air, I sighed before flicking my eyes to the side at Nalithor's spear. The weapon had grown warm in my grip and had begun to tremble with power, reaching for me again with darkness. I turned my attention to the shoreline below, wondering if perhaps the weapon had sensed something that I couldn't see. Even after switching my vision, there was still nothing. I sighed.

Moments later I felt that massive, overwhelming power of his radiating from somewhere behind me. I pivoted to look over my shoulder in surprise, only to discover there was no one there. The burst subsided as quickly as it had come. Muttering to myself, I leapt into a nearby tree and focused my gaze toward the waterfall that fed the one beside me.

Above the second, larger, waterfall I spotted the shine of flaming carnelian trees rising high into the air. Ellena and the others had warned me to keep my distance from the forest, but *that* was where Nalithor's power had come from. To the hells with their warnings. '*An Aledacian Forest, eh? He went there, of all places?*'

Without hesitation, I darted through the trees and sped toward the Forest of Fire. I would have to learn its name later. For now, finding Nalithor was the most important thing on my mind. The past few days had been rather lonely without him by my side, and I intended to fix that. Of course, I found myself concerned about him too.

When I reached the second waterfall, I barely paused to summon a series of shadowy platforms before leaping up them. The cliffs were slick with water and moss, so I knew it would be too risky for me to climb them. The spray of water made me a little more cautious than normal, but I planned to make up for lost time once I was on solid ground again.

As with Sihix and Ceilail, this forest's trees were crystalline in construction. Wisps of flames danced inside the trees and in their leaves. I was surprised to find that I didn't feel heat radiating from the flora. What I *did* notice concerned me.

The forest's inhabitants had all collected along the outermost rim to hide inside trees or high up on the branches. Some of the smaller creatures were huddled under bushes or behind mushrooms. If they could use it as a pseudo-shield, they were doing so.

"Beasts?" I kept my tone conversational as I approached the tree line, watching as several of the fiery inhabitants turned to examine me and then the spear that I carried.

"Your Brands…" A nymph murmured, drifting out from within a tree near me. Her expression was thoughtful as she traced my form with fire-like eyes. "You may help him. We will not interfere."

I nodded to her and then took off at a sprint through the trees, weaving my way through them with ease. While running I shifted my vision briefly so that I could examine the forest's magic, but it glowed with such intensity that it brought tears to my eyes at first. Once my eyes adjusted, I leapt high into a tree and pressed my palm against the massive trunk. The area hummed with an unfathomable amount of energy, but it also felt as if it was *breathing*.

No wonder so many people believed that these forests were cursed.

*'This one hasn't been corrupted by anything—yet.'* I flicked my gaze around, examining every tree within range. *'Everything I touch shifts to the color of my flames. Hmmm... Can I find Nalithor by looking for blue-white things, then?'*

Every single living thing that belonged to the forest was huddled along the outskirts. People, creatures, animals—everything. From the largest creature to the smallest insect, everything had taken to hiding in whatever nooks and crannies they could find. They were so panicked that many were at the risk of stumbling out of the tree line entirely. Several watched me with fear in their eyes as I walked deeper into their home.

The stench of Chaos Beast blood was almost overwhelming.

*'Is someone killing them? Can't tell...'* I grimaced, putting more distance between me and the cowering creatures. It felt as if there were hundreds of Chaos Beasts in the forest. Every fiber of my being ached to hunt the creatures down, to tear their flesh apart with blade and claw. To paint the flora with their blood and decorate the trees with their copses. I shivered and shook my head hard. *'I have to find Nalithor.'*

The local Lari'xan's energy interfered with my altered senses more than I had anticipated, making it difficult for me to spot anything other than their aether. Sihix and Ceilail were like children when compared to the power of this Lari'xan, and it gave me the impression that this one had never been bound or corrupted in the way the other two had.

I kept my movements quiet while I crept from branch-to-branch at a careful pace. It wasn't long before I was deep enough into the forest that there wasn't so much as a hint of its native creatures around me. Even the young had cooperated with their parents and elders to flee. While I could sense them far behind me still, their presences were beginning to get drowned out by the Lari'xan. However, their fear still clung to the air even so far in.

Minutes passed before I encountered a new, unfamiliar, scent. I stopped on a limb and crouched, sniffing at the air. This one wasn't a Chaos beast, but I wasn't certain what—

"Reltyir, Reltyir?" A voice queried from beside me, making me jump and whip around.

I just stared at the voice's source for a moment. *'A red fox, in a kimono, and standing on his hind legs? Am I... Am I truly losing it?'*

"Please, please, Reltyir, can you help Rely'ric?" The fox spoke again, tugging at one of the platinum chains around my hips. "You know him don't you? You have something of his. I can smell his magic on you. You are friend, yes?"

"His magic...? Yes, I brought his spear. He dropped it." I sighed, looking at the panicky fox. "Yes, I know him. He's my—"

"Yes, yes!" The fox nodded excitedly, his bushy tail whipping back and forth. "Rely'ric has been fighting too long. Far too long. He's injured. You can help, yes? Yes?"

"He's…hurt?" I stared at the fox, a pulse of rage shooting through me when he nodded his head and pointed deeper into the forest with a forepaw. "Then, the reason I can't sense his power aside from small bursts…"

"Yes, yes. Rely'ric is almost completely drained, yes." The fox nodded again before hopping back and forth, rapidly, on his hind legs. "Thousands of beasties he's killed here! But still too many alive. Too many. Being pursued. Chased. I can show you the way. Please, please. You will help, won't you?

"Your Brands are like his. Reversed. Mirrored. You carry his scent. His spear. You *must* be friend, yes?"

*'Nalithor is hurt?'* Rage crept through me again, causing the spear in my hand to tremble and release a low hum. I glanced deeper into the forest for a moment, before looking at the fox. "Can you show me where he is *without* getting hurt by the beasts yourself?"

"Yes, yes. Beasties can't see me." The fox chuckled, beckoning to me. "I've been hiding his trail. Hiding his blood. I will show you, only you. You can follow even if you lose sight of me. Please, prepare yourself to fight. Careful for yellow blood. Yellow is poison. Rest is just stinky. Can't have you both hurt. Both hurt would be bad, very bad."

I adjusted my grip on Nalithor's trembling spear and then nodded to the fox to indicate I was ready. Seeming satisfied, the fox took off at a run through underbrush. I broke into a sprint and followed from higher up in the branches, soon finding the first hints of Nalithor's bloody rampage as the fox's magics dissipated. Corpses of beasts littered the forest floor. Some even dangled from the branches above me. There were bodies from the size of a rat to the size of a cottage. If it was a beast, he had utterly destroyed it.

The carnage made me wonder if, perhaps, his usually calm demeanor had slipped.

Shaking my head, I refocused my attention on the speedy fox and followed him ever deeper into the fiery forest. When a beast leapt out from around a tree, I slashed it in half in one swing of Nalithor's spear and resumed my chase. He was right—they didn't appear to sense him at all. Interesting. I pushed my curiosity from my mind and cut down several more beasts. They seemed intent on slowing me down, but I refused to let that happen. Eventually, I summoned an array of flaming orbs behind me and lobbed them through the beast's skulls while I made my way through the stragglers. I couldn't afford to waste time on them.

From the sheer number of corpses, I could only assume that Nalithor had been fighting for days. I followed the fox, at a run, for at least twenty minutes before catching my first whiff of Nalithor's scent. Somehow it was stronger than I had ever smelled before. The notes of sweet spices, sandalwood, and musk more apparent than ever. There were new undertones alongside it that I couldn't identify. It felt as though it carried faint traces of his power, which only served to make his weapon vibrate more. I gritted my teeth—it didn't matter. I now had another way to track him. Something told me I *had* to find him, and soon.

"Reltyir, Reltyir! Can you heal? Can you fight?" The fox inquired from ahead. "Rely'ric is hurt badly."

*'He's asking that* now?' I cut through another small group of beasts, causing Nalithor's weapon to sing with anticipation for more blood. "I can, and I can. Just how many beasts *are* there...?"

"Few left, few left." The fox giggled at me. "Up ahead—clearing. I must fetch Yumeko. We need her help."

*'Yumeko?'* I pursed my lips, dashing past the fox. *'A female? That had better be another fox.'*

I growled at my own jealousy and shoved it aside before leaping into a new, higher, tree. Slowing my pace, I tilted my head and listened when I caught the sound of voices. I slinked my way along the maze of branches, then darted up a neighboring tree while making my way in the direction of the closest beast I could sense. Soon, I slowed to a stop above a clearing that had a river running through it. A small caravan of what appeared to be slavers had set up camp on the shore of the deep, clear river.

"Just how fast can that bastard run?!" A male whined. "The poison *or* the beasts should have crippled him by now!"

"I'm going to break that ass in before we sell him!" A second male snarled, causing a scowl to split my face. "A god should be able to take quite the pounding, right? Hahaha!"

*'They're…talking about* Nalithor?*'* A twitch ran through my grip on the spear. My blood ran cold as I surveyed the clearing. These "people" were little better than animals. My prey. I would hunt down and gut every last one of them like the savages they were. A shiver ran through me, causing me to shake my head. Darkness poured from Nalithor's spear again and pulled at me, urging me to act out on my desires. *'I'm not going to lose to a fucking weapon, of all things.'*

"Hah! To think we'd find a god *here*. It must be our lucky day!" A woman released a fanatical laugh, turning to grin up at the towering beast sitting in their camp. "You were right, Boss! This was the perfect place to search!"

*'Boss?'* I stared at the woman and then the beast in disbelief, sneaking closer. Nalithor's foxy friend had hidden in the bushes below me and was tracking my movements with wide eyes. *'How in the hells is the beast their* boss?*'*

"Tch, Melody, can't we just kill him already?" The first male whined.

"Dumbass!" The woman snapped, hitting the man upside his head. "We don't have a *Godslayer*—we *can't* kill him! We *can* capture him for the Exiles, though! We'll be rich!"

"Yes, yes. You Humans *do* love your money, don't you?" Another male voice spoke, bored. I bit back a snarl when the Angel strode into view. "Don't get cocky. You were lucky to find him while he's drained of power, but he is still much stronger than a Human, and you still have to capture him."

"Of course, you were kind enough to provide us beasts to wear him down with!" The second Human male laughed. "So…you're saying that, no matter what we do to him, he won't die—right?"

"That is correct," the Angel responded, his tone full of distaste as he watched the Human fiddle with his belt. "Tch. Disgusting creatures. Melody, keep your men in line. I am still an *Angel* you know. Their filthy behavior is unforgivable."

"Ugh, you prick!" Melody backhanded the second male, dazing him. "Keep it in your pants! You can fuck all the slave boys you want when we get our reward! For now… Let's see how much damage it takes to incapacitate a god!"

Something inside me snapped, and I was on the woman in an instant. I grabbed her by her hair and used it as a handle to smash her face into a boulder by the river's edge. Her skull shattered in one blow, sending bits of bone and clumps of grey matter across my leather armor and the surrounding terrain.

The beast was the first one to react, but it didn't matter. None of them were allowed to escape. Especially not the Human men.

I ducked under the beast's swipe, then leapt into the air, tearing its undersized head clean from its shoulders. When it didn't stop moving, I tore its limbs away one-by-one. Frustrated, I finally punched a hole through the creature's chest with Nalithor's spear. Finally, with the beast ended, its screaming stopped, and I turned on the remaining Humans.

"Don't just stand there, you fool! Kill her!" The first Human male yelped at the Angel, who just rolled his eyes as if a stubborn child had addressed him.

I wasn't going to give them a chance to move. Spear in hand, I fell on the first of the Human men and beheaded him with a single stroke. Next, I turned on the second filthy Human. Darkness flowed outward from me to grasp the bastard's ankles, wrists, and head. He screeched in terror, trousers growing dark with urine when I tugged at his limbs. Shadows spiraled outward from Nalithor's spear to join mine. The man was so terrified that I couldn't understand a single blubbered word.

Every time I pulled at his limbs, he shrieked again.

Finally bored of his terrified sounds, I tore my blade through his groin and let him scream in agony for a moment. Satisfied, I ripped his limbs and head from his torso with a single, savage, yank. I grinned when his blood sprayed into the air from his ruined body and stained my armor, skin, and hair crimson. The lack of beast blood intermingled with his blood surprised me on some minor level—but I had more prey to kill.

I twirled Nalithor's spear into an offensive stance as the combined darkness returned to me, then leapt at the Angel with glee. He was quick to pull a longsword to hand, but it didn't matter. The spear sliced through the sword and then his forearm, severing both in half. My blade hummed with pure delight and shivered in my grip when the Angel's blood poured over it. Darkness flowed from the pale blue gems once again and wrapped around both my wrists. It felt just as thirsty for blood as I was…and seemed somehow approving.

"Stop that pitiful wailing," I ordered, grabbing hold of one of his wings. "It's just your arm. Ah, but if I do *this*…"

He screamed when I ripped the wing from his back. He crumpled forward on the ground, twitching in pain. I slammed the heel of my boot into the side of his skull to put him out of his misery. His head burst like a fruit beneath the force. For a moment, I considered ripping him into smaller pieces—but there were more slavers to kill.

*'I guess all the screaming woke them up.'* I bit my lower lip and shivered, turning to face my new prey.

"T-the bitch is insane!" One of them shrieked. "No one told me we'd be dealing with a god *and* his goddess—I didn't sign on for this!"

*'Hmmm, that seems like an increasingly common assumption,'* I mused, leaping forward to butcher the remaining Humans.

Once all of the slavers were dead, I stalked over to their supply wagon and began rummaging through their belongings. The fox from before approached me, looking startled by the amount of bright red blood that coated me and his master's spear.

"Reltyir, Reltyir, what are you looking for?" The fox hopped back and forth on his hind legs. "You aren't injured, are you?"

"Not my blood. Mine is black," I murmured before motioning at a piece of one of the men. "They said something about poisoning Nalithor. I came across a lot of soldiers on my way here—they died from poisoning. These people should have an antidote if they're responsible, right?"

"Poison? Poison? Poison is bad!" The fox exclaimed, darting forward to search as well. "Rely'ric's veins were growing dark. Poison? Poison's doing? Hurry, please. Hurry, please. I will look for the antidote."

I glanced at the strange fox for a moment before nodding and speeding away from the slaver's camp. I followed the trail of blue-black blood through the trees with growing concern, ignoring the humming of Nalithor's bloodthirsty weapon. The sheer amount of blood he was losing was dangerous. Had one of the beasts injured him so badly, or was something else to blame? God or not, losing so much blood had to have been dangerous. *'I will rip whoever is responsible apart!'*

Shoving my bloodlust away, I paused to rest the shaft of the spear on my shoulder and then began running again. Following Nalithor's scent and his trail of blood was a simple matter for me. I sensed that the forest itself was watching as I leapt between its trees, branches, and underbrush without care. For some reason, I felt compelled to help the Adinvyr even though I had felt so cross about being left behind at first. Well, being left behind *and* the thoughts he had left me with.

*'Perhaps it was a good thing I stayed behind,'* I considered, frowning while I wove my way through the trees. *'If I had come as well...who would bail the both of us out of this mess? I'll... I'll have to worry about whether or not he'll accept me later.'*

The sound of splashing nearby caught my attention, causing me to pause and listen. Nalithor's spear grew hot and shuddered beneath my grip again, releasing a shrill sound. I glanced to the side at the weapon and then shook my head before leaping up several trees. Placing my free hand against the tree's trunk, I leaned around it to peer at the source of the splashing sounds.

Several yards ahead was another clearing, but this one was much smaller and had a thin waterfall pouring off nearby cliffs and into the basin which fed the stream that snaked through the clearing and out into the forest. However, what had my attention was Nalithor's tall, muscular form. He waded into the water with his clothes, armor, and all still clinging to his body. His back and arms were gashed open to the bone in several places, with many more lesser wounds marring his skin. The veins beneath his pale skin had grown noticeably dark, but they weren't black—yet.

The water behind Nalithor turned opaque blue-back when he waded deeper into the stream, making me grit my teeth to stifle a snarl.

"'You really are in a sorry state, aren't you?'" I quoted his own words back at him as I sat down on the tree branch. He turned his head slightly, but his long hair still obscured his face. "I'm not as good of a healer as you are by any means… But, would you like some help with that? Ah—and you dropped this."

I hefted the spear and threw it blade-first into the gravel by the shore. The weapon turned to darkness before even hitting the gravel and flowed up Nalithor's form to disappear into one of the crystals in his jewelry.

"What…are you doing here?" Nalithor asked. I tilted my head in response to his strangely strained and husky tone. After a moment he sighed and shook his head. "Ugh…never mind that, for the moment. Yes."

I slid off the tree branch and landed in a crouch. Shrugging, I strode across the clearing and tossed my traveling coat and pack aside. Nalithor flinched when I reached up to pull his hair away from his back and shoulders. It only took a moment for me to pin his hair up and out of my way, but it still caused him pain. I grimaced, examining the lacerations across his back. Not all of them were from beasts—some were undoubtedly from weapons.

"You smell different…" Nalithor murmured, beginning to pivot toward me.

"And *you* need to stay still if I'm going to help you," I responded firmly, summoning shadows around my hands. "If this hurts, I'm sorry."

Without waiting for his answer, I allowed my shadows to flow freely from my hands. I shut my eyes and concentrated on knitting his wounds back together. Although I wasn't good enough to heal him completely, I knew enough to stitch his severed muscles and blood vessels back together. He had sustained so many wounds that it was necessary for me to pace myself—otherwise, I would have run out of energy before seeing to all his injuries.

I doubted I would be able to heal him beyond starting the process. Even with my affinity for darkness, *that* much healing was draining. Just *looking* at his wounds made me want to tear into new prey with reckless abandon.

Stitching *skin* back together was the most difficult thing to me...but I knew he could handle that later. I just had to stop the bleeding.

His scent, and the scent of his blood, were distracting as ever and threatened to dull my senses to all else. I shoved both from my mind the best I could and held back a shiver. I had to force myself to concentrate on healing.

"You're bleeding as well. Are you alright?" Nalithor questioned while I drew my darkness-encased fingers along his skin.

"Just a few scrapes from the underbrush," I replied dismissively, gnawing on my lower lip while assessing the remainder of damage on his back, then moved to his left side. "Arms."

"You..." Nalithor trailed off, staring down at me with a stunned expression. "You are absolutely *covered* in blood. Just what, exactly, did you kill the damned things with?"

"Eh?" I glanced down at myself and then sighed. "Hmmm, maybe I should restrain myself more next time."

"That isn't beast blood." Nalithor gave me a firm look as I raised my fingers to his left bicep. "What—who—did you kill? *Why are you here?* You were supposed to wait in Draemir until I—"

"I decided to make use of being your *partner* while it lasts!" I retorted hotly, silencing him in an instant. "*You* were being pursued by a caravan of slavers, I'll have you know! They were quite cross that their poison and beasts hadn't forced your submission yet. The blood is *theirs* and—"

"There was an Angel with them?" Nalithor frowned, leaning down to sniff at me. "What is this about being my partner 'while it lasts?'"

"Yes. There *was* an Angel." I huffed, moving to his other arm. "He screamed quite nicely when I ripped his fucking wings from his back!

"And before you complain about it—no, I didn't exactly have *time* to 'wash off their unworthy blood.' Chasing down your poisoned ass seemed more pressing."

Nalithor arched an eyebrow at me, so I growled and bared my fangs at him before refocusing on his right arm. I was already beginning to feel faint from using so much power to heal, but I still had his chest to take care of. The Adinvyr watched me for a moment when I moved to stand in front of him. I lifted my hands to his bloodied chest and bit back a grimace when the scent of his blood threatened to draw me in again.

"You didn't answer my other question," Nalithor stated, placing a hand on top of my head, which earned a brief pout and glare from me. "You...*really* shouldn't venture so close to a hungry, *wounded*, Adinvyr, Arianna..."

"The results of my tests *and* our orders arrived this morning," I replied flatly, reaching up to his face with both hands so that I could heal the gouges he had sustained to his otherwise flawless face. "We've been assigned to work together, but I know you tend to detest having partners. So—"

"So, you're *mine* then?" Nalithor interjected, catching me by my wrists. He pulled my hands from his face and watched me with an unreadable expression. "I smell Daijiro on you. Where is he?"

"Daijiro? Ah. You must mean *him*," I grumbled, attempting to reclaim my wrists. "He's searching for the antidote in the slaver's belongings. He— Eeek!"

Nalithor slipped an arm around my waist and hefted me into the air, tossing me into the deepest part of the basin. I grit my teeth, shivering as the surprisingly cold water engulfed me. The Adinvyr grinned at me when I broke the surface of the water to glare at him.

"It's *cold* you know!" I pawed the water out of my eyes.

"You're covered in so much blood that I can barely make out that succulent flesh of yours," Nalithor countered sweetly, earning him another glare. "Ahhh...speaking of which, how many of my countrymen must I kill for laying their hands on you while I was away? Hmmm?"

"No one." I shrugged, grimacing while I looked down at my clothing. After a moment, I ripped off my clothing in irritation, including undergarments, and dove back into the basin. After several moments I resurfaced and pushed my soaked curls out of my face. "They're all too frightened to knock on my barriers anymore, let alone *attempt* to lay a hand on me."

"You're shameless," Nalithor commented, observing my nude form with an expression that I could only describe as hungry. "Didn't I *just* warn you—"

"Rely'ric, Reltyir!" Daijiro darted out from the trees as I wrung pink water from my curls. "More beasts are—"

"Arianna, my dear, would you mind if I borrowed some power from you?" Nalithor inquired smoothly, tracking my movements as I summoned a towel from my shrizar. He looked more than a little disappointed when I wrapped the towel around myself. "Daijiro, you can return on your own, can you not? Have Yumeko prepare a room for the lady and draw her a bath."

"As you wish, Rely'ric." Daijiro bowed, then vanished in a vortex of blue fire.

"I didn't say yes yet, now did I?" I arched an eyebrow at Nalithor. "What about the poison in your veins? The antidote?"

"You were going to," Nalithor responded with a playful smile. "Feeding will be sufficient. Had I been feeding properly in the first place... Suffice to say that their poison would have done nothing, and we wouldn't be in this mess. *So,* where would you like me to bite you?"

"You've already decided *that* as well, haven't you?" I scoffed, crossing my arms at him.

"Aw, you're no fun tonight." Nalithor smiled at me, then cast a displeased grimace towards the trees. "Fast bastards... Very well. Come here."

Nalithor pulled me into his chest and nuzzled into the left side of my throat. He took a deep, shaky breath as his lips parted against my skin. His fangs sunk deep into my flesh, my vision spinning in an instant. Nalithor's grip was tight enough to keep me upright as he crushed me to his chest, drinking greedily from my throat. My thoughts began to blur as I realized just how famished he was. The blood loss had taken a much greater toll on him than I had anticipated.

I was certain that it should have hurt. In reality, it was far, far from it. It felt so good that I could barely form a coherent thought aside from wanting *more*. I was unbearably aroused, aroused to a point that hot wetness trickled down my inner thighs. My perked nipples sent shudders through me each time they rubbed against Nalithor's chest. Nothing I did, and nothing I thought, could help me regain control of myself.

His deep, contented, groans saw to that.

When he withdrew his fangs, it sent an involuntary shiver through me. He chuckled, then ran his tongue up my neck before nibbling at my earlobe.

*"Sleep,"* he commanded.

I was vaguely aware of the patter of approaching feet as Nalithor lifted me into his arms, but my consciousness fully slipped before he even finished adjusting his grip on me.

# CHAPTER ELEVEN
## *Vigilant*

I cradled Arianna's unconscious form in my arms and cast a glare over my shoulder at the pack of approaching beasts. The damned things snarled and snapped their maws at us, their vile stench distracting me from the rather exquisite woman I had just partaken of. Were it not for their interference, I likely would have taken more of her blood.

Alas, such things had to wait.

*'Silly little thing, dropping her towel...'* I shook my head, choosing not to reclaim it. We were losing time.

Shifting my gaze away from Arianna's nude form, I summoned a ring of darkness around our immediate surroundings. The beasts yelped and shrank back when my power stung at them. Whilst they were distracted, I shut my eyes and focused. Neither Arianna nor I could fight the beasts in our condition.

The only option was to take her to my domain until we were both fully recovered. Under other circumstances, I would have hesitated to bring *anyone* to my private domain…but this woman was an exception I was willing to make. Not only because she had healed me, but because she was willing to give me her blood so that I might save us both.

It took me mere seconds to grasp onto a thread of my territory's power. I reached out with practiced ease and conjured a shadowy doorway up from the ground before me, feeling my senses sway even after such a simple use of magic. The beasts hissed and screeched in terror, shrinking away from the darkness. They didn't appear to be of X'shmiran origin, so I found their response intriguing.

Not intriguing enough to stick around, however.

*'Damn it.'* I dropped to one knee as the dark portal wavered and then disappeared behind me. *'Perhaps…the poison took more of a toll than I thought.'*

My gaze shifted down to the petite woman slumbering in my arms when she nuzzled into my chest with a sleepy grumble. Keeping my gaze restricted to "proper" places was…difficult. The delightful little moans and whimpers she had released while I drank from her were distracting enough *before* her perked nipples or the sweet scent of her arousal.

The delicate Brands of Divinity dancing along her skin seemed to taunt me. They drew my eyes to, and accentuated, regions of her body that I likely should have refrained from looking at.

*'Perhaps another taste…'* I paused with my lips against her throat and shivered. *'If only these marks were my claim on her. It's a shame I had to feed from her before having my chance to…'*

I grew still, feeling Arianna's pulse quicken and my fangs pressed against her throat. I couldn't recall preparing to bite her again. Had I been so enraptured by her taste and scent? By my desire to claim her? I groaned. I knew better than to feed from a slumbering woman, and yet I was still considering doing just that. Transporting us to my domain was taxing at best, and the taste of her blood…

*'She already drained herself too much by healing me. I can't take more,'* I reminded myself, straightening as I shifted my gaze away from Arianna and up at the tiered palace before me. *'I should entrust her to Yumeko and the others before I give in to temptation.'*

My increasing desire for her made everything difficult. I had opted out of using my venom when I bit her—I didn't want to risk it warping her mind, no matter how temporary. Even so, she had reacted like *that*. I let out a sigh and shook my head as a shiver ran down my spine and through my tail. "Difficult" wasn't a strong enough word for this woman anymore.

I slipped past the main entry of my domain, blind to my surroundings. Bringing Arianna into the palace itself was the first, crucial, step. My own arousal made it difficult for me to focus, and difficult to walk. Armor-plated leather trousers were *not* the most comfortable method of constraining my growing desire, but I couldn't simply set the princess down and rearrange myself either.

*'First her antics upon arrival in Draemir, then at dinner, and now this...'* I shook my head and surveyed the courtyard, searching for my servants. *'It's a shame I didn't get to claim her before leaving, as I had planned to... At this rate, I will throw caution to the wind and* train *her to take me.'*

"Reltyir? Reltyir? Is Reltyir alright?" Daijiro's voice from behind me startled me from my thoughts, causing me to turn and look down at him. "Rely'ric, I brought her things from the clearing. Ruined. Ruined. All of it ruined. Beastie blood."

Daijiro's fluffy tail thrashed behind him as he hefted Arianna's blood-soaked leather pack. He opened to reveal that both beast and Human blood had pooled inside with her belongings. I grimaced when the stench reached me.

"See if the others can purify it." I shifted my attention away from Daijiro when I caught the sound of more clawed paws approaching, finding a group of female Vulin approaching us. "Yumeko, you made the necessary preparations for Arianna-z'tar's stay?"

"Yes, and the men have prepared your rooms and a bath for you as well." Yumeko nodded and then reached up to me expectantly, her attention focused on the nude princess in my arms. "You are both in such terrible shape! Honestly, my lord, just what—"

"Rely'ric, Rely'ric, where are you going?" Daijiro panicked when I turned to leave the palace after handing Arianna off to the Vulin women.

"There is still the matter of my men who fell during our skirmish near Suthsul," I replied. Several more Vulin darted out from nearby to block my path alongside Daijiro. "As the general in charge, it is my duty to—"

"No, no." Daijiro pressed his paws against my knee and shook his head hard. "Reltyir found bad things there. Bad things. Not safe. Not yet.

"I followed Reltyir while she searched. Searched for you, searched for beasties. Rely'ric is far too damaged to fight bad things in this state. Reltyir is too weakened to help. Rely'ric can't fight the small ones waiting in Xiinsha. Rely'ric should wait."

"For once I agree with the rambling one," Yumeko chimed in. "You had to borrow power from this woman in order to return to your own domain, didn't you, Rely'ric? Heal. Rest. Once you have both recovered, *then* your mind will be clear enough to deal with your tasks."

I released a heavy sigh and then pivoted to look back at Yumeko and the other women with her. They didn't waste any time—they had already wrapped Arianna in a robe and pooled her long hair on top of her torso so that they could carry her with ease. Yumeko shot me a firm look before motioning to the women with one paw. The bossy fox led them up to whichever floor they had prepared for their guest, leaving me half regretful for allowing them to separate us.

They were attempting to hide it, but I knew they were excited to have a guest.

"Rely'ric," Daijiro called, his tone concerned as he came to stand beside me. "Poison fading? Diminishing? I found antidote. Many antidotes. Many poisons. Alchemists examining them now. Healers examining now, too."

"Many antidotes *and* poisons?" I glanced down at the panicky Vulin. "Feeding appears to have chased away the poison…but keep me informed. I am going to bathe and then rest."

*'Among other things…'* I sighed to myself as I made my way to a nearby staircase and ascended them in search of my rooms on the top floor. *'The sooner I get these accursed trousers off, the better.'*

"Rely'ric, Rely'ric, one more thing. One more." Daijiro called from behind me, making me twitch. "Reltyir is guest? How to treat? Never have guests. What should I tell the others?"

"How to treat her?" I considered it for a moment, a strange sensation passing through my chest. "Tell them… Tell them that Arianna-z'tar is to be treated as if she's the lady of the house. She is—"

"Important to Rely'ric? Important, yes?" Daijiro sounded a little *too* enthusiastic. "I will let others know! Others excited to have guest. Will be more excited about *important* guest! Feast? Party?"

"Don't get ahead of yourself." I sighed, shaking my head. "If she came across something as 'bad' as you claim, we will likely need to hunt it and return to Draemir as soon as we've both recovered.

"Those matters aside… Seal my domain off from the other gods. I don't want anyone dropping by while Arianna and I recover. Not even my family."

Daijiro nodded his understanding and scampered off to see to his duties, allowing me to resume my ascent upstairs. As concerned as I was about what had happened along the Draemir Barrier, and to the men in my command, I was now more concerned about what Arianna could have come across during her search. If it passed through the barrier while we were recovering... I shook my head. I knew better than to try poking around inside her head for information at this point.

However, the fact that she not only encountered, but tore into, Human slavers and an *Angel* concerned me. She should have been at least a *little* averse to hunting people, but it was clear by her demeanor and the blood coating her that she had reveled in the slaughter.

*'Didn't she say something about them "being upset that the poison and beasts hadn't worn me into submission?"'* I pursed my lips while striding down the hallway to my rooms, fiddling with the belt of my armored trousers as I went. *'They were involved with what happened? I suppose questioning them isn't an option now. Not if her rampage was anything like it was in Ceilail.*

*'She's...my partner now.'*

I hesitated outside my rooms when the thought crossed my mind. In all honesty, I had thought that at least one of the Oracles would deny my demands and assign someone else as Arianna's partner. Knowing them, I doubted they "let" Lucifer pair us without a fight. Regardless of whether any of them truly knew who she was, the Oracles were trouble. They had a direct connection to the Elders, and they had been obsessed with me for decades—even before I had become a god.

Curling my hand into a fist, I pivoted and walked away from the door to my suite. Finding Arianna's assigned rooms didn't prove difficult—I could sense the Vulin and the princess herself in the bath down the hall. I strode into the room without hesitation, earning gasps and mutters from the female Vulin. Several voiced protests, but I raised a hand to silence them.

"Yumeko." I settled my gaze on the fox, watching as she grew still, and her eyes widened. "Show me which rooms you chose to give to Arianna."

"M-my lord?" Yumeko stuttered, blinking at me. She glanced to her fellow Vulin before standing up and scurrying over to me. "This way, Rely'ric. Is something the matter?"

"I want to take extra precautions," I answered, following the fox down the hall. "It occurred to me that our mutual enemy may have discovered who Arianna is...and it wouldn't do if they realized she's here. Not while we are both weakened."

"*Them...*" Yumeko bristled, her snout wrinkling. "Here, Rely'ric. I thought it best to have her on the same floor as you."

I slowed to a stop outside of the room, noting Yumeko's expectant look. The Vulin hated the Elders almost as much as I did, and with good reason. They, at least, I could trust. They were beyond those bastard's reach.

Sighing, I shut my eyes and placed a hand against the door. Power snaked from my fingers and trailed over the door and through the walls, creating a web of dark magic around the suite. Each passing second made me feel more and more faint, but it was necessary. I couldn't rest if I wasn't certain Arianna was as protected as possible while here.

However, I knew better than to stop at protective wards. Knowing Arianna, she would be itching for a hunt the moment she woke up, regardless of how drained she might be. I resolved to add one final enchantment to the room—one to make sure that she rested undisturbed until she was healed to a certain point.

I staggered back from the door with a wince when pain shot through my temples. Even if I wanted to add more enchantments, I couldn't without risking the stability of my domain. My power was spent.

"Rely'ric?" Yumeko grabbed me around the calf as if it would help steady me. "You must rest, my lord! The vixens are almost finished caring for Reiz'tar. Please, return to your rooms and recover. You will find a bath waiting in your suite. If you keep pushing yourself in this way—"

"See to it that Arianna isn't disturbed," I interrupted, earning a wide-eyed look from the fox. "She gave much so that we could escape, and to heal me. If she wakes too soon, she will try to find a way back to the forest so that she might finish the beasts herself—distract her if that happens. Do what you must to keep her from—"

"Rely'ric!" Yumeko summoned her power and braced me with it when I staggered. "To your rooms, now! We will care for Reiz'tar—

and for you."

The fox prodded me down the hallway with her power, not content until she had ushered me into my suite and shut the doors behind me. I placed my hands flat on a nearby table and leaned against it, closing my eyes as I willed my head to stop spinning. Now the both of us had overdone it. But…she was safe now. My knees hit the floor, sending a jolt of pain through me. Enough to force me to regain consciousness. I bared my fangs and slammed my fist into the floor, frustrated.

*'What in the hells did they* use *in that poison?!'* I growled as my vision swam. "Daijiro!"

The fox appeared in front of me from a burst of flames, looking taken aback when he spotted me.

"Rely'ric? Wrong? What's wrong?" The fox panicked, waving his front paws at me.

"Help me…to the bath." I shoved my pride aside, gritting my teeth. "*That fucking poison* has—"

"Here, here." Daijiro rushed over to me. "Bad poison? Should I fetch antidote after all?"

"See to it that our alchemists bring me a list of the ingredients used in that vile substance as soon as they have it." I snarled, allowing the Vulin to use his power to help me to the bath. The strength had almost left my limbs entirely, but I couldn't just go to bed bloodied. Nor could I use magic to cleanse myself. "If I'm correct, that poison…"

"No words, rest, rest." Daijiro shook his head hard. "Will tell them to bring to you when they have it. Rely'ric needs help? More help?"

"Yes…" I sighed, sinking into the bath with a wince as the water stung my wounds. *'I must grow stronger…but I can't do that without feeding. But…I can't— I won't—feed from someone else.'*

❧

A day and a half had passed since bringing Arianna to my domain. While I had mostly regained my strength already, the princess still showed no sign of waking. She had spent much more of her power than I first realized, and feeding from her had brought her magic dangerously low. However, I couldn't bring myself to feel guilt. Had I not fed from her, we wouldn't have had the *chance* to recover.

I wouldn't have been able to live with myself if my own cowardice led to Arianna's demise.

I looked up from my book and over to the slumbering princess, unsure what to make of her. Once I was capable of moving again, I took to sitting in her rooms and reading while waiting for her to wake. I wanted to be there when she woke up. Surely, she had known the risks she was taking, and yet she had retained her playful nature.

A sleepy grumble distracted me from my thoughts, causing my heart to skip a beat—had she awoken? Alas, no. She rolled onto her side so that she was facing me, her body curling into a ball around her pillow as she hugged it to her chest. I breathed a sigh, disappointed. I should have grown used to it by now. Every time I came to her suite, it was never long before she shifted in her slumber so that she was facing wherever I had chosen to sit. She never drew close to waking, nor did she reach for me, but her power was another matter.

Her darkness coiled around me like a living creature, tempting and drawing me ever closer to her. Had she not been so weakened, it might have succeeded.

*'She shouldn't be recovering so slowly.'* I frowned, setting my book aside. *'Is this because of the curses that bind her?'*

"Rely'ric," Yumeko spoke quietly and tugged at the sleeve of my robe. "Daijiro has left to speak with your people and Reiz'tar's Guardians. You're certain you don't wish for them to know where you are?"

"We can't risk the wrong ears hearing." I shook my head and glanced at the bipedal fox. "I would deal with the remnants of battle on the southern border myself if I could but…I want to be here when Arianna wakes."

"Poor thing truly drained herself," Yumeko murmured, tugging the blankets up over the slumbering princess' shoulders. "She should have known it was dangerous to give so much!"

"I'm sure she did." I closed my eyes for a moment and sighed. "Her antics distracted me. If only I had been more focused, I wouldn't have—"

We both went silent and fell still when Arianna grumbled something and turned onto her stomach. She stretched out and then sunk into her pillow again, remaining fast asleep. Her dreams and thoughts were growing ever more active, but her breathing indicated that she was in a deep sleep. Nothing appeared to be wrong with her, aside from her weakened magic, but it still worried me.

Yumeko motioned for me to follow her into the hallway so that we could continue our conversation, and after a moment of hesitation, I complied. My wards around the room shimmered when we passed through them, then fell back into place. I was tempted to increase their strength every time I came to Arianna's rooms but doing so would have defeated the purpose in recovering.

"I came to give you these, my lord." Yumeko reached into one of her sleeves and pulled out a small stack of papers. "A page for each of the poisons. We believe we know which one was used against you—and which antidote is for it. Due to the ingredients we recommend—"

"Vralsium?!" I demanded, skimming the sheets. "Where in the hells did slavers get their hands on that accursed substance?"

"We need to get you back to bed immediately." Yumeko crossed her arms at me. "The antidotes will cure the other trace ingredients, but we *must* remove the vralsium before it weakens you further, my lord. For them to combine vralsium and beast blood—"

"They knew they were hunting a deity." I bristled, crushing the papers in hand. My anger paused, briefly, when I glanced over my shoulder toward Arianna's rooms. She had likely been exposed to the toxins as well, but vralsium's existence was still classified within Vorpmasia. If she didn't remember what we had discovered in V'frul, then I couldn't tell her. "Yumeko, extract the vralsium from Arianna first."

"My lord?" Yumeko asked, staring at me. "She isn't a deity—*you are*. First, we must—"

"*Arianna first*," I reiterated, pivoting to walk back into Arianna's rooms. "She is still a demigod—Lucifer's daughter. Vralsium could cripple her powers, and faster than it would on me.

"Fetch the alchemists immediately."

I strode toward Arianna's bed and sat on the edge, peeling the sheets back from her shoulders. A brief pulse of magic guaranteed that she wouldn't wake from her slumber yet. I pulled one of her arms out from beneath her pillow and released a growl upon seeing her Brands. Although her veins were not growing dark, her divine markings had grown dimmer and blurred. *'I should have noticed it sooner!'*

Vralsium was a rare but foul substance. In its natural form, it was a dark green metal found deep beneath Avrirsa's crust. Few species could venture deep enough toward the planet's core to mine for the material, and fewer still were stupid enough to do so. The Elders refused to explain why or how they had allowed such a metal to exist— and it had already caused us many problems over the past two centuries.

The metal had the ability to utterly negate divine powers, and the nobles of V'frul had turned it against their own deities *and* ours. They had taken the Elven and Akor deities as slaves to be sold at auction, with plans to enslave many other racial gods from the surrounding countries. It was shortly after discovering their plot that we learned of vralsium and the manner in which it could be used—I had found the documents myself while Arianna slaughtered the nobles for their crimes.

A small smile twitched across my face as I reached out to stroke Arianna's cheek. Even so long ago she had been like a goddess of death. It truly seemed to be her gift.

"Rely'ric, do you intend to remain here?" A male voice startled me into turning.

"I will not be satisfied until every trace of vralsium and toxins have been removed from Her Highness," I answered, tensing my jaw. "She—"

"The procedure takes hours, Rely'ric!" Yumeko exclaimed. "If we treat the both of you at once, it will significantly expedite the process!"

"You understand that we cannot let her know of this, don't you?" I sighed, turning to look at the small gathering of Vulin behind Yumeko.

"Of course." Yumeko rolled her eyes and crossed her arms within her kimono sleeves. "If she knows naught of it, she's less likely to draw the attentions of those who wish to know more of it. What do you intend to tell her? She will know she has been weakened significantly."

"That I took too much of her blood," I answered, glancing away from the Vulin and Arianna both. It pained me, but I couldn't see any other option. Arianna needed a believable excuse for why she was weakened, and I couldn't risk letting her know about vralsium. Not yet. Not while she was still forced into Human form. If someone truly wanted to press her for information, she would have no chance against them.

"Rely'ric, you should rest while we work," one of the male Vulin spoke, narrowing his eyes at me. "You've already pressed yourself much too hard in order to protect our guest. If you do not pace yourself, the both of you will be stranded here for moons to come."

"Then I will rest here." I snorted, pulling myself fully onto the bed before stretching out alongside Arianna. "Once you have finished, and only then, will I return to my rooms."

"Rely'ric! That is incredibly inappropriate!" Yumeko chastised. "If she were to awake—"

"I can assure you that Her Highness wouldn't mind," I murmured, focusing my gaze on the ceiling above the bed. "Work quickly. If we take too long, Arianna's Guardians and my parents will be the last of our worries.

"The Elders won't tolerate a 'mere mortal' in my domain for long."

# CHAPTER TWELVE
## *A God's Domain*

*'Mmm…smells good.'* I purred and nuzzled my face into a soft pillow. *'Wait. Forests aren't this cozy, and they don't smell like…*

"Nalithor?"

I cracked an eye open and pushed myself a few inches off the bed. A shiver ran through me when the satin sheets slid down my back and exposed me to the cool air. Looking around, I found that the room was coated in darkness aside from a few flickering candles, and the pale light of the moons that filtered in through a nearby wall of windows. My expression fell, and my pulse calmed, when I realized that I was alone.

Despite the strength of his scent lingering in the air, Nalithor wasn't there.

After shifting into a sitting position, I surveyed the room again and then lifted a hand to the side of my throat. Sure enough, my fingertips found the indentations that Nalithor's fangs had left behind. A brief tingle of residual pain shot through the healing wounds when I prodded at them again to be certain.

*'So, I wasn't dreaming.'* I shut my eyes for a moment and let my hand fall to my side. *'This obviously isn't the Forest of Fire. Where am I?'*

I hesitated before swinging my legs over the side of the bed. Once standing, I snatched up a robe that was waiting for me on the back of a nearby chair and pulled it on while walking toward the wall of windows. The architecture was much the same as the tiered and lacquered buildings in Draemir, yet this was clearly not the same place. Forests spread as far as I could see, and there was no sign of a lake.

Wherever I was, it was much like Lysander and Ellena's palace but on a much larger scale. Unlike their palace, this one appeared to be comprised of a single building instead of many smaller ones.

There was no doubt in my mind that it was beautiful, but it was also very foreign. The clear trace of Nalithor's scent was the only thing keeping me from drawing a weapon and tracking down someone to beat information out of. From my rooms, I spotted gardens, ponds, and massive blooming trees sprawling out beneath the endless night sky. I remained at the window for several minutes, entranced by the pale flowers swaying in the breeze.

Magic hummed through everything. I didn't even have to shift my vision in order to determine that much. There was enough power in the air alone to make my skin prickle in response. It was very, *very* different from Dauthrmir, Draemir, and the Abrantia Valley.

I turned away from the windows and refocused on the room I had awoken in. After fumbling around in the dark for a few minutes, I managed to find a Magitech switch on one wall and pressed it. I winced and shielded my eyes when the lights sprang to life.

Once my eyes adjusted, I took a better look at "my" room. It was massive and luxuriant, decorated in varying shades of red and cream. The furniture was a mixture of Dauthrmiran and Draemiran styles, all carved from dark reddish-brown wood. I had thought my rooms in Draemir were extravagant, yet this place blew them completely out of the water and without contest.

What I had done to deserve such beautiful accommodations was beyond me.

It took me longer than it should have to realize that the door to the bedroom *slid* open instead of pulled. I grumbled curses at my grogginess and pawed at my eyes before stepping into the adjacent room. The sitting room was just as lavish as the bedroom and was decorated in a similar fashion—complete with several large sofas, chairs, and an intricately carved coffee table. Three of the four walls were lined with floor-to-ceiling bookshelves. The one empty wall was home to a chest of drawers with a large, carved mirror on top of it.

I pursed my lips and glanced between the three doors, unsure of what to do. There was nothing to indicate where I was, the way out, or if I needed to act with caution. A quick peek through the door next to the chest of drawers revealed a large but empty walk-in wardrobe. The second door was the one I had come out of, so it was pointless to check that one.

'*So…the third must be the exit, right?*' I padded across the room and slid the third door open, poking my head into the hallway. After glancing both ways, all I could do was blink and attempt to contain my curiosity. There was an upright fox strolling down the hallway toward me and, unlike Daijiro, this one was sandy brown in color. By the *very* proper white and pink kimono the fox wore, I could only assume it was a female.

"Reiz'tar, you're awake already?" The fox smiled up at me, her tone confirming my assumptions. "My name is Yumeko. I-I hope your rooms are to your liking, Reiz'tar. It is so unusual for the master of the house to bring home guests!"

'*Master of the house? Nalithor?*' I wondered, blinking down at Yumeko when she giggled at me. '*Well, at least she turned out to be another fox and not competition.*'

"It's lovely," I replied, examining the fox for a moment, finding myself still a little unsettled by…whatever they were. "Ah, but I was wondering…"

"Clothes?" Yumeko giggled, raising a paw to her mouth. I just nodded in reply. "Your clothes were ruined beyond repair. However, I'm certain I can conjure something suitable for you. Here, let's see."

Yumeko shooed me back into the room and kneeled at the edge of the door to close it, then turned to look at me with a thoughtful expression on her face.

"So that's why I didn't see my bag anywhere. I thought maybe I'd left it in the forest." I sighed, running a hand through my curls. One of my bracelets banged into my nose, making me scrunch my face. "Who bathed me and changed me out of my armor, then?"

"That would be myself and some of the other vixens," Yumeko answered with an amused smile. She motioned for me to remove my robe and continued, "Your Brands really are quite similar to his, aren't they?

"What colors do you like, Reiz'tar?"

"I like blue, and white... Black, silver, platinum. Umm..." I mumbled, counting off on my fingers as my thoughts trailed off. After a pause, I motioned at the room around us. "Scarlet as well. Oh! But what about my armor?"

"You don't need your armor here." Yumeko giggled, then motioned at me with her paw. "Taking your shinies into consideration, I think we'll go with something like *this*."

I let out an unladylike yelp when a thong snapped into place between my legs. I whipped around to see if someone had managed to sneak up on me, but I only found floating stretches of cloth. Yumeko burst into laughter and gave me no time to question her. The chortling fox summoned a loose, low-cut outfit similar to what I had worn to dinner in Draemir.

*'Does this fox take after Ellena and Erist? Honestly...'* I bit back an irritated sigh and glanced down at my cleavage, and then the slit in my

skirt. *'Well, it is pretty.'*

"Hmmm, you *are* pale, aren't you?" Yumeko murmured, tracking me while I examined the blue outer layer and cream inner layer. After a moment the fox clapped her paws, causing the colors to change. "What about this? I'm sure that, as a Lyur'zi, you tire of wearing black all the time…but I think it contrasts quite nicely."

"It's very pretty," I replied, examining myself for a moment before tapping my bare toes against the floor. "Do I not need shoes?"

"Not unless you decide to wander outside of the palace." Yumeko shook her head, then shot me a firm look. "You should take things slowly, Reiz'tar, and wait for your magic to adjust to this place. Rely'ric had to take a lot of energy from you in order to bring the both of you here. It may take a few days yet for you to return to your full strength."

"Where is 'here' exactly?" I asked, watching as the fox hopped up onto the dresser and pulled my hair into a loose bun. She pinned my hair in place with a few hair sticks that she had conjured.

"This is *his* domain. He created it," Yumeko replied. She tugged at a few of my curls and arranged them to her liking. "There…that should do it. Do you like tea? Are you hungry? I can show you to one of the lounges if you would like to view the gardens while you dine."

"Ah…yes, please," I replied, moving to follow Yumeko. The fox knelt at the edge of the door and slid it open, motioning for me to go first. *'Is that how they're supposed to be opened and closed? Hmmm…'*

"As you will see, the only people in Rely'ric's domain are Vulin like myself and Daijiro—whom you've met," Yumeko began while leading me down the hall. "We're all terribly excited to have a guest. I hope you will forgive us if we seem rude, Reiz'tar. Our kits aren't accustomed to seeing people who aren't Vulin so they may ask strange questions. Rely'ric makes a point of rarely allowing anyone aside from Vulin and himself here."

"Please call me Arianna." I frowned, turning to follow the fox down a flight of stairs. "I apologize, I forgot to introduce myself."

"Rely'ric made certain that we knew who you are." Yumeko giggled, shaking her head.

I fell silent and followed the quick "Vulin" through the palace. The structure was much larger than what the glimpse from my room had implied. It took several minutes of walking before Yumeko led me into a spacious room adjacent to a rose garden. Once there, she instructed me to get comfortable wherever I liked and motioned to the piles of pillows and throws that covered the room. I decided to kneel at the low table in the center of the room and tucked my legs beneath me, letting the skirt of my kimono-like attire fan out around me.

Oddly, I found myself thankful to be seated again. Walking through the palace had left me feeling far more exhausted than it should have. I kept my expression passive, but I didn't quite feel like myself. Feeling so faint was a foreign concept to me. I didn't think that I'd expended so much energy while fighting through the slavers and their beasts. *'Did Nalithor really take that much power from me?'*

The wall of sliding doors to my right was open and gave me an unobscured view of the rose gardens just outside the lounge. Their sweet scent was carried by a mild breeze that drifted through the room and into the hallway I had entered from. A stone path wound through the flora and out of sight, likely curving through more gardens if my view from upstairs was anything to judge by. Massive magnolia, cherry, and wisteria trees were in full bloom within the property and intermingled with the forest surrounding the palace grounds.

Dozens of other plants and trees, many of which I had no name for, were also in full bloom beneath Avrirsa's three moons.

'*He* made *all of this?*' I wondered, staring out at the glowing flowers. My attention snapped back to Yumeko when she tugged at my left sleeve.

"How do you like your tea, Reiz'tar? Black or sweet?" The Vulin looked a little distressed when she spoke, but I wasn't sure if it was because I had zoned out, or if she was just *that* nervous about having a guest.

"Sweet," I replied with a smile, hoping a pleasant expression would calm Yumeko's nerves. "I really enjoy sweet things—perhaps a little too much."

Yumeko nodded her head rapidly and then disappeared from the room, so I glanced out to the gardens once more. It was gorgeous here. I had no words for it. The air was a little on the cool side, but it was comfortable. Cool enough for hot beverages and blankets, but warm enough to go without. Aside from the occasional whiff of flowers from outside, *everything* smelled like Nalithor, and I found it incredibly distracting.

I released a small sigh and shifted my gaze to my hands, twisting one of my rings around my finger while staring at it with a blank expression.

*'Yumeko said that he makes a point of not bringing anyone here?'* I gnawed on the inside of my cheek while thinking. *'I wonder why that is? Doesn't he want to show off his creations? Ah... Or does he want to keep it as his own private hideaway? Am I intruding?'*

*'It seems like I can't even access my shrizar here. I'm not that weakened—I think. Did he limit the usage of magic here somehow?'*

"Arianna?" His voice interrupted my thoughts, causing me to turn my attention from my hands. Glancing toward the gardens, I found Nalithor striding up the stairs of the raised porch that encircled the palace. "You're awake? For how long?"

"Not long," I responded, my eyes drifting down his exposed chest briefly. Snapping my gaze back to his face, I watched as he slid off his sandals and moved into the room with me. "Are you alri—"

I fell silent when Nalithor closed the distance between us with a few long strides and dropped to his knees beside me. He pulled me from my seat and tight into his chest, burying his face into my exposed shoulder and squeezing me tight against him. One of his arms wrapped around my waist while his other hand rested against the back of my neck.

It was almost as if he was making sure I was real.

My heart raced, but I still hesitated before wrapping my arms around Nalithor's torso, unsure if it was the appropriate response. I laid my hands flat on his back and leaned into him, basking in both his warmth and his scent. Even though only a few days had passed since he'd left Draemir, it felt like too long since I had last seen him.

"I've been so worried about you," Nalithor spoke in a low, soft tone. He loosened his grip enough to bring one hand up to cup my face and traced my lower lip with his thumb. "Are you alright? I thought you would be asleep for at least another few days. I didn't take too much—"

"One question at a time." I shook my head at him and reached up to his wrist, pulling his hand from my jaw and mouth. I shot him a crooked smile. "I'm fine—for the moment at least. What about you? Are your wounds—"

"You're certain you're alright?" Nalithor pressed me, his expression full of concern. He laced his fingers and breathed a relieved sigh when I nodded my reply. A small smile tugged at his lips as he glanced down at me. "You...look incredible."

"Oh please." I laughed, turning away from him a little. "How long have I been asleep, exactly? I feel *creaky*! And...famished."

I tugged my hand out of Nalithor's grip and then paused, surprised when I spotted the crestfallen look that flashed across his face. He was quick to smooth his expression over, but not quick enough.

"A day or two. Perhaps three," Nalithor replied, reclaiming my hand. "You lost a lot of blood, Arianna. I thought it best to let you recover here where the Vulin and I could keep an eye on you...instead of in Draemir. Your barriers weakened more than I thought they would after I—"

"Rely'ric, please!" Yumeko chastised the Adinvyr when she returned with a tea tray. "You should change into something more appropriate before conversing with a *lady*! Reiz'tar, don't hesitate to slap him if he misbehaves."

*'Says the one that dressed me like* this.' I arched an eyebrow, watching Yumeko set the tray on the table in front of me.

"I don't think she minds," Nalithor remarked, tilting his head to the side as he examined me. He suddenly pulled me backward against his chest and chuckled. "But if I do *this*...then she doesn't have to look!"

*'Maybe I* want *to look...'* I pouted, drawing my legs into a more comfortable position as Yumeko snorted and retreated from the room once more. I glanced up and over my shoulder at Nalithor, hesitant. "Are you...going to let me be your partner?"

"I would have to be *mad* to say no to having you as my partner, Arianna," Nalithor murmured, planting a soft kiss on the side of my neck. He rested his head on my shoulder and rubbed his cheek into it, releasing a contented sigh. "I'm going to have to keep a careful eye on you. I won't tolerate anyone trying to steal a taste of you.

"Hmmm... Neither you nor your power taste even *remotely* Human. Whatever binds you must be powerful magic."

"I'd argue that we're both a little mad," I pointed out, arching an eyebrow when his grip on my waist tightened. "Enough about me! What about your wounds and the poison you were exposed to?"

271

"Your *delicious* blood finished the job you started." Nalithor purred, sliding his tail up my skirt to wrap around one thigh. He lifted one hand to my chin and tilted my head to the side, exposing more of my throat. "You made the most *amazing* pet sounds, you know." He paused to run his tongue up my skin and released a devious chuckle before continuing, "I do hope you realize that as my *partner* you will be serving as my *food* more often."

"Speaking of food," I grumbled, flushing darker when his tail slipped further up my thigh. "How am I supposed to have breakfast like *this*?"

Nalithor chuckled. "Very well. I will pester you *after* you've had your breakfast."

He gave me another squeeze before releasing me and rising to his feet. I watched him with a small pout as he strode around the table and perched on the opposite side of me to recline against a pile of pillows.

For some reason, Nalithor tracked my movements with unusual intensity while I poured myself tea and made myself comfortable again. He seemed worried still but had relaxed a little.

"Rely'ric, when will the two of you be returning to Draemir?" Yumeko inquired, returning with several Vulin and many platters of food in tow.

"As soon as I'm satisfied that Arianna is well enough to handle the beasts that stand between us and home—and the pestering of my countrymen," Nalithor replied. His gaze trailed down my throat and to my cleavage while he watched me pour a second cup of tea, which I slid across the table to his side. "My dear, do you have a copy of your results with you? I would like to see precisely what was said. I have a difficult time believing the Oracles didn't put up a fight."

"Mmm... I would if I had access to my shrizar here," I murmured while stirring honey into my tea.

"Ah yes, I suppose that *would* be a problem." Nalithor smiled and shook his head. "I suppose I can make yet another exception for you...and that adorable pouting of yours. Try now."

I huffed at him and then reached out in search of my shrizar. Once I found it, I pulled a thick stack of papers and offered them to Nalithor. He arched an eyebrow and accepted it, but remained silent as he settled back against his pillows to read.

Glancing from Nalithor and then to my plate, I sighed and decided to focus on my breakfast instead of the muscular deity before me. Partially because I was still cross about him leaving me behind in Draemir, and also because of the sexual frenzy he had left me in.

Much of the results made little to no sense to me, in large part because the Archmagi and Oracles were confused themselves. My species? Undetermined. My power? Rivaling that of Nalithor's—a god more powerful than the Upper Gods.

They were of half a mind to forgo assigning me a partner in favor of attempting to determine who—and what—I was. Someone had changed their minds, and I could only assume that it was likely Lucifer who was responsible. I doubted there were any other deities in Vorpmasia who were inclined to interfere in such a way, and Nalithor hadn't been involved with analyzing the tests.

*'I shouldn't be so close to him in power unless...'* I tensed my jaw and gripped my fork and knife harder. *'My potential role was given to him. Even if I once had a chance at becoming a deity myself, that role is his now. Yet he is nowhere near the strength that he should be...'*

"Have you gotten the chance to explore Draemir yet?" Nalithor's question startled me into looking up from my food, only to find his focus was still on my test results.

"Your mother and 'Auntie Erist' attempted to drag me shopping with them, but I declined," I answered while pouring myself a second cup of tea. "I've spent most of my time reading, or kicking the asses of the Draemiran soldiers."

"Shopping?" Nalithor set the papers aside and arched an eyebrow at me. "Why *shopping* of all things?"

"They're *still* dissatisfied with my wardrobe." I shrugged, pulling another ham steak and several more pancakes onto my plate. "I insisted that I didn't need—or want—their company, but they seem intent on pestering me."

"What of my father and Arom?" Nalithor questioned, tilting his head as he examined me with an unreadable expression. "I'm sure at least my father must have provided you with a challenge."

"He hasn't challenged me yet." I huffed dismissively before stabbing a piece of meat with my fork. "Arom and Erist have been trying to get me to visit them at their temple. I've *politely* refused."

"Has 'The White Fox' slipped back into her antisocial habits?"

Nalithor teased, smiling as he scooted closer to the table and reached for the tea that I had poured him earlier. "Do I need to prize you out of your self-imposed cage once more?"

"I prefer to surround myself with *pleasant* company." I pouted and pointed my fork at him. "Since *you* went off to hunt without me there hasn't been anyone pleasant to keep me company. Ah…that reminds me."

Nalithor shot me a questioning look when I fell silent and frowned. I ignored him for the moment and thought back on my search of Draemiran lands, the border with Suthsul, and my trek through the Forest of Fire. Sighing, I returned my attention to Nalithor with a small frown on my face.

"What, exactly, did you fight with on the edges of Suthsul?" I asked, shooting the Adinvyr a concerned look before quickly taking in what parts of him were exposed—he looked healthy enough. "It struck me as strange that you left your spear behind, and what I saw lurking along the edge of the Draemir Barrier didn't help matters…"

"Angels attacked us." Nalithor spat with distaste, a pained look crossing his face. "Like the ones you saw in Abrantia, they were working with beasts. Not Dux-class ones, but still cause for concern— they fled the battlefield soon after fighting broke out.

"The Angel's weapons were poisoned, and they all appeared to be corrupted. A few non-corrupted ones appeared and attempted to stop their former brethren—they failed. I'm sure you found some hint of that. What did you see that made you concerned?"

"Hmmm... C'mere," I grumbled around my fork, beckoning him with my free hand. He was quick to oblige me, and promptly lifted me into his lap once seated on my side of the table.

"Now *that* is an invitation I can't refuse." Nalithor chuckled, slipping his hand into mine. He rested his other arm across my lap and shot me a smile when I gave him a questioning look. "Let's see what made you so cross on your approach through the forest, hmmm?"

Something about Nalithor's hand in mine made my pulse quicken. I bit the inside of my cheek and forced myself to cast the feeling aside for now. Instead, I focused on calling forth the memories of my search through Draemir's southern outskirts. Nalithor nuzzled into my shoulder with a contented sigh as I led him through my memories and let him see what I had discovered along the Draemir Barrier—as well as my encounters in the Forest of Fire.

Nalithor's grip on me tensed when my discovery of the slain soldiers came. I sensed some portion of his grief, but he said nothing. I couldn't relate to feeling loss over the life of one's soldiers—it was difficult for me to feel anything for the X'shmirans. Nalithor, however, seemed to take some manner of comfort from embracing me. I decided it was best for me not to say anything about the loss of life—or my inability to relate.

"That beast..." Nalithor murmured with unease. "Beasts tend to balk at even the slightest hint of pain. For it to willingly drag itself against the barrier... You were quite the whirlwind of death, weren't you?"

"They…might have made me a little angry," I muttered, reaching for my tea. I took a sip before continuing, "Still, we should return to Draemir and report what I saw, shouldn't we? A beast like that, Angels, poison, and—"

"We also still have a festival to attend," Nalithor interjected, lifting me off his lap. "I still need to show you around Draemir as well, don't I? You'll be a welcome distraction from the damned trainees at any rate."

"Trainees?" I inquired.

"Father wants me to provide some of his newer recruits with training while we're in Draemir." Nalithor sighed and rested his palms flat on the floor to either side of my hips, leaning toward me. "How am I supposed to go from *our* sparring sessions to training weaklings like—"

"You don't know for sure that they're weaklings until you actually meet them!" I laughed, shaking my head. "Really though, have you grown a little spoiled, Nalithor? Hmmm?"

"Spoiled and…a little hungry perhaps," Nalithor murmured, nuzzling into my throat. "Or perhaps I am just addicted to your taste. I'm not certain."

Before I could reply Nalithor pinned me to the floor. An amused expression spread across his face while he watched me attempt to scoot away. I wasn't quite sure just *what* the Adinvyr was thinking, and not knowing just made my pulse race faster.

"You shouldn't say—" I cut myself off when he leaned down and nuzzled my throat again.

The sensation of his torso pressed against mine and his lower body nestled between my legs proved to be distracting as ever. Perhaps even more so than usual. Heat rose in my body, my pulse quickening further as he nibbled at the side of my throat. In my hesitation, he had taken the opportunity to pull one of my legs aside with his tail.

Nalithor's scent alone was enough to drive me mad in my current state *without* him teasing me in such a way.

"Aaah, you really smell *too* good…" Nalithor groaned into my throat, tilting my head with one hand to expose more of my throat. "It truly is a struggle to behave myself around you."

"You must…be really hungry still." I bit my lower lip hard when Nalithor's mouth traveled over the weakest part of my neck. Some part of me refused to make it obvious that *that* spot was weak. "How are we supposed to return to Draemir if—"

"May I?" Nalithor asked quietly, his fangs grazing the side of my throat/

Somehow, I could hear *his* racing heartbeat over mine.

"Since you asked so *nicely*…sure," I replied with little hesitation. *'Why do I* want *him to*—'

Nalithor sunk his fangs into me a little sooner than expected, startling a whimper out of me. Somehow it felt even more amazing than the first time he'd fed from me. It was euphoric, a sensation I could see myself becoming addicted to. Biting back my whimpers and moans of desire proved ever more difficult as he massaged his tail along my inner thigh.

I couldn't recall a time when I had been so aroused, but that could have been to blame on my inability to think straight while Nalithor was feeding on me. How being bitten could bring me so much pleasure was beyond me.

At some point, my hands must have wandered off because, the next thing I knew, Nalithor had caught both of my wrists and pinned them to the floor above my head. He withdrew from my neck just enough to speak.

"Now, now," Nalithor began, his voice husky. He flicked his tongue over the wounds he had left and shivered. "*Food* shouldn't be so…encouraging."

"B-but…" I protested, my face growing hot as Nalithor let out a chuckle that sent a shudder through me. "You're— Aaah…"

I struggled when Nalithor buried his fangs in me again, this time piercing my weak spot. This time I really did go blind with pleasure, unable to form even half of a coherent thought.

"To think you find it so enjoyable *without* the presence of my venom…" Nalithor chuckled, withdrawing from my throat. He flicked his tongue over my lower lip and then smirked. "You are going to be quite entertaining, aren't you? Have you been hiding a bit of a masochistic streak from me, Arianna?"

"A-as if you don't know," I grumbled, averting my gaze when I felt my face growing even hotter.

Nalithor just chuckled and then planted a brief kiss on my lips before letting me up and rising to his feet. He shot me a sultry, knowing smirk again while he watched me. His tail swayed behind him in a manner that made it seem like he wanted to pounce on me.

"After you have finished *your* breakfast, I will consider returning us to the forest," Nalithor informed me, examining the way I was still laying on the floor. "If there are any beasts lingering, we will have to kill our way out of Xiinsha. I don't plan to take any risks."

'So that's the forest's name then? "Xiinsha?"' I wondered while pulling myself into a sitting position. "Good. I didn't get to savor my adventure through there the first time. Finding your self-satisfied ass seemed more important."

Nalithor laughed and shook his head at me before strolling out of the room. Once he'd disappeared around the corner, I released a small sigh and raised a hand to my throat to prod at the tender puncture wounds. They were already healed over and, now that my thoughts were clearer, I could sense Nalithor's magic clinging to me.

I knew full well that he could've healed them completely—so why didn't he?

'Is he...marking me?' I twitched, sending my fork clattering across my plate. 'Why in the hells am I okay with that?!'

I chose to devour my food instead of dwelling on the Adinvyr. It seemed like a good way to distract myself from the lingering sensation of Nalithor's lips and fangs alike—let alone the remaining arousal that didn't seem like it would go away anytime soon.

A while later, Nalithor's arms slipped around my waist, and he pulled me off the floor. He startled a yelp out of me because, somehow, I didn't sense him coming. His laughter sounded rather triumphant.

"My servants are *terribly* distressed that I might take you away from them already." Nalithor nuzzled me, chuckling when I squirmed in his grip.

"You haven't had enough yet?" I questioned as he continued to nuzzle me. He coiled his tail around my legs and released a purr into my throat, making me shiver.

"There's no such thing as having 'enough' of you *or* your blood," Nalithor informed me, his voice little more than a husky growl. "I want more of you…but that will have to wait. For now."

"If we are going to fight our way through the forest you need to put me down." I pointed out as his tail crept up my thighs. He bristled and let out a displeased growl.

"I'm of half a mind to keep you here and never let you leave," Nalithor grumbled, pouting into my shoulder. He squeezed me much like I was a stuffed animal.

"It *is* quite lovely here," I remarked thoughtfully, feeling his head turn, indicating that I'd grabbed his attention. "I don't intend to let anyone steal the rights to you, or your attention, away from me. You don't need to *imprison* me to keep me to yourself, you know."

"Are you certain you're well enough to leave?" Nalithor turned me so that I was facing him and narrowed his eyes at me. "If the beasts were truly hunting for me, we can expect that they and their masters may have set up camp in the clearing we left from. When we return, it will be to the exact area we left from."

"I'm…probably fine." I tilted my head, thinking. Nalithor didn't look convinced, but neither was I. All-in-all, I still didn't fully feel like myself yet. It was as if something other than Nalithor's feeding had caused it, yet I had no idea what the culprit could have been. "Hmmm, since you're so concerned—shouldn't you have asked that *before* feeding from me?"

"I have to be able to fight after taking us back." Nalithor arched an eyebrow at me. "You are not convincing me that you're prepared to return."

"How about taking me for a walk through the gardens?" I suggested abruptly as I turned to face the Adinvyr. "I've barely done anything since waking up—I can't honestly claim whether I'm fine or not."

"A walk?" Nalithor tilted his head, skeptical. "Not a sparring match?"

"After *just* eating?" I shot him a look.

"I certainly won't complain." Nalithor smiled, offering me his arm.

Nalithor called for one of the Vulin, who quickly conjured sandals for me to wear outside in the gardens. Once the Vulin and Nalithor were both satisfied, Nalithor led me out into the cool air by the arm and down the nearest stone pathway. I took in our surroundings in awe.

The flowers, the sparkling ponds, the night sky, and even the palace itself were all like works of art. I could have spent hours just basking in the atmosphere and taking in the beauty.

*'Looking up is making my head spin...'* I shut my eyes briefly and refocused my gaze forward before glancing to the side at Nalithor to see if he had noticed the brief discomfort that had overcome me. If he had noticed, he was hiding it well.

"What—" Nalithor started when I tugged him to a stop and leaned into his chest. "Arianna?"

"I...don't think I'm ready to return yet after all," I grumbled, closing my eyes as I rested my cheek against his chest. "Maybe another day or two...just to be safe?"

"If *you* of all people are being cautious, you likely need at least a week." Nalithor sighed, wrapping both of his arms behind my back. "I *did* take too much, didn't I? Had I exercised more restraint—"

"Don't think it's that..." I murmured, nuzzling him while listening to his pulse quicken. "I'm tired still, and just...don't feel well."

Nalithor paused with one hand flat against my back and released a small pulse of power. Seconds later he breathed a sigh of what sounded like relief and began stroking my back.

"Shall I carry you back upstairs? You seem exhausted." Nalithor's soothing tone threatened to lull me to sleep then and there.

"Mmhmm." I nodded into his chest and shut my eyes. *'Comfy...'*

"My lord?" Yumeko voice startled me enough to make me realize I had drifted off at some point and that Nalithor was carrying me through the hallways of his palace.

"Arianna and I will be staying for another day or two," Nalithor addressed the fox, then glanced down at me with a smile. "Go back to sleep, Arianna."

# CHAPTER THIRTEEN
*Misunderstandings*

I opened my eyes and then grew still, surprised by the scattered white hair less than a foot away from me. Nalithor was slumped over with his torso on the edge of my bed and appeared to be sound asleep. His arms were crossed, and his head rested on them, but his hair was *everywhere*. Hesitant, I reached out and nudged his forearm. No reaction.

*'Books, papers, a few cups... Was he worried about me?'* I surveyed the mess around Nalithor, on the nightstand, and what had fallen to the floor. My joints weren't stiff, and I didn't hurt anywhere, so I knew damned well I couldn't have been asleep for long. Yet the Adinvyr seemed to have been watching over me while I slept. *'It's not like I was ill. Just tired. Perhaps I'll just let him rest.'*

Shaking my head, I slowly slid out of the opposite side of the bed and then glanced over my shoulder to see if I'd woken Nalithor. Still nothing. He was completely out. I covered a yawn, creeping out of the bedroom, and left my suite. I didn't know what time it was, but I could tell my stomach would start rumbling for food soon enough.

*'Ah... Clothes?'* I paused in the hallway and then glanced down at myself, befuddled. *'Not a dress... One of Nali's shirts?'*

I lifted one sleeve to my nose and sniffed before nodding to myself. It had to be one of Nalithor's shirts. Why I was wearing that instead of something more suitable for a woman was beyond me. It may as well have been a nightgown on me. Sighing, I reached out to find my shrizar but was met with nothing. The corner of my eye twitched in irritation.

*'It's not like I'd go off and hunt those beasts while he sleeps!'* I huffed to myself and stalked through the palace. *'Maybe. I have no idea how to get out of his domain anyway. Though I suppose not being able to access my shrizar* does *make me less likely to attempt finding a way out of here...maybe I should find a way out just to spite him.'*

"Arianna-z'tar?" Yumeko looked up and blinked at me when I rounded a corner. "Are you looking for something?"

"Food," I grumbled, sounding much more tired than I felt. "Figured if I wandered around for long enough, I'd eventually find the kitchen."

"The kitchen?" Yumeko shook her head hard. "That is hardly a place for someone of your rank! Where would you like to eat? I will have someone bring you breakfast at once."

"It's quite alright, I can cook—" I tensed and took a step back from the Vulin as she bared her fangs at me. "Okay, okay! Uhm... Is there anywhere to sit in the gardens? I'd like some fresh air."

"Of course." Yumeko nodded, her demeanor shifting back to tranquil. "Tea? Coffee?"

"Tea, please." I paused and glanced over my shoulder. *'I could have sworn I just felt...'*

"Kaho, see Arianna-z'tar to the gardens." Yumeko turned to look at a nearby potted plant, then sighed. "Stop hiding! She's our guest!"

A smaller Vulin with chocolate-colored fur peeked out from behind the pot and stared at me for a moment with watery eyes. I had to bite the inside of my cheek to keep from making an excited squeak. The Vulin were too godsdamned adorable—especially a young one. I doubted picking up and snuggling one would go over well.

"T-this way." Kaho stuttered, stepping out from behind the plant fully. She pawed at the sleeves of her pale green kimono and then took off at a hurried pace down the hall, her tail flitting behind her. "W-what kind of flowers would you like to sit by?"

"Hmmm, how about under a mrifon tree? Or by roses?" I murmured. "I'm sorry, I don't exactly know what my options are."

"Tree? Tree near roses with bench!" Kaho mumbled mostly to herself, nodding her head so hard that her ears flopped around. "Good perch. Books with it. You like books?"

"I love books," I replied, earning a less fearful look from the small

Vulin. "There're books *outside*?"

"Mmmhmm!" Kaho nodded her head several more times. "This way!"

The young Vulin took off at a full run, causing me to chase her barefoot through the palace and outside through the gardens. It took a few minutes for us to arrive at the base of a gargantuan mrifon tree and the sitting area beneath it. There were chaises, chairs, a coffee table, and several bookcases nestled beneath the tree. The bookcases were enclosed by glass etched with aetheric symbols. I didn't recognize the type of magic, but I could only assume it was something to help protect the books from the weather.

*'Does this place even* have *weather?'* I wondered, glancing up at the sky. *'Hmmm… There* are *a few clouds now.'*

"This good?" Kaho tugged at my leg. "Did Kaho do good?"

"Kaho did very well!" I smiled at the small Vulin and then crouched down, so we were closer in height. "Do I need a key for the bookcases?"

"Key? No key." Kaho shook her head. "Kaho can go back to Momma?"

"Sure." I nodded at the small creature, watching as her face lit up. "I wouldn't want to get into trouble for keeping you from her too long!"

Kaho giggled and took off across the gardens, soon fading from view. I shook my head to myself and then walked over to the bookcases, now more curious about them than I was about the Vulin.

The leather-bound tomes seemed to be in excellent condition, but I didn't recognize any of the titles. One case appeared to be dedicated to fiction, while the other was filled with an eclectic collection of non-fiction books.

Looking between the two bookcases, I had no idea where to start. While I wasn't quite in the mood for a novel, I wasn't awake enough to absorb information either. I crossed my arms and skimmed the titles of the books, noting that some were in languages I didn't even know the names of. Most seemed to be about beliefs and customs outside Vorpmasian borders. Many referenced Elves, some referenced Humans, and none referenced Vampires.

*'I suppose Vampires are a more "modern" phenomenon.'* I tilted my head, glancing between the Elven tomes. *'Hmmm, no books on the Kelsviir either—is that because they're native to Vorpmasia? Or…are these tomes pertaining to potential enemies?'*

I pursed my lips. That didn't sound like a correct assumption— Balance's only enemies were people who threatened the balance between powers. Anyone and everyone had the potential to make Balance their enemy. As the God of Balance, Nalithor shouldn't have had any strict affiliations with *any* world power—not unless they were so weak that they needed an extra push. It struck me as strange that the "Elders" had let Nalithor maintain his relationship with the Vorpmasian Empire.

*'Ceilail or Xiinsha—or one of the others—should have been able to intervene as well.'* I plucked a novel from one of the bookcases and then

made my way over to a chaise. *The Vorpmasian Empire seems powerful. That they're part of the Rilzaan Alliance makes them even more powerful. How has their agreement not drawn the Elders' ire?'*

"Reiz'tar?" Yumeko called, her tone indicating that it wasn't the first time. "Are you alright?"

"Sorry, I was thinking." I glanced to my left, finding that the strawberry fox had brought me tea already. "Ah, thank you."

"Would you like warmer attire, Reiz'tar?" Yumeko tilted her head at me. "I would be happy to conjure you something more suitable."

"Mmm? I'm warm enough." I shook my head. "If anything, maybe a blanket."

Yumeko conjured a fluffy blanket for me and then disappeared in a puff of pink smoke before I could thank her.

Sighing, I set the book aside and opted to drink my tea instead. I didn't feel as if I could relax. There were too many things for me to contemplate and I rarely had time to do so. Nalithor still made little sense to me, deity or otherwise, but particularly as a deity. He seemed to truly have the role, and yet his interactions with others made no sense to me.

*'Then again... I can't claim to know the intricacies of deities.'* I gnawed on my lower lip, thinking. There was no way for me to know for certain what Nalithor's role as the God of Balance entailed, yet I was confident thinking or speaking as if I knew every little detail. Like I knew what he should have been doing, what he wasn't doing, and what could get him into trouble. *'Ceilail did say it was supposed to be*

my *role…but it isn't. I couldn't possibly know anything about it.*'

The patter of approaching feet made me smooth my expression over and redirect my attention to the nearby pathways. Moments later a small group of Vulin, led by Yumeko, strode around a wall of hedges and approached me with a few platters. They set their cargo on the nearby coffee table and lifted their covers to reveal meats, pastries, fruits, and a variety of bowls containing other breakfast foods. It seemed as if instead of asking me what I wanted, they chose to prepare *everything* instead. A growl from my stomach made me question if I could consume it all.

"Did you happen to see Rely'ric on your way downstairs, Arianna-z'tar?" Yumeko inquired as her companions retreated through the gardens.

"Hmmm? He was asleep in my rooms," I answered, pausing mid-reach for a plate. "Looked like he fell asleep read—"

"Honestly! When will he learn it isn't appropriate to barge into your rooms uninvited?!" Yumeko huffed, her fur standing on end. "I will go drag him out of your rooms by his tail immediately!"

"That isn't—" I started, but the fox had already disappeared. "—necessary. Well, I doubt he'll be sleeping through *that*."

I stared at the assortment of food before me and then sighed, feeling my heart fall in my chest. Alone with breakfast. The disappointment was frustrating, and the blame was fully on myself. I could have tried harder to wake Nalithor, but I didn't. As difficult as he was to deal with, it would have been a significant improvement over eating alone.

*'Not like I can find my way back to my rooms to pester him.'* I glanced up at the looming palace for a moment, then at my surroundings. *'I don't think this is even on the same side of the palace as my rooms, but I can't tell. Tch.'*

Since procrastinating would have just made me feel lonelier, I chose to stuff myself full of food instead. What was the "appropriate" way to interact with a deity was still beyond me. His intentions seemed a little clearer at least, even if I didn't understand his interest in *me*. Or how to react. Or if it was even "okay" for him to pursue me. *'Damn it, Ari! Just stop thinking!'*

I shut my eyes and took a deep breath before refocusing on my food. There was nothing here for me to hunt, yet that was the only thing I could think of doing to collect myself. At least the gardens weren't so steeped in the Adinvyr's scent. My mind seemed to clear more the longer I sat outside. However, my shrizar was still out of reach.

After devouring my fill of breakfast, I swung my legs up onto the chaise and hefted the novel I'd selected before. I had to do something, anything, to keep my mind off Nalithor, off the beasts, off everything. That he hadn't come found me likely meant he'd evaded Yumeko and/or wasn't interested in my company yet.

*'Shut it, Ari.'* I gritted my teeth and growled at myself. *'Nalithor likely has many other things to attend to before we leave here. I'm not the center of the universe!'*

Sometime later, the sound of careful footsteps approaching caught my attention, causing me to grumble and turn my head away from the noise. I didn't recall falling asleep, but I was incredibly comfortable. The small sigh I heard made me crack an eye open to find Nalithor surveying the area as if looking for something. He looked relieved, yet cautious. I shut my eyes again and pretended to be asleep, attempting to quell my increasing pulse, cursing myself for being happy to see him.

"I know you're awake," Nalithor commented dryly, making me tense. "Shall I carry you back to your rooms?"

"No…" I grumbled, sitting up. After pawing my hair out of my face, I turned to look at Nalithor. "Ate too much. Made me sleepy. Did Yumeko fetch you?"

"Fetch me?" Nalithor arched an eyebrow, then shook his head and perched on the chaise beside me. "You know, it's quite worrying to wake and find you missing."

"This is *your* domain," I pointed out. "What, exactly, is going to happen to me here?"

"Aside from being my breakfast?"

"You know damn well what I meant."

"And I know 'damn well' that you are itching for a hunt."

I huffed and crossed my arms, turning to look away from Nalithor. He didn't seem like he was content with me redirecting my attention and was quick to slide an arm around my waist, pulling me closer. He planted a kiss on my left shoulder, making me realize that my shirt—his shirt, whatever—had slipped from my shoulder. A small purr rumbled in his chest before he chuckled and squeezed my waist.

"I half-expected to have to go hunting for you in the forest," Nalithor remarked, earning a brief glance from me. "Did you sense that there's nothing here for you to hunt?"

"Of course." I scoffed. "Restricting my access isn't enough to keep me from hunting. I could conjure a blade if I needed something other than my fists. But it's obvious there's nothing here *to* hunt! It's beautiful and all, but don't you—"

"Sometimes a quiet place to rest is needed," Nalithor interjected, gripping my chin and turning my head so that I had to look at him. "Are you cross with me? Making certain that you recover seemed prudent. If you, of all people, admit that you need time to recover... Well, you likely need *weeks'* worth of recovery, don't you?"

"*Weeks?* Hardly!" I exclaimed, pivoting so that I was fully facing him. "And I'm not cross with you. Whether or not *I* like it, we both needed to recover. I just get antsy if I haven't hunted in a few days. Not sensing *anything* to kill is a little...disconcerting."

"You don't have an 'off switch' at all, do you?" Nalithor laughed. "It will likely be a few more days before—"

"I am *not* waiting that long!" I growled at him and pinned him to the chaise, which only made him laugh more. "*I mean it.* If you refuse to take me somewhere to hunt, then I'll just have to kick your ass first!"

"And how does this help you with kicking my ass?" Nalithor smirked, running his hands up my thighs and to my hips. "Perhaps if you ask me *nicely,* I will take you hunting soon."

"Take me *now* or—" I paused tilting my head. "That didn't sound quite right."

"*I* think that sounded *perfect.*" Nalithor chuckled, sitting up with me still on his lap. He nuzzled into the left side of my throat and kissed me where he'd bitten me previously, eliciting an involuntary shiver from me. I gritted my teeth and growled at him, trying to think of the quickest way to redirect his attention to *hunting.*

*'It doesn't help that he sees* me *as prey.'* I bristled and grabbed Nalithor's braid when he grabbed two handfuls of my butt. "Since you're so feisty this morning—fight me."

"Fighting you isn't quite what I had in mind," Nalithor spoke into my throat, making my heart skip a few beats. I didn't know quite what to think about the rather erotic tone his voice had taken, let alone what he'd actually said. In a way, it was worse than if he'd explicitly stated what he was thinking. Instead, my mind wanted to try filling in the blanks.

"How am I supposed to prove to you that I can hunt if you won't fight— Nnngh, stop that!" I shivered as he drew his tongue over the healed-over puncture wounds. My throat was already sensitive enough before he'd left *those* there. Now it was even worse.

"You turn this into a form of combat too, you know." Nalithor chuckled, withdrawing from my throat. "It's a fight you want, is it? And if you lose?"

"It's not about winning or losing!" I pointed my finger against his chest and shot him a glare. Something about his expression made me think I failed the "glare" part. "We can't leave until I 'prove' that I'm well enough to fight, right? If I *don't*—"

"Are you truly so eager to leave?" Nalithor interjected, his quiet, disappointed tone surprising me almost as much as his averted gaze. "I know you live for the hunt, but..."

"You have things to do, don't you?" I sighed at him, crossing my arms. "Do you really expect me to let you return to Dauthrmir *without me*? Your domain is beautiful, but if you leave me alone here—"

"Perhaps I don't want to share you with the other dignitaries and festivalgoers," Nalithor suggested, shifting his unreadable gaze back to my face. "Regardless, *straddling me* isn't conducive to fighting me, and you are much too petite for it to be construed as intimidating."

"I can be intimidating if I want to!" I bristled, flames licking along my forearms. "We're supposed to be *partners*, Nalithor! That means if one of us is going back to Draemir, *we're both going.* Even if you tie me up here—"

"Tie you up? Mmm... That *is* a good idea." Nalithor purred, leaning in closer with a mischievous smirk. "I wonder where you got that idea? This is all you can summon for flames, yet you wish for me to let you return?"

"I don't *need* magic in order to fight." I snorted, pulling myself off him. Once standing, I crossed my arms again and turned my back to the Adinvyr; he looked disappointed, but I didn't intend to let his expression sway me. "My physical strength and a blade are plenty to deal with the beasts—especially now that there's two of us. I can't in good conscience remain here for days on end without reporting my findings to your parents, nor should I make Djialkan and Alala wait too long to discover my whereabouts."

"I could have the Vulin bring them here." Nalithor trailed his fingers down my spine and sighed. "You may be ready to return, but I am not. There is more that I would discuss with you and, as you mentioned, I don't intend to let you leave until you've proved that you're well enough to fight."

"Then let's *fight!*" I pivoted to look up at him, then paused when I caught a glimpse of the forlorn expression on his face. *'Did I...*

"You *can* bring me back here any time you like, can't you?"

"Let's go back inside. We can discuss things there." Nalithor turned away from me and began walking toward the palace.

I stared after him for a moment, a pang of guilt shooting through me. It really seemed as if I'd managed to upset him, or at least hurt his feelings a little. That hadn't been my intention. Not at all. I bit the inside of my cheek, feeling a lump forming in my throat. I was useless with people, especially people who seemed interested in me.

"I'd rather—" I started, but Nalithor kept walking.

Instead of following him, I plopped back down on the chaise and stared at my feet. Had I been too pushy about the matter? I *knew* we needed to return, soon, but Nalithor seemed totally uninterested in doing so. It seemed likely to me that, if he felt so strongly about staying, he had probably attempted to use his power as an Adinvyr to seduce me into staying.

I hadn't felt even the slightest trickle of his power. The only thing I had felt was my growing attraction to and desire for Nalithor.

*'Which is troublesome in its own right...'* I shut my eyes and breathed a heavy sigh. *'Is he upset because I won't bend to his will, or did I... Was he being genuine, and I hurt his feelings? What if he won't let me be his partner after all?'*

An unwelcome spike of fear shot through my chest, making me clench the edge of the chaise.

"Arianna?" Nalithor's voice made me glance up, but his posture and crossed arms was almost enough to make me flinch. "Are you going to make me carry you inside?"

"I'd rather stay out here," I grumbled, looking away from him.

"Why?"

"Because it's pretty..."

"It's cold." Nalithor's footsteps drew closer, and after a moment he reached for me, but I shied away. "If you stay out here dressed like that, you'll only end up more—"

"Nalithor, I'm a warrior too. I don't need you to coddle me." I glanced at him briefly and then turned my gaze away again. He still looked hurt, and I sighed. "Isn't having a 'mere mortal' in your domain just going to cause you problems with the Elders? It's already my fault that we haven't reported to your parents yet. I don't want to also be the reason—"

Nalithor's arms wrapped around my torso moments before he rested his head on my shoulder. He hugged me tight, nearly causing both of us to topple onto the chaise in full. I froze, unsure of what to do with my arms or hands. *'Is it…is it even okay for me to embrace a deity? Why did he hug me? Hells, why does he…anything?'*

"We can remain here as long as we want—or need," Nalithor ran one hand down my back before lifting me off the chaise and ground both. "I can send Daijiro to Draemir if we find ourselves needing to stay here longer. The Vulin can come and go freely. Whereas I…"

"You have to transport us back to the same place you came here *from*, right?" I mumbled, now unsure what to do with both my arms *and* legs. "I… I can walk, Nalithor."

He paused for a moment, then just kept walking. This time, however, his destination didn't seem to be the palace. After covering more ground, Nalithor set me down and shot me an unreadable smile. Somehow it made me feel worse. I didn't like that he'd withdrawn in such a way, but I didn't know how to fix it.

"You wanted to fight, didn't you?" Nalithor motioned around us. "I will use my full repertoire; you will use your physical strength and a blade."

"But—" I started to protest.

"This is what you wanted, isn't it?" Nalithor shot me a strange look.

"You need to let me access my shrizar first! Otherwise, there won't *be* a blade." I sighed, bringing my fingers to my temples. "And I can tell you're upset with me. Which thing did I do that I shouldn't do again?"

"Arianna, you push yourself without regard for your own safety."
Nalithor gave me a firm look, but his tone was soft. "One moment you
appear open to my attentions, the next you balk at even the slightest
touch. Furthermore, you are not a 'mere mortal,' as you put it. You
are—"

"*You* are a god, and *I* am trash as far as the Elders are concerned!"
I pointed out a little more bluntly than intended, causing the Adinvyr
to growl at me. "I doubt they'd take kindly to me being here. And as
far as *I* know, whether the information is accurate or not, gods aren't
supposed to act like—"

"—like *we* are people?" Nalithor's dangerous tone made me stop.
"And? My other answers?"

"I wasn't saying you're not—"

"Then why are you so skittish?"

"Why are *you* so...physical?" I countered, exasperated, bringing
my fingertips to my temples. "I... I don't know how to react to
physical contact. What is appropriate? What isn't? People in X'shmir
won't even look at me, let alone touch me. And they're *mortals*. Most
of them would laugh their asses off if someone told them a *god* wanted
anything to do with me!"

"I would argue that I'm a man before I'm a god." Nalithor crossed
his arms at me. His tone was dangerous again, but I didn't feel as
though it was directed toward me. "You are over-thinking things,
Arianna. There are no restrictions on what deities and mortals can do
to or with each other. The only thing that you're correct about is the

Elders, potentially, being quite cross about me bringing you here. Unlike the rest of the deities, the Elders don't understand...attachment or loyalty. *They* would have just left you behind for the beasts."

"You could have as well," I pointed out, perhaps a little too seriously. "You would have preserved more of your strength—"

"Do you truly think I would abandon you in such a way?!" Nalithor demanded, flames bursting to life around him. "Do you trust me so little?"

"I trust you with my life; otherwise I wouldn't have let you feed from me—and we would both still be stuck with the beasts." I snorted, shaking my head as Nalithor's flames reached for me. He shot his own power a strange look while I continued, "Well—*you'd* be stuck with the beasts. I'd be dead. Probably. I can be stubborn."

"'Can be?'" Nalithor gave me a sideways look.

"Details." I waved a hand dismissively. "I trust you, Nalithor, I do. But that doesn't mean I understand you or why you act in certain ways. I've lived my life as an outcast. The only people I've ever had *any* kind of positive attention from are my Guardians and the people in Sihix— most of which are too reverent to treat me like I'm one of them."

"*I refuse to abandon you*," Nalithor reiterated, backing me into a tree's trunk. He placed a hand above my head to brace himself so he could lean down, growling. "I will not lessen my actions just because the X'shmirans treated you like you're less than a person.

"When I get my hands on the X'shmirans I am going to tear them limb from limb. I won't be satisfied until I have butchered every single twisted bastard—"

Nalithor shut his eyes and inhaled deeply to calm himself. It didn't seem to help much because, when he opened his eyes, I could still see his simmering rage. The other emotions in his face were difficult for me to grasp—if only because they were directed at me.

"Is *nervousness* the only reason your heart races when I..." Nalithor stopped mid-reach for my face and averted his gaze before turning fully away from me. His pained expression broke something in me. "I...have paperwork to attend to. We can spar some other time."

I stared after him, unable to think of something to say. That was the last thing I'd meant to imply, yet it seemed to be all he took from my explanation. I bit my lower lip hard as a lump formed in my throat again and my vision blurred. How else could I explain it to him? My frustration made it even more difficult to find the words to express myself.

"Th-that's not why..." I stopped myself when my voice cracked, but it was too late. Nalithor stopped and stiffened, his head turning slightly. Before he could fully turn to face me, I took off at a run for the forest, unwilling to let him see me cry. I was torn, I was frustrated beyond belief, and I didn't know how to express myself to him. At all.

Coming to his domain had reminded me, blatantly, that he was a deity.

An "Evil Mage" like me wasn't worthy of a deity's glance, let alone their interest.

The rough forest floor cut my feet open, but I didn't care. I needed to put some distance between Nalithor and myself so that I could regain some semblance of composure. I knew the entire situation was my fault but that didn't make things any better—nor did it tell me how to fix things. This was one of the rare times I wanted to be alone, but the Adinvyr wasn't having any of that.

A few dozen feet into the forest, I hit what I could only describe as a wall of aether. Everything went blank for several long seconds when I collided with it—my sight, my thoughts, my hearing. It was like my senses were filled with nothing but white. Moments later I regained some grasp of my senses, enough to realize that I was caught in a web of Nalithor's darkness. He was pulling me back out of the forest. The moment I realized my face was still wet with tears I attempted to pull out of his grip so that I could run again.

"You should be more careful." Nalithor sighed, but I kept my gaze averted. "Let me see your feet. You're bleeding everywhere."

I flinched and pulled away when he reached for me, feeling tears welling up again. It was more because of pain than anything, but the look on his face made it clear he thought I was rejecting him. He recoiled and took a step away, his tail dropping slack behind him.

"...I'll go...fetch the Vulin healers." Nalithor shut his eyes in pain and turned away from me. That alone was enough to make the tears start falling again.

"N-no! Don't leave!" I ran after him and buried my face in his back, ignoring the jolts of pain shooting up from my feet. "W-wrong.

You're wrong about—"

"You shouldn't be standing!" Nalithor pivoted to catch me as my legs gave out to agony. "Let me fetch—"

"No!" I protested, burying my face into his chest. At least this way he couldn't see my face. "Y-you can heal me. Just hurts. Lots."

Nalithor's heart skipped several beats beneath my cheek, but he hesitated to move his hands anywhere as if doubting what my reaction would be. I tried to think of a way to explain to him other than saying "you're wrong" repeatedly, but an upset mind never functions well.

"Is that…why you flinched?" Nalithor asked quietly. He paused when I nodded into his chest. "Is that all I'm wrong about?"

"No," I mumbled into his chest, shaking my head this time. "I'm…I'm supposed to be a w-waste of your time because I'm—"

"According to who?" Nalithor bristled, grabbing me by my face and forcing me to look at him. His expression softened the moment he laid eyes on my tear-stained face. He sighed and gave me a sad smile. "My misunderstanding upset you this much?"

"I didn't mean to imply—" I started, but Nalithor leaned forward and silenced me with a hesitant, brief kiss.

"Sit. I won't have you suffering a moment longer." Nalithor pointed at the ground and then sat down himself. "You can try, again, to explain if you like."

The Adinvyr held out a hand expectantly, glancing from me to my foot and back once. Actually moving my leg so that he could work on healing my foot was a contest of wills I almost lost. *Won't be running barefoot through a forest again any time soon...'*

"What I was trying to explain is why I...why I struggle to react or reciprocate," I muttered, glancing away from him. "The only times a X'shmiran ever embraced me or touched me was when they were trying to kill me. I've seen them interact 'normally' with each other, but... I don't know what's appropriate, regardless of 'rank.'

"The way X'shmirans depict deities doesn't help. According to *their* beliefs, the only reason you..." I took a deep breath and then sighed, attempting not to struggle while he healed my feet. "To them, the only reason you could possibly have for so much as *looking at me* would be to execute me. Part of their confusion with you is the fact that you haven't slaughtered me for talking to you."

"You are not making a good case for letting them live," Nalithor commented, flames appearing in a circle around him. Luckily for me, their heat was pleasant to the touch. "So even though the X'shmirans are so far removed from the rest of Avrirsa, they too fail to see deities as 'people.'"

"To be fair, they fail to see people as people too," I pointed out, earning a brief glance and smile. "I... I really didn't mean to upset you, Nalithor. I just don't want to be a burden. I shouldn't get in the way of your duties as a general or as a deity, yet that seems to be exactly what I'm doing. How can I call myself worthy of being your partner if I'm this weak?"

"Weak?" Nalithor shook his head but didn't turn to look at me, choosing instead to focus on his healing. "Arianna, most people would still be asleep from the *first* time I drank you. That you would sacrifice your strength, albeit temporarily, to allow us both to escape is admirable.

"You are not getting in the way. If anything… I should be the one apologizing. After all, *I* made *you* cry. Not…the other way around."

"I started it…" I mumbled, deciding to stare at my lap instead of at him.

"Your pulse is racing again." Nalithor glanced at me, his expression passive. "Do I truly make you that nerv—"

"*You don't make me nervous, damn it!*" I snapped, my face burning hot. "Unless 'nervous' and 'flustered' are the same thing. But they're not. And stop gloating! I *will* kick your ass if you—"

"Says the princess that can't draw a weapon here." Nalithor caught my leg when I went to kick him, then smirked and moved to pin me to the ground. "Oh? You got away? Have you found someone other than me to practice your grappling skills with?"

"No one else will practice with— Hey, t-that's cheating!" I yelped when his darkness lashed out and dragged me back to him. "At least fight me fair if you're going to fight me at all!"

"I'm an Adinvyr, this *is* fair." Nalithor looked down at me approvingly as he pulled my legs to either side of him, his gaze wandering to where my shirt had slid up to my waist. "For such an 'innocent' 'X'shmiran' girl, you certainly know how to choose enticing undergarments."

"Is it really alright for you to act like this, as a god, with a mortal?"

I asked, attempting to readjust my shirt.

"Of course. Where else do you think the Elders would expect unmarried deities to look for a mate?" Nalithor tilted his head, watching me with a predatory expression. When I couldn't think of a response, he smiled. "You wanted to prove that you're ready to return to Draemir, did you not?"

I opened my mouth to tell him off but fell silent instead when he summoned his spear and stabbed it into the ground next to my head. However, he seemed more interested in keeping my legs spread to either side of him than he was in fighting me. No matter how I moved, he wouldn't let me reclaim my legs just yet.

"You shouldn't have been able to wield this." Nalithor motioned at the spear, pausing to track the tendrils of darkness that were flowing from it towards me. "Hmmm... You are a strange one aren't you, Arianna?"

"Humph. *Strange*? I prefer 'unique.'" I rolled my eyes before reaching up and pushing at his lower abdomen. "Let me up."

"*Make me.*" Nalithor challenged, leaning down to nuzzle my throat. "Perhaps I should add another set of marks if you fail..."

"Speaking of which, why didn't you heal these fully?" I questioned, attempting to ignore his mouth teasing along my throat.

"Perhaps I enjoy the reminder." Nalithor withdrew from my throat with a smirk and then drew his claws down the side of my throat. "Besides, it should function as suitable discouragement for any of my countrymen that might want to step out of line."

"Smug." I snorted, earning a grin. "Aren't we supposed to be fighting each other?"

"I suppose…" Nalithor rested his hand on one of my thighs instead of letting me up. "I'm not giving you access to your shrizar quite yet. You will wield the spear instead since it seems to accept you. I would prefer to avoid drawing unwanted attention by having you summon any of Aurelian's creations for you here. The change in the aether wouldn't go unnoticed."

"But fighting is fine?" I arched an eyebrow at him.

"You're not allowed to use your magics." Nalithor shook his head at me. "Fight me using pure strength. It is likely that you will have to fight magical attackers when we return to Xiinsha—I want to make certain you've recovered enough to handle them."

"You *do* have to let me up first." I sighed, shooting him a look.

"I did say '*make me*,'" Nalithor slid his hand up my thigh and to the waistband of my panties, tugging at it. "Do you need some encouragement, my dear?"

"I'm going to—" I didn't get to finish before Nalithor rose to his feet and pulled me up with him. The speed of which made my head spin. "Let's see who can kill more beasts on the way back to Draemir, hmmm?"

"You're that confident that you're ready to return?" Nalithor asked, tracking me as I moved to dislodge his spear from the ground. "I suppose we can make a contest of it regardless of the 'when.' What if I win?"

"Don't you think you've already won enough for a month?" I countered dryly.

"Nowhere *near* enough," Nalithor informed me. He came to stand beside me and gripped my hip before leaning down to kiss me on top of the head. "If I win, mmm, I'm sure I can think of *something* I desire as a prize."

# CHAPTER FOURTEEN
## *Camaraderie*

"You really want me to wield one of your weapons instead of mine?" I crossed my arms and looked from Nalithor to his spear, and back.

"If you can quell its power while dealing with fighting me, that will be sufficient proof that you're ready to fight our way back to Draemir." Nalithor tilted his head slightly and glanced from me to his spear, tracking the wisps of shadows that were reaching for me. "I'm also hoping that we'll discover what's causing the weapon to act this way. It should have burned you when you fetched it from the sand, let alone how long you carried it with you. Instead... Well, I have no idea *what* it is doing, to be quite honest."

*'How did he recover so fast from all of...that?'* I bit back a sigh, my

shoulders slumping. How he had managed to switch back to his usual teasing self was beyond me. Personally, I felt awful for upsetting him. *'And why is he so adamant that I need to "prove" I'm ready to go back to Draemir? Feeding from me didn't weaken me all that much. I wonder what's really bothering him.'*

Resigned, I gripped the spear in my left hand and pulled the blade out of the dirt. Darkness burst into life around the length of the weapon and flowed up to encase my entire arm up to the shoulder. It startled me, but it didn't feel threatening. Just...strange. A shiver ran down my spine when I sensed bloodlust from the blade. I knew *that* power, yet the Adinvyr who owned the weapon seemed just as surprised as me.

"Now *that* is interesting," Nalithor murmured, his gaze tracing down my arm before flicking back to my face. "Shall we, my dear?"

"No magic on my end, right?" I pouted, testing the weight of the spear. Nalithor just smiled, nodded, and waited. "I'd like to eat after I defeat you. I'm still hungry."

"You won't defeat me—not in your condition." Nalithor shot me an odd look. "Alas, winning isn't your goal."

"Right, right. Prove that I'm not a burden." I snorted and then shifted my stance.

"I didn't mean—"

I darted forward and slashed upwards with the spear, forcing Nalithor to leap out of reach. The weapon was much heavier and longer than what I was accustomed to wielding, but it felt almost as if the darkness flowing from it was attempting to strengthen my grip. It hummed with excitement as I chased after its rightful owner. I intended to end the fight as fast as possible—the spear's seeming sentience was a bit unsettling.

Nalithor blocked my next strike with one hand and used the other to channel flames at me. Both of us paused for a moment to stare at the spear—it hadn't even given me a chance to dodge or block the flames before engulfing them in such thick darkness they were snuffed out. In seconds the bloodlust emanating from the weapon spiraled to new heights, urging me to draw Nalithor's blood. I bit the inside of my cheek and shivered. The idea was…tempting. But not in a manner I was accustomed to. This wasn't a desire to cause harm.

"Shall we stop?" Nalithor rubbed his chin in thought, watching me and the darkness.

"I see no reason to," I answered shaking out my left arm. "You've infused the weapon with your darkness? I see no other reason for it to seem so…sentient."

"Some of my power is stored within my weapons—a failsafe in case I run into a nasty foe." Nalithor made a vague motion with one hand. "The Exiles can't be expected to adhere to the same morals as the rest of the world does. What may be forbidden arts to us is free game to them."

"Storing power in case of emergency, huh?" I murmured, glancing down at my shadow-encased arm. "Is this where you say, 'most people would have fled?'"

"Something like that." Nalithor shot me a rather cheerful smile. "For someone who is supposedly unsure of how to interact with a deity, you are certainly comfortable with my power. Do you truly understand how much the weapon is using to shield you?"

"Mmm..." I tilted my head and looked at the weapon for a moment, then back at Nalithor. "Enough to blow X'shmir out of the sky in its entirety.

"Enough talking! If you want to chat, we can do it over lunch."

"You don't wish to be—" Nalithor cut himself off and darted out of my way when I closed the distance between us. "—alone?"

The weapon sang in my grip, eager for blood. Eager for contact. Nalithor's brow furrowed as he continued to evade me, and the darkness around my arm and the spear grew. I could tell that he was using my attacks as a means to gauge the weapon more than he was gauging me. Even if it was understandable, I found it frustrating. He should have been more concerned with fighting me than he was with inspecting his own weapon.

A pulse of irritation drove me to attack the Adinvyr at a faster pace. I would *make* him focus on me.

Nalithor summoned a slender sword and blocked my next strike with ease, a smirk settling on his face. His tail swished behind him for a moment while he examined me, watching as I attempted to physically overpower his stance. Seconds passed before he lashed out with fire and sent me flying backward, but I landed on my feet. I launched myself at him again, this time shifting my grip on the spear lower for extended reach.

The spear grazed up Nalithor's abdomen and chest as he darted backward, spilling his blue-black blood along the blade and his skin. His amused smirk shifted into a broad grin mere moments before he disappeared from sight entirely. A prickling sensation down my back was the only warning I had for his strike. I turned in time to block him with the shaft of the spear, but his kick hit with enough force to send me stumbling back.

"I thought the weight of the weapon would slow you down, but you're fast as ever!" Nalithor laughed, twirling his sword in one hand. "You seem disturbed. What's the matter?"

"Why does your spear desire..." I trailed off, staggering back as I shook my head. The weapon's desire for blood was almost enough to overwhelm me. It was if it were trying to invade my senses and direct my desires to be in line with its own. I closed my eyes for a moment and took a steadying breath, pushing the spear's power further from my mind. Once satisfied, I fixed my gaze on Nalithor—he looked far too pleased with himself. "Shouldn't your blade desire to spill the blood of your prey, not *yours?*"

"So, blood is what you want, is it?" Nalithor chuckled, motioning at his bloodied torso.

"No, the *spear* wants—" I cut myself off and shot the weapon a sideways glare when its power nudged me again. The entire weapon suddenly burst into shadows and rushed back to Nalithor, absorbing into his jewelry. I bristled and bared my fangs at him. "Hey! We're not done fighting yet!"

"I'm satisfied that you're well enough to return," Nalithor stated as he strode towards me. His smirk grew when he caught me watching the blood trickle down his chest, so I huffed and looked away from him. "Now, now, you know we will both need our strength for the return trip. The beasts will still be waiting for us—perhaps even their masters."

"We haven't had a good sparring session in a while though..." I sighed and shook my head before glancing at him. The scent of his blood struck me as more alluring than usual, and he still hadn't cleansed himself of it. Nor had he healed the deep wound I'd left.

"You know," Nalithor gripped my chin and made me look at him, a smile playing on his lips. "I won't blame you if you give in to your hunger. I might even encourage it..."

"Hunger?" I placed a hand on his abdomen to keep him from pulling me closer—and ruining my clothes. "If anyone is 'hungry' the way *you're* thinking of, it would be you. Especially if you aren't going to stop the bleeding."

"I was considering having you take care of it," Nalithor murmured, tracing his thumb over my lips. "Or are you still cross with me?"

"You don't seem to *want* me to use my magic here quite yet," I pointed out before glancing down at his torso again. "Hmmm, I didn't think I'd cut you so deep. Will you be alright?"

"Of course I will be." Nalithor chuckled, shaking his head at me. "I can tell just how...'entranced' you are, Arianna. Does the sight of my blood truly excite you so?"

"You smell like dessert," I informed him. "And I want lunch. Can you blame me for being a little distracted?"

"Very well, I won't tease you." Nalithor smiled and released me so that he could tend to his wounds. "You didn't answer my other question; are you still upset with me?"

I contemplated his question for a moment then shook my head and answered, "Upset? No. Perplexed? Yes."

"Care to elaborate?" Nalithor hesitated, then offered me his arm. "Assuming you don't mind me joining you for lunch, that is."

"I *will* be cross if you *don't* join me..." I grumbled, accepting his arm. He seemed to relax a little. "I'm perplexed because... To put it bluntly, coming here has reminded me that you are indeed a deity—a powerful one. It's made me wonder if, perhaps, the way I've been treating you and the way we've been interacting really *is* inappropriate. I thought people were being nosy when they claimed we weren't behaving properly."

"That you've treated me as an equal is one of the reasons I'm drawn to you, Arianna," Nalithor stated, his tone firm. "Most people who know that I'm a god treat me with an unearned reverence that I abhor. The ones who know my role are even worse. *You* never seemed to care before whether I'm a deity—nor do you put much stock in X'shmiran beliefs. I suppose you could say that *I* am perplexed by this shift."

"An 'unearned reverence?'" I asked, looking up at him.

"Mindless admiration based solely on the fact that I'm a deity."

Nalithor shook his head and sighed. "I'm...the God of Balance. If Vorpmasia grows too strong, it will be *my* duty to...'level the playing field.' Most people, even among the Royal Families, seem oblivious to the very real threat that my role could turn me against them.

"My role could brand me as a traitor to the people I used to protect and, that aside, I have yet to do anything *as a deity* that deserves such degrees of admiration from the people."

"So, *you* would prefer that I treat you like an equal..." I murmured, catching him nod in my peripheral vision. "Is that socially acceptable? Or do I need to mind how I act around other people? I wouldn't...I wouldn't want my declaration when we arrived in Draemir to cause you unnecessary trouble."

Nalithor slowed to a stop and tugged at my arm, but I didn't look at him. Instead of trying again, he spoke, "If anyone takes issue with your declaration or the way we act with each other, *they* are the ones in the wrong. Should anyone voice such opinions or attempt to intervene, *I will put them in their place.* If you truly desire my company—and exclusive access to it—for Faerstravir, it is yours."

"You're sure?" I grumbled.

"Absolutely."

"I'm...not a burden?"

"Am I going to have to claim you for myself in order to get the point across?" Nalithor nudged me, chuckling when I flushed. "Arianna, you are far from being a burden in any situation we have faced thus far. It goes beyond whatever you are beneath all those seals.

Even the highest of gods can be useless or a 'burden.' You have drive—
a desire to act, to improve. And a rather endearing hunger for my blood
as well, it would seem."

"I-I do not!" I protested, shooting him a pout. "That was your
weapon's—"

"The power was reflecting the wielder's desires." Nalithor shot me
a knowing smile. "Regardless, I believe lunch is in order before we leave
for the Xiinsha Forest. The Vulin will be upset to see you leave so soon
but, alas, we *do* have duties to attend… You're certain that you don't
wish to stay longer?"

"Tempting… But you still need to show me around Draemir," I
murmured, shaking my head. "I want to see what Faerstravir is like as
well. We don't really have festivals in X'shmir."

"Not even for the harvest?" Nalithor inquired, shooting me a
curious look as he led me toward his palace once more.

"No. Most festivals were done away with when an earlier
generation of royalty decreed the gods to be 'false,'" I answered,
contemplating X'shmiran traditions for a moment. "They attempted
to replace the original festivals with ones that had no ties to deities, but
it was soon after that the Chaos Beasts truly became a problem in
X'shmir. After the X'shmirans realized that the large, raucous festivities
drew beasts to the city they stopped allowing parties or festivals of any
sort."

"X'shmir is such a strange place." Nalithor grimaced. He lifted me
off my feet and carried me the rest of the way into the palace, chuckling

at the look I shot him. "How have they survived for so long without mages existing prior to you and Darius? How have you managed to protect the city on your own? Why are there so many beasts, and where do they keep coming from?"

"Many things about your 'homeland' make little sense. If the sky wasn't so unnerving, and the people so foul, I'd be far more likely to remain there for a few months to study the beasts and any other phenomena that I could find."

"Mmm? Unnerving?" I glanced over my shoulder at him when he pulled me onto a pile of pillows with him. He seemed intent on keeping me on his lap. This time, I decided to say nothing of it. "The Mists *did* seem to interfere with your senses quite a bit. They rather like to watch, too…"

"Yet you seem unaffected by it." Nalithor grumbled, nuzzling into my shoulder. The motion caused the shirt to slip from my shoulder again, allowing the Adinvyr to rub his cheek into my skin. He released a contented purr before continuing, "This belief the X'shmirans have that a god would pay no attention to an Umbral Mage… I would like to know more of it."

"More?" I murmured, falling silent for a short while as I wracked my mind. Nalithor stayed quiet and let me think. He seemed content to do nothing but nuzzle my shoulder and hold me. "The X'shmirans fear deities—which is strange if you consider their insistence that deities don't exist. They don't believe that the gods have roles. Rather, they think that all gods exist to force conformity to 'the great design.'

"'Evil' Mages are considered a flaw in that design. I hate to draw the comparison, but X'shmirans see Umbral Mages the way people here see the Exiled Gods. Beings to be exterminated for their crimes— regardless of intent or proof. Since we're supposedly a flaw in 'the great design'…"

"…the X'shmirans would believe it falls to the gods to eliminate any Lyur'zi they find," Nalithor spoke, nodding his understanding into my shoulder. "Tch… You should pledge yourself to *me* instead of those foul creatures."

The Adinvyr growled his frustration and squeezed me tighter. His words came as a surprise to me, but I couldn't help but shake my head and smile.

"You make it sound far easier than it actually is." I nudged one of his wrists, earning a huff. "I know you're procrastinating, Nalithor. You should call your foxes so that we can eat and then get going. As beautiful as it is here—"

"So, you do approve of my domain?" Nalithor's question surprised me, but I couldn't turn to shoot him a look with the way he was holding me. "I'm…not going to be able to convince you to stay, am I?"

"Mmm? And let you have all the prey to yourself?" I demanded, shaking my head. "I know you can bring me here any time you like until ordered otherwise. There's no reason to keep me hidden away here now that you know I can handle myself in battle still.

"Unless…you're hiding something from me?" I paused, feeling

Nalithor tense. His grip on my waist twitched tighter, causing his claws to dig into my skin. "Well, Nalithor?"

"I can't tell you." Nalithor's grip went slack, allowing me to turn slightly. He looked rather torn, as if struggling to determine what he *could* say. "I... Suffice to say that one of the poisons brought by the slavers had affected you to a minor degree. The Vulin and I made certain that every trace of it was gone."

"One of the poisons?" I probed. His expression was too worried for me to be cross with him—yet. "So, they had more than just the one that darkened everyone's veins? What—"

"I can't give you any details about it, Arianna." Nalithor shook his head and attempted to pull me even closer, but I was already as close as I could get. "The poison is a vile, vile substance and the reagents are...classified. Even if you were an officer in the Vorpmasian military, you likely wouldn't be on the list of people allowed to know of it. If I chose to disregard protocol and tell you, you would be in great danger. I will not expose you to that threat if I can avoid it."

"A need-to-know basis, is it?" I sighed, contemplating it. The Adinvyr tensed as if expecting me to lash out in anger, but I shook my head. I could understand all-too-well. After all, there were plenty of things I couldn't tell him either. "And if we find ourselves in a situation where we've confiscated these poisons, or the substances used within them?"

"I would be hard-pressed to tell you unless one of us was infected with the substance," Nalithor murmured, bringing one hand to my face. He stroked my cheek with his thumb while he searched my face. "If we come across more slaver camps on our way back to Draemir, the Vulin will confiscate everything in them after we've executed the slavers themselves. The Vulin are better equipped to handle such things for us and will be able to make off with the poisons before prying eyes, or fingers, get to them. You...seem accepting."

"Well, I'm not Vorpmasian, and the X'shmirans aren't exactly endearing themselves to the empire," I pointed out with an amused smile. "I know better than to pry about classified information, Nalithor. Especially something that sounds so...sensitive. My only question would be; is the empire responsible for the substance's existence?"

"No." Nalithor shook his head. "Devillians pride themselves in physical and magical prowess, not poisons. Well...unless they're an Imviir."

"I think an Imviir's venom would count as 'physical prowess' since it's *their* venom." I arched an eyebrow at the thoughtful man. "Your venom would probably fall under the same category too, though I somehow doubt you would use it in combat situations."

"Only if I found myself needing to subdue you," Nalithor answered dryly. "Seeing as you appear immune to my other powers."

"Well, since you can't tell me of this mysterious poison I was apparently exposed to, hmmm..." I tilted my head, thinking for a moment. Nalithor looked wary about what I planned to ask next. "How about the Vulin? I've never heard of anything like them—what are they?"

"Ah…they are difficult." Nalithor relaxed a little and nuzzled into my shoulder once more. "The Elders claim that the Vulin are 'leftovers' from a previous world and aren't meant to exist in this one. They planned to eliminate every Vulin in Avrirsa…but I intervened and took them in. What remains of their species lives here, in my domain, and they help me with all manner of things. Not just maintaining the palace and its grounds."

*'Leftovers from a previous world?'* I wondered, listening as Nalithor purred into my shoulder. He seemed so content now despite how we had upset each other. I shivered when Nalithor began planting kisses on my shoulder and then up my neck, one of his hands coming up to grip the other half of my neck. His darkness coiled around both of us lazily while his attentions threatened to draw me in. "This isn't—"

"But you're so fun to tease." Nalithor nipped at the side of my throat once before straightening and moving away from my throat. "I suppose it's for the best that I call the Vulin. Far be it from me to make you fight on an empty stomach. All I ask is that you take great care. You should still be bedridden…yet you appear fine aside from weakened aether."

"I'll be cautious if you manage to entertain me to make up for it," I suggested, shooting him a look over my shoulder. His startled expression and the slight flush to his cheeks made me smirk. "If I'm going to take it easy, there had better be something worthwhile for me to watch."

"Must I prove myself worthy again?" Nalithor arched an eyebrow at me.

"Not quite what I had in mind," I answered with an amused smile. "I haven't truly had a chance to admire you at work yet. This seems like an excellent opportunity to see how my partner deals with his prey."

"And if *you* are my prey?" Nalithor countered.

"I wasn't aware there was an 'if' there," I answered in a tone dripping sarcasm. He just chuckled and shook his head, so I nudged him. "Lunch and a day full of slaughter await us. I'm going to grow agitated if you make me wait much longer to hunt."

"You certainly know how to get an Adinvyr's attention." Nalithor chuckled. "As you wish, *Your Highness*. We can converse more after we've returned to Draemir."

Nalithor and I had clad ourselves in armor and readied weapons after finishing lunch. Soon after, the Adinvyr deity had brought me to a portal beyond his palace's grounds. Everything had spun for a few seconds before I found myself standing in the Xiinsha Forest once more. The scent of beasts and blood ignited my instincts as a huntress immediately. I wanted to revel in the slaughter to come.

"Don't be so hasty, my dear." Nalithor caught me around the waist with his tail and pulled me behind a tree. "If there are *this* many beasts loitering, we may have an even larger problem on our hands than I thought. Stay close."

"But—" I trailed off into a grumble and pouted when Nalithor placed his hand over my mouth.

The now-focused Adinvyr picked me up and leapt upwards through the tree to a higher perch. Once he released me, I let out a small sigh and slumped back against the tree. Nalithor had a displeased expression on his face when he crouched on the limb and tracked the movements of the beasts in the clearing below us. From the look of things, the monsters were following the remaining traces of Nalithor's blood. Why they had remained for *days* to do so was beyond me.

*'They should have given up by now,'* Nalithor remarked as if responding to my thoughts. *'Someone is using them like hunting dogs.'*

*'Xiinsha's inhabitants are still hiding in the forest's outskirts,'* I muttered, pivoting to survey the area around our perch. There were even more beasts filtering through the trees and toward the clearing below. *'I think they're looking for you. If someone is using them to hunt…'*

*'I'll observe them while you work,'* Nalithor tapped me on the shoulder, causing me to glance at him. *'Don't overdo it. As much as the Vulin and I would like you to remain in my domain longer, we really should report your findings.'*

*'I'll be fine as long as I don't need to share my sight.'* I breathed a sigh after settling into a cross-legged sitting position.

Nalithor nodded at me and then shifted his piercing gaze back to the beasts. I watched the swaying of his tail for a moment while he stalked them. Even though he said I shouldn't be hasty, *he* looked ready to pounce into the middle of all the beasts by himself. Now that he had fed from me twice, and wasn't attempting to snuggle with or seduce me, he seemed much more alert and focused. However, I got the feeling that he was still hungry.

I shut my eyes and took several deep breaths to still my thoughts. When I opened my eyes, streams of glittering red and gold magic arched through the air surrounding us. The magic twisted, turned, and danced around the trees and their branches. The ground moved and warped with so much power that I couldn't even make out the shape of Xiinsha's underbrush or the massive tree roots.

*'Is there any corruption?'* Nalithor asked.

I blinked a few times, watching as ripples of pale blue-white power laced with darkness ripped outward from Nalithor when he spoke. The wisps drifted around and past me, carried by the lazy breeze blowing through the forest. *'Nalithor's words didn't carry power before. He's…getting stronger? Then why does he seem so hungry still?'*

*'Arianna?'* Nalithor probed. *'You look much like a distracted cat. Too many pretty lights?'*

*'Very funny,'* I muttered, shifting my attention away from the ripples of his power. *'Xiinsha doesn't show any sign of corruption. Sihix, for example, still has discernible scars. This forest seems as if it never waned. Or rather, if it did, it must have been very long ago.'*

*'Any sign of our prey?'*

*'Give me a moment—and stop talking.'* I sighed, pivoting to poke his swaying tail. *'Your thoughts carry power with them now—it's distracting me from my search.'*

Nalithor swatted at my hands with his tail and shot me a fang-filled grin. I shook my head at him before switching my attention to my search. Hundreds of beasts prowled through Xiinsha, hunting. Their foul magic left trails of oily magic behind them. They were so intent on their hunt that they ignored all else—even the easiest of meals.

A deep frown formed on my face when I came across another type of magic, followed by another, and another.

'We have a problem.' I stood and allowed my vision to return to normal. 'How much fighting are you capable of in your current condition?'

'I should be quite fine. I'm more concerned about you,' Nalithor answered, flicking his gaze to me.

'The Angel I killed seems to have had friends.' I sighed, irritated. 'I think they have more slavers with them, but I'm uncertain. At any rate, their accomplices don't seem to be Human—they're leaving trails of dim magic through the forest.'

'How many beasts?' Nalithor inquired, tracking me as I shifted from foot-to-foot. 'You look eager.'

'Too many beasts... They're hunting,' I muttered while fidgeting with my vambraces. 'Hundreds of them. Small ones, no Dux, no colossal ones. Don't think they're Rilzaan beasts.'

"Calm down." Nalithor pulled me up against his side and gave me a smile, his voice low.

"Easier said than done..." I grumbled.

Nalithor ginned and patted me on top of my head. I shot him a look before turning to stare at the beasts gathered in the clearing, and then at the tree we had perched in. The tree's color had turned a maelstrom of blue-white and cobalt blue in response to our individual powers. The beasts below us didn't seem to notice, but I doubted it would be wise for us to remain for long.

'*Are the beasts colorblind?*' I nudged Nalithor with my elbow and then pointed at our perch once I had his attention. '*I don't think the Angels or their accomplices will be.*'

'Ah, would you rather turn the hunters into the hunted?' Nalithor smirked at me. 'We could always lie in wait for them here.'

'*Xiinsha will change color wherever we go.*' I grimaced, nudging the tree trunk. Spirals of cobalt flame sprouted from where I touched it and rushed through the crystalline bark. '*As pretty as this is, it isn't conducive to a stealthy strategy…and weren't you already calling the "hunters" our "prey" anyway?*'

'Can you leave at least some of the slavers—or an Angel—alive?'

'Why should I?'

'I would like to "question" them.'

'They don't deserve to live.'

'Corpses don't speak.'

'*But they* need *to die!*' I snapped back.

'You can play with them after I get information out of them—or with me, if you so desire.'

I pouted and huffed, pivoting to look away from the grinning Adinvyr. He had a point, and I knew it. He looked like he *knew* I knew it too. Frustrating as it was, I nodded my head in reluctance. '*Fine—*

*but if they make a wrong move, I will kill them.'*

*'That's fair.'* Nalithor smiled and ruffled my curls. *'Let's begin with the beasts here.'*

*'Careful.'* I caught him by the arm when he moved to leap from the tree. He shot me a questioning glance, so I continued, *'All the beasts I sensed or spotted were all moving to this location. They seem to be tracking your blood.'* I motioned at the bloodstained grass below. *'Since Daijiro isn't hiding it anymore the beasts have a free pathway here.'*

*'You said there weren't any Duxes,'* Nalithor pointed out. *'We should be fine—we just need to take them out quickly. After we take these out, we'll hunt the Angels you sensed.'*

Nalithor slipped from my grip and leapt from the tree with a grin plastered on his face. Before the beasts could turn, the Adinvyr had already drawn and brandished his spear. Several of the creatures toppled to the forest floor in halves before Nalithor's feet even touched the ground. The air around him shimmered, briefly, when his jewelry repelled the spray of corrupt blood.

I sighed before sliding out of the tree as well. After drawing a pair of swords, I watched the creatures turn and leap for Nalithor. Several rushed past me and went straight for Nalithor, ignoring me entirely. When I looked over my shoulder, I found more enemies speeding through the underbrush, their sights set on the clearing. Two more darted past me, oblivious to my presence.

*'So, they* are *looking for him.'*

Another beast chose to leap over my head instead of skirting around me. I flipped my grip on one sword and tore the damned thing open lengthwise, spilling its innards to the ground. Several others slowed their approach and began stalking me with drool dripping from their lipless snouts.

Darkness burst through the clearing while Nalithor tore through his opponents. The ones stalking me flinched and turned tail to scamper away from the pulsating shadows, their cries of fear filling the air.

"X'shmiran?" Nalithor inquired conversationally.

"I don't think so," I answered, shifting my attention to another fleeing beast. "They aren't Dux, nor do they look like stitched corpses."

"I'm impressed you haven't run off," Nalithor commented, resting his forearm on my shoulder. He smiled, watching me as I flicked my attention from beast-to-beast. "What's on your mind?"

"Something is off," I muttered, narrowing my eyes.

"What...?" Nalithor trailed off once he shifted his attention to them.

Most of the creatures had huddled together during our brief exchange. Their eyes were wide with fear as Nalithor's dark aura continued to swirl through the clearing. However, what I found most unsettling was that the beasts looked as if they were discussing something. Although they made no noises, their eyes kept flicking to each other and then back to Nalithor and me. There was a little too much intelligence in their gaze, and their huddling didn't look like it was out of fear.

'*A new breed then?*' Nalithor asked, slowly moving his arm around my waist. '*How many did you say there were?*'

'*Hundreds—but there could be more.*'

'*How many Angels?*'

'*Half a dozen, perhaps. The rest are probably Elves and Devillians.*'

'*All of these beasts were like these?*'

'*No other types,*' I confirmed. Nalithor's grip tightened as he pulled me a few paces away from the edge of the clearing, but I kept my attention focused on the strange creatures. '*What are you thinking?*'

'*Their attention has shifted to you,*' Nalithor stated, digging his claws into my hip as he drew me further backward.

I pursed my lips and examined the beasts. Their eyes were darting between Nalithor and I only now, their expressions holding a hint of confusion. Several of the larger ones kept lifting their heads and sniffing at the darkness. Their distress seemed to worsen as they tried to figure out…something.

'*What do you have in mind?*' I questioned when Nalithor slowed to a stop. I felt him turn to look over his shoulder before he answered me.

'*Can you tell if the Angels or the slavers are the ones issuing orders?*' Nalithor sighed when I shook my head. '*If we try to deal with the beasts, we will wear ourselves out long before reaching the Angels.*'

'*Straight to our pursuers then?*' I asked. Nalithor's hand grew hot against my hip, causing me to shoot him a questioning look over my shoulder. '*You're not seriously—*'

Nalithor's flames engulfed the both of us a split second before he pulled me backward into one of Xiinsha's trees. His power took my breath away for a moment, but the beasts charging the tree forced me to regain focus. The creatures slammed their heads into the bark and bounced off it, yelping in pain before scrambling to their feet to claw at the tree. Yowling, they began circling the tree and sniffed around its base.

Their quick switch to analysis was more than a little unnerving.

*'Traveling through the trees as flames seems easier than searching for shadows,'* Nalithor pointed out, pulling me along with him. Our combined flames dyed the trees varying shades of blue in our wake. Under other circumstances, I would have taken the time to admire it. *'Tch... Hold on a moment.'*

I glanced around from within the tree we had stopped in, then frowned when I looked at the ground several yards below. The beasts had managed to keep up with us even though they seemed colorblind. They sniffed around the base of our current tree and began circling it while more of their brethren appeared from the underbrush. There were at least eighty of the damned things by now.

Nalithor startled me when his power interlaced with mine. He chuckled and pulled a small amount of mine away. Before I could question him, he released a burst of our combined powers rushing through the forest. I stared at the trees, bewildered, as everything in my line of sight turned blue.

The beasts pursuing us bolted in different directions and attempted to follow the power that Nalithor had spread through the forest. They seemed oblivious to the fact that Nalithor had already withdrawn it, or that we had begun moving again. He released a boyish laugh as we flowed through the trees. His pulse raced with excitement while we sped through the forest, and I found it strangely contagious.

'Left,' I spoke when we neared one of Xiinsha's empty villages. 'Follow the stream.'

'Good girl.' Nalithor laughed, veering off according to my directions.

'It's hard to tell if you're being sarcastic, teasing me, or serious when you say it like that.' I sighed at him, surveying our surroundings while he pulled me along. 'I hope you have a plan.'

'We are going to pounce on them before they have a chance to notice the changing color of the trees,' Nalithor offered. 'If they don't have proper lookouts stationed, that is. Are you ready?'

'The sooner, the better I suppose.'

Nalithor laughed in delight and increased our speed. His pulse spiraled out of control when we finally caught the scent of the Angels nearby. His bloodlust swirled from his flames and into mine, threatening to overwhelm my senses. It was far worse than what I had felt from his spear while sparring earlier that day, and there was something different about his bloodlust this time.

It was as if his power was an uncontrollable raging beast intent on destruction, and it was trained on the Angels ahead of us.

'There's no way they're oblivious enough to miss that,' I thought to myself within my deeper barriers, shivering as Nalithor's flames raged wilder. *'That sensation is familiar. Exquisite... It's like—'*

**'Wait here.'** Nalithor commanded, separating his flames from mine. He burst out of the tree and into the Angels' camp, his fangs bared in a snarl. *'You can't involve yourself with this one.'*

I suppressed an irritated sigh and watched Nalithor dive into the group of waiting Angels. The winged men had most definitely sensed the God of Balance's bloodlust on our approach. They had attempted to ready themselves for a fight, but they were no match for a wrathful deity. Nalithor sliced the first one in half in the same motion as leaping from the tree. He squared off with the rest of them, darkness raging around his form. The Angels held their weapons before them, but their hands shook.

"Here's one of the false gods!" An Angel with creamy chestnut wings snapped, his grip on his longsword visibly twitching. "Where's the other one, trash?"

*'False? Other one?'* I frowned, sizing up the Angels for a moment before flicking my gaze to Nalithor. *'Hmmm, I know they're no match for him but...'*

A ripple of power drifted through the trees, making me freeze in place when it crept through me. I stared, dumbfounded, when I sensed Nalithor's racing pulse. His desire to execute the remaining four Angels before him. His unadulterated *fury* over something I couldn't determine. The overwhelming urge to fix...something.

Had I been standing, the brunt of his power and maelstrom-like thoughts would have knocked me from my feet.

*'W-why am I sensing all of* that *from him?'* I drifted a few inches away from the outside of the tree, hesitating to switch to my magical vision.

My world slowed to a stop the moment I *did* switch. Tendrils of darkness, flames, and frost stretched between the both of us. They swirled in a lazy dance and connected from the left side of his chest to mine. Within his chest was a familiar glow—two crystalline hearts hovered within his chest.

Multicolored magics intertwined and flowed through both hearts before spreading throughout the Adinvyr's limbs. The lotus-like one was mine. The other one was like a mrifon and shone much brighter. His divine heart seemed as if it was feeding magic into mine. Mine, in turn, reached tendrils of power out to me.

*'Gods…have crystalline hearts,'* I reminded myself, struggling to separate Nalithor's bloodlust from mine. *'How would* fake *Elders make someone into a* real *god? Wait… Didn't I say there were* six *Angels?'*

I pressed myself against the inside of the tree and searched for the remaining Angel. The bastard had to be somewhere nearby. I could worry about the tendrils of magic and the *two* divine hearts later.

"You still can't accept that a *Devillian* holds a role above Lesser?" Nalithor sighed. His condescending yet commanding tone sent a spike of desire through me, but I shook it off. "Tch, I was considering letting you live—if you cooperated. However, meddling with the affairs of a—"

*'There.'* I glanced upward, spotting the final Angel high above

Nalithor.

I sent myself spiraling high into my tree and then leapt for the winged asshole. The bastard shrieked in terror when I barreled into him with flames still licking along my skin. I gripped his sword arm and tore the weapon away from him, but he managed to kick me hard in the ribs, sending me flying back into another tree.

Something about *this* Angel was different, but there was no time for me to analyze it.

He aimed an ax kick for my shoulder, but I rolled out of the way. I flipped my grip on his sword and grimaced—another *Godslayer*. Useless against his kind.

Shrieks from below split the air when Nalithor tore into the four Angels on the ground, causing the one before me to snarl like an animal. Instead of moving to assist his comrades he summoned light in both hands and chucked both orbs of it at me.

'*Hate it.*'

I growled and summoned one of my own swords in my free hand before dashing after him when his orbs missed me. A twisted grin crossed his face as he released a maniacal laugh. My sword grazed his chest when he darted backward, spilling golden blood onto the tree branch. The bastard didn't even flinch—instead, he summoned chains of light.

'*Snuff it out.*'

"So, this is where the fake goddess was hiding!" The Angel sneered, spinning the chains.

*'Pathetic creature. What did it sell itself to?'*

Searing pain lanced through my back and knocked me to my knees. I doubled over, coughing, when an unfamiliar power spread through my veins and ignited my rage. My urge to kill the laughing bastard reached new heights, but even the smallest of movements caused me agony. Blood splattered from my mouth when I coughed in pain, my chest constricting as the Angel's power raced through me.

*'Kill him, tear him to shreds. Pluck his wings*—break him.' I growled when my vision swam, consumed by both rage and pain. There was little else.

A roar of pure fury broke my thoughts. An immense darkness rushed upward from the forest floor and then tore through every trace of light, obliterating it as it collided with the crazed Angel. I heard the crunch of breaking bones when the darkness slammed the wretch into a tree. Darkness blotted out almost everything other than my pain.

The winged bastard screamed in terror and what was likely much more pain than what I felt. Then, I heard a sickening crunch. Two more followed and the screaming stopped.

"I told you to stay in hiding!" Nalithor's hand rested on my back, making me flinch.

"Bastard thought he was being sneaky." I spat, glancing to the side at the shadows swirling around Nalithor's form. "He was planning to— Jich! *Dehsul*."

I slammed my fist into the branch beneath me when pain lanced through my back again. I continued to spew curses in both Draemiran and the common tongue, dropping both of my swords so that I could dig my fingers into the bark. It was all I could do to keep myself from turning and retaliating in response to the pain. Nalithor's power spread through my skin while I muttered curses. A feral snarl escaped me when he pulled something sharp from my back.

Nalithor's shadows twisted and grew with every curse and whimper of pain that escaped me.

"The *Godslayer* is his?" Nalithor nudged me gently, his tone indicating he'd asked several times.

"Yes," I answered, terse, as I watched several shards of light drop from Nalithor's hands. *'Tch he left the bastard alive? I should skin—'*

"You *know* the weapon can't harm me, I'm—"

"He wasn't aiming for yours. He wanted the other one."

"The other...?" Nalithor gripped my shoulder and pulled me into a sitting position. "What do you mean the *other one*? How did you know—"

"I can see the magic from—" I cut myself off with a shriek when Nalithor pulled another shard from my back. I devolved into a slew of curses all over again, feeling blood trickling down my back.

"You were saying that you can see the magic of both hearts?" Nalithor asked while shadows drifted upward from my clenched hands. "For how long?"

Growling, I engulfed the shards of light with darkness and snuffed them out. They crunched like glass before disappearing altogether. Satisfied, I answered Nalithor, "Since now. Their glow is bright enough for me to make out the shapes and their elements. I assume that— *Fucking son of a—*"

Nalithor sighed as I doubled over coughing again. He rested his palm on my back and stroked me carefully while waiting for me to finish. I shot a glare off to my left when I heard maniacal, but pained, laughter. The Angel bastard was pinned to a tree with several of Nalithor's weapons piercing his broken and battered wings.

"Oh no you don't. You've already overexerted yourself by using magic when I told you not to." Nalithor's tail coiled around my waist when I moved to tear the Angel apart. "I had to kill the other ones in order to stop your fight. That leaves me with only *him* to question. You can kill him *after* I'm done with him—if he survives."

"If he…?" I turned to question Nalithor but trailed off when I saw the anger in his eyes.

The Adinvyr's tail snapped sideways and slammed into the branch when his gaze drifted down to my bloodied mouth, and then to where my blood had stained the branch black. A pulse of unhindered power rippled outward from Nalithor when he shot the laughing Angel a murderous look. Nalithor's Brands rippled and grew brighter while his aura threatened to overwhelm the feeling of everything else nearby.

"Stay here." Nalithor growled, grabbing my face in both hands. He planted a firm kiss on my mouth before abruptly releasing me.

He leapt from the tree and toward the Angel. An opaque orb of darkness erupted around me when I moved to watch the enraged deity. I placed my hands against the shadows and then sighed—it was solid and reverberated with more magic than I could hope to break through. Nalithor's darkness stuck to my palms when I pulled away from the shell, sliding over the Brands on the back of my hands for a few moments before returning to the barrier.

Pouting, I crossed my arms and drilled my fingers against my right arm. This was hardly a show or entertainment. Nalithor's darkness was so thick that it blocked out *everything* beyond it—sights, sounds, smells, and other power. Switching to magical vision was pointless, but it didn't take long for me to grow impatient. I began feeling around in search of gaps or weak points in the barrier so that I could slip free. I had a morbid fascination with watching Nalithor work, and I intended to indulge in it one way or another.

This time, Nalithor's darkness was *not* calming or arousing by nature. I could feel the anger and hatred that he channeled toward the Angel somewhere beyond the barrier, and had to wonder if the Adinvyr knew that I found that attractive as well—albeit in a different manner. Try as I might, no word strong enough for his rage came to my mind. Hells, I wasn't even certain what had pushed him to such a point.

I was like a leaf, and he was a maelstrom.

"Of course you tried to escape." Nalithor sighed, his dark barrier dropping to the branch around me like liquid to reveal that I'd been crawling around in my search. I looked up at him, sheepish, to discover a sad expression on his face. "Am I that frightening?"

"Frightening?" I asked, disbelieving. "No, you're not scary. You didn't have to seal off sounds and smells too, you know! It's really disorienting when I can't— You're covered in blood. Why is their blood *gold*, anyway? Don't the others have red blood?"

I rose to my feet and glanced around to find that the Angel was in much worse shape than before. His body was so broken that, for a moment, I thought Nalithor had killed him after all. However, the shallow rise and fall of his chest revealed otherwise. A shiver ran down my spine. *'Mmm, I want to watch Nalithor execute this bastard.'*

"You can wait to kill him," Nalithor stated, backing me into a tree. His firm gaze made me bristle. "They're here to bind this forest's Lari'xan, slay me, and slay *you*. He called Xiinsha an *Elder*. Something you need to explain to me, Arianna?"

"I can't." I pursed my lips as he braced an arm above my head. His other hand came up to grip my chin. "It's best if—"

"I don't like secrets." Nalithor growled, lifting my face toward his.

"Would you rather be Exiled instead?" I countered, reaching up to grip his wrist. "Just as you have something *you* can't talk about, I can't—"

"You're both false gods anyway!" The Angel spat. "Who gives a damn if either of you is Exiled?! You should be executed instead!"

Before I could retort, Nalithor vanished and then reappeared in front of the Angel. The angered Adinvyr slammed his fist through the bastard's head, shattering his skull and leaving a hole in the tree. Nalithor shook the gore from his arm before turning to look at me with his fiery gaze.

"You believe I will be Exiled if you share your information with me?"

I crossed my arms, watching him leap back to my branch. "I *know* you will."

"What if I 'acquire' the information from you?" Nalithor tapped one of my temples lightly. Anger flashed in his eyes again when he glanced down to my bloodied lips.

"And if the Elders decide to poke around inside *your* head?" I countered, prodding his blood-coated pecs with one finger. "*How* you learn of it doesn't matter. Learning about it at all will get you Exiled— simple as that."

"According to who?" Nalithor caught my hand by the wrist and pulled it away from his chest.

"Djialkan, Ceilail, and—"

"Djialkan wouldn't trust the ones who created him?" Nalithor frowned, searching my face.

"They offered to 'replace' me as his ward, didn't they?" I pointed out, watching as Nalithor bared his fangs and growled. "That would require killing—"

"I won't allow it." Nalithor snarled and pulled me into his chest. "You don't want me to be Exiled... I can understand that. However, keeping secrets—"

"*She is in a position to look into matters that you cannot.*" A male voice snorted. "*If you would force her to tell you, despite the risks, you are a fool undeserving of your title.*"

"Xiinsha." Nalithor growled, a twitch running through him when he turned to glare at the fiery male. "What in the hells is going on?"

*"He truly seems eager to become an Exile like those that he* should *be hunting, does he not?"* Xiinsha looked toward me, his eyes flicking down my bloodied form. *"Cease your growling, Adinvyr. Honestly, you are always such a headache when you show up.*

*"Even so, I will echo Ceilail on this matter. Drop your inquiries, Nalithor. If you become an Exiled God, this woman, whom you desire so fervently, will have no one to turn to. It would be a death sentence for the both of you."*

"If it's so dangerous for *me*, how can it be any safer for her?!" Nalithor rounded on Xiinsha, his face twisted with fury. "The Elders—"

*"Are fools that you cannot trust,"* Xiinsha replied with a dismissive wave of his hand. *"Arianna is not a goddess. Therefore, she is in a unique position to deal with certain matters for Ceilail, Sihix, and I. However, she cannot disclose such information to you until she knows more...and you have grown stronger."*

"You're *using* her?" Nalithor snarled, pulling me into a possessive embrace. "Why should I let—"

*"We are 'using' her to fulfill a role of Balance that you cannot,"* Xiinsha stated flatly. *"Until she and Djialkan have finished their investigations it is not safe for you to know of it. Arianna will bring the matter to your attention when it is time.*

*"Correct, Arianna?"*

"That's the plan..." I grumbled into Nalithor's chest as he

tightened his grip on me. "Nalithor, the Angel blood—"

"You will tell me the *moment* you are able?" Nalithor demanded, lifting me off my feet so that our eyes were level. "You have only been hiding it to protect me—and my position?"

"Yes, and yes." I pouted as he studied me. "I don't *like* hiding things! Especially not from my partner. I'll understand if you don't want me to *be* your partner anymore, but...we both have something to hide from the other. Both for protective reasons. I would hope that you can understand."

*"Are the two of you going to stand here all day, or are you going to go deal with the other intruders in my forest?!"* Xiinsha snapped. *"I refuse to deal with them by accepting them into my territory. Get rid of them."*

"That one is as pleasant as ever..." Nalithor muttered, watching as the fiery Lari'xan disappeared into the trees.

"Nalithor..." I trailed off when Nalithor set me down and walked away from me to pick up the discarded *Godslayer*.

"That bastard knew you feared light." Nalithor's voice was little more than a growl. He spun the sword a few times before incinerating it. "That's why he tried to poison you with it. Taint you. And then *kill—*"

He interrupted himself and slammed his fist into the trunk of a tree, his tail whipping back and forth. Palpable fury rose within the Adinvyr again, radiating around him while he muttered curses and continued to growl. When I didn't say anything, he turned to look at me. His expression softened, a little, when he saw my uneasy shifting.

345

"Does it still hurt?" Nalithor closed the distance between us.

"No…" I mumbled, looking away from him. "Whatever it was, I think you got it all."

"No more coughing up blood?" He brought his hand up to my face and stroked my cheek.

"No." I shook my head. "If…if you can't trust me to be your—"

"I believe you, Arianna." Nalithor sighed. "I still refuse to let anyone else be your partner, I refuse to let anyone touch you or harm you. I'm considering beating that corpse a few more times for what he did to you. I'm also considering eviscerating all the Lari'xan so that you belong only to—"

Nalithor cut himself off and looked away from me, his face gaining a hint of pink.

*'He…wants me to himself that badly?'* I blinked at him.

"Loathe as I am to admit it, Xiinsha is right. We should get to work." Nalithor sighed, shifting his hand to wipe the blood from my mouth. "Since I executed the Angel you're still—"

"I'm not cross because of that." I shot him a look. "Locking me in your darkness wasn't necessary. I couldn't see, hear, smell, or sense anything!"

"That was the point," Nalithor replied dryly, tapping my nose. "Overhearing my questions or seeing my methods could present us with problems with the Elder Gods. I was questioning the bastard as the God of Balance, not as General Vraelimir of the Vorpmasian Empire."

"Fine." I released a heavy sigh. "I don't feel like arguing about it. At least leave me some of the slavers to kill?"

"Perhaps..." Nalithor murmured, a smile stretched across his face. He pinned me back against the tree, a devious glint in his eyes. "Tell me, my dear, just what is that *exquisite* desire I see in your eyes? You should have been frightened, and yet you're looking at me like *that*..."

"You were supposed to *entertain* me," I reminded him after a moment of hesitation, feeling myself growing hot with embarrassment. "I...wanted to see you 'work'. I wanted to see you execute that bastard—"

"To be fair, you *did* get to see me kill him," Nalithor interjected, pressing his thumb over my lips to shush me. "Did I not *satisfy* you, *Your Highness?*"

"You killed him too fast." I bristled when he chuckled at me. "I wanted to see you take your time, make him suffer, make him—"

Nalithor cut me off with a deep kiss, his hand drifting down to rest around my throat. When he withdrew, he settled a self-satisfied smirk on me.

"Let's see how quickly we can finish hunting our prey—preferably *before* you run off to tear into them without me." Nalithor's hand fell away from my throat. He smiled and offered it to me instead, though his eyes betrayed his mixed desires. "We still have much to attend to before returning to Draemir and, the longer we stay, the more likely we are to attract more Angels.

"I'll try to make certain you don't grow bored this time. If all else fails… Mmm, I believe I may have a few solutions for when we return…"

"A few more…?" I shook my head hard, earning a chuckle. "Killing first, teasing later."

Nalithor and I set off through the forest in search of the slavers I had sensed earlier, and it didn't take long for us to find the first group. We tore into them with mutual glee. I struggled to keep myself from tearing them apart with magic. I wanted to ruin their corpses and leave nothing behind but scraps. Alas, Nalithor was insistent that I shouldn't use magic unless we found ourselves in an emergency again—and it didn't seem wise to go against his wishes.

"Bah! That tasted terrible!" I whined, spitting out a mouthful of blood before kicking aside the corpse of a scarred Devillian.

"Oh? Is the blood of an Adinvyr not to your liking, *Your Highness?*" Nalithor teased, tugging at my curls briefly before leaning down to nuzzle my cheek. "You seemed like you rather enjoyed it when I gave you a taste of *mine.*"

"*His* is bitter." I pointed down at the dead Adinvyr. "And I didn't *want* a taste anyway! It's not my fault he bled everywhere when I… Okay, maybe it *is* my fault that he bled everywhere. But—"

"Adorable." Nalithor planted a kiss on my cheek and then stood tall once more. "Let's move on to the next group. After, we can check the situation at the edge of the Draemir Barrier."

"Not adorable," I grumble while following him. "We need to figure out what to do about the beasts. They're catching up."

"They'll be a simple matter once we lure them from the forest." Nalithor shot me a grin over his shoulder. "Once we lure them out into the open, I can take care of them, and give you the show that you so desperately crave."

I shifted my vision and examined the glow of our hearts within Nalithor's chest while I chased him through the forest. Tendrils of power still stretched from my heart and to me, seeming unbreakable even while we ran. I struggled to believe that someone as powerful as Nalithor hadn't noticed the behavior—especially when his own power seemed to be growing.

*'If he's figured out who I am, then why hasn't he said anything?'* I wondered, allowing my vision to shift back to normal. My gaze trailed down Nalithor's back and to his buttocks. *'Humph, at least his ass looks good in that armor. Following him certainly has its perks.'*

"The false gods are here!" A lookout cried as we rushed toward his camp. "Capture them!"

*'Leave one alive for questioning,'* Nalithor spoke, leaping into the air to decapitate the lookout. *'I want to know what this "false god" nonsense is about—and what it has to do with slavers.'*

*'Fine...'* I nodded, darting into the camp with my blades drawn. *'I think the other caravan fled. I don't sense them in Xiinsha anymore.'*

I tore through the nearest Elf and spilled his organs onto the forest floor, leaping for the next before the corpse had finished falling. Several more fell before one finally managed to nick me. I grimaced when I felt blood trickling down my upper arm. The slavers weren't as skilled in combat as I would have liked, but it seemed as though I was more weakened than I'd wanted to believe. I likely wouldn't have been able to deal with more skilled men.

*'What's to blame—Nalithor's feedings, the mysterious poison he mentioned, or that damned Angel?'* I pondered it as I slew the offending slaver. Shaking my head, I pivoted to search for more prey. My thirst for combat still wasn't satisfied.

"You should have left that one for me." Nalithor huffed as he dragged another slaver across the encampment and towards me. "I'm certain that I could have found a fitting punishment for him."

"It's not his fault that my reaction times are slow right now." I tilted my head, glancing between the terrified slaver and my alluring companion. "The stupid flappy one is to blame for that."

"You brought a *woman* with you, too?" The slaver snorted. "Looking like that… She'd fetch almost as a high of a price as we'd get for you! More if she's the fake goddess whore—"

Nalithor struck the slaver across the mouth, stunning him into silence. I bit back an amused smirk and watched as the twitching of Nalithor's tail grew more and more agitated.

"Who would be stupid enough to purchase a *deity?*" Nalithor arched an eyebrow, his voice deadly calm.

"There's plenty of clients who would be happy to own a *fake* god!" The delirious man cackled. "Our client believes slavery is the fitting punishment for filth like—"

"Tch, the arrogance." Nalithor sighed, tossing the man aside. In the same motion, the slaver burst into blue-white flames.

"Aw, where's the flair?" I teased as Nalithor strode toward me. "That would have been an *excellent* opportunity to begin your show for me."

"This is partially my fault as well, isn't it?" Nalithor spoke softly, placing a hand over my bleeding wound. His eyes searched for others, but there were none. "I *did* take too much, didn't I?"

"I'm fine," I replied with a small smile. "Even if it was too much, it was necessary. *I* don't think it was too much, but I'm not exactly an expert on the matter."

"We're lucky that you recover so quickly," Nalithor stated. He removed his hand from my now-healed wound and brought his fingers to his lips. I noticed a small shiver run through him when he lapped my blood from his fingers. "Come, we should leave before Xiinsha decides to throw us out himself.

"When we get back to Draemir I want to examine your back. I want to make certain that I removed all of that bastard's magic."

# CHAPTER FIFTEEN
## *Temptation*

I sat with my back against the trunk of a tree and sipped from a waterskin while I watched Nalithor tear through beast after beast. He had been insistent that he didn't need my help—that I should rest and let him do all the work—and it stung a little. Nalithor felt responsible for my weakened state and wanted to keep me out of harm's way. Although I appreciated his concern, I wanted to help anyway. I wasn't yet satisfied with our hunt.

*'Though I do have a nice view of his ass from up here...'* I tapped one of my feet in the air while examining the Adinvyr below. *'It's been at least, what, two hours already? Just how many of the damned things did they send after him?'*

The grassy field below me was strewn with corpses and stained with their foul blood. However, Nalithor was all I could bring myself to focus on. His graceful yet deadly movements, the glint of his spear before tearing into a beast's flesh, and that broad boyish grin that adorned his face. Even though the monstrosities were far too weak to provide the deity with a challenge, it was clear that Nalithor was in his element.

It struck me as strange how they continued to adapt and adopt new strategies against Nalithor. I had never witnessed such intelligent Chaos Beasts before, nor ones that communicated so "openly" with each other. Despite their apparent intelligence, they stood no chance.

*'They haven't even* begun *to tire him yet.'* I pursed my lips while looking between the happy Adinvyr and the snarling beasts. *'I doubt the Exiled Gods would create "useless" creatures, let alone send them after a stronger target. So, what is their real purpose? Are they meant to challenge mortals to grow, or are they there to distract deities from whatever it is the Exiles are up to?'*

My eyes snapped back to Nalithor when a gleam of moonslight reflected off his spear. The weapon still had wisps of darkness coiled around it and, every now and then, those wisps reached for me. I had begun to suspect that there was something more to it than his weapon just "liking" me—even the darkness of his aura reached for me on occasion.

I gnawed absentmindedly on the mouth of the waterskin while I watched Nalithor's unending fight. Even though I found his typical Draemiran attire rather alluring, his armor was also quite a treat.

Unlike his usual wardrobe of loose and airy garments, his armor hugged his muscular body like a glove. His current set consisted of leather with plates of armor sewn into strategic locations. It accentuated his long legs and round ass quite nicely.

Of course, his upper half was quite nice too.

*'Hmmm, I quite like his tail as well.'* I decided while examining the glinting veins of platinum amongst his tail's otherwise obsidian scales. *'Tch. How much longer until he runs out of beasts? As much as I enjoy the excuse to stare at him…we can't stay here all day.'*

I sighed and shifted my attention away from Nalithor to survey our surroundings. From my perch, I could make out the sands of Suthsul to our south and the orange glow of the horizon beyond. The treetops obscured any trace of the trail of destruction I had found several days prior, and I couldn't seem to find the slave caravan that had escaped our grasp either.

"Am I not putting on a good enough show for you, Arianna?" Nalithor teased.

"You can only entertain me for so long when you're not being challenged," I called down in reply, shifting to a more comfortable position. "I'm long past bored. Are you sure I can't kill a few myself?"

"It wouldn't be so bad if they at least attacked at once." Nalithor chuckled while spinning his spear through the umpteenth beast. "There shouldn't be *that* many left to kill. I'm sure you can be patient and watch me some more."

Nalithor shot me a knowing smirk and turned, flourishing his tail.

The corner of my eye twitched in irritation even as I watched him leap into the fray once more. I wanted to kill things too. I wanted to help. Studying his lithe form could only provide me with so much entertainment—when he had his clothes on, at least.

*'He's so distracting…'* I sighed and moved to my feet, dismissing my waterskin into a shrizar. Busying myself seemed like a needed course of action.

I shifted my attention away from Nalithor and refocused on the magic surrounding us. Now that we were away from the Xiinsha Forest the glow of magic was dimmer and less concentrated. Beasts were still closing in from all around us, but their numbers had thinned.

It wouldn't be long before the last ones arrived, and I couldn't spot any subsequent packs beyond the stragglers.

When I looked to the delighted deity again, I pursed my lips. Darkness, blue-white fire, ice, earth, and black lightning swirled around his form. Over the past several hours his strength had increased instead of lessening. Both hearts within his chest glowed with brighter magic now and seemed as if they had begun feeding each other instead of the one-sided taking mine had been doing.

I shook my head and let my vision return to normal. Even if the elemental cacophony that was his aura wasn't visible to the naked eye, his opponents could certainly sense it. As could I.

My gaze traveled down Nalithor's shoulders and back, and I found myself cursing the armored jacket he wore. It obscured his pale skin and muscles from view. I found myself wishing I could see through it.

Or strip it off him myself. Either would have worked—I was quite bored.

He'd made it quite obvious that he knew I was watching him—perhaps a little *too* closely—but I didn't care anymore. I needed to keep myself entertained, and he was amazing to look at. Maybe, if I lavished him with enough attention, he'd finally get the hint that I enjoyed his advances.

Once the beasts appeared to be defeated Nalithor leapt up to my perch and dismissed his weaponry. A confident smirk stretched across his face as he examined me, his tail swishing behind him a few times. He looked like he was thinking about something, and I wasn't quite sure if I wanted to know the specifics.

"You're something else," Nalithor remarked, taking a few steps toward me. "How am I meant to focus on the hunt when you're watching me so…*intimately?*"

"Are you complaining?" I crossed my arms and settled a defiant glare on him when he came to a stop in front of me.

"What did I do to 'earn' such thorough attention?" Nalithor tilted his head and let his gaze trail down my bloodied form. "Were you that bored?"

"Why can't it just be that you're nice to look at?" I countered dryly. "Besides, you *exist*. Isn't that enough of a reason to look at you?"

"Perhaps…but not with a gaze like *that*," Nalithor replied, bracing his forearm against the tree trunk above my head. "I'm flattered by your attentions, of course. I'm simply concerned that you seem a little… 'hungry.'

"Are there more beasts coming?"

"Not in my range of vision, no," I answered with a small shake of my head. "We should be fine to continue making our way to the barrier. There's— What? What's that look—"

Nalithor released a devious chuckle and leaned down to plant a kiss on my lips. He seemed hesitant to withdraw but, before I could react, he made up his mind. After straightening to his full height, he smiled down at me and tugged at my curls.

"I've decided that I don't want to wait until we return to Draemir to reexamine your back," Nalithor informed me, pulling me away from the tree's trunk. "Let's get some of this blood off of you so that I can look."

"You're still worried about that?" I arched an eyebrow at him when he hoisted me up and then leapt out of the tree.

"Of course I am," Nalithor answered, setting me down on my feet. "We need to keep each other safe, do we not? I want to make certain that I destroyed every scrap of the light that bastard tried to infect you with."

I sighed and chose to oblige him. Several minutes passed in silence while Nalithor led me through the forest and toward a series of rivers and streams that flowed through both Xiinsha and Draemir. Once we reached the base of one of the many waterfalls in the area, Nalithor pulled off his armored jacket and draped it over a low branch.

"I'll have to wash off the blood so that I can see what I'm doing."

Nalithor tapped my spine as he passed me and moved to the water's edge.

'*What a pain.*' I perched near the basin and watched Nalithor as he soaked a cloth prior to wringing it out.

"Do you...truly believe that I'm too weak to be let in on this 'matter' you're investigating?" Nalithor asked, coming to stand behind me. "Ah... You will need to remove your armor. Your jewelry shouldn't get in the way much."

"Whether or not you're strong enough isn't the problem!" I huffed while pulling both my armor and undershirt off. Once off, I clutched them over my bare chest. "I just don't want to get you Exiled. I don't like secrets either, but sometimes that's the only way to keep someone safe, isn't it?"

"Even if the Elders choose to Exile me, I would still deal with X'shmir for you." Nalithor sighed as he moved my hair out of his way. "So, you don't need to worry about—"

"To the hells with X'shmir!" I turned to shoot him an indignant glare. "I'm not worried about whether or not you will conquer them. That's absurd! What I'm concerned about is *you*.

"If those bastards Exile you, we won't be able to see, speak, spar, or work with each other anymore! Exiled Gods are cut off from everyone aside from each other, right?"

"You're..." Nalithor flushed and glanced away from me when I leaned toward him. "The Exiled Gods *do* have mortal followers and 'Chosen,' as normal deities do."

"Oh, and where are they?" I demanded pointedly. "Hunting down the Exiled Gods is supposed to be one of your primary duties, isn't it? The easiest way to get to your prey would be to capture and 'interrogate' one of those mortals. How long would one of them last?"

"Not…for long," Nalithor muttered, his gaze flicking back to me. "Even so, shouldn't I be concerned about your goals? If the Elders would go as far as to *Exile* me over your information, it can't be something good."

"They also haven't made a move against me, and *you* aren't drawn to kill me like the other 'problems' that show up," I countered with a slight pout.

"Yet you won't let me help you." Nalithor sighed and set the damp rag aside before lifting his hands to my face, his expression pained. "You're letting the Lari'xan *use* you. I don't like it. Wouldn't…wouldn't your task be at least a *little* simpler with my assistance?"

"No, because then you'd be Exiled," I reiterated, exasperated. "It's more complicated than 'oh, Ari-mrii, the Lari'xan are using you!'" A small smile tugged at Nalithor's lips when I failed to mimic his accent. "Djialkan and I are *both* wary of the situation. He's looking into related matters for me so that we have a better foothold moving forward. We have to know who we can trust, and who is telling the truth—he's finding those things out for me."

"You should just let me help you," Nalithor stated, stroking my cheek with his thumb. "I can be quite stealthy, you know. I'm—"

"I'm not willing to risk the Elders looking in your head!" I leaned farther forward and gave him the firmest look I could muster. "If they look in your head and take you away from me because of what they see there, my focus will change to taking out *them* instead of—"

My eyes widened when Nalithor pulled me fully against his chest and kissed me. The passion I sensed from him was *not* what I expected, causing me to nearly drop my clothing in surprise. It wasn't long before his kiss swept me away and I found myself kissing him back as he attempted to pull me ever closer.

After several long moments, he withdrew just enough to speak.

"Promise me that you will fill me in the *moment* you are able." Nalithor's voice was low as he searched my face. "Or if you run into 'trouble.' I refuse to lose you to the Elder *scum*—" he shut his eyes for a moment and took a deep breath to calm himself before continuing, "They took everything from me once before. I *will not* allow it to happen again."

"I promise." I nodded subtly. "Even if the Old Ways rear their ugly head and try to prevent it, I'll make sure Djialkan and Alala know to do it for me. I—"

Nalithor silenced me with another brief kiss. He pulled away with a smile on his face and chuckled. "Here, let's get you taken care of before I decide to kiss you again."

I obliged him and adjusted myself so that my back was to him once more, my pulse racing. At this point, I was so hot that I wondered if I was flushed from head to toe. I had surprised myself with my statement, but it was true—if the Elders tried to take Nalithor away from me, I would kill them. All of them.

*'I can't pretend to be surprised by his hatred of the Elders, either.'* I flinched a little when Nalithor lifted the damp cloth to my back. "That's *cold!*"

"Now you understand why I didn't suggest we bathe here." Nalithor chuckled while carefully washing the blood and grime from my back. "Do your best to sit still. I'll try to make this quick."

Sighing, I focused my attention forward and stared at the dark scenery before me. Nalithor's hands dancing along my back was incredibly soothing, causing me to zone out while I waited for him to finish searching for remnants of foul magics...or to at least speak.

Warmth radiated from his hands and through my skin as he traced my back. Magic seeped from his fingers while he searched. He seemed as though he was trying very hard to not graze me with his claws—I even felt him flinch a few times when they touched lightly against my skin.

*'He really can be quite cute sometimes,'* I mused, the warmth of his magic threatening to lull me to sleep. *'Bah... Maybe we* should *have stayed in his domain for a few more days. I'm sleepy.'*

"Ahhh... That's a relief." Nalithor sighed, startling me when he rubbed his cheek between my shoulder blades. "No remnants of that bastard's magic on you... How are you feeling?"

"A little tired," I replied, shivering when the Adinvyr trailed kisses down my spine. "You're very...affectionate, after we've been out hunting."

"I won't hunt with just anyone." Nalithor purred into my back, one of his arms hooking around my waist. "Adinvyr desire hunting and combat prowess, bloodlust, power, passion, loyalty, and camaraderie from their potential...mates. You display all those traits in splendid fashion. It's difficult to *not* be drawn in by you."

"Passion?" I arched an eyebrow when Nalithor nodded into my back. "What—"

"I understand if it makes you uncomfortable," Nalithor interjected, planting one last kiss on the back of my shoulder before releasing me. "It isn't easy to remember that we have been raised in very different environments. The desires and interests of Adinvyr are, admittedly, vastly different from those of Humans."

"It doesn't bother me." I glanced over my shoulder at him before pulling my clothing back on. "It's much better than the X'shmiran way of money and rank.

"Though, I'm not sure if I would refer to myself as 'passionate.' There are a few too many things you could mean by the word."

"You're passionate when you hunt." Nalithor chuckled, looking down at me with a mischievous twinkle in his eyes. "You're passionate when you dispatch of non-beast threats, and when it comes to protecting your brother. You were passionate when we kissed, when I fed from you, and when we spar.

"You're passionate when it comes to protecting *me*, apparently... Which is a whole other level of endearment to my kind, you should know."

"You're leaving very little room to argue." I shook my head while fastening my vambraces back into place.

"That's because you're not supposed to argue when someone pays you a compliment!" Nalithor grinned and ruffled my hair. "Since I'm always forgetting that you are new to our culture, let's make a deal. If you are unsure of—or curious—about something, just *ask* me. You can ask me anything. In turn, I can ask you anything. Does that seem fair?"

"Anything?" I tilted my head as he stroked my curls.

"Anything."

"You *do* realize that I've now forgotten *every* question I've ever considered asking you, right?"

"You'll remember eventually." Nalithor laughed. "Are you ready? If we hurry, we should be able to take a proper bath before worrying about dinner."

"Even if we help each other I'm not sure how we're going to get all of this off." I grimaced, nudging at one of my blood-caked curls before moving to follow Nalithor. *'Wha… He's blushing again?'*

"Before I forget, again," I paused to reach into my shrizar and withdrew a strip of platinum chain, "part of your jewelry broke during your skirmish by the Draemir Barrier. I found this around the time I found your spear."

"Ahhh, so the vixen *does* find and hoard shiny things?" Nalithor teased, taking the broken chain from me. "Aurelian will be quite cross that one of his creations was damaged. Hopefully, he can determine the 'why' and 'how' of the matter quickly."

"Next time you'll have me to watch your back." I nudged him in the ribs, grinning when his face reddened, and he sighed at me. "What? Now that I know being protected by someone isn't a problem, I don't need to be so hesitant about voicing it. Were you X'shmiran, not only would you be furious about someone wanting to protect you, you would be steaming mad that it was a *woman*."

"X'shmirans aren't known for making much sense." Nalithor huffed, his tail snapping behind him while his face continued to redden. "You shouldn't tease me."

"You tease me all the time."

"That is different."

"It really isn't." I laughed. "You're—"

Nalithor picked me up by my waist and slung me over his shoulder, but his rumbling chuckle and the swishing of his tail gave away his amusement. He placed one hand over my ass and gave it a firm squeeze before beginning to walk again.

"You're making it more and more likely that I will simply take you back to my domain." Nalithor informed me. "Be a good girl and search for traces of Angels while we travel, won't you? The less time we spend by the barrier, the better."

*'He gets flustered by someone wanting to protect him?'* I wondered with a small smile, shifting my vision to comply. *'It must hold special meaning or importance to him.'*

"Hmmm? What's that smell…" I mumbled, lifting my head to

look around.

"P-p-ple-please forgive me, Lord Balance!" A young male voice yelped, accompanied by the beating of wings. "I know these are Devillian lands, but—"

"Explain yourself," Nalithor ordered as he set me down. His grip tightened around my waist when I pivoted to look at the young Angel. "After the past few days, you would be lucky if neither of us—"

"Queen Gabriel sent me to find the traitors!" The Angel boy yelped, dropping to his knees. He touched his head to the ground and drew his quivering grey wings tight against his back. "They poisoned the nobles of Leryci while court was in session! Gabriel has been trying to save her subjects for *days*."

*'Don't kill him.'* Nalithor gave me a sharp squeeze and coiled his tail over my hips. "What's your name, boy?"

"I-Iltaery, Lord Balance!" The boy whimpered, his shaking worsening. "Th-that's the blood of a noble on your armor, is it not? P-please don't kill—"

"Arianna, be a dear and *gently* show the boy what happened in Xiinsha." Nalithor nudged me, giving me a look that was likely meant to discourage me from taking the boy's head.

"A-Arianna? As in—" Iltaery's eyes went wide when he lifted his head and looked up at me. His hazel eyes fastened on the Brands of Divinity that encircled my throat. "Y-y-y-you have Brands like Queen G-Gabriel and…"

"You…want me to be gentle with him?" I mumbled, shifting my

gaze from the Angel and to Nalithor, finding an oddly sad smile situated on my companion's face. "But he's—"

"Y-y-you're Arianna Jade Shujare, right?!" The boy exclaimed, making me flinch and shoot him another look. "Daughter of Lucifer Shujare and Gabriel Xodit, twin sister of the Holy Prince, Darius Raisur Shujare. Heiress to—"

*'Daughter of Lucifer and...who?'* I stared at Iltaery, my pulse leaping into my throat.

"Former heiress to the Dauthrmiran throne and the opposite of Darius, who was heir to the Leryci throne," Nalithor injected, stopping the Angel's rambling. He pulled me closer to his chest and ran a hand down my back as if to soothe me. "Calm down, Arianna. We can discuss it later—either before or *after* I skin Djialkan for not telling you. For now... Iltaery needs to learn of what the traitors did in our lands."

I opened my mouth to speak and then let out a heavy sigh instead. My heart pounded in my ears, and a slight tremble had entered my limbs. I clenched and unclenched my shaking hands a few times before shifting my gaze to the wide-eyed Angel boy. For some reason, he was staring up at me with reverence instead of fear.

He didn't smell or feel wrong like most other Angels I'd met...but he had a big mouth.

"I-I'm sorry, Princess, did I say something I shouldn't have?" Iltaery turned to face me fully, still on his knees, as his eyes teared up.

"It's fine, I've known for quite some time." Nalithor placed a hand on top of my head and smiled at me for a moment before shifting to look down at the frightened boy. "However, Iltaery, you *must* keep her existence quiet. For now. You may tell Gabriel about the twins, but only if you can do so *without* being overheard. No one else may know. Not yet."

"I-is that an order as the God of Balance?" Iltaery whimpered, looking to the Adinvyr for confirmation. Nalithor simply nodded. "I-I understand, my lord. I'll k-keep quiet."

*'Arianna, calm down,'* Nalithor reiterated, giving me a comforting squeeze before releasing me. *'Show the boy what he needs to know about the Angels we faced. The sooner he leaves Vorpmasian lands, the better. He may be a child, but the other generals will not be so merciful to him.'*

*'How…long have you know?'* I grumbled before crouching down in front of the awestruck Angel and lifting my fingers to his temples.

*'No two people smell alike. It wasn't exactly difficult to tell,'* Nalithor replied dryly as I eased memories of the past few days into the Angel's mind. *'Accepting it was more difficult than figuring it out. For quite some time I was concerned—perhaps even convinced—that you might have been a fake created by the Exiled Gods. However, you haven't changed as much as you may think. You've left little room for doubting your identity. However, I do wonder why you and Djialkan both decided not to tell me outright.'*

"M-may I go now? T-those men were…" Iltaery gulped when I moved my fingers away from his temples. "The queen needs to know of this immediately!"

"You had best go straight to her then." Nalithor nodded to the boy, tracking the child's movements when he bowed to us both. "Inform Gabriel that I may require her assistance with Darius. His new 'home' has not been good to him."

Iltaery nodded his head several times in rapid succession and then took off through the trees, his petite grey wings stretched wide behind him. Before I could turn to address Nalithor, he pulled me back against him and hugged me tight.

"I'm just glad you're *alive*, Arianna." Nalithor sighed into my shoulder. "That…is good enough for me."

"How long…" I trailed off when Nalithor nuzzled me and tensed his grip.

"It wasn't until recently that you made it so undeniably clear who you are. However, I had already decided to make you mine *before* I realized that you're truly…you." Nalithor rubbed his cheek against my neck before continuing, "Why didn't you or Djialkan tell me?"

"Who I was in the past shouldn't matter…" I grumbled, wringing my hands together while I struggled to find the words to explain myself. "Without my memories, I'm not the same person I used to be, right? But I have new memories now, so I'm different. Ceilail… Ceilail offered to restore my memories, but—"

"But?" Nalithor prompted, turning me to face him. "I doubt you would have been so foolish as to deny such an offer!"

"If I had accepted, I would have lost all the memories and knowledge I've gained since being taken from Dauthrmir." I shot

Nalithor a firm look as he stared down at me. "I wouldn't remember why X'shmir needs to be punished; I wouldn't remember the things I've learned about magic, beasts, or combat. I certainly wouldn't remember any of our interactions from the past few months. Does that seem like a fair exchange to you?"

"That is a *terrible* deal..." Nalithor relented, a small sigh escaping him as he studied me. "One at the cost of the other isn't fair at all. I want you to remember our past...but not at the expense of everything else."

"I'll just have to get to know you again, right?" I tugged at the hem of his armored jacket, a small smile on my face. "As for Djialkan, he's told me almost nothing about the past. It's frustrating, but I'm sure he has his reasons. We should really get going though, shouldn't we? That boy delayed—"

"Yes. We can discuss this later." Nalithor pulled me into a firm hug again and nuzzled the top of my head. "We need to keep your identity quiet for now, but..."

"You're glad that you don't have to hide the fact you know, and I don't need to hide it from you?" I offered as he squeezed me harder.

"That sounded needlessly complicated." Nalithor chuckled, releasing me so that he could examine me with bright eyes. "Shall I carry you again? You are quite tiny after all."

"I can *walk*." I prodded him in the chest.

"Can you walk *and* search for traces of magic at the same time?" Nalithor smirked when I faltered.

"You're just *looking* for an excuse to carry me!" I prodded him again, this time while pouting. Perhaps if I was 'cute' I'd get my way. "I'm not *that* weakened. You don't have to—"

Nalithor grinned and scooped me into his arms despite my protests. As soon as he was satisfied that I was secure in his arms he burst into a sprint through the forest, his vigor renewed. It seemed as if a weight had been lifted from his shoulders…and I would have been lying if I claimed I didn't feel the same way.

Several hours later, Nalithor and I found ourselves strolling through Draemir's streets at a leisurely pace. The excited citizens called greetings to their returning prince but kept their distance—the amount of blood we were covered in shocked even Devillians.

Our visit to the Draemir Barrier had been short. Upon arrival, we had found that soldiers and scholars from various parts of Vorpmasia had already arrived and begun their work. After briefing the soldiers on what had transpired, Nalithor's temper had risen again. The soldiers urged us to return to Draemir so that we could rest, and the angry deity seemed eager to do so.

It had taken him half of the several-hour walk to calm down. He seemed most livid about the Angel I had fought but any attempt Nalithor made to discuss it devolved into cursing and tail thrashing.

We didn't run into any more Angels, friendly or otherwise, the rest of the way to Draemir. However, we did find several stragglers from a slave caravan. They didn't last long. *'At least he's fun to watch even when the bastards are too easy to kill.'*

"We are *covered* in blood," I commented, cozying up tighter against Nalithor's side while taking note of the stares that the tourists, and even a few Devillians, shot our way.

"It suits you." Nalithor teased, sliding his hand from my waist and down to my hip. "Perhaps we overdid it a little?"

"There were a *lot* of things to kill," I pointed out with a small smile, shooting him a sideways glance. "What makes *this* blood more worthy than what I've been covered in before, hmmm?"

"It all depends on whether or not I have the honor of washing it off of you," Nalithor replied innocently.

I laughed as he pulled me into the palace and along a series of corridors. Unlike the citizens in the city itself, the Vraelimir Family's servants seemed accustomed, even approving, of our gory appearance. They just giggled, laughed, or murmured words of encouragement before returning to their duties.

At least the blood had dried long ago—I would have felt a *little* guilty if we made too much of a mess.

"By the Elders, you two!" Lysander exclaimed when Nalithor pulled me into the Draemiran's equivalent of a throne room. "What happened to killing *beasts*? Not...other things?"

"There were quite a few of those as well," Nalithor replied so seriously that I couldn't help but snicker at him. "You should know as well as I do that Aurelian's gifts do not repel the blood of people, Father, no matter how inferior the creatures may be."

"It really should," I pointed out as Nalithor traced my hip with his claws. "Slavers are little better than beasts. I'd imagine Aurelian could be convinced to make a few *minor* adjustments to his designs."

"Arianna, be a good girl and show them what you saw." Nalithor purred, a smile settling on his face when he looked down at me.

Instead of speaking, I decided to shove the memories of my search at both Lysander and Ellena. I ignored their startled expressions and pivoted into Nalithor's chest instead. He moved his hand to my bare waist to stroke my bloodied skin, a low chuckle rumbling in his chest. His parents were *furious* when they reached the portion of the memories that dealt with the first group of slavers—and what the men wanted to do to their son.

Glancing between Lysander and Ellena, I wasn't sure which one wanted to kill something more—they looked equally pissed. '*As they should be.*'

The Adinvyr beside me, however, seemed content to caress me.

"If that's all that happened, where have the two of you *been* for the past few days?" Ellena demanded. "The other gods and dignitaries have been demanding the presence of *both of you*! We're beginning to run out of excuses!"

Ellena shot me a strange look when I slipped my arm behind Nalithor's back and rubbed my cheek against his blood-soaked chest. I ignored her expression, choosing to listen to Nalithor's quickening heartbeat beneath my cheek instead.

"We have been at *my* palace while recovering from our wounds,"

Nalithor answered. Something about his tone made me giggle again. "I had hoped that the beasts and our other pursuers would give up but, as you can see from the state we are both in, they did not.

"Is that all? I would rather like to cleanse this unworthy blood from Arianna."

*'Oh, so* now *it's unworthy?'* I bit back a laugh. *'Getting this muck off does sound like a good idea though.'*

Nalithor gave his parents no chance to respond and instead guided me out of the room and through the palace grounds. His grip was firm enough to make me shoot him questioning glances, but he seemed oblivious to them. We cut through several sections of palace and across multiple gardens before reaching his wing. He showed no sign of slowing, even once we entered the corridor that housed our rooms.

I yelped when Nalithor hoisted me into the air and tossed me into the deep end of the bath, barely giving me time to dismiss my armor. The instant I broke the surface I pushed my hair out of my face, shot him an indignant glare, and then attempted to cover myself with my arms. I shifted away from him with a crimson face, my thoughts entering a chaotic spiral.

My own nudity was the *last* reason for my flushing. The glimpse of Nalithor's dick had been brief, but he was *massive* to a degree that I couldn't wrap my head around. I glanced down at one of my forearms, attempting to process the information—but it was impossible. *'Those jokes about "breaking" me weren't really jokes, were they?'*

"You don't have to pretend to be modest." Nalithor chuckled from the opposite end of the bath while I floated in the deep end. "I think a bottle of mri'lec is in order. Or perhaps some varikna if you would like something stronger?"

"Because of our hunt, or because—" I ducked instinctively when I heard a splash. The resulting waves nudged me closer to the line of windows nearby.

"We *are* quite bloody, aren't we?" Nalithor laughed from somewhere behind me.

I glanced down at the water around me, a crooked smile forming on my lips. "Well, at least your kind seem to have found some way to purify us *and* the water... Though I'm still not sure what you want to celebrate."

"Our successful hunt, the fact we managed to return to the city *before* the festivities began," Nalithor began. I snuck a peek over my shoulder at him and admired his sculpted buttocks before he pulled a towel around his waist. "Mmm... I would also argue that getting to drink *you* is cause for celebration.

"Once you've rinsed the rest of the blood off, join me. I hardly expect you to spend your time treading water, nor do I believe I've quite earned the right to assist you."

I stuck my tongue out at his back and took one more glance at his alluring physique before dipping under the surface of the water. Once I was sufficiently soaked, I scrubbed the blood and grime off my skin, turning the water around me a myriad of pinks and blacks. A few seconds passed before the water seemed to "pop" and returned to its normal hue.

After a moment of hesitation, I summoned a thin cotton dress around myself so that I was at least *somewhat* covered. Satisfied that I wasn't exposed anymore, I swam my way back to a section of the bath where my feet could actually reach the bottom.

"*That* is more distracting than if you had remained nude," Nalithor informed me dryly, tracking me as I strode to where he sat reclined on a marble chaise that had been carved into the pool's wall.

"Is it?" I questioned, glancing down at myself. I had to catch myself on Nalithor's shoulders when he pulled me onto the chaise with him, my legs across his lap. "Or were you just distracting me so that you could pounce, hmmm?"

"Perhaps a bit of both." Nalithor smiled and handed me a glass of mri'lec. "Regardless, I intend to keep an eye on you. Not only because you're quite lovely to look at, but also because I don't trust anyone else with you. Speaking of which... Have any of the bastards begun testing your barriers again? They're certainly focused on mine."

"Mmm? They're still leaving me alone," I replied, tilting my head when Nalithor released a displeased sigh. "Did you not put on enough of a show for them when you arrived at dinner a few days ago?"

"I will have to remedy that as soon as possible." Nalithor sighed again, slipping his free hand behind my back. "Until then...there's the matter of your results from the tests. You shouldn't be so powerful, but..."

He trailed off, his expression one of intense curiosity as he examined me. I decided to take a few sips of my mri'lec while waiting for him to finish his thoughts. His tail slowly coiled around my thighs while he studied me, making me wonder just *what* he was contemplating so deeply.

"Perhaps…" Nalithor placed his glass aside so that he could lift a hand to my face. "Hmmm… *They* must have never taken away the power They gave you and Darius.

"You and your brother, amongst others, were all 'marked' as candidates for the role of 'Balance.' If you and Darius survived, I have to wonder if others did as well."

"Others were hunted?" I questioned as he stroked my cheek with his thumb a few times, before trailing his fingers down to the Brands around my neck.

"Yes…and then the role was given to *me* because your heart supposedly changed me in some way." Nalithor nodded, but his attention was on the delicate markings around my throat and jugular. "You…are completely unfazed by my touch, aren't you?"

"*Unfazed?*" I asked in disbelief. I couldn't help but break out into a grin and giggle at his crestfallen expression. An Adinvyr, of all people, struggling to tell what I thought or felt struck me as hilarious. "Do you really have that difficult of a time with gauging me, Nalithor? *Hmmm?*"

"What…" Nalithor trailed off when I leaned forward to kiss his cheek.

A grin tugged at my lips again when a bashful expression crossed Nalithor's features, and he averted his gaze, his face turning a surprising shade of pink. Thoroughly amused at this point, I shifted my lips to the side of his neck before speaking again.

"I don't think you have room to claim I'm 'unfazed' after your comments, and subsequent *stunt*, at dinner the other night." I purred sweetly, smiling into his skin when I felt his pulse quicken beneath my lips, and his tail tighten around my leg.

*'I want to take a bite…ugh.'* I pulled away before the temptation could grow stronger. Opting to take a sip of my drink instead, I glanced to the side at Nalithor. He seemed adequately flustered, which was a nice change of pace—even if short-lived. A few moments of silence passed before he let out a slight sigh and shut his eyes for a few seconds. He seemed much more focused when he reopened them, and shot me a sultry smirk.

"If you *are* affected, then…" Nalithor purred, pulling my drink from my grip and setting it aside. He pulled me closer with his other arm, studying me with a predatory look. "Just how long did it take for you to work off my…ahhh…'*suggestions?*' Hmmm?"

Nalithor brought his hand up to my flushed face, his lips hovering over mine. Something about his expression made me realize that he didn't think the thoughts he'd sent me the other night affected me at all—nor did he think I was going to answer him. Instead, he thought he was just going to kiss me and that would be that.

"*Seven hours*, give or take a few minutes," I countered just before he could kiss me. He froze, making me smirk. "With all the teasing you do…did you *really* think those thoughts wouldn't do anything?"

"Seven…" He blinked, pulling back a few inches. "Just how much pent-up—"

Nalithor fell silent when I closed the distance between us and planted a timid kiss on his lips. Blushing, I pulled away and attempted to calm my racing pulse. I wasn't sure how he would react to *me* kissing *him*, and the concept was more than a little nerve-wracking. *'I should've thought about that* before *kissing him! Damn it. What if he gets mad? He's a dominant, right? So he might be particular about—'*

I squeaked in surprise when Nalithor lifted me up and set me on the edge of the bath, his eyes fiery and his expression devilish as he drew closer. He nudged my knees apart and rested his hands to either side of my hips. I scooted back across the marble as I went to question him, but it was pointless.

His lips met mine as he pulled himself fully out of the bath and pinned me beneath him. Nalithor's desire wrapped around me like a blanket. I soon found myself returning it in kind, all too eager to give in to our mutual hunger. I wrapped my arms around the back of his neck without hesitation.

We explored each other's mouths as he pulled my dress down, the teasing and dancing of his tongue drawing me further into his grasp. His hunger matched my arousal as he left my lips and kissed down my throat. I couldn't help but squirm in response to his touch as his hands roamed along my torso, as eager to explore my flesh as he was to taste it.

Nalithor chuckled deviously when his tail sliding between my legs caused a whimper to escape me. The motion was agonizingly slow. I wanted more than that—*far more* than that.

"*Patience.*" Nalithor growled, kissing from my chest and up to my throat again. "I think first…"

"Why do you have to tease me so— Ahhhnnn…" I shuddered when his fangs sank into the side of my throat and his tail pressed against my slit firmly once more

My back arched as Nalithor's hands explored my body, tugging, stroking, and teasing everything he could reach. He groaned with desire when I tugged at the towel around his waist, attempting to pull it from him. Instead of stopping me, Nalithor nudged my legs further apart and ran his fingers along my slit, taking care not to graze me with his claws. He withdrew his fangs from my throat and ran his tongue over the puncture wounds.

"W-what are you two doing?!" An all-too-familiar voice yelped. "A-Ari, bathing with a *man*, l-let alone…let alone *that!*"

'*Nngghh, I'm going to* kill *whoever let him in here…*' Nalithor growled into my throat, shifting to glare toward the room's entrance. "*Get out.*"

"No. I need to talk to you. *Now.*" Darius snapped, his face growing scarlet when he looked toward where Nalithor's towel had loosened. "If anyone is going to 'get out,' it will be Ari."

'*Does he realize* who *he's talking to?*' I bit back a growl of my own.

Nalithor shot my twin a murderous glare before shifting his attention to me and pulling me into a sitting position. The Adinvyr ignored Darius for the moment, instead shifting my dress to cover my breasts again. My brother let out an indignant shriek when Nalithor learned down to kiss the blood away from my throat. Nalithor squeezed my thigh and shot me a knowing look while I considered ripping my twin to shreds.

"I'll be in my rooms if…you want to continue, Nalithor," I stated, tracing my fingers down his chest as I looked up at him. "I don't have the patience to deal with my brat of a brother right now—especially not if he's forgotten his manners."

"C-continue?" Darius stuttered, watching Nalithor help me to my feet, "*Continue?!* Why in the hells would he want—"

Without another word, I strode away from Nalithor and past my brother. Darius flinched away from me when flames swirled around me briefly. I swept out of the bath and down the hallway outside, satisfied that I was dry. It would have taken a *lot* more mri'lec to keep me in the same room as my brother. *Especially* if I had to deal with the lustful looks he tended to send Nalithor's way.

I was liable to tear my twin's throat out if he so much as *looked* at Nalithor the wrong way again.

Alala and Djialkan both went running when I stormed into my suite. I slammed the sliding door behind me, nearing an uncontrollable level of *pissed. 'Why in the hells is my brother here?! Who the fuck let him into Nalithor's section of the palace? I'm going to fucking wring their throats! We should have stayed in his domain.*

*'I finally had Nalithor all to myself and in "private"—of course,*

*Darius just* had *to show up and fucking ruin it!'*

I stalked into my wardrobe in search of lacy undergarments and a satin baby doll nightie. I didn't plan on going *anywhere* for the rest of the afternoon. Not with my brother lurking in the palace.

If Nalithor took too long, perhaps I would send a servant to bring me food.

*'Darius better not keep Nalithor away from me for too long.'* I huffed, plopping onto a sofa and grabbing the nearest book. *'Honestly! Is some alone time with Nalithor too much to ask? I-I just want...'*

I sighed heavily and flipped open the book, staring at the pages without really seeing them.

*'Do I...need to be more forward with Nalithor?'*

# CHAPTER SIXTEEN
*Timing*

I conjured a sphere of flames in my left hand and watched the dim magic swirl for a few seconds before extinguishing it. Somehow, I doubted that Nalithor's feedings were solely responsible for my lessened power. While it was coming back, it seemed to be returning much slower than whenever I overexerted myself against beasts.

*'What was in that poison he said I was exposed to?'* I narrowed my eyes, shifting my vision to examine my own aura. *'Or is that Angel bastard's light magic at fault?'*

Sighing, I pivoted away from the windows and glanced at my bed and then the door. I had woken up alone. Nalithor hadn't come by my rooms the prior night, not even to take me to dinner. I had thought that my invitation was quite clear.

*'Maybe he came by when I'd already fallen asleep?'* I gnawed at my lower lip while walking through my rooms and to the wardrobe. The more I accepted my attraction to Nalithor, the more I found myself wanting to draw his attention. Considering what *almost* happened between us, and my raunchy dreams, I was relatively confident he felt similarly.

Even so, I wanted to entice him. His reactions alone made it worthwhile.

*'I could just be assuming that he's responsible for my dreams.'* I pouted, thinking for a moment before shaking my head and lifting the lid of a trunk. *'That really isn't too crazy an assumption at this point.'*

Deciding what to wear, without Alala nosing through everything to help me, was a little more difficult than I expected but I eventually settled on something between formal and casual. I wasn't sure if and when we—or I—would be expected anywhere, but I didn't feel like draping myself in endless layers of brocade either. The deep neckline would leave my neck, collarbone, and cleavage exposed while not showing *too* much.

*'Then again… What is "too much" cleavage anyway?'* I tilted my head for a moment, thinking on it. Shrugging to myself, I adjusted the long skirt so that the slits were even on each side. The split skirt would give me full range of motion if I wanted to kick the living hells out of something—like my brother, for example. I wasn't sure how much trouble I'd get in for kicking Darius' ass, but the prospect was seeming better all the time.

*'Who in their right mind let Darius into* Nalithor's *section of the palace anyway?'* I grimaced at my reflection while pulling my hair up. *'Hells! Why is Darius in Draemir to begin with? I thought he was meant to stay in Dauthrmir and attend to his studies?'*

I gave myself a brief look-over in the mirror before applying a little bit of makeup. Satisfied, I made my way out of my suite and through the palace in search of breakfast. Servants and guards milled about the lush grounds, but that didn't seem to dissuade them from calling to me with exclamations about my attire or jewelry. I wasn't sure how to deal with the attention or take the compliments, so I just mumbled my thanks and hurried toward the main palace.

"Ah, Arianna-jiss!" A busty Adinvyr woman with pastel pink hair grinned at me when I slunk into the kitchens. "Ellena-z'tar is looking for you.

"Oi, Asha! Show Her Highness to Ellena-z'tar's lounge, would you?"

"Wha? But—" I protested when the younger Adinvyr, Asha, grabbed me by the sleeve and tugged.

"I'll have Asha bring you food and tea, don't worry!" The pink haired Adinvyr laughed, shooing me.

Before I could protest further, Asha pulled me out of the kitchens and through the palace. The bouncy young girl didn't say anything to me, just grinned and hurried me in the direction of Ellena's lounge. I wasn't sure if I wanted to deal with the Goddess of Adinvyr so early in the morning, but it was clear I didn't have a choice in the matter.

"Ah good! Someone caught you before you could slip away!" Ellena grinned when Asha tugged me into the *very* pink lounge. "Thank you, Asha-mrii. You can go back to Dovsdra now—I'm sure she needs your help."

Asha giggled and ran off with a bashful expression on her face, leaving me to examine the two women waiting for me. They made me want to dart off myself, but for different reasons. It was far too early in the morning for me to feel like dealing with both Ellena *and* Erist. They both had sly expressions on their faces and seemed insistent that I should sit with them.

"Bah! That boy of mine didn't even bother to heal your throat?" Ellena huffed. She rose to her feet and swept toward me, motioning at my throat. "Typical man! Takes after his father, that one. Probably sees it as marking his territory. Humph!"

"Good job on not killing your brother though, Ari," Erist added with a grin. "I thought Nalithor was going to kill everyone in the palace last night when he dragged Darius into the throne room! Did the boy interrupt something?"

"…you could say that," I muttered before batting Ellena's hands away from my throat. "Gah, cold!"

"Here, take a seat!" Ellena grabbed me by the shoulders and steered me toward the sofa. "From what Nali said last night neither of you were expecting Darius' presence here. Is that true?"

"The X'shmiran Royal Family decided that they wanted to attend the spring festivities," Erist began before I even had a chance to respond, so I just sighed and plopped onto a seat. "According to Lucifer and the Oracles, Dilonu and Tyana *insisted* that Darius should be allowed to come as well. The Oracles decided to oblige…by having *all* of the 'struggling' classes flown to Draemir for Faerstravir."

"The 'struggling' classes?" I frowned at Erist before glancing to Ellena when she sat to my right. The Goddess of Adinvyr seemed a little *too* interested in me this morning.

"Yes. Classes that struggle with both magic *and* other cultures," Ellena replied dryly while fidgeting with the skirt of her kimono. "It sounds as though Darius must have thrown a spectacular tantrum or pulled some political strings. I got the feeling from the Oracles that they sent multiple classes so that Darius wouldn't think he'd 'won.'"

"That boy went running off through the palace grounds in search of you two as soon as he arrived—surprisingly slippery, that one," Erist muttered with a grimace. She swished her pale green drink around its glass for a moment and then shook her head. "When Nalithor dragged him into the throne room, the boy was spluttering something about how 'inappropriate' it was for Nalithor to let *you* corrupt *him*. I haven't seen Nalithor so enraged in a long time."

"Oh of course. It's so *terrible* that I *forced* Nalithor to feed from me, right?" I rolled my eyes and slumped back against the sofa. "I'll be impressed if my brother doesn't get himself killed while here."

"Unfortunately this means that you will have to deal with your brother *and* those…'people,'" Ellena pointed out with a small frown. "There's going to be a great deal of Lesser Gods, royalty, nobility, and demigods in Draemir for the next week. I even received word this morning from Leryci that Gabriel will be coming as a show of respect."

"Nalithor had one of those little cuties of his bring antidotes for the Leryci nobles." Erist half-shrugged in response to my questioning look. "Devillians and Angels haven't gotten along with each other for a *very* long time. However, Gabriel also isn't the sort who would ignore a gesture of goodwill either. Especially not from a far superior deity."

"If that's the case, then how did Lucifer and Gabriel end up..." I fell silent when Ellena hushed me.

Asha and several other servants arrived with food and drink moments later. I remained silent, aside from a few utterances of thanks, while the servants laid out food and tea on the table for me. Once they were finished, they left, and Ellena both closed and locked the lounge doors behind them. The Adinvyr matriarch returned and released a heavy sigh while I poured myself a cup of tea.

"Lucifer and Gabriel aren't on friendly terms—let alone anything more—and never have been," Erist began as I piled food onto a plate. "The Elders wanted to see what a union between two very different races would create. From what I understand, it ties into their desire to create a 'perfect' God of Balance. Most other races perceive Angels as being of the light, and Devillians as beings of darkness."

"Both of them agreed to it, of course. Though I'm not sure if anyone would have argued with the Elders about such a matter anyway," Ellena muttered, her voice full of distaste. "Gabriel chose to raise Darius as the heir to the Leryci throne since he was born as an

Astral Mage. Lucifer raised you as heiress to the Dauthrmiran throne."

"Gabriel wanted to keep Darius as far from darkness as possible while raising him," Erist added, making a sour face. "Thankfully she still understood the bond between siblings—especially twins. She brought Darius to Dauthrmir for short visits every now and then.

"Do you know if Darius has any memory of the past?"

"If he does then he's been very good at hiding it." I shook my head. "That, or Fraelfnir could be helping him. However, Fraelfnir claims that Darius has zero memories prior to X'shmir."

"Bah, enough about that brat!" Ellena snorted, crossing her arms and her legs with a flourish. "He's lucky my son didn't shred him into ribbons for the intrusion. Only a fool interrupts a warrior's post-victory bath or meal!"

"Post-victory…" I started laughing at the indignant goddess. "I would hope that I'm at least a little more than a 'meal,' you know. I'm pretty sure I'm at least a *little* more valuable than—"

"Of course, of course." Erist giggled, flapping her hand at me. "The Royal Family, and the nobles, don't feed on just *anyone* you know. I'm sure Nalithor has dropped plenty of hints that you've simply *missed* because you're no longer familiar with Draemiran ways.

"Which reminds me, Ellena! Didn't you ask for Arianna's presence here so that she could *ask* you about such things?"

"Ah, that's right!" Ellena beamed at me and clapped her hands together. "If there's anything you need to know about Draemiran ways—courting rituals or more mundane things, even—feel free to ask us! That boy of mine probably hasn't explained even *half* of his actions to you, has he? Besides that, depending on *your* intentions, there are some things you can't outright ask him anyway!"

"Hmmm..." I mumbled around my fork, considering it for a moment. Their expectant looks made me hesitant. "There *is* something I wanted to look into, but I wasn't sure how to go about it.

"Those little ornaments that some warriors fasten to the hilt of their weapon... What are they called?"

"Oh? Why? Are you thinking of getting my son one?" Ellena asked with a sly grin. The tip of her silvery tail flitted from side-to-side as she leaned towards me. "You know, many have *tried* to gift him one but—"

"It depends on which type you're referring to," Erist interjected, causing Ellena to cross her arms and pout. "The ones for a family member are 'zrintor,' and the ones for a lover are 'zrintaas.'"

"Zrintor and zrintaas, hmmm?" I murmured while stirring sugar into my tea. "How do you tell the difference between the two? What's the significance?"

"How do you tell..." Ellena blinked at me. "Do you *have* one? Did someone other than my son give you—"

"She's not obsessed with her family *at all*." Erist rolled her eyes at the Adinvyr before shifting her attention to me. "It honestly depends on whether or not we're talking about custom-made or mass-produced ones, Ari-mrii. As for the significance—"

"Who gave you one?" Ellena demanded, rounding on me with fiery eyes. "When did they give you one? Was it just out of the blue? A holiday? Were you leaving to hunt? Were—"

"No one gave me one!" I yelped, shrinking back from the angry Adinvyr matriarch while attempting to shield my food *and* scoot away from her. "Someone in Sihix made me one to give away, but I don't know what kind it is or what—"

"Let me see it," Ellena demanded, outstretching her hand. "I'll be the judge of whether or not it's good enough for my son."

"Who said she was going to give it to Nalithor?" Erist snickered, causing Ellena's tail to smash into the side of the sofa. "Maybe she was going to give it to Darius if it's for family? Or perhaps there's another cute Devillian in her life she wants to give it to? Eyrian has become quite the handsome man too, after all."

"Y-you two are impossible!" I fled from the sofa and over to a chair instead, bringing my food and drink with me. "This is why I don't ask questions—people jump to conclusions about *everything*!"

"But you *do* want Nalithor," Ellena pointed out flatly, causing my face to grow hot. I wasn't sure what to do about being confronted by his *mother* of all people.

"Maybe we should answer her questions about significance *before* you start trying to play matchmaker, Ellena?" Erist rolled her eyes at the eager Adinvyr. How the *Goddess of Love* was more reasonable than the Goddess of Adinvyr was beyond me. At least *someone* was willing to focus. "Zrintor are simple, Ari-mrii. They're gifted by a family member and are basically a charm for good luck. For example, parents often give their children a zrintor before they're sent off for their first hunt—or when they come of age."

"Zrintaas have deeper and varied meanings," Ellena continued after sticking her tongue out at Erist. "Giving one to someone on a 'normal' day is like when a teenager asks to be your boyfriend or girlfriend. It's cute, maybe even endearing, but not likely serious in the long run. If it's on a holiday, hmmm... How to explain it?"

"If single, it's like a more serious way of asking to be in a relationship. It's more serious, more respected and, generally speaking, is the ideal way to go about it," Erist offered after a moment, leaning against her armrest while she thought. "If the two people are already involved with each other, it's like saying 'you're mine.' It's like when Human men begin buying expensive jewelry for their women—except zrintaas aren't trivial or materialistic items."

"What *are* they then?" I frowned. "The ones I've seen look like jewelry for weapons. Though, I suppose weapons are rather important in most Devillian circles, given the importance put on 'hunting.'"

"Zrintaas usually carry a piece of the person who gifted it," Ellena offered. She summoned a slender sword to hand and nudged the small silver zrintaas that dangled from the hilt. "Lysander infused the crystal in this one with power, memories, and emotions. They serve as a charm for luck, a reminder of the connection between two people, and as comfort when separated."

*'Infused? Hmmm...like mine then,'* I thought while nibbling at my food. *'Corentine said not to give it to anyone or use it for myself. I guess it*

*makes sense now. She didn't say I couldn't show anyone... Though I suppose she did say that I should keep it in my shrizar...'*

"The best way to give away a zrintaas is when someone is going to war, of course," Ellena continued, breaking my train of thought. "It's the most meaningful way to gift one. If you give someone a zrintaas before they go to war, it represents the desire to enter a long-term and exclusive relationship. The only thing more meaningful than that would be outright asking for someone's hand in marriage."

"You really don't know what type you have?" Erist questioned with a frown. I shook my head in reply since my mouth was full. "How did you wind up with one then, exactly? You said that someone in Sihix made it for you?"

"Corentine, Sihix's High Priestess, took a crystal that I used during training and made it into one of those decorations," I replied, shifting in my chair. "She said that I wasn't to use it myself and that I couldn't give it away until I 'fully understood' what such things were for. However, she neglected to tell me what they're even called. So, I've been mostly in the dark aside from seeing them here and there Below."

"Then let us see it." Ellena held out her hand again and gave me a firm look. "What sort of crystal did you use for your training? I hear X'shmir's soil is rife with dark and wind aspected crystals."

"Ah... It *used* to be unaspected," I mumbled, opening my shrizar with reluctance before pulling out a lacquered box. "I'll show you two *if* you promise not to tell anyone else about it. Corentine didn't say that I *couldn't* show anyone, but—"

"But if you *do* decide to give it to Nalithor, you want it to be a surprise?" Erist grinned at me. "I sure won't tell him. His reaction to such a gift would be priceless. Oh please. Don't give me that look. Who else would you be considering giving it to?"

"She has a point." Ellena giggled, poking one of my flushed cheeks. "*I* won't tell him either. Not only do I want to refrain from getting his hopes up, but it's also a very…personal experience. I wouldn't want to rob him of something he thought he'd never have."

"Never have?" I shot Ellena a frown, confused. "But I saw one of his students attempt to gift him—"

"Ah, so he hasn't properly expressed how much you meant to him when you were children," Erist remarked with an oddly sage nod of her head. "I will put it like this, Ari-mrii, cheesy as it may be. You and he were like two halves of a whole. It's what made you two work so well together.

"When you were taken away…it took him well over a century to learn how to fully function without you by his side. It took several decades more for us to get him to feed in *any* sense of the word."

"Even as a child he was convinced that you were *his* and that no one else could ever hope to have you," Ellena added with an amused giggle. "Enough about the past. Show us this trinket of yours already!"

I sighed and set my cup of tea down so that I could nudge open the box's lid. The two goddesses both crowded around me and exchanged a look before plucking the box out of my lap and lifting it so that they could see it better. I pursed my lips and batted down my nervousness while waiting for them to finish. I didn't like hearing that Nalithor had struggled so much after I was taken away, and it was difficult for me to fathom being *that* close to someone.

Being important to him was nice and all…but something about Erist's tone made me think that, perhaps, Nalithor had taken my "death" dangerously hard.

*'He…he didn't try to end himself, did he?'* A sharp pang shot through my chest at the thought. *'I know we were just children back then. Could we really have been* that *close?'*

"Well it doesn't seem like you infused any of your memories into the crystal at least," Erist remarked, causing me to shift my attention to them again. "We were worried that your memories of Limbo might have slipped their way into it, but that doesn't appear to be the case."

"It's definitely a zrintaas—zrintor aren't this ornate," Ellena added, offering the box back to me. "Your friends in Sihix must care a great deal about you. This is an exquisite piece. I would very much like to see if the creator would be willing to do business with us…"

"They're more like family than anyone in X'shmir itself has been, at any rate," I replied, taking back the box. After nudging the zrintaas around and arranging it how I wanted it, I returned it to my shrizar for safekeeping. "That's including Darius, mind you. Djialkan and the people of Sihix have been…everything, really. They're one of the few reasons I don't want to see X'shmir completely blown out of the sky."

"We both have to return to preparing for tonight's feast, but let us know if there's anything else you need to ask, alright?" Erist grinned at me, placing her hands on her hips. "We're more than happy to help you re-acclimate to Draemiran ways—even Dauthrmiran ones, if you need help with that as well."

"I know you'll be able to pick the best time to give that zrintaas to Nali!" Ellena teased, turning to follow Erist toward the door. "We'll see you later, Ari-mrii. Try not to murder your brother, alright?"

I sighed at them and then returned to finishing my breakfast. When I was done, I decided to leave the palace and wander through the gardens while thinking. I wasn't quite ready to track Nalithor down yet. Not after all the information that had been dropped on me.

When Corentine had told me that it was an "important" item, I had never thought she might have meant something like *that*. Now that I knew the significance of a "zrintaas," I didn't know what to think—let alone what to do. While it was true that I'd been considering giving it to Nalithor, the new information was making me reconsider.

Timing seemed important, and to know which timing was needed in our case, I would have to think about it more. Just up and giving it to him no longer seemed like a good option, but that left a holiday or "war present" as my remaining options.

Much more thought was required before I could make that decision.

*'Well, there's a few days before Faerstravir officially begins...'* I drummed my fingers against my forearm, oblivious to my surroundings. *'I just want to keep Nalithor to myself at this point.*

*Though, I suppose he's required to attend tonight's feast. Hmmm…*

*'I will give it time. This won't be the only holiday—and this seems like something I shouldn't rush.'*

# CHAPTER SEVENTEEN
*Importance of Acceptance*

I didn't really know where I wanted to go, so I settled on wandering aimlessly across palace grounds and eventually down the road that led through the military district. Squadrons of soldiers and mages were sparring, practicing their techniques against dummies and targets, or involved in some kind of meditation-like practice that I didn't recognize.

Most of them seemed sloppy in their movements, and those who were meditating were clearly dozing off. Some of the mages were levitating off the ground while meditating—several of which received a rude awakening when they dozed off and dropped themselves on the ground.

*'New recruits? It's so difficult to gauge Devillians' ages…'* I pursed my

lips.

"There you are," Nalithor called, startling me and causing me to shift my attention away from the training recruits. "I was wondering when you were going to…"

Nalithor fell silent while looking down at me. For some reason, he seemed surprised by my attire and my cleavage—but mostly my attire. He continued to examine me in stunned silence, his tail swishing slowly behind him. After letting him enjoy the sight for a few more seconds, I closed the distance between us and pointed up at my face.

"*Nalithor*, I'm up here." I smirked when his eyes snapped back up to my face. "See? That wasn't so difficult. I'm sure Shir and Gari will be overjoyed that you approve."

'*He may be surprised by my attire…but his isn't anything to sneeze at either,*' I mused, giving him a quick looking over. '*I doubt he's dressed like that for his students. Though, I'm certainly not complaining. Would it be a bit much if I asked him to turn around?*'

"Shir and… Ah, so this is another creation from your friends in Sihix?" Nalithor inquired. He gripped my chin lightly and turned my head to the side, examining the crystal-studded ornaments in my hair. "And these too, hmmm… Where were you heading?"

"Nowhere in particular." I shrugged, shooting Nalithor a smile when he released my chin and offered me his arm instead. "Did you have something in mind?"

"The slow return of your power gave me an idea," Nalithor answered, a small smile forming on his face when I accepted his arm.

"Have you heard about the students the Oracles sent here?" He paused and waited for me to nod my reply before continuing, "I'm expected to teach this morning's class. They are supposed to be learning the importance of accepting their nature—and their magic alongside.

"Since you have a unique grasp on such matters…perhaps you'll be willing to lend me your assistance with this one?"

"Hmmm, not *quite* what I had in mind," I answered in a teasing tone. I squeezed up against his side and shot him a look, slipping my free hand into the folds of his kimono. A small growl escaped him as I ran my nails down his muscular abdomen. "I'm sure it wouldn't be *too* dangerous to leave them on their own for the day, right?"

"*Don't tempt me.*" Nalithor smacked my ass with his tail and shot me an entertained look. "While I would love to escape them, it's for the best that we deal with them as asked. The sooner we do, the sooner you can have me to yourself."

"I suppose I can help then," I replied after a moment of consideration. Sighing, I pulled my hand from his robes and shot him a questioning look. "What are you planning, hmmm?"

"I'm going to share some of my power with you," Nalithor answered as he led me down the road. "I think that will be the most effective way to get my points across to the students, and the state you're in certainly gives us the excuse to utilize such a method.

"Djialkan and Alala are watching over the class at the moment since I was coming to fetch you."

"Fetch me?" I asked as he pulled me into a building and then up a flight of stairs.

"Yes. I sensed that you were awake, and I want to keep an eye on you while you recover," Nalithor answered with a nod and an unreadable smile. "And…perhaps I'm still a little miffed that our time together yesterday was cut short. I thought Djialkan was going to incinerate me when I dropped by. He said you needed sleep. Did you rest well?"

"You're impossible. But yes, I did sleep well." I shook my head at him and then scented the air, frowning. "Darius is in your class too, huh? Wonderful…"

"All the more reason for such an obvious method, don't you think?" Nalithor chuckled. "Thankfully, his rooms aren't in our section of the palace but…his presence is still unwelcome."

'So Nalithor is displeased as well.' I observed with a small sigh of relief, shifting my gaze away from the Adinvyr. 'A little "miffed" that we were interrupted… After what Ellena and Erist told me, I think that's putting it lightly.'

I bit back another frown when Darius' fear washed over me. I glanced to the side at Nalithor and caught the agitated expression on his face. The muscles in his torso and arms tensed. He didn't look at all pleased as we approached the classroom.

Maric and the rest of Darius' escort saluted when they spotted us, but tension was clear on their faces too.

'Darius has been like this since learning what today's subject matter is,' Nalithor offered as he nodded to the soldiers. With a reluctant sigh, he pushed open the door and led me into the classroom by my arm.

Darius looked up from his desk with a venomous expression when he spotted us. He looked positively murderous, causing me to flinch and hide behind Nalithor's arm by instinct. The Adinvyr beside me simply slipped his arm around my waist and led me toward the front of the room with him. The protective action made me feel a little better, but not by much.

"Alala, Djialkan, have they been behaving themselves?" Nalithor inquired while pulling me over to the massive, ornate desk that sat at the front of the room.

I perched on the edge of the desk while Nalithor settled into the oversized chair behind it. I crossed my legs and shifted to examine the class, attempting to determine just how much I would have to restrain myself. As usual, the class consisted of Astral, Umbral, Shadow, and Light Mages. None of them appeared to be in touch with their respective elements, and all of them stunk of fear.

I wasn't sure if it was Darius' demeanor that was frightening them, or if they simply shared his fear of their own powers. However, there was something "different" about these students compared to Nalithor's usual classes.

*'All of them are blocking themselves the way Darius is?'* I frowned. *'Also...why are they looking at me like that?'*

*'You are quite the sight to behold, sitting there like that,'* Nalithor replied with a devious chuckle. I pivoted to look at him, earning a smirk. *'If you* must *know, most of them are imagining what you would*

*look like pinned to the desk beneath them.'*

"Arianna-z'tar's recovery, and your studies, are connected today," Nalithor addressed the class, drawing most of the students' attention to him. After a moment, he stood and came to lean against the desk beside me. He pulled me towards his chest and then made a small motion with one hand, rendering my aura visible in the air around me. "Who among you can see what is wrong with Arianna's magic?"

*'So, he can't see magic, but he can make it visible to the naked eye?'* I bit back my questions and glanced to the side at Nalithor as his hand came to rest on my hip. *'Hmmm... Or can he see the magic in people but not in "things?" The environment?'*

"A lots been drained," one student offered.

"I know you're a prince too, Professor, but is it *really* appropriate for you to grab Her Highness like that?" An Elven student asked, his face twisted in confusion.

I had to bite back a laugh when I felt Nalithor twitch.

"I'm sure that, as my *partner*, Arianna would be swift to protest if she believed I was being inappropriate," Nalithor replied innocently. I felt him shift to look in Darius' direction when my twin's pencil snapped. *'Oh? No one told the boy? It's a shame the marks from my fangs have already healed. I'm certain that his reaction would have been well worth the headache it would give us.'*

"*Focus*, Nalithor." I teased, nudging him with my elbow before I settled my eyes on the classroom. "But yes—you're correct. My power isn't where it should be, and recovery is a gradual process."

"Were she suffering from blood loss due to battle," Nalithor continued, "a simple transfusion from the healing staff would help remedy the problem. As you know, restoring magical power is not so easy a task.

"Loss of power can be just as life-threatening to a mage as losing blood, yet there aren't many ways to restore lost power.

"Can any of you name methods for restoring it?"

There was only silence while the students thought. I studied them while they attempted to determine what Nalithor was referring to. Several of them looked as if they may have realized it, but they doubted their answer—likely due to their fear of magic.

Nalithor grew more impatient by the second and soon shifted his hand to stroke my spine while he waited for the students to stop fighting themselves. I glanced at him, but he just shot me a smile and remained silent.

"Drawing energy from elemental crystals wouldn't be enough, would it?" Darius offered after nearly two minutes. He looked as though his rage had subsided—for the moment. "If the problem is similar to the loss of blood, then she would need a 'transfusion' of magic, right?"

"That's correct, Darius," Nalithor replied, nodding. "However, there are two major problems that must be factored in. First, there is the issue of elements. The power Arianna receives must be of an element that she is aligned with. In Arianna's case, that would be fire, ice, shadow, or wind. For most mortal mages, there are only one or two elements to choose from.

"Second is the problem that you are all in this class to study; the acceptance of your own nature, magic, and power. For example, if Arianna wasn't in tune with her elements and I tried to loan her my power on the battlefield, her body would reject my magic, and we would both be weakened for it. Whatever I tried to loan her would simply return to Avrirsa."

"If that happened, it would put both of our lives at greater risk," I continued after Nalithor nudged me. "And if we're working with any other teams, it would put their lives at risk as well."

"For another example," Nalithor spoke, tugging at one of my curls absentmindedly. "If she were drained to the point that she couldn't move, I would have to give her so much of my power that we would have to support each other afterward in order to *walk*."

"If his magic evaporated because I didn't accept my elements, or was frightened of magic, then neither of us would be moving anywhere," I added. "We would be at the mercy of whoever or whatever we had been sent to fight, incapable of defending ourselves or each other."

"The problem applies to those of you studying to become healers as well," Nalithor murmured, before glancing at me. "Arianna, your hand please?" He took my hand and lifted it so that my palm was facing the ceiling, then addressed the class again, "Darius, what do you think would happen if I cut your sister's hand and then tried to heal it with magic that I feared?"

"It would lose its integrity and do nothing?" Darius frowned, clearly unsure, before shaking his head.

"It would damage her," Nalithor replied, earning startled looks from most of the students. "When you're untrusting of your own magic, it tends to do the opposite of what you're trying to accomplish. Whereas if you trust it..."

Nalithor took a step away from me and pulled my hand with him before abruptly slicing my palm open with a slim dagger. Black blood splashed to the floor, earning startled shrieks from every non-Devillian and non-Vampire in the class. More yelps followed, this time from the entire class, when Nalithor coated his freehand in darkness and healed the wound.

"If you trust your magic, then you can stitch wounds back together or heal them completely depending on your knowledge of anatomy and how well you've learned to See the nerves, blood vessels, and other important bits that have to be put back together," I added as Nalithor released my hand, an amused smirk on his face. "My specialty is inflicting wounds—not healing them. You'll have to forgive my crude explanation."

*'I'll have you know that you are quite the proficient healer.'* Nalithor chuckled, squeezing me. *'Certainly, the most tasty one too.'*

*'You make it incredibly difficult to tell when you're actually hungry,'* I informed him dryly.

"Of course, healing is a simple matter since only the mage doing the healer needs to be in-tune with their own power," Nalithor continued, moving to stand behind me. "The element of the healer's magic doesn't matter because their magic won't be lingering in the body of their patient.

"Which brings us back to the matter of 'transfusions.' As you know, Arianna and I are both Umbral Mages. As such, darkness is an obvious choice. We also share the elements fire and ice, so I could utilize one of those instead.

"However, her affinity for darkness is the strongest—as is mine. This is part of why the Vorpmasian Empire pairs mages of the same 'type' with each other. They're guaranteed to share at least one element so, if an emergency arises, there is a fix for the problem."

"Partnership is also important. Both mages *should* know and trust each other enough to understand each other's elemental preferences," I added before pointing a finger at the class. "Given what we've said so far, I don't think I need to explain to you what would happen if a solitary mage came across another and attempted to 'help.'"

"How are we supposed to learn to accept our magic though?' A female Elf frowned, glancing between Nalithor and I as if it would give her answers.

"Fearing whether or not your skill is at an acceptable level is fine—natural, even," I started after a moment of thought, then made a vague motion with one hand. "If you're scared about being able to do something, it shows you have the desire to learn and improve. You can't learn if you don't have the desire to, and the same applies to improving.

"The problem is when you misdirect your fear to the elements or your power itself. Magic is reactive, almost sentient. If it senses you're scared of it, it will feel 'hurt' and run away from you."

"Wild like an animal and fragile like a kitten?" Nalithor teased, earning snickers from the students and a dry glare from me.

"Are you talking about magic, or me?" I retorted, crossing my arms. I shot him a defiant look, causing several students to laugh outright.

"You're more of a fox than a kitten," Nalithor replied, smirking, before shifting his attention to the students. "Are you all going to go screaming and searching for cover again, or can you actually *focus* and *learn* from me sharing my power with Arianna?"

"You're going to show us?" A Sundreht asked, his feline ears perking forward with interest.

In response, Nalithor simply leaned down and nuzzled the side of my throat. A few students' faces drained of color in response to whatever look the Adinvyr shot their way. However, Nalithor didn't give them much time to be frightened. He summoned dense, warm darkness around both of us, eliciting whimpers of fear from several students.

As with the last time I'd felt so much of his power, it seemed as though it was able to slide over my skin and ignore my clothing entirely. He chuckled deviously when I squirmed in response to his shadows squeezing my thigh. It must have been the reaction he was looking for, because after he finally let his darkness seep into my body

409

and disappear.

*'Better?'* Nalithor released me and returned to his seat, shooting me an innocent smile.

*'Was the* groping *really necessary?'* I countered as Alala wiggled out of hiding and leapt into my lap. *'Also... Didn't you say it would take a long time to recover the amount of power you took? I'm rather certain I was on track to recover in the next week or so...'*

*'Perhaps you have a little bit of Adinvyr in you after all.'* Nalithor teased.

"Now, as you can see, Arianna's magic has been replenished. Not fully, but close," Nalithor stated, motioning to the magic that still hung in the air around me. "Normally it would take weeks or months to replenish the amount she lost—perhaps even half a year were she a normal Human. However, because she is so accepting of darkness, she is able to take mine and instinctively convert it into her own.

"Such an ability has other applications in combat as well, but that's a lesson for another day. Once Arianna is feeling strong enough to spar, perhaps we will grace you with a demonstration."

*'You should grab a chair, you know,'* Nalithor commented while instructing the class to open their tomes. *'As much as I enjoy seeing you perched on my desk in such a way, our students are not the only ones who find it distracting.'*

*'Still insist that I stay so that you can "keep an eye on me?"'* I asked. I picked Alala off my lap and then slid off the desk, noting the way Nalithor's eyes drifted down to my thigh when the slit in my skirt

pulled higher up my hip.

*'Most definitely...'* Nalithor replied, tracking me as I moved past him. *'I'm not letting you go* anywhere *by yourself when you look that delicious. Weakened or otherwise.*

*'Selfish reasons aside, it's important to keep an eye on you in case you begin to shift back to whatever you truly are. Darius isn't supposed to know who or what you two are yet—if Fraelfnir's words can be trusted.'*

I chose to relent for the time being and pulled a chair up beside Nalithor's desk. Alala and Djialkan both curled up in my lap as soon as I was situated, so I decided to pet them while watching the students. Darius still looked pissed off, but his anger was slipping deeper and deeper into confusion while he and his fellow students worked, questioned Nalithor, and studied.

As time went on, I began to get an idea of what problem many of them faced.

*'Nalithor,'* I called, breaking my extended silence. Nalithor stopped his pacing between the students and pivoted to shoot me a questioning look. *'I think I've realized what most of them are struggling with.'*

*'Do you have a solution?'* Nalithor countered, his tone full of curiosity as he turned and strode toward me.

*'I think so. Assign them into pairs; one healer with one warrior. Astral with Astral and Umbral with Umbral, and so on, if there are enough,'* I began, causing Nalithor to arch an eyebrow at me. He was patient enough to wait, even if his expression was rather expectant. *'Give them each an unaspected crystal and tell them to infuse it with "themselves." We*

*can go from there if their results prove my theory correct.'*

Nalithor seemed intrigued and moved over to a nearby cabinet to fetch a tray of small, clear crystals. He moved through the classroom and called out names of students, pairing them up. They looked startled by the strange request but hurried to obey. Soon enough the class was split into twenty-five pairs.

*'And now?'* Nalithor asked, leaning on the back of my chair. *'What are you up to, hmmm?'*

*'Usually,* I'm *the impatient one. Watch,'* I replied, biting back an amused giggle.

It didn't take long before the students said they were done and they turned their gazes to Nalithor, expecting further instruction from the Adinvyr.

"Trade crystals with your partner," I stated flatly, causing several students to flinch outright. "Inspect the energy they infused into their crystal."

*'Ah. That's why you wanted to pair mages of the same type.'* Nalithor murmured. *'They're rather terrified of their partners, it would seem. What are you thinking?'*

*'It would appear that they don't understand the multifaceted nature of elements,'* I offered, glancing upward when Nalithor shifted his hands to my shoulders. *'Look at Darius. He's* terrified *to handle the energy of someone who is a destructive Astral Mage, but confusion is taking over.*

*'The Old Ways may mostly be dead, here, but it would appear that some people still believe that darkness is evil and light is good—and that*

*the same concepts can be applied to destruction and healing.'*

"As you can see," I started aloud, "the magic you infused feels the same as your partner's does—magic is a neutral power. It is the people who wield it that make it do things you perceive as 'good' or 'evil.' If darkness and light followed the beliefs you are accustomed to, and were it not neutral, shadows like Nalithor's wouldn't be able to heal—and light would be incapable of destruction.

"Light can be just as damaging or corrupting as darkness, and darkness can be just as healing, soothing, and calming as light."

"Light and darkness share the same purpose," Nalithor added, ruffling my curls. "But, as with any element, they choose a person based on factors of their personality. Light and darkness are the only elements with direct ties to healing, while the rest of the elements are used for destruction, utility, or creating—such as building cities or forging items from metal and flame.

"Being chosen by light doesn't inherently make you a good person, and being chosen by darkness doesn't make you a bad or evil person. It's how you choose to use your power that determines that."

"What about healers compared to fighters?" Darius demanded, curling his hands into fists. "Hurting people is bad, isn't it?"

"Well, if someone was threatening to kill you or the people you love," I started, turning to look at my twin, "would you; A) protect your family? B) Let the scoundrel kill them and potentially *you*?"

"Wha...?" Darius blinked at me for a moment before slumping back in his chair. "But people are—"

"What about Chaos Beasts, then?" I offered, earning a blank stare from Darius. "They've hurt and killed thousands, if not millions, of innocent people. There's a difference between killing for justice, killing for revenge, and killing for the sake of killing."

"Killing for revenge is a poor solution to an often very real problem," Nalithor remarked, pulling Darius' gaze to him. "For example, if someone killed one of my younger siblings, it's quite likely that I would hunt down whoever was responsible and exact revenge.

"While that isn't inherently wrong, at least not in Draemiran culture, the socially acceptable method would be to leave it to the government or to the Goddess of Justice."

"Whereas killing for justice—and protection of others—is what the soldiers of the Vorpmasian military and the mages of the Alliance do," I elaborated, motioning to Nalithor and then to myself. "We're duty-bound to protect the people of Vorpmasia, or whichever allies we're sent to protect. It's in the very contract that we sign. Neglecting our duty would mean loss of life, and we would be responsible for it as if we had killed the citizens ourselves."

*'At least they've stopped ogling us so much and have begun paying attention instead,'* Nalithor mused, rubbing my shoulders. *'Though I'm not certain they understand quite yet. It will likely take time.'*

"Let's look at it from another perspective..." I tilted my head, thinking for a moment while examining the students' faces. "To our healers in the class; would any of you refuse to use your abilities on a patient?"

There were quite a few confused glances exchanged, as well as a healthy mix of "yes" and "no" answers.

"Why?" I probed, motioning at the closest person that answered affirmatively.

"If the person killed a lot of people, then he shouldn't live." The male Elf snorted.

"On the other hand, what if you later learned he was innocent?" I countered with a smile. "Refusing to heal him would have denied him a chance to prove his innocence because *you* let him die. You would be responsible for having played the role of executioner—and unjustly so. It would then be *your* life that hung in the balance, and you would be charged for murder.

"Girl with the pigtails, why did you say 'yes'?"

"If the person were beyond saving, then it would be better to conserve my power for those that *could* be saved," the pigtailed Sizoul replied, frowning at me for a moment before shifting her eyes to Nalithor as if begging him to agree with her.

"Another reason that healers also work in pairs…" Nalithor mused, shaking his head. "It's difficult for any mage to understand how much power they have, but your partner is capable of seeing it more clearly. Your partner in work, when you're assigned one, will be able to see your limits better than you can. It's difficult to view oneself without bias.

"One of the biggest mistakes new healers make is underestimating their ability—and skipping a patient entirely because of it. This is why we pair new healers with veteran ones both in hospitals and in the field. Patients won't get passed over and die due to the neglect of uncertain healers that way, and the new healers are exposed to advanced techniques that aren't easily taught in a classroom."

"So, basically every gods-damned thing we've worried about has *nothing* to do with the elements themselves?!" Darius demanded, slamming his fists onto his desk.

*'What made you realize it, my dear?'* Nalithor asked.

*'The tension between the students,'* I replied, stretching before continuing, *'Some of them were just scared of the light versus darkness issue. However, a lot of the healers, like Darius, seem to have muddled their sense of "right" and "wrong" along the way. They've confused healing and fighting as matters of morality instead of necessity.*

*'Darius wasn't the only one flinching or looking disgusted at the prospect of touching the crystal of someone who is destructive.'*

"Arianna-jiss, how did you come to accept your darkness then?" One of the female Umbral Mages, another Elf, inquired with a small frown. "You didn't receive formal training in the way we did, right?"

"Sometimes extreme circumstances come along," I started, tilting my head in thought as Nalithor's grip on my shoulders twitched and grew tense. "I found out the hard way that darkness was safer and more comforting than light, and wrapping myself snuggly within that darkness is what kept me sane. Mastering fire, ice, and wind came afterward for me—the reverse of how it is *meant* to progress."

"How did you learn to fight without anyone to teach you?" It was a Rylthra Astral Mage who spoke up this time, his fluffy ears perked and flared to show his interest.

"Instinctively." I laughed. "Trial and error. I couldn't stand the smell of the palace in X'shmir, or the smell of the city. So, I'd often leave the city and go into the wilds surrounding it. The Chaos Beasts smelled at least a *little* bit better.

"I learned through observing the creatures of the forest while they defended their homes—and from my fumbling attempts to defend myself against the beasts. Djialkan, here, used what power he could, and Darius' scaly friend helped with some of the worse wounds. Isn't that right, Fraelfnir?"

*"You are lucky that Djialkan did not rip your legs off himself to keep you from wandering into trouble all the time!"* Fraelfnir spat, materializing on Darius's shoulder. His golden eyes were aflame with irritation. I just grinned at him.

*"Children have terrible consistency,"* Djialkan retorted with disdain, earning laughter from the students. *"Too fatty."*

"He has to watch his womanly figure, obviously," I offered with a sarcastic grin as Djialkan snorted shadows at me.

"Professor, why is she able to fight you evenly if she's had no formal training?" Another male student asked, befuddled.

"Because the way Arianna-z'tar trained is more...natural. It honed her instincts in a way that formal training does not." Nalithor laughed, his eyes bright. "Experience in the field trumps orchestrated training exercises. She can determine the movements of her opponents based on the slightest changes in their muscles, shifting of their weight, or shifting of their grip. She can also detect the disturbances in the air and the flow of magic by sheer instinct. Most warriors would have to use their magic to test such things first, which is time wasted.

"That is why our magical duel was fiercer than our physical matches. Arianna combined magic with her instincts, and it made her a force to be reckoned with."

I watched in silence as Nalithor redirected the class's attention away from me and began dishing out homework for the lot of them. Finally, he sent them on their way to their next class. By the sound of matters, it would be the first of *many* culture-related classes. Nalithor sounded relieved that he wouldn't have to deal with it.

Darius shot us both a strange look before leaving, but at least it wasn't another glare.

"That went surprisingly well," Nalithor remarked, offering me a hand. "I suppose we will know soon if your words stuck with them. We have a few hours before we're expected anywhere. Do you have plans?"

"I don't make plans—and luckily Ellena and Erist refrained from making any *for* me." I shook my head before accepting Nalithor's hand and letting him help me to my feet. "To be honest, I'm quite cross that I don't have you all to myself. *Again.*"

"But you *do* have me to yourself." Nalithor purred. He embraced me and buried his face into my shoulder, releasing a contented sigh. "I'm *yours* for the remainder of our stay here, if that's what you still desire. The rest of *that one's* classes are with other teachers—and this was the last class I was asked to teach. You were still asleep for the others."

"You've fulfilled your obligations then?" I questioned with a small pout.

"Indeed, I have." Nalithor chuckled as I pivoted to look up at him. "What do you want, hmmm? It's still a little distressing that I can't see into that head of yours..."

"Is my sister troubling you, Nalithor?"

*'Nggghhhh, I'm going to fucking kill...'* I trailed off as Nalithor pulled me into his chest, closing my eyes. I inhaled his scent and forced myself to relax in an attempt to calm down.

"Actually, *you* are interrupting, Darius. *Again*." Nalithor growled, making a show of running his hands down my back and to my ass. He grabbed both of my butt cheeks firmly enough that I almost squeaked in surprise. "*You* have classes to attend. Arianna and I have *each other* to attend to... **Run along.**"

Darius released a feral snarl and went to say something, but Nalithor wasn't having it. Before my brother could form a full syllable, Nalithor scooped me up, and my two Guardians leapt into my lap. Everything spun for a moment as the irritated Adinvyr sunk into the shadows and transported us all the way back to the palace, leaving my brother behind.

Alala and Djialkan promptly dropped from my lap and scampered off in search of lunch.

"Ah…if only we had more time before we're expected at tonight's feast." Nalithor sighed, setting me down and pulling me into his chest again. "Perhaps I should take you into Draemir to explore since I don't have enough time to '*savor*' your company before the party, hmmm?"

"I do hope you'll accompany me *personally* this time, Nalithor," I remarked, earning a startled look from him.

"Is that an invitation?" Nalithor asked, coiling his tail around my hips.

"I would like to say it's a *demand* but…" I smiled and rose up on my tiptoes, linking my hands behind his neck. "Yes, it's an invitation. I know I've already 'claimed' rights to your company for the duration of our stay, but… Will you be my date, Nalithor?"

He looked so incredibly surprised that, for a moment, I feared he might reject me. Instead, he lifted me off the floor and gave me a long kiss, crushing me against his chest.

"Your blushing when you are being forward is *adorable*," Nalithor informed me, withdrawing from the kiss. "I will *gladly* accompany you. Seeing as I must wear divine attire for the night… I do hope you have something suitably formal?"

"I can think of a thing or two to pour myself into, yes," I replied with a crooked grin as he carefully set me down on my feet once more. "We must deal with other deities again?"

"And their 'Chosen,'" Nalithor replied with disgust, shaking his head. "The way they treat their Chosen feeds into why I dislike the term 'slave' for submissives. I think you will understand when you see them yourself. For now, how about I take you into the city for some lunch? Perhaps I will show you around afterward, if we have time, and we don't receive too many challenges."

# CHAPTER EIGHTEEN
*Enthrallment*

"Let me spoil you." Nalithor pulled me closer by my hips and grinned down at me. "You know, I'm quite cross that *those women* attempted to lure you into the city while I was gone. I thought I made it quite clear that *I* intended to be the one to show you around."

"Spoil me?" I protested, glancing away from him. "Are you sure that *this* suits me? I mean…it's kind of frilly. I—"

"It suits you perfectly," Nalithor assured me with a smile. He seemed to take my flushing as an invitation to tease me more. "The only thing that would be *more* fitting is a nice collar around that dainty throat of yours."

"D-dainty?" I sighed at him, feeling my face grow hotter. "You know, *none* of this is practical for combat. Should you really be wasting—"

"You're not going to be fighting *all* the time," Nalithor countered with a smirk. "We should return to the palace soon, I'm afraid. I'll wait for you at the front of the store while you change."

Nalithor released me and stepped away, allowing me to retreat into the boutique's changing rooms. I glanced at myself in the mirror, unsure of what to think of the frilly pale blue dress. I shook my head and took it off so that I could slip back into the sultrier attire I'd chosen that morning.

Once finished, I crept out of the changing rooms and looked around for Nalithor. I found him speaking with the store owner at the front. Judging by the mischievous expression on his face—and the delighted expression on the owner's face—Nalithor was ordering something.

The slow swishing of Nalithor's tail furthered my suspicions.

"You are being surprisingly cooperative," Nalithor remarked, sliding an arm around my waist. He shot me a smile before leading me out of the shop. "I was under the impression that you loathed shopping."

"It's not so terrible when in good company," I pointed out, motioning at Nalithor. "Besides, I was beginning to grow accustomed to having you all to myself…and then my brother showed up."

"You truly dislike sharing, don't you?" Nalithor chuckled,

"Do *you* like sharing?" I countered.

"No, I do not." Nalithor shook his head and grimaced. "A bath in acid would be more pleasant. Although I could say the same of your brother's company."

"He does seem like he's grown worse," I murmured, letting Nalithor steer me through the streets while I thought. "Did the Oracles or anyone indicate that something may have happened while we were gone?"

"Nothing," Nalithor replied. "Maric reported that the prince grows brattier and more demanding by the day, but that isn't something that comes as a surprise to us. Come, we should hurry. It wouldn't do for us to run out of time to prepare—or for us to be late."

"Nali, Nali, Nali!" A group of young voices clamored for my companion the moment we neared palace grounds.

Three boys came rushing out of the palace gates. The smallest two both reached up to Nalithor as soon as they came to a skidding halt in front of him. The third boy looked roughly fourteen to fifteen—so about one hundred and fifty years of age for a Devillian.

All three were excited to see Nalithor, but the oldest was quick to smooth his expression over, cross his arms, and turn away from us with a small "humph." Nalithor just chuckled and picked up the two young ones and lifted them on to each of his shoulders, a broad grin spreading across his face.

The youngest boy had pale blue hair and silver eyes, his older brother had pewter hair and eyes which gradated from blue to silver. The oldest of the trio had white hair with streaks of blue running through it, and his left eye was blue, the right one silver. All three of them shared similar horn styles to their parents and Nalithor, as well as silver- and platinum-scaled tails.

"Nali! Mommy won't let us come to the party tonight!" The second-oldest whined.

"Nali, skip the party and play with us instead!" The youngest tugged at one of Nalithor's earrings. "The servants are boring!"

"Oh? Are these the precious siblings I've heard about?" I looked between the boys on Nalithor's shoulders and then over to the grumpy teen. The teen just huffed and looked away again with a pink face.

"I'm Rhylt!" The youngest beamed at me.

"Eildr." The second-oldest flushed and looked away.

"The cranky one is Lyt," Nalithor added when the teen refused to speak. "You know that I have to attend tonight's party, Rhylt, Eildr. It wouldn't do to let Arianna-jiss contend with our guests all on her own."

"She's pretty, so she can come play too!" Rhylt pouted. "The other gods are mean and boring."

"Ijelle isn't back from the Nrae'lmar Expedition yet, Lyt?" Nalithor looked over to the cranky teen, who let out a heavy sigh.

"'Jelle probably won't be back 'til after the festival has already started," Lyt grumbled. He fidgeted with his hair while shifting back and forth on his feet. "Storms over the Gal'edean delayed their flight back—they're waiting for fairer weather."

"She said she'd bring presents!" Eildr's face lit up with excitement. "Nali, you should bring us presents more often too! You always find fun stuff."

"Boys!" Ellena's firm tone made me shift my attention over my shoulder. Their mother looked rather cross at first glance, but the twitching corners of her mouth when she spotted the young ones on Nalithor's shoulders gave her amusement away. "Nalithor, you know you shouldn't indulge them at times like this!

"Our guests have already begun to arrive. Rhylt especially doesn't need to see the 'Chosen' being paraded through palace grounds like livestock!"

"But, *Mom!*" Lyt snorted, pivoting to look at Ellena. "We already *know* how those stupid gods—"

"And *that* is exactly why you boys should return to your rooms for the evening." Lysander stepped out of the shadows beside his wife. He shot his sons a tired but unyielding look. "Say goodbye to Nalithor and Arianna-jiss for the evening. They need to prepare for tonight's festivities and don't have much time left to do so."

"Mother and Father are right—Arianna-mrii and I need to be off." Nalithor chuckled, setting his pouting siblings down. "We can play some other time, alright?"

"Fine…" Rhylt pouted and kicked at the ground.

Nalithor chuckled and then led me across the palace grounds, his arm around one of my shoulders. His expression was mirthful, but he remained silent. After several minutes we entered his section of the palace and parted ways to prepare ourselves for the night's festivities.

I found Djialkan and Alala napping in the sitting room together, so I did my best to move quietly while making my way to the wardrobe. I had a good idea of what I wanted to wear to the party, but taking a bath first seemed prudent. However, there was so little time left that I chose to lay out my clothing beforehand.

———— ❧ ————

*"Have you given him your gift yet, Arianna?"* Djialkan questioned, tracking me as I paced through my suite.

"Gift? Ah… You mean the zrintaas?" I murmured, distracted while I rummaged through my drawers in search of hair sticks.

*"You* did *decide you wish to give it to him, did you not?"* Djialkan tilted his head at me when I strode past him for the umpteenth time. *"Alala and I will be remaining in your rooms. Will you be alright without us?"*

"Mmm? You don't like the deities either?" I shot him a glance before sitting down at my vanity and pulling several drawers open.

*"I share Nalithor's displeasure regarding the Chosen and how they are treated."* Djialkan nodded, then shifted into the form of a small Devillian boy. He twirled a pair of hair sticks around his fingers and grinned at me. *"Are these the ones you are looking for? Allow me."*

I shot the thieving fae-dragon a disgruntled look and then pulled several sections of curls up. Djialkan carefully wove the ornaments into my hair, looking terribly amused by something the entire time. However, I couldn't determine what had him in such a mood. He still had the same amused look on his face once he'd finished placing the ornaments in my hair, so I wasn't sure if it was his thieving that had him so tickled, or something else.

Once the ornaments were in place, I finished applying makeup around my eyes and to my lips. Satisfied with my appearance, I shifted my attention to my jewelry and shifted a few chains and bangles to more comfortable positions.

"I think I'll be fine," I commented while glancing down at my blue nails to make sure the polish hadn't chipped. "And to answer your first question, yes. I did decide to give him my zrintaas. Just not yet."

*"You intend to make it a 'going-to-war' gift, Arianna?"* Djialkan shot me a small frown, tracking me as I rose to my feet. *"To give the charm to him in that manner is—"*

"More meaningful? I know. Giving it to him now just doesn't 'feel' right. Either I give it to him then, or I wait for another festival to come 'round," I replied, turning away from the mirror. "What are you and Alala going to do about dinner?"

*"We have already made our desires known to the servants and chefs."* Djialkan snorted at me, shaking his head. *"You had best hurry. The weak ones have already begun making their entrances."*

I tugged Djialkan's silver hair over his eyes before he could shift back to his draconic form and snickered when he shot me a disgruntled glare.

*'Nalithor probably thinks I'm going to slip into another one of those regal kimonos...'* I smirked while making my way down the hall.

Of course, I couldn't just go with what he likely expected. I had chosen to go a much different route instead. As far as I was concerned, the lightweight gown I wore was suitable for a goddess attending a festival. Its soft black fabric clung to my curves and accentuated them without being skintight and it provided a nice backdrop for my ever-present platinum jewelry.

Thin straps held the dress up and connected to a low neckline. Several pieces of my sapphire-studded jewelry around my hips kept the skirt of the dress in place, keeping the hip-high slits from letting me flash *too much* skin.

*'Perhaps it's somewhere between dancer, goddess, and "pet."'* I bit back another smirk when I caught Nalithor's scent nearby. *'Maybe he's right. Perhaps I am a little* too *"accepting."'*

"There you...are..." Nalithor trailed off when he turned to look at me. Within seconds he closed the distance between us, pinned me back against a wall and lifted my chin. A husky growl rumbled deep in his chest, almost causing me to giggle at him. "Looking like *that*... I should claim you right now!"

"I take it you approve, then?" I asked innocently, smiling as his hand slid from my chin and down to my throat.

"You are *impossible*." Nalithor growled, his grip twitching around my neck. "I can't decide if you do this to get a rise out of your brother...or *me*."

"*Your* reaction is the only one I find myself caring about," I informed him, reaching up to tug at the hem of his armored kimono. "I can always change into something else if you don't *like* my dress."

"You are to stay by my side at all times." Nalithor's grip on my

throat tightened slightly, causing me to flush. "I will not have *anyone*—
"

"Anything else?" I interjected, sliding both my hands up his exposed abdomen. "I don't know about you, but *I* don't intend to leave my date's side. If you grow tired of my company, you will have to get rid of me yourself." I paused and dug the tips of my nails into his chest, shooting him a sweet smile. "And if you decide to do *that*… I will make you fight for it."

"You're…" Nalithor trailed off into a growl, his tail thrashing behind him a few times. He leaned down with a dangerous, mischievous glint in his eyes. "At this rate, I won't let you leave my side *ever again*, Arianna. Just how far do you intend to test me?"

"I suppose we'll just have to wait and see," I replied sweetly, sliding my hands back down his torso. My nails grazed across his skin along the way down, making him growl at me yet again. "Those growls of yours are quite enjoyable, you know. You're only encouraging me."

Nalithor caught me by the wrists when my hands wandered a little *too* low for his tastes. I shot him another innocent smile as he pulled my hands back up. After a moment he let out a sigh, offered me his arm, and smacked my ass with his tail once I'd accepted it.

I considered praising his ability to spank "properly" but instead remained silent. I'd teased him enough—for now.

'*You are not wearing anything underneath,*' Nalithor pointed out. I couldn't help but laugh when I spotted the flush in his face.

'*What, exactly, would I wear when the slits are* this *high?*' I countered,

431

jutting one leg and part of my hip out from behind the fabric. Nalithor's face flushed a shade darker as his eyes traveled up my thigh.

*'You* definitely *need to remain by my side,'* Nalithor stated, shaking his head. *'As forw our entrance... We need to make a strong impression, don't we?'*

*'What do you have in mind?'* I inquired. Nalithor tensed, causing me to glance around in search of what could have caught his attention.

*'First, I have a request.'* Nalithor stopped and turned to look down at me. He raised a hand to brush a stray curl from my cheek. *'I would prefer it if you didn't use your power to buffer* Darius' *display when he arrives. He needs to understand just how lacking his abilities are, and—'*

*'And you want me all to yourself for the night?'* I offered with a smile when Nalithor hesitated. *'You don't need to be so reserved with me, Nalithor. Speak your mind.'*

A small smile crept across Nalithor's lips as he nodded. Satisfied, he led me by my arm to a massive courtyard where the night's dinner was being held.

There were blooming plants and soft decorations everywhere I looked. Dozens of large tables were strewn throughout the area, many of which already had people sat around them. Judging by the number of deities, royalty, and nobles present, Faerstravir was quite popular with foreign gods and dignitaries alike.

*'What's wrong?'* Nalithor glanced down at me when I flinched.

*'I hope you won't need me to see magic for you at any point tonight. Too bright,'* I grumbled, shutting my eyes and shaking my head. *'With*

*this many deities in one place, it's nothing but color and light. Can't even make out shapes.'*

*'You shouldn't need to use your vision tonight.'* Nalithor shook his head at me. *'I don't want you to strain yourself, either. Perhaps I should have you teach me to "see" magic one of these days.'*

While nearing the queue of people waiting to enter the courtyard, I ascertained why Nalithor disliked the term "slave" for submissives so much. It was obvious that the deities and their Chosen were much of the reason. Only a handful of Chosen stood behind their deity's seat, their bodies clad in regal armor—the way they were meant to be.

The vast majority of "Chosen" wore little to no clothing, and kneeled or laid subserviently by their god's or goddess's feet. Many wore simple collars or, in some cases, even shackles. A few bore bruises or lacerations that likely came from the treatment they received at the hand of their "owners."

It made my stomach turn. Chosen were meant to be warriors and helpers that assisted their deity with their duties. Not…this. I sighed to myself. That information was likely something I wasn't "supposed" to know already, but my gut told me it was true.

*'You dislike them because they make a mockery of your preferred type of relationship?'* I asked bluntly, cutting my gaze to the side to look at Nalithor. His face flushed as we joined the queue of dignitaries, and struggled to think of a reply.

*'I never said I—'* Nalithor cast a murderous glare over his shoulder at someone.

'You hide your dominant tendencies about as well as I hide my excitement to hunt beasts,' I offered in a very serious tone before breaking into a smile. 'In all seriousness, is that why? While I don't necessarily see anything wrong with them kneeling at the feet of—'

'Becoming a deity's toy isn't why any of them wished to become "Chosen,"' Nalithor interjected with a small smile. He motioned subtly at a nearby table before continuing, 'Though you are right—they do make a mockery of such relationships as far as I am concerned.

'Erist'il and Arom'il are both a piece of work. Part of their "laws" regarding relationships between deities is that if one dies, both die. They consider it a "mercy." Unfaithfulness is punished by death...so I'm sure you can see how the prior rule can become a problem.'

'So, the deities are using the Chosen as a loophole to acquire playthings.' I nodded my understanding while glancing around at the number of Chosen I could spot in the courtyard. 'The ones in armor and are standing behind or beside their deity, are the legitimate Chosen then. The collared ones are the toys?'

'You spotted the genuine Chosen already?' Nalithor arched an eyebrow at me. 'You shouldn't be able to sense the contract between them and their deity. Did your sight allow you to spot them?'

'No—as I said, the magic is too bright here.' I shook my head. 'They just didn't strike me as normal guards, soldiers, or mercenaries. Of course, I doubt that deities would need an escort anyway. Hired or otherwise. ...is that really considered appropriate behavior, though?'

I turned my gaze away from the nearest table of deities, startled by the glimpse of what I'd seen. In total, there were six Chosen with their deities at that table, all of varying race. At first glance, nothing seemed too different about them compared to the other Chosen in the courtyard. However, a second look revealed they weren't *just* nude.

All six of the Chosen were fastened into rough iron collars and shackles. The males and females all had piercings through their nipples, with weights hanging from the rings. The men had rust-coated chastity devices fastened around their manhoods.

Several of the deities had deigned it fitting to attach leashes to the nipple piercing instead of the collars, and seemed fond of yanking on said leashes every now and then while conversing.

*'It gets worse…'* Nalithor sighed, pulling me closer to his side. *'As you saw in the residential district, public displays are not frowned upon in Draemir—if they don't take place in areas such as the merchants' or military districts. You are likely to see worse by the end of the night.*

*'The other Lesser Gods do not comprehend the… "depth" of Adinvyr relationships. They believe displays, such as what you just saw, are the appropriate way to display power and status. The fools think it makes them seem desirable, and like they are "good" masters and mistresses.'*

*'Bah it's always about power and status, isn't it?'* I huffed, rolling my eyes. *'If they can't grasp anything beyond that, to the hells with them! They clearly aren't meant to be masters or mistresses if they can't understand the true dynamics.'*

"What do you *mean* 'release all your power upon arrival?!'" Darius whined from somewhere behind me. I tilted my head slightly, listening. "Is that why there's been so many shockwaves? Tch!"

*'Speaking of releasing power...'* Nalithor chuckled and shot me a devious grin. *'I think we should release our power together. What do you think?'*

I couldn't help but be affected by his contagious grin. *'You* want *to terrify the poor bastards, do you?'*

*'I wouldn't want any of them to continue believing that either of us is approachable,'* Nalithor answered with false innocence.

*'I would hope that I'm at least a* little *approachable.'* I sniffed, focusing my attention forward again. *'I must say, I'm a little miffed that my twin considers* these *shockwaves. I hadn't really noticed them.'*

*'You should only be approachable by* me,*'* Nalithor informed me, releasing a growl as he slid an arm around my waist and pulled me tight against his side. "Darius, since you're so *nervous* you may go ahead of us if you like."

I glanced up at Nalithor, intrigued, and studied the strange smirk on his face. I wasn't sure just what he was up to. The Adinvyr shot me a smile and rested his hand on my exposed hip, stroking my skin. If Darius' scowl was any indication, he had noticed.

Darius' date, *Xander* of all people, redirected my twin's attention and shooed him past us.

*'Xander, hmmm?'* Nalithor murmured, watching the pair cut into the line in front of us. *'You seem unsurprised.'*

*'Actually, I was curious about that one,'* I murmured, examining Xander's back for a moment. *'During our excursion to Abrantia he*

sustained a lot of damage, but I got the impression that it was intentional. Is he…is he just that into pain, or—'

'Ah, I suppose you could say that Xander has a few wires crossed.' Nalithor chuckled, squeezing me. 'Pleasure is the only thing that Xander can feel—physical pain doesn't exist for him. Being a Vampire only serves to enable him, seeing as their kind are incredibly difficult to kill. For example, he rather enjoys being run through. Xander only ever dodges lethal strikes.'

'In that case, I suppose caning and the like would only qualify as teasing for him. Darius must be delighted.' I snorted and rolled my eyes before shooting Nalithor a questioning glance. 'What? What's so funny?'

'You are more observant about such things than I gave you credit for.' Nalithor teased, tracing one of his claws along my hip. 'Perhaps you really are an Adinvyr under there.'

'Since you know who I am, shouldn't that make it easier to determine what I am?' I asked with a small frown, pivoting to look up at him. 'If Lucifer and Gabriel are my—'

'Lucifer is "unique."' Nalithor half-shrugged, shaking his head. 'Each Devillian race was created from an aspect of Lucifer, but none of us are biologically related to him.

'You, however, are his child by blood. There is no way of knowing for certain what you are. When we were children, you were more like your father than Darius was. Your horns and tail were similar to Lucifer's, when you weren't hiding them. You almost always hid your Brands, however.'

437

'So, it's entirely possible that I have traits from multiple races or even none of them?' I asked, pausing when Nalithor nodded his agreement. 'I take it that Gabriel must be rather "unique" herself if the Elders chose to pair her with Lucifer.'

'Darius is more like her,' Nalithor muttered with distaste. 'Lucifer raised you, and she raised Darius. But…because you are twins, you were close. She often brought Darius to Dauthrmir to visit you. However, the visits were always short-lived because she feared our "dark ways" would taint her precious son.

'The Oracles always suspected that you wound up with the Devillian traits and that Darius received the Angelic ones. However, no one ever proved it. Your twin also had horns and a tail of his own, so I doubt their theory.'

"Ari, I'm totally going to show that I'm more powerful than you!" Darius sneered over his shoulder, making the corner of my eye twitch. "Dressed like *that*…you're just food for him, aren't you?"

Nalithor's grip tightened as I considered ripping Darius' head from his shoulder. I bit back a shiver when the Adinvyr's hand drifted lower, his claws tracing where my thigh and torso met. He chuckled when I shot him a disgruntled glare.

'When you are that red, your glaring just becomes more adorable.' Nalithor teased, digging his claws into my tender skin. He smiled when I flushed, and my pulse sped up. 'Ahhh… who am I fooling? You are worthy of adoration regardless.'

Several minutes passed before it was Darius and Xander's turn to make their entrance. I watched with faint interest when Xander released his power first. He, at least, had a significant amount compared to the other nobles. It wasn't enough to draw my full interest, but it was still much more interesting than those who had gone before him.

For some reason, Darius seemed startled by Xander's power. Alas, I chose to ignore my twin and focused on Nalithor instead. My rather delicious-smelling date was still tense for some reason, and I hoped to alleviate that.

'*What*—' Nalithor began to question when I shifted in his grip to rest my cheek against his chest.

'*These people are terribly boring,*' I informed him, nuzzling his chest for a moment. '*What did you have in mind for our display?*'

'*You're…going to indulge my request?*' Nalithor gripped my chin and lifted my head up so he could study my face.

'*Indulging you is* much *more rewarding than pampering my twin,*' I replied simply, earning a surprised look from the Adinvyr.

'*In that case,*' Nalithor began, his tone contemplative. '*Mmm… Let's see which one of us can exert more power.*'

'*Shouldn't* you *be the one with more power?*' I shot him a sly look before glancing toward my brother. '*Well, if* that one *doesn't stop procrastinating, we'll never find out.*'

"Darius, were you not going to show your sister that you are more than 'food?'" Nalithor inquired, his tone surprisingly haughty. He slowly slid his hand just low enough on my hip to be inappropriate, causing me to squirm and flush.

"Ari, are you really going to just let him grab you like that?" Darius demanded, a nasty scowl settling on his face.

"If you keep us waiting, he may shift to something other than *grabbing* in order to ease our boredom," I replied with a poisonous smile. I had to suppress a shiver when Nalithor coiled his tail around my thigh as if to prove my point further.

Darius turned a brilliant shade of red when he failed to determine where the tip of Nalithor's tail had disappeared to. Nalithor was actually keeping his tail in an appropriate place, but the skirt of my dress hid that fact. My date chuckled when Darius turned abruptly and stalked into the courtyard. Darius released his power in an angry fit but, since he was more healing-minded, his power simply made most of the remaining plants burst into full bloom.

I watched with amusement as several fountains flowed faster, and then my brother's failed control over lightning gave him a sharp zap. Being the *good sister* that I was, I managed to hold back my laughter. Darius' power had little effect on the floating Magelights that lit the courtyard, which I found a little strange. I didn't spot so much as a flicker or pulse from them.

"Shall we, my dear?" Nalithor chuckled, pivoting to look down at me. "Mmm... Or are you '*just food?*'"

"I'd like to think that I'm dessert, actually," I informed him as he withdrew his tail from my leg, but not before I felt it twitch. Smirking, I added, "Or did you find my taste to be more savory than sweet?"

"You are most certainly sweet, Reiz'tar." Nalithor purred, pulling me past Xander and my shocked twin, "I find myself wanting to feast on *you*..."

I smirked when I felt Nalithor's power trembling just beneath the surface. I obliged his prior suggestion and released my power alongside his as we strode through the courtyard and toward the head table. The whirlwind of our combined powers sent many people shrieking and ducking for cover, including my twin.

Nalithor's power took on the form of dragons as it raged alongside my more vulpine elements. However, the display didn't distract from me or my attire for long.

"Lord Nalithor, surely you don't intend to keep such a troublesome woman to yourself?" A male voice commented. I shot a sideways glare at the unfamiliar deity that had spoken. "I would be *happy* to lend you my expertise in training such an unruly creature. She should know better than to compete with your release of power!"

"Are you suggesting that I am incapable of handling this *delicious* morsel myself?" Nalithor countered, pulling me to his chest possessively. He wrapped one hand around my throat and made a show of caressing my inner thigh with his tail, startling a whimper out of me. "Ahhh...you *are* such a good girl, aren't you, Arianna?"

Nalithor didn't give me enough time to think of a retort and, instead, adjusted his grip on me and guided me to an oversized chaise behind the head table. He drew me onto the chaise with him so that I was laying alongside him atop the fluffy pillows and throws. I had to shift my position carefully in order to keep from flashing my groin at anyone.

Once I was comfortable, I glanced to my right and examined Nalithor's rather self-satisfied expression. Somehow, his commanding presence and the darkness of his aura didn't dissuade further interruptions.

"M-my lord, shouldn't you at least have her kneel at your feet like a proper slut?" It was a female deity to question him this time, and her comment made many of the present Devillians—Adinvyr or otherwise—bristle and snarl.

Nalithor made a simple motion with his right hand and lifted the cheeky goddess into the air with his shadows. She gasped for air and clawed at Nalithor's power, her face beginning to grow red as she struggled.

"How many of you intend to question me and my preferences?" Nalithor's dangerously calm tone and the rippling darkness around him made the foreigners freeze and grow pale, while the Devillians nodded their approval. "Arianna-z'tar could crush any one of you like an ant, and I am inclined to let her if *any of you* continue to speak to either of us with such disrespect."

"The *princess* is my son's date," Lysander spoke up, his chilling tone making several people flinch. He swept a murderous glare over the courtyard. "Her 'place' is by his side. You would do well to remember that Nalithor is the God of Balance before he is a Prince of Draemir. If you would not say it to the Elders, then you should not say it to him."

*'I see the deities are as desperate to have you as the mortals are.'* I teased Nalithor, shifting my focus to him. He twitched when I drew my hand down his chest, and I leaned in closer to whisper, *"I don't think that* bitch *has earned the right to have you choke her, do you?"*

My comment startled Nalithor enough that he must have dropped the goddess—I heard her collide with the floor, followed by screeching and coughing. Nalithor, however, was quick to recover. His surprised expression shifted to a sultry smirk as he slipped an arm around me and rested his hand on my hip once more.

"You are a terrifying woman, Arianna," Ellena informed me, her tone one of disbelief. "That much power should be—"

"Impossible?" I offered with a laugh, motioning at Nalithor with one hand. "This one seems to find me quite impossible, at least."

"Not that I *mind* by any stretch of the imagination," Nalithor added, chuckling as he trailed his claws over my hip. "Still, making even *gods* want to fight me over you… I really am going to have to make sure you stay with me all night, aren't I?"

*'Are you certain it's* me *they're after?'* I inquired, relaxing against Nalithor's side. *'I would've thought you to be their focus.'*

*'They find you fascinating, as they should,'* Nalithor replied, studying me with an unreadable expression. *'Still… I should apologize, shouldn't I? I never asked your permission to handle you in such a way, and—'*

*'I like to think that the fact I haven't eviscerated you yet shows that I enjoy your attention,'* I interjected with a pointed glance, before shifting

my attention to Ellena. She was approaching us with a drink in each hand and glancing between us like she couldn't make up her mind about something.

"I don't know which one of you is going to kill someone first!" Ellena exclaimed, shaking her head before offering us each a drink. "I *was* going to ask my son to attend to his duties as a prince...but you aren't going to let him, are you, Arianna-jiss?"

"She is considering killing you for even *suggesting* it," Nalithor answered as I opened my mouth to state as much. My face flushed and I snapped my mouth shut. "Was the X'shmiran's presence here *your* doing, Mother?"

"Hardly." Ellena flapped her hand at us and grimaced. "With their sins and what is on their minds? Convincing our men to *not* act against them has been difficult.

"The X'shmirans, apparently, wish to learn more about the nations they allied themselves with. The Oracles suggested that they should attend Faerstravir...and should be arriving soon.

"Gabriel was delayed and won't arrive for several days yet." Ellena shook her head and then shifted her attention to me. "I'm surprised by the tension between you and your brother, Arianna."

"His behavior regarding Nalithor and I both has been incredibly inappropriate," I replied with a small sigh. "The rumors he has been spreading about his supposed 'relationship' with Nalithor makes me angry enough as it is, and who knows what sort of tales he's come up with about me."

"He's the one half of the twins that I *don't* want obsessed with me," Nalithor added, shooting me a smirk. "I actually find myself feeling bad for his 'date,' however. One would think that he'd focus on Xander's willingness instead of shooting glares our way."

"Darius flip-flops between wanting to compete with me and wanting to be a 'good brother.'" I shrugged before taking a sip of my drink and glancing out from our perch. "I would argue that my brother isn't the only one neglecting his date. Even the 'Chosen' are sending rather strange looks our way."

"They can't figure you out." Nalithor grinned. "They're attempting to determine if you're my Chosen, a goddess, or something else entirely."

"I would say most of our fellow deities are suffering the same problem," Ellena murmured, a small frown on her face. "Even I'm not sure just *what* exactly…"

Ellena shook her head and then returned to her seat beside Lysander, so I refocused my attention on Nalithor. He still seemed terribly pleased with himself—aside from the warning glances he kept shooting toward different tables on occasion.

I found the way he continued petting my hip to be incredibly distracting. At this point, I was convinced that my face would remain flushed for the evening. Perhaps the consistency, at least, would fool onlookers into believing it was my makeup.

It wasn't long before Dilonu and Tyana arrived, accompanied by a mixture of X'shmiran and Vorpmasian guards. Nalithor released a low growl, his grip tensing, when the king and queen made their way straight to the head table. Neither of them paid any heed to the other dignitaries in the courtyard, nor did they show their respect to Lysander and Ellena upon stopping before the table.

"'*Lord*' Nalithor, you still haven't purchased Arianna from us." Dilonu sneered, crossing his arms. He stared at us with a look that made my skin crawl. "Unless you intend to pay for her, I suggest that you take your hands off—"

"If he won't let a *god* challenge his possession of her, what makes you think he will heed a mortal?!" The God of Elves snapped, fastening a murderous glare on Dilonu. "Lord Balance is second only to the Elders, *Human*. If he wants that woman, then she is his. That he has yet to take your head should be payment enough!"

'*For once the Elf says something that makes sense,*' Nalithor scoffed, settling a dangerous look on the X'shmiran king and queen. "If you intend to disrupt the feast, I will be happy to silence the both of you permanently.

"This woman is *mine*, whether you approve or not. Should you attempt to interfere, I will destroy every last shred of your soul until there is nothing left of you for the Elders to reincarnate."

"How *dare*—" Tyana began, but a sharp backhand from a new female shocked her into silence, nearly knocking her to the floor.

"Lysander, Ellena, Nalithor," The new female bowed her head to the deities she addressed. "I will see to it that these two lost children are re-educated in the ways of our people. It pains me to see my kin

446

act in such shameful fashion."

*'Hadyn, the Goddess of Humans,'* Nalithor offered as I slid my gaze between the blonde Human and the spluttering X'shmirans. *'They should be capable of instinctively recognizing their matron deity...but I am unsure of anything when it comes to those two.'*

*'Watching you destroy them has its own appeal.'* I smiled, nuzzling into Nalithor's chest again. Dilonu and Tyana spouted a new round of protests in response, but I ignored them. *'Hey... Watch where you're sliding your tail! We haven't even had dinner yet, and this skirt is—'*

*'It would be much easier to hide if you had chosen a less delicious dress...but I can't honestly complain.'* Nalithor sighed, settling for lacing his tail around my thighs.

I fell silent and observed the partygoers, taking in the variety of gods and races present. However, it wasn't long before I shifted my attention away from them and back to Nalithor. His power and scent coiling around me made it difficult to focus on anything else. The occasional teasing of his tail along my thighs, and his hand stroking my hip, only served to distract me further.

Dinner provided a very brief distraction from Nalithor's attention, but I found myself *missing* his attention while we ate. I was more than happy to return to cuddling after we had dined.

*'Ahhh... What am I going to do with you?'* Nalithor sighed and pulled me into his lap, nuzzling the crook of my neck. *'You are still drawing so much attention. The thoughts these bastards are having about you makes me want to kill them all.'*

'Is it really that bad?' I asked, shifting my legs into a more comfortable position. The jingling of my jewelry caused several of the closer groups of dignitaries to shift their attention to us.

'They're so focused on how delicious you look that it hasn't even occurred to them that your jewelry was forged by Aurelian,' Nalithor muttered irritably, planting a kiss on my shoulder. 'They think you're wearing slave jewelry. I question Aurelian's choice of bells, even though I...'

'You approve of them?' I offered, amused. 'Aside from the obvious problem of your parents' guests, I do like it here. I can see why you're so proud of Draemir.'

'Our "guests" are wearing on my patience,' Nalithor grumbled, nuzzling my shoulder again and nearly displacing one of my straps.

'If you keep that up, they're going to become a bigger nuisance,' I pointed out, reaching back to tug at his braid. 'That's at least the fifth time you've almost knocked my strap off. I don't think you want me to flash them, given your distaste for their ways.'

"You've barely even given me a glimpse," Nalithor whispered into my throat, his power rippling over my skin, followed by a sigh. "At the very least, I should get to 'appreciate' them before anyone else."

"Alright, that's enough!" Darius exclaimed, storming toward us. He didn't stop until he was a few feet away from the front of our chaise. "Ari, I want him. Give him to me."

"That's my boy!" Dilonu cackled from the X'shmiran's table. "Show the Evil Mage who is—"

"You're challenging me *again*?" I questioned, tilting my head. Nalithor's grip on me tensed as he released a feral growl.

"Since *I* want him, that means he likes *men*," Darius stated as if it was the most obvious thing in the world. "Clearly you've used your power to influence him. I'm not going to let you take someone that doesn't want you!"

"That's not how it works, boy!" Erist sighed, exasperated. She turned in her seat to look at my twin, shaking her head. "That's not how *any* of this works!"

"There's no reason for someone like Nali to be interested in a worthless, selfish bitch like—" Darius snarled in protest, but my anger drowned out the rest of his sentence.

*'Arianna, calm down—'* Nalithor started to warn me, but it was too late.

With a flick of my wrist, I sent Darius flying backward to the courtyard and crashing into the base of a tree. To my surprise, his skull didn't crack when it slammed into the trunk, nor did he lose consciousness. I would have to try harder.

I moved to stand up and pursue my brother, but Nalithor tightened his grip and kept me trapped on his lap. Darius stormed back to us with a crazed look of rage on his face.

"How *dare* you raise a hand against an Astral Mage?!" Darius shrieked. I just snarled at him and attempted to pull myself out of Nalithor's lap.

"Darius, do you *really* think that your sister—or anyone else, for that matter—is capable of casting a spell strong enough to affect someone of *my* rank?" Nalithor inquired dangerously, making my brother flinch. "Didn't you hear? My rank is second only to the *Elders*, boy. I can't decide what to be angrier over; the fact that you believe me to be so weak, or that you think your sister has to resort to such methods to attract a mate."

"He's right, boy." Someone snorted from the Elf god's table. "She may be powerful but, unless she's an Elder, she has no power over him."

*'Let me up.'* I growled, struggling in Nalithor's lap. My pulse raced; my body was hot with rage. *'I'll tear that fucking brat limb-from-limb! Then we won't have to deal with his bullshit anymore.'*

"Have you forgotten just *who* I've chosen to conquer for?" Nalithor questioned Darius, shifting his tail to bind my thighs as he spoke. "Arianna... Am I going to have to subdue you in order to keep you from killing your brother?"

"Why do you give her *all* of your attention then?!" Darius whined. "She's just an Umbral Mage—she's not worthy!"

"***Because I want her.***" Nalithor snarled at Darius. "I am an Umbral Mage as well, lest you forget. However, as badly as I want her...it is *nothing* compared to how much she wants to *kill you* at the moment.

"Arianna, you will have to forgive me for this later."

I started to turn to question Nalithor, but his hand wrapped around the front of my throat. He gripped my jawline between his thumb and index finger, turning my head a little to the left. Without missing a beat, he sunk his fangs deep into the right side of my throat, his other arm encircling my waist.

Warmth spread from his bite and flooded my veins. In an instant, my vision blurred and my strength disappeared. I let out a gasp, attempting to struggle out of his hold. However, the angry racing of my pulse only served to quicken the pumping of my blood into Nalithor's greedy mouth.

Fire raced through my veins, attempting to shatter every single resistance I had left.

"N-Nalithor, stop it—" I finally managed to speak, but I trailed off into an involuntary moan as he tightened his grip on me. He buried his fangs the rest of the way into my flesh, causing me to twitch and shudder. *'I-I wasn't so angry that you needed to use…venom…'*

Nalithor seemed oblivious to my attempts and prying his grip loose from my waist and jaw, but soon enough it didn't matter. My struggles soon turned into ecstatic writhing as arousal leaked down my thighs, and my breath became short. I no longer cared that he was feeding from me in front of others, or that he'd used his venom against me.

*'Calm down.'* Nalithor growled as I attempted to fumble my way to his pants.

*'Take me,'* I countered desperately, earning a low groan from him. Another wave of his venom rushed through my system, making me shudder. *'I don't care if you break me! Make me—'*

**'I said calm down.'** Nalithor's voice was still husky, but firm

451

enough this time to make me pause.

'B-but…' I trailed off into a whimper when Nalithor's grip on my throat tightened, and I felt his tail sliding up my thighs.

'Nnngh… *Most people would be little more than a doll after so much venom, yet you're still so disobedient,*' Nalithor chastised me, pulling away from my throat. He ran his tongue over the puncture wounds, slowly, and chuckled when I shuddered. '*If you are not going to calm down, then…**sleep**.*'

'*But I want you to*—' I attempted to protest even as my vision grew dark, my pulse still tracing.

Despite my blinding desire to have Nalithor take me right then and there, my body was eager to obey him even if my mind wasn't. His power slid over me, leaving my skin tingling in its wake. Nalithor's desire hit me like a wall as my consciousness continued to slip. What I sensed was a mere *hint* of his lust and frustration, yet it was far greater than mine.

If it was meant to serve as a warning, it did no such thing. His power and desire only served to further my blind hunger for him.

**"*I said* sleep, Arianna."**

His dangerous growl made my heart stop for a moment when the full brunt of his power rushed through me. Everything spun as I lolled to the side in Nalithor's grip. Vaguely, I caught the sound of what might have been arguing. My mind was too far-gone to identify any of their voices.

All I could think of, as my mind drifted off to sleep, was Nalithor and I exploring every inch of each other's bodies.

*'I'm…hungry.'*

# CHAPTER NINETEEN
*The Would-be Hero*

"Nali, you shouldn't swallow her blood! Spit it out!" I pleaded with Nali as Ari collapsed in his arms. Small traces of her poisonous blood trickled from the wounds in her neck, capturing the attention of several other Adinvyr. "An Umbral Mage, like her, is nothing but poison!"

Nali's pale eyes snapped up and glimmered with hatred when he looked at me. Darkness burst out from his feet as he stood up and continued to whirl around him like a storm. Six pairs of massive, feathered wings appeared from his back as the air around him twisted and warped with power. The ground beneath us trembled as dark energy crackled and crept around everything.

My heart raced with fear, the pressure of Nali's power pressing me back. Shining platinum armor ran along the upper ridges of his glossy obsidian wings, matching the armor that protected portions of his body. His white hair whipped around his shoulders, carried by the immense power radiating from him. It was a stark contrast to the color of his wings.

He was so incredibly beautiful but fearsome.

I forgot to breathe while looking upon the enraged deity. My limbs shook and sweat beaded across my skin. If I moved, I might die.

*'B-but... Nali is an* Astral *Mage, right?* **They** *wouldn't lie about something like that!'* I reminded myself, shivering. *'I have to save him from her blood before it poisons him. That armor should be* gold! *His wings should probably be white too then, right? How could she corrupt him so fast?'*

"L-Lord Balance, please!" A Sundreht stuttered, kneeling before the head table. I just stared at him for a moment. "I beg you, do not punish us *all* for the reckless actions and words of this youth! Your claim on that woman is indisputable!"

*'Balance? Nali's role is* Balance?' I looked between the Sundreht and the glowering deity. *'All the more reason he couldn't possibly be an* Umbral *Mage! Such dark creatures couldn't* possibly *fathom how to perform that role!'*

"His *claim?*" I snapped, turning to glower at the cat-eared bastard. "Why would *Balance*, one of the most *holy* roles, want—"

*"In case you have forgotten, brat,"* Nali began, his voice reverberating with power and murderous intent. My body froze, and my heart stopped, too scared to move. *"I too am an Umbral Mage. Your insults*

*toward* my *character and honor I can ignore. However, your treatment of Arianna is something I will not allow."*

Nali didn't make a single move, aside from the continuous thrashing of his tail, yet something threw me across the room. My body slammed into a table and slid across the ground several feet before one of the X'shmiran guards caught me. I scrambled to my feet and braced for another hit but found that Nali had turned so that his back was facing the courtyard. All I could see of my stupid sister now was one of her hands dangling to the side, devoid of strength.

He seemed to relax when he looked down at Ari, but it didn't last for long.

"We'll go with you." Ellena rose from her feet and looked up at her son, her expression softening for a moment before she turned to address another woman. "Erist, your drink can wait until later! Arianna-jiss is more important than your booze right now!"

"*Fine.*" Erist huffed, slamming her tankard down. "Arom, grab the boy and take him back to the temple. Make sure he stays there."

The golden-blonde man to Erist's right let out a heavy sigh and rose to his feet. When he turned toward me, I felt my heart leap into my throat. His cold green gaze and chiseled features were *almost* as amazing as Nali's. This "Arom" fellow wasn't quite as well built, and nowhere near as tall, but I wouldn't have minded having him beneath me either.

He was paler than Xander, so his skin would show bruising and the mark of whips much better.

"You still have not paid us for our daughter, yet you *bit* her?" Dilonu snarled, slamming his hands down on his table. I jumped and shied away from the X'shmirans, then glanced around nervously at the Devillians—they were *not* happy. "I refuse to let you take both of our children off to—"

Dilonu screamed when an unseen forced ripped his torso open and sent his blood splashing to the floor. Arom clamped a hand on my shoulder when I turned to approach Nali again. His grip rooted me in place—he was much stronger than he looked.

I couldn't fathom why Nali didn't just kill Dilonu. The bastard wouldn't stop screaming—but killing him would have solved so many problems.

A shudder ran through Nali's wings and tail when he shifted his attention over his shoulder. His vicious expression made everyone flee from Dilonu's side. If Arom hadn't kept me in place, I would have run too.

"No god needs to *buy* his prospective mate." Arom's smooth, cold voice made me tense more than his strange response did. "Your rights to Arianna-jiss ended the moment Nalithor-y'ric chose to acquire her assistance with the beasts, and his choice to pursue her as more than just a tool cemented your loss of her.

"Dilonu, Tyana, if either of you attempts to interfere, or force Nalithor-y'ric to buy the princess, your lives will be forfeit. As the God of Love, I will end your pathetic existences myself—the same goes for you, *boy*."

"I said that I want her," Nali stated, shifting his murderous gaze to me. "If you are incapable of respecting that, then I have no desire to be in even the same room as you. Nor will I subject Arianna to your vile, childish presence any further."

"Enough talk, let's go." Erist patted Nali's arm. "If your display doesn't make its point, they don't deserve to live anyway."

*'W-what in the hells does he mean? "He wants her?!"'* I clenched my fists at my side and glanced around the room, frantic for a distraction. *'I can't let him take her away somewhere they'll be alone! Shit, shit, shit!'*

I gathered light around my forearms and took a step forward, but searing pain shot through my shoulder from Arom's hand. His impossibly pure light pierced through me and took over my power, wresting it from my grasp with ease. I dropped to my knees with a strangled scream of pain.

Shifting my gaze upward, I snarled when I caught sight of Nali crouching slightly seconds before bursting into the air on his multiple pairs of wings. Erist and Ellena darted after him on foot, soon disappearing from the courtyard.

My attempts at reaching Nali with my light were useless. I brushed against a solid wall of darkness, like a void, and cold terror overtook me. My dinner and drink threatened to come back up.

Arom's power burst through me again, yanking me away from the abyss of Nali's darkness and tearing through me like a knife. Everything went blank as I collapsed into a pit of fear, desperation, and overwhelming light. How could my sister consort with these people without pissing herself?

*'T-They need to give me more power. More power, so that I can...'*

If anyone said something to me, I didn't hear it. I was aware, on some level, of Arom steering my shaking body out of the courtyard. My breath came in panicked gasps, burning my lungs as my chest constricted. Darkness crept around my senses, making me jump at the slightest of things.

Nali's power blanketed the palace grounds like dense snow. Cold. Suffocating. Silent. Threatening.

Warmth didn't tint his aura until he shifted it away from me and to my damned sister. How had she entranced him, a god, in such a way? *'They swore that he would be mine! What in the hells did she do to lure him away from me? They are so much more powerful than anyone else—they promised him to me!*

*'They wouldn't lie to me. Ari did something. I'll... I'll find a way to save Nali from her!*

## CHAPTER TWENTY
### *Disquiet*

*'That stupid boy should be grateful that I didn't tear him apart.'* I cast one last glare at the courtyard before flying away, my grip tightening on Arianna. *'I'm not certain I can keep* both *of us from destroying him for much longer…'*

I tensed, a cold chill running down my spine. Darius' desperation and lust didn't feel…*right*. His thoughts were a jumbled mess. Half of them were directed toward me, whilst the other half appeared focused on something else.

A brief flare of murderous intent, directed at Arianna, made me stop. I hovered midair for a moment, considering taking out the spoiled brat once and for all.

*'I'll have their heads if they lied to me!'* Darius' thought made my

blood run cold. His presence was like thousands of spiders were crawling across my skin. *'They promised that they were powerful enough to make Nali* mine—*!'*

Darius' thoughts spiraled into an unintelligible cacophony again moments before Fraelfnir shielded Darius' mind once more. I had heard enough—few beings could claim to be *that* powerful. However, the Elders weren't the sort to make deals with mortals—nor were they the sort to interfere with the roles of "lesser" deities.

I attempted to reach out to Fraelfnir, question him as to why he had let me hear his ward's thoughts, but the fae-dragon was unresponsive. All I could sense was his disgust with his own ward.

*'The Elders…'* I released a low growl and resumed my flight across the palace grounds. My grip tightened on Arianna's thigh and shoulder, rage creeping through me. *'First, they try to take Arianna away from me, then they lie about her death…and then Djialkan claims that he "does not know these Elders." I don't like this.'*

"Nalithor, wait up!" Erist huffed from behind me when I landed outside my portion of the palace.

"I don't need your help." I spat, turning to glare at both Erist and my mother. "I can take care of Arianna myself. I won't leave her alone after *those bastards*—"

"You intend to bathe her yourself? Not happening!" Mother shook her head and stalked toward us. "If she wakes up, she's going to eviscerate you."

"I did what was necessary to keep her from killing *her own family*."

I growled, pivoting to shift Arianna out of their view. "Your assistance isn't—"

"We'll return her to you after you've calmed down, and after she's been changed," Erist interjected. She narrowed her eyes at me, her expression uncharacteristically serious. "Someone was sending spiked drinks her way, Nali. The servants intercepted quite a few, but we don't know if any got through. Ellena and I want to check her for drugs and poison while *you* calm down."

"Spiked..." My tail smashed through a wooden column behind me, my blood igniting.

"Poison, we think, but we're not certain." Erist outstretched her arms, an expectant look on her face. "Let us see to her bath and a change of clothes. *You* should calm down before you take another bite out of her.

"I couldn't hear her thoughts, but she clearly said something that flustered you. You've never been one to expend *all* of their venom on their prey, yet that's precisely what you did, didn't you?"

"She wouldn't *obey!*" I tensed, shaking my head hard. "Even now she's—"

I cut myself off with a heavy sigh. Both women just continued to stare at me with firm expressions while I clutched Arianna's unconscious form. Arianna's skin was flushed, and her breaths were still short. Her pulse raced beneath my hands as she fidgeted in her slumber.

It didn't appear to matter how much darkness I wrapped her in, or how much of my venom I had used against her. She continued to struggle against my enchantment, threatening to awaken.

Erist was right—I had spent nearly all my venom while attempting to subdue Arianna. It wasn't a conscious choice, and Arianna shouldn't have been resistant enough to require *that much* of it.

Yet, between that and my power, I had barely managed to subdue her.

"You very obviously want to take another bite out of her—if not more." Mother's voice snapped me out of my thoughts, causing me to shift an icy glare at her. "Go calm yourself before you do something stupid. We'll have her back to you within an hour."

I hesitated a few more moments before finally relenting. Erist and my mother took Arianna from my grasp, taking care not to wake her, and then rushed her past me and into the palace. Sighing, I turned and stepped inside as well.

Arianna's scent clung to me, making my thoughts hazy as I strode down the hall to my rooms. I wanted to wrap myself in her and her presence, but… *'No. I can't do that right now.'*

I stalked into my rooms and leaned on the back of a sofa, attempting to regain some semblance of self-control. Arianna's power was taking its sweet time dissolving into mine. It swirled through me at a lazy pace, caressing my senses and drawing me toward her.

The first few times I drank of her, her power hadn't affected me in such a way. However, this time her blood, and the power carried within it, brought intense lust with it. A lust I had somehow…missed.

Did she truly have such a hunger for me, or was my venom to blame?

'*I didn't taste any poison…*' I brought my fingers to my lips and thought, beginning to pace around my rooms. '*Darius continues to interrupt us at every chance he gets. Even the other gods wish to interfere and get her under their control. Are they just intrigued by her power, or have they begun to realize* who *she is?*'

'*And then there are the Elders… Arianna and Djialkan don't trust them, yet they won't let me know* why. *The Elders offered to find Djialkan a new ward. In order to do that, they would have to slay his existing ward. Are they…*'

I slowed to a stop. Only the Elders could assign a ward to a fae-dragon, meaning they *knew* who Arianna was. They should have had the power to destroy her with little-to-no effort. Yet, they hadn't. If they knew who she was, and still wanted her dead, then why hadn't they acted?

The Elders should have been powerful enough to destroy the both of us.

'*But, from what I have seen, they aren't very powerful.*' I grimaced, tapping my claws on my forearm. '*So, Arianna and Djialkan don't believe the Elders are who they claim to be. They want to investigate.*

'*Then what? What do they plan to do if they're correct?*'

I frowned. Arianna was as powerful as ever, and the Elders hadn't taken her ability away. Nor had they taken away the Brands that marked her as a candidate for the role of Balance. Yet, she wasn't a deity. '*But…she is close.*'

"Are you going to stand there all night, or are you going to put her to bed?!" Erist demanded from behind me, causing me to stiffen and pivot to look at her. "Try not to let her kill you when she wakes up."

I muttered a few curses under my breath and swept across the room to pluck Arianna from Erist's arms. I shot the Goddess of Love a filthy look and then turned away from her, carrying the sleeping princess toward my bedroom. Erist and my mother had dressed Arianna in fluffy pajamas and pulled her hair into a loose braid, which was draped over her shoulder. However, she didn't appear to have calmed down in the slightest while away from me.

"*Oh*? You're taking her to *your* bed, Nalithor?" Mother called slyly, making my tail jerk sideways into a chair. "You know, if we'd known *that* was your plan, we—"

"*Do you really think I will let her out of my sight after you mentioned someone attempting to* poison *her?!*" I pivoted to glare at both of them, darkness rising upward from around my feet. They both exchanged a look and took a step backward. "Arianna will be staying with me until you've discovered who wanted to poison her—and *why*."

Another wave of darkness erupted from around my feet, making both women scramble out the door and down the hall. I huffed and used a tendril of darkness to slide the door shut before carrying Arianna deeper into my suite. At some point, she had shifted to nuzzle my chest. She was still asleep, but the attempted drifting of her hands made me wonder.

"You're impossible…" I murmured when her nails dug into my

skin.

I attempted to deposit the sleeping princess on the mattress, but her arms looped around my neck as soon as I tried to pull away. Her strength surprised me. Arianna pulled me into bed with her and promptly nestled her head near the crook of my neck, an aura of darkness drifting freely from her as she pressed herself closer to me.

I bit back a shudder when her plush lips brushed against my throat. *'She shouldn't be this active in her sleep. She—'*

Startled, I reached down and caught her forearm. I didn't think that her aura had drawn me into such a deep haze, and yet I hadn't noticed her hand traveling downward. However, Arianna's firm grip on my shaft and her fangs grazing my throat were *impossible* to ignore.

Prying her grip loose proved more difficult, and more disappointing, than it should have been. She couldn't even fit her hand completely around my manhood, but that certainly didn't keep me from responding to her touch.

*'This woman...'* I sighed, prying Arianna off me so that I could scoot off the mattress. *'Let's see how much of her power I drained this time...'*

After pulling the blankets over Arianna, I made a small motion with one hand and summoned her aura into the visible spectrum. I paused when she shifted and grumbled something in her sleep, turning onto her side so that she was facing me. My gaze drifted down to her throat, finding that *those women* had already healed the marks my fangs had left.

*'Tch. Maybe I really should collar her.'* I huffed, returning my gaze to her aura. My tail snapped back and forth in irritation. *'Ugh... Why must it be so difficult to focus around her?'*

I took a few deep breaths and shook my head, attempting to regain my focus. Arianna's aura hadn't diminished near as much as I had expected. After taking so much blood from her, and injecting her with nearly all my venom, her aura should have been nonexistent.

It had weakened a little, certainly, but it was the equivalent of a light sparring session.

*'Even so, I should at least fix it before she wakes up...'* I perched on the edge of the bed and cupped Arianna's face in one hand, summoning darkness to give her. *'Ah... While I'm at it...'*

I withdrew my hand from Arianna's face and pressed my fingers to the left side of my chest, summoning her heart from within me. The crystalline lotus danced with a bright array of elements and burned hot in my hand. It was brighter than I had ever seen it.

Never before had I seen the faint trail of darkness that extended between Arianna and her heart.

*'It's... connected to mine as well?'* I frowned, tracing the pathways of darkness. *'I'm wasting time.'*

I reached out to Arianna and held her heart by her chest. Their beats were in sync, their power a perfect mirror of each other. However, it refused to return to her. I gritted my teeth, my tail snapping from side to side. After all this time separated from her, why wouldn't it return to its rightful owner?

*'Am I doing something wrong? It should return to her as soon as it's brought close enough. Perhaps— Gods damn it, woman!'* I tensed and hurriedly returned the crystal to my chest. Reaching down, I gripped both of Arianna's wrists and prized them away from my groin.

At least, this time, she hadn't snuck her hands *down* my pants. However, her touch was distracting all the same. She had already aroused me enough during dinner. I didn't need the added distraction.

*'My venom must be to blame, but— Ah.'* I sighed, pulling away from the handsy princess and retreating to the nearby sitting room. *'She wasn't under the influence of my venom when she submitted to me in the bath. Nnngh, I really will kill Darius if he interferes again.'*

*"I sensed her heart. You attempted to return it to her?"* Djialkan slid open the door and strode into my suite in his Devillian form. He looked mildly interested. *"How did that go for you?"*

"It still won't return to her. I'm assuming you know why?" I growled at him while stalking into my wardrobe to pull off my layers of royal finery.

*"I do not believe that her body can handle the power of a deity's heart,"* Djialkan answered plainly, shrugging.

"You believe it's protecting her, then?" I muttered in displeasure, searching for looser trousers and a robe. "So, the 'Elders' still want her dead, someone in Draemir attempted to poison her, and Darius still has an unhealthy obsession with me. What are we going to do about this?"

*"Poison?"* Djialkan frowned. *"I will speak with Fraelfnir about*

469

*Darius. As for the Elders, you know that Arianna and I do not wish for you to—"*

"You think that you're the only ones who've noticed they are weak?" I asked, turning to glare down at Djialkan. He took a step back, bristling. "For now, I will refrain from interfering, Djialkan. However, if she finds too much trouble—"

*"I do not wish for harm to come to her either, Nalithor."* Djialkan hissed at me. *"Alala and I are her Guardians before all else. One of us will inform you as soon as she stumbles too deep into this matter— regardless of her wishes.*

*"Until then, you should worry about how to keep Arianna from killing you when she wakes. Do not give me that look—I can smell your venom quite clearly."*

Djialkan scampered out of my suite before I could wring him by his neck, eliciting another growl from me. I closed the door behind him and then paused, listening for any sign that the noise might have awoken Arianna.

Once I was satisfied that she was still asleep, I released a sigh of relief. There was a great deal of frustration for me to work off before I could handle explaining myself to Arianna, let alone what to do about the elders.

*'Nnngh... I need more than just a bite of her at this point. Blood just isn't enough anymore.'*

# CHAPTER TWENTY-ONE
## *Conflicting Emotions*

"Mmm…" I purred, nuzzling into my pillow and running my hands over the satin sheets beneath me. "Smells good. Comfy…"

Groggy, I nuzzled deeper into the mattress. It wasn't until I began drifting back to sleep that I realized *why* everything smelled so good. I couldn't remember what I had dreamed about, but I was plenty aware of what had happened at the party the previous night.

*'Honestly, venom?! I wasn't really going to kill Darius. Well, maybe I was going to kill him a* little *bit.'* I clenched my teeth to stifle another growl and examined the variegated blue and black satins, leathers, and velvets that adorned the room. *'Humph, he may have good taste, but I'm going to have his head for—'*

I winced when everything spun, making me shut my eyes and lift

471

a hand to my forehead. Nalithor's scent and power clung to *everything*, even me. It hadn't been so strong before.

*'What in the hells happened after he made me sleep? His power is drowning out* everything...'

I glanced down at myself to find that I was wearing fuzzy pajamas. Since it was "safe" to get out of bed, I crawled across the massive mattress until I was on the edge of the damned thing. I couldn't fathom why anyone needed a bed so large, but at least it was comfortable. Even if *he* wasn't in it.

*'Damn it!'* The corner of my eye twitched as I slid off the mattress and onto my feet. *'Angry, Ari, you're supposed to be* angry! *Not* horny. *Urgh! Venom? Yeah, must be residual venom.'*

Mumbling to myself, I stumbled through Nalithor's suite but found no trace that he had been there recently. It seemed like a prime opportunity to bathe in peace before he returned. *'Maybe that'll help me calm down.'*

I crept out of his rooms and walked quietly down the hallway to the bath, but whatever notion I had of "calming down" shattered the moment I caught the sound of Nalithor's enraptured moans. Everything in my head stopped for a few seconds before whirling into a maelstrom.

I needed to know what in the hells was going on in the bath. Was he pleasuring himself? Was he fucking someone else? Had someone seduced him? *'If someone else is in there, I'm killing them both.'*

I pressed myself against the wall by the door and shifted so I could peer through the crack. My heart raced with apprehension, but I would have sworn that it stopped altogether the moment I peered into the bathroom.

Nalithor was stretched out on one of the chaises, fully nude, with his tail woven around the length of his manhood. He was writhing in ecstasy while he used his tail and hands both to please himself. I couldn't do anything but stare for several long moments, entranced as I watched him massage his balls and shaft alike. It took what seemed like an eternity for me to realize that, even erect, he wasn't much larger than what I'd glimpsed before.

Given the size…I found it to be a strange relief.

*'Shit, I need to sneak off before he notices I'm—'*

My mind went blank when Nalithor's euphoric moans reached a new height. I couldn't help but watch as he came. His back arched and his muscles strained as both his tail and manhood released what seemed, to me, like an impossible amount of come…and what looked like small obsidian eggs.

*'D-did I forget something I read in those tomes? Or is that some kind of…uhm, toy?'* I inched away from the door, still transfixed by the climaxing Adinvyr. *'Damn it! He's going to be done soon. I need to go. Need to go. Uh…uhm…'*

I froze in place, stunned when Nalithor began pleasuring himself all over again. A Human would have been done after coming once— let alone *that much*. However, when his eyes shifted sideways toward the door, I would have sworn that I caught a smirk.

Biting back a startled yelp, I dispersed into the shadows and fled to my room. I stifled a curse and came to a stop in front of the door, finding it locked from the inside with a note attached to it.

*You are under Nalithor's protection whilst I investigate new matters that have arisen. Stay with him at all times. Otherwise, remain in his rooms until he can come fetch you.*

'R-really?' I ripped the note off the door and skimmed it a few times. 'But...if he actually noticed me watching him... Ugh, gods damn it all!'

Fidgeting with my pajama sleeves, I stalked back to Nalithor's rooms. Pale blue energy shimmered and drifted through the hallway, emanating from the bath. It coiled and twisted around me as I passed through it and into the suite I had woken up in. A shiver ran down my spine as I tried to block out the scent of Nalithor's power.

It was difficult to describe, but it smelled similar to how his blood tasted.

'His blood...' I bit my lower lip and shook my head hard as I strode into the bedroom. 'Ugh, I'm hungry. Where's a servant when I need one?'

I conjured a book from my shrizar and stalked toward the bed to sprawl across it once more. Reading something, *anything*, seemed better than dwelling on Nalithor's anatomy at the given moment. His sculpted body, his long shaft, his girth, and the obscene amount he had—

Cursing, I flipped the book open and began reading. There was no telling how long it would take for him to truly finish, and I wasn't sure if sneaking off was a good idea. While I didn't care if I made the Adinvyr angry at the moment, Djialkan was another matter entirely. The fae-dragon would have roasted me if I ignored the note he left me.

A while later I felt my anger simmering again. Not only had Nalithor used his venom against me, but he had done so in front of *people*. Deities, royalty, nobility, and servants had all been privy to my...pleasure. And then he had the gall to deny my desire for him to take me! *'Though, that could be because of the venom. He probably didn't even take me seriously. Bah! That just makes me angrier!'*

Snapping my book shut, I tossed it aside and looked over at the clock. It was still late at night. Nalithor's aura drifting through the palace had grown even stronger while I attempted to read, and was now at a truly intoxicating level. I couldn't think straight anymore. His power pulled me and caressed me like a living thing, threatening to make me lose control once more.

*'D-damn it...'* I shivered and slipped under the covers, attempting to block out the sensation of fingers traveling along my inner thighs. *'At this rate, I'm going to sneak back to the bath and watch him. Ugh, no. No, no, no. That's the venom talking, right?'*

I yanked the covers over my head and bit my lip to stifle a whimper. If Nalithor's power was capable of teasing me in such a way, I wasn't sure if I wanted to even *think* about what the Adinvyr himself was capable of. Especially not when I was still tipsy from his venom.

*'Just go back to sleep, Ari.'* I told myself, turning onto my stomach and crossing my arms beneath the pillow. *'At least I confirmed he wasn't taking someone other than me. I shouldn't worry, for now.'*

———⟐———

"Finally awake?" Nalithor questioned when I slid open the door to the sitting room. "I promise that I was a *perfect* gentleman while you slept."

"If you hadn't been, I probably wouldn't be able to walk right now with how—" I cut my snappy retort off with a sigh, covering my face with one hand. Nalithor's rumbling laughter didn't help with my embarrassment. "I need tea…and why am I in *your* rooms instead of *mine?*"

Maybe if I pretended not to have left his rooms last night, or woken up for that matter, I could avoid having a conversation about what I'd seen.

"My own paranoia," Nalithor replied before motioning for me to sit near his perch. "The servants intercepted a number of poisoned drinks that were meant for *you*. Combined with the issues of your brother, our guests, and the Elders' repeated sketchy behavior… Well. Suffice to say that I've decided to make it difficult for *any* of them to gain access to you."

"Did you really have to use your venom?" I crossed my arms and sunk into the massive chair, shooting Nalithor a look. "Also, I'm cold. Blanket, please."

"Yes. It seemed like the best way to subdue you. Even with it, you were still...difficult." Nalithor rose to his feet and then glanced down at me. "I was concerned that I might have taken too much, yet you seem fine. However, my venom should still hold some sway over you...that much of it should have kept you subdued for *at least* four—"

"Cold," I reiterated, shooting him a grumpy pout.

Nalithor released a small sigh, looking down at me with an unreadable expression while he examined me. It wasn't until he turned away and walked toward a dresser that I realized just how little he was wearing. A pair of loose Susthulite trousers hung low on his hips, revealing a questionable amount of his "v." I rather liked the sight...but that just made me grumpier.

He pulled a large, soft-looking navy blanket from the dresser and then returned to offer the blanket for me. His tail began swishing back and forth while waiting for me to take it.

However, I doubted he was prepared for what I had in mind.

"What—" Nalithor trailed off when I gripped him by the wrist and yanked him down onto the chair. "Arianna, what are—"

Nalithor went silent as I straddled his lap and brought a dagger up beneath his Adam's apple. I heard the low rumble of a growl from his throat, but I was too angry to care. His hands came to rest on my hips, earning him a sharp glare. He looked more amused than threatened despite his growling.

"Apologize," I demanded, bracing myself against his chest with one hand as I pressed the blade against his throat for emphasis. "You put me in a compromising situation in front of *people*! The least you...could do..."

I watched, transfixed, as Nalithor pulled the dagger up from his throat and to his mouth. He ran his tongue up the blade, slicing it open just enough to make blood well up and coat his tongue. My anger vanished as I watched a few beads of the obsidian liquid trickle down my otherwise platinum blade.

When the scent finally registered, my concentration lapsed, and the dagger disappeared back into my jewelry. *'I-I want a taste...'*

"See something you like, my dear?" Nalithor asked innocently, gripping my chin. He chuckled, a mischievous smile spreading across his face. "Poor little thing. Do you want a taste that badly?" He paused and wrapped one arm behind my back, pulling me closer. His lips brushed against mine as he spoke again, "Mmm... Though, you *are* cute like this too..."

"N-no. I don't want a taste. Don't tease me," I muttered, turning my face away from him. "I'm still angry with you. You—"

"You are a *terrible* liar," Nalithor informed me, turning my face so that I had to look at him again. "Come here."

"I'm already—"

Nalithor cut me off, pulling me into a deep kiss. The instant I tasted his blood all else seemed to stop. His blood was sweet, rich, and had near-unfathomable power coursed through it. I wanted it. All of it.

I wrapped my arms around Nalithor's neck and pressed myself

against him close as I could get. My heart raced as he kissed me at a tortuously slow pace. I wanted so much more than that, yet he seemed content with teasing me. However, that certainly didn't stop him from sliding his hands down to my ass and giving it a firm squeeze.

"Mmm... How is *that* for an apology?" Nalithor purred, pulling away to study me, a playful smirk on his face. "How long have you been craving my blood in such a way, my dear?"

"Craving?" I paused when he leaned forward to nibble at my lower lip. "A long time, I suppose. But you..."

"Am I the White Fox's version of catnip?" Nalithor teased, moving his hands up to my face. He chuckled when I gave him a confused look. "Your pupils are dilated, much like a very pleased cat."

Nalithor just chuckled when I glared at him. He lifted me off his lap and then set me back on the chair before fetching the discarded blanket. Offering it to me again, he smirked, his tail swishing back and forth. Perhaps he was expecting me to draw a blade against him again, but this time I had something else in mind.

I caught him by the wrist and averted my gaze when I felt my face growing warm.

"This chair is big enough for two, and our cuddling was interrupted last night..." I grumbled quietly, my grip on his wrist twitching when I felt my pulse quickening again. *'Damn it. Why am I so flustered? Is some of his venom still— Oh. That's right. A lesser amount is carried in his blood too. Fuck.'*

It appeared that no further invitation was needed. Nalithor looked a little startled, but a pleased smile soon took over. He scooped me up in the blanket and then nestled me alongside him on the chair. I snuggled up against him and laid my head on his chest as he put an arm around me. I could both hear and feel his elevated pulse beneath my cheek. It surprised me on some level but in an endearing sort of way.

"I *thought* you were angry with me?" Nalithor questioned, stroking my side. "Considering that I bit you in such a way—in *public*—I would understand if you—"

"Normally, this is where I'd say you can make it up to me..." I grumbled, draping an arm across him before nuzzling deeper into his chest. "I think, *this time*, I'll let you get away with it. I can't deny that their shocked expressions were terribly entertaining. I may not like it, but I *do* understand that you were trying to keep me from making a mistake."

"I'm rather certain that I should still make it up to you in some way." Nalithor chuckled, stroking my back. "How about—"

"Maybe *I* will just have to feed on *you* once I shift," I stated, listening with satisfaction as his heart skipped several beats. "That seems fair, doesn't it?"

"*Cheeky.*" Nalithor laughed, coiling his tail around one of my legs. "Now, now. You aren't going back to sleep already, are you? What happened to wanting tea?"

"I'm not going to sleep, you're just comfy," I informed him. "Besides, *you* are always nuzzling *me*. It's my turn for once."

"Still, I can't very well find us tea *or* breakfast like this," Nalithor mused, continuing to stroke my back. However, this time my heart dropped, and I pouted.

"If you don't want to cuddle, I can just get up…" I sighed, disappointed, as I shifted to remove myself from his lap.

"You want to stay?" Nalithor questioned, catching me around the waist. He fell silent until I nodded my answer. "I *want* you to stay as well. We can find breakfast later, or I can send someone trustworthy to fetch food."

"In that case, I want to eat in one of the gardens by the lake," I informed him, looking up at him. "I take it you'll be joining me *personally* since you're seeing to my protection or whatever?"

"Either way I would want to accompany you." Nalithor smiled and adjusted himself a moment before resting both his hands on my hips. "Before I get *too* distracted by how adorable you are, there is still the matter of your brother."

"Ahhh yes. How are we going to get the little bastard off your tail?" I questioned, startling a laugh from the Adinvyr. "*Also*! Who bathed and dressed me, hmmm?"

"Erist and my mother *refused* to let me see that succulent body of yours." Nalithor teased, digging his claws into my hips. "As adorable and soft these pajamas of yours are, I was *hoping* they would at least slip you into something a little more…"

"Sexy?" I offered when I caught the sound of his pulse quickening again.

"Yes, sexy," Nalithor replied with a sheepish smile. "*Thinking* it doesn't sound nearly as selfish as *saying* it.

"As for Darius, Erist and Arom have taken him to their temple and intend to keep him there for some time. I'm not certain what they think they can teach him and, if I am being honest, I don't care to know.

"I hope that my display scared some sense into that boy and into those filthy X'shmirans...but I am unsure."

"Scared some sense into them?" I questioned, tilting my head. Nalithor's face reddened, and he glanced away from me. "What, exactly, did I miss?"

"I was...a little angry," Nalithor muttered, squeezing me much like a stuffed animal. "Dilonu attempted, *again*, to make me buy you. I injured him for it. I wanted to kill him, but until I know more about this 'curse' that was placed on you—"

"Well, if we're lucky, this means we won't have to deal with Erist *or* the X'shmiran royalty for a while," I pointed out, looking up at Nalithor. "There's more to the spring festival than fancy parties and rude deities, right? Will you—"

"I would be happy to escort you." Nalithor smiled at me.

"I was going to say, 'be my *date*.'" I pouted, averting my gaze when I saw the expression that formed on his face. "You don't have to look so surprised! I-if you don't *want* to, I understand, but..."

"You are making it difficult for me to allow *anyone* other than myself near you," Nalithor interjected, his tone contemplative as he cupped my face and made me look at him again. "I know you are not under the influence of my venom anymore. Why are you spoiling me so much?"

"I'd argue that I'm spoiling myself," I commented, watching as, for some reason, Nalithor grinned and laughed. "What? I'm serious! It's not like I'm actively *trying* to indulge either of us. I just...I enjoy your company."

"You're bashful." Nalithor smirked. "Always so blunt, yet when it comes to an admission like *that*, you turn such a lovely shade of pink and begin acting so shy. Watching you go from bloodthirsty huntress to bashful vixen is quite endearing.

"That aside; *of course* I will be your date. However, we still need to discuss what we're going to do about you when we return to Dauthrmir. You will be expected to come live with me, but you will also still be expected to work."

"Bah! You'd think that killing beasts would qualify as work." I bit back a purr when Nalithor resumed stroking my back.

"Mmm... I still believe you should come work for me at *The Little Orchid*," Nalithor remarked, giving my leg a squeeze with his tail. "However, I find myself unwilling to let you call anyone 'Master' or 'Mistress.'"

"*Oh*? You won't *let* me?" I teased. "How am I supposed to interpret that, hmmm?"

"I don't want to let anyone else have you," Nalithor stated, lifting me fully into his lap. He pulled me back against his chest and then nuzzled my shoulder, sighing. "I don't want to give them so much as a *chance* to pretend that you're theirs, either. Ah... I really am growing quite selfish when it comes to you, aren't I?"

"To be fair, if you *wanted* to share me in such a way, I would take your head," I pointed out quite seriously, but he started laughing anyway. "Still, that poses a problem, doesn't it? If I worked for someone else—"

"I won't allow it," Nalithor grumbled, his grip tightening on me.

"Tsk, tsk, being so possessive." I couldn't help but giggle at him. "What am I supposed to think about this? If you're *this* possessive over me, I assume there's a *reason* you haven't asked me to be your 'Chosen' or something yet?"

"The rules regarding Chosen are strict." Nalithor sighed into my neck, making me shiver. "If you were to become my Chosen... That is all you could ever be. You would never be permitted to become my..."

"Goddess?" I inquired when Nalithor's grip twitched tighter, and he hesitated to finish his sentence. "I see. So that must be part of why the other deities are able to use the Chosen as a loophole so easily? Hmmm..."

I opened my mouth to speak again and then abruptly shut it when I felt my stomach rumble beneath one of Nalithor's hands.

"Breakfast, then?" Nalithor laughed, scooping me into his arms before rising to his feet. "Let's see... You wanted to eat in the gardens? I should probably let you get dressed."

"I also want to spar," I added to the growing list. Grinning, I reached over his shoulder and tugged on his braid a few times. "Will you *indulge* me with a sparring match or ten after we eat?"

"That can certainly be arranged." Nalithor laughed, setting me down. "I will go send a servant to inform the cooks that you desire breakfast. Do *try* to stay out of trouble while you get dressed? Ah, and before I forget, your clothes are in my wardrobe."

"If you take too long I will have to find some way to entertain myself," I pointed out as he walked off, smirking when I saw his tail twitch to the side and graze the corner of a bookshelf. "I meant *reading* of course. What were *you* thinking?"

"If I told you that we wouldn't leave my rooms for *hours.*" Nalithor chuckled, shooting me a sultry glance over his shoulder. "*Behave.* I will be back soon."

I admired his muscular back and long hair as he strode toward the door, then shook my head and turned away to search for the wardrobe. Now that we weren't under the blanket I was growing cold again, and more clothing seemed like a good idea.

'*Hmmm... I'm still a* little *annoyed with him,*' I considered, crossing my arms as I padded around the suite. '*Using his venom against me, in public no less... Perhaps I should use our sparring matches to get my revenge? Though, that could be difficult giving the current record. Might be an interesting challenge, though.*'

Shaking my head, I decided to think on it later. Nalithor's heart was in the right place, even if I didn't approve of his actions. Letting

485

me kill my brother would have been stupid, especially if Nalithor was as attached to me as he led me to believe.

*'If I'm telling the truth, I'm* impressed *that he refrained from killing Dilonu,'* I nudged open a few doors until I found Nalithor's wardrobe. *'Although, for now, we need to let the bastard live for the same reasons that* I *need to not kill* Darius.*'*

Looking through my clothing, I settled on something comfortable and proceeded to pull it on while waiting for Nalithor to return. My attire took up a mere corner of Nalithor's wardrobe, and it looked as though some of his had been pushed out of the way to make room for mine.

It was no wonder that Ellena and Erist thought I owned "too little" if even a male of the family had so many clothes to choose from. Though, I had to wonder how much of it was because Ellena was a doting mother versus Nalithor purchasing things for himself.

*'I guess this will do if we're going to spar later.'* I bit back a yawn and pulled on a pair of knee-high boots over my breeches. *'I'm not "on duty" as an Umbral Mage right now, so I can wear whatever…right?'*

I straightened and returned to the sitting room in Nalithor's suite. There were dozens of tomes and scrolls scattered everywhere, many of which looked as though the Adinvyr prince had read them many times. Most appeared to be on the subjects of deities, Exiles, the Elders, or the Aledacian Forests.

In particular, the books about the Elders looked more beat-up than most.

*'Hmmm, the Elders huh?'* I picked up one of the books and leafed through the pages. *'I guess he* does *have many reasons to not like them either.'*

"Good, you didn't wander off," Nalithor remarked when he slid the door open and walked into the room, his expression rather serious. "I'm afraid that breakfast in the gardens will have to wait."

"Did something happen?" I tilted my head, watching as he swept past me and into the wardrobe.

"I'm expected to have breakfast with my parents, several Upper Gods, and Gabriel." Nalithor grimaced as I leaned against the doorway. "They asked that I bring you along as well, if you'll agree to it."

"Well, I *am* under your protection, aren't I?" I asked, tracking his movements as he pulled layers of dark brocade from one of the closets. "It doesn't really seem appropriate for me to attend, but I suppose it can't be *that* bad if they requested my presence."

"They likely wish to discuss the matter of Darius, and X'shmir," Nalithor muttered.

"I'm sure there are plenty of other things they need to talk to you about." I shook my head, turning so that my back was to the wardrobe and I was leaning against my other shoulder. "What happened after you 'subdued' me last night?"

"Darius began screeching for me to spit your blood out," Nalithor replied with a snort. "He claimed that the blood of an Umbral Mage is 'nothing but poison.' Erist had Arom restrain your brother." The

Adinvyr paused a moment before sighing. "Dilonu thought it was a prime opportunity to speak up about the fact that I 'have not paid them for you, and yet I bit you anyway.'"

"Sounds about right." I rolled my eyes.

"I tore the bastard's chest open," Nalithor spat, his tail smashing into something. "Arom informed Dilonu *and* your brother that a deity does not need to *buy* their prospective...mate. Darius was quite upset.

"For some reason, as I flew you away from the courtyard, Fraelfnir let some of Darius' thoughts slip through to me. Someone 'promised' Darius that they had the power to make me *his*. The rest of his mind was in disarray, but his desire to kill them if they had lied was quite clear."

"Someone strong enough to..." I frowned, thinking on it for a moment. "I don't like the sound of that. You're sure that's what he was thinking?"

"It was undeniably clear." Nalithor sighed. "Shall we?"

Before I could turn to look at him, he looped his arm around my waist and pulled me to his side. Nalithor's power blanketed my senses momentarily, and I had to bite back a shudder when the desire to take a bite out of him surfaced again. The taste of his blood still coated my mouth, and I wanted more. So much more.

"I suppose I can have you treat me to breakfast in the gardens some other time." I sighed as Nalithor's hand slid down to my hip and squeezed before releasing me. "Where's Alala? I saw that Djialkan left a note about investigating 'new issues,' but I haven't seen the fluffy one."

"She's roaming around being cute and listening in on our 'guests,'" Nalithor replied, a devious smile settling on his face. "I have some matters that I wish to look into, and her cuteness makes it easy for her to assist."

I fell silent and let Nalithor lead me out of his suite and through the labyrinthine collection of buildings that made up the Draemiran palace. The further we walked, the more I formed an idea of just how angry Nalithor had been the previous night. Trails of shimmering blue power still drifted across the palace grounds, and hints of dark energy crackled in the shadows where Magelight couldn't reach.

*'Was it necessary to put* this *much power into your display?'* I questioned, hurrying after the Adinvyr. *'Everything is—'*

*'They needed to learn a lesson.'* Nalithor huffed, his tail twitching as he glanced over his shoulder at me. *'What do you mean by "this much power?"'*

*'Here.'* I fell into step with him and grasped his hand. *'Look.'*

Nalithor sighed after a moment and looked down at me with a small smile. *'I did mention that I was a little angry.'*

*'I'd argue that you had to have been more than "a little" angry.'* I rolled my eyes at him and released his hand, but he was quick to reclaim it and pull me toward him.

*'I am tired of people who wish to interfere or otherwise take you away from me,'* Nalithor stated, his expression firm. *'Testing me is not beneficial for their longevity. If they wish—'*

"Nalithor, Arianna!" Ellena called from a doorway ahead, a bright smile on her face. "I was beginning to think you wouldn't come! Your tea is already here."

*'Be careful of what you say. I do not trust these gods—even if they do work for me.'* Nalithor sighed, offering me his arm.

I accepted his arm and let him lead me into the large, formal room that his mother and father were waiting in. Aside from Ellena and Lysander, there were six other deities present. I recognized Sebastian, the God of Chaos, from our previous yet brief meeting. Near him was the giant of a man that was Aurelian, the God of War.

Aside from them, there were four females that I couldn't identify.

"Oh my, you look so different without horns..." A woman with golden hair and chartreuse eyes murmured, examining me. "Nalithor, you didn't tell me that *both* of my children were bound into new forms."

*'Children...? Great.'* I bit back a glare as Ellena shooed me to a seat alongside the long, low table and away from Nalithor.

"Is it really alright to let Arianna-jiss attend?" Aurelian questioned, pushing his shaggy burgundy hair out of his eyes.

"I believe the 'Elders' already know who she is," Nalithor replied, adopting a formal tone as he strode to the head of the table and sat with his parents to either side. "We ran into the Elders while in Abrantia. They offered to assign Djialkan a *new* ward."

"And only the Elders can assign wards, to begin with." A woman with pewter hair and golden eyes frowned. She flicked her gaze to me, revealing diamond-shaped pupils. "I am Llrissa, the Goddess of Justice. You should try to rein in that temper of yours, Arianna-jiss. Dead men don't talk."

*'Neither do dead deities,'* I considered, bristling as I knelt at the table and pulled a cup of tea toward me. "If I torture them, they will just say what they think I want to hear. False information is worse than *no* information."

"I'm Aurelian, and this is Elise," the burgundy-haired giant offered with a broad grin, revealing upper and lower fangs. He fastened his golden gaze on me, then gave me an approving nod. "Looks like you've been taking good care of my gifts. Are the blades holding up well?"

"*Our* gifts," Elise corrected her husband, elbowing him in the ribs. "Honestly, Arianna, this oaf would have had you running around in heavy *men's* jewelry if it wasn't for me!"

"I am Ceres, the Goddess of Nature," the woman with leaves and flowers for hair added with a warm smile. "There are a few more of us who have allied with Nalithor-y'ric, but they were unable to join us today. However, we comprise the majority of his accomplices."

"I...am Gabriel," the golden-haired woman spoke with a small frown as she examined me. "I suppose, given the circumstances, I can't expect you to call me Mother..."

"We can save the pleasantries for later," Erist spoke from beside me, her expression serious. "The Exiles are acting up again, and I think we should discuss that before we address the matter of Arianna and Darius." Erist turned to me with a small smile, nudged me with her elbow, and pointed at the nearest plate. "Eat up, girlie. You're stuck with us for a bit."

*'Humph. Why couldn't Nalithor at least sit with me?'* I suppressed a pout and began piling food onto a plate, aware of several deities tracking my movements. *'I'm going to kick his ass later.'*

"Sometime last week," Lysander began, shifting a stack of papers, "a group of Exiles attacked the westernmost border of the Suthsul Desert. They left the trading caravan alive...but slaughtered dozens of Chaos Beasts."

"*More* Exiles?" Nalithor sighed heavily, lifting his cup of tea. "You know the Elders have forbidden me from acting out against the Exiles. Why aren't you out there dealing with the Exiles yourse—"

"*This* is why," Lysander interrupted, handing his son a sheet of parchment.

I watched, curious, as Nalithor skimmed the document. His anger grew worse by the second. Darkness crept outward from him, coating the room like a warm blanket.

By the expressions and shivering of the deities present, they didn't agree with my sentiments.

"The Elders have ordered that *no one* is to interfere with the Exiles?!" Nalithor snapped, his tail thrashing into something behind him. The other deities shrank back. "Eliminating the Exiles is *supposed* to be one of my duties! They've taken everything else away, what are—"

"The trees still refuse to acknowledge the Elders," Ceres

murmured, swaying in her seat.

"Those Angels who remain loyal to me agree; there is something amiss with the Elders," Gabriel spoke with a small frown, lifting a delicate glass. "We all know it, and yet—"

"Are you all *trying* to get Exiled?" I asked, the corner of my eye twitching. I set my plate down on the table in front of me and shot them a glare.

"Arianna…" Nalithor sighed, pushing his hair back between his horns.

"We have all noticed our powers waning." Aurelian turned to me, his expression firm. "As our powers wane, the Elders have taken away duties from more and more of us."

"The Elders forbade me from overseeing trials." Llrissa grimaced.

"The Elders forbade me from planting new forests…" Ceres sighed.

"The bastards forbade me from making things interesting." Sebastian pouted.

"We're not allowed to train warriors." Elise motioned between Aurelian and herself.

"And the role of Balance has been demoted to that of a babysitter," Nalithor added dryly, shifting his gaze away from the deities and settling it on me instead. "Balance is *supposed* to seek out and destroy—or imprison—the Exiles, find a permanent solution to the Chaos Beasts, and manage relations between the Upper Gods; particularly Good and Evil.

"However, the Elders have been taking away my obligations one-by-one. All that I am permitted to do now is maintain relationships between the deities, keep mortals from skewing the balance, and kill beasts."

*'Even his previous duties are a mere fraction of what Balance is meant to do...'* I thought, picking up a muffin to nibble on. *'Though, I suppose it's entirely possible that he didn't feel the need to list everything. Even so, how does he keep himself from seeing to his "forbidden" duties anyway?*

*'I suppose some of those duties are the reason Sihix, Ceilail, and Xiinsha said I can do things that Nalithor can't.... Hmmm.'*

"Why do you think the Exiles would be *killing* their pets?" Ellena frowned, shifting to look up at her son. "As far as we know, this is the first time something like this has happened right?"

I listened in silence as the deities around me discussed what could cause such strange behavior. None of their theories seemed probable to me—they were thinking of Exiles as some mysterious existence, not like the former gods they were. Former people. These gods would make little progress if they couldn't understand that the Exiles weren't much different from them.

While they talked, I ate my breakfast and then proceeded to feel out the power that radiated from each of the deities. They were all strong, certainly, but I couldn't shake the feeling that they should have been far more powerful. Nalithor's strength had been growing as of late, yet the people around us seemed so weak. The difference between the Lesser and Upper Gods was negligible.

Nalithor, however, was stronger than all of them combined.

*"What is this? You're letting a mortal mingle with you?"* The male voice made my blood run cold. It took all of my self-control to keep myself from drawing a weapon. *"Whose toy is she? No one informed Us that one of you had decided on a Chosen."*

"She's my son's *potential mate,* and she is our *guest,*" Lysander stated with a snarl, bristling when a blade came to rest alongside my throat.

"Arianna-jiss is under my protection and isn't to stray from my side," Nalithor added, shooting a dangerous glare over my head at the owner of the sword. "Someone attempted to poison her. I intend to keep her alive and *by my side.*"

*'It needs to die.'* I clenched my hands in my lap, a shiver running down my spine. *'Feels wrong, so wrong. Corrupt existence. Needs to die. Weak. So weak, perhaps if I'm fast enough I can—'*

*'Nnngh… Calm down.'* Nalithor growled, shooting me a warning look. *"Elder,* to what do we owe this appearance?"

*'Elder? What? No way in the hells is* that thing *an Elder!'* I clenched my jaw as Nalithor wrapped his power around me, dulling my senses. *'You aren't helping.'*

*"Prospective* mate?" The Elder's frown was audible, but I didn't dare turn with a blade pressed to my throat. *"Why have you not simply taken her, then? If you wish for her to be your goddess, then all you have to do is fuck her to prove it."*

"Such behavior is atrocious in our culture." Nalithor's threatening tone made me fidget in my seat. "As the ones who *created us*, I'm certain you can understand."

*"Bah! I will never understand your aversion to taking what you want."* The Elder scoffed, moving the sword away from my throat. *"I have been trying to contact you for days. Why have you shut me from your mind?"*

I shifted my gaze to the side as the Elder walked away from me and strode toward the head of the table. Goosebumps prickled along my skin, and I suppressed a growl. I would have known *that* Elder anywhere. He was one of the bastards responsible for taking me away from Dauthrmir. *'What does he want with Nalithor? Why hasn't Nalithor torn that fucking trash apart?'*

Erist patted my leg and shot me a look, shaking her head subtly.

"I am not in a state that the mortals of Vorpmasia can handle," Nalithor responded, shooting the Elder a sideways glare as he approached. "I have blocked everything so that my presence does not cause problems."

*"All the more reason to take the woman, no?"* The Elder sneered at me over his shoulder before returning his attention to Nalithor. *"I'm sure, after a few minutes, she won't mind anymore."*

Nalithor shot to his feet with a feral snarl, his tail thrashing behind him, and grabbed the Elder by the front of his robes. Darkness burst through the room anew, coating everything and eliciting shrieks from the few deities in the room that weren't comfortable with the element.

I simply picked up my plate and continued my breakfast, observing the exchange in silence. Nalithor was furious, and I knew better to tease someone who was *that* angry.

*"I should destroy you."* Nalithor's tone gave me pause, making me glance away from my food for a moment.

*"Oh, so you're serious about this one, are you?"* The Elder laughed, caring little for the Adinvyr's suffocating rage. *"Good, good. We have grown tired of waiting for you to choose a goddess. We were preparing to assign you one if you did not show any sign of—"*

"If you 'assign' him a goddess he won't get a chance to destroy you before I do it myself," I stated conversationally. The bastard grew pale and simply stared at me for a moment. "I assume you fouled our breakfast for a reason?"

*"You* dare *speak to an Elder in such—"* The Elder cut himself off when more power gathered in Nalithor's hands, causing the dishes on the table to vibrate. *"For* you *of all deities to raise your hands to me... The threats against your prospective goddess are sincere?"*

"I am tired of the weak ones attempting to wrest her from me." Nalithor fastened a condescending glare on the Elder. "Now there is also the matter of bastards trying to poison her, and the X'shmirans attempting to *sell* her to me. Your added insinuations and suggestions are unwelcome."

*"Bah! Your kind are so difficult."* The Elder sighed. *"Alas, it is a good thing she is here. I have a question for her. Arianna-jiss, what do you know of Kalenek?"*

I glanced to the side briefly, noting that Sebastian stiffened and grew pale, before returning my attention to the Elder.

"That's the Exiled God of Chaos, isn't it?" I tilted my head, watching as Nalithor set the Elder down and returned to his seat. "I've learned precious little about him since coming Below. All I know is that he's an Exile, and is responsible for the creation of Vampires."

*"X'shmir is built of architecture unique to Exile strongholds,"* the Elder began in a lecturing tone. *"We have reason to believe Kalenek himself was there at one point. Perhaps you knew him by another name? Does 'Lehrr' ring a bell?"*

My grip on my cup twitched tight enough for a split second to shatter it, sending shards of ceramic slicing through my palm and fingers. I was oblivious to the pain and simply stared at the Elder, dumbfounded.

"*Lehrr?* You're telling me that *Lehrr* is the former God of Chaos?" I demanded as Erist turned and took my lacerated hand in both of hers. "You've *got* to be kidding me. There is no way in the hells that *he* is—"

*'Your pulse has quickened...'* Nalithor murmured, his expression unreadable. *'Was he...a lover?'*

"Lehrr was a servant in the X'shmiran palace!" I shook my head hard. "He was the only one who attempted to stop the X'shmirans from 'cursing' me, if you will. Dilonu and Tyana had him thrown over the edge of the island for interfering."

*"Thrown over..."* The Elder's eyes widened, though this time the other deities present seemed to share his astonishment. *"You are*

*certain? Do you know where X'shmir was located at the time?"*

"The Mists are far too thick for me to have known, even if I *wasn't* in the process of being tortured at the time." I snorted while Erist attempted to mend my hand. "This was a little less than twenty years ago, mind you. I'm not sure how durable you deities are but…that's quite the fall."

"You could break every bone in our body, and we still wouldn't die." Sebastian grinned mischievously. "How *very* interesting. Perhaps we *will* find my predecessor sooner rather than later…"

*"This is a problem…"* The Elder muttered, turning his attention back to the grumpy trio of Adinvyr at the head of the table. *"You are serious about this woman then, Nalithor?"*

"That is a stupid question," Erist stated dryly, making the Elder twitch. "You know their kind. He wouldn't have reacted in such a way to *an Elder* if he wasn't serious."

*"I will see to it that the other deities understand the situation."* The Elder sighed with clear distaste. *"You could have at least chosen one with a proper fear of the gods, Nalithor. This one is too headstrong."*

Without another word, the Elder vanished from sight. Most of the deities present erupted into a string of curses. Surprisingly, Chaos was the calmest among them. He looked lost in thought, yet extremely amused with himself.

It seemed like a miracle that Nalithor, Ellena, and Lysander managed to avoid breaking anything with their thrashing tails. Erist cursed like a sailor while she finished mending my hand. I remained silent and wiggled my fingers a few times to make sure they all still worked, then poured myself a new cup of tea.

*'You didn't answer my question,'* Nalithor stated, jealousy and rage tinting his presence. *'Was Kalenek your—'*

*'I did say it was around twenty years ago,'* I interjected, stirring honey into my tea before shooting Nalithor a sideways glance. *'Unless you think a six or seven-year-old Human would have—'*

*'X'shmir is a strange place.'* Nalithor huffed.

*'Hmmm, you do have a point there, I suppose,'* I remarked, tilting my head. *'In that case, no. He wasn't a lover. However, he was one of my direct servants in the palace during his time there. Starting from before I came into my powers as an Umbral Mage.*

*'Djialkan, Fraelfnir, and I knew Lehrr wasn't Human. However, we never sensed anything "strange" or "wrong" about him either. He was a gentle, kind soul. It's difficult to believe Lehrr and Kalenek are the same person.'*

"Nalithor, you're hiding your thoughts from the Elders?" Ceres inquired.

"I would wager that they only noticed because I didn't respond to their summons," Nalithor murmured, his tone thoughtful as he tapped his claws against one arm. "The bastard didn't even notice when I said something to Arianna over our private connection—or when she replied. He should have caught the reverberations."

I released a small sigh when the deities began discussing business again. They were all upset that the Elders had banned them from the very things their roles presided over, and I couldn't blame them. However, I found it terribly boring to listen to deities I barely knew complain about their problems. I just wanted to snuggle with Nalithor, sleep, rest in the gardens, or fight something.

By the pacing of their conversation, I could tell none of those things would happen soon. That I had to sit so far from Nalithor wasn't helping matters. Erist was alright to sit beside, but she was no Nalithor.

"Arianna, how is your brother doing?" Gabriel questioned quite some time later, examining me with a worried expression on her face. "Has he... Has he been cursed by our kind as well?"

"If he's been bound by Angelic magics, I'm not aware of it," I replied with a shake of my head. "He has plenty of other problems to deal with. The X'shmirans weren't good to me by any stretch of the imagination, but I would argue that their treatment of Darius is many times worse."

"Your situations are vastly different and equally reprehensible." Nalithor shot me a firm look. "Both of you have been tortured, just in different ways."

"I deal with it better than he does," I pointed out, tilting my head. "For now, I'm more concerned about the thoughts of his you said you heard."

"I have already informed Gabriel," Nalithor stated, shaking his head. "She is here for a different reason."

"I need to 'see' the Angels responsible for the things that have happened to you," Gabriel began, her worried frown deepening. "I'm also going to remove what I can of the Angelic magic that binds you. As their matriarch, it should be a simple matter."

*'Remove…the curses?'* I paused mid-sip and looked at Gabriel for a moment, then glanced at Nalithor and back.

"Show *all* of us the Angels," Aurelian spoke up, tapping his temple with one finger. "Now that we're all on such a tight leash there's little fun for us to have. Tracking down these bastards should provide us with *some* entertainment, at least."

"Aye, it could be quite fun," Sebastian remarked, his tone sing-song.

"…fine. I sighed, summoning several dozen statues of ice around the room. "Will these suffice?"

"This…many?" Color drained from Gabriel's face as she looked around the room.

"Not counting the ones that are dead for certain," I replied, shifting in my seat to get more comfortable. "Nalithor. Which of the Elders was that one?"

"One of the ones responsible for my promotion." Nalithor sighed heavily, leaning back on his palms. "The two you saw in Abrantia were part of the group who don't believe a God of Balance is needed."

"You have your deities flipped," I stated icily, shooting him an icy glare. "Show me your memories of when I was taken from Dauthrmir. Now."

"What—" Nalithor growled, his tail smashing through the wooden floor behind him. "You're doubting my recollection—?!"

"*That one* is the one I saw arguing with Lucifer while the Angels dragged me away!" I growled back at him, ignoring Gabriel's startled gasp. "So, either *your* memories have been tinkered with, or *mine* have! I'm more inclined to believe *yours* have been—"

"I refuse to make either of us relive that," Nalithor stated, power shimmering around him as his anger grew. "Which one of them did what doesn't matter. They all deserve to die."

"Humph, we can agree on that last part at least." I huffed and crossed my arms. "I still don't like the idea that one of the bastards responsible for stabbing me is also behind your 'promotion.'"

"If you are right."

"I *am* right."

"You don't know that for sure."

"I nearly killed him the moment I smelled him!"

"You could say that about a lot of people, Arianna."

"That doesn't make it any less true!"

"Are you two quite finished?" Gabriel interjected dryly, looking between us as we both snorted at her. "Yes? Good. Now, Arianna, hold still while I work. I need to get a good look at what magic was used to 'curse' you—and how."

I looked away from Nalithor with a small "humph" and focused my attentions on a wall instead. My increasing boredom and the lack of interesting distractions was making my temper rise. He'd bitten me in front of people. He had used his venom against me, in front of said people. Then he refused to fuck me. I really didn't *care* anymore if his reasoning was valid. The more I thought about it, the angrier I grew.

I shelved my anger, for the moment, and did my best to hold still while Gabriel examined the magics that bound me to X'shmiran ways. My instincts screamed at me to run away from her light-aspect magics, but my brain knew that would have been stupid. However, that didn't make it any easier for me to keep from fidgeting.

"How long until you can safely kill the X'shmiran royals, Nalithor?" Gabriel turned to look at the now-pacing God of Balance, her voice terse.

"Unless something drastic comes to our attention...several months at best," Nalithor muttered, pulling at his braid. "For it to happen sooner, they would need to declare war on us, violate our treaty, or the Elders would have to lift the restrictions they have placed me under.

"As of now, we do not have the specific type of evidence the Elders require. They do not believe the events thus far are...punishable."

"I've removed most of your restrictions, Arianna," Gabriel began with a small frown, turning to look at me. "However, I can't remove the one that would slay you and Darius if you were to kill the king and queen of X'shmir. The magic used for that is volatile—and not of Angelic origin. I do not recognize it. The safest way to remove it is to wait for the king and queen to die of natural causes...or wait for someone else to kill them. However, if you are near them when that happens...you and Darius will still die.

"It's a good thing you and your Adinvyr haven't bedded each other yet. There was also a restriction that would have killed you for having sex."

"Tch, of course, there was," I muttered, feeling my face growing hot and I heard Nalithor's pacing halt.

*'You haven't...'* Nalithor trailed off when I shot him an embarrassed glare.

*'What, exactly, am I supposed to fuck in a country of people who hate me? Hmmm?'* I snapped.

*'Hmmm, I will have to be extra careful with you then,'* Nalithor mused, his tone rather serious as he examined me. *'Perhaps I will start with—'*

"Now then. If Darius is truly in an even worse state than Arianna, I should get to him right away," Gabriel began, turning to look at Nalithor. "Where is my son?"

"Arom and I have him locked up in our temple right now," Erist offered with a grimace. "He can't know you're his mother, yet. That you're a goddess and an Astral Mage should help gain his trust. I hope."

I watched as Erist stood and escorted Gabriel from the room. After a moment, I sighed and returned my gaze to the empty plate before me. Although I hadn't expected much out of meeting my real mother, I couldn't help but be disappointed. She acted concerned, but I didn't sense any genuine worry from her at all unless she was speaking about my brother.

It was a little upsetting since I was already stung by Nalithor's rejection.

'Ugh, really though?' I wondered, pouring myself yet another cup of tea. 'The X'shmirans wanted to keep me from having sex entirely? They should die for that alone!'

"Ceres, Sebastian, will you be able to continue the tasks I assigned you?" Nalithor questioned the two deities, both of which exchanged an uneasy glance. "If not, there is something else I would like you to look into for me."

'You don't strike me as the sort to delegate tasks,' I remarked, watching as Nalithor's tail twitched. 'Does this have something to do with the Elders' "meddling?"'

'We have been looking into the issue of the Elders ever since we noticed their power waning alongside ours,' Nalithor muttered irritably. 'The Elders themselves do not understand what "Balance" is meant to do. Or, if they do understand, they are intentionally keeping me from doing my duty. I cannot act without the threat of being Exiled hanging over my head.'

"Now then, for the matter of the festival—" Lysander began.

I tuned them out and bit back my increasing frustration. At the rate they were going, I wouldn't even get to kick Nalithor's ass before dinner. The deities seemed intent on talking for what seemed like an eternity. That Nalithor was sitting with his parents instead of with me added insult to injury. I hated it.

Had it been anyone other than his family, I would have killed them long ago and drenched the room in blood. It seemed like the appropriate way to get my point across.

'Who would've thought being in a room of people could feel so lonely?'

I bit back an exasperated sigh and considered pouring another cup of tea. *'Bored... Maybe I should just leave.'*

"What do you mean the poison was *Adinvyr* venom?!" Nalithor's enraged roar snapped me from my thoughts in time to watch him slam his palms down on the table. He glowered at Lysander, bristling. "An *Adinvyr* had the audacity to—"

"Aye, one of the women was hoping to bed Arianna-jiss before you could." Ellena teased with an entertained smile as Nalithor twitched and shot her a glare. "Of course, the fact that Arianna has been sitting here so nicely proves she's rather resistant to even *your* venom. Someone lesser wouldn't have—"

"It doesn't matter if they *would have* affected her!" Nalithor stated with a savage snarl. "I will have the bitch's head for even *trying* to—"

"You know the woman you're getting riled up and possessive over?" I snapped, giving Nalithor a sharp glare. "She's sitting right here, and she can hear you. She's also going to kick your ass from here to Abrantia if you continue acting like she's not here. If you go and chase down the Adinvyr bitch that offended you...well...

"How well can you swim?"

"Oh? Have you been neglecting your quarry, Nalithor?" Lysander arched an eyebrow at his son.

"I haven't—"

"He clearly has, if he's made Arianna *this* angry." Ellena giggled.

"No, I haven't! We just—"

"I'm quite certain we raised you better than that, boy!" Lysander slapped his son's back and released a hearty laugh. "We're done for now. Let my men do the hunting, Nalithor. Punishing the woman can wait. Her Highness, however, is losing her patience with you."

"He's lucky I lasted this long!" I huffed, rising to my feet and stalking toward the door.

"There wasn't anything shiny here to distract you," Nalithor commented dryly, appearing beside me and placing a hand on top of my head. "Do you still wish to spar?"

"Are the moons round?" I batted at his hand, pushing it off my head. "I'm not an armrest!"

"Come, I'll take you somewhere safe to spar." Nalithor chuckled, slipping an arm around my waist and pulling me out of the palace. "We should be—"

"What, exactly, is *safe* about sparring?" I demanded, dislodging his arm from my waist and taking several steps away from him, crossing my arms. "*Safe* is boring. *Safe* is for those rookies you detest so much. *Safe* is—"

"*Safe* meaning that we can both unleash our full power without disturbing the Draemirans," Nalithor stated, gripping my chin and pulling my face upward, making me rise on my tiptoes. "What has you so agitated, hmmm? You weren't so—"

"Full power?" I asked with a begrudging pout.

"Yes, our full power." Nalithor tilted his head and examined me. "You're not angry with me because of who that Elder *might* be, are you?"

"No," I muttered, reaching up and attempting to dislodge his hand from my chin. "Let go. We're never going to go spar like this."

"Tell me why you are angry, then," Nalithor spoke conversationally, seeming oblivious to my nails digging into his wrist.

"No."

"Then we won't spar."

"But—"

"I'm not going to indulge difficult behavior."

"I'm not *difficult*, I'm—"

"Then tell me why you're upset."

"I'm not *upset*, I'm *angry*. There's a *difference*! It's just... Did you really have to sit *all the way over there*? It's not like I—"

"Sometimes it isn't 'appropriate' for you to sit beside me." Nalithor smirked, pressing his other hand against the small of my back. "Mmm... Instead of sparring, we could always do something *else* to work out that frustration of yours..."

"Nope, you haven't earned it." I huffed, wriggling out of his grip and moving away with my arms crossed.

"But, the other night, we..."

"If you want to make up for lost progress, spar with me," I stated, shooting him an indignant glare.

"Fine. You want to spar?" Nalithor growled, closing the distance between us. He hoisted me up without warning and settled me over his shoulder. "Then we will spar."

I yelped when he slapped my ass hard. A split second later he leapt into the air, his black feathered wings sprouting from his back and nearly smacking me in the face. The ground rushed by beneath us at an alarming pace, soon giving way to the lake itself. For a few minutes, I forgot my anger and stared in awe at the sparkling lake and glowing forest that bordered it.

Soon, Nalithor landed on a secluded beach and dumped me unceremoniously on my rump.

"No rules," Nalithor stated as his wings vanished into dark energy and absorbed into his back.

"Good. Perhaps this will be interesting enough to keep me from tracking that elder down," I muttered, pulling myself to my feet. "No rules at…all…"

Heat rose in my body as I watched Nalithor slowly strip off his overrobes, leaving only his pants and shoes on. Despite my anger, I wanted to close the distance and run my hands over every inch of his sculpted torso. The swishing of his tail and his smug expression indicated he probably knew it, too.

"Mmm…." Nalithor turned to examine me, a smirk forming on his face. "Perhaps, if you manage to win, I'll treat you to another show."

# CHAPTER TWENTY-TWO
*Modesty*

"A s-show?" I took a step back, my face burning scarlet. I drew my scythe and leveled it at him, bristling. "What makes you think I would want something like *that*?!"

"Oh, isn't that what it was? Or…" Nalithor grinned at me and summoned his spear, resting it on his shoulder before continuing, "Perhaps you were hoping I'd invite you to come join me instead, hmmm?"

"*T-that's not it at all!*" I snapped.

Nalithor shot me a knowing smirk, irritating me further. Darkness burst outward from me when I rushed him. The blades of our weapons crashed together, the harsh sound ringing in my jaw as the force of my strike traveled down my arms. A triumphant grin crossed Nalithor's face as he shifted his stance and swung the shaft of his weapon toward my ribcage.

I dispersed into the shadows for a few seconds before leaping at Nalithor from the side. My overhead strike grazed down his shoulder and chest as he leapt away. He laughed, flashing his fangs as a playful expression settled on his face, and he tracked my movements. I, for one, didn't care about what he found so amusing.

The scent of his blood was hypnotic—I needed to end our fight before I lost myself to it.

"Mmm... You scratched me already?" Nalithor drawled, lifting his free hand to the wound. He examined the blood that came away on his fingertips and then shot me a smirk. "Was that wise?"

"Stop playing around!" I swung the point of my scythe's blade into the ground and growled.

Jagged pillars of ice erupted from the ground and raced toward the playful Adinvyr. Pale flames burst out from Nalithor but only bounced off the approaching spikes. He vanished into darkness just before the spikes impaled the spot he'd been standing in.

A sudden wave of bloodlust from my right was all the warning I had before he reappeared.

The blade of Nalithor's spear tore down my right bicep, ripping through clothing and skin alike. It stung, but there was no time for me to nurse the wound. Nalithor sprang into action again, chasing me across the beach, his slashes and jabs pressuring me backward.

Despite my familiarity with scythes, it was too cumbersome to use against his faster weapon. I let my blade disappear into my jewelry and summoned a longsword instead, then leapt away from the Adinvyr for the umpteenth time.

"Don't you think you're being a little too—" Nalithor cut himself off and winced when I ducked under the swipe of his spear. I darted past him, slicing him across the abdomen. "—vicious?"

"You said no rules," I pointed out. "So, stop going easy—"

I brought up my sword to block his spear. My joints creaked beneath the strength he exerted. I gritted my teeth and pushed back with a growl. Nalithor smirked in response to my glaring. His eyes almost seemed to glow in the dim light. I couldn't quite understand why he seemed so smug.

Perhaps it was time that I *made* him stop fooling around.

Nalithor staggered back a few steps when my foot slammed into his ribs. I flipped my grip on my sword and chased after him. We exchanged a flurry of blows before the rumbling of the earth made me leap away. The ground split open where I had been standing, and the newly formed fissure followed me as I retreated.

*'Tch, what a pain.'* I sped away and jumped into a tree before glancing around in search of the pesky Adinvyr. *'Where did he—'*

I yelped, startled, when a tendril of water wrapped around my ankle and yanked me from the tree, throwing me clear over the open surface of the lake. Without thinking, I froze the immediate surface of the lake and slammed back-first into it. The wind left my lungs, making me gasp and cough for air as I slid to a halt.

Nalithor gave me no time to recover. I rolled out of the way and onto my feet mere moments before his spear buried into where I had been laying on the ice. He grinned and turned to examine me, his gaze trailing along the bloody nicks that covered my skin. Finally, he lifted his gaze to my face and smirked.

"You're faster than I gave you credit for. Still not ready to surrender...yet...?" Nalithor trailed off, watching as I lifted the back of one hand to my mouth and flicked my tongue over a gash. "At least *share—*"

"I was wondering what about my taste had you so interested." I tilted my head to the side, watching as pale magic danced around Nalithor's form. He growled, his tail thrashing behind him as I continued, "Mmm... Why should I share? Didn't I say you have to earn—"

Magic exploded around Nalithor, sending particles of frost and wisps of darkness into the air and surrounding the length of his weapon. He swung for me, leaving an arc of elements in the air. I stuck my tongue out at him and danced away from his strikes, freezing more of the lake as we went.

We were far enough from the shore that the glowing flora provided us with no light. Only the moons, starlight, and my ability to see magic allowed me to track the Adinvyr's movements. Without all three I would have lost long ago, and I knew it.

That was part of the fun.

*'Hmmm, he's been holding back even when we fight beasts.'* I

summoned several dozen swords of ice and leveled them at Nalithor. "You're cute when you're frustrated."

"I am going to spank that sass right out of you." Nalithor growled, bursting forward in a maelstrom of pale flames.

"You have to catch me first," I answered sweetly before dispersing into the shadows and returning to the forest.

It took Nalithor mere seconds to catch up to me. We clashed again, adding to the collection of scratches and scrapes. A few of his strikes dug deep, but I didn't care. It was nowhere near as distracting as the scent, or sight, of his blood. I wanted another taste. I wanted it so badly that my anger had dissolved quite some time ago.

"For you to be fighting me like *this*... You must really want another show." Nalithor chuckled, eliciting a growl from me.

"I'm not going to just *let* you win!" I snapped, deflecting another spike from his spear.

I spun into a kick and slammed my shin into Nalithor's bloodied abdomen. He staggered back, wincing, so I took the opportunity to kick his weapon from his hand. I ducked under his counterstrike and swept his legs out from under him. He summoned boulders in the air above us as he fell and landed hard on his back. I pinned him and placed the tip of my sword against his jugular. Magic shimmered around his hands, indicating that he was preparing to toss the chunks of earth at me.

"Will you crush us both?" I tilted my head, watching the trickle of blood that my blade drew. "Or— Hey! Watch what you're grabbing!"

"I know *exactly* what I'm grabbing." Nalithor purred, squeezing my ass and pulling me down against him. "Mmm...I would argue that *I* won this round."

"I'm the one with a sword." I growled at him, but he seemed content to dig his claws into my hips anyway.

"And *I* am the one with a beautiful woman straddling me," Nalithor countered, smirking, as he smoothed his hands down to my thighs.

"Seeing as I don't want a woman *around me* let alone *on top of me*, I don't think that logic counts," I retorted. The corner of my eye twitched when the Adinvyr chuckled at me. "You are far too comfortable with—"

"Mmm, how should I reward you?" Nalithor removed his hands from my thighs and reached up to grip the blade of my sword. "Is *this* really necessary still?"

"I never said I wanted a reward," I muttered, huffing as I lifted the blade away from his skin. Ignoring the trickle of blood down his throat proved difficult. His pale skin and the contrasting liquid called to me. "I'm not satisfied yet. Let's spar some—"

A yelp escaped me when Nalithor knocked the sword from my hand and then rolled me onto my back in the same motion, pinning me to the ground beneath him. We were both worse for wear. Our clothes were in tatters, and our skin was smeared with each other's blood, stemming from dozens of nicks, gouges, and scrapes.

Blood trickled down Nalithor's skin in places still, even though most of the wounds had begun to close.

"We should probably return to the palace," Nalithor murmured, studying me. "Or do you intend to try fighting me when you can't even concentrate anymore?"

"I can focus just fine!" I growled at him as he lowered his head, his lips just out of reach of mine. "Let me up so I can—"

"One victory isn't enough?" Nalithor questioned, nuzzling into my neck. He ran his tongue over a cut that I hadn't even noticed, startling a squeak from me. "Ahhh… You taste—"

"What were you saying about returning to the palace?" I rolled my eyes at him and then suppressed a shudder when I felt his fangs graze my throat. I almost *wanted* him to take a bite out of me. *'That won't do…'*

"It's true that we're still expected to attend the nightly dinners." Nalithor sighed into my throat. "However, I tire of such things. I would rather—"

Nalithor trailed off into a throaty growl when I pressed my lips to his bloodied neck. The scent was driving me crazy. Even if it was just a small taste, I wanted it. There was no way I could focus on conversing with him when his sweet-smelling blood was so close. Rather, I *couldn't* focus on anything.

I wanted to sink my fangs into his skin. I wanted to—

"*Enough*," Nalithor groaned, wrapping one hand around my throat and prying me away. "Your control is lapsing. You haven't shown any signs of reverting to your true form and yet—"

"My control isn't 'lapsing!'" I protested, growling at Nalithor as he studied me. "Let me up."

"We still haven't agreed on how I should reward you for winning," Nalithor countered with false innocence. "The offer of another 'show' is still on the table, you know." He paused to trail his claws down my throat and to the buttons of my blouse. "Or did you have something *else* in mind?"

"I-I said I wasn't *looking* for a reward!" I protested, batting his hand away from my chest. "B-besides, I didn't *mean* to see that y-you were..."

"Whether you meant to or not, you liked what you saw." Nalithor smirked. "Oh, don't worry, I'm not cross with you...at least, not for *peeping*."

"Come along. We should bathe and heal each other before we're expected anywhere."

Nalithor pulled me to my feet and into his chest. The proximity of his bloodied skin threatened to draw me in again, so I turned away with a small "humph," earning another chuckle from the difficult Adinvyr. I went to move away from him, but Nalithor was quick to lift me into his arms instead.

"You don't need to carry me. I can walk."

"But you can't fly."

"We don't *need* to fly, though, we can walk."

"The longer we take to get back, the more likely you are to take a bite out of me," Nalithor spoke dryly. He strode toward the lake's shore where there were fewer trees and shook his head. "Despite your 'cravings,' I don't think you have shifted enough to benefit from feeding."

"If I even *do* shift," I grumbled, crossing my arms.

"You will. We just don't know how to trigger it," Nalithor replied. He readjusted his grip on me before taking to the air. "If my blood were a catalyst, you would have shifted the first time I let you have a taste. Since it didn't, all we can do is assume that something else is required."

"Well, it may be a good thing that it isn't so simple." I sighed, resting the side of my head against his chest. "After all, Darius still doesn't know about the past, and Fraelfnir seems to think it needs to stay that way. I'm not sure how well Darius would handle—"

"I, for one, don't care anymore if that brother of yours has a meltdown." Nalithor growled, his grip tightening enough to make his claws rip my clothing. "The longer you stay in this muddled form, the more at risk you are.

"Your heart refuses to return to you while you're like this—I tried to give it back to you. Djialkan believes that it won't return until you're in a form that's capable of handling that amount of power."

"And yet I can handle fighting you," I pointed out, tugging at his braid.

"Yes, cute little deadly thing you are." Nalithor smiled. "A few times there I thought you were trying to *kill* me, you know. You play rough."

"You *did* say no rules." I pouted, shifting my gaze away from him and to the fast-approaching Draemiran palace. "Besides, you were taking me more seriously than you take beasts—*and* you never gave either of us the chance to dull our weapons."

*'Looks like we don't have time to ourselves just yet.'* Nalithor growled, tucking me toward his chest in a defensive manner.

Darkness flowed around both of us as Nalithor's rage began to simmer. I shivered and nuzzled my face into his skin. My thoughts and vision blurred momentarily when his power flowed over me, threatening to lure me in. The combined scents of his blood and power were almost enough to drown out the traces of my brother and the four deities accompanying him.

I shifted just enough to shoot them a sideways glare when Nalithor landed on the ground outside of his portion of the palace.

"W-what in the *hells* happened to you two?" Darius demanded, his eyes wide. He took a step back when Nalithor's darkness rounded on him with a hiss.

"We were sparring," Nalithor stated coolly. "I assume you lot are standing here for a reason?"

"Sparring? With *that* many cuts?" Erist sighed, shaking her head. She raised her fingertips to her temples before continuing, "Darius needed proof that Arianna's blood didn't 'poison' you. Apparently, he *genuinely* thought that—"

"Umbral Mage blood is poison!" Darius argued. "I can't just *let* her poison a god."

"By that logic, Nalithor's blood should be poison too." I purred. Turning, I made a show of running my tongue along a gouge on Nalithor's chest. It took most of my self-control not to laugh when I heard his tail twitch into something behind him, and the rest of it to keep myself from biting him. "Mmm… Nalithor tastes *incredible*, you know. I won't mind if he's 'poison.'"

*'Behave.'* Nalithor growled, his grip twitching.

*'That isn't very specific,'* I countered innocently.

"He's not *supposed* to be an Umbral Mage!" Darius snapped, his face scarlet. "You shouldn't grow attached to someone you can't have!"

"I've never *been* an Astral Mage, boy." Nalithor's condescending tone made me smile. "Arianna and I are busy. If that was all you wanted to discuss with us, then *be gone*."

Nalithor turned on his heel and carried me toward the doorway to his part of the palace. I flinched when I felt the familiar hum of light magic in the air. A savage snarl escaped Nalithor's lips as he pivoted, darkness erupting around us both. His darkness devoured Darius' pathetic attack and then slung it back into my brother.

Darius screamed in a combination of terror and pain as the orb of light threw him off his feet and crashing into a stone lamppost. Darkness raged around Nalithor while Gabriel and a deity I didn't recognize both rushed to my brother's side and helped him back to his feet. I could feel Nalithor gathering more of his power as he considered lobbing it at my brother, who already appeared to be in agony after being hit with his own power.

"Let's not waste our time on them." I rubbed my cheek against Nalithor's chest and shifted my gaze away from both Darius and the deities. I trailed my fingers down his abdomen and to the waistband of his trousers, eliciting a sound somewhere between a purr and a growl from him. "We're both in desperate need of a bath."

"A b-b-bath? Together?!" Darius yelped. Nalithor simply ignored him and turned to walk toward the doors again. "I won't allow it! Ari, you're no longer allowed to talk to Nalithor! You're not allowed to see him, be near him, touch him, or— H-huh? W-why isn't it working?!"

*'Did he just try to* kill *you?'* Nalithor's chest rumbled beneath my cheek, but I just continued to trace my fingertips along his skin. *'First, he attacks you with* light, *then he attempts to reinstate restrictions—'*

*'The more time you waste on him, the higher the chance of me growing cross again becomes,'* I interjected, examining the blood that came away on my fingertips before lapping at it. *'Hmmm... I think you taste much better than I do.'*

A small smile crossed my lips when Nalithor twitched. He was so much fun to tease at times.

"Get Darius out of my sight before I decide to execute him for interfering," Nalithor spat, shooting an icy look at the small group of deities. "I won't tolerate any more interference from the deities, let alone a mortal. If you intend to keep him alive, see to it that you at least get some useful information out of him."

Nalithor didn't bother giving the deities a chance to respond. He stalked into his section of the palace and used tendrils of shadow to slam the door shut behind him. I purred and nuzzled into his chest again, drawn by the sensation of his darkness. His pulse sped up when I snuggled closer, and after a moment he released a sigh.

"I thought you would be cross with me because I threatened your brother," Nalithor commented as he carried me through the doors that led to the bath. He hesitated a moment before setting me down on my feet.

"I would've been cross if you *hadn't* threatened him," I replied while pulling my tattered blouse over my head and tossing it aside.

Nalithor opened his mouth to say something but instead fell silent, watching as I stripped off the remainder of my torn clothing before striding towards the bath nude. I felt his eyes tracing down my back, and it was only a matter of seconds before I heard him approach me. Before I could turn to question him, he lifted me off the floor and nuzzled the back of my right shoulder, releasing a low purr. He carried me the rest of the way into the bath, his lips traveled along one of the many cuts I had sustained.

"Perhaps I should have gone easier on you," Nalithor murmured, his grip on my waist tensing. He ran his tongue over the wound before adding, "Seeing you injured is *unacceptable.*"

"I would be *very* angry if you went easy on me while sparring." I pouted, tugging at his arm. "You don't need to carry—"

"We need to get your desires under control," Nalithor groaned into my shoulder. "You shouldn't be able to affect me this much..."

"Affect...?" I trailed off when he released me, and I attempted to battle the urge to turn and peek at him. "Why, exactly, do you think that I shouldn't 'affect' you?"

"My dear, I'm an *Adinvyr*. *I'm* supposed to be the one affecting *you*." Nalithor chuckled, running his hands down the sides of my torso and to my hips. "I'm disinclined to attend dinner tonight. Perhaps we should skip it?"

"Well, I'm not sure how much more I can take of mouthy deities and royals," I commented dryly, glancing over my shoulder at him. "Though, seeing the X'shmirans squirm might be worthwhile."

"Mmm... I am not in a sharing mood," Nalithor muttered, moving his hands from my hips so that he could trace a few of the wounds on my back. "I suppose, before we make any decisions, we should bathe and heal our wounds. Here, let me see."

"See? I-I don't need help with—" I flushed when Nalithor tugged at my shoulder, indicating that he wanted me to turn toward him. "I can heal myself!"

"I will never understand the aversion to nudity that Humans raise their young with." Nalithor sighed, lifting me up by my waist. He hauled me over to the edge of the bath and set me on it so that our faces were level. "Is it a concern that nudity is ugly? Humans seem rather preoccupied with such notions. Or is it some twisted perception of 'purity?'"

"It's about *modesty*," I retorted, attempting to cover myself. "Showing ourselves to anyone other than—"

"*I* think you are just shy," Nalithor stated, placing his hands on the floor to either side of my hips as he leaned toward me. "Or…are you insinuating that I *still* haven't 'earned' it?"

"That's not what I was saying." I shivered when Nalithor pressed his lips to my left shoulder. "Y-you're…*really* covered in blood, you know."

"So are you." Nalithor purred, kissing down to my collarbone. "What are you going to do about it?"

"Weren't we supposed to be taking a *bath* and not—" I bit down on my lower lip, hard, when Nalithor ran his tongue from my collarbone up to the underside of my jaw.

"I may have had something *else* in mind as well." Nalithor chuckled deviously. "However, we don't have much time before *I* have to join the festivities."

"Before *you*… What about me?" I demanded. Nalithor withdrew from my throat and shot me a smirk before grabbing my hips and pulling me back into the water with him. *'Tch. Complains about me trying to cover myself, yet he has a towel on!'*

"I can always remove it, if you prefer." Nalithor smirked at me. "Are you struggling with yourself a bit, my dear? How adorable."

"I'm not adorable!"

"To answer your question, I've decided that you are going to stay in my suite for the night." Nalithor motioned loosely with one hand. "My venom clearly still affects you—at least a little bit. I can't have you beheading the guests just because they looked at me the wrong way."

"I don't have to be under the influence of your venom in order to behead people for *that*.' I snorted, crossing my arms over my chest as I looked away from him.

"You're much more likely to act on it while—" Nalithor grinned crookedly when I shot him a glare. "Are you going to let me help you or not? I can't heal you sufficiently when you are attempting to cover yourself."

"…fine," I mumbled, flushing brighter when I let my arms fall to my side. "Do I really need to stay in *your* suite, though? Isn't mine sufficient?"

"Fear not, I'll be a gentleman and sleep on a sofa in the sitting room," Nalithor replied dryly, lifting a hand to my shoulder. "I prefer to keep an eye on you myself. Alala should be able to guard you until I return from dinner, but I prefer to keep you close by."

"You don't *have* to sleep on the couch…" I grumbled, averting my gaze. "I can behave myself at dinner, too. You don't need to lock me in your rooms to keep me safe."

"I didn't think you would take kindly to sharing the bed with me, considering you can't even look at me while I'm nude." Nalithor released a dejected sigh, causing me to pivot and look up at him in surprise.

"Didn't we *just* go over the whole 'Human modesty' thing?" I prodded him in the chest and pouted. "Didn't you wonder *why* I was scared you'd be angry with me for peeping, no matter how short-lived?

"Besides, our snuggling keeps getting interrupted. People like

Darius keep pissing us *both* off. And to top it all off, that stupid fucking 'Elder' implied that you should rape—"

"He deserves the most painful death I can give him, for that." Nalithor growled, shifting his hands to the next set of wounds.

"Darius, or the Elder?" I inquired dryly, earning a laugh from the Adinvyr. "I'm rather certain that I can behave myself at dinner. You don't need to keep me in your rooms."

"That's assuming we make it to dinner at all." Nalithor sighed, studying me. "I will admit, you are much more distracting than I thought you would be. Perhaps it is because I am hungry but, hungry or not, you are quite pleasant to look at."

"Hungry? Already?" I questioned as he motioned for me to turn my back to him.

"Blood as sustenance only works for so long," Nalithor replied, drawing his fingers down my spine. "Tch, I didn't realize I had wounded you this deeply."

"How deep—" I winced when Nalithor lifted me and pressed his mouth to a wound partway down my back.

"Here, sit," Nalithor stated, lifting me out of the water entirely and onto the ledge of the bath again. "I'll be able to mend your wounds better if I can see them."

*'Says the one that's intentionally drawing this out as long as possible.'* I rolled my eyes and sat on the floor. "Better?"

"Much," Nalithor replied, nudging my soaked hair the rest of the way over my shoulder. "As far as dinner is concerned, I doubt your ability to restrain yourself at the given moment."

"If I'm 'affected' by your venom still, you can just *order* me to behave, can't you?" I smirked when his fingers twitch against my back. "From what I understand, I should be 'pliable,' correct?"

"In that case…" Nalithor murmured, nuzzling the back of my shoulder. "You are to refrain from attacking *any* of our guests at dinner. You are to stay by my side at all times, and—

"What are you giggling about?"

"*No*." I smirked at him over my shoulder.

"*No*?" Nalithor stared at me for a moment, disbelief apparent on his features. "*No*? If you are saying '*no*,' then you are no longer under the influence of my venom. But, I used so much… You—"

"You shouldn't make assumptions," I informed him, earning a heavy sigh.

"If you're not affected by my venom anymore…" Nalithor purred into the crook of my neck and slid his hands around to the front of my torso, trailing them a little too low for comfort. "Are you really *that* cross with me for not sit—

'*Damn it. They just don't know when to leave us alone, do they?*'

Nalithor shifted and wrapped an arm across my chest and settled the other low across my hips. His chest rumbled against my back as he pulled me closer and rested his head on my right shoulder. I heard his tail cutting through the water behind him in an agitated manner while he continued to growl. Nalithor's grip tightened when I squirmed, his claws digging into my skin until I stopped.

*'Visitors?'* I asked when I caught the sound of the door sliding open, and Nalithor's growling became more savage.

"So, this is where you two were!" Ellena snapped. "Nalithor, you're already running late as it is! You can spend time to yourselves later. For now, our guests are quite cross that you two have yet to make an appearance!"

"I don't particularly feel like sharing Arianna with our guests at the moment." Nalithor huffed, nipping at my shoulder.

"You don't have much of a choice now, do you?" Ellena countered dryly. "You're still here as a prince, and Arianna is your guest…but she is also a foreign dignitary. Both of you are expected to join us for dinner tonight, seeing as the festival begins in proper tomorrow. *Not* coming to dinner will raise more problems than it will solve."

"But…" Nalithor trailed off into a growl and shifted me further from his mother's view, bristling. "I refuse to share—"

"You won't be 'sharing' me if you keep me by your side," I pointed out, causing Nalithor to squeeze me tighter. "Don't you want to silence the mouthy ones once and for all?"

"Nnngh… But I would *rather*—"

"Time is ticking!" Ellena huffed. "I dropped off appropriate clothing for Arianna in your suite, Nalithor. See to it that you're both dressed and at dinner in fifteen minutes, or you will *both* have a new slew of wounds to heal!"

I listened to the click of Ellena's heels as she stalked out of the bath and then slammed the door behind her. Nalithor sighed heavily into my shoulder and nuzzled me again, darkness flowing freely from his hands to spread across my skin. Once pressured for time, he seemed to take healing me more seriously.

Finally, he released me and tugged at my curls.

"My turn," Nalithor stated when I turned to look at him. "Let's hurry, before she comes back...and before I choose to ignore her warnings."

# CHAPTER TWENTY-THREE
## *Discordance*

"Don't you think this is a bit too fancy?" I grumbled while adjusting a brocade sash.

Nalithor chuckled from somewhere behind me as he reached up to brush a few curls away from my throat. He elicited a startled squeak from me when his lips, and then tongue, grazed over the side of my neck.

He grinned when I whirled around to glare at him.

"Missed a spot."

"Missed…?" I sighed at him. "You could have just cleaned it *normally*."

"And miss out on those adorable noises you make? Hardly." Nalithor's grin broadened while he examined me. "As for your attire, my dear, 'fancy' is the point. The spring festival begins in earnest tonight for the Draemiran nobility, royals, and our divine guests. For the rest of Draemir, it starts tomorrow.

"Here... I suppose it would be best if you pinned your hair up."

I tilted my head and watched a brief pout cross his lips before he conjured several of my platinum hair sticks, and other ornaments, he had lifted from me on previous occasions. Nalithor's face held poorly concealed disappointment when he offered the decorations to me.

Instead of taking them, I turned so that my back was to him and lifted a few sections of curls into a messy bun. "Since you've decided to give them back to me, I suppose I can let you return them to their rightful place as well.

"I get the feeling we're running even later than we were before. We should probably hurry."

"I suppose we should..." Nalithor sighed and then wove a few of the ornaments into my hair. "Are you certain that you wouldn't prefer to remain here?"

"What happened to showing me off, *hmmm*?" I shifted to nudge him with my elbow. "Don't worry; I'll try not to kill anyone too important."

"It's comments such as that, that worry me," Nalithor stated dryly, offering me his arm.

I grinned and took his arm, allowing him to lead me out of his suite. We passed the occasional patrolling guard or busy servant while making our way across the palace grounds. Nalithor maintained a brisk pace, but that didn't stop him from the sporadic glance down at me. I couldn't tell if he was checking to make sure I wasn't going to run off and kill something, or if he was admiring my attire.

The heavy layers of obsidian and sapphire brocade made me feel out of place. It was far more ornate than anything I was accustomed to wearing, and the fact it matched Nalithor's attire made me uneasy. I couldn't help but suspect that Ellena was up to something—especially since *she* was responsible for selecting my finery.

*'Why did Ellena want me to wear something so formal?'* I gnawed on my lower lip, glancing to the side as Nalithor led me past a group of chatting Elves. *'I suppose the other guests are wearing formal attire as well...but Nalithor and I both seem overdressed by comparison.'*

"Nali!" An unfamiliar voice called when we entered the dining hall.

A young woman with long white hair came barreling across the wooden floor at us, her bright orange eyes fixated on Nalithor. The deity promptly released me, blocked a punch from the Adinvyr woman, and then tossed her a few yards away as if she weighed nothing. A savage grin spread across the woman's face as she charged Nalithor again, her tail whipping behind her in delight.

"Ah, ah, ah." Nalithor caught me around the waist with one arm when I moved to kick the woman across the room. He grabbed her with his free hand and gave us both a look. "Arianna, this is my sister— Ijelle. Ijelle, this is—"

"Let me go, Nali!" Ijelle protested, clawing at his arm. "It's been months! We haven't fought in—"

"Mmm? Sister? So, I shouldn't kill her then?" I sighed, pouting before glancing toward the white-haired woman. "I suppose I can see the resemblance. That said, she's wearing far too much clothing to identify her Brands."

"Too much cloth—" Ijelle trailed off when she finally looked at me. Her face grew a bright burgundy when her molten-colored eyes dropped to my cleavage. "U-u-uh…um…"

The Adinvyr woman's silvery tail stopped swishing entirely for a moment before she pulled out of Nalithor's grasp and retreated to the crescent-shaped table at the back of the room. Ijelle was flushed all the way to the tips of her pointed ears, and promptly clenched her hands in her lap when she plopped down at the family table.

I wasn't sure if it was even *possible* for her to grow redder.

*'My sister isn't as good with beautiful women as I am.'* Nalithor smirked at my confusion. *'Come, let's make ourselves comfortable. We will likely be stuck here for several hours.'*

*'The only "beautiful woman" you need to be "good with" is* me,*'* I informed him as he steered me past dozens of tables and to the head table. *'I still don't think this attire is appropriate. It's even fancier than your sister's, and she's the only Draemiran princess!'*

"You are *late*." Ellena huffed, shooting us a look when Nalithor escorted me around the side of the table and to our waiting seats. "Arianna-jiss, is my son being too greedy?"

"Hardly. I think I'm even growing accustomed to his attentions," I answered with a crooked grin.

"Besides, Arianna won our match earlier," Nalithor added, sitting down and pulling me to his side. "I should be catering to *whatever she desires*, so there is no room for me to be 'greedy' this evening."

"You *let* her win?" Ijelle demanded from her seat on the right half of the table.

"Not necessary." Nalithor shook his head. "Arianna can be quite ferocious when something she wants is involved."

"I said I *didn't* want—"

"You can't fool me, my dear." Nalithor chuckled and then squeezed my waist when I huffed at him. "Mmm...since we haven't had dinner yet, how about some tea?"

"Sure..." I trailed off and glanced toward the other half of the table when I caught Ijelle growling at us. She had her arms crossed, and her expression was rather unpleasant. *'What is she so upset about?'*

*'Ijelle and I have always had similar taste in women,'* Nalithor replied, pulling a pair of cups toward himself. *'Of course, seeing as she is my only sister, I have probably spoiled her a bit. She is accustomed to sitting by me at these affairs.'*

I fell silent while Nalithor prepared tea for the both of us and began surveying our surroundings. It was easy, even as an outsider, to spot the foreigners at many of the tables in the massive room. They all fidgeted at their low tables in a poor attempt to find a comfortable way to sit or kneel.

Many of the deities among them were visibly displeased that they couldn't force their Chosen to sit at their feet. Some of them were even flushed with anger in their attempts to arrange their Chosen into more submissive positions. *'I'm impressed you haven't killed the bastards yet, Nalithor.'*

*'Don't tempt me.'* Nalithor shot me a sideways glance before returning to preparing our tea. After a moment, he sighed. *'The Elders do not like looking for replacements. Rarely does a Middle or Upper God misstep to a degree that allows me to act.'*

*'A pity, that,'* I murmured, glancing from table to table once more.

This time, the Chosen and the other servants were clothed. The majority of foreign dignitaries appeared unfazed by the way the Chosen were treated. I couldn't determine if they approved of the vile behavior, or if they had simply come to accept it as something they couldn't change.

To my surprise, the X'shmiran delegates looked horrified by the situation with the Chosen. Their discomfort was clear on their faces, even on the handful of servants that were fawning over Dilonu. The bastard's torso was visibly bandaged beneath his layers of royal finery. Everyone at the X'shmiran table looked out of place when compared to the other guests.

The X'shmiran's attire and jewelry was nothing compared to that of the other dignitaries, let alone that of the gods. It made me even more uneasy about the attire Ellena had brought to Nalithor's rooms for me. The only women at the party who came anywhere *close* to my level of adornment were Erist, Ceres, Llrissa, and a few other female deities I didn't recognize.

I may have been Nalithor's date, but I wasn't his goddess. Being equally adorned didn't seem appropriate, and it had certainly begun to catch the interest of some of the guests.

*'Is it normal for Lucifer and Gabriel to share a table?'* I asked, glancing up at Nalithor when he offered me my cup.

*'No. Gabriel usually doesn't attend such affairs.'* Nalithor looked toward the opposite end of the table and then shifted his attention back to me. *'Most Devillians and Angels don't get along well. Angels have treasured the light over all else for a very long time. Those born with dark abilities were treated as outcasts and only allowed to perform certain jobs or tasks.*

*'It wasn't until more recently that Gabriel began pushing for change. She believes her people's biased treatment is what caused their current divide—and other issues. It is also why you were never permitted to visit her and Darius in Leryci.'*

"Arianna, does your kimono fit alright?" Ellena inquired sweetly.

"Yes...thank you," I replied, shooting her a suspicious look.

"Isn't Arianna-jiss one of the X'shmiran royals?" Ijelle inquired, a small pout on her lips. "Why isn't she sitting with *them*?"

"Arianna-z'tar is my partner," Nalithor replied, his tone dismissive.

"But she's still the X'shmiran princess, right?"

"She is, but that doesn't matter."

"Aren't dignitaries supposed to remain at their family's table?"

"Since Arianna-z'tar is my prospective mate, that rule doesn't apply."

"Y-y-your *what*?!" Ijelle yelped as my face burned hot. "Since *when*? Why wasn't I informed of this when I arrived this morning?!"

"Perhaps if you hadn't slept the day away, you would have learned of it sooner," Lysander chastised the flustered princess, his expression one of amusement. He didn't seem at all concerned about his son's proclamation and instead directed an approving nod in Nalithor's direction.

*'Why aren't you denying this whole "prospective mate" thing they've been going on about?'* I questioned, feeling my face growing hotter when Nalithor arched an eyebrow at me. *'I mean, you didn't really say that you want—'*

*'You aren't denying it either.'* Nalithor smirked and pulled me closer, his tail coiling around my hips. *'You know, I told myself that if I ever discovered you had survived... I would see to it that you weren't dragged back into the role of Balance.*

*'Yet here we are, finding ourselves in a situation where you could become the Goddess of Balance.'*

*'If you tried to go with your prior plan, I would kick your ass for it,'* I grumbled, glancing away from him. *'Even so... You've never really made your intentions clear to me. It came as a surprise when—'*

*'As if I would let anyone else have you!'* Nalithor huffed, allowing his hand to slip to my hip. *'I fully intend to win you and make you mine.'*

"I think Ellena and I finally figured out a way to get the weak ones off your tails." Erist grinned, pointing at us. "Nalithor, how much protection would we need to erect in the city if we wanted you and

Arianna to spar each other at full power?"

"Sparring?" I perked up and glanced toward Erist. "What kind of sparring? I like sparring. Full power for us, or full power for 'normal' people? Weapons? Limited weapons? No weapons? When can we—"

"Calm down, she clearly doesn't mean right now." Nalithor chuckled at me before shifting his attention to Erist as well. "As the excitable one asked; do you mean our legitimate full power, or do you mean the power the citizens would expect of us?"

"Your actual power," Ellena answered, flourishing with one hand. "We don't want to leave any room for doubt in their minds that the two of you are well beyond their reach."

"Then there is nothing you can do to protect the city or the onlookers." Nalithor shook his head.

"What if we—"

"You cannot simply shield the power of the God of Balance—let alone *two* of us."

"But she *isn't*... Or at least, she isn't *yet*—"

"She is close enough to be capable of defeating me on occasion."

"You both also forget the affect my son's power will have on the people of Draemir," Lysander interjected before either of the women could argue further. "We can also assume that Arianna-z'tar's power is likely to have some effect on the citizens as well—and possibly our guests. A fight at their full strength is unwise."

*'Bored already?'* Nalithor inquired when I nuzzled my cheek into his chest.

*'If we can't fight at full power, I don't need to listen to their plotting much,'* I replied, shifting so that my chest was pressed against his side. *'If we're going to be here for several hours I may as well get comfortable.'*

*'Ah...how even the most innocent of actions enrages some of our guests.'* Nalithor chuckled, stroking my hip. *'Such a pity that the Elves are incapable of seeing you as anything other than Human. Their complaints would be far fewer in number if they could discern that simple fact.'*

*'They don't seem to like Humans much at all.'* I glanced at the room, observing the varying tables of Elven dignitaries. *'I suppose the Kelsviir are closer to Devillians in their customs than they are to their Elven brethren. Who are the other Elves that don't appear livid?'*

*'Raogsur—Ocean Elves,'* Nalithor answered. His grip twitched when I rested one of my hands on his thigh, but he continued as if nothing was amiss, *'The Kelsviir and the Raogsur are more agreeable than the other Elven races. There are six Elven races that we're aware of, though the Elders have hinted at the existence of more.'*

*'You don't know?'* I pursed my lips while examining the six tables of Elves.

*'Well...you are aware of which Elders I speak of.'* Nalithor sighed. *'They tell us nothing. They simply wait for us to discover things on our own.*

*'At first, we believed it was because they wanted us to live and experience Avrirsa in the manner mortals do. However, now we aren't so sure.'*

*'They've hinted that they simply don't know themselves?'* I questioned.

It didn't come as even the slightest surprise to me that those bastards didn't know what they were talking about. It *did* strike me strange that they'd been careless enough to indicate it to the other deities, however.

*'Precisely,'* Nalithor confirmed. He seemed as though he was going to continue, but instead his grip on me tightened, and a growl rumbled in his chest.

I shifted my gaze to the area leading up to the table and quickly spotted the source of Nalithor's discontent. Rabere Inej Derkesthai, the Beshulthien Emperor—and Nalithor's "former" brother—was approaching the head table with several young Elven women in tow behind him.

The woman hanging on Rabere's arm, in particular, looked quite full of herself. Her skin was barely covered by the burgundy dress she wore. She was pale, brunette, and adorned with almost as many pieces of jewelry as her Emperor. The way she carried herself was the sort that made me want to punch her on sight.

How she managed to ooze more arrogance than the Beshulthien Emperor was beyond me.

"Ah, you still have the fake by your side, Brother?" Rabere questioned, a smug smirk settling onto his features. He and his women stopped in front of us—none of which took the time to acknowledge the other royals or divinity at our table.

"*That's* the girl he thinks is me?" The Elf on Rabere's arm demanded in disbelief. She placed a hand over her chest, feigning her best expression of shock. "Really, Nali, you believe that I was reincarnated as a *Human*? Just what sort of sense of humor do you think the Elders *have*?"

*'Don't.'* Nalithor squeezed me hard with his tail. *'It would be best if we let him pretend.'*

*'But she smells* foul!' I grit my teeth, glancing between the Elven women in rapid succession. *'Don't like it. Something is wrong with them. Are you sure I can't kill them?'*

*'For now,'* Nalithor answered.

"Now, now, Arianna—remember, he's the *God of Balance*." Rabere smirked down at his Elven companion. "As you can see, Brother, I've found the *real* Arianna. Not some Human whore that has fooled you by taking on the same name."

"By taking on the same name? *Really*?" I laughed incredulously. "Arianna is hardly an unusual name, and it's not my fault that Dilonu and Tyana Black chose to name me after a figure of Dauthrmiran history. I'll have you know that I never claimed to be the same woman. It's a shame your sniveling companion was also given the name. She doesn't appear worthy of it."

"You will address His Excellency with the proper respect, whore!" The Elven Arianna screeched at me, summoning near-intangible wisps of darkness around her hands.

"Respect is earned, not given." I tilted my head and examined the Elf, watching as she grew paler. "You call *that* darkness? Are you even old enough to be playing escort?"

*'I do so love that deadly aura of yours.'* Nalithor purred, smoothing

his hand from my hip and down my thigh. *'Still, we should take care not to provoke them* too *much.'*

"Your Excellency, it is true that we named her after the late Dauthrmiran princess." Tyana flinched when the Vampire turned to shoot her a glare. "W-we heard that she achieved much in her short life, and we hoped to bestow those blessings on—"

"You must not have loved Arianna the way I thought you did," Rabere remarked conversationally, refocusing his gaze on Nalithor. His statement earned snarls from several people seated at our table. "I thought you would fight me for the right to the *real one* the instant you saw her."

"We were children when she died." Nalithor's terse tone and dangerous glare made several of our companions inch away from us. "Neither of us were old enough to grasp such a concept; especially not you. To claim that either of us loved her at such an age is as ridiculous as—"

"I'm hurt!" The Elven woman exclaimed with a horrified gasp. "Don't you care about me *at all?!*"

*'Ohhh? The bloodsucker is directing her in what to say?'* I mused while the air reverberated with poorly-shielded telepathy. Smiling, I glanced up at Nalithor. *'Are you* sure *I can't kill them? Hmmm?'*

*'Don't...tempt me.'* Nalithor sighed when I trailed my fingertips along his thigh. He shot me a warning look before settling a frigid look on his brother again. "*This one* is who I desire. Nothing more, nothing less. The past can remain in the past—it *has* been two centuries after

all. I was bound to move on at some point."

"B-but *I* am the one—" The Elven woman stuttered, looking toward the Vampire beside her for reassurance.

"I'm disappointed in you, Brother. I never would have thought you'd abandon Arianna like this." Rabere smirked, continuing to ignore my presence. "Have you finally lost whatever remained of your sanity? You would make a *Human* your goddess? Are you mad?"

*"Nalithor has chosen who he desires to pursue."* A female voice chastised, causing many of the divine guests to stiffen and grow pale. *"You have no right to challenge him on the matter."*

I bit back an aggravated sigh when the air rippled, and a female Elder appeared. Her white robes fluttered around her before settling into place. She flipped her blonde hair over one shoulder before taking a moment to survey the room. She smelled just as vile as the other Elders I had seen, but something about her power made me more uneasy than the other ones.

*This one* was attempting to exert her power but appeared oblivious to the subtle looks of confusion that the deities present shot her.

"Pursue?" Rabere sighed, shaking his head. "Pointless."

"I would say it's far from pointless." I huffed, turning to nuzzle into Nalithor's chest. I danced my fingertips along his thigh again, listening to his pulse quicken. "The chase can be quite enjoyable for both people involved, you know."

"You've conditioned her to your ways already?" Rabere snorted in disbelief. "How did you manage to get *livestock* to—"

"Watch your tongue, young one!" A woman from a table near the X'shmirans snapped. "Humans are not your livestock, and neither are the Elves. You would do well to remember that before *you* become the hunted."

"Of course, Hadyn." Rabere rolled his eyes without turning to look at the Human Goddess. "I simply meant that *this one* is livestock. Not *all* Humans."

Before anyone could react, Nalithor had left my side and launched himself over the table. The Elven women screamed in terror and fled from their emperor's side when the enraged Adinvyr collided with the smug bastard. Both men went tumbling across the wooden floor. I released a bored sigh when Nalithor landed on top of his brother—I doubted it would be much of a fight, and no one present seemed stupid enough to interfere with a brawl between brothers.

The crunch of Nalithor's fist smashing into Rabere's face was quite satisfying, but even more amusing to me was the frightened looks of the Vampire bastard's Elven women.

"This is *your* fault!" The Elven Arianna turned to point at me, her green eyes alight with hatred. Thin tufts of darkness swirled around her. I was quite certain even my brother would have been able to kick her ass.

"Am I really going to have to put you in your place?" I sighed, shooting the woman a bored look. "I much prefer challenging prey."

"*Me?* In *my* place?" She shrieked, her shrill voice causing my teacup to rattle in its saucer. "*I'll kill you!*"

*'What a boring creature.'* I rolled my eyes and directed my shadow toward her. My darkness engulfed the Elf until the density of magic surrounding her muffled her screams.

The Elf's inability to struggle within my shadows earned a disappointed sigh from me. I had hoped she would squirm at least a little bit, but she couldn't even twitch—voluntarily or otherwise.

I decided to release her from my grasp when her heart began to race uncontrollably and started skipping beats. She toppled to the floor unconscious, her burgundy dress soaked with vomit, urine, and feces.

"Oh? She tried to use darkness when she's *that* frightened by it?" I tilted my head and examined the Elf for a moment before returning my attention to the brawling brothers. "Nalithor, are you going to leave me alone all night? I'm bored already."

"*This bastard called you livestock!*" Nalithor snarled, lifting his bruised and battered brother by the throat.

"Yes, yes, and I'm sure I've been called worse," I stated, watching Nalithor's tail thrash into the floor. "At this rate you will need to change into new clothing, leaving me *bored* and *alone* for even longer.

"You should just have the disagreeable one take the smelly one away before she ruins our appetites."

"The smelly...?" Nalithor glanced over his shoulder at me, his expression one of confusion until I pointed down at the unconscious Elf. "Rabere, *clean **that** up.*"

Nalithor tossed the Vampire at the soiled Elf like a rag. I tracked Nalithor's movements as he walked around the table and returned to his seat to my right. Rabere hadn't even managed to scratch him. The Vampire himself, however, was quite the mess. It appeared that, brother or not, estranged or not, Nalithor hadn't held back in beating his brother senseless.

*'His blood smells like shit,'* I stated, holding a napkin out to Nalithor so that he could wipe off his hands. *'His Elven pet almost smells better.'*

*'At least you didn't kill her,'* Nalithor muttered dryly. *'I might kill her myself for pretending to be* you. *That, at least, isn't something Rabere is forcing her to do.'*

"*Rabere, do not interfere with Nalithor and his prospective mate again.*" The Elder placed a hand on her hip and glared at the Vampire. "*You are young, but that is no excuse for your behavior. It does not matter who* the young woman is. *What matters is that Nalithor chose her and is happy with her. There is more to life than one girl you both knew two centuries ago. You should respect him for being able to move on.*"

"But she is a *fake!*" Rabere snapped.

"*Her name alone does not prove that. Many young boys and girls were named after Lucifer and Gabriel's children.*" The Elder sighed, pressing her fingertips to her temples. "*And what of it if she were? Would you give your Elf up to Nalithor?*"

"Never!" Rabere snarled, his face twisting in anger. "He can't have *any* of my—"

"Why would I *want* any of your women or men?" Nalithor glared at his battered brother. "It's difficult enough to give *one* woman the attention she desires, let alone—"

Nalithor twitched and looked down at me, his face growing pink when I hooked my left leg over his. His pulse raced when I traced my fingernails down his abdomen. I rested my other hand on the floor behind him so that I could prop myself upright and glare at the God of Vampires and his harem of Elven women.

Darkness swirled around me as I examined them, contemplating if it was worthwhile to kill a few of them in plain sight. Only a few of them seemed to sense what I was considering.

*"Didn't he tell you to clean* that *up?"* I asked, settling my icy gaze on Rabere. He stiffened, color draining from his face.

*'Watch where you're...'* Nalithor trailed off into a growl when I slipped my hand beneath the folds of his kimono and trailed my fingers down to his hips. *'What happened to* behaving yourself?'

*'We never established what counts as "behaving,"'* I replied innocently.

Nalithor gripped me by the chin and pulled me upward, giving me a firm look.

*'Keep that up, and neither of us will be having dinner,'* Nalithor stated. He looped his other arm behind my back and pulled me fully onto his lap, making it impossible for my hand to wander further.

"You're going to let her talk to another deity like that?!" Rabere snapped from somewhere behind me.

Nalithor ignored his brother entirely and pulled me into a deep kiss instead. I pressed myself closer to him and relaxed into our kiss as his tail draped around my hips. Several indignant shrieks and growls echoed through the room, but I didn't care. Nalithor's tongue snaked past my lips, his darkness enveloping us.

The taste of his blood surprised me for a brief moment before overtaking my senses.

*"Enough,"* Nalithor commanded in a quiet growl by my ear, gripping one of my wrists tight.

"What...?" I trailed off with a small shudder when his lips brushed against my throat.

*'You get quite handsy when you lose yourself to your hunger.'* Nalithor drew his fangs over my skin. *'Mmm, we need to work on your lack of control.'*

Nalithor shifted me in his lap, drawing me back against his chest. With my thoughts clearing, I realized that my pulse was racing so fast that a slight tremor had entered my hands. A quick glance at our surroundings revealed that Rabere had retreated to the Beshulthien table, and his horde of Elven strumpets were nowhere to be found.

*'Where did that Elder go?'* I asked, tilting my head back to look at Nalithor.

*'She left quite some time ago,'* Nalithor replied dryly. *'I suppose I should be flattered that you find me so distracting.'*

"Nalithor, I would like to ask Arianna a few questions," Gabriel spoke, a slight frown on her face as she examined us. "I assure you it *is* important."

"Very well." Nalithor sighed, resting his free arm across my lap and lifting his cup of tea with the other. "Anything to distract her from her desire to kill those people is a good start."

"Does…does Darius get his way frequently?" Gabriel's expression twisted with immense concern while she wrung her hands.

"Yes. He throws quite the tantrum if he doesn't." I nodded.

"He *did* manage to get the Archmagi to test him again, after all," Nalithor added while pouring me another cup of tea. "They aren't known for being agreeable."

"I am concerned that Darius may have the power of persuasion." Gabriel sighed, her expression downcast. "We all knew that bringing him to check on you, Nalithor, was not a good idea—yet we did it anyway. Telling Darius that you were fine should have been sufficient. Instead…we brought him to see you. And then he attacked you, Arianna. Darius' behavior is unacceptable."

"If the boy has *that* power it must be dealt with at once," Nalithor muttered. He slipped his tail beneath the skirt of my kimono and coiled it around my bare thigh before turning his attention to the worried Goddess of Angels. "Has Darius shown any sign of knowing that he has such an ability?"

"The boy hardly knows that he can heal!" Gabriel shook her head. "I have found deities willing to help me seal that power, if we can prove he has it. However, I wanted to be certain first…and of course, acquire your permission."

"You have it." Nalithor nodded at Gabriel. "That type of power is too dangerous in anyone's hands—let alone someone with his state of mind."

*'The power of persuasion?'* I inquired, curious. *'I get the feeling you two aren't referring to the effect Adinvyr have on people.'*

*'The Elders call it a "leftover" power from one of the previous worlds,'* Nalithor replied, bristling. *'They claim that they are incapable of removing these "extra powers" despite the fact that they are supposed to be the ones who created the universe, to begin with. I'm sure you can see why many of us were already suspicious.'*

*'Yet they haven't caught on to your suspicions?'* I asked, watching the veritable army of servants moving throughout the room, carrying platters of food and drink. They all seemed so happy—a stark contrast to the servants back in X'shmir.

*'Yes, which only serves to further our suspicions,'* Nalithor confirmed, sighing. *'I suppose I should let you up so that we can dine...'*

*'We can cuddle later.'* I shot him a smile when he lifted me off his lap and sat me down beside him.

*'Cuddling seems to be one of the last things on your mind.'* Nalithor smirked, tracking me as I reached for a plate. *'How long until you lose yourself completely to that hunger of yours, hmmm?'*

*'Humph, if you're correct in your assumption that feeding won't help me yet...'* I trailed off, thinking while pulling a variety of meats onto my plate. *'We had best hope that "losing myself" to hunger is a long way off.'*

*'My blood would excite you more than it already does if you could benefit from feeding,'* Nalithor mused, slipping his tail around me again. *'Tch. That Vampire bastard is still—'*

"Nali," called a familiar male voice, causing me to look away from the Adinvyr and to Eyrian. "I challenge you for the right to Arianna-jiss."

"You *what?*" Nalithor sighed heavily and ran a hand back through his hair, settling his gaze on the Draekin. "Are you serious?"

"Of *course* I'm serious." Eyrian bristled, narrowing his eyes at Nalithor. "I won't stand by and *let* you—"

"Me too!" Ijelle rocketed to her feet, turning to look at us. "I can't just sit by and let my brother claim such a hot woman without a fight!"

"*Both* of you?" Nalithor's tail twitched around my waist.

"Me three," Xander piped up, grinning as he rose from his seat beside Ijelle. "Perhaps the three of us can take Nalithor out. After, we can fight amongst ourselves for the right to Arianna-jiss?"

*'Stay here.'* Nalithor glanced down at me as he stood. *'I won't have anyone else attempting to make off with you while I deal with the cheeky ones.'*

*'If you take too long, I'm going to grow very cold and very angry,'* I stated, watching Nalithor's tail jerk to the side and his muscles tense. *'Not to mention lonely! Who will I snuggle with if you take your time fighting them?*

*'After all, if you take your sweet time like you did with* healing me *earlier, you won't return to my side until well after dinner is over.'*

*'I will make quick work of them.'* Nalithor's form shimmered with pale blue frost and tendrils of darkness as he approached his three challengers. Divine armor rippled into existence around his body as he

walked, giving his royal finery a much more imposing look.

Xander's playful expression dropped to one of seriousness as he exchanged a wary glance with Ijelle. Neither of them seemed to know what to think of Nalithor's demeanor. They both took a step back when power burst out from Nalithor at the same moment he summoned his spear.

I watched with vague interest as Nalithor leveled the weapon with them—he didn't even bother dulling the blade before leaping into his first attack.

*'Eyrian is the only one that's serious...'* I glanced at the Draekin, catching him looking at me. Arching an eyebrow, I rested my chin on one hand and pointed at Nalithor. Eyrian's face reddened, and his eyes snapped away from me, focusing on the Adinvyr instead. *'Hmmm... I believe he said something about being close to "the princess" when he was young too. Is Nalithor not the only one that knows who I am?'*

Ijelle and Xander both darted off in different directions, expressions of shock on their faces. Nalithor's spear cut through the air where they had been standing, leaving a trail of black lightning in its wake. Nalithor's jaw was set with determination as he whirled around and slashed downward at Ijelle's shoulder. Her eyes widened as she summoned a rapier to block the strike.

The strength of Nalithor's attack sent his smaller sister skidding across the room, and the Devillian guests into a flurry of whispers. Even the Adinvyr present seemed surprised by their crown prince's ferocity.

Xander jumped at Nalithor next, a pair of daggers in hand. However, Nalithor had already turned to deflect the Vampire's attack. His spear tore down Xander's torso, drawing a line of scarlet blood from one shoulder to the opposite hip. Xander's face flushed and he bit his lower lip in a poor attempt to stifle an enraptured moan. His odd pleasure gave Nalithor an opening to toss the Vampire across the room like a ragdoll, trailing droplets of blood through the air.

*'His blood smells different from that of other Vampires...'* I pursed my lips, watching Xander's blood splash to the ground. He was bleeding so much that I was almost concerned for him. *Almost. 'His blood smells good. Why would it be so much different than his maker? Hmmm. Is something wrong with Rabere, or is Xander the one that's an oddity?'*

"So, you really are—" Eyrian ducked under a slash of Nalithor's spear, his eyes narrowing. "—serious."

"As are you, if you waited for them to fail at their plan." Nalithor's tone sent chills down my spine, but Eyrian didn't back down. "If it is a fight you want, then you shall have it."

"Well then, Arianna." Ellena shifted to smile at me. "What do you think? Would you be willing to spar with Nalithor during the opening ceremony tomorrow, even if it can't be at full strength?"

"Well, the closer to full strength the better," I murmured while pulling two rolls onto my plate. "I don't need an excuse to want to fight Nalithor. If he agrees to it, I'll happily oblige."

I shifted my attention away from Ellena and back to the fight when

I caught the scent of unfamiliar blood. Not only had Xander sustained a new wound during the brief chat, but Ijelle was also bleeding profusely from her upper arm. Ijelle's tail snapped wildly behind her while she growled at her older brother, her face twisted with rage.

"Oh? He's serious enough to injure his precious younger sister?" Aurelian laughed. "It's been years since we've seen Nalithor this lively! I'm liking his new fervor."

"Arianna-jiss, are you going to just *let* him tear his friend and siblings to shreds?" Lucifer asked dryly, shooting me an amused, sideways look.

"Sib*lings*?" I arched an eyebrow at him.

"Xander is our adopted son." Lysander chuckled while pouring himself a large glass of blue wine. "Ijelle is young and doesn't know what she's gotten herself into. Xander, however, knows full well."

"You shouldn't need to interfere. Nalithor won't kill them."

The clang of metal drew my attention again. I watched for a moment as Nalithor and Eyrian clashed, their respective elements whirling around them. Eyrian had summoned armor and a pair of spiked gauntlets. Although Aurelian had made both men's armor, Nalithor's was by far more ornate.

However, Eyrian didn't seem concerned about facing off against a deity despite being "lesser" for being a demigod. I couldn't help but wonder if it was because they were friends, or if the Draekin was just that fearless.

Both of them were holding back power. I could feel it, and it made me bored with their fight. *'A shame they have to worry about the state of the guests and the palace...'*

"You *do* want him to yourself don't you, Arianna?" Gabriel questioned with a small smile, earning a surprised look from several of the Devillians at our table. "If I haven't forgotten Devillian ways entirely, Arianna is the only one allowed to interfere, yes?"

"You are correct..." Lucifer frowned, glancing at Gabriel and then me.

Sighing, I rose to my feet and swept around the table. My heavy attire swished around my legs, joining the musical jingling of my jewelry as I strode across the floor. I summoned darkness around myself before approaching Nalithor and his challengers.

My approach caught Ijelle's attention first. Her face turned scarlet despite the glint of fear in her eyes.

"Do I have to wait for you to kill each other?" I demanded. Both Eyrian and Nalithor froze mid-strike, their tails dropping to the floor behind them. For a moment, neither of them dared move.

"Oh? The cutie is bold, hmmm?" Xander grinned as my gaze flicked to his bloodied chest briefly. "We won't be much longer, sweetheart. Just let us finish kicking Nali's—"

"I'm not interested in the attentions of other men—let alone a woman," I interjected, striding up to Nalithor's side. I pushed his spear arm out of my way and came to stand before him, slipping both my arms around his torso before shooting a glare over my shoulder at his challengers. "If you three keep him from me for any longer I will kill you myself."

"I'm not done putting them in their place." Nalithor growled, his tail snapping back and forth as he looked down at me. "They should know better than to—"

"And *you* should know better than to leave me to my own devices." I gripped him by the front of his kimono and yanked him down, rising onto my tiptoes to further make up for the difference in our heights. "Let's return to our seats before I have to find some other way of entertaining myself, hmmm?"

"I knew it! She's a domme, right?" Ijelle sounded a little *too* excited. "Nali, let me have her, I'm sure she can—"

"Arianna, what happened to behaving yourself?" Nalithor brought his free hand up to my chin, his expression unreadable. "Didn't you say you could—"

I cut him off with a soft, brief kiss before releasing his kimono and settling back onto the flats of my feet. Nalithor stared down at me for a moment with a look of surprise on his face, but I just shot him an innocent smile and waited. His sister seemed unable to formulate a response other than stuttering, her face growing redder by the moment.

Eyrian and Xander both looked miffed, though Eyrian more so.

"Even *if* they won, *you* are the one I'm interested in," I stated once the silence had dragged on. "I don't think Draemiran ways would *force* me to indulge one of them, right?" I paused to draw my fingertips down Nalithor's skin where his kimono had gaped open.

"Besides…you don't actually want to kill them, do you?"

"I don't, but they—" Nalithor growled, shooting a glare over my head.

"You don't like dommes right, Nali?" Ijelle asked with a hopeful grin.

"If you think that *this one* is a domme, you still have much to learn." Nalithor dismissed his weapon, shook his head, then lifted me off my feet. "Very well, Arianna. You desire my undivided attention for the evening? Let's see if you can handle it."

"We aren't finished yet!" Eyrian protested, snarling, as he adopted an offensive stance.

"I don't know about you, but *I* don't want to upset the feisty one here." Nalithor chuckled, causing me to shoot him a pout. "She is quite ferocious when angered. It wouldn't do for *all* of us to be sent to the healers."

"I wouldn't mind having her punish me." Xander grinned and then lapped some of the blood from his fingers. "Having a tiny little thing like her break me has its own appeal, you know."

"Breaking you isn't difficult to begin with, Xander." Nalithor rolled his eyes before turning to carry me back to our seats. "Alright, Arianna, you have my attention. Now what?"

"Arianna said that she would fight you during tomorrow's ceremony if you agree," Ellena spoke up as Nalithor nestled me down beside him. "What do you think, Nali? It would be an excellent way to stop the citizens from bothering you both with—"

"They haven't bothered us in quite some time now," Nalithor interjected. He slipped his tail under my skirt and wrapped it around my thigh as he continued, "That said, I'm more than happy to spar with Arianna. Our fights are always quite interesting, even when we must restrain ourselves.

*'You waited for me before touching your food?'*

*'I wasn't going to eat alone,'* I grumbled, flushing.

*'That is* incredibly *endearing,'* Nalithor informed me, leaning down to kiss my cheek.

Dinner managed to pass without any more interruptions, much to my relief. The guests seemed more interested in the parade of performers and guzzling down drinks. Even most people at our table left us alone—aside from the occasional glance or attempts at smalltalk.

I caught snippets of conversation between Gabriel and the others, which was mostly focused around what to do about Darius. They seemed quite concerned about the power he might possess, but I was more interested in my date than I was in their conversation.

"Here, try this." Nalithor pulled me into his lap and then lifted a small dessert plate, offering it to me.

"What is it?" I nudged one of the doughy, sugarcoated balls.

"Something sweet." Nalithor chuckled at me when I sniffed at it. "Ah, and it's cold."

"Hmmm..." I lifted the fork from the plate and then poked one of the balls a few times. "I do like sweets..."

"It isn't going to bite you." Nalithor teased, squeezing my waist.

"Though…*I* might."

"Humph. With you, it's a question of 'when.' Not 'if.'" I rolled my eyes before stabbing the sweet with my fork and taking a bite.

Within the flaky dough was an orb of frigid ice cream. The color of the ice cream was bright purple, but I had no name for the flavor. However, it tasted amazing, and I promptly set about devouring the rest of the ones on the plate.

"At least give me one." Nalithor laughed, nuzzling into the side of my neck.

"Okay…" I pouted and then offered him the fork.

He set the plate down on the table before taking the fork from me. After eating the last one, he returned the fork to the plate and then pulled over another platter of unfamiliar sweets.

"Mmm… You like pastries too, right?" Nalithor murmured while selecting several small but colorful desserts. They looked more like artwork than food, but they *definitely* smelled like food. "What would you like to drink? More tea, or perhaps mri'lec? Varikna? Ah… Perhaps you would like some fiirzik?"

"Fiirzik? I'm not familiar with that one," I commented, watching as Nalithor set the dessert plate on my lap.

"It's sweet, has little alcohol content, and is consumed hot," Nalithor replied. He motioned a servant toward us and requested they bring us some of the liquor.

"I assume you want some too?" I asked, lifting the plate off my lap. I twitched a little when Nalithor nuzzled into my shoulder yet again.

"You know, I'm starting to think that you want to expose my skin for all to see."

*Your kimono gets in the way of what I want,'* Nalithor grumbled, nipping at my earlobe. *'I'd much rather have you for dessert.'*

I suppressed a startled noise when Nalithor's tail ran between my legs, causing me to jerk and almost drop the plate of pastries. The mischievous Adinvyr chuckled into my throat as his grip on my waist tightened, and he slid his tail over my slit again. This time, however, he didn't remove it.

*'W-what are you doing?'* I flushed when I felt my nipples straining against my bra. *'This isn't—'*

*'As I said; your kimono is in the way of what I want.'* Nalithor teased, curving his tail down the front of my panties. *'We're trapped here for several more hours yet. At the very least we can enjoy ourselves, hmmm?'*

*'This is hardly the time or place to...'* I shuddered when his tail massaged over me again. *'Save it for later! Hiding what you're doing simply isn't possible!'*

*'So sensitive.'* He purred as he withdrew his tail, smirking into my throat when I shivered again. *'Very well. I'll behave myself—for now. However, I can't say the same for when we return to my rooms.'*

"Rely'ric, Reiz'tar, your fiirzik." The servant bowed deeply when he returned to us with a small platter, carrying two tall glasses and a bottle of shifting orange liquid.

"Ah, thank you. Set it there—I can pour it myself," Nalithor addressed the servant.

I fidgeted for a moment on Nalithor's lap when he coiled his tail around my thigh again. He chuckled deviously before pouring us both a steaming glass of fiirzik. My frustration grew to new heights when I realized that I was *missing* his tail's presence between my legs. Dinner, around dozens of people, was *not* the time for such things. Not by a long shot. Yet I was still disappointed that he had done as I asked.

"Here." Nalithor offered me one of the glasses. *'I didn't detect any form of poison or drugs. We should be fine.'*

*'You're still worried about that?'* I questioned, accepting the glass.

*'Look at how many people are present—of* course, *I'm concerned.'* Nalithor sighed, shifting me so that I was sitting between his legs. *'It doesn't help that we are going to be here all night. We can't sneak off easily, either...'*

*'And* because *we can't sneak off, you shouldn't tease me so much!'* I twitched, feeling his tail wandering higher up my thigh.

*'But you are so adorable when flustered.'*

*'Do you really want any of your guests picking up on my excitement?'*

Nalithor growled and pulled me back against him, his tail squeezing tight. I rolled my eyes and then lifted my drink to my lips, taking a small sip to determine if it was too hot or not. Nalithor should have thought of such things *before* teasing me in such a bold fashion.

"Now that dinner is over, Nalithor, we should discuss preparations for your match tomorrow," Erist began with a bright smile. "Oh, Ellena, perhaps we should take bets on their fight. What do you think?"

"I'm certain the two of you can think of a healthier way to handle prizes." Lysander sighed at the women, shooting them a tired look. "We hardly need people gambling on—"

"Ah! How about—" Ellena began with excitement.

I tuned them out and returned to sampling the variety of desserts before me instead. Nalithor's tail petting my thigh being rather distracting, but nowhere near as much as his more intimate antics had been. It was comforting, in a way, and he seemed to be content with behaving himself for the most part. I was glad to eat and drink with limited surprises.

*'Getting drowsy, my dear?'* Nalithor questioned me sometime later, startling me when he plucked my glass from my hand and set it on the table. *'Ah, you nodded off entirely?'*

*'They're* boring...' I grumbled, shifting to rub my cheek against his chest.

*'Shall I carry you back to my rooms?'* Nalithor stroked my back as I shut my eyes. *'Ah, and am I still invited to—'*

*'Warm...'* I purred, nuzzling his chest again.

"If you will excuse us, I believe my vixen is well past her bedtime," Nalithor addressed the others at the table while shifting me into his arms. "I will regale her with the details of our fight in the morning.

*'You didn't answer my question,'* Nalithor added, rising to his feet.

*'If you sleep on the couch, I will kick your ass...'*

563

# CHAPTER TWENTY-FOUR
*The Way to an Adinvyr's Heart*

When I awoke the next morning, I found myself in a surprising but comfortable situation. I didn't recall undressing and crawling into bed the night prior, yet there I was. Nalithor was sound asleep behind me and was clutching me against his chest like an oversized stuffed toy. One of his hands had shifted to grab one of my breasts, but I wasn't bothered by it—it was endearing in a way.

*'Hmmm, how to get myself out of this one?'* I nuzzled into the pillow and sighed. The slight movement was enough to disturb the Adinvyr, causing his grip on me to tighten and his tail to coil around one of my legs. *'I wanna go get food!'*

A soft warble drew my attention. Shifting my gaze to the side, I watched Alala as she padded across the top of the bed and came to stand on my hip. I attempted to pull myself from Nalithor's grip, but he released a low growl in response and tightened his grasp, nuzzling the top of my head. Sighing, I looked over to Alala with a small pout when she warbled again.

After some trial and error, I managed to free myself from Nalithor's grasp without waking him. I danced back a few paces from the bed when he reached out to catch me. The Adinvyr grumbled something in his sleep and gripped the pillow I had been using. He pulled it tight against his chest and nuzzled his face into it, purring, as the pleased swishing of his tail dislodged the sheets from his shoulders

*'Yep—more cat than dragon,'* I mused, kneeling on the edge of the bed so that I could pull the sheets over his shoulders. *'Maybe he'll be awake after I'm done with my bath...'*

I slipped out of the bedroom and made my way to the wardrobe to select a change of clothing. Alala followed me to the bathroom and, once I opened the door, went flying across the floor to dive into the steaming water.

*'Ugh. I almost wish he'd taken my bra off.'* I grimaced and pulled the contraption off before prodding the red marks it left behind. *'Damn things are* not *meant for sleeping in!'*

My stomach growled as I approached the edge of the water. Sighing, I decided to make it a quick bath instead of relaxing—food sounded much better.

No matter how hard I scrubbed, I couldn't seem to get Nalithor's scent out of my skin and hair. Eventually, I gave up and cleaned Alala's fur before getting out of the bath. I let my hair hang down my back in damp curls while pulling on my change of clothes. Putting on actual daytime clothes seemed like too much effort, so I was content to stick with a short babydoll and a slightly longer fluffy robe.

"Come on, Alala, let's see if he's awake yet." I grinned at the fox when she poked her nose out from beneath a towel. "Maybe if we're *really* cute he'll treat us to something fun, hmmm?"

Alala yipped and swished her tail excitedly before darting out from under the towel and over to the door. She pawed at the base of the door several times until I strode over and slid it open. I grinned, watching her scamper down the hallway to run circles outside of Nalithor's suite.

My amusement was soon replaced with disappointment.

*'He's still asleep?'* I pouted, perching on the edge of the bed.

Nalithor barely stirred when I reached out to tug at his long hair. Next, I reached out and pulled at his cheeks. Again, almost no response. I nudged him a few more times while Alala pounced on his tail—still nothing. The only reaction I managed to get aside from mumbling was a brief nuzzle of my hand.

Alala huffed in indignation and pouted on Nalithor's ankle. I watched the Adinvyr for a moment while attempting to decide what to do. He wanted to keep me by his side—and therefore safe—but I was *hungry*.

I pried my hand out from beneath his head and then crept into the adjacent sitting room. Alala followed me once more, this time with a firm expression. Well, as firm as a little fox could manage, at any rate.

"I'm hungry." I pouted at Alala when she moved to block the door and geckered at me. "You want breakfast too, don't you? How about we both go?"

Alala remained silent for a moment before huffing and moving out of my way. After sliding my feet into a pair of sandals, I strode down the hallway with Alala scampering along beside me. The only indication of the time of day—or night—was the low number of servants and guards making their way across palace grounds. It had to have been early morning or late at night still.

To my surprise, no one scolded me for being dressed for bed.

"Ah, Arianna-jiss!" The pink-haired Adinvyr chef exclaimed when I walked into her kitchens. "You're up early!"

"Morning, Dovsdra." I nodded while Alala warbled her own greeting.

"You hungry, girlie? If you're in the mood to wait I can..." Dovsdra trailed off and shot me a curious look when I shook my head.

"Actually—if it isn't too much trouble—I'd like to cook for myself," I mumbled, tucking a damp curl behind my ear. "I wanted to—"

"Ahhh, you going to try winning his heart through his stomach?" Dovsdra grinned at me. "I didn't think a foreign princess would be able to cook! You sure you can make breakfast for three *without* destroying my kitchen?"

"Oh, I had to cook a lot for myself in X'shmir. I'll be fine," I replied with another small shake of my head. "I'm just hungry... I wasn't trying to 'win' *anything*."

"But you were gonna make some for him too, right?" Dovsdra's grin broadened when my face reddened. "I'm short on staff this morning—so you can use the ovens over there." She paused to point her spatula at the corner behind me. "We have plenty of ingredients in stock but, if you can't find something, holler for Asha or me."

"Thanks." I nodded to the Adinvyr chef and then made my way to the corner of the kitchen. "Alala, behave."

The fox froze midway through her motion to steal a piece of bread from a nearby table. Alala huffed and followed me over to the ovens, continuing to grumble the whole way. Once I was satisfied that Alala was safely curled up out of everyone's way, I began gathering what I needed for making fluffy fruit-filled pastries.

I was aware of Dovsdra watching me from time to time, but I chose to ignore it—she was likely just concerned about whether or not I was going to destroy her kitchen.

"Here." Dovsdra set a bowl of unfamiliar blue, purple, and red fruits on the counter beside me. "His Highness is rather fond of these. I assume you'll be needing a pitcher of iridesci as well?"

"Iridesci? What's that?" I turned to look up at Dovsdra, earning a grin.

"It's a morning drink that our warrior-men are fond of." Dovsdra laughed, hands on her hips. "I'll grab you a shot of it—you can decide for yourself if you want to bring him some."

A few minutes later, Dovsdra returned with a large pitcher of pale liquid that swirled blue and lavender. The scent was citrusy, but it smelled as though it was mixed with something else. I half-expected it to be a liquor. However, the stinging smell of alcohol wasn't present.

Dovsdra poured a shot glass of the bi-colored liquid and offered it to me, smiling. The refreshing taste reminded me much of orange juice, yet the flavor was more subtle—and somehow invigorating. Alala yipped with excitement when Dovsdra placed a saucer of the liquid on the table for her as well. The fox was more than happy to lap up the drink, turning the fur of her muzzle blue and purple in the process.

"It's quite good." I set the empty glass down and then motioned to the bowl of fruits. "What of these fruits? Do they require any special preparation?"

"Treat the red and purple ones like oranges, the blue ones like apples." Dovsdra pointed at the massive fruits in turn. "Tastes similar too. If you need more, somehow, we've got plenty. Need anything else? Ah, meat perhaps?"

"I'll start on the meat once the pastries are in the oven," I replied with a shake of my head. "Besides, I don't want to eat up more of your time. I'm sure you have plenty of other things to do."

"It's fine!" Dovsdra grinned, smacking my back. "We're all just happy to see someone willing to take care of the prince—instead of the other way around. He deserves to be spoiled by a beautiful woman after all the help he's given his parents with the young ones."

*'Spoiled? But I'm not spoiling him, I'm just making breakfast!'* I

pouted, turning to the fruits so that I could prepare them as filling for my pastries. *'Besides! He beat the shit out of his brother last night for me. The least I can do is...'*

I sighed at myself and shook my head. Perhaps I wasn't *trying* to spoil him, but using ingredients he liked wouldn't hurt. After all, I didn't want him to hate what I fixed us for breakfast. Hells, he'd probably be cross that Alala and I had snuck off without him. Anything to get back on his good side would be welcome.

*'What am I trying to convince myself about anyway?'* I shoved several trays of pastries into the oven and then turned to search for meats.

"Ah, Arianna!" A familiar female voice called from behind me.

I pivoted to look over my shoulder at Ijelle, watching as her eyes snapped up from my bare legs and to my face. She flushed bright red and shot me a sheepish smile, clearly unsure of what to say.

"Morning," I stated, turning back to my cooking.

"Oooh, breakfast? Did Dovsdra cajole you into working the kitchens, Ari?" Ijelle inquired, leaning against the counter to my right. "Oh! Iridesci too? Can I have—"

"I'm cooking breakfast for Nalithor," I pouted, nudging the pitcher away from the perky Adinvyr princess. "That's for Nalithor too."

"For Nali?' Ijelle blinked at me, then glanced around. "Where is he, anyway? I didn't think he'd let you out of his sight after what Bear-Bear did last night."

"Bear-Bear?" I couldn't help but laugh at the name, even as I turned to look at the flushed princess. "Really? *Bear-bear*? Isn't that a little too cuddly-sounding for *that one*?"

"Enough about last night!" Ijelle shook her head abruptly. "Are you really Nali's partner? I mean, I know there's no way in the hells that my brother is a submissive by any stretch of the imagination... But I can't see you as one either—you seem so strong! So, how in the world did you two wind up as partners?"

"Because Arianna-jiss is the submissive one." Xander laughed, catching the chatty Adinvyr by her shoulders and steering her over to a table. "Nalithor was right. You still have a long way to go when it comes to identifying such things, 'jelle."

"You thought I was a 'mistress' too." I pointed a spoon at Xander.

"You give off a strong 'alpha female' vibe." Xander grinned, flashing his fangs. "Ijelle, you know better than to bother someone while they're cooking. Dovsdra kicks your tail for it all the time—do you really want to add Arianna-jiss into the mix?"

"What *I* want to know is why you two challenged Nalithor last night." I shook my head and resumed cooking. "Surely you didn't think that you'd be able to beat him?"

"I can take care of a woman way better than he can!" Ijelle declared, thumping her chest once. "He can have anyone he wants, yet he chose to pursue someone as difficult and dominatey as you. I don't get it. How can he expect to take care of his needs *and* a domme's needs?!"

"Getting Nalithor to fight us seriously is next to impossible," Xander answered, making a vague motion with his hand. "I know that stealing you away from him is impossible, tempting as it may be. However, that doesn't mean I can't use his attachment to make him fight me properly. If there's one thing I know about Nalithor, it's that he will do *anything* to keep *you* safe and by his side, *Arianna-jiss*."

"Why'd you say her name all weird like that?" Ijelle demanded, rounding on the amused Vampire. "Unless you're trying to say she's— Oh, oh my... I-is she really—"

"Keep the chatterbox quiet will you, Xander-zir?" Dovsdra called dryly, shooting the prince and princess both a look. "Never know who's listening in this time of year. Understand, *Ijelle-jiss*?"

"Y-yes, Dovsdra!" Ijelle yelped before turning to look at me. "S-so, what you're saying is...I have no chance of winning you over, Arianna-jiss?"

"Even if Nalithor wasn't in the equation, I don't like women," I pointed out, shaking my head at the pouting Adinvyr. "I can barely even *get along* with women, let alone something more!"

"Why are the pretty ones always straight?!" Ijelle huffed, frustrated. "And, if Nali *is* 'in the equation,' why hasn't he been feeding properly? I can tell he's drained!"

"He's...worried about breaking me." I tilted my head to the side, thinking for a moment before shifting to look at Ijelle. "You *do* realize how much smaller than him I am, right? Hells, I'm quite a bit smaller than you, too."

"B-break..." Ijelle's face grew redder by the moment, her gaze drifting down my body for a moment. "W-well, I guess you *are* a lot shorter than he is but—"

"Arianna-jiss is also 'mostly Human,'" Xander interjected with a crooked grin, watching the blushing Adinvyr princess. "Let's allow her to return to her cooking, hmmm? You still need to regale me with the tale of your adventure to the Nrae'lmar Continent. Your report will help determine if we should send another expedition there soon."

A little over an hour later, Alala and I made our way back to Nalithor's suite. The fox trotted along behind the cart of food and warbled to herself as we went. Most of the servants we passed seemed to know Alala already and were quite enamored with her. Several stopped us so that they could pet her, while others just called things to express their adoration of her.

I pulled the doors to Nalithor's part of the palace open with my darkness. The moment I nudged the doors shut, Nalithor's power rushed down the hallway and swirled around us like a storm. It was so dense that it lifted the skirt and sleeves of my robe into the air. After a moment his power subsided, but the Adinvyr himself had already swept out of his suite.

"Arianna, where have you *been*?" Nalithor sighed in exasperation as we approached him. "Alala, didn't I say not to let Arianna wander off on her own?"

"Alala came with me." I tilted my head, admiring Nalithor's exposed torso for a moment before motioning to the cart of food in front of me. "You didn't seem like you wanted to wake up, so I decided to go get us breakfast."

"Breakfast?" Nalithor paused and sniffed at the air before glancing down at the cart. "Iridesci?"

"And more," I replied dryly. "You're blocking the way, though."

"Ah…" Nalithor stepped aside so that I could pass and then fell into step with me, tugging at the sash of my robe as we walked. "You let others see you like this? Do I need to kill anyone for looking at you the wrong way?"

"Barely anyone is even *awake*." I shook my head at him. "Here, hold—"

"Don't wander off like that again." Nalithor lifted me up by my waist and nuzzled into my shoulder. "If something had happened to you, or that bastard took you somewhere, I would have—"

"Couldn't you have just used your power to figure out where I went?" I arched an eyebrow at him once he set me down. "Or spoken with Alala? Did you *just* wake up?"

"I've been up for…a little while." Nalithor flushed and glanced away. "What's for breakfast? Dovsdra's cooking is usually—"

"*I* cooked it." I shot him a sideways look before pushing the cart into his rooms and walking past him.

"Oh? You weren't going to let someone else cook for us?" Nalithor chuckled, pulling my sash loose. "Here, it's much too warm for this."

Nalithor tugged my robe off my shoulders, earning him another pout. He tossed my robe over the back of a sofa and then examined me with a sly grin. Something about his expression made me grow hot, so I moved away and began placing the covered platters of food on a table.

The mischievous deity settled onto one end of the sofa and tracked my movements while Alala claimed a chair all to herself. I sat down across from Nalithor and began piling food onto my plate but, after a moment, he rose to his feet and plucked me off the chair. He carried me over to the sofa, set me down beside him and shot me a grin.

"As much as I love looking at you, this is far cozier," Nalithor stated innocently. "Besides, I have to show my appreciation somehow." He paused to slide an arm around me and gripped my left thigh, pulling me closer. "Mmm... Can I convince you to fix me a plate as well?"

"Someone feels like being pampered, huh?" I asked dryly before setting my plate down and pouring him a glass of iridesci. "Alright then—what would you like?"

"Hmmm..." Nalithor murmured, slipping his fingers under the waistband of my panties. "How about the adorable chef herself?"

"Not what I meant."

"Just a little taste?" He purred, leaning down to nuzzle me.

"And let us *both* be weakened for our duel tonight?"

"Your resistance is maddening at times."

"If I didn't resist, Alala would eat all the food I made!"

"Very well." Nalithor sighed, straightening. "I'll take some of everything."

"Here." I handed him the glass of iridesci.

"Cooked me breakfast *and* poured me a drink?" Nalithor

questioned while stroking my hip. "What did I do to deserve so much of your attention, hmmm?"

"Do I need a reason to give you attention?" I countered while piling warm pastries and steaming meats onto a plate for him. "Though, I will admit that I appreciated your reaction to *that one's* taunting at dinner last night."

"He deserves a harsher beating than what I gave him." Nalithor growled, bristling. "Next time I see him I will—"

"Behave yourself so that you don't get Exiled?" I offered him his plate of food and gave him a sharp look. "You wouldn't do something stupid enough to make the Elders take you away from me…*right?*"

"I'm quite certain that you are more frightening than they are when angered," Nalithor mused, accepting the plate with a smile. "Oh? You woke up early enough to make pastries? You should have woken me. I wouldn't have minded."

"We tried." I motioned between Alala and myself. "You were *out*. I thought you might be up after I finished my bath, but I underestimated how early it was. Since our prodding and nudging didn't wake you up, I decided to make breakfast while waiting."

"All I ask is that you do not wander off like that again." Nalithor squeezed me and shot me a concerned glance. "That Vampire bastard can't be trusted. I wouldn't be surprised if he attempted to kidnap you right off the palace grounds. So, please—"

"Okay." I nodded and then leaned forward to finish putting food on my own plate. "In that case, I may have to be more violent in my attempts to wake you."

"Mmm, you are quite the good cook, aren't you?" Nalithor murmured after swallowing a bite of food. "Just what will it take to have you cook for me more frequently?"

"I'm not *that* good." I shook my head and then shot him a smile, settling back against the sofa. "Flattery never hurts though. So, if you're looking for more pampering, you're off to a good start."

"I wasn't *looking*—" Nalithor sighed when Alala warbled at him.

"It's not like I mind!" I laughed, scooting a little closer to him. "You're usually the one giving me all the attention. It's only right that I give you some in return. Besides, you seem like you enjoy it."

"I would argue that *I* should be lavishing *you* with attention," Nalithor mused.

"That's not an argument I'll let you win." I glanced at him before reaching out to pour my own drink. "Ah, before I forget, I ran into Ijelle and Xander in the kitchens. Your sister seems quite convinced that I'm a domme…and Xander is quite cross that he has to resort to challenging you for me to get you to fight him seriously."

"Xander just wants more pain." Nalithor grimaced, shaking his head. "Ijelle has much to learn. She's the equivalent of a Human twenty-year-old—thinks she's an adult now, yet fails to act like one most of the time. However, she *is* powerful. One of the youngest Archmagi in history. It's one of the reasons she was sent on the Nrae'lmar Expedition."

"Someone is a proud older brother." I smirked at him as he flushed.

"So, she can handle traveling to unknown lands, but she can't handle a 'pretty woman?'"

"I'm proud of both her and Xander," Nalithor stated, relaxing against the sofa. "Xander may not be family by blood, but he's been a brother to me all the same. He and Ijelle both became Archmagi at relatively young ages. With Rabere cast out of the family, Xander and then Ijelle are the oldest after me—with Ijelle being heiress to the throne."

"I can't imagine having so many siblings," I remarked while cutting up my food. "Just dealing with Darius is enough of a hassle, and I can't help but think of multiples of him when it comes to siblings."

"Darius is a special case—and I don't think *anyone* could handle more than one of him," Nalithor replied dryly before pausing to snatch up several more pastries. "The X'shmirans didn't adopt any other children?"

"No. Supposedly they were only 'allowed' to have Darius and me." I shrugged. "That's one of the oddities that Djialkan, Fraelfnir, and...*Lehrr* picked up on."

"You seem to have difficulty accepting that Lehrr and Kalenek are one and the same." Nalithor pursed his lips and examined me for a moment. "I know you said that you were too young to be lovers, but you were obviously close to him in some way."

"I would probably be locked up in the X'shmiran dungeons, or dead, if it wasn't for Lehrr." I sighed, glancing to the side when Nalithor's grip on my hip twitched. "The palace servants were forbidden from helping me or cooking for me when it was first 'discovered' that I'm an Umbral Mage. Dilonu and Tyana intended to deny me of everything—food, drink, education, contact with others…

"Lehrr was among the few servants who snuck things to my rooms. He was the only one willing to speak out or try to defend Darius and me from the more painful plans the X'shmirans had. He seemed genuine in his desire to help us, and both the fae-dragons trusted him. So….the idea that Lehrr is the First Exile is strange."

"So, I have an Exiled God to thank for your wellbeing." Nalithor sighed. "If no one was originally permitted to help you…what changed?"

"The 'curses' that the Angels placed on me," I replied, lifting the pitcher of iridesci so that I could refill Nalithor's glass. "Dilonu and Tyana didn't want to put their *precious* Astral Mage at risk."

"Of course not." Nalithor rolled his eyes and then set his glass down to the side. "Well, I promise to take *much* better care of you than any of them ever could or will. *Especially* if you're going to spoil me like this. Hmmm… Now, how to show my appreciation?"

"You could just say 'thank you,'" I laughed, watching as he placed his empty plate on the table. "It isn't that complicated."

"Actions speak louder than words, and I wouldn't insult you by doing something less meaningful." Nalithor huffed, lifting me into his lap. "Mmm… We have a few hours before we're expected anywhere. What would you like to do?"

"What would I like…" I flushed when the idea of Nalithor taking me back to his bed flashed through my mind.

"There's not enough time for *that*." Nalithor purred, taking my plate and setting it aside. "Well, my dear? Aside from your more *pleasurable* ideas—"

"It's still *morning*," I protested, reddening further. "Surely we have plenty of time."

"Not if I'm to explore you properly," Nalithor interjected in a teasing tone and smoothing his hands down my thighs. "You know, if you're going to *think it,* you may as well *say it*. Remaining silent does nothing to hide those delicious thoughts of yours from me."

"Not *my* fault we keep getting interrupted..." I grumbled when he shifted me to face him. "What do *you* want to do? I'm sure you have friends to see or duties to attend to instead of— Eek!"

Nalithor gave my ass a firm squeeze. My face burned hot when he smirked at me. His expression changed to a grin as he snaked his tail between my legs.

"I could just tease you until we have to leave. That seems like a reliable way to secure my victory," Nalithor remarked with false innocence as he smoothed his tail along my slit. "Mmm, you make the most adorable expressions."

"Not adorable!" I protested before biting my lower lip hard in an attempt to suppress a shudder.

"You didn't have to bite yourself *that* hard..." Nalithor murmured, pulling me closer. "At the very least, you should share."

Nalithor flicked his tongue across my bleeding lip before pulling me into a kiss. After a few short seconds, he withdrew and chuckled, squeezing my ass again. I wasn't certain if my heart could beat any faster, or if my face could grow any redder.

"As much as I would like to spend the day devouring you," he ran his tail over me again for emphasis, "again we have the issue that one or both of us would be weakened for tonight's fight. You can't feed from me reciprocally, if you can feed at all."

"And yet you tease me incessantly!" I prodded his chest hard while he coiled his tail around my hips. "Don't give me the innocent look! You know damn well that you—"

"Mmm, I will be quite happy when I finally get the chance to claim you." Nalithor smirked, pulling my legs around his waist before standing up. "Do you think you can behave yourself long enough for us to go into Draemir?"

"Define behave?" I asked, the corner of my eye twitching.

He carried me into the wardrobe and set me on top of one of the counters before shooting me a smile.

"If you can keep yourself from *killing* anyone, I'll bring you with me to the training grounds outside of Draemir." Nalithor chuckled and reached back to grasp my ankles. "Of course, you will have to let me go first."

"I'm waiting for a good reason to." I dug my heels into the small of his back.

"I feel like flaunting you today," Nalithor replied, lifting a hand to brush his fingers against my cheek. "We don't have any more parties that we are *required* to attend. Now that the festival has begun in earnest, we're free to do as we like—aside from our little sparring match tonight, of course. However, I do still need to give my father's recruits their testing…"

"So, you want to see if they can even *pretend* to focus with me around?" I arched an eyebrow at him.

"Plus, I *did* say that I wish to keep you with me." Nalithor tapped my nose and smiled. "You asked what *I* would like to do, yes? Can I convince you to play along with my schemes for the day?"

"What schemes?" I asked, twitching a little when Nalithor's hands came to rest on my thighs.

"Let me choose something *enticing* for you to wear." Nalithor grinned, running his hands up to my hips before tugging at the hem of my babydoll. "I want to make certain that the citizens, and our guests, realize that you are *mine*."

"You want me to play trophy?" I tugged on his braid and nudged him with my heels again. "What's in it for me, hmmm?"

"In the short term, you get the satisfaction of indulging me." Nalithor chuckled, placing his hands on the counter so that he could lean over me. "Beyond that…I suppose it depends on how well you perform during our sparring match tonight.

"Until then, let's see what kind of trouble we can get ourselves into. I haven't had the chance to show you the training grounds *or* the city in proper."

After a moment, I nodded my acceptance and let him pull my legs from his waist. I tugged his braid once more before releasing it. I watched him as he moved through the wardrobe to search through my corner of clothing. He was smiling to himself, making me wonder just what else he may have been plotting.

Something about the swishing of his tail made me want to pounce on it. By the look of things, Alala felt the same way, and it wasn't long before she acted on the urge. Nalithor didn't even have to turn to look at the fox in order to swish his tail away from her grasp. Eventually, Alala gave up and leapt up onto the counter to sulk next to me.

"Want another glass of iridesci?" I asked, tapping my nails on the counter.

"If you are attempting to win me over, it's working." Nalithor shot me a grin over his shoulder.

"I'll take that as a 'yes.'" I slid off the counter and soon returned with both of our glasses refilled with the pale drink. "So why, exactly, do you want me to play trophy today? Is there another nuance of Draemiran culture that I'm missing?"

"Not at all." Nalithor shook his head without turning. "I like to show off what is mine, it's as simple as that.

"It's a shame your presents aren't here yet... Here, this will have to do."

"Presents?" I tilted my head and examined the flowy dress he'd selected—it was similar to the one I had been wearing when he had to bite me publicly. *I'm still not sure if I kicked his ass hard enough for that.'*

"You didn't think that I would take you shopping and *not* get you anything, did you?" Nalithor countered with a mysterious smile before laying the sapphire dress on the counter beside me. "Here, I'll help."

"Okay…" I grumbled, unsure what to think of him buying me anything.

Nalithor chuckled at my blushing and helped me pull my nightie over my head. I caught him admiring my cleavage for a moment before he turned and picked up the gown he'd chosen. He took the opportunity to grope me a few times and laughed when I shot him a dry look.

"Hmmm, corset?" I asked, moving toward my corner of the wardrobe.

"No. Stay like this." Nalithor caught me around the waist. "Your jewelry will keep it in place just fine." He tugged at the platinum chains encircling my hips. "I'll get dressed, then we can leave."

I hopped up on the counter again and took a few sips of my iridesci while I watched Nalithor undress. He didn't seem to mind at all, so I took the opportunity to admire his muscular back and buttocks. His tail swished a few times when my thoughts threatened to run off without me, but he didn't comment.

It was frustrating, but I could barely keep my mind off Nalithor and how much I wanted him to take me.

"Hunger and lust are a troublesome combination," Nalithor teased, casting a smirk at me over his shoulder. "Do you really find me so interesting to look at?"

"Is that really such a strange concept?" I countered as he shrugged on an overrobe, obscuring my view of his back.

"The fact that you're resistant to my power *and* smitten is what I find strange," Nalithor replied, amused, as he reached around me to pluck his glass off the counter. "Now, now, don't make that face. Your blushing just makes you all the more adorable."

"Not adorable!" I huffed, crossing my arms and glancing away from him.

"You *are* adorable, and you are *mine*," Nalithor stated, cupping my face in both his hands. "If anyone tries to take you away from me, deity or otherwise, I will shred them. If I catch anyone's scent on you, other than mine, I will—"

"I'm not complaining," I interjected, placing my hands on his chest. "Are you sure that you want to be so possessive over *me*, though?"

"Who else would I want to possess?" Nalithor blinked at me, genuine confusion on his face.

"Well, I know you could have *anyone* you want, so I—"

"I don't want 'anyone.' I want *you*, and I intend to have *you*," Nalithor interjected. He hefted me over his shoulder and walked out of the wardrobe, continuing, "Even if I have to train you to take me, I will still have you eventually.

"Normally I would say that this is where you tell me if you *don't* feel the same way, but your wandering thoughts and that *twitch* make your desires quite clear.

"Alala, watch our rooms while we're gone. I won't have anyone rifling through our things. Not even servants."

"At least let me walk," I sighed, "and grab sandals."

"Perhaps I intend to carry you all day."

"That isn't really conducive to flaunting my assets." I snorted at him. "Speaking of which, they're threatening to fall out of the dress *you* picked. Is that what you wanted to show off, hmmm?"

Nalithor's tail jerked to the side and thudded into the edge of the sofa as he came to an abrupt halt. I grinned and shook my head when he set me down with a begrudging sigh. He watched me carefully as I returned to the wardrobe to slip on a pair of sandals, and he slid an arm around my waist the moment I returned to him.

"If we are lucky, we will make it out of the city without anyone pesky interfering," Nalithor murmured, leading me down the hallway and out into the open air.

"Now that you've said that, someone *will* bother us."

Flowers, lanterns filled with multicolored Magelights, and multitudes of shimmering decorations hung everywhere I looked. Men, women, and children in the residential district were busy decorating their homes and lawns with ornaments. Most of the women and children had flowers woven into their hair or jewelry. The men wore a mixture of formal-looking brocade kimonos with carved leather armor or, sometimes, plate armor nestled over the top.

Even the Draemiran soldiers and guards wore fancier armor and robes than normal.

Most of the Adinvyr we passed nodded or bowed to us briefly before returning to their tasks. Nalithor looked quite pleased with himself and had an almost boyish bounce in his step. In contrast, I felt a little nervous while I hung on his arm and hid a little behind his bicep.

I wasn't sure why we were getting so many looks from the citizens, and I was beginning to feel out of place again without any flowers or ornaments in my hair.

*'You don't need to be so shy.'* Nalithor smiled at me when I ducked behind his arm again. *'It's not like they're going to bite you—nor would I let them if they tried. Besides, you could handle them with ease if they tried something.'*

*'They keep looking at us,'* I mumbled, rubbing my cheek against his arm. *'I can't promise that I would handle them without killing them, either...'*

Nalithor laughed and pulled me down a cobblestone walkway that had fewer people traversing it. I released a small sigh of relief and nuzzled a little closer to Nalithor as we passed many blooming parks and the ornate fences that bordered them. Magefire lanterns dotted the fences and the branches of our heads alike, illuminating what would have otherwise been a very dark pathway.

*'This way.'* Nalithor lifted me over a fence and then pulled me down an alley. *'There isn't really a shortcut from the markets to the city gates, but we can avoid the nobles and residential districts this way at least.'*

*'Everything is just so* busy!' I exclaimed as he slid his arm behind my

back. *'I assume there's a reason you didn't just opt to fly or travel through shadows?'*

*'We'll draw* more *attention if we do that,'* Nalithor stated as we spilled out of the alley and into a crowded street. *'Traveling by such methods isn't allowed during festivities such as this, unless you're part of the Royal Guard or the Vorpmasian military. Since we aren't on duty, we would be intercepted by one of the patrols.'*

*'And explaining our way out of it would just eat more time.'* I sighed and squeezed closer to the Adinvyr when the crowd surged toward the western half of the main plaza. *'Bah, the more people I see, the more out of place I feel.'*

*'You haven't changed much,'* Nalithor mused, causing me to glance up in surprise.

*"Isn't that the X'shmiran princess with Nalithor-zir?"*

*"Her? Are you sure? She doesn't look like a Human."*

*"Why doesn't she have any mrifon in her hair? I thought her relationship with His Highness was just a rumor."*

*"It's Faerstravir! Even though she's a warrior, she's still a woman. She should have mrifon or rozntaar in her hair!"*

*'Pay them no mind.'* Nalithor squeezed me and guided me through the crowd, passing several groups of Adinvyr who were watching us with a curious expression on their faces. *'Hmmm...I wasn't expecting you to draw* this *much attention to us.'*

*"Nalithor-y'ric, Arianna-z'tar!"* An airy female voice called to us.

*'Of course...'* Nalithor sighed, turning to look up at the nearest tree.

"What is it, Ceres?"

*"Why did a goddess refer to that girl as -z'tar?"* The people closest to us begun whispering, their murmurs soon spreading throughout the crowds.

"I apologize, Nalithor-y'ric, but we require your assistance." Ceres leapt gracefully from the tree and then bowed to us. "Arianna-z'tar's presence would be most helpful as well."

"Can't it wait?" Nalithor pulled me against his side as the whispering of the crowd grew. "Arianna-z'tar and I were on our way to meet with the Draemiran recruits."

"It would be best if we did not wait," Ceres replied with a small shake of her head, dislodging a few leaves from her "hair." "I will send one of my messengers to inform the recruits that you will be late. We should not require you for long."

Nalithor sighed again but nodded his acceptance. To my displeasure, Ceres began leading us toward Erist and Arom's temple. Citizens and tourists alike scurried out of Ceres' and Nalithor's paths, but that didn't stop them from gawking at me. Judging from the people's whispers, it was very unusual for them to see Nalithor in the company of someone other than members of the Royal Family or Draemir's allied deities.

"Oh good! You found them!" Erist looked up from a vase of flowers and grinned brightly when we walked into the rather lavish temple.

The floors, walls, and ceiling were *all* covered in rose marble. Intricate carvings and inlays of gold filigree made the walls and pillars even more opulent than the stone did on its own. Heavy velvet curtains hung over the stained-glass windows and were held back by golden ropes. Incense smoked in intricate golden burners that lined the hallways, filling the air with a strong but sweet musky scent.

Adinvyr and a few Elves rushed around the entry hall, their pale pink robes fluttering around their forms as they saw to whatever tasks their deities had assigned to them. Each of the individuals who wore pale pink robes also wore golden jewelry with pale pink crystals set into them. A few women wore wristlets or anklets, another wore a pair of earrings, and the males wore thick bracers or large rings.

*'Erist and Arom's Chosen,'* Nalithor stated, drawing my attention back to him. *'The deities in my immediate circle of trust have taken proper Chosen under their wing. Erist and Arom, in particular, require...many.'*

*'Their jewelry hums with magic similar to Aurelian's.'* I observed, glancing to the side when several more Elven Chosen rushed by us.

*'That's because he made it.'* Nalithor shrugged, leading me toward Erist. *'We wanted to make certain that the Chosen could defend themselves. As such, Aurelian and Elise have been working with the other Upper Gods to properly train and equip the Chosen with armor and weaponry that suits them.'*

"Ahhh, Ari-mrii you just get cuter every time I see you!" Erist exclaimed with a huge grin, before turning to shoot Nalithor a chastising glare. "Honestly, boy! No mrifon? No rozntaar? She needs at least *something* in her hair if you wish to avoid—"

"Perhaps Nalithor does not want to dissuade challengers?" Ceres interjected, thoughtful. "Adinvyr do rather enjoy proving that they deserve the attentions of their desired mate, yes? Faerstravir is just another excuse for their kind to challenge each other to battle, is it not?"

Nalithor huffed at Ceres' remark, but I got the feeling she wasn't wrong.

"None of the rozntaar bushes around the palace are in bloom yet," Nalithor replied, wrapping an arm and his tail around me in a possessive manner. "However, I doubt you called us here to discuss flowers or Faerstravir. Isn't this a busy time of year for you, Erist? What could you possibly require us for?"

"We need your help with Darius." Erist made a sour face at Nalithor. "We are having a hard time convincing him that his 'special' power is one that needs to be sealed. We were hoping that Arianna can talk some sense into him."

"It looks like we are well past that." Gabriel sighed heavily as she and Lucifer swept around a corner and moved toward us.

"Darius refuses to speak with Arianna." Lucifer shook his head, throwing his hands into the air. "He's convinced that Arianna has done something to 'taint' Nalithor."

"*Taint?*" I arched an eyebrow. "Is he *still* going on about Nalithor being an *Astral* Mage?"

"Whoever has been telling Darius these things seems to have a strong hold on him." Gabriel crossed her arms, her brow furrowing. "I refuse to believe my son is *this* ignorant. He trusts these people too much if it blinds him to the obvious facts before him—how they won, or took, his trust is another matter. The boy needs his reality shattered."

*'Is that really something a doting mother would say?'* I wondered, examining Gabriel for a moment, though I didn't disagree. *'Humph. I still have no idea what to think of her...'*

"What did you have in mind?" Nalithor's grip on me tensed.

"Darius needs to understand that you are truly a creature of darkness," Lucifer began thoughtfully, stroking his chin as he examined me for a moment, then flicked his gaze upward to Nalithor, "and that Arianna's blood hasn't poisoned you. We've attempted to teach him that blood simply doesn't work in the way that he suggests, but he is rather devout in his beliefs."

"He won't tell us who gave him these ideas either," Erist added, leaning against a fluted pillar. "Arom even tried sweet-talking the boy—he still won't budge. Just tried to get in my husband's pants instead."

"You want me to give him a scare, then?" Nalithor sighed, shaking his head. "Simply displaying my power over darkness is something that could wait until after Arianna and I fight tonight."

"No... It will take more than that." Gabriel shifted from foot-to-foot a few times before continuing, "He needs to understand that your affinity with darkness is strong, but the point will not get through his skull unless..."

"Darius needs to see you as a more powerful being than his sister," Lucifer stated firmly, narrowing his eyes at Nalithor. "*Temporarily.* I'm aware that I haven't yet earned the right to act like a father again, but Arianna is still my—"

"Arianna would have to agree to this method regardless," Nalithor interjected, holding up a hand to stop the conversation. "I can't simply take her over with my power, darkness or otherwise. We are too…even."

"Even though her godhood was taken?" Lucifer frowned at me as I glanced between them.

"Will *one of you* clue me in?" I sighed at them. "I can't agree *or* disagree to do something if you won't tell me what you're planning."

"They want you to let Nalithor use his darkness to take you over and control you—temporarily." Ceres motioned to the Adinvyr and then to me. "Even your brother knows that only very powerful beings can take control of someone. He believes this is what you have done to Nalithor."

"So, you lot want to prove your point to my brother by showing him the polar opposite?" I arched an eyebrow when several of them nodded, and then shifted my gaze to Lucifer and Gabriel. "You know, suggesting something like this doesn't help to earn my trust at all."

"Do you have a better idea?" Lucifer questioned, crossing his arms over his chest. The faint sadness in his eyes was upsetting.

"Aside from kicking Darius ass? No…" I mumbled with a pout, glancing away. "Sorry…"

"Darius is frightened of darkness as you are of light, yes?" Ceres spoke up in a neutral tone. "To a lesser extent, perhaps, but frightened all the same. Directing darkness at him would not be helpful."

"We considered having Nalithor take over someone else but—" Erist grinned when flames crackled around me, and I shot her a glare. "Exactly—you wouldn't allow it. So, you see our dilemma."

*'She didn't have to be so blunt about it!'* I grumbled, the corner of my eye twitching. My flames subsided as I let out a sigh, but the heat in my face did not.

*'Shall we put them in their place for suggesting such a troublesome method?'* Nalithor offered as Gabriel and Lucifer turned to discuss something with Erist.

*'I meant it when I said that I couldn't think of an alternative,'* I replied, pivoting to look up at Nalithor. *'My question is how this connects to sealing his ability.'*

*'The Elders* want *everyone with the power of persuasion to have their ability sealed,'* Nalithor murmured. *'You would think that alone would be enough to convince Darius.'*

*'Nalithor...'* I stared at him, surprised. *'You mean to tell me that the Elders are worried about—'*

*'I know what you're thinking.'* Nalithor chuckled, tapping the tip of my nose. *'Do you truly think we could get that brother of yours to cooperate with us* against *the Elders? There are too many risks. Letting Darius keep an ability like that, when he is already so warped, is not a wise move.'*

*'I wasn't going to claim it was a* wise *move, but it's still an*

*interesting...*' I trailed off into a pout when Nalithor shook his head.

*'No wonder both the old and current Gods of Chaos favor you,'* Nalithor stated dryly, a smile tugging at his lips. *'I don't think anyone is ready for the sort of trouble your brother would cause if we let him loose with this sort of power.'*

"How does giving Darius a start lead into our goals?" I shifted to address the other deities, watching as Lucifer's dark tail twitched before he turned to frown at me.

"He's so worried about Nalithor that he won't even discuss anything else." Gabriel flourished one hand, her tone one of exasperation. "Even when the three of you were children, Darius was never *this* fixated on Nalithor—nor was he at odds with you for any length of time."

"His power of light is slipping closer and closer to darkness," Ceres added, procuring a small crystal from her shrizar and holding it aloft in her palm. "His inner turmoil about the Adinvyr, and his jealousy toward you, is tainting his magic."

"It's become that bad then, has it?" Nalithor sighed heavily. "Very well, I agree we need to do something about it but—"

"Fine. What do I need to do?" I interjected.

*'Arianna, I would be—'*

*'It's kind of like being your pet, except you would be fully pulling the strings. Right?'* I shot him a sideways glance and watched as he mouthed a few times, his facing pink despite his concern. *'Ah, I suppose marionette would be a better term.'*

*'Yes, you are right, but there* must *be a better option!'* Nalithor protested with a low growl. *'As…appealing…as it is to have you as my* pet, *having you act as my puppet is not something that I want to—'*

"Since the two of you are so close in power, it is unlikely that Nalithor can make you do something you don't *want* to do," Erist spoke up with a broad grin. "If you were weak, then there'd be some concern over what he could make you do. However, unless someone *really* likes killing everything they come across, no one can force them to kill something even if they've been taken over. Their psyche will shut down their body completely, breaking the connection."

*'You know, being your pet doesn't sound half bad,'* I added when Nalithor opened his mouth to speak. I shot him a sly smirk when he snapped his mouth shut. *'You really should stop reacting like I see it as a bad thing. Making assumptions, especially about that, will just make me angry with you.'*

"Since you both have a strong affinity for darkness," Lucifer began with displeasure, "Nalithor would need full access to your mind. You would have to let him through all of your barriers so that he could properly overtake your darkness with his."

*'All of my barriers?'*

*'Now you're concerned?'* Nalithor chuckled.

*'…you will need to stay away from anything in my mind that has to do with Limbo or X'shmir.'*

*'You don't trust me to let you keep such things private?'*

*'It's because I trust you that I'm concerned.'* I turned to glare at him.

*'Even if it's by accident, I trust you to get pissed at the X'shmirans—maybe even enter a blind rage. It wouldn't do for you to kill them while they're this close to Darius and me.'*

*'I wouldn't intentionally search your memories without your—'*

*'Then stay only to the sections of my mind that relate to pulling strings,'* I stated, crossing my arms as he frowned at me. *'Don't search, don't wander, and don't drift. I want to avoid accidents if possible.'*

"Very well." Nalithor sighed and pushed a hand through his hair, his shoulders slumping. "We *are* running out of options for dealing with the boy. If you are all certain, and Arianna is willing, then I will play along."

*'Will this interfere with our sparring match this evening?'* I inquired as the other four deities turned to discuss something with a servant.

*'No, it shouldn't.'* Nalithor lifted a hand to my face, his expression one of reluctance. *'I may need to wait until we leave the city to release you. It depends on how Darius handles this. Is that alright?'*

*'I'm sure you'll take good care of me, won't you?'* I teased with false innocence and a few bats of my eyelashes. *'Mmm, I bet I could pull this off without you having to take me over.'*

*'Although it's tempting...'* Nalithor brought his other hand up to my face as well. *'Let's do this the safer way, shall we? Preferably* before *lunchtime would be nice.'*

*'Aw, but I get so few opportunities to fluster you.'* I grinned as he pulled me closer with his tail. *'Fine, fine. The sooner we get away from Darius and his fucked-up power the better. Ready?'*

'*I will re-shield your mind immediately,*' Nalithor stated with a slight nod.

'*Alright... Let's see if this is enough to knock some sense into my brother.*'

# CHAPTER TWENTY-FIVE
## A Foolish Notion

"Darius," Ceres' soft voice called, "Nalithor is here."

I looked up from my book and grinned at the smiling Goddess of Nature. She tried to say something when I rushed past her, but I ignored her. I didn't care what she had to say. Nali was here!

*Someone* had to take the proper precautions and check him for poison, and get rid of it if it was still there. Since Nali was a healer, I could only assume that Ari's poisonous blood was mind-altering. There was no way Nali was too weak to detect something making him sick.

My excitement was short-lived. Darkness permeated the hallway, making my breath stop short. Adrenaline shot through my system, making me tremble as I considered running away. The shadows shifted and churned like a living creature as I crept through them. I knew this power—it was Nali's. For some reason I couldn't detect even a hint of my sister's power alongside it, tainting it.

*"The two of you are sparring for tonight's opening ceremony in the plaza, aren't you?"* Erist's cheerful voice drifted to my ears while I inched past the darkness, *"You're not going to let her win, are you?"*

*"Perhaps if she is a* very *good girl..."* Nalithor's sultry tone sent a shiver down my spine.

*'So, Ari's here? Why didn't Ceres say any...'* I pursed my lips and crossed my arms. *'Hmmm, maybe that's what she was trying to tell me. Maybe I should've listened. Well, I can deal with this. I just have to—'*

My blood ran cold when I caught the sound of Ari purring like a cat. There was no one else that voice could've belonged to. I couldn't understand why I was unable to sense her power or her mind. *'Did she cut me off entirely?'*

I clenched my teeth and stalked down the hallway. When I reached the lounge they were resting in I felt like someone had hit me in the gut. Nalithor was sitting on one of the sofas, darkness coiling around him in a serpentine manner. The shadows writhed and slithered around both Nali and...Arianna.

My sister was sprawled across the couch and had her head in Nali's lap. The Adinvyr deity was stroking her hair in an absentminded manner while he conversed with the other deities in the room. Arianna, however, seemed oblivious to everyone else.

"W-what is the meaning of this?" I demanded, curling my hands into fists. "Arianna, get off Nali at once!"

Arianna didn't even flinch when I drew light around my hands. Instead, she shifted in Nali's lap to look up at him as his tail draped over her hip. If she said something to him, it was too low for me to catch. My eyes widened when I saw the collar of darkness that encircled her throat.

However, it was hidden from my vision when Nali brought one of his massive hands up to my sister's much smaller throat.

"*Stay,*" Nali commanded, using his grip on Arianna's throat to make her lay down again. "Darius, refrain from giving *my* pet orders. She is no longer yours to command."

"Pet…" I trailed off in disbelief, watching as Arianna brought both her hands up to Nalithor's wrist and pulled his hand back to her throat with another purr. "Ari, what in the hells did you do?"

Her gaze flicked toward me briefly but it was like she couldn't see me at all. Her pupils were dilated so far that they had lost their slit shape. Another squeeze of her throat snapped her attention back to Nali, and after a moment she shifted so that her back was facing me.

I bit back a growl, watching as my sister traced Nali's muscular abdomen with her fingers. *'Is she trying to taunt me?!'*

"It's about time you got her under control," Gabriel remarked from her perch on a chaise. "Are you certain that she's been good enough to join you on the sofa, Nalithor-y'ric?"

"I wouldn't reward bad behavior." Nalithor shot the Goddess of Angels a condescending look. "Now, where were—"

"Ari, I told you to get away from him!" I snarled, conjuring a bow and aiming at them both. "He doesn't belong to—"

Before I could finish my sentence, Ari had leapt from the sofa and severed my bow in half with a slender sword. Nali caught her around the waist and pulled her several feet away from me when she went to run the blade through my jugular. I froze, having felt the cold blade nick my skin.

Ari's eyes were still unfocused and her face expressionless. Nali leaned down and said something by her ear and, once he finished speaking, the sword disappeared into one of the bracelets around my sister's wrists.

"You should know better than to threaten a pet's owner, Darius," Erist chastised, grabbing me by the shoulders and steering me to a chair. "He could have let her kill you!"

"Ari wouldn't kill me!" I protested, plopping down in the chair after a few prods from the goddess. "She's not *supposed* to be with—"

"*Behave,* or I will have you sit at my feet." Nali's tone made me flinch and turn to look at him and my sister.

Nali's hand had encircled Ari's throat again and was squeezing, lifting her to her tiptoes. Instead of appearing frightened or intimidated, Ari was flushed, purring, and leaning into him. The scent of blood drew my attention down to where her long nails had sliced Nali's abdomen open.

It took several more seconds before Arianna seemed to notice.

*'What's wrong with her? She's usually quicker than me...'* I stared in

confusion as Arianna lifted her bloodied fingers to her lips. She seemed entranced. *'We're Human! Why does she seem so enthralled by his blood?'*

"Ah, ah, ah. You haven't earned that." Nali caught her wrists and pulled her fingers away from her mouth. "Come."

The irritable god perched on the sofa once more and then conjured a shadowy leash, pulling Arianna to him. She didn't even hesitate to lay with her head in his lap and didn't even bother readjusting her dress or hair. Nali murmured something along the lines of "good girl" and began petting her again.

"From what I understand, Darius, you are being difficult." Nalithor's firm tone and frigid gaze made me tense. "Why haven't you let them seal that troublesome power of yours yet?"

*'R-right. This power...'* I bit my lip and clenched my hands in my lap. *'M-maybe I can use it to—'*

"Master, I'm bored..." Arianna's low murmur made my thoughts grind to a halt. All I could do was stare at her in disbelief as she pressed herself against Nali's chest. "When can we— Ah!"

Her face turned bright pink, and she shuddered when Nali's tail disappeared up the skirt of her dress. I expected her to slap him, punch him, or roast him—*something*. Instead, she cuddled into his lower abdomen and shivered again as Nali stroked the back of her bare shoulders.

"T-that's my *sister*, you know. I can't just let you—" I gulped when Nali's dangerous gaze settled on me and darkness swirled around him anew.

"Darius, how much longer do you intend to dance around the subject of your power?" Nali questioned, his power causing a layer of frost to form over the room. "The Elders have given me permission to seal *all* of your magic by force if you refuse to cooperate. *That* power is not meant for this world, and I will remove it without your consent if you push me."

"Why don't the Elders do it themselves, then?!" I retorted, crossing my arms and attempting to ignore Ari's catlike attempts to regain Nali's attention.

"Because dealing with a spoiled prince is not within the Elders' job description," Nali stated flatly, shooting me a bored look. "You should be grateful that they aren't here to deal with you in person. If you had managed to create a mess big enough to draw their personal attention, losing your powers would be the least of your worries."

*'Fraelfnir?'* I reached out timidly.

*'Nalithor bridges the gap between the Elders and the Upper Gods.'* Fraelfnir snorted at me. *'Do you truly wish to anger someone who could destroy you without moving from his seat?'*

"Are you sure you can't just let me keep it?" I shot Nali a warm smile. "I'm sure we can come to some sort of agree—"

I yelped when Nali crossed the distance between us and pressed the blade of his spear against my throat, firm enough to draw a trickle of blood. Ari let out a displeased sigh and rolled onto her side, nuzzling into the cushion Nalithor had been sitting on. She tracked us with her hazy gaze, but I wasn't certain if she saw us at all.

It was her duty to keep me safe, yet she did nothing.

'Fraelfnir sighed. *'Did you* really *think your power would work on the God of Balance?*

"Do you truly wish to obtain what you want without regard for others?" Nalithor growled, his eyes fiery. His tail thrashed behind him like an angered beast. "Would you truly become like the X'shmirans in order to get what you want? Do you simply not care about how others, even your own flesh and blood, think or feel?"

*'Like...the X'shmirans?'* I stared at Nali in disbelief. "How *dare*—"

"What else would you call taking someone's right to choose away from them?" Nali huffed at me and dismissed his spear, pivoting to return to Arianna. "Oh? You kept my seat warm for me? Good girl..."

"You speak of the 'right to choose' when you've obviously done something to force Ari to act like *that*? There's no way an alpha female like her would willingly—" I yelped and shrunk in my chair when darkness burst out from Nali, blanketing the room until I couldn't see anymore.

My heart leapt into my throat as shadows pushed down at me from all sides, suffocating me within Nalithor's power. What normally seemed warm and comforting had turned cold and threatening. There wasn't even the smallest hint of Arianna's power mingled with his. It was *all* Nalithor's, and it was vaster than I could comprehend.

This, truly, was the power of a god. A god that I had angered.

I couldn't find my way out of it and began to tremble and shake in my desperation.

"Ahhnn, Master's power is the best..." Arianna purred from somewhere.

I could sense her moving. My first instinct was to lash out at her with light, but Nalithor's darkness devoured it whole. To him, my power was as trivial as an ant was to a Dux.

After what felt like an eternity, the shadows bucked and flowed back to Nalithor. My heart sank with a mixture of jealousy and fear when the darkness dispersed enough to reveal the Adinvyr and my sister. They were in the middle of a questionably intimate kiss—I couldn't believe that she was letting him explore her in such a way in front of *people*.

Arianna looked more like a toy in his lap than a person. She was too tiny by comparison to him, and too entranced, for me to see her as anything else.

*'Why... Why won't any of my boyfriends kiss me like that?'* My mouth twitched into a scowl as I watched them.

"W-won't having my power sealed away hurt?" I raised my voice in hopes it would at least get them to stop making out. "It's part of me, right?"

"It won't hurt." Lucifer shook his head at me. "It's more like sectioning off a particular part of your mind—a quarantine, if you will. Your other abilities should actually improve without *that* power distracting and warping them."

I opened my mouth to protest more but snapped it shut when I caught the scent of Nalithor's blood again. Arianna was kissing down a series of small, bloody cuts covering Nalithor's chest and abdomen. His blue-black blood stained her lips and the corners of her mouth. The Adinvyr watched her with an amused, approving expression and then pulled her hair back just enough to force her to look at him.

"She *is* a good girl, isn't she?" Erist giggled when Arianna pouted up at Nalithor. "The Oracles were right about her being a submissive after all! Took you long enough to tame her.

"Have you picked out a proper collar for her yet?"

"I have a few in mind," Nalithor answered, lifting Arianna up until her chest was level with his face. "Are we done here? I didn't have enough of her for breakfast, and we still have errands to run."

"Ari, are you going to just let him treat you like a *thing?*" I exclaimed when the Adinvyr nuzzled into the top of Arianna's breasts. "You're an *alpha*, remember?! You—"

"M-Master, please don't tease me!" Arianna's whimper cut me off. All I could do was stare when she reached her hands up to Nalithor's face and pulled him into her bust.

"Of course, Nalithor-y'ric." Ceres bowed her head. "We wouldn't want to keep you longer than necessary. I'm sure the recruits are growing anxious for your arrival."

"But—" I shrunk back in my seat when Nalithor shot me a venomous glare. "I need to talk to Arianna about something!"

"We don't need any further distractions from our errands." Nalithor shook his head and lifted Arianna off his lap before rising to his feet. "Besides, I am not inclined to let you talk to her. You've proved, many times, that you are more likely to attack her than you are to speak with her.

"I won't have you frightening my pet, nor will I have you harm her. Until you can prove that you don't intend to do either, I refuse to leave her alone with you."

Nalithor pulled Arianna to her feet and tucked her against his side. I mouthed at their backs for a moment as they walked toward the gilded doors, then leapt to my feet. Darkness rooted me in place when I moved to chase after them. Nalithor shot me a murderous glare over his shoulder when I summoned light in an attempt to free myself from his grasp.

*'Wha... What has he done to Ari?!'* I demanded of Fraelfnir. *'There's no way she'd let him treat her like that! They told me he isn't a dominant! So why is he—'*

*'Nalithor is a god, and you are a mortal,'* Fraelfnir reprimanded me. *'What right have you to question him or to interfere? He is second only to the Elders! Furthermore, I showed you both of their test results. When will you accept that Nalithor is not a beta—'*

*'What did he do to her?'* I flinched away from an encroaching tendril of darkness.

*'What do you mean "what did he do to her?"'* Fraelfnir sounded exasperated with me. *'Enough of this. We can discuss it after the Upper Gods have sealed that accursed ability of yours.'*

*'I'm so sorry, Ari.'* I stared after her as Nalithor pulled her out of the lounge and out of sight. *'I thought* you *were the one corrupting, Nalithor*

*but…it's the reverse, isn't it? They told me that* you *were the one I had to stop b-but it's clearly…'*

My thoughts trailed off when I was met with silence. Her mind was completely closed to me. Not even the smallest crack was available for me to reach her through. Nalithor's power was like an all-consuming void around her mind.

I curled my hands into fists at my side and took a deep breath. 'They *have questions to answer for me. Just…just hold on, Ari. I* will *save you!'*

'*A foolish notion.'* Fraelfnir snorted. '*He is the God of Balance. Did you* truly *expect him to be all light and goodness?*

'*Balance can be the brightest and kindest of the roles, but it can also be the darkest and cruelest. Arianna is…very close to that role. It only makes sense that she would be drawn to him in such a way.'*

'*No. There's no way she'd submit to someone.'* I shook my head hard. '*Not after being a slave to X'shmiran ways for so long.'*

# CHAPTER TWENTY-SIX
*Distractions*

Nalithor's scent was the first thing to catch my attention when my senses began to clear. A few moments passed before I realized that my head was nestled against his shoulder and that the side of his throat was mere inches away from my lips. The Adinvyr's pulse was racing beneath my cheek, and he had an arm behind my back as if to brace me.

Judging by the breeze, and the muffled sounds coming from below us, I could only assume that we were still outside. It sounded like Nalithor was rummaging around in a bag with his free hand.

I stared at his vulnerable throat for a moment before shifting and nuzzling into his skin. A low growl rumbled in his chest in response to my nibbles.

"Nnngh, *stop that*." Nalithor wrapped a hand around my throat and pulled me away from his. "I told you to behave…"

Nalithor trailed off and stared at me for a moment. His eyes widened for a split second before his expression shifted into a smirk. I suppressed a startled squeak when his tail coiled around my hips and pulled me tighter against his torso, making me realize that I was straddling him.

When I glanced back up, I discovered that Nalithor had leaned in closer and his lips were just out of reach. His hand twitched around my throat and my pulse sped up. It proved difficult to not fidget on his lap.

"You should still be under my sway…" Nalithor murmured, his lips brushing against mine. "You were being such a good girl, too."

"A…good girl?" I blinked at him as he released my throat and trailed his fingers down to my chest, tracing my Brands. "What do you mean by '*good girl*,' Ma—"

I cut myself off, my face burning hot. Nalithor grinned and pulled on a dark leash, drawing me closer until I had to brace myself by placing my hands on the tree trunk behind him. The shadowy leash was connected to something around my throat but, once he stopped tugging on it, I couldn't feel it anymore.

*'W-why in the hells did I almost call him "Master?"'*

"You're still a *little* under my sway then." Nalithor purred. He nuzzled into the top of my bust and kissed up to my jugular. "What sort of delicious thoughts have you been hiding from me, hmmm?"

"What do you mean by 'delicious thoughts?'" I bit down on my lower lip hard when his hands gripped my ass, and his fangs grazed my throat. "I haven't been 'hiding' any—"

"You started calling me '*Master*' on your own," Nalithor interjected, releasing a husky chuckle. "I could certainly get used to having such a *loving* pet..."

"I-I started calling you...?" I trailed off, my face growing hotter when Nalithor withdrew from my throat to look at me.

Nalithor studied me shortly before lifting me off his lap and turning away with an amused expression on his face. When he returned his attention to me, he offered me a steaming cup of floral-smelling tea.

"Try not to make any abrupt movements—or pounce on me." Nalithor smiled, tracking me as I accepted the cup from him. "It *should* take you a while yet to regain full clarity. Although...I'm uncertain if you should have regained your *stubbornness* so quickly, either."

"Humph. What's wrong with pouncing?" I muttered, lifting the cup to my lips.

"I would rather you pounce on me while *not* under my power's influence," Nalithor replied dryly. He turned and began rummaging through something beyond my view again. "We can't linger for long. If necessary, I will carry you until you've fully recovered."

"I should be fine." I glanced to the side when a flash of blue and white caught my eye. "Mmm? What are those?"

"Rozntaar," Nalithor replied, an unreadable smile on his lips. "I found some blooming on our way through the city. Since it's Faerstravir, and you are my date, I—"

"So *those* are rozntaar?" I interjected, my curiosity getting the better of me. I placed my cup aside and then leaned across Nalithor's lap to get a better look at the flowers. "Oh? Cherry blossoms, magnolia, and—"

"Your hair ornaments, please." Nalithor outstretched a hand and smiled at me.

"For me?" I blinked at him, pointing at the flowers with my free hand.

"As I was saying, you *are* my date." Nalithor chuckled and placed a hand on top of my head, ruffling my curls. "I was going to wait until I was certain you were no longer under my influence, but you are more alert than I thought."

"But, really, for me?" I asked again, this time shifting my gaze to the amused Adinvyr. "Is that really okay? I'm a least a *little* familiar with rozntaar. They're usually given to women by—"

"Yes, for you." Nalithor nodded. "I *did* tell you that I intend to make you mine."

"Mmm..." I murmured, shifting so that my torso was across his lap and I could nudge one of the brilliant blue flowers. "All yours?"

"All...?" Nalithor trailed off with an amused laugh and placed a hand on my back, stroking me. "We did agree that neither of us is keen on sharing, did we not?"

"It was a 'yes or no' question." I glanced at him.

"Then, the answer is 'yes.'" Nalithor laughed again. "When you grin like that your nickname becomes even more fitting."

"Which nickname?" I rolled my eyes before obliging him and procuring several of my hair ornaments.

"You're going to have to get off my lap if I'm going to help place these in your hair," Nalithor commented dryly, tapping my back with his claws.

"But you're comfy…" I pouted, resting my chin on his thigh.

"At the very least, you need to *sit* in my lap instead of lying across it." Nalithor brushed my hair away from my neck and traced a claw along my throat. "We must leave shortly anyway. How about I let you cuddle with me while we oversee the recruits, hmmm?"

"Promise?" I shifted to look at him.

"Of course." Nalithor chuckled. "How could I say 'no' when you're so adorable and when you've been such a good girl?" He paused to help me sit up and then nestled me between his legs. "Aren't you going to ask how our little plan went? Or how your brother took it?"

"I don't really care." I tilted my head, considering it.

"You almost killed Darius." Nalithor purred, rubbing his cheek against the side of my head. "I intervened, of course, *like the good Master I am.*"

"See? Nothing to worry about," I murmured distractedly, watching Nalithor's tail swish alongside us. "I knew you wouldn't just *let* me do something stupid— Ah ha! Gotcha!"

I lunged forward and grasped Nalithor's tail in both hands,

tumbling out of his lap. I landed on my back with a good portion of his tail clutched in my arms. The heat of his tail surprised me, but his laughter distracted me from my own curiosity.

"What's so funny?" I demanded, tightening my grip. "You—Hey!"

Nalithor smirked and conjured the shadowy leash again, tugging it. Another firm tug made me release his tail so that I could sit up and dig into the tree branch. I reached up with one hand and grabbed the shadowy collar that encircled my throat, but it wouldn't budge.

However, the collar was forgotten the moment I saw his tail swishing in my peripheral vision.

"Enough of that, '*kitten.*'" Nalithor chuckled when I moved to snatch his tail again. "Come here."

He pulled me back to his lap despite my muttered protests and hooked his fingers under the collar once I was within reach. I growled and dug my nails into his wrist when he lifted me onto his lap again, but he just laughed and pulled me closer.

"Perhaps you are a Sundreht and not an Adinvyr or Rylthra?" Nalithor teased, coiling his tail around my hips to keep me from wriggling away. "Didn't I tell you that we don't have time to linger? Be a good girl and let me put these in your hair—then we can leave."

"Only if I get you to myself," I grumbled, glancing away from him.

"Let's see if you feel that way *after* my power dissipates, hmmm?" Nalithor tugged on one of my earrings and smiled. "Now, now, no pouting."

"What makes you think I'm still under your influence?" I crossed my arms, watching him as he wove flowers into my hair ornaments.

"Your pupils are still a little dilated, and you are too easy to distract." Nalithor squeezed me with his tail as if for emphasis and then released me. "Besides, you almost called me 'Master' again, didn't you? Now then, turn around so I can place these in your hair. We can leave after."

Nalithor shot me a questioning look when I leaned forward on all fours instead. I nuzzled his neck and listened to his pulse race, a smirk stretching across my lips. After Nalithor released a shaky sigh, I nipped at his earlobe and then purred, "As you wish, *Master*."

I gave Nalithor an innocent smile as I pulled away, then turned to oblige his request. His tail made a faint scratching noise as it swished in agitation, but he kept it from my view this time. A few seconds passed before he let out an exasperated sigh and lifted his hands to my hair to place the ornaments.

*'Hmmm, this will be fun.'* I considered. *'He's probably going to tease me incessantly about calling him "Master" anyway, so I may as well beat him to it.'*

"What are we going to do about lunch?" I asked while walking two fingers along Nalithor's thigh to entertain myself.

"I already picked up lunch for us from one of the cafes. It's all in my shrizar—aside from your tea, of course," Nalithor replied, running his fingers down my back. "Mmm... All done. Shall I reward you for being such a good girl?"

"Are you teasing me again?" I grumbled, my pulse quickening. *'Ugh… Maybe I am still under the influence of his power. I shouldn't be so happy to receive praise. At least, not that kind of praise.'*

"There will be plenty of time for teasing later." Nalithor chuckled. He turned me to face him and examined me for a moment. "Come here."

Nalithor pulled me close and pressed his lips to mine. The instant I tasted his blood both my thoughts and vision seemed to go blank. I sunk into his kiss, oblivious to all else as the taste of the power running through his blood threatened to intoxicate me all over again. One of his fangs sliced my tongue open, adding my blood into the mix and eliciting a groan of desire from the Adinvyr.

When he pulled away, I found myself incredibly disappointed. He kept a hand loose around my throat as I leaned in and licked the blood from the corner of his mouth.

"Why did you *stop*?" I sighed, laying my head on his shoulder to sulk.

"We *do* have to get to the training grounds at some point," Nalithor replied, stroking my back. "Shall I carry you, or do you think you can walk?"

"You're actually giving me an option?" I snorted. "I would *prefer* to walk."

"Yes, this time." Nalithor laughed and lifted me out of his lap. "Hmmm… Perhaps I should have had you wear a kimono today. Although, it certainly would have made your antics at Erist's temple more difficult…"

"Antics?" I tilted my head and looked up at him. "Do I even want to know?"

"Fetch your tea." Nalithor motioned to my left after he stood up. "I will let you walk, but I won't let you leap down without my assistance. You *should* be a bit wobbly still—assuming you don't get distracted by my tail again."

"I wasn't watching it!" I snapped, flushed, before whirling around to collect my tea.

"You're not fooling anyone." Nalithor grinned. "Ready?"

Nalithor lifted me by my waist once I reached him and then he leapt into the narrow street below us. After releasing me, he shot me a boyish smile, offered me his arm, then proceeded to guide me through the outskirts of Draemir. The tone of the citizens' whispering had changed to something more pleasant now, but I wasn't able to focus enough to hear what they were saying.

In fact, it was difficult for me to focus on anything other than Nalithor. I wanted to nuzzle back into his chest or throat and just take a nap while he oversaw whatever duties he needed to tend to. Nalithor's scent and power were teasing me, luring me even with my shields back in place. *'Honestly! Just how does taking over someone work? If I called him* that *without him telling me to… Well, it isn't like I haven't thought about it before. But…'*

*'Are you certain I don't need to carry you?'* Nalithor interrupted my thoughts. He lifted me over a curb and out of the street as a patrol of

mounted soldiers clopped by.

'*You're* distracting,' I grumbled, crossing my arms and looking away from him.

'*And it is quite endearing that you think so.*' Nalithor smiled, shaking his head. '*Let's hurry. I don't want to linger in the Scarlet District any longer than necessary.*'

We hurried down the streets at a quicker pace. At our new speed, I had little time to dwell on Nalithor's power or scent, and for that I was grateful. As enjoyable as both were, it was far too hypnotic for me to handle in the state I was in. I needed something to distract me from him, and a run through Draemir seemed like a solid way to do so.

The colorful decorations and the smells of cooking food blurred together as we neared the main street that ran through the Scarlet District. Shining ornaments of silver and pastel colors hung everywhere, flowers and ribbons coiled around both balconies and lampposts alike. Mrifon, rozntaar, and many more flowers I didn't know the names of adorned both the buildings and the women's hair.

While mrifon were like a cross between a rose and a spider lily, rozntaar were more similar to magnolia. However, unlike magnolia, rozntaar had many more layers of petals and bloomed in rich colors. Most of the other flowers used for the festival were pastel or white, so spotting the rozntaar was easy even if they were few in number.

'*Don't touch that.*' Nalithor caught me around the waist when I went to pick up a large flower that had fallen from above us.

'*But it's so pretty—*'

*'Do you want the prostitutes to think you're coming back to partake of their services later tonight?'*

*'W-what?'*

'Ahhhnnn? Is the spoiled prince not going to share?" A male voice teased from above, eliciting an irritated growl from Nalithor. "Ari-mrii is so adorable—you shouldn't keep her all to yourself."

"Cyrr, you shouldn't push him." A male with sandy-brown hair sighed.

"He's right though, Ari-mrii is quite cute..." A third male murmured. Long purple hair fell around his shoulders and obscured half of his face as he leaned on the balcony railing to examine us.

"See? Prisshin agrees!" The first, green-haired male grinned. "The nobles and royals can be so dull can't they, Ari-mrii? I assure you than Prisshin, Llan, and I can show you a *much* better time. You're so cute, I'd even do it for free."

"I should tear—" Nalithor pivoted, snarling.

"Let's go," I interjected, sliding an arm behind Nalithor's back before nuzzling into his chest. "I want lunch, and we still have much work to do."

"Lunch? Pah! Neither of you have even been feeding the other properly!" Cyrr snorted.

*'Come on.'* I rubbed my cheek against Nalithor's rumbling chest. *'Do you really see them as competition?'* A small smile crept across my lips when he twitched. *'If you do...I'm going to have to kick your ass well before our scheduled match.'*

"Reiz'tar has no need of your services," Nalithor spoke coolly, darkness rippling around us both. "We have somewhere important to be."

Nalithor's hand came to rest on my hip, eliciting aggravated snarls from the male prostitutes above us. They were smart enough from attempting to use their power to lure me, it seemed, even if they weren't smart enough to keep their interest in me to themselves.

I could still hear low rumbling within Nalithor's chest while we walked, and his grip on my hip was almost tight enough for his claws to draw blood.

Several more prostitutes, male and female alike, attempted to gain our attention as we wove through the throngs of people. Nalithor ignored them all, keeping his eyes focused forward and his grip tight. I kept a careful eye on our surroundings and nuzzled closer to the angry Adinvyr when I caught the scent of familiar Humans.

I wanted nothing to do with the X'shmirans.

"A-ah... L-Lord Balance..." Tyana gulped, exchanging a look with Dilonu and the nobles accompanying them. "I d-didn't think we would see you in this section of the city."

"My ayraziis and I are on our way to the training grounds," Nalithor replied, his tone frigid as his claws dug into my hip. "Excuse us."

"Y-Your?" One of the nobles spluttered with wide eyes, while the king and queen simply looked confused.

I kept my mouth shut and let Nalithor lead me along the streets once more. My face burned so hot that it was probably close to the lanterns that hung from the nearby brothels. Of all the things Nalithor could have called me, *that* was the last one I expected. Ayraziis didn't have a direct translation in the common tongue, but the Adinvyr of Sihix Forest had explained to me what it meant.

It was much more serious than simply calling me his girlfriend.

*'Do... Do you mean that? Or...'* I flushed hotter when Nalithor glanced down at me.

*'Of course, I do—I wouldn't have called you my ayraziis otherwise,'* Nalithor informed me, before glancing at our surroundings. *'Ugh... These people. Let's hasten our pace again.'*

Nalithor pulled me away from an encroaching group of Elves and down the street again. I couldn't think of a response without growing redder, so I remained silent the rest of our way through the city. My heart refused to stop racing.

While I had grown used to him saying that he would make me "his," calling me his ayraziis wasn't something I thought he would do lightly.

The scent of blood stirred me from my chaotic thoughts, causing me to tense and survey our surroundings. I kept pace with Nalithor while attempting to determine the source of the offensive smell. It was close. It was stalking something. Murderous intent radiated from an alleyway to my left.

*'Arianna?'*

*'Beast blood.'*

I peeled away from Nalithor and leapt into the alley, drawing a slender sword while I ran. A terrified scream caught my ears, followed by the scent of Devillian blood. Turning the corner, I found a creature that didn't even look much like a person anymore. Its dark gooey skin was coated in the blood of the young boy it had injured.

Gripping the shadows, I wrapped them around the...thing, before adjusting my grip on my sword. It screamed, writhing within the darkness, incapable of chasing its prey. I tore its throat open with a single strike, then grimaced when its blood splashed across my dress and skin.

*'The crystals didn't shield me from its blood?'* I frowned, kicking the motionless corpse over before sniffing at the bloodied blade of my sword. The creature's overall shape was humanoid, but nothing else about it was like a person at all. It made my skin crawl.

"W-what in Avrirsa was that thing?" The boy yelped, seeming oblivious to Nalithor attempting to calm him down.

"Arianna?" Nalithor probed.

"Not sure..." I outstretched an arm without turning. "The jewelry didn't block its blood. Now that I'm closer, it doesn't smell *quite* the same as a beast's."

"It didn't block... Are you alright?" Nalithor grasped my wrist, came to stand before me, and sighed. "Well, at least none of it got in your hair or the flowers. Here."

Nalithor's magic engulfed me for a moment and then dissipated. I glanced down at myself and blinked at the new clothing he had summoned around me. The black dress was like a cross between Draemiran and Dauthrmiran styles, giving me better range of movement than a pure kimono would have. A questionable amount of my cleavage and throat were displayed, but that was likely Nalithor's intent.

"R-Rely'ric, Reiz'tar, w-what was..." The boy trailed off and turned cherry red when I turned to follow Nalithor over to the boy.

"Run along home and stick to the main roads." Nalithor ruffled the hair between the boy's short white horns, shooting him a smile.

The boy glanced at me, his face turning red even to the tips of his ears. He turned after a moment and ran through the alley and toward the main street, quickly disappearing from view.

*'At least his wound wasn't deep,'* Nalithor murmured, moving past me to examine the dead creature. *'However, this...*thing...*is an issue.'*

*'What is it?'* I questioned, moving a few paces away from the growing pool of blood beneath it. *'Can I kill it again?'*

*'Come, we're leaving.'* Nalithor turned away from the corpse and scooped me into his arms. *'A patrol will be here momentarily to collect that. Hold on tight.'*

*'Hold on to what?'* I yelped and buried my face into Nalithor's chest, startled by the sudden burst of power around him.

We sunk into the shadows and raced the rest of the way out of the city. Nalithor's power made my head swim. I staggered when he set me down but managed to catch myself on the trunk of the tree we had stopped by. My pulse raced, my breath short. Before I could fully recover, Nalithor's arms slipped around my waist as he nuzzled into my shoulder.

"Still a little intoxicated, my dear?" Nalithor's sultry purr elicited an involuntary shiver from me, threatening to make my mind go blank entirely. "Ahhh, you are such a fun one."

Nalithor planted a kiss on the side of my neck and released me. I sighed, nudged my hair ornaments to make sure they were still in place, then moved to follow the playful Adinvyr. His tail swished from side-to-side as he walked, and a boyish bounce had entered his step again. I tracked his tail for a moment before lifting my gaze to his back, the corner of my eye twitching—I got the distinct feeling that he was trying to bait me into pouncing again.

I shook my head and breathed another small sigh before picking up my pace. My senses were quicker to recover this time, at least, so I surveyed our surroundings while we walked.

It was much quieter outside the city. There were few people on the roads. Only a few patrolling soldiers, a handful of farmers and fishermen, and the occasional traveler. The soldiers saluted us, while the others bowed deeply before hurrying on their way. They made it quite clear that they were acknowledging *both* of us. I didn't know how to feel about people knowing who I was just by looking.

"Feeling better?" Nalithor asked, shooting me a smile when I looked up at him. "Well, your pupils are no longer dilated at least."

"I wasn't feeling 'bad' or 'off' in the first place." I tilted my head, examining the faint look of surprise that he attempted to hide. "Mmm?

Should I have felt ill or something?"

"No… It's just…" Nalithor sighed and ran a hand through his hair. "Never mind. Shall we quicken our pace? We're almost there."

"Don't forget your promise." I wrapped both of my arms around his left one and nuzzled into his bicep.

"Promise…? You still wish to cuddle?" Nalithor questioned, his tone carrying a hint of surprise.

"Mmhmm. You called me your ayraziis," I pointed out, noting his face growing pinker. "After that, you're not going to get rid of me *that* easily."

"Get rid of…" Nalithor shot me a firm look. "That is the *last* thing I intend to do! I—"

"There you are, General!" An unfamiliar voice called. "Is everything alright?"

"We ran into some matters we had to address in the city." Nalithor's tone shifted to one of formality as the soldier fell into step with us. "I trust you kept the recruits entertained while waiting?"

"Yes, sir!" The soldier grinned. "I wasn't aware General Black would be joining us as well. Shall I have one of the men fetch a chair for her?"

"No need." Nalithor shook his head. "Bring the recruits to the main training yard and tell them to prepare to fight. I intend to see how they fight *before* wasting my time on the finer details."

The soldier saluted us and then scampered off to do as he was told. Nalithor grumbled a curse and led me into a massive, walled-in courtyard. Most of it was covered in sand. A raised walkway of laid stones bordered it, leading to a thick stone platform at the very back of the courtyard. Several large chairs rested on top of the platform, all but one of which was occupied.

"Yo, Nali!" Sorr grinned when he spotted us. "What's this my men are muttering about? You two found a 'thing' in the city?"

"Well, it *was* a thing. Now it's a dead thing," I stated, my eyes flicking between the other five males present.

"It smelled bad, and so she killed it," Nalithor added dryly.

Xander and Eyrian I recognized, of course. Sorr as well, with his bright red hair and bronze horns. The other three men were all Adinvyr and dressed in similar fashion to Sorr, indicating that they were all Draemiran generals.

One of the men had sand-colored hair and brass horns. The second had dark brown hair and obsidian horns. The third had mint green hair and white horns. Their scaled tails were the same color as their horns, and all three of them had the black sclera and slit pupils that I had grown accustomed to since coming Below.

Recruits had already begun to file into the courtyard, so introductions were kept brief. The man with mint green hair was named Thys, the sandy one was named Rhyr, and the brunette was Belttur. They were all close in age to Sorr and had grown up together with him in Draemir.

Nalithor had been responsible for training all of them, but apparently, he wasn't much older than they were.

*'Come here.'* Nalithor tugged my sleeve and moved toward the empty chair in the middle. *'We can cuddle, but… I do need you to pay attention to the recruits as well.'*

*'Did someone grow too accustomed to having a pet?'* I teased before curling up on the empty portion of his chair, against his left side.

"So, it's true, Nali?" Rhyr grinned, rubbing his chin. "Arianna-jiss really *can* make you, of all people, blush!"

"I'm not…" Nalithor sighed at his cackling friends. "Can any of you honestly claim you wouldn't have a reaction to her attentions? Or to her teasing?"

"You two still plan to duke it out at tonight's ceremonies?" Sorr leaned forward in his seat, eager.

"If Arianna feels up to—"

"Even *consider* canceling it, and I will kick your ass right now." I prodded Nalithor in the chest, shooting him a glare. "I cooked you breakfast! The *least* you can do is—"

"I'm more curious about the rozntaar in Arianna-jiss's hair," Eyrian remarked with a huff, shooting Nalithor a sideways look. "You didn't tell me you were that serious about her."

"I haven't had time to tell anyone much of anything, between keeping this one out of trouble and dealing with matters in Xiinsha," Nalithor responded with a huff, pulling me tighter against his side.

"Generals," a soldier began, saluting us, "these are all of the recruits. How would you like—"

"And she's off again…" Nalithor sighed as I darted from his chair and sped through the ranks of recruits. "Arianna dear, bring them back *alive* this time, won't you?"

*'Alive?'* I sighed to myself. *'I guess that can be arranged.'*

I skidded to a halt and drew shadows to me, plunging them into the ground. I smiled when the sound of several recruits screaming caught my ears. Turning, I sauntered back to the generals with a bounce in my step. The screams muffled and then disappeared, dragged into the shadows.

Once I reached the platform, I ripped the recruits out of the shadows and dumped them on the ground in front of the generals.

Nalithor tracked my movements with an amused, predatory expression on his face. The others appeared more wary. I sat alongside Nalithor again, but this time I hooked my left leg over his and turned so that my torso was pressed against his side. It was much easier for me to nuzzle him that way.

"So, you *can* restrain yourself." Nalithor chuckled, draping his tail over my hip. "Good girl."

*'I'd argue that* you *restrained* me, *"Master,"'* I teased, smirking when his tail twitched.

"Dare I ask why you wanted to kill them, Arianna-jiss?" Rhyr inquired, rising to his feet to approach the nearest captive.

"They don't smell right," I replied, drawing one of them up with tendrils of shadow. "See? Veins and eyes don't look right either. Their presence is weird, too."

"Presence?" Belttur arched an eyebrow.

"Their aura," Nalithor offered before turning to an armored Adinvyr nearby. "Rinzci, take them to the prisons and find out where they got their claws on such detestable substances—and see if any of the healers or alchemists can determine *what* it is."

*'Awww... But I wanted to play with them.'* I pouted, nuzzling Nalithor's chest. *'Can't I at least—'*

*'No, you may not.'*

*'Just one?'*

*'No, we need information from them.'*

*'But—'*

*'I'll find you something fun to play with later,'* Nalithor interjected, tightening his grip. *'Perhaps if you're* very *good, I will let you play with me.'*

*'Play with...'* I stopped attempting to chase after the foul-smelling things that I wanted to execute. *'When you say "play with you"...'*

"Hmmm, we truly do have a lot of hopefuls, don't we?" Nalithor glanced to either side at the other generals. "What do you think, Eyrian? A free-for-all?"

"You're just trying to avoid more work." Eyrian sighed, shaking his head. "I, for one, don't want Lysander-y'ric to tan my hide."

"But you're already tanned." I tilted my head.

"You know what I meant!" Eyrian huffed.

"We have mages this year too, huh..." Thys murmured, tapping his claws on his armrest. "We don't have enough officers on hand to make everyone spar at once—most of them are busy in the city."

"Having Arianna or Nali spar them wouldn't be fair either," Xander piped up, grinning. "Besides, you two want to conserve your strength for tonight right?"

"Making them fight *any* of us wouldn't be fair," Nalithor muttered, bored already. "I suppose we will have to do this the slow way."

*'Hmmm, no female recruits?'* I questioned, relaxing into Nalithor's chest once more.

*'Mother has her own personal army—of women,'* Nalithor answered dryly as he rested a hand on my thigh. *'My mother takes all of the female Adinvyr, and the occasional Vorpmasian Elf. She is…quite particular. She wishes to preserve the more feminine combat arts that she and Erist have developed over the years and passes them down to the women who join what is essentially "the Queen's Guard." Father accepts both men and women into our army, but… There's a certain level of prestige associated with the Queen's Guard.'*

*'Well, with a name like that I'm not surprised,'* I mused, before shifting my attention back to the recruits. *'These greenlings seem less distracted and more experienced than their counterparts in Dauthrmir. Perhaps this won't be as bad as you seem to think?'*

*'Draemiran children are raised to hunt and to fight.'* Nalithor twisted his tail around my thighs while speaking. *'In Dauthrmir, due to the mixture of cultures, children often have a more passive upbringing unless they belong to the noble class—or if their parents are Adinvyr or Draekin.'*

"Nali, what're your plans after tonight's opening ceremony?" Sorr asked, a huge grin plastered on his face. "We've got a room reserved at—"

"Arianna-jiss is welcome to join us as well, of course," Thys stated after smacking Sorr upside the head.

*'Would you like to?'* Nalithor questioned, glancing down at me. *'If not, we can find elsewhere to dine.'*

*'They're your friends, right?'* I traced my fingers along his abdomen while thinking. *'Go without me? I'm not sure if I feel comfortable around them yet. But I also don't want to keep you from your friends. You haven't seen them in a while since you've been working out of Dauthrmir, right?'*

*'I would like you to come,'* Nalithor stated simply.

*'I'll consider it.'* I purred and snuggled deeper into his chest. *'Maybe that can be your reward if you best me during our match tonight.'*

*'Oh? I had something else in mind for my reward.'* Nalithor chuckled and nudged my inner thigh with his tail. *'Let's focus on the task at hand, shall we? After your antics earlier...you are* much *too distracting.'*

"It depends on the outcome of our fight, Sorr. I have to keep her on her toes somehow."

Nalithor stroked my thigh as we fell silent and watched the recruits spar each other one-by-one. It was still difficult for me to focus, especially with Nalithor petting me. I found myself relaxing against him and enjoying his scent much more than the fights going on before us.

Even without him attempting to take me over he was magnetic in his own right.

"Hmmm... What are *they* doing here?" Rhyr's disconcerted mutter drew my attention a while later.

"What do you want, Rabere?" Nalithor sighed, irritated, as he pulled me closer to his chest. "Didn't I make it clear that I am uninterested in you and your whore?"

"D-did he just call me a whore?!" Elven-Arianna shrieked.

"Your ears are quite large—I'm rather certain you heard him clearly," I muttered, shooting her a sideways glare.

"*My* Arianna insists on challenging *your* Arianna." Rabere sighed, holding his fingertips to his temples for a moment before lowering his gaze to me. "She thinks you...cheated."

"If she is *really* royalty, then she should be able to duel me!" Elven-Arianna declared with a haughty sniff. "Unless you Humans are still too barbaric to—"

"Do I *look* Human to you, wench?" I shot the Elf a condescending look and then pulled myself off Nalithor's lap. "Fine. If you want to soil yourself in fear again, I will oblige you."

"Don't take too long." Nalithor smacked my ass.

*'Was that necessary?'* I glanced over my shoulder at him.

*'Absolutely.'* Nalithor smirked.

"You're going to fight in *that*?" Rabere glanced down at my attire before lifting his molten eyes back to my face.

"Human..." The Elf tilted her head and examined me. "I suppose not. However, you and Darius-zir are the X'shmiran's children, are you not?"

"*Adopted* children," Xander corrected, earning a glance from his maker and the Elf alike.

*"We get to see Arianna-jiss fight?"*

*"Awesome! We'll get to see how different her fights between this chick and Nalithor-y'ric are!"*

"Well then, you wanted to fight as 'royalty?'" I questioned, placing my hand on one hip while the closest recruits scampered out of our way. "What shall it be?"

Instead of answering me, the Elven woman smirked and summoned a pair of fans to her hands. She made a show of spinning around with them like a dancer before striking a pose and snapping both open to reveal bladed edges. I sighed when the ground beneath my feet trembled, and the scent of poison reached my nose.

*'Zrityr... Have you learned to wield those?'* Nalithor sounded concerned.

"A Wood Elf then, are you?" I rolled my eyes and conjured cobalt flames around my fingertips. "Sorry for this, then."

I pointed downward and sent my flames piercing into the soil beneath my feet to meet the roots that were rushing toward me. Whatever creature was attached to the other end of the roots screamed in agony from nearby before recoiling and retreating.

Satisfied that the creature wouldn't come to its mistress's aid again, I summoned a pair of my own zrityr.

"Y-you *bitch!*" The Elf shrieked, tears streaming down her face.

*'Did you...kill her familiar?'* Nalithor questioned in a surprisingly

wary tone.

I sidestepped a swipe from the Elf, observing as she flailed wildly to attack me.

'*I considered it,*' I replied, drifting away from another erratic slash. '*It's a little singed, but it will be fine. It did run off though. Perhaps it was a young familiar?*'

"Didn't I say not to kill her, Arianna?" Rabere appeared between us and caught the Elf by both of her wrists, twisting until she dropped her zrityr. "I don't recall you asking for permission to poison your blades, nor did I give it to you."

"But she—" Elven-Arianna fell into stunned silence and staggered back when Rabere slapped her, hard, across the face.

I took a few steps back and shut my zrityr. The Adinvyr present all appeared ready to pounce on the Vampire and rip him to shreds for slapping the woman. Nalithor's arms slipped around my hips, pulling me further away from the Vampire. I glanced down when Nalithor nuzzled my waist and growled at the two Beshulthiens before us.

'*She kinda deserved it.*' I flicked the tip of one of Nalithor's horns, drawing his attention.

"I'll still fight her if she has a pair without poison," I called, twirling one of my zrityr in one hand.

"Until she learns to behave, she will not be fighting anyone." Rabere grimaced. He fetched the Elf's zrityr and threw them into a shrizar. "Come. We are leaving, and *you* are staying in the manor until you learn to behave better than a wild animal.

"Nalithor... You should take better care of yourself. With a willing meal by your side, you shouldn't be this weakened."

*I'm a "meal," huh?'* I rolled my eyes before glancing down at the growling deity.

*'It's true that you're food...'* Nalithor muttered, squeezing my hips tighter. *'But you are also much more than that to me.'*

"What was that woman *thinking?*" Sorr sighed, slumping back in his chair. "Poison in front of eight generals, her emperor, and this many soldiers? Is she mad?"

I arched an eyebrow at him. "She's a woman, and you're asking *that?*"

*'Come here...'* Nalithor grumbled, a small pout on his face as he pulled me fully onto his lap. *'I really can't stand that bastard so much as looking at you.'*

"So, it's true that Rabere is causing trouble again?" Belttur motioned at Nalithor's sulking expression. "I'm almost impressed that Rabere is *still* obsessed with *that* Arianna-jiss." He paused, a look of recognition crossing his face before he looked down at me. "Ahhh... That *is* a problem, isn't it?"

*'Still obsessed with me?'* I nudged Nalithor.

*'When we were children, Darius was obsessed with me, and my brother was obsessed with you.'* Nalithor grimaced, shaking his head. *'I...may have been overprotective of you. You were very shy and skittish. As such, I kept you mostly to myself.*

*'Eyrian trained with us at times, but for some reason, I never trusted*

*anyone else around you. He…still holds a bit of a grudge due to the way I acted.'*

*'Hmmm… Speaking of obsessions…'* I relaxed against Nalithor once more and released a contented sigh. *'I didn't really think about it before, but what are we going to do about my brother? He's going to expect me to act as your* pet *all the time now.'*

*'You're probably right about that.'* Nalithor sighed. *'…I may have mentioned something about having a few collars in mind for you as well.'*

*'You…'*

*'What? Your pet "act" was very convincing.'* He shot me a smile before shifting his gaze to the recruits once more.

I nudged him a few times for elaboration, but he remained silent aside from a devious chuckle or two. Once I realized he had no intention of explaining himself further, I laid my head on his chest and pouted. Nalithor was far more interesting to me than the recruits, but he was finally focused on observing them.

*'Pet "act" huh…'* I pondered, suppressing a purr while Nalithor petted my back. *'I wonder if he really thinks it's just an act?'*

It wasn't until well into the afternoon that the throngs of recruits began to thin out. Even during lunch, I got to remain on Nalithor's lap, so I didn't really mind. The generals, including Nalithor, mostly conversed among themselves while overseeing the many sparring matches.

I remained silent, and they didn't see fit to address me. Under other circumstances I might have been miffed about it, but since

Nalithor continued to pet me…

*'Damn it! His attention isn't the only thing I care about.'* I pouted to myself before glancing upward at him and pausing. *'Why does he look sad?'*

Without a second thought, I shifted on his lap and nuzzled into the crook of his neck. I felt his pulse quicken in response. He moved his hands to my hips as I pressed the length of my torso against him.

*'What…'* Nalithor trailed off when I rubbed my cheek against his neck. *'Are you going to try taking a bite? Here?'*

*'You looked mopey,'* I informed him.

*'I'm not…'* Nalithor sighed. *'Perhaps a little. I dislike the methods we resorted to using against Darius. Taking over someone isn't my ideal course of action, nor would I ever want you to* pretend *to be my…'*

*'Pet?'* I finished, smiling into his neck when his hands twitched. *'I think we can both agree that there wasn't an obvious course of action that was "desirable." As for pretending…did I give you any indication that I* would *have* to pretend?*'

*'You…'* Nalithor trailed off into a growl when I kissed his neck. I just smiled and settled back into my spot.

"Well, that turned out better than expected," Rhys muttered, riffling through a stack of papers.

"You two really should join us for dinner after your fight," Eyrian remarked, rising to his feet before shoving his aqua mane out of his eyes. "Ijelle isn't going to want to leave Arianna alone once she sees her fight for real."

"You do have a point there," Nalithor spoke dryly. *'Have you at least recovered from—'*

*'I've been "recovered" for a while.'* I huffed as he lifted me off his lap and nudged me to my feet. *'Do you really find it so strange when your ayraziis is affectionate?'*

"Whatever you two were discussing, you clearly lost, Nali." Sorr laughed, clamping a hand on Nalithor's shoulders. "No way are you the winner if she made you turn *that* red."

"You two will be fighting in the plaza between Erist and Aurelian's temples, right?" Xander grinned, looking between us. "My bet is on Nali—I don't see him letting Ari-mrii win."

"It depends on what they're fighting for." Eyrian crossed his arms, shaking his head.

"Regardless, we should hurry back to the city so that we have time to prepare ourselves." Nalithor turned and motioned for me to follow him in the direction of the gates. "Hopefully, after this, my mother and Erist will let us be."

"It's Ellena and Erist—the chances of that happening are zero." Thys snorted. "Try not to strain us too terribly with your match."

"I dunno, trying to shield the city from a deity and an anomaly's power sounds like fun!" Sorr grinned, punching one hand into the other. "It's about time we had something challenging to do!"

"Anomaly, huh?" I rolled my eyes and hurried after Nalithor. *'We're going to fight in front of the temples?'*

*'Unfortunately.'*

'So…we can assume Darius will be watching.'

'Yes… Our little ruse may be unraveled after all.'

'Oh? Are you not up to the task of being a Master?' I asked innocently, shooting him a sly smirk when I passed him.

'Don't tease me.' Nalithor crossed his arms and shot me a firm look.

'Who said I'm teasing?' I stuck my tongue out at him, watching a look of surprise wash over his face. 'Catch me if you can!'

'Catch…? Nnngh, get back here!'

I just laughed and slipped into one of the shadows just before he could grab me.

'If you can catch me, perhaps I'll let you select two prizes for winning our fight.'

'Now you definitely aren't getting away.' Nalithor's husky growl made me grin.

# CHAPTER TWENTY-SEVEN
## *Faerstravir*

*'There're so many people...'* I leaned against the balcony railing and looked out over the plaza. A large platform had been constructed for the opening ceremonies of Faerstravir, and around it, every inch of space was filled with people. Small Magelight lanterns flickered everywhere, hanging from the trees and bobbing along to the flitting movements of those who carried more.

Despite our rush to return to the palace and be on time, two and a half hours had passed since Nalithor and I had dressed and arrived at the plaza. We had to wait for other formalities and performances to finish, resulting in us sitting through speeches, dances, and other colorful displays of both culture and tradition. The crowds were just as eager for Nalithor and me to fight as I was at this point.

I just wanted to *fight*. I had to win *something* today.

*'Not that it's bad he managed to catch me.'* I tapped the claws of my gauntlet on the railing, my gaze flicking across the gathered crowds. *'He wasn't very specific about how he wants to feed from me, though. Bah, I'll just have to make sure I win our fight. I can't just* let *him get away with making up the rules as he goes along!'*

"You were right about the boy," Nalithor stated from somewhere behind me. "Now that his power is sealed, Erist and Arom have deemed it 'safe' to allow him back into civilized society."

"That was cold!" I exclaimed, shying away from his armored fingers.

"Any brilliant plans for dealing with the brat?" Nalithor smiled and reached up to nudge one of my hair ornaments.

"We should have considered that *before* having you take me over," I muttered, shaking my head. "Darius doesn't understand those sort of relationships—or any sort, probably. There's no telling whether his lack of knowledge will work for or against us."

"I'll take that as a no, then." Nalithor chuckled as he leaned on the railing beside me. "In other news... That *thing* you killed was apparently a person at one point."

"A person? *That?*" I glanced up at him. "It didn't even smell remotely like a person!"

"It appears that someone thought mixing beast blood and the poison we ran into near Xiinsha would be a good idea." Nalithor grimaced, his icy eyes fixated on the crowds below us. "The blood and the poison interacted with each other and twisted someone into...*that.* Our scholars are still attempting to determine if the creature was Human or Elven—they've ruled out the other races."

"And the soldiers are trying to figure out how it got into the city— and if there's more?" I motioned toward a patrol that had peeled away from the plaza and was moving for the Scarlet District.

"Ah...is *that* what you meant about your brother not understanding?" Nalithor murmured, tilting his head to the side as he examined something. "Perhaps it would be best if you *didn't* look."

I followed Nalithor's gaze anyway and grimaced when I spotted Darius. My brother had Xander and a Rylthra male, whom I didn't recognize, sitting at his feet. Darius had them on a leash, and their "clothing" amounted to little more than metal devices locked around their otherwise exposed nether regions. The Rylthra man seemed to be struggling to keep his fluffy vulpine tail from being stepped on by other festival-goers, but my brother was oblivious to his plight.

Both Xander and the Rylthra male had piercings that came as a shock to me. In X'shmir it was rare enough to see someone with their ears pierced—I'd never even considered that people might get other things pierced as well.

The thing that struck me as the strangest was Darius' partner, Vivus. The cherry-haired Vampire was standing off to the side of the trio and looked incredibly uncomfortable. I knew his pained, distraught expression well—Vivus was jealous. Jealous to the point of emotional distress.

Why he felt so strongly about my brother was beyond me. How my brother could act in such a way in front of someone who clearly cared about him was another thing entirely.

"Is it really alright for him to have them exposed in such a way?" I sighed, surveying the plaza once more. "Even the deities who had nude "Chosen" with them at dinner have them clothed now."

My question went unheard. Darius shifted to kick Xander across the face, sending him toppling from his kneeling position and onto his side. Nalithor released a vicious snarl and leaned forward against the railing, the wood cracking beneath his grip. He looked ready to launch over it and tear into my brother.

Several nobles and royals turned to chastise Darius, and a group of guards began making their way towards him as well. I brought my fingertips to my temples and sighed.

'Right. Xander is the Vraelimir Family's adopted son…' I bit back a groan and shifted my attention to the angry Adinvyr beside me. "That's…just a fraction of what I mean when I say Darius doesn't understand. He—"

"He is a fool." Nalithor growled, his tail thrashing behind him. "I only allow him to live because harming him may yet pose a threat to you—Gabriel failed to specify if she had removed *that* restriction as well. Someone needs to kick that brat's—"

"Jumping down there yourself won't make things better," I stated, catching Nalithor by his arm. "As much as I would like to watch you beat the snot out of him, like you did with Rabere, we have our own fight to prepare for."

Nalithor sighed, his shoulders slumping for a moment before he turned to look at me. His expression softened. "The guards and nobles will deal with him better than I can at the moment."

I watched him walk away from the balcony, for a moment, and studied his white and platinum armor. Even without switching my vision, the pale blue topaz set into the armor and his jewelry held the obvious glow of magic. Unlike his other sets, this one covered his skin from the throat down. There was a helm to accompany it as well, but he had placed it aside while we waited.

"Hurry up, Nalithor!" Ellena demanded from somewhere behind me, causing me to pivot and look at her. "You two can chat later. I still expect you to put on your usual performance before you fight Arianna-jiss!"

"Very well..." Nalithor sighed, picked up his helmet, and then strode toward me. *'Be a good girl and stay up here until it's time for our fight, alright? It will be our turn once I get this out of the way... Step back.'*

I shot him a brief pout and then moved out of his way, watching with fascination as his wings appeared from a burst of shadows. Armor covered the upper ridges of his feathered wings and matched his body armor perfectly. His ebony feathers had an iridescent sheen, but I didn't get to admire them for long.

With a graceful leap, Nalithor hurtled over the balcony railing and glided through the air to the platform below. Cheers and screams of delight ran through the spectators when they spotted the regal Adinvyr approaching.

I had grown so used to people fawning over him that this more genuine, adoring reaction from his people surprised me. The citizens were ecstatic to see their prince—it was mostly the tourists who seemed more taken with his Adinvyr charms. I crossed my arms and examined the faces of the festival-goers in thought.

*'Hmmm, are Adinvyr even affected by each other's natural power?'* I wondered, unsure what to think of the clamoring crowds. *'They certainly adore their prince…but this is much different from the attention he gets in Dauthrmir.'*

"Don't let his sighing fool you—he looks forward to this every year." Ellena giggled, coming to stand beside me at the balcony. "Both of you loved Faerstravir as children. It was your favorite time of year. Though, he always had you choose what song you wanted him to play for his performance.

"What did you decide for him this year?"

"Song? He didn't ask me." I shook my head and then glanced at Ellena.

"Oh? I wonder what he's up to then…" A small frown touched Ellena's lips when she shifted her gaze down to her son once more. "Well, the two of you will be fighting next. Did you two decide how you're going to make your entry?"

"Mmhmm. His suggestion makes much more sense now that I know he's going to be on stage before me." I paused when I spotted

Alala trotting up to sit beside Nalithor as he procured his violin—much to the crowd's delight. "Alala… Should I fetch her?"

"She's going to assist the Archmagi with protecting everyone from your sparring match." Ellena shook her head and turned away from the balcony. "See the daises surrounding the stage? Once the Archmagi and Alala are in place, that's your cue to make your entrance."

Both of us snapped our attention back to Nalithor when he began to play. I didn't recognize the song. A ripple of hushed murmurs spread through the crowd like wildfire. Some of the Devillians and even a few guards motioned up toward the balcony Ellena and I were on. Even the tourists appeared awestruck, though I wasn't certain if it was for the same reasons the Devillians were.

"Oh my…" Ellena's eyes widened as she looked from me to her son and back a few times. "The noblewomen are *not* going to be happy. I have to go speak with Lysander at once!"

"What—" I didn't even get to finish my question before Ellena had disappeared out the door and down the hallway.

I pursed my lips at the door and then returned my attention to the performance below. Onlookers were still murmuring amongst themselves, but no one seemed capable of pulling their eyes away from Nalithor and his violin anymore.

It didn't matter where any of us were from—the whimsical, sweet melody of a love song was something we could all understand. The pure emotion with which Nalithor played was something anyone present could sense.

Even Darius had stopped making a commotion and was watching with an astounded look on his face.

*'Then... Nalithor really meant it when he called me his ayraziis?'* I stared at the Adinvyr deity, speechless.

"You had best put all of your strength into your fight with him, Your Highness." One of the guards by the balcony door laughed. "If you don't display your full power after making a warrior fall for you, you'll be in quite the mess."

"I really don't understand Draemirans." I huffed, stalking over to pick my helm off the table.

*"It is an invitation for you to prove to the people that you are powerful enough to be his 'queen.'"* Djialkan snorted, swooping down from somewhere above to land on the balcony railing. *"Alala called me back to assist. This is not what I was expecting. Nalithor has begun calling you his 'ayraziis' then, has he?"*

"Queen?" I arched an eyebrow at him.

*"A warrior does not simply make a romantic gesture in front of thousands of people."* Djialkan shifted to the form of a boy and then rolled his eyes at me, placing one hand on his hip. *"Furthermore, he was heir to the throne before he became a god. The people of Draemir still expect him to follow the customs he was raised with. Being a deity does not change that he is an Adinvyr."*

"A little warning would've been nice..." I grumbled, tugging my helm over my burning hot face. *'Put all of my power into our fight? We were supposed to restrain ourselves...'*

*"Fight him like you are trying to kill him. Anything else will be insulting."* Djialkan hopped down from the balcony, dropping several stories, and then made his way toward the stage. *'I will help Alala and the Archmagi with the barrier. Knowing the two of you, this fight will get out of hand.'*

When the song ended, the crowd erupted into elated cheering. Even the foreigners who didn't understand the significance of the gesture were roaring and throwing things into the air with the rest of the Draemirans.

Despite Ellena's concerns, the nobles looked quite pleased.

My heart pounded in my throat while I watched Nalithor dismiss his violin. The sideways smirk he shot toward the balcony before turning to fetch his helmet did *not* help matters. I had no idea how to handle or what to do about such an overt display.

It seemed to take forever for the twenty Archmagi, Alala, and Djialkan to take their places on the series of glowing daises. Xander had donned a loose overrobe and joined the procession of Archmagi as well, leaving my brother with just Vivus and the Rylthra man for company.

The crowd burst into a new flurry of whispering while waiting. However, most of the non-Draemirans looked confused as to why Nalithor was still on stage. The Adinvyr in question seemed quite content with himself as he pulled his hair up and then tugged his full helm on. His tail swayed behind him at a relaxed pace while he pulled on his gauntlets and adjusted their fit.

*'Tch. At least I don't have to deal with stupid lines or formal announcements.'* The corner of my eye twitched. I hopped onto the railing of the balcony and adjusted my own gauntlets one last time.

**"Would you all like to meet my ayraziis?"** Nalithor's purred question nearly stopped me in my tracks and ignited my face once more. *'You are so very easy to fluster, my dear.'*

The instant the Archmagi erected a barrier around the stage, I pulled darkness under my feet and launched myself from the balcony. Wind whipped around my armor, accompanied by cobalt flames and wisps of shadow. The crowds below shrieked in excitement and fear when they noticed me.

Nalithor darted away a split second before my ax kick would have met his shoulder. My heel slammed into the ground, sending dirt and an explosion of elements into the air around me. I rushed after Nalithor as soon as both feet hit the ground. My knee grazed across his abdomen. Our armor screeched in protest, ringing in my eardrums for a split second before Nalithor danced out of reach again.

*'You've grown faster.'* Nalithor chuckled.

In a single motion, the Adinvyr summoned his spear and slashed for my throat. I blocked it with my forearm, grabbed the shaft and yanked it toward me, slamming my foot into Nalithor's ribcage in the same motion. He stumbled, giving me time to draw my scythe and pursue him.

Frost trailed behind me and formed into slender blades of ice, following me as I ran across the stage. Nalithor cut the first several in half when I lobbed them at him, but I had already closed the distance between us. Our weapons collided with a deafening clang that traveled down my arms.

The ground beneath us rolled, making me stagger backward and allowing Nalithor to dodge the remainder of my frosty blades. I sensed something behind me and to my right, making me retreat into the shadows. Seconds later, sharp rocks rained down from above.

When I exited the shadows, Nalithor's shin snapped out across my stomach. The force sent me flying back-first into the barrier.

*'Fuck! That actually hurt!'* I dropped to the ground, coughing, before darting away from the downward slash of Nalithor's spear.

*'That's one weapon down,'* Nalithor remarked, motioning to where my scythe laid by one of the Archmagi. *'Let's see how many you have, hmmm?'*

I danced away from Nalithor again and then countered with a kick to his wrist, sending his spear flying into the air. His wings burst from his back as he chased the weapon, but I was quicker. I arced through the air, carried by shadows, and snatched his spear from him.

The weapon was heavier than what I preferred to use, but I could make it work.

Nalithor dodged my strikes with ease and attempted to disarm me. Tendrils of darkness seeped upward from the weapon to prod at my gauntlets, making me curse to myself. I had forgotten his spear's strange fascination with me.

I leapt away from Nalithor again and then turned, chucking the spear as hard as possible at the nearest dais. The blade cut through the barrier as if it were paper and landed blade-first beside Sorr, making the Adinvyr general yelp and scramble backward. The other Archmagi were quick to repair the barrier as Nalithor and I charged each other once more.

Black lightning crackled around Nalithor's fists. He flew into the air high above me and hovered there. I made an upwards motion with two fingers and summoned an angled wall of ice to block the first arrow he fired from his bow. The delay was brief, but it was enough for me to pull new weapons from my jewelry.

*'Flying is cheating,'* I informed him.

*'Against you, it isn't.'* Nalithor laughed.

I crouched briefly and then launched upwards in a whirlwind of darkness, pulling my left hand back to strike. Flames ignited along the edges of both the katar I had summoned. Lightning-infused arrows whizzed past me as I charged straight toward the flying Adinvyr. Nalithor swerved away, so I conjured a platform of shadow and kicked off it to chase him through the air.

Nalithor dodged my strike but flying while holding a bow left him open. My foot hooked around his neck when my kick landed, and the force of my strike sent him hurtling toward the ground. He chose to furl his wings rather than soften his fall. The ground cracked and heaved around where he landed. I caught the sound of him laughing between coughs for air.

If he was laughing, then he was fine.

I flipped in the air and crouched on the underside of one of my platforms, hanging upside-down. Flames trailed behind me when I shot downward toward Nalithor with one of my katar pulled back and ready to strike. A boulder lifted from the ground as I bore down on him, forcing me to turn and destroy it instead of continuing toward Nalithor.

The air reverberated with the familiar sensation of shadowstepping. I managed to turn in time to block Nalithor's strike, but one of his new blades slipped between two plates of my armor and nicked my shoulder. It stung, but it wasn't deep. I could ignore it.

*'Daggers, huh?'* I pulled the blade from where it was still pinched between the plates of armor and then tossed it aside.

*'This armor is cumbersome against you,'* Nalithor spoke in a conversational tone and flipped his remaining dagger in one hand. *'I think we should say to the hells with Mother's suggestion to wear "fancy" armor. What do you think?'*

*'Forget cumbersome. It's too* hot *for this!'* I huffed. *'I don't know about yours, but* mine *is lined with* fur!*'*

Nalithor chucked, his form rippling as he summoned light armor around his body. He looked much like an amused cat while he spun his dagger between his fingers and waited. His hair was still pulled up instead of hanging down his back. I didn't like it. Perhaps I would make fixing that my next goal.

*'That suits you much better.'* Nalithor smirked once I had shifted to my own set of light armor. *'Perhaps one of my prizes should be to have*

*you dance for me? After all, you clearly have the attire for—'*

He trailed off into a laugh and blocked my strike. His expression was positively devious while I chased him across the stage again. Blood dripped from a variety of wounds on both of us, and every strike and counter added new ones to at least one of us if not both.

What must have been several minutes later, a mountain of our weapons laid outside the barrier with the Archmagi. I was down to a pair of zrityr, and Nalithor had summoned two katana. Without any other weapons left to use, I had to either rely solely on magic against his longer weapons…or do what I could with my zrityr's much shorter range.

*'You could just admit defeat.'* Nalithor purred, his eyes tracking the trickle of blood from my throat and down to my chest. *'I can't have you losing too much blood.'*

*'Or* you *could admit defeat,'* I stated, tensing my jaw and shifting into an offensive stance.

*'Very well. If you insist on being stubborn…'* Nalithor darted forward, a smirk on his face as he judged my stance.

I dipped under his strike and slashed upward with my left zrityr, countering his other katana with my right. The edge of my weapon drew a long gash up his torso and sent more blood trickling down his torso. The scent was making my concentration lapse.

Our fight had drawn on far too long and, if it lasted much longer, my growing hunger was going to make me do something stupid.

Nalithor's armored shin lashed out at me, making me backpedal mid-strike. He pursued me and rained down both lightning and shards of rock. It was obvious he was trying to push me somewhere. I wasn't going to let him herd me into a trap.

I slipped into the shadows and dismissed my zrityr before motioning the darkness to lash outward with me when I leapt for the Adinvyr. Tendrils of darkness coiled around his blades and ripped them from his grip, sending them flying out of the barrier in opposite directions. I barreled into Nalithor, knocking him clean off his feet, and sending us both toppling to the ground.

I winced when my head slammed into the ground. My spine and the back of my skull screamed in protest. The impact didn't knock the air from my lungs, but my head certainly hit the soil hard enough to daze me. It took me several long seconds to register Nalithor's hand around my throat and the victorious smirk on his face.

*'You miscalculated your jump.'* Nalithor chuckled, leaning over me.

*'As if that wasn't obvious,'* I grumbled, glancing between us to find that he had nestled himself comfortably between my thighs. *'I guess I won't be kicking you off me.'*

*'Are you going to try to fight me if I let you up?'* Nalithor paused, studying me as his blood dripped onto my face. *'Ahhh... Someone is hungry I see.'*

Nalithor rose to his feet and pulled me with him. He looked like he was going to say something but fell silent when I rose onto my tiptoes to reach behind him and pull his hair tie loose.

"That's better." I smiled, letting his hair fall down his back and around his shoulders. "I can't have my *nylziis* hiding his hair when he makes such a fuss over mine, now can I?"

"We should see to our wounds before I claim my prizes." Nalithor grinned before turning to address the Archmagi. "You may lower the barriers now."

"You both fight like monsters!" One of the next performers exclaimed when we strode by.

"Of course they do!" A man snorted, rolling his eyes at the woman. "How else would they fight *against* monsters, hmmm? Use your head!"

"You are both an absolute mess!" Ellena swept toward us, her delighted expression contradicting her firm tone. "Arianna, I didn't know you knew how to wield zrityr! You should spar with me some time—I would love to see how much you were taught."

*"Ellena is right; you are both filthy,"* Djialkan stated, approaching us while carrying Alala in his arms. *"Fraelfnir tells me you did something foolish while I was away. However, it appears that Darius has not caught on quite yet."*

"We fought like *that,* and the boy's suspicions weren't piqued?" Nalithor turned to frown at Djialkan.

*"Whatever sort of performance you two put on at Erist's temple..."* Djialkan sighed, his shoulders slumping as he shook his head in disbelief. *"Darius now believes that you have taken control of Arianna completely. Mind and body. He believes that Arianna has gone from being a X'shmiran slave to a god's slave."*

"Bah, that boy!" Ellena huffed, crossing her arms.

"We should—" Nalithor started.

"—enjoy your night while you can." A male voice interjected from behind us. "You are leaving first thing tomorrow morning."

We both turned to look at Lucifer as he approached us. The nearby soldiers saluted him as he passed, while Ellena nodded her acknowledgment of the emperor. Lucifer was dressed in full imperial regalia and yet still managed to move with feline grace despite the weight. Silver armor glinted along his forearms, shoulders, and the front of his high boots. His bi-colored eyes were alert and focused as they flicked around our surroundings.

After a moment, Lucifer lifted a hand and dismissed the guards. Once they were gone, the air around us rippled and shimmered as a barrier settled into place around us.

"What do you mean?" Nalithor questioned, frowning. "I thought Arianna and I weren't leaving for our post until after Faerstravir ends?"

"That *was* the plan, but we have a new problem," Lucifer replied, shaking his head. "Tomorrow morning you are to leave for the western edges of Vorpmasian territory. The group of Exiles that attacked Suthsul's western borders were spotted heading north and toward the empire.

"We're shifting our forces to protect Ryrun, Ee'nir, and Krae'lh. I want the two of you to scout past our borders and see if you can determine whether or not the Exiles have set up a hole for themselves in Falrrsald."

"Falrrsald? Are you certain?" Nalithor crossed his arms, his brow furrowing.

"The tribes still want nothing to do with us. They said that they will allow you into Falrrsald, but they are unwilling to share their hiding places." Lucifer sighed, his pose pensive. "Chaos Beasts will be the least of your concern while traveling. I would rather not send Arianna with you to such a dangerous place, but…"

"But there are no other demigods crazy enough to venture into Falrrsald in search of Exiles, right?" Nalithor asked dryly before turning to look at me. "I doubt you would allow someone else to accompany me anyway."

"Not happening," I confirmed. "We fight well together. Throwing in someone new would just be a hindrance for you."

"Separating a nylziis from his ayraziis would enrage the Draemiran nobility," Ellena added with a deep frown. "They are much more old fashion in that regard than the commoners. Arom would probably throw a fit as well—and Erist by extension."

*'Didn't the Exiles attack beasts? Not the Suthsul borders themselves?'* I glanced at Nalithor.

*'The Elders won't question my interference if we're there to protect Vorpmasia,'* Nalithor answered, sighing. *'Exiles have been known to sway mortals and bring them into the fold—that is something the Elders want stopped at all costs. Tribal villages make good prey for the Exiles.'*

"Falrrsald is dangerous, Arianna." Lucifer turned to look at me with concern. "You will need to be on guard at all times and stick close to Nalithor.

"I would have preferred that you did not go to such a place while still sealed. However, of the remaining pairs available for me to send, the two of you are the strongest."

*"Alala and I will discuss how best to handle this situation,"* Djialkan stated, shooting Nalithor and me a look in turn. *"The two of you should heal yourselves, bathe, and then determine how you are going to spend the rest of your evening."*

"Djialkan, I wish to speak with you anyway." Lucifer turned to look at the fae-dragon. "We can discuss the particulars of their mission afterward, and then you can pass it on to them."

*"Very well."* Djialkan nodded and then strode over to the emperor. *"Alala wishes to hear the details as well."*

After a few murmured farewells, Ellena left to rejoin Lysander in overseeing the festivities and Lucifer, Djialkan, and Alala left for the emperor's Draemiran estate. I let out a small sigh and then turned my attention to Nalithor. We both still had blood trickling from some of our deeper wounds, but the flow was sluggish at this point.

"Shall we?" I took a few steps toward Nalithor and nudged his bloodied arm. *"Before* I bite you wherever I please?"

"You're not even the victor, and you're considering taking a bite?" Nalithor arched an eyebrow at me and then smiled. "Very well. We can't properly enjoy Faerstravir while we're both a mess." He paused and glanced to the side, a grimace flashing across his features. *'Strange... Vampires shouldn't be drawn by your Devillian blood. Come here, I'll fly us back to the palace.'*

*'Isn't it poison to them?'* I frowned and moved closer to the Adinvyr, allowing him to pick me up.

*'They rather desperately want a taste of your blood…and other things.'* Nalithor's grip on my thigh twitched. He growled and shot a glare toward a nearby structure. *'Hold on tight.'*

I tucked myself into Nalithor's chest as the ground grew distant. It took most of my concentration to keep myself from taking a taste of the blood running down his skin. His chest rumbled with laughter when I turned my face away. I pouted, gnawing the inside of my cheek.

All I could really do at this point was hope that we arrived before I gave into temptation.

*'Will we be passing through Krae'lh, Ee'nir, or Ryrun on our way to Falrrsald?'* I inquired, attempting to distract myself.

*'That depends on whether Lucifer sees fit to have an airship shuttle us to our borders with Falrrsald,'* Nalithor answered, his tone contemplative. *'Ee'nir is Rylthra territory, Krae'lh belongs to the Jrachra, and Ryrun belongs to the Imviir. They are all Devillian races loyal to the empire, but traversing their lands can be…a chore.'*

*'How long do you think we'll be away for?'*

*'If we don't take an airship it will take at least a week just to get to Falrrsald.'* Nalithor sighed as he landed outside of his section of the palace. He nudged the doors open with one foot before continuing, *'Ryrun is mostly swamp and jungle, Ee'nir is all jungle. Krae'lh borders both territories and extends into the Suthsul Desert itself.'*

*'So none of them are pleasant to walk through on foot.'* I grimaced.

*'You think Lucifer might send us on foot anyway?'*

*'It depends on how much investigating he wants us to do—and where.'* Nalithor snorted. *'He may want us to look for traces of Exile interference in those territories on our way through. If not...we are still looking at a very long airship ride.'*

"In other words, I will be either very bored or sleep a lot," I mused as Nalithor pushed open the door to the bath and carried me in.

"How's your back?" Nalithor asked, setting me down with care.

"Might have a few bruises." I dismissed my armor into my jewelry as I walked toward the edge of the bath. "Though that's probably true for both of us, hmmm?"

"You were quite rough." Nalithor laughed. "If anyone challenges either of us after *that* display... I do believe we can dismiss them as incredibly stupid."

"We weren't doing that already?" I glanced over my shoulder at him before wading into the bath.

"Let's make this quick," Nalithor stated as he stripped off his own armor. "I wouldn't want you to miss out on enjoying at least *some* of what Faerstravir has to offer."

In some ways, Nalithor seemed even more distracted than me while we healed each other and bathed. I couldn't determine if he was just feeling affectionate, or if he was hungry, but he kept nibbling and kissing my damp skin while healing me.

Eventually, we were both healed, and I hopped onto the ledge of the bath to wring the water from my curls.

Once finished, I shifted to pull my legs out of the water and stand up. Nalithor, however, seemed to have another idea. He gripped my hips and scooted me closer to the edge instead. I didn't know what to make of the mischievous expression on his face.

"What...?" My face reddened when Nalithor nuzzled into my stomach.

"I'm hungry..." Nalithor purred, sliding his hands down my thighs and to my knees. "I think it's time for my first prize."

Nalithor pulled my legs apart and chuckled deviously before kissing down to my inner thigh. I wasn't sure what the Adinvyr was planning to do with me, and that only served to spur my mind into running through the possibilities. Nalithor lifted my leg over his shoulder and nipped at my inner thigh, chuckling when I twitched in response.

"W-what are you doing?" I managed to ask. My face grew hotter when Nalithor shot me a suggestive glance.

"I decided this is where I'm going to bite you next." Nalithor paused to run his tongue over a patch of skin surprisingly high up my thigh, then smirked at me again. "Do you have a problem with that?"

"N-no, it's just—" I bit back a gasp when his fangs sunk deep into my skin.

It wasn't long before he withdrew to lap at the trickle of blood, a low purr rumbling in his throat. However, I wasn't prepared for his fingers to trace down my slit. He managed to startle a squeak out of me, earning him a sharp glare.

"Mmm... I *was* going to take a taste of *that* instead, but then we would be here all night." Nalithor teased. He released my thigh and pulled himself out of the water until his face was level with mine.

"You say that like it's a bad thing." I pouted, glancing to the side when he planted a kiss on my cheek.

"I'll take the time to 'savor' you later." Nalithor laughed and moved away from me, heading for the stairs that led out of the bath. "Let's get you dressed, then we can go back into the city."

"You still haven't told me what you want your other prize to be." I pulled myself to my feet and then glanced down at the indentations his fangs had left behind. *Well, I guess it will be easier to cover than if he'd bitten my throat again... B-but really, a taste of that instead? I can't tell if he's just teasing me again or if he's serious!'*

"Hmmm, my second prize..." Nalithor murmured to himself while pulling on a pair of boxers.

I dried myself off and pulled on a fresh set of undergarments while Nalithor thought. When he still didn't say anything, I glanced over to see that he appeared lost in his thoughts. His tail swayed slowly behind him while his eyes ticked back and forth as if he was reading something.

"Shall we accept Sorr's dinner invitation?" I asked, watching as Nalithor's tail jerked and he turned to look at me with surprise. "You haven't gotten to talk to your friends much since coming home, and we have to leave in the morning. I'm sure you'd like to spend at least *some* time with them."

"Not as my second prize," Nalithor stated as I strode past him and headed for the doors. "For my second prize, let's see…" He paused as we left the bath and walked down the hallway to his rooms. "I want you to share my rooms and my bed with me in earnest, and not just because I'm protecting you."

"Share…?" I glanced over my shoulder at him, surprised.

"Not just here in Draemir. I want you to share my bed when traveling and when in Dauthrmir as well," Nalithor confirmed with a small smile. "Do you really think I would want my ayraziis to sleep away from me?"

"Well, when you put it that way…" I murmured, adjusting one of my bra straps while we walked into his wardrobe. "Are you certain that's what you want as your *prize*? All you had to do was ask me. You could choose something else as your prize. Either way, if that's what you want as your prize, I'll happily accept."

"Mmm, good." Nalithor lifted me up by my waist and nuzzled into my shoulder, purring. "Are you certain you don't mind coming to dinner with us? I know you said before that you were unsure about it."

"I don't want to leave you alone, and I don't want to be left alone." I pouted when he set me down and turned to the nearest rack of clothes. Sighing, I hopped up onto the counter.

"Alright." Nalithor chuckled. "We'll get dressed in something appropriate for the festival and then we can leave. Let's take care not to stay out too late—we'll want to get an early start tomorrow morning."

*'Krae'lh, Ryrun, Ee'nir, and Falrrsald huh?'* I mused, swinging my legs back and forth while watching Nalithor search for clothes. "Traveling on foot might not be so bad, but I get the feeling that Lucifer wants us to be in Falrrsald as soon as possible. I assume we will be walking anyway once we arrive, right?"

"Yes, and we will have to be careful while there," Nalithor answered without turning. "The monsters that roam Falrrsald are arguably more dangerous than beasts are. From what we understand, the tribes have hiding places that the monsters are incapable of reaching or fitting into. However, the tribes are not keen on Devillians and do not wish to share such places with us. We will have to find an alternative."

"Do we need to worry about the tribes picking a fight with us?" I frowned at Nalithor, tracking him as he turned to set a few garments on the counter beside me.

"They will believe we are both gods when they see our Brands." Nalithor pivoted to rummage through the wardrobe again. "In some regions I may have to shift and disguise myself as a Human or an Elf. As for you..." He paused to glance at me. "Hmmm... They will probably think that you are only part Devillian. You might need to masquerade as my slave in those situations."

"Slave-slave, or...?" I tilted my head.

"Yes—slave as in an *actual* slave." Nalithor sighed, grimacing. "I'll have plenty of time to regale you with the details on our way to Falrrsald no matter which method of travel we take. For now, let's focus on Faerstravir and enjoy ourselves.

"The festival will be long over by the time we return to Vorpmasian soil."

# CHAPTER TWENTY-EIGHT
## *Friends and Family*

"Hey, you two made it!" Sorr grinned and waved for us to join him.

Incense burners within the private room released tendrils of smoke coiling through the air, filling the room with a rich floral scent. The room was warmed by a crackling fire. Plush furniture surrounded the fireplace, creating a welcoming nook. Furs and leathers gave the room a cozy feel despite the hints of richness that came from the occasional hints of brocade, velvet, and gleaming metal or crystal fixtures.

The Adinvyr, as a people, seemed to have a penchant for mixing their hunting culture with hints of extravagance and art. I certainly didn't mind—it gave Draemir a much different air than Dauthrmir.

Aside from Sorr, Belttur, Thys, Rhyr, Eyrian, Xander, *and* Ijelle were all present. They had changed out of the more formal, armored robes they had worn during my fight with Nalithor, and now wore casual attire.

Well, as casual as I'd ever seen a Devillian wear, at least.

Most of them seemed alert, perhaps even a little on edge, but Xander and Ijelle were both engrossed by the scantily clad Devillian dancers present.

"Xander, you alright?" Nalithor called to the Vampire.

"Hmmm?" Xander glanced away from the dancers when they flinched and stopped dancing. "Oh, you saw that? Our favorite bratty prince couldn't kick his way out of a paper bag. Figured I'd make it more dramatic for fun."

Nalithor sighed and shook his head at Xander. The Vampire just grinned and returned his attention to the dancers; one of whom approached me with a nervous look on her face.

"R-Reiz'tar, we didn't know you would be coming," the Adinvyr woman stuttered, bowing deeply. "Shall I fetch some of our male dancers for you?"

"Not necessary." I shook my head and then motioned to Nalithor. "I hardly need more entertainment when I have this one around."

"I-if you insist, Reiz'tar..." The dancer looked to the side at the Adinvyr generals and wrung her shaky hands. She looked as if she wanted to say something but instead returned to the other dancers.

"I didn't think you two would make it," Eyrian remarked, shooting Nalithor an irritated glance.

"Right? How are you two not exhausted after a fight like that?" Ijelle piped up.

"Hmmm? But that was just light sparring..." I tilted my head and looked at Ijelle. "Besides, there's no time to be tired when fighting beasts. If you think our fight was tiring you might want to consider working on your stamina."

"Nalithor spoils her too much," Rhyr stated in a matter-of-fact tone.

"She hasn't gotten to fight any beasts by herself yet." Thys nodded his agreement.

"T-there were plenty of beasts on the Nrae'lmar Continent!" Ijelle snapped.

"Did you fight any on your own?" Belttur cut his gaze to the side at Ijelle.

"Of course not! We had an army of Archmagi and soldiers with us!" Ijelle huffed.

"So they are right—you haven't fought any beasts on your own yet." Nalithor chuckled and ruffled Ijelle's hair as he strode past her. "You still have a great deal of training to complete before you can fight the way Arianna and I do.

"Now that you're back from your expedition, you can return to training at the academy in Dauthrmir. You *are* powerful, but you have a way yet to go before you master that power."

"That aside, your fight was hardly 'light sparring,' Arianna-jiss." Sorr shot me a grin. "When you smacked into the barrier, I wasn't sure what would break first—you or the magic!"

"I've been thrown harder by beasts. I'll manage." I shrugged.

"Should I be offended?" Nalithor arched an eyebrow at me.

"I suppose that depends on how severe a sadist you are," I answered with an innocent smile.

'I can assure you that I am not that cruel,' Nalithor responded dryly before settling on a sofa by the fire and making himself comfortable.

"Rely'ric, do you require—" One of the dancers started to sashay toward the sofa.

"Do I *look* like I require your company?" Nalithor bared his fangs, growled, and pulled me down onto the sofa beside him. He maintained a threatening glare on the dancer throughout the display.

The dancer shrieked and ran across the room to rejoin her fellow entertainers. Darkness rippled around Nalithor as he continued to growl. He pulled me closer to his side and tensed his grip, making me wonder just what had him so on edge. Nalithor's possessive behavior sent the dancers into a flurry of hushed whispers, but I couldn't hear them over the music or over the conversations our companions were having.

"So, what brings you two here after *those* displays?" Sorr leaned forward in his chair and grinned, resting his elbows on his knees.

"We need some privacy." Nalithor turned his gaze toward the dancers—all of whom froze like frightened deer.

"Y-yes, Rely'ric!" The dancers yelped and fled from the room so fast that they almost tripped over each other in their haste.

*'Is there a reason they're so frightened of you?'* I glanced at him when he chuckled.

*'They are scared of* you, *not me,'* Nalithor answered. The moment the women were out the door, he made a motion with one hand and conjured a shimmering barrier to coat the walls of the room. "There... That's better."

"Awww, but they were fun to watch!" Ijelle pouted and slumped back in her seat.

"You'll have plenty of time for performers later." Nalithor shook his head at his sister before turning his attention to the generals. "Lucifer cut our vacation short—Arianna and I will be leaving for Falrrsald in the morning."

"You're going *where*?!" Eyrian shot to his feet, his draconic tail sending his chair toppling over. "I don't care *how* proficient you two are in combat. Going to Falrrsald as a pair is far too dangerous! Unpleasant natives aside, the monsters are like to crush you both!"

"At the very least, Lucifer should assign another pair or two to accompany you." Thys frowned, tapping his claws against his crossed arms. "You can disguise yourself as a Human, but Arianna-jiss can't. If the natives think she is of mixed blood—"

"*When* they think she's mixed blood," Belttur corrected.

"—you're going to have to fight off an entire village of savages!" Thys continued, his face twisting in distaste. "They're already difficult enough with their fears of Devillians and deities. Yet, if you stay out in the wilds..."

"Staying in the wilds is questionable at best," Rhyr muttered in thought. "Of course, the Elders would have a conniption fit if you utilized your personal domain as a 'camp' every night. Are you certain that Lucifer will only let the two of you go?"

"We're the only ones he can spare to go to Falrrsald." Nalithor nodded before reclining beside me and stretching before continuing, "It may not be ideal, but I believe Arianna and I can manage by ourselves. That said, Faerstravir will be long over by the time we return—and we will have to make our way straight to the capitol to report."

"Tch. So, you two are going to Falrrsald, and I'm going to X'shmir." Eyrian grimaced, drawing my attention to him. "Just what did we do to get stuck with assignments like these?"

*'You're quiet. Are you still paying attention?'* Nalithor nudged me with his tail, his gaze flicking to the side at me before refocusing on our companions. After a few moments, he held a drink out to me.

*'I'm still listening.'* I accepted the glass from him and then settled into my corner of the sofa. *'Falrrsald sounds interesting... However, I'm a little more concerned about how my brother will handle being in Dauthrmir on his lonesome.*

*'I also had a thought about Darius, but I'm not sure if the Archmagi can take much more of his whining. Hells, I'm his sister, and I know I can't.'*

"Is that all the confidential talk you had in mind, Nali?" Sorr motioned at the wall closest to him. "Our servers will get cross if they can't, ya'know, serve us."

"Arianna?" Nalithor nudged me, earning curious looks from our companions. *'They* are *all Archmagi, after all.'*

"I want my brother tested again now that his power of persuasion is sealed," I stated flatly, causing a few of the men to stare at me in surprise. Xander simply sighed and reached for his drink. "Call it a hunch if you like, but I believe that Darius' results were actually higher than they should have been. I also don't believe the Oracles were correct in their assessments."

"Was his power really *that* strong?" Thys looked to Nalithor, frowning.

"Darius' power of persuasion was strong enough to lure Middle and Upper Gods to do his bidding." Nalithor made a sour face, shaking his head. "I know the brat has been tested twice already, but Arianna's concerns are valid. It's quite possible that Darius' ability skewed his results. Intentional or not."

"I'm inclined to agree," Xander muttered after taking a large swig of his drink. "He isn't in any of my classes, so I can't speak much in regards to his power aside from what I've heard from you and Vivus.

"However, Vivus and I both noticed that Darius' behavior doesn't quite match up with the Oracles' 'assessments' as the princess put it."

"Spare us the details." Nalithor shot the Vampire an annoyed glare.

"Hells, I'm still stuck on the fact you two are going to *Falrrsald!*" Ijelle sighed, throwing her hands in the air. "I've barely seen you this past year, Nali, and now you're going to *that* place? Not only that, but you're taking this dainty little thing with you? Beasts and monsters aside, you're looking at so much trouble just from the natives and slavers in the region. *Furthermore*, Arianna's seals are weakening aren't they? What will you do if—"

'*Well, she has a point there,*' I thought to myself. '*The fact that Gabriel removed my seals could pose a problem—but Lucifer knows that. Either the situation in Falrrsald is important enough to risk it, or he doesn't think it will pose much of a problem...*'

"We will have to address those issues if and when they arise." Nalithor shook his head at his sister. "For now, I would like to enjoy what little of Faerstravir I can with friends and family."

After a few mumbled protests, the generals and Ijelle relented. Nalithor sighed and let his barrier fall before pivoting to pull me closer to his side. I managed not to spill my drink when he slid me across the sofa, but I shot him an irritated look anyway. He just chuckled and nestled his arm behind my back, allowing his hand to come to rest on my hip.

'*Something bothering you?*' I asked, tracking several tendrils of magic as they slipped away from Nalithor and slithered out the nearby window.

'*I dislike the number of Vampires in the city,*' Nalithor murmured, glancing toward the wall of windows and then over to Xander. '*I had Xander look into it—they don't appear to be allied with Beshulthien, and it's unlikely they're allied with Vorpmasia.*'

'*Aren't you supposed to be* relaxing *instead of looking for trouble?*' I nudged him and then flourished my drink. *'Also, are you* trying *to get me drunk? This is very strong.'*

*'We won't have time for drinking while in Falrrsald. We may as well enjoy ourselves now.'* Nalithor chuckled. *'However, varikna* is *quite strong. Would you prefer something milder?'*

*'Too late. You'll just have to take responsibility for me if this makes me hammered,'* I informed him.

"Arianna, is there anything I should know before going to X'shmir?" Eyrian questioned. His expression was unreadable when he looked between Nalithor and me a few times.

"Aside from the fact you'll want to kill everyone?" I tilted my head, watching a small smile tug at the Draekin's lips. "It's difficult to say. Before Vorpmasia landed on our doorstep, most of the commoners believed that gods were incorporeal—or that they didn't exist at all. The concept of demigods has been lost to history.

"How they react during your extended stay honestly depends on how much they've learned over the past few months—and when Dilonu, Tyana, and the nobles are returning to the city. Most of the commoners are terrified of the royal court. They'll be less scared of *you* than they are of Adinvyr…but they will still do their best to avoid you. More so once the royal court has returned to X'shmir."

"We're still not permitted near Sihix, either." Eyrian sighed and ran a hand through his shaggy hair. "Is there any way for us to contact the people of the forest from outside? Or…"

"Not that I can disclose." I shook my head. "You could try sending a message with their next round of supplies, but there's no guarantee they'll be willing to speak with any of you. There's also the issue of whether or not you can get to any of their meeting places discreetly."

"Bah, enough serious talk!" Sorr slammed his tankard down on the table. "If we're all separating again, we should make the most of Faerstravir!"

"In other words 'let's get drunk' in Sorr-speak." Xander grinned.

"Or 'let's get fat.' He does love his food," Rhyr offered.

"It's Sorr, it's both," Belttur and Thys stated in unison.

"It's what festivals are for!" Sorr huffed, his face turning a red to rival his hair. "Nali, Ari, when you two come back from Falrrsald you better invite us all to your hunt celebration. Got it?!"

"When you return, you're both required to fight us the way you fight each other." Belttur shot Nalithor a sharp glare. "I didn't think Xander was serious when he told us that you fight Arianna more seriously than any of us, but your display proved he's right."

"I'm with Belttur on this one." Rhyr growled, his cup cracking in his hand. "We should challenge you two right now!"

"There's nowhere *in* the city where we could fight them, Rhyr." Thys grinned and clamped a hand on his friend's shoulder. "We'll just have to be patient and train until Arianna-jiss and Nalithor come back."

"So, no more fighting tonight?" I grumbled, slumping against Nalithor's side. "I could go for a few more rounds. It's not really a problem as long as we can find somewhere to fight."

"We'll be doing plenty of fighting in Falrrsald—save your strength." Nalithor laughed and squeezed me once before picking up a bottle of varikna. "Very well. When Arianna and I return, we can have a proper celebration—brawls and all."

"I want in on it too!" Ijelle leaned forward, grinning. "The way you fight with Ari makes it look like you're handling an *infant* when you spar me! I won't stand for that."

"But—" Nalithor started with a sigh.

*'They'll never improve if they don't get their asses handed to them on occasion,'* I interjected, pulling my legs up on the sofa before leaning into Nalithor's chest. *'It's better for them to get their tails kicked in a controlled environment instead of by beasts—or worse—right?'*

"Very well." Nalithor sighed again. "If that's what you want, then—"

"I thought you two were going to *kill* each other, you know," Ijelle interrupted, pointing between us and narrowing her eyes. "Now you're being all cozy as if nothing happened! Your strikes were aimed at each other's vital points, so why—"

"You'll understand if you ever find your own ayraziis, Ijelle." Rhyr patted the princess's head, earning an irritated growl from her. He ignored her growling and looked back to Nalithor and me instead. "Under other conditions, the two of you would have fought even rougher than that, wouldn't you?"

"And without Mother's 'rules' that were made for the sake of entertainment," Nalithor muttered, nodding once.

"Well, it's no secret that Ellena-z'tar can be a bit…pushy." Thys shook his head and grimaced. "Still, it was an interesting experience. You're both formidable in your own right. I'd be curious to see what you two can do without restrictions."

"Aye. Quite a few times there I thought Arianna-jiss was going to be the victor." Sorr grinned broadly. "It's refreshing to see a woman that fights with real weapons. Too many women these days rely on daggers and poison."

"Let's hurry with dinner and then go see what Faerstravir has to offer us this year, hmmm?" Nalithor offered with a small smile. "Preferably *before* Sorr and Eyrian get too drunk."

*'Or before I get too drunk to remember any of it,'* I added dryly, glancing at Nalithor when he slid his hand from my hip to my thigh. *'That said, is it alright for us to take the night off like this? Shouldn't we be preparing?'*

*'It will be fine.'* Nalithor chuckled, smoothing his hand along my leg until I twitched. *'You can sleep on the airship—if we take one. Otherwise, I can just carry you while you rest.'*

"O-oh… You're *all* here?" Darius' uneasy comment caught my attention, making me glance away from Nalithor and to the doorway. "Ari, I really need to talk to you about—"

"I'll allow it. Make it quick." Nalithor cut my brother off and shot him a murderous glare. "I'm already of half a mind to kill you for your treatment of Xander—my brother. If you try anything with Arianna, I will have you begging for death."

"She's my *sister*! I wouldn't try to hurt—" Darius protested.

"You've already tried to hurt or otherwise kill her several times that I am aware of." Nalithor snarled his response. He shifted his focus to me and pulled me closer, lifting my face toward his. ***"Don't let him keep you from me for long."***

Nalithor gripped my jaw and pulled me into what I could only describe as a "possessive" kiss. It made me disinclined to leave his side. Instead, I leaned in for another kiss, earning a devious chuckle from the Adinvyr. He shifted his hand to my throat and kept me just out of reach.

"Now, now. Go deal with your brother first." Nalithor purred, studying me. "Perhaps after you return you can earn another."

*'You enjoy pissing my brother off a little too much,'* I informed Nalithor before pulling myself off his lap and striding over to my fuming brother.

*'Not as much as I enjoy your taste, I assure you,'* Nalithor teased.

Darius grabbed me by the arm and pulled me down the hall to an empty room. He suddenly embraced me, squeezing me so tight that my spine popped. He was shaking. I just stood there for a moment and waited for him to let me go. Nothing I could think of was reason enough for him to hug me like *that*.

"Ari, we've gotta get you away from Nalithor as quickly as possible." Darius gripped my shoulders and held me at arm's length. "He's been using small tastes of his blood—and thus his venom—to enslave you! The other Draemirans seem swell enough, but *he* is—"

"*Enslave* me?" I demanded in disbelief. "Coming from the one who doesn't know how to be a proper dom? Don't give me that look; I *saw* you kick Xander. You *do* realize he's technically part of the Vraelimir Family, don't you? You kicked a *prince*."

"You called Nalithor '*Master!*' He said you're his pet!" Darius argued, stomping his foot. "The Ari I know wouldn't let anyone enslave her like that. Not after all the X'shmirans have put us through. You—"

"*Slave* and *pet* are two very different things, Darius." I sighed at him, lifting my fingers to my temples. "Hells, even the type of 'slave' you are thinking about is *entirely* different."

"*You are attempting to compare* real *slavery with a type of* willing *submissive, Darius,*" Fraelfnir snapped. The white fae-dragon appeared on *my* shoulder of all places and glowered at my twin. "*I told you this before we came here! A 'pet' is loved, cherished, protected, and cared for by his or her 'owner' or 'master'. It is a deeper and more trusting form of relationship than even some marriages back in X'shmir. A pet is a* willing *submissive and* not *a slave of any sort.*"

"Like the shiny one said." I scratched Fraelfnir's chin, arching an eyebrow when he purred.

"You still expect me to believe that *you*, of all people, are a submissive?" Darius crossed his arms.

"Only when someone's earned it—along with my trust and respect." I shrugged the shoulder opposite to Fraelfnir. "Whether you like it or not, I won't be leaving Nalithor's side any time soon. Not only do I *want* to remain with him, but we've been assigned our first mission. We leave in the morning."

"A mission?" Darius' eyes widened. "Take me with you! Someone has to keep that monster—"

"Ahhnn? Monster?" I grinned crookedly. "Did you really expect the God of *Balance* to be *all* good? If 'Good' begins winning too much, it's *my Master's* job to fix the problem, you know.

"Ah… Or were you referring to *that?*"

"That?" Darius paused. His face burned scarlet when he realized what I was referring to. **"No, I wasn't talking about that at all, you pervert!"**

I laughed when Darius bolted out the door and slammed it shut behind him. Fraelfnir nosed my cheek to draw my attention to him, so I stifled my laughter and looked to the scaly one.

*"I will do what I can to keep the boy from ruining our relations with the Rilzaan Alliance."* Fraelfnir sighed and hung his head. *"He is in contact with someone who appears to be feeding him misinformation. For some reason, I am incapable of listening in on their conversations. However, Darius appears to trust this person more than anyone else.*

*"Be careful on your mission, Arianna. Your seals are…almost nonexistent. They will not take much more stress."*

"Fraelfnir," I called when the fae-dragon lifted into the air from my shoulder. "Darius' sealing was successful?"

*"Aye, it was."* Fraelfnir nodded to me. *"I am to report to the deities if the seal is damaged, breaks, or vanishes."*

"Darius is going to be tested for a third time at the academy," I informed the fae-dragon, watching a thoughtful expression cross his scaly features. "Would you do me a favor and accompany him? I want us to be entirely certain that nothing is interfering with his tests, the Archmagi, or the Oracles."

*"Very well,"* Fraelfnir agreed. *"I intend to keep a close eye on the boy anyway, as does his new escort."*

With a few mumbled goodbyes, Fraelfnir and I parted ways. The fae-dragon's behavior struck me as odd—normally he didn't want to be near me or my darkness. I shoved the matter to the back of my mind while approaching the room Nalithor and his friends were in.

When I nudged open the door, I found that Nalithor had already grown irritable. He was still lounging on the sofa, but his arms were crossed, and the lower half of his tail was twitching.

"That *brat* thinks that I've been *drugging you* with my blood?" Nalithor growled, his rising anger causing the fireplace's flames to turn pale blue and flare upward.

"So you *were* listening." I nodded and slid the door closed behind me before returning to the sofa.

The moment I was within reach, Nalithor grabbed me and pulled me onto his lap. He nuzzled into my shoulder with another low growl and coiled his tail around my hips. Nalithor crushed me against his chest for several long moments before loosening his grip enough for me to settle into a more comfortable position. Once I stopped readjusting myself, he offered me a new glass of varikna.

"Nalithor is scary when it comes to you." Eyrian shook his head, then sighed. "Can't say I blame him either. Not with the way Dariuszir has been behaving."

"Are you sure I can't squash that brat like a bug?" Ijelle growled, looking over my head at her brother. "Someone needs to teach him some respect!"

"Not yet." Nalithor chuckled. "I will get around to it eventually."

*'You're comfy...'* I rubbed my cheek into Nalithor's shoulder.

*'Not going to sleep already, are you?'* Nalithor paused, tensing when my lips brushed against his throat. *'Now, now... None of that. I can't have you taking a bite out of me while you're in that form. Nor is it the way I would* prefer *for you to feed.'*

*'Not my fault you smell like dessert.'* I shifted so that I was no longer facing his throat. *'Just how long do we have to wait for dinner to get here? We have a lot of stuff to go see, don't we?'*

*'Yes, we do,'* Nalithor confirmed, petting my waist as he spoke. *'Performers, artisans, games, grand displays of culture and battle... Don't eat too much, you will want to try some of the street food, I assure you.'*

"Where do you think we should start, Nali?" Sorr waved a map at us. "Near the Scarlet District, then work our way inward to the rest of the city?"

"That would probably be best," Nalithor replied, nodding. "However, we shouldn't stray too close to the Scarlet District. Several of the workers have already shown an unhealthy amount of interest in the violent one here."

"Unhealthy amount of interest?" Eyrian arched an eyebrow and glanced down at me. "For her or for them?"

"They offered her their services for free." Nalithor huffed, pulling me close and tightening his grip. "That they would be willing to pursue her when not on the job is—"

"She's cute *and,* she's dangerous. We're Adinvyr. Are you really that surprised?" Belttur interjected, giving Nalithor a look. "If you hadn't already claimed her as your ayraziis, everyone in this room would likely be—"

"I'm not *cute!*" I snapped, shooting Belttur a glare. "Not cute. Not adorable. Next person to call me either of those things is getting torn into tiny little—"

"But you *are*—" Nalithor didn't get to finish his sentence before I had shifted and pinned him to the sofa. I dug the nails of my free hand into his chest and steadied my drink with the other. "Come now, it's a *good* thing, Arianna. I don't mean it as—"

"Not. Adorable." The corner of my eye twitched when Nalithor lifted his hands to grip my hips. "I can kill things larger than *buildings* for fuck's sake! 'Cute' or 'adorable' isn't really a fitting term for someone capable of that!"

"Small things are adorable, and you're small." Ijelle pointed between Nalithor and me when I shot her a glare. "I mean, look at you two! You're— Eek!"

Ijelle leapt away from her seat by the fire when the flames turned cobalt and lashed out at her.

'*Behave.*' Nalithor chuckled, sliding his hands up from my hips and to my waist so that he could lift me off him. '*Belttur is right—we are Adinvyr. Those things make you adorable to us. Worthy of adoration, admiration. Attractive.*

'*Perhaps Humans use it in a different way than we do?*'

I huffed at Nalithor as he sat me down beside him once more. If I hadn't been holding a glass in one hand still, I would have crossed my arms. I couldn't think of an argument if he and the others meant "adorable" in the literal sense of the word. Nalithor was correct, however—I was used to hearing it in a patronizing way and not in a genuine one.

Thankfully, dinner arrived soon, and my frustrated outburst was soon forgotten. I was famished and set about devouring everything in sight the moment I was able. My companions seemed content to eat at a slower pace and converse with each other.

No matter how much Draemiran cuisine I ate, it seemed like I couldn't get my fill.

'*Tch, that's a problem...*' I grumbled to myself while picking through a platter of desserts. '*Just how much food do I need? Or is it...*'

My thoughts seemed to pause when Nalithor drew his fingers down my spine and nuzzled into the crook of my neck. The varikna had already made my thoughts fuzzy, but even without it, Nalithor was a difficult man to ignore. I glanced to the side at him when he pulled me closer, the sudden motion almost causing me to drop my plate of desserts.

*'What happened to "behaving?"'* I suppressed a shiver as his lips traveled down my throat. *'This isn't conducive to seeing what the festival has to offer.'*

*'Only because you are so sensitive.'* Nalithor teased when I shied away from his nibbling. *'You can bring your sweets with you. We should get going before you get any more distracted.'*

*'Says the one who distracts me on purpose!'* I huffed, tucking my sweets into a colorful bag. *'Ah, drinks?'*

*'We'll find you something interesting to try with the street food.'* Nalithor chuckled, tousling my hair as he stood and walked past me. *'I can't have you getting too tipsy yet.'*

With another huff, I rose to my feet and followed Nalithor, Ijelle, Eyrian, Xander, and the four Adinvyr generals out of the restaurant and into the streets of Draemir. The sounds of music, cheering, and elated banter echoed off every surface. Before I even had a chance to acclimate to the noise, Nalithor pulled me to his side and led me through the streets with his friends in tow.

Draemir was alight with colored Magefire lanterns, fire dancers, musicians, and a wide assortment of mages who were performing tricks or complex magics for the entertainment of onlookers. There were artisans selling Draemiran wares for both battle and home. Male and female warriors displayed their honed bodies and refined combat abilities against training tools or each other, enthralling tourists everywhere.

It amazed me that the Draemirans managed to blend art, battle, and hunting so seamlessly into their culture. Their art often reflected scenes of battle or the hunt, but their weapons and armor were works of art themselves. Even their fighting methods seemed like art in a way.

*'I can see why Faerstravir lasts for so long,'* I mused, glancing up at Nalithor. He seemed delighted to be among his people, and in the company of his close friends. *'Even a week isn't enough to visit it all!'*

*'The entire city is filled with this—from the Scarlet District and all the way to the walls that surround the palace grounds,'* Nalithor informed me, grinning. *'Let's go see if you still have obscene luck with the games in the parks.'*

# CHAPTER TWENTY-NINE
### To Falrrsald

I glanced down at Arianna when her arms squeezed around my thigh and she nuzzled her cheek against me. Despite the amount of food and drink she had consumed the previous night, she was restless in her slumber. However, I did learn that alcohol made Arianna *very* sleepy.

Toward the latter half of the night she had dozed off on me while our mottled group watched the fireworks displays, and she had barely woken long enough to undress for bed.

She had awakened briefly this morning on the way to the airship. Once she put on her headphones and began listening to music, she fell asleep almost instantly. The volume was turned up so far that I caught sounds and phrases from time to time. I couldn't blame her; this airship's engines were obnoxiously loud.

*'Djialkan got to your domain safely,'* Alala stated while pawing at Arianna's hip. *'Bah! Is Ari ever going to wake up? I wanna play!'*

*'Let her sleep.'* I smiled and reached out to the impatient fox, ruffling the fur on her tiny head. *'She will need as much sleep as she can get before we arrive in Falrrsald. We won't be able to stay in one place for long once there.'*

Alala snorted and rested her head on Arianna's hip, her tail swishing in displeasure.

To my surprise, Djialkan had insisted that I allow him to work from my domain whilst Arianna and I were away from Vorpmasia. Yumeko and the other Vulins were happy to have a guest and quickly agreed to play host to the fae-dragon.

Djialkan had transported all of Arianna's belongings to my domain. Once done, he had proceeded to link all her shrizars to their storage space while she slept. I was a little impressed that the magical intrusion wasn't enough to rouse her from her slumber.

Apparently, Djialkan and Alala had agreed that one of them would accompany us to Falrrsald and the other would look into other matters. They both refused to tell me the details of their investigation into the Elders, but Djialkan had at least informed me that his search had broadened to include whatever was going on with Darius—and that Fraelfnir would be assisting him.

*'I don't like the idea that someone is manipulating that boy...'* I flinched and glanced down when Arianna's teeth sunk into my thigh.

'She's still *asleep?*'

I managed to pry Arianna from my thigh, then shifted her so that she was laying on her back. Her fangs would have broken skin if I hadn't already changed into my leather traveling armor.

At first, she became more restless and attempted to turn again. However, I was able to soothe her with darkness. Once she relaxed into her slumber once more, Alala hopped up and curled up on Arianna's stomach.

*'You will need to stay with Arianna or me at all times, Alala.'* I looked down at the pouting fox. *'It's even more dangerous for you in Falrrsald than it is for us. The tribes will think you are just an animal—they do not know what Guardians are.'*

Alala made an indignant noise and turned her head away from me. The fox had been cranky all morning, but I hadn't been able to identify the cause. I could only hope that it wasn't a reflection of the mood Arianna would wake up in. She had been in a relatively good mood the previous night despite the surprising amount of varikna and mri'lec she had consumed.

*'A hangover, perhaps?'* I wondered, reaching down to stroke Arianna's hair.

The slowing of the airship's rumbling engines drew my gaze to the nearest window. My stomach sank with apprehension. Open plains and small hills stretched into the distance as far as the eye could see, interrupted on rare occasion by a cluster of trees or by monolithic stones.

A long stretch of flat, hand-laid river rocks signified the border that the natives didn't want us to cross.

*'Arianna.'* I nudged her shoulder gently and watched her stir for a moment. *'We're here.'*

She grumbled something unintelligible and kept her eyes shut. I sighed and, after brief contemplation, pried her headphones from her ears. Alala warbled at Arianna the moment I set aside the headphones, but Arianna just muttered something and attempted to shift onto her side again.

"Don't you want to slay some beasts?" I questioned. A small smile formed on my lips when Arianna's shifting paused, and she cracked an eye open. Just the mere mention of beasts was enough to make bloodlust tinge her aura, despite her groggy state. "We've arrived on the border with Falrrsald."

"Already?" Arianna pulled herself slowly into a sitting position and yawned.

"It's been nine hours," I informed her, rising to my feet. "Grab a snack from the kitchens on our way through the ship. We have a few hours of walking before we reach anywhere we can stop and rest—let alone cook."

"A few hours?" Arianna picked up Alala and then moved toward the window, her jaw going slack as she stared at Falrrsald's eastern plains. "It looks so *desolate*! Hmmm, but there's magic everywhere…"

"Magic?" I glanced over my shoulder at her while tugging on a long leather traveling coat. "As in the natural aether currents, or something else?"

"No, as in someone's been *using* magic near here." Arianna turned from the window and followed me through the ship at a brisk pace. "Or maybe *something*. That much magic seems strange. Were they fighting something? Hmmm… Or perhaps these 'monsters' use magic in some way? Oh! Maybe, since it's so desolate, someone was practicing experimental spells here?"

Arianna continued to ramble to herself while we walked through the ship. Her face grew ever more alert as her remaining grogginess dissipated. However, I had to bring her to the kitchens myself because she was so distracted by whatever her vision let her see. She ate while we walked, devouring her food so fast that I wondered if she even tasted it.

"Rely'ric, Reiz'tar," a soldier bowed to us as we approached the ship's off-ramp. "Be careful out there. We'll be patrolling the border if you need us to bail you out, but we can only go so far without drawing the dragons' ire."

I nodded to the soldier and then strode past him. If I had my way, and Arianna could maintain pace, we would be well out of "rescue" range before making camp. The faster we traveled, the sooner our business in Falrrsald would be over, and the sooner I could take Arianna somewhere safer.

The temperate winds of Falrrsald rushed around me upon exiting the ship, filling my senses with the smell of sweet grass and freshly churned earth. Arianna's muttering ceased when she stepped out of the airship. I watched her for a moment as her bright eyes darted around the scenery.

She was obviously taking in something I couldn't see.

"What's wrong?" I asked when a frown tugged at the princess's lips.

"The magic here is strange." Arianna tilted her head. "It looks kind of like the corrupted magic that was sealing Sihix and Ceilail…but something is eating away at it."

"Show me?" I stopped beside her and glanced down expectantly.

Without a word or motion, Arianna sent several images to my mind. Pale magic twisted through the air with such density that I almost couldn't make out the sky behind it. Sections of the energy dripped with a dark oily substance.

When she said something was "eating away at it," I hadn't thought she meant it so literally. Sections of the magic had full bites taken out of them or had been munched away entirely.

"When you said eating…" I sighed and then adjusted my coat. "I guess this will be an interesting trip after all."

# END OF BOOK THREE

Thank you for reading!

**Also:** Please take a moment to leave a review!

Reviews are the lifeblood of any indie author and can make or break the success of a book. It doesn't need to be long, it could be a few words saying what you liked or five things you think could have been done better. Even a sentence or two would mean the world to me and would help me continue to write books in the future.

CONTINUE READING FOR HOW TO CONNECT WITH THE AUTHOR, UPCOMING RELEASES, AND MORE!

# BOOK THREE GLOSSARY

## HONORIFICS

| | |
|---|---|
| Chrot'zi | The Draemiran form of address for an Astral Mage. |
| Lyur'zi | The Draemiran form of address for an Umbral Mage. |
| Reiz'tar | A formal way to address women of high status. It is used similarly to "my lady."<br><br>Also used when addressing someone whose name is unknown to you, or if it isn't appropriate to speak someone's forename—such as an Empress. |
| Rely'ric | A formal way to address men of high status. It is used similarly to "my lord."<br><br>Also used when addressing someone whose name is unknown to you, or if it isn't appropriate to speak someone's forename—such as an Emperor. |
| Mrirtec | "Young Master" or "Little Master" in the Draemiran tongue. |
| -jiss | A Draemiran honorific suffix used for |

| | |
|---|---|
| | daughters of royal and imperial families. |
| -tyir | A gender-neutral Draemiran honorific suffix that is used to formalize addressing someone. |
| Reltyir | The formal version of -tyir. |
| -y'ric | A Draemiran honorific suffix derived from Rely'ric, -y'ric is most often attached to the given name of the person being addressed. |
| | Although it is most often used for men of high status, it is not uncommon for people to use –y'ric as a form of address for a man they are courting. |
| -zir | A Draemiran honorific suffix used for sons of royal and imperial families. |
| -z'tar | A Draemiran honorific suffix derived from Reiz'tar, -z'tar is most often attached to the given name of the person being addressed. |
| | Although it is most often used for women of high status, it is not uncommon for people to use -z'tar as a form of address for a woman they are courting. |

## PLACES

| | |
|---|---|
| Beshulthien | An empire founded by the patriarch of the Vampire race. |
| Vorpmasia(n) | The Vorpmasian Empire was founded by the Devillian patriarch, Lucifer. Vorpmasia is made up of eleven separate territories, with a central capitol. |
| Dauthrmir | The capitol of the Vorpmasian Empire. |
| Draemir | The territory of the Vorpmasian Empire that is overseen by the God and Goddess of Adinvyr. |
| Gal'edean Ocean | The vast ocean to the east of the Rilzaan Continent, the Gal'edean Ocean is ruled by a variety of sea-faring and aquatic races. |
| Suthsul Desert | A large desert to the south of the Vorpmasia Empire, and home to the Vunsori—Desert Elves. |
| V'frul | The Vunsori capital deep within the Suthsul Desert. |
| X'shmir | A human city-state located on one of Avrirsa's many flying islands. Ruled by the Black Family. |

## RACES

| | |
|---|---|
| Adinvyr | A Devillian race with strong ties to sex |

| | |
|---|---|
| | and sexuality. In order to survive, they must periodically feed on sexual energy which they can take from their prey in various forms. |
| Akor | A Devillian race characterized by their stone-colored range of skin tones and fiery appearance. The Akor have a close relationship with volcanic areas due to their need to drink and bathe in lava. |
| Imviir | A Devillian race with humanoid torsos and faces but are like a serpent from the waist down. They prefer to live in humid jungles. Imviir possess both fangs and venom like a snake. |
| Jrachra | A Devillian race that lives and breathes everything arcane. From a young age they paint aether-infused sigils on their bodies. The number of sigils on a Jrachra indicates power and age. The brilliance of the aether indicates status. The color(s) indicate elemental affinity. |
| Kelsviir | Also known as "Dauthrmiran Elves," the Kelsviir are fiercely loyal to the Vorpmasian Emperor and treat him with the same respect afforded to a race's |

| | |
|---|---|
| | patriarchal and matriarchal deities. |
| | Unlike the other Elven races, Kelsviir have skin tones similar to the colors of stones, ranging from pure white like marble to pitch black like obsidian. All tones between are varying shades of grey. |
| | Due to the environment and the prevalence of dark aether, they have evolved to have dark sclera like Devillians, and parts of their bodies can contain bioluminescence. |
| Oelerran | Also known as "Wood Elves," this race was conquered by the Beshulthien Empire and brought under its yoke. Despite this, they retain their haughty nature and blind hatred for Humans. |
| Raogsur | Also known as "Ocean Elves," this race is native to the Gal'edean Ocean, making their homes on and within its turbulent waters. Though they are not part of the Beshulthien or Vorpmasian Empires, they often do trade with both and assist those who get lost in their territory. |

| | |
|---|---|
| Rylthra | A Devillian race with the characteristics of a fox. Although their faces and bodies are similar to that of Humans and Elves, Rylthra have ears and tails like foxes. Their fur and hair color are sometimes mismatched.<br><br>Rylthra are capable of shapeshifting into the full form of a fox. The number of tails is indicative of age and power.<br><br>Those with multiple tails often become priest(esses) or Oracles. |
| Sizoul | A Devillian race which lives in an isolated, northern part of the Suthsul Desert that technically belongs to the Vorpmasian Empire. Sizoul have an appearance similar to that of the Desert Elves, but retain the horns, tails, claws, fangs, and black sclera of the other Devillian races.<br><br>Unlike other Devillians, Sizoul's horns, tails, claws, and eye colors take on the appearance of precious and semi-precious |

| | gems. |
|---|---|
| | While the other Devillian races take interest in war, Sizoul prefer to make and create things. |
| Sundreht | The shortest of the Devillian races, Sundreht have ears and tails like a cat. Despite their comparatively small stature, Sundreht are one of the more battle-oriented races. |
| Vampire | A sanguine race created by a twisted god who preyed on a Devillian prince's wish for more power. Despite the prince's desires, Vampires are weaker than Devillians. |
| Varjior | A race of shapeshifters that can take on animal form. Although often confused for Devillian, they are something else entirely. |
| Vulin | A race of bipedal fox people that Nalithor saved from execution. Not much is known about them, aside that they're a remnant from a previous world, and that they serve the God of Balance in a similar fashion to familiars. |
| Vunsori | The proper name for "Desert Elves." |

# DRAEMIRAN LANGUAGE

| | |
|---|---|
| shrizar | A Draemiran term that was popularized during the foundation of the Vorpmasian Empire.<br><br>A "shrizar" refers to the pockets of magic a mage can create and utilize for the storage of items. |
| fiirzik | A strong alcoholic beverage that is served hot. |
| Faerstravir | Draemir's spring festival. |
| varikna | One of the strongest forms of liquor to ever come out of Vorpmasia; even a few sips of this drink is too much for most Humans and Elves. |
| mrilec | A sweet, wine-like beverage popular among Draemirans. It is a brilliant blue color. One of its primary ingredients is taken from the mrifon tree. |
| mrifon | A type of tree native to Draemir. It has dark bark with brilliant blue veins of bioluminescence running through it. Though "mri" loosely translates to "small," the flowers the tree produces in the spring are the size of dinner plates. |
| Groslturvir | Draemir's winter festival. |

| | |
|---|---|
| Lari'xan | A Draemiran term than can be translated as Elemental Gods, Local Gods, or Aetherial Gods. |
| dehsul | A Draemiran curse word that's used in a similar fashion to "fuck!" |
| iridesci | Iridesci is a portmanteau that quite literally translates to, "iridescent drink." This morning beverage is light, refreshing, and citrusy in taste. It is named for its dual blue and purple colors, and the slight shimmer it has when exposed to light. |
| jich | A Draemiran curse word that's used in a similar fashion to "shit!" |
| sh'rlic marnas | A command which roughly translates to "break apart." |
| throstor | A Draemiran word with combined meanings: "die" and "get out of my sight." |
| toryn'xir | A potent sedative that is opalescent lavender in color. Though strong, it remains weak enough that you will still wake the next morning. |
| vralsium | A metal that is seen as poisonous to deities and their offspring, not much about it is public knowledge. |

# Available Now

Of Astral and Umbral

*Beneath the Mists*

*Courting Balance*

Deck of Souls

*Fateseal*

# Upcoming Works

Of Astral and Umbral

*Book 4, TBD*

Deck of Souls

*Book 2, TBD*

*Book 3, TBD*

New Series

*Shatterpact, TBD*

*The Dragon Emperor's Pearl, TBD*

# About the Author

Bonnie L. Price was born in 1990 and has lived in four different states. At the age of twelve, while living in rural Upstate New York, she turned to writing as a way to entertain herself. Without internet or TV, there was little else to do during the long, cold winters.

What started as a way to amuse herself soon became a passion, and she's been writing ever since.

**Want to connect with Bonnie?**

Fan Group:

facebook.com/groups/blp.demonden

Discord: https://discord.gg/gRuGc2r

Author Page:

facebook.com/BonnieLPriceOfficial

Twitter: https://twitter.com/Bonnie_L_Price

# ILLUSTRATION

In love with the cover illustration? Want to see more from the artist? Check out the links below for how to follow her!

DEVIANTART.COM/LAS-T

LAS-T.ARTSTATION.COM/

FACEBOOK.COM/ThanderLin.Illustration

CPSIA information can be obtained
at www.ICGtesting.com
Printed in the USA
BVHW082054010120
568263BV00001B/41/P